THE SOURCE

MARLIN 1, RADAR SITE
SOUTH FLORIDA

"Inform, Ironman. Three Russian aircraft at 30,000."

"Yes, sir. It's the monthly resupply flight. They must be getting low on vodka."

"Probably!" The captain goes back to reading his newspaper, more concerned about where the Heat is in the NBA standings. The sergeant watches the sweep of the scope a few more times, then picks up the yellow handset on the console.

"Ironman, this is Marlin 1. We have three Russian aircraft at 30,000. We ID them as a Condor and two Fulcrums in escort. Their flight path suggests they are heading for Malangas, east of Havana. Over."

"Roger, Marlin 1. We have them at 0145 Zulu, on 2-18-00 at 30,000. Over."

"Roger, Ironman. Marlin out."

IRONMAN, GULF REGION COMMAND CENTER
PENSACOLA, FLORIDA

"Sir, that was Marlin 1. They are reporting three Russian aircraft south of the Keys."

The officer of the day walks by and looks over the operator's shoulder at the scope. The sweep picks up the three aircraft in a tight "V" formation. Picking up a clipboard, he quickly flips through the papers. His fingers stop on a flight form. It shows that the transport would be flying with an escort. Putting the clipboard down, he rechecks the designation on the screen of the two aircraft flying with the transport. "It seems a little out of character to have two Mig-29s escorting a 124 on a resupply flight, which it would normally fly alone."

"You're right, sir."

The captain shrugs his shoulders. "Well, log it and make sure it gets out with the morning traffic to Ultima."

"Yes, sir."

ABOARD THE AN-124
JUST NORTH OF CUBA

The many dial lights in the cockpit shine off the visor of the pilot as he leans forward to adjust his seat belt. Quickly looking around at the others, he again takes a drink of coffee. They have been in the air now for fourteen hours, including four air tanker refuels for the fighter escorts. The two fighters have moved just ahead of them in the bright moonlight. Con-trails stream back, looking like crystal cloth as they flow away from their wings. Looking back along his own wings, he can see the frosty stream flowing away.

"Comrade Captain." He keys his mike.

"Da, Comrade Navigator."

"The moon has a perfect twenty-one-degree halo. I thought it might remind you of your home in Siberia. It means trolls are about this night."

Others on the net chuckle. "You're right, Comrade." He leans forward and looks up at the moon. The circle surrounding it sparkles in the clear sky. It looks like a huge lens held up to magnify the silver-blue light. "It does remind me of home, and the fun of chasing trolls in the night." His eyes trail back to the fighters. "If by chance we meet some trolls, we have the perfect companions to deal with them." The pewter grays of the fighters' skins glow in the freezing light. Rechecking the instruments, he turns towards his co-pilot.

"Yefimov, contact the fighters. We will begin our descent in about fifteen minutes." He gets a thumbs up as the co-pilot turns to look out the window, and he keys his mike. Recouping his oxygen mask, the pilot again keys his mike. "Comrade Sergeant."

"Sir." The reply is instant from the bowels of the aircraft.

"Inform the lieutenant that we are about thirty minutes out so he can get his men ready."

BACKFIRE

An Echo One Intrusion

BY
STEVE SIMMONS

HATS
OFF™

Backfire: An Echo One Intrusion

All Rights Reserved.
Copyright © 2003 Steve Simmons

No part of this book may be reproduced or retransmitted in any form or by any means without the written permission of the publisher.

Cover illustration by Michael Hall.

International Standard Book Number:
1-58736-125-6
Library of Congress Control Number:
2001119033

Published by Hats Off Books™
610 East Delano Street, Suite 104
Tucson, Arizona 85705 U.S.A.
www.hatsoffbooks.com

ACKNOWLEDGMENTS AND DEDICATIONS

To my four sons and their wives: Steve and Pricilla, Brad and Sue, Jason (still looking), Zack and Lisa. They have read portions of the story and helped with suggestions, and they have just been there for the long haul.

To my mom, Myrtle, for her encouragement to be a free thinker and for always being there to support me, and to my dad, Richard, for planting the seed of interest in military history and for his dedication to duty in two wars.

To the ex-employees of Price Club/Costco in Texas who wanted their names used in the book, you'll find them there.

To Louis Sanchez, who looked for a reference book on Russian military weapons. He found it in six months and overnighted it to me.

To Tom Swanton, retired air force colonel. He took the time to read the book in its roughest form, and he gave suggestions and kind words to keep it going.

But most of all, I would like to thank my wife, Susie. She really believed that the project would come this far. She kept me on course and allowed me the time to chase a dream. She is the backbone of our family, the strongest visionary, the warmest love, and is always willing to give in order for others to achieve. Through her, I could see a thousand worlds, and she lifted me up to see beyond the veil of tomorrow.

"Da, sir." Walking alongside the stacked pallets of equipment, the sergeant works his way to the front of the cargo bay. As he approaches the front, a guard standing near the pallets watches him. Even in the red glow of the lights along the passage, the figure is hard to make out. He is stopped, and the man goes to get his lieutenant. A large wooden crate on a four-wheeled dolly sits alone in the first fifty feet of the cargo bay. Around it, men in gray-black camouflage lie on the floor or sit with their backs against the side of the plane. The guard and another man make their way over to him.

"Da, Comrade?"

"Sir, the captain wanted me to tell you that we will be landing in about thirty minutes."

"Thank you, Sergeant."

As he makes his way back down the side of the bay, the sergeant looks back towards the front. The men who had been lying on the deck have formed a line along the side of the bay. Each has a pack at his feet, and his weapon hangs from the strap around his neck. Suddenly a black form appears from the crates and blocks his view. They stare at each other for a microsecond; he turns and quickly moves into the back of the plane.

The pilot watches out the window as the two fighters break to each side. They barrel roll out away from his front. Ribbons of crystal intertwine as they streak away. Coming back around, they again form up into a "V" formation. The captain looks over to his co-pilot. "These young fighter pilots sure like to play with their toys."

"Da, sir. I'm beginning our landing pre-checks."

"Good." The pilot switches his frequency, and keys his mike.

"Malangas, tower. This is flight R009 inbound. Over."

"Roger, flight R009. This is the Malangas tower. Over."

"Malangas, we are three aircraft approaching at 30,000 feet, on a heading of 265. Over."

In the tower, with the green glow of the scope on his face, the operator checks the time on his clock at 0215 Zulu. He keys his mike. "Roger, flight R009. I have you at 30,000 on heading 265. Come to heading 255 and begin your decent to 10,000 feet. Call when you have reached the outer marker. Over."

"Roger, Malangas. Turning to heading 255 and descending to 10,000. Over."

"Roger, R009. Malangas out."

The pilot checks the two fighters off his wing tips as he slowly pushes the yoke over and forward. The huge transport slides to the left and begins to descend. The two Migs drop in unison with him. He and the co-pilot continue their pre-landing checks.

The men in the cargo bay can feel the plane turn to the left and then begin to descend. Their lieutenant grabs on to the dolly as he continues his last minute instructions before they land.

As they descend, the pilot can see the lights of towns and small villages on the dark mass to their left. On the waters below, boats with lights shining seem to be sailing on an undulating sea of nickel. The silver-gray from the moonlight gives the water a metallic glow.

The fighters have broken off at 10,000 feet. They circle above like worker bees around their bloated queen. Their radars scan the skies for any possible intruder.

"Malangas, this is R009. We are at the outer marker. Over."

"Roger, R009. Come to a heading of 110 and begin your decent. You are cleared to land on runway eleven."

"Roger, Malangas. Come to 110. Cleared to runway eleven. We will begin our decent."

"Roger, R009. Welcome to Cuba. Over."

As they begin their descent, the pilot pushes the lever forward to deploy the landing gear. Under the belly, twelve sets of wheels begin moving into position. The heavy thud is felt throughout the plane as they lock into position.

MALANGAS AIR BASE
CUBA

"Sir, the planes are at the outer marker."

General Quintano looks at his watch, and pushes a button on the bezel of the Tag Hure. The blue light glows in the darkness of the jeep. As he releases the button, a smile crosses his face. He remembers Paris, where his father gave it to him on the trip after his graduation from the university.

"It's 0245, and they're right on time, Sergeant Rio. Contact the other jeep, and have them standing by." He calls to the other jeep as Quintano climbs out. As Quintano straightens his jacket, his eyes are drawn to the north, up the main runway. Three sets of lights over the Gulf begin turning towards him. Rio climbs out and joins him, looking up the runway.

"Sir, the men are out of the other jeep and are standing by."

"Good." Quintano adjusts his field jacket collar as a cold wind blows in from the Gulf. A glowing ring around the moon highlights the chill.

"Excuse me, sir, but it seems a little odd that we are out here at this hour for a Russian supply flight. Why were we held back 200 feet from the hangar?"

Quintano's eyes continue following the lights out over the water as they continue to get larger. "The Russians are bringing in some kind of optical aircraft camera. They have asked us to stand by in case of any problems."

"Sí, General. The only problem is that we're all going to freeze out here." He slaps his gloved hands together.

"That's true, Sargeant. It is cold out tonight. I'm going over to the hangar. After they have secured the cargo in the hangar, have the other jeep join up with you. And head back to the barracks. Tell Captain Vargas that I'll see him there."

"Yes, sir." The words hang in the cold wind as Quintano begins walking towards the partially opened doors.

The wind pulls at his jacket and pushes his trousers tight against his legs. Holding his hat, he looks back up the runway, as the rumble of powerful engines seem to fill the frozen air. Someone in the darkness near the edge of the runway strikes two flares. He begins waving them from his chest out to the full extent of his arms. The figure glows red in the darkness. The two escort fighters fly down the length of the runway, as the transport touches down. They cross over the man with the flares and over the hangar with a compression of the air and the howl of raw power. Breaking to the left, they swing around to land behind their charge. As they turn, Quintano can see the cones of flames protruding from their engines. As they cross the face of the moon, they look like black paper cut-outs. He pauses for a second.

"Mig-29s—quite a fighter to be escorting the big cargo plane." He shrugs and continues on towards the two men standing at the edge of the hangar doors. Their gray and black camies blend well with the shadows. Their eyes have been on him since he left the jeep. Waiting until he is about ten feet away, the tall blond acknowledges him.

"Good morning, Comrade General."

Quintano smiles as he reaches them. "Good morning, Comrade Brock, and also to you, Comrade Val." They both nod their heads.

Even at six feet tall and in good shape, he is dwarfed by the size of the two Russians. They had all worked out in very intense exercises. But the Russians had moved into the range of huge as opposed to athletic. Brock extends his hand and engulfs Quintano's; it is like shaking hands with a bear. "You still wear that blue light watch, my General?"

"Sí. I should have known you would pick that up."

Val reaches over and shakes his hand. "Good morning, Comrade General." Quintano can feel the strength being held back in these powerful handshakes. "We also recognized your walk, from your wound in Kabul. But you were always a Cuban who would do well in the Spetsnaz."

"Thank you, Comrades."

Their attention is drawn to the runway, as the huge cargo plane touches down. In the darkness, the huge plane has the appearance of a fat bird with its wings slumped down at the tips. When it comes to a stop, it slowly begins moving along the side of the runway, towards the man waving the flares. As it reaches the man, its nose is bathed in the red light of the flares. The huge plane dwarfs the man as it follows his directions to the front of the hangar. The three cover their ears as the plane comes to a stop in front of them. The engines are spooled down as the huge nose of the plane begins to lift up out of the way. During this process, the two Mig fighters have landed, and taxied to a hangar further down the field.

As the nose lifts up, red and green lights from the interior of the plane ooze out into the darkness. A ramp begins sliding forward and is lowered into place. As it makes contact with the tarmac, it sends a metallic clank into the darkness. The sound draws the attention of the Cuban guards, who look back towards the plane.

At the margin where light and darkness form a perfect line, dark forms kneeling in a line from the plane to the hangar doors appear. Back lit by the soft red and green lights of the cargo bay, the forms seem like stone statues caught in moonlight. They do not move as a motor mule drives up the ramp and into the belly of the plane. The Cubans look away as if some evil has come suddenly from the darkness.

Quintano had watched the men deploy from the sides of the plane and form the two rows. Their AKS-74 weapons aimed outwards, their dark gray and black camies seem more a part of the night than of cloth. No sounds are made as they wait for any unexpected action.

"Do you remember Kabul, Raphael?"

Quintano smiles and looks up into the cool blue stones of Brock's eyes. "I do, amigo. It was my first time working with you and the Spetsnaz. But then we were under fire. I was amazed at the level of ability of these men. They are still impressive."

"Thank you, General. The men will appreciate your comment."

The mule appears at the top of the ramp and slowly drives forward, dragging out the large crate on the dolly. When it reaches the bottom, it pushes onto the tarmac and begins heading for the hangar. As it passes, the men on each side rise and slowly begin backing into the hangar. Two men near the door take up positions at the opening, their rifles pointed out board. As the dolly crosses the threshhold of the hangar doors, they begin to close.

Quintano and the two Russians move in behind the moving screen. As they reach the side of the dolly, a hollow thud fills the hangar as the doors close behind them. In the back of the hangar, one of the men opens an iron gate. He walks in and opens two large iron doors built into the back wall of the hangar. As he turns on a light switch, the white-painted interior dazzles in the overhead lights. The dolly is turned and begins backing through the gate, and into the missile storage room.

Quintano reads the Russian TAC marks on the side of the box, which contains optical camera equipment. The word "secret" has been stenciled on all sides of the crate. Once inside, the dolly is disconnected from the mule and it drives back into the hangar. Val takes a quick walk around the box and then turns the light off as he leaves. The steel doors are closed behind him. A new cipher lock had been installed on the right door; as the doors meet, a green light appears on the lock. He leans down and punches in a series of numbers. The light goes red. Moving back out of the gated area, it is closed and two large locks are put onto the welded hasps. Val secures them, and two of the armed escorts take up a position on each side of the gate.

The lieutenant joins Val as he walks back to Brock and Quintano in the center of the darkened hangar. Val hands him a sealed envelope.

"Here are your orders, Comrade Lieutenant Vortusha. This part of the operation is now in your hands."

Taking the envelope he delivers a smart salute. "We will execute our assignment to the last, Comrade Colonel. Please excuse me. I will see to my men." He turns on his heels and moves back towards the door leading to barracks at the back of the hangar.

Quintano assesses this young lieutenant, who wears no unit patches on his fatigues. His AKS-74 hangs down his back, and he has the true sign of the Spetsnaz units—the always-present entrenching tool. He looks back at the guards. The muted light of the hangar throws shadows over each fold in the guard's form. Their faces, colored in dark grays and black, causes the eye to look twice to see human forms. His thoughts are brought back by Val's voice.

"Thank you, Comrade General. Air Marshall Shagan expresses his thanks for letting us store this equipment in the missile bunker."

"This is no problem, mi amigos. Will you be staying for a while, perhaps dinner tonight?"

"We're sorry Raphael. We are to leave for Archangel later today. But the next time we are here, we will look forward to an evening with you, Comrade, and your wonderful family." They walk to a small door inset into the huge hangar door. Both men again shake hands with Quintano.

Brock opens the door back out onto the tarmac. "We will make it a point to spend some time with you on our next trip. Da svidaniya, Comrade."

"Adiós, amigos. Have a good flight." He steps out the door and back into the morning darkness. The cargo plane is gone. It has been moved to another hangar near the two Migs.

A team of forklifts moves pallets of cargo into the open hangar. He looks once more back at the hangar he just left. It is as if nothing had happened there. Only the far-off sounds of the unloading and the wind make any noise.

"It's strange?" His voice is blown away in the cold wind gusting off the tarmac. The chill in the wind burns his eyes, and he looks forward to better weather coming soon. Strolling across the open tarmac, he is soon lost in the darkness.

CHAPTER 1

Cool winds off the mountains of eastern Senegal blow over the warm moist air of the plains below. The turbulence causes warm air to rise in a swirling column. Clouds build in a massive cylindrical formation, the warm air raising miles into the atmosphere, forming huge cauliflower formations. As it reaches the base of the troposphere, it spreads out to form a huge anvil with lightning striking from its base. It swells with the rising moisture, until the bulk of the storm can no longer support the huge anvil crown. Villagers west of the mountains begin driving their cattle and goats into pens, and quickly work to get their houses ready for the coming storm.

The darkening clouds fall towards the west, plunging into the valleys and crevices of the surrounding mountains. The huge cloud mass assaults the city of Dakar. The sky turns ink black as the rain beats down on the defenseless city. The concussion of the thunder shakes the city to its foundation. The rain falls in sheets that seem to beat at the roofs and windows like gravel.

Slowly the storm moves on to the open sea, where it is nurtured into a huge pillar of slowly turning clouds. It continues to build and expand as it moves farther out to sea.

The National Weather Bureau tracks it across the Atlantic Ocean, where it turns into a tropical storm. They pulled the next name up in their computer. The storm was code-named *Evita*.

PENTAGON WEATHER ROOM
WASHINGTON, D.C.

The big screen at the front of the room bursts to life; colors fill the semi-dark room. As the computer displays the intensity of the storm, reds and yellows appear at the core, surrounded by shades of blues and greens. Evita swirls and turns, its evil black cores like an eye looking into the room. On smaller screens around the room, the world's weather is being received and analyzed. Any weather disturbance in the world could be thrown up on the big screen for closer analysis. "Sir, were getting the latest pictures of Evita."

Captain Emmett looks up at the screen as his assistants join him. They are all bathed in the changing hues of color. "She could be a mean one, sir."

"You're right. The test will come when it passes over Cuba. With luck it will spend itself against the mountains."

"Sir, we have the latest predicted track. I'll bring it up on the screen."

A white overlay of western Cuba appears in the middle of the screen. Emmett looks around. "Bring it in closer." The image is enlarged and a series of purple dots cross the island.

"Sir, we believe the center of the storm will cross the island at around 0230 Zulu, about sixty miles east of Havana."

Emmett turns his back to the screen to face the others. "Ladies and gentlemen, we will need to maintain a close watch on this storm. With the large disparity in temperatures between the southern ocean and the Gulf, she could explode into a very dangerous lady." Emmett looks at his watch. "Damn, it's 8:40 P.M. My wife is planning on some guests at 9:30. I have to run." He picks up his coat and his briefcase. "But I want to stay informed on Evita. Remind the late watch officer to call me, whatever the time, if she begins to break loose in the Gulf."

When he reaches the door, he turns back towards the screen. The colors and form of the storm move and change on the screen, reflecting his thoughts. He closes the door, and leaves the center for home.

Evita moves over the Isle of Pines off the southern coast of Cuba. It heads across the open water towards the main island. Heavy gusts of wind and surging waves trumpet the arrival of Evita on the southern coast of Cuba. With bursts of torrential rain, the storm sends out tentacles of clouds to probe the ridges and valleys of the mountains before it. The reaching arms seem to pull the storm forward as they lock in combat with the raising landmass. Soon rifts in the mass of stone are found, and the probing arms race forward. They pull the bulk of the storm against the mountain. Its fluidity allows it to flow around hard spots. Its forward elements suck it through the passes. Heavy rains mark its passage.

When the forward elements of the storm breach the mountains, they stall in the hot moist air. They wait patiently for the full girth of the storm to join them. The mountains have taken a toll on the slashing storm. It has compressed the size, but not the fury. Evita finds new life in the hot moist air. It seems to sense the presence of the Gulf ahead, and races down the mountainside towards the northern coast. Rain quickly fills dry streambeds. Water fills every depression, crack and crevasse. Run-off begins moving towards the coast. Soon creeks and streams merge with rivers. The water begins leaving a path of destruction in its wake, as it races into villages and fields. The works of man are quickly breached and pushed aside, as roads and bridges are erased in swirling waters. The passage of Evita across Cuba will not be easy.

MATANZAS AIR BASE
CUBA

The hot still air fills the rooms of the technician shop. A man sits in a chair; his feet resting on the top of a desk. He leans back precariously in the dark. Another man lies on a sweat-stained cot. Neither are quite at the full embrace of sleep, but rather are trapped in the twilight zone of exhaustion. Their minds race through the events in their past which have brought them to this place and time.

Both had come out of the Cuban school system and had gone on to the University of Havana to pursue advanced studies in electronics. As their senior year was ending, their instructors had approached them to do advanced electronic training with the Russians. Their training included the repair and upgrading of the electronics of the fighters and other Soviet aircraft flown by the Cubans.

The face of the man on the cot contorts. His dream seems to cause him pain as his body moves to a new position. The wall fan plays over him, but beads of sweat trickle down his cheek. Vaguely his mind can hear the man in the next room. Miguel rocks the chair down on all four legs. Standing, he picks up his coffee cup and walks across the room. Standing in the light from a bulb outside the window, Miguel checks his watch. "Shit." Time seems to drag on. They just have to wait a little longer, and their task would be completed.

He checks his watch again. The second hand seems to crawl across the face of his Russian watch. The red star on its face glows. It was a gift from one of the air crews he had worked with. He had been up all night on that one, fixing their radar so that they could return home. Miguel looks around the tech shop. Small colorful lights glow from the workbenches. The coffee seems to be eating into his stomach, but he must be awake and alert. Their time was near, and no mistake such as sleep must interfere. His hand raises once more to look at his watch; ten more minutes and he would wake up Luís. He walks back to his chair and sits down in the dark.

From a drawer near him, Miguel pulls out a bottle of dark rum and pours some into the coffee. His drink is long, his exhale is loud, and the fire from his cup dashes into his system as he leans back in his chair. His eyes close as the whirring of the fan pounds on his thoughts. All is done, all is ready. Folding his hands behind his head, his thoughts go back in time.

His mind's eye sees the happy times at the university. They had excelled in their classes for advanced studies under the Russians. They had become the wizards of the black boxes, radars, missile tracking systems, and other electronic wonders. But soon after they began working at the base, their illusions fell away. They were programmed into their jobs, and the world passed them by. They earned just above the wages of the laborers on the base. The regime under Castro was outdated and needed to change.

Friends from school who had escaped to America sent word back of their success. They earned big money, both legally and illegally. Even drug runners needed their radar and other equipment modified to evade detection. Both he and Luís had turned to Libertal, a reactionary group opposed to the regime in Cuba. Meeting others who shared their frustration with the government, they were welcomed into the group. The group found their access to the weapons of the Russians an added plus. They had been experimenting with different ways to sabotage the complex black boxes for months.

Diagrams and plans were funneled through the group to the Americans. This was to be their final act. They had saved the money needed to get to America. Libertal had set up the trip, and they would leave late that day. Their dreams were full of their forthcoming successes in America.

His right arm rises into the air, as if it had a mind of its own. Leaning his head forward, he scans the face of the timepiece. The hands rest on 1:00 A.M. "It is time."

Miguel walks over to the door of the storeroom. "Luís, Luís. Wake up. It is time." Luís hears the words, but his mind doesn't want to let go. "Luís, wake up." A hand grabs his shoulder and shakes him. "Come on, we have to get going."

His eyes slowly open. "All right, all right. I'm getting up."

He swings his feet to the floor, and rubs his eyes. The light from the other room makes him blink, as he slowly rises from the cot. His stretch is long, and his first steps are unsteady. Entering the room, Luís searches for his cup. Miguel is leaning over the work-bench, getting his tool case ready to go. "Come on, Luís." Miguel looks back over his shoulder. "The plane leaves in forty-five minutes."

Luís sees his cup near the coffee pot. He loads it half full, and walks back to the desk drawer. Filling the other half with some rum, he drinks the contents down. The cup slides away as a short breath exhales from his lips. His eyes focus on the workbench as Miguel steps back. Next to the tool case is a black box with connector ports on each end. The box is four inches wide, four inches high and eight inches long. It looks like others on the shelf above the bench. Luís moves next to Miguel at the bench. His hand lifts the top of the box back.

Inside two blocks of plastic explosive rest along its length. A timer built by Miguel sits in the center of the blocks. Luís holds the lid, as Miguel adjusts the timer. "The capacitor on this thing should give it all the boost it needs. OK, four hours and forty-five minutes. That should put it out over the Atlantic. All they will ever know is that the plane just disappeared. Then they will search and find the wreckage with a hole blown in the side of it. And Libertal will take credit. To show that the fight to free Cuba is not over." Miguel lowers the lid and tightens the screws to seal the box.

Luís looks into Miguel eyes. "But do you think we are still doing the right thing?"

"Sí, mi amigo. With the Russians pulling out of Cuba and Fidel's resistance to deal with the Americans, Cuba can only become like Haiti and the other islands, with their broken economies, forced to take hand-outs from the super powers."

"I guess you're right. Things are getting worse."

"I know I'm right." Miguel puts his hand on Luís's shoulder. "Remember my friend. As soon as you can, get to Playa Blanco. The boat to the United States will leave at sunset. Do not miss that boat. Because of the two Mig-29 escorts, they might guess what happened. They will guess that it was probably us who put the bomb on board."

"I understand, Miguel. We both need to make it to the boat."

Miguel picks up the box as Luís unplugs the coffee pot. "We don't want to burn the place down, right?"

"Right." Miguel nods his head. Luís grabs the tool case off the bench and they head for the door. As Miguel opens the door, the warm night air blows in. The light outside of the tech shop throws a yellow arch across the ground. Luís turns off the lights and closes the door. The sound of their shoes on the gravel walkway is the only noise they hear. The stars are beginning to disappear as they walk into the darkness. The glow from another light ahead forms a circle on the path.

"The night is warm, huh Miguel?" He looks up at the sky. "Yeah, a lot of clouds are beginning to come in. Where is that storm that is coming at us?"

"I don't know. The last I heard, it had turned northeast, heading towards the outer islands. They said it could be a big one." As they pass under the light and round the corner of the building, they catch their first site of the Tupolev bomber. The long slender body of the plane is silhouetted in the glow of the hangar lights. A guard stands near its tail.

They have to cross a dark area to reach the plane. The noise from their feet changes as they leave the gravel area and walk on the concrete tarmac. As they walk through the darkness, a bright beam of light hits them in the face. Both men stop in their tracks, the light moves closer.

"Miguel and Luís. What are you doing out here at his time of the morning?" The light pays up and down each figure, and stops at the black box. "You need to fix something on that plane?"

"Sí, Felix. You scared the shit out of us." Miguel shakes his head. Luís catches his breath. "We didn't see you standing there."

"I know. I saw you looking around. What, one of their magic boxes not working?"

"Yeah. They're leaving this morning, so we had to work late to get it fixed."

"OK. You had better hurry because the crew just went to have breakfast. And the others will be loading some cameras or something. They don't want anyone around the plane."

"All right, Felix. Thanks."

As they move towards the plane. Felix yells to the guard by the hangar door. "Pablo, Miguel and Luís are going on the plane to fix something."

"Sí." He walks out under the wing to meet the two approaching figures. "OK, Felix. Get me some rolls with my coffee, OK?"

"All right, Pablo. I'll be back in a few minutes."

Pablo meets them near the front access door to the plane.

"Hey, Pablo. How are you doing?"

"Ah, fine, Miguel. You guys need to go onboard?"

"Yeah. We need to replace this piece." Miguel holds it up for Pablo to see.

He shrugs his shoulders. "Hell. They all look the same to me."

"Yeah, but they have different jobs to do."

"OK, but those Russian guys will be back soon. And they don't want anyone near this plane. So hurry the job up."

"Just give us five minutes, and we'll be done."

Luís drops the door, and uses the ladder to climb up into the plane. Miguel hands the box up to him, and then climbs up. Red security lights lead them up to the crew area. Miguel throws a switch on the panel in front of him, and the cockpit lights up.

Luís looks out of the front windows above the pilot's seat. The sky continues to darken.

Directly behind the captain's chair, Miguel gets on his back under the console of the radar officer's seat. "All right. Hand me the box." Luís can only see the lower half of his body and the outstretched hand.

"Here you go, hurry." He puts the box in his hand.

"It will only take a minute." Miguel slides the box into a slot on a rack of other black boxs. "All right, give me the connector pieces."

Luís removes four foot-long pieces of braided cable from the tool case. Each has a connector at one end. Miguel grabs them and screws the connectors into the box; he takes the tails and feeds them into the cable channel. He ties them into place, then runs the beam of his flashlight over the box.

"Well?" Luís looks into Miguel face.

"It is done, Luís. Even the builders of this thing could not tell it didn't belong there." They hear Pablo talking to someone outside. Quickly they pack up their tools and get ready to leave. Someone is in the door climbing up.

"What are you doing in here?" A husky Russian voice resounds in the cabin. He quickly reached them. "What is going on? Who told you that you could come on board?"

"We're from the tech office. We're Luís and Miguel."

"I know who you are. But what are you doing here?"

"We had to fix one of the transponder boxes." Miguel points towards the console.

"I'll have to check this with the captain. I was told that no one would be on the aircraft at this late hour."

The Russian moves back down the ladder to the ground. Miguel and Luís follow him out of the plane. At six feet, six inches, he towers over the two techs. His muscles ripple under his stripped naval tee-shirt. His small flashlight plays over their faces. Taking a walkie-talkie from his belt, he turns it on. First there is static and then the sound of another Russian talking to someone.

"Val, this is Brock. Is the captain having breakfast with you?"

The radio goes silent and then leaps back to life. "Yes, Comrade. Captain Mikulin is eating with us. What is the problem?"

"I'm at the plane. The two Cuban techs, Miguel and Luís, were on board fixing something. Did you or the captain know anything about it?"

"Hold on, Brock." Val turns to the men eating at the table across from him. "Excuse me, Captain. Were you aware of any repairs on the plane that the Cuban techs would be fixing tonight?"

Mikulin looks up from his meal. He looks at Val and then to his radar intercept officer next to him. "Kosa, didn't they say one of the transponders was acting up?"

"Yes, Comrade Captain. They asked if they could replace it as soon as they got done."

Mikulin looks back at Val. "Yeah, Val. We were aware of it."

"Thank you, Comrade Captain. Next time please inform us of these late night repairs." The captain nods his head towards Val.

He keys the mike. "Brock, this is Val."

"Yes, Comrade," the voice booms back.

"Apparently the air crew was aware of this last minute repair. It's all right."

"OK. Brock out." Brock lowers the walkie-talkie. Silently, he looks the two men up and down. "This just seems odd that you would be out this late, Comrades."

Luís looks up into the man's face; the light from the hangar shines through his short-cropped hair. "We just wanted to be sure that everything was all right before they left."

"All right, Comrades. Another time, we would have sat down and had a long talk about this. You can go." They walk away from the lone figure. In the darkness, they can feel his eyes burning into their backs. "You." Brock motions to the guard. "Come here."

Pablo walks up to him. "There are supposed to be two of you out here. Where's the other guard?"

"He went to get some coffee for us, señor."

Brock keys the walkie-talkie. "Val, this is Brock."

"Yes, Comrade, what now?"

"Is there a guard in there getting coffee?"

Val looks back at the coffee pot and sees the guard getting two cups of coffee. "Yes, he is getting some coffee."

"Well, that's the other asshole who is supposed to be guarding this plane. Could you ask him if he could get back to his post so we don't have any more night visitors. These guys couldn't guard their own asses if you tied them together."

"OK, Brock. I'll send him back out. Remember, they are our Latin Comrades."

Brock's voice comes back on the air. "Yeah, I remember, so fuck them."

Val shakes his head as he sets the walkie down. He can hear the air crew chuckling. "Comrade guard." Val turns towards the man at the coffee pot. "Are you guarding the plane?" The man nods his head. "I think you better report back to your post."

"Sí, señor. I was just getting some coffee."

Val turns back to his food, and waves his hand in the air.

Felix carries the two coffees and rolls out into the night, and heads for the plane. As he walks back, two men pass under a light on the side of a building. Felix nods his head as Miguel and Luís disappear back into the shadows. As he nears the hangar, he can see two men standing in front of the doors.

"Pablo, here is your coffee and rolls."

He takes them. "Gracias, Felix."

"I didn't know you were out here, señor, or I would have gotten you one also."

Brock shifts his stance. "The hell with the coffee. I want both of you right around this plane. We had two guys go on the plane."

"Sí, señor. It was Miguel and Luís. They had to fix something on the plane. Did you know about it?"

Brock looks deeply into his eyes. "I didn't." Brock turns on Felix. "Anyone getting near this plane will be checked by me. Do we understand each other, Comrades?"

"Sí, señor. It was so quiet, and there is a new feel in the air."

"Fuck the air. You don't leave this post until you are relieved. We will be taking over that duty in about thirty minutes. Can you hang on that long, Comrades?"

"Sí, señor Comrade."

Brock looks them both over and walks towards the mess hall, shaking his head. They watch him leave. Felix leans over and whispers to Pablo, "What an asshole."

"Sí, Felix. They all think something is going to happen all the time." They both walk out to the front of the plane. Sipping their coffee, they stop under the sharp nose.

Felix looks up at the sky. The clouds have blocked out the stars. "Do you feel something, Pablo?"

"Sí. The wind has stopped, and it is getting cooler."

"But also listen to how quiet it is?"

"That storm has changed its direction." They move over and stand in front of each wing.

"Yeah, I think the storm is coming." Pablo nods his head.

Meanwhile, as Brock enters the mess hall, the others look up and then go back to their breakfasts. He gets some coffee and walks over to sit next to Val, who looks up and smiles.

"Are the guards OK now, Comrade Brock?"

"Shit, if these assholes knew what they were guarding, they would shit their pants."

Val puts his hand on Brock's shoulder. "Enough Comrade, they are to have no idea of what is out there. We should not speak of it here."

Brock takes a sip of coffee, and nods his head.

"A pastry, señor?" The mess hall worker offers some to Brock.

"Have a pastry." Val nudges Brock's arm. "We have about twenty minutes before we meet everyone in the hangar."

Brock looks over the tray and takes two cinnamon rolls. "Thanks, Comrade."

He nods and moves over to the four men finishing their breakfast. The captain and the radar officer wave him off, but the others each take one. "These jelly ones, Comrade Captain, are great. You should try one."

"I'm afraid to. If you add very much more weight, we won't get off the ground." The air crew laughs together as the radio operator finishes his roll. Captain Mikulin pushes back his chair and gets up. He checks his watch.

"Comrades, we have about fifteen minutes to finish getting ready and meet the others in the hangar."

"Yes, Comrade Captain." The others push back from the table and follow him out the door.

Val finishes and stands up to leave. "Brock. We will assume the guard in about fifteen minutes at the plane, right?"

"Yes. And I will feel a lot better about it." As Val leaves, Brock gets up and walks over to the food counter and takes one more roll. Then he leaves to join the others.

Luís opens the door to the tech shop and throws the tool case in on the floor. He locks the door and rejoins Miguel on the path to the front gate. "You have everything packed. Right, Luís?"

"Yes, I will pick up my bag and catch the bus at 2:10."

"Good. Move quickly, my friend. Because they will begin a search immediately when the plane goes down. That Russian bastard will see to that."

As they continue to walk, Miguel checks his watch. "It's 1:45; we'll have a four and a half hour head start on them. Remember, the boat will be there at 6:00 P.M. If you miss it, you're on your own."

"I know, Miguel. You make sure that you get there on time."

"Right." He looks around to be sure they are all alone. They walk up to the front gate and show the guard their ID cards.

"You guys are working late, huh?"

"Yeah, we had to fix something on one of the planes."

"Here you go, Miguel. And you too, Luís. Go home and get some rest."

"Yeah, thanks, Juan. See you tomorrow."

When they reach the street, they turn and face each other. "For freedom my friend." Luís extends his hand.

"For freedom." Miguel clasps his hand and they shake. They move away from each other in opposite directions up the street. Their pace is quick. As Luís moves up the street, his eyes scan everything around him. Few people are out at this hour, just one or two heading home or going to work. But one never knows. That thought races through his mind.

"Want to have a good time, señor?" A figure steps out of a doorway and catches Luís by surprise.

"What the hell?" Luís looks into her face. "No, not now. Don't bother me." He pushes her aside.

"All right. No need to get rough. It could have been great." She laughs as she steps back into the shadows of the doorway. Luís draws a deep breath.

"Settle down," he tells himself. He looks down the street to the corner. A figure stands under a streetlight reading a paper. He looks up from his reading. His eyes look over the man passing near him on the sidewalk. Luís looks back over his shoulder, to make sure he is still there. The figure's head drops back to reading his newspaper. He picks up his pace as he moves down the street. Only two more blocks to the apartment.

As he rounds the corner, the sound of music drifts to him from a club up the road. Ahead of him, a group of people is drinking on the steps of one of the apartments. As he nears, two girls get up and move towards him. "Hey, señor. Want a good time?"

"No, not now. Let me by."

The three men on the steps get up and join the girls. "Señor, what's the matter? These girls not good enough?" They box him in as he approaches.

"No. They're fine. But I'm in a hurry." The smell of the rum they are drinking fills his nostrils.

"I don't think you like them." A hand pushes on his chest. "Or are you more interested in boys, señor?"

"I don't have time for this. Leave me alone."

"Ah, a man who has no time for pussy." The hand tightens on his arm. "Now this is some sort of man. One who needs no women." The men laugh as another hand grabs his other arm and they spin him around. The two girls stand facing him.

"A man who does not like these." She lifts her tee-shirt to expose her breasts. Luís strains at the hold on his arms, his eyes fixated on her breasts.

"Yes, but not now. I must be going."

She spins around, humming a tune, her breasts swaying to her movements. The other girl reaches down and grabs the hem of her skirt. Slowly she rises it. "Maybe this will change your mind."

Luís looks past her as she lifts her skirt. A police car slowly rounds the corner. The men see it too. "Maria, policía." She drops her skirt, and the other one pulls her tee-shirt down, as the car rolls to a stop at the curb beside them. A bright light from the car baths the small group. "Any problems here?"

"No, señor, just playing around." The hands move away from Luís's arms.

"We were just having some fun with this man, who is in such a big hurry."

The light falls on Luís. He hears the car door open. "Well, señor. What is so important at this early hour? May I see your papers?"

Luís's palms are sweaty as he takes his papers out of his pocket. The officer shines the light down on the papers, then back into his face, to check the photo.

"Is everything all right, Luís? You seem to be breathing hard, and your hands are sweaty."

"I'm fine. These ladies were showing me their wares. I guess I got a little excited." The light plays over the two women. Their tee-shirts are pulled tight over their breasts.

"I see what you mean." He hands back the papers. "Well, have a good night." The officer gets back in the car, and it slowly moves down the street.

The three men drink from a bottle being passed around. They offer Luís a pull on the bottle. "No thanks." He moves down the street at his former pace. "Shit." His mind rolls. "They almost got me picked up." Using his sleeve, he mops his forehead. "Just a little further," he mumbles. Reaching the steps, he takes them two at a time. With one more quick look down the street, he races up to his apartment on the second floor.

As the door closes behind him, he leans on its cold surface. Crossing the room, he turns on a small lamp. His duffel bag is laying near a chair. Quickly he moves into the bathroom to relieve himself. His reflection stares back at him from the mirror over the sink.

"Did we do the right thing?" His mind seems clouded. Turning the faucet, he splashes cold water over his neck. Another scoop by his hands brings cool relief to his heated face. "I have to get going." His eyes follow the rivulets of water running down his face.

Removing his shirt, he grabs a clean one and walks back into the main room. Stopping at a nightstand next to the bed, he pulls the drawer open. "I'll need this." His hand picks up a pint of rum;

he slips it into his windbreaker. Grabbing his bag, he goes to the door and takes one last look around the apartment.

"This was good. But it would be better if we were free." When he reaches the street, he quickly checks his watch. "Good, I have time to get to the bus stop and sit down for a few minutes." Looking both ways, he heads for the bus stop.

Back at the base, the air crew heads for the hangar. As they cross the dark tarmac, two figures go racing by, heading for the mess hall. "Good morning, Captain Mikulin."

"Good morning, Lieutenants. You have fifteen minutes to make the meeting in the hangar."

"Yes, sir." We'll be on time." They call back over their shoulders as they reach the mess hall.

"Do you think they will make it, Captain?"

"Yeah, Nikie. These young fighter pilots are always on the run." The crew laughs among themselves as they move towards the hangar.

As the young pilots enter the mess hall, they look around for the coffee pot. "Ski, here is our savior. I'll get you a cup." He watches as Norba fills the cups.

"Thanks, I need it." They set their cups on a table and race down the serving line, loading their plates. They quaff their food down in a manner of minutes. Norba pushes his plate away and looks at his watch. "We need to get to the meeting in just a few minutes, Ski."

"Yeah, I know, Norba. We will get there on time." He looks up at his friend. "Norba, the woman I was with last night. What can I say? She knew things that would make Satan blush."

"Well, that's good, Ski. But we need to get going."

"Yeah, I know. But what a woman." They drink down their coffee, and head for the donuts. Each of them grabs three donuts and a cup of coffee to go. They leave the mess hall and head for the hangar.

Brock stands in the darkness at the front of the plane. He watches as the two Cuban guards are relieved. His platoon of special forces Spetsnaz begins moving out of the hangar in their shadow gray camies. Four of them take up positions around the bomber; each is carrying an automatic weapon. At each side of the open hangar door, machine guns are carried in.

Val joins Brock at the front of the plane. "I feel better now that we have taken over the guarding of the plane." Brock takes a deep breath. Val nods his head. "I must agree with you, Comrade Brock. I do feel better now."

They move under the wing of the bomber. Val checks the guards around the plane and at the hangar doors. As they enter the hangar, more guards stand in the back, outside a fenced area.

Val nods to Mikulin, as they walk up to join him and his crew. The two fighter pilots come into the hangar and move quickly over to join them. Mikulin smiles. "Well, you made it, Lieutenants. I was beginning to wonder."

"Yes, sir. We just wanted to grab some breakfast."

Mikulin looks over the two young fighter pilots. Each has three donuts and a cup of coffee in his hand. As always, they are moving at high speed. He checks his crew as Val steps in beside him.

"Gentlemen," Val addresses the group to get their attention. "The time has come to complete our mission here in Cuba. We will start loading to get you out of here by two o'clock." Brock looks at his watch; it reads 0130. They were right on time.

"Gentlemen, Comrade Mikulin will brief you on your flight." Val motions to Brock. They move to the back of the hangar.

"Gentlemen," Mikulin gathers the air crew and fighter pilots around him. "As you know, we will be loading the plane with some top-secret equipment. We will be ferrying back to Volstad air base. We'll take to the air at 0200. From here we will fly the Delta-1 route with our escort. This trip has been cleared with the Americans. It is considered a goodwill mission. We are the last of the offensive bombers to leave Cuba as part of our disarmament plan. I now suggest that we begin our preparations to depart at 0200 hours."

"Yes, sir." The men move away from Mikulin to begin their pre-flight checks. The two fighter pilots move back into the darkness and head for the next hangar. As they eat their donuts, they watch the sleek predatory birds gleaming in the lights from the hangar. The ground crews are making their last minute checks on the Mig-29s. Flashlight beams dance around under the two planes. The crew chief sees them coming and walks out to meet them. "Good morning, sirs." A quick salute passes in the dark. "Good morning, Comrade Sergeant. Are they ready to go?"

"Yes, sir. We completed all the loading last night. We're finishing up the routine checks."

"Would you like a donut, Sergeant?"

"Yes, sir." Ski hands over a glazed one. "We have the coffee pot going in the back, if you would like some more."

"No thanks, Sergeant. We need to get ready."

"Yes, sir. We'll see you back out here in a few minutes."

"Thank you, Sergeant." They head into the hangar to get their flight gear on. As they enter the hangar, Ski looks back at the bomber. Ground crew personnel are moving around the plane, but they are not flooding the area with lights. He can see the machine gun crews at the side of the door. "That's strange," Ski thinks to himself. "Whatever it is they're loading must be important."

As they enter the hangar, the sudden bright lights makes them squint. "Hey, Norba. Isn't it funny that we're on a peace flight, but both planes are carrying a full combat load of missiles?"

"I guess I have just enjoyed the chance to fly to Cuba."

"Well, Norba, whatever they're carrying in the Tupolev must be important."

He shrugs. "I guess." They enter the ready room and begin putting on their equipment.

Mikulin watches as the ground crew begins going through their final checks.

"Comrade Captain." The radar officer walks up to him.

"Yes, Kosa."

"Sir, I'm going over to the weather office to make a final check. That storm has changed direction and is now coming in from the southeast. We may encounter it earlier than we thought."

"Good, we don't want a sudden surprise to hit us."

"Yes, sir." Kosa disappears into the darkness, heading for the tower. The co-pilot and the radio officer are climbing up into the plane to begin their pre-flight checks.

"Comrade Captain." Val walks up to Mikulin. "We are ready to begin loading."

"All right, Comrade. Everything looks all right."

"Yes, sir." They move back to the fence gates, accompanied by to armed guards.

Val takes a key from around his neck. He inserts it into the top lock of the gate. Mikulin removes a key from around his neck, and places it in the lower lock. They both turn the keys in unison. The gate pops open.

"Thank you, Comrade Captain. We will get you loaded as soon as possible."

"Good. I'll get the ground crew ready." Mikulin walks back to the plane as Val motions to the men to move the tow vehicle up to the gate doors. Val walks up to the large metal door and wipes off the digital lock. He punches in a series of numbers. He works through the combination, and when the green light comes on, he reaches over and pulls the two steel handles. In a few seconds, the latches are thrown, and he pulls the large doors open. Entering the room, he turns on the lights. A large box sits on a dolly in the middle of the room. The smell of dampness fills his nostrils.

"Damn." He waves his hand in front of his face. "Bring the tow in."

The tow is backed in and the tongue on the dolly is snapped into place. Val steps aside as the large box is extracted from the vault. The box is marked with large red words in Russian: AERIAL CAMERAS—TOP SECRET. It is moved directly to the plane. Val has his Makarov 9 mm in his hand; it hangs at his side. Four other men, who are carrying assault weapons, join him.

Mikulin puts on a headset and plugs it into the plane. Nikie, his co-pilot, is doing routine checks on the equipment.

"Nikie, open the bomb bays."

"Roger." A green light goes on as he flips the switch. Under the plane, the doors slide apart. "We have a green light, Captain."

"Roger." Mikulin waves the tow driver into place. "Bring it in."

When he gets to the right position, he holds up his hand. "All right." He draws his hand across his throat. Two men climb onto the dolly and begin prying off the top of the container. Another man with the controls to the dolly waits next to Mikulin for orders. The top comes off in two sections; it is passed to men on the ground and moved away from the plane. The light in the bomb bays shines down on their faces.

"Nikie, stand by to load." A quick "roger" comes into his headset.

Mikulin looks over at Val and nods his head. Both men look around the area. Val gives him a thumbs up. He turns to the man with the dolly controls. "Bring it up halfway." The man nods and pushes a button. The dolly begins to scissor. It lifts the box upwards. The operator moves nearer to the dolly and squats to look up into the open bays. At the halfway point, the operator stops the lift. "Sir, it's in position."

"Very good." Mikulin puts his hand on the operator's shoulder and squats down next to him. "Remove the sides of the box."

The men on the dolly begin prying off the sides of the box. Others below them help pull the sections out and onto the ground. Mikulin watches their progress. "Nikie, lower the connectors." A special frame in the bay is lowered over the cylindrical object. The men on the dollies snap the connections in place on the smooth top portion.

"We're connected, Comrade Captain." They give him a thumbs up.

"Nikie, check your panel."

"Roger." His eyes go to the bomb display. "Sir, we're showing green on the connections. Loading frame is in a down position."

"Roger. We're going to pull it on board."

"Panel shows clear."

Mikulin taps the operator and the dolly lifts higher. The two men climb down as it is pushed upwards into the bay and stops. They walk around the load, and give Mikulin a thumbs up. "Nikie, bring the load on board."

"Roger." The frame moves up into the bay and sits suspended above the dolly. "Sir, we have green across the board."

The dolly is lowered and towed out of the way as everyone clears back from the plane. Mikulin, Val and Brock walk in under the open doors for a final check. They look up at the large white cylindrical load. Mikulin checks around the sides, and gives Val a thumbs up. Val shakes his head. "I'll be glad when this delivery is over."

"Agreed." Brock takes a last look.

"Gentlemen, we need to clear this area. And get the doors closed," Mikulin says as they walk out under the wing. "Nikie, close the bay doors."

"Roger." The doors slowly close, and darkness creeps back under the plane.

"Sir, we are secured."

"Roger. I'm disconnecting." Mikulin takes off the headset and rolls the cord up. He hands it to the dolly operator.

"Good job, gentlemen."

"Thank you, sir." The ground crew moves away from the plane. Only the guards around the perimeter of the plane remain.

Val puts his hand out. "Good luck, Comrade Captain."

Mikulin smiles and they shake. "Thanks for the help on this mission, Val. And you too, Brock."

"Thank you, sir." Brock shakes his hand. "Have a good flight."

Right. How soon will you guys be leaving?"

"We're flying out on Friday with the rest of the recovery team. We should see you back in Archangel in about a week."

"Excellent. We'll meet at the coffee shop and laugh at this whole affair."

Val smiles. "Very good, my friend. We'll see you soon." Val and Brock head for the radio room at the side of the hangar.

Mikulin makes his final check of the aircraft, talking briefly with the ground crew. He is just walking up to the hatch to get on board when Kosa walks up.

"Captain, we have a situation. That storm is coming in right behind us. In about another hour, nothing will be leaving this island. The storm has been raised to possible level two hurricane."

"Well, let's not wait around here." He gestures for Kosa to get on the plane. Once up, Mikulin secures the hatch, then makes his way up to his seat. After belting in, he puts on his helmet and begins checking his instruments.

"Captain, pre-flight checks are completed."

"Thank you, Nikie. Everything looks good."

The radar officer takes his place and begins turning up his instruments. "Sir, this is radar."

"Roger."

"Sir, that load we have is displaying a full weapons load."

"Yes, I know. Is everyone up on the intercom?"

"Yes, sir."

"Good, gentlemen. I will now give you the last portion of our pre-flight briefing. Our load is not camera equipment. It is a full nuclear load."

"But, sir—" a voice cuts into the net.

"All right, just let me finish. It was thought best not to tell anyone about our load until now. The reason is that these weapons should not have been here. Since this is a goodwill mission, knowledge of our load was restricted. We will fly the Delta route with our escort, being duly gracious to our American escorts. On our final turn on the route, we will refuel. From there our course will be back across the Atlantic, to arrive in Volstad. This way the Americans will never know of the weapons being here, and we will rejoin our comrades. I ask only that we all do our jobs, and we have a good flight. Also, the fail-safe system is locked in the guarded position; the weapons cannot be armed. Are there any questions?"

"No, sir." The response comes from each of the other positions.

The airman at the front of the plane signals the start up of the engines. "Number one coming up."

Mikulin's hand flips some switches, and moves the throttle forward. "Roger. Number one up."

"Number two coming up." The huge engines roar into life. Both pilots check the gages in front of them. The glow from the gages shines off their helmets and visors.

"Sir, Raven 1 is calling."

"OK, tie us into the TAC net."

"Roger, sir." As his words die away, the voice traffic rushes into the headset.

"Bear 117, this is Raven 1. Over."

"Roger, Raven."

"Sir, we are cleared to taxi. We will meet you at altitude. Over."

"Roger, Raven 1." Mikulin looks out the right side window and watches as the two Migs move away from the hangar and head for the main runway. As the fighters turn, two red and orange eyes appear at their tails as they taxi towards the runway.

"Flight 117, this is the tower. Over."

"Roger, tower."

"You may begin to taxi. There is traffic in front of you. Over."

"Roger, tower. Have traffic in sight."

Mikulin looks down at the man in front of the plane. "Sir, have a good flight. Ground out."

"Thanks, we'll see you in Volstad."

The airman disconnects his headset and walks to the left front of the plane. He raises two red flashlights and begins waving the plane forward. It begins following a bright yellow line. After a short distance, the line takes a long curve and runs beside the main runway. The airman with the lights brings both of them together and aims them along the line. As the plane passes, he salutes. Mikulin returns the salute as they move down the taxi strip.

They listen as the two fighters are given final OK to take off. The two jets stand frozen in position as tongues of flame roar from their exhaust. Suddenly they vault forward at ever-increasing speed. About halfway down the runway, they pull their noses up to the stars. They rocket into the sky.

"Flight 117, you are cleared to take off. Over."

"Roger." Mikulin turns the bomber onto the runway and lines it up. The path through the cold air by the fighters can still be seen in front of them. Mikulin makes a last minute check of his gages and pushes forward on the throttles. The bomber shudders slightly as the power is turned on, and then begins moving down the runway.

"Half flaps, Nikie."

"Roger. Half flaps."

The wings at their full forward position cut through the cold air. The engines gobble up the cool morning air and push more power out the exhausts. As they gain forward speed, the nose slowly begins to rise with a slight pull backward on the yoke. It seems to just suddenly be airborne. The stars now begin to appear in the front windshield as they rise higher into the sky.

"Radar is clear, sir."

"Roger, Kosa."

"Tower this is 117. Over."
"Roger, 117."
"Proceeding to cruise altitude."
"Roger. Have a good flight."
"Roger, tower. Flight 117."
The nose of the plane continues on a slight vertical heading as Mikulin begins a slow left-hand turn. "Radar, do you have our two young friends on the scope?"
"Yes, sir. They are at 25,000 feet and circling."
"Good. Raven leader, this is Bear. Over."
"Roger, Bear."
Mikulin looks out the windows but cannot see anything, except the ground lights growing smaller. "Raven, join on me. Over."
"Roger, Bear. Beginning turn to join on you now."
Mikulin watches the altimeter climb past 25,000 to 30,000 and level off.
"Sir, come to course 345 northwest."
"Roger. 345. Any sign of our friends?"
"Yes, sir." Nikie points out the side window. As Mikulin looks out his side, the sleek form of the Mig hangs in the air off his wing tip. He smiles to himself.
"Nikie, give me wings back a half."
"Yes, sir. Wings back a half." He looks out his side as the wings move back. Moisture in the air sweeps off their tips.
Mikulin keys his mike. "Raven leader, we are on a heading of 345 northwest at 450 knots. Over."
"Roger, Bear. 345 northwest at 450 knots. Over."
"Roger, Raven leader. Do try and keep up. Over."
"Roger, Bear. We'll do our best. Raven out."
The three begin the first leg of the Delta route. They move north to run along the coast of Florida. At a land radar site on the tip of Florida, the three have not gone unnoticed. Their direction and speed are duly noted. The operator keys his mike.
"Sir, three bogies leaving Cuba. Heading 345, air speed 450 knots. I believe our Red friends have just left Cuba."
"Roger. Vector interceptors into escort position." Two F-16 fighters lift off of the south Florida mainland and rise quickly into the night.

CHAPTER 2

OVER THE GULF

As Mikulin looks out his side window, he can spot the lights of ships in the Gulf. The weather is clear, and the star's blaze above them like diamonds. This is the time the captain loves. He enjoys the sound and feel of the plane, and the sky like an endless path in front of him.

"Sir."

Mikulin comes back from his thoughts. "Yes."

"Sir, I have two bogies coming in at three o'clock."

"Roger, Kosa. That should be the American jets coming up."

"Yes, sir. Large radars have swept us since we left Cuba. These two are also sweeping."

"Roger."

Mikulin looks out the side window; the nose of the Mig is pulled up a bit.

"Raven, this is Bear. Over."

"Roger, Bear."

"I know you have also picked up the two bogies. Over."

"Roger. We're on infrared. Over."

"We will continue our flight with no overt gestures. Over."

"Roger, Raven." Nikie looks out his side window to try and catch a glimpse of the approaching jets.

The two F-16 fighters climb into the clear night sky. The lead pilot keys his mike. "Lands End, this is Falcon leader. Over."

"Roger, Falcon."

"We have three boogies at 30,000 feet. We'll break at three miles and take up a twelve o'clock position at their rear. Over."

"Falcon, we will turn you over to Top Hat in one hour. They will be taking up a position northwest of your flight. Over."

"Roger."

"Lands End, contact Top Hat in one hour. Over."

"Falcon, we have you five miles for visual contact."

The two F-16 fighters begin a slow right turn at three miles. They take up a position above and behind the three jets. As they ease up behind them, they finally get a view of the group. They had only seen these types of aircraft in films and photos.

"Axeman, this is Rapper. Over."

"Roger, Rapper."

"If I'm not mistaken, we have two Mig-29 Fulcrums up here with us."

"Roger that."

Mikulin waits until they are in position behind them. He keys his mike on the American TAC frequency. "Falcon 1, this is Bear. Over."

Axeman looks ahead at the three aircraft. "Roger, Bear. Falcon 1."

"Good morning, sir. This is Captain Mikulin aboard the Tupolev."

"Good morning to you, sir. You picked an early start for your flight."

"Yes, it is less busy, and the weather was getting pretty bad."

"Roger that, Bear."

"Falcon, we will make a course adjustment at 0245. That will take us to Point B. Over."

"Roger, we were told that this is the last flight of the Delta Route. Over."

"Yes, we will end another piece of the cold war. And we look forward to many years of peace in the world."

"Roger, Bear. We both share that dream. Falcon out." The five continue through the night. At 0245, they execute a slight turn and continue into the night sky.

Norba looks forward at Mikulin and out the front of the plane. "Sir, we will be coming into a front."

"Roger, I'm beginning to see the clouds ahead." Mikulin makes some adjustment to the trim.

"It seems to be a trailer from the thunderstorms coming in from the southwest. It looks to be just rain squalls."

"Roger, Kosa. What's the status of the storm coming in from behind?"

"It looks big. It was making twenty knots, but when it hit the island it slowed down."

"Good. We'll be joining the Badger in-flight refueler east of its path, and then continue back home. Our two little gas guzzlers will like that."

"Yes, sir." Kosa goes back to his scope, rechecking their location and watching the storms around them.

"Sir, we're receiving a communications burst from the satellite."

"Roger. Break it down and let's see what they want to know."

"Yes, sir." The communications officer runs the message through a decoder and puts it up on the screen next to Mikulin. "Sir, it's a message from the air marshal in Moscow. Comrade Val has confirmed the loading and security at the base. He is aware of the storm hitting Cuba and requests a mission status."

"Roger. Send this: mission is progressing as planned, will bypass sever storm. Will keep with ETA Volstad. Looking forward to dinner in Archangel."

The communications officer sets his equipment, and sends a burst back to the satellite.

At the war room in Moscow, the message is received and decoded. The operator carries it down the hall to the air marshal's office. He knocks and goes in.

"Sir, we have the reply back from Cuba, flight 117." He hands it to the man behind the large desk.

"Thank you, comrade." His eyes read the message and he reaches for a nearby phone. "Comrade Secretary, please. This is Air Marshal Shagan."

"Yes, sir. He has been expecting your call."

Shagan holds on the line, and rereads the message.

"Comrade Shagan, it is good to hear from you."

"Sir, the Archangel flight is proceeding according to plan. I have just received confirmation from Captain Mikulin. I knew you were concerned about the weather."

"Yes, I was briefed on the storm. It looks like everything will end well."

"Yes, Comrade Secretary."

"Please call me if any changes or problems develop."

"Yes, sir."

They both hang up, and Shagan dials another number. The officer in the communications center answers the phone. "This is Marshall Shagan. If there are any changes or any more communications with flight 117, I want to be informed immediately."

"Yes, sir."

Shagan hangs up the phone, and turns his attention to other matters.

REGIONAL COMMAND CENTER
PENSACOLA, FLORIDA

The night duty operators watch the progress of the five planes. The watch officer walks up behind him at the console. "That's the Russian flight in the Gulf, huh?"

"Yes, sir. They're on course. I've been watching them since our fighters left Lands End." His finger points to the blips on the screen. "These are the two Falcons escorting. Apparently there are two Mig-29 fighters with it." They watch as the images move on the map of the Gulf. "They're right on the Delta route." He flips a switch and superimposes the route in red on the screen.

"Well, everything looks nice and peaceful." He pats the operator on the shoulder. "I'm going to run down to the mess hall. Do you want anything?"

"No, sir. But thanks."

As the officer goes to leaves, he scans the images on the map once more.

RUSSIAN BOMBER
NORTHERN GULF AREA

"Captain, we're going to be—" The words are cut short as the plane suddenly buffets in the air. Kosa looks forward at the back of Mikulin's seat. He watches as his helmet turns in his direction. "As I was saying, sir, we're going into some turbulence from the storm." He sees the twinkle in the eyes between the helmet and his oxygen mask.

"Roger, Kosa. That was a pretty good call."

Mikulin turns back to the front, and keys his mike. "Raven leader. Over."

"Roger, Bear."

"We're going to cut back to 400 knots and extend our wings."

"Roger, Bear. We'll be moving out and back a bit for more room. Over."

"Roger, Raven." Mikulin adjusts his radio. "Falcon, leader."

"Roger, Bear."

"We will be extending our wings because of the turbulence and dropping back to 400 knots. The fighters will be moving out and back for safety, in case we need to maneuver."

"Roger, Bear. We are repositioning now. Out."

Mikulin watches as the jets begin repositioning themselves away from the bomber. "OK, Nikie. Wings at full extension. I'm powering back to 400 knots."

"Roger, Captain. Wings forward and locked."

As the planes move about, they are shaken by the turbulence. Mikulin's hands grip the yoke harder. The plane is suddenly pushed one way and then the other. Lightning streaks through the sky to the left of the planes. The silver-blue light illuminates the group as the boom of the thunderclap shakes the planes. "Sir, I'm picking up three bogies due north of our position at different altitudes."

"Roger." The yoke jerks in Mikulin's hands. "That's outbound traffic from Pensacola."

Nikie looks out his side as another flash of lightning streaks across the sky. He can tell that the fighters are having a time of it in the turbulence. The lights flicker around the cockpit. "Sir, going to combat lights."

"Roger, Nikie. The blinking lights are a distraction." The cabin area is now bathed in a soft red glow. Mikulin checks the flight panel. "That's better."

Nikie turns facing back into the cabin. "Kosa, check the fuses on the overhead lights. We may have blown one."

Kosa turns to a panel behind him. Finding the culprit, he resets the switch. "Found it. It's reset." As he looks back to his scope, the flashing lightning flares across the screen.

"Bear, this is Falcon. Over."

"Roger, Falcon."

"Sir, we are about to turn you over to the navy. We're being ordered back to our base because of the hurricane coming. We should be picking them up as we pass south of Mobile. They will escort you on the completion of your route."

"Roger, Falcon. It is getting a little testy up here. It was good flying with you, gentlemen. Bear out."

"Good luck on the rest of your flight, sir. Falcon out."

Mikulin turns towards his co-pilot. "Nikie, would you take the controls. I need to check something."

His hands grab the yoke, the plane shakes for a second. "Got it."

"Thank you." Mikulin picks up a small bag next to him, and checks a small map enclosed in plastic. He lifts his head and looks out the window. "Kosa."

"Sir."

"I see us at a position just south of Pensacola."

"Roger, sir. These head winds are costing us in both fuel and time."

"Roger." Mikulin checks his watch. "It's 0345; we're doing all right. Make the fix for the south-bound leg."

"Yes, sir. A question, sir? Why do we have all of this tracking radar, when you have your little maps?"

A smile comes across Mikulin's face. "I just can't give them up; they make me feel more in charge of my own destiny."

"Roger, sir. I'm computing our turn and fuel amounts."

"Raven."

"Roger, Bear."

"We are computing our upcoming turn and fuel now. How are you doing?"

"The head wind is causing us to use more fuel, but we'll be OK to the Badger. Over."

"Raven, you heard that we will be getting a new escort soon?"

"Roger. My sweeps say they're on their way now, about ten kilometers northwest of us. Over."

"Roger, Raven. Contact confirmed. Bear out."

Two F-14 Tomcats cut through the morning sky; they sweep the formation as they climb. Their wings tucked back, they throw swirls of condensation as they maneuver in the humid air. "Falcon leader, this is Shark leader. Over."

"Roger, Shark. Welcome to the formation."

"Falcon, we will move into your slots as you pull out. Over."

"Bear, this is Falcon."

"Roger, Falcon."

"Sir, our replacements are here. We will be breaking off. Good luck in this weather, and have a good flight back home. Falcon out."

"Roger, Falcon. Good flying to you also. Over."

The two Falcons rise up out of the formation. They form up and take a left turn. They are quickly gone into the night. The two Tomcats ease up into position just outside of the Migs. The formation is flying in a wide "V". The Tomcat pilots and the Mig pilots look each other over in the light from lightning strikes.

"Shark, this is Bear. Over."

"Roger, Bear. This is Shark leader. Over."

"We welcome you out into this less than favorable weather."

"Roger, Bear. So you're the last? Over."

"Roger. Let's hope so, Shark. We will be making our final southern turn in fifteen minutes. Over."

"Roger, fifteen minutes to turn. Over."

The Tomcat leader adjusts his radio to another frequency. "Top Hat, this is Shark 1. Over."

"Roger, Shark 1."

The big E-3 Sentry AWACS flies its oblong route off the Florida coast.

"Top Hat, we are assuming escort of two Mig-29 fighters and one Backfire bomber at 0345 hours. Over."

"Roger, Shark. Assuming escort at 0345 hours. We have you 5/5. We'll be orbiting at Catfish station. Over."

"Roger, Top Hat."

A navy E-2 Hawkeye takes up its position off the southern Louisiana coast. It begins tracking air traffic in the western Gulf. It contacts Ironman, and sends its updates to the command center. The sergeant in the control room at Ironman watches as the two Tomcat fighters replace the Falcons. He puts the weather overlay on the screen. "Damn," he says to himself. "That weather sucks big time." Using the new power of the Hawkeye on station, the overall picture of the area gets a lot clearer.

"Sir, we will be turning in two minutes, on the last leg of the route," says Kosa. "At that time, we will be directly south of Pascagoula, Mississippi."

"Roger, Kosa. Turn in two minutes." Mikulin looks over the gages and over at Nikie who is still flying the plane. Everything seems to be going well except for the weather. Just then, an invisible hand smashes into the side of the bomber. The big ship shudders.

The shuddering movements of the plane have caused the quartz timer in the black box to break its solder joint. It slides side ways and hits a capacitor next to it. It bends slightly on its soldered wire ends.

"Making turn to new heading now." The five aircraft make a slow left turn and begin the south run of the route. Nikie brings the plane level just as another gust of wind shudders the fuselage. "OK, Nikie. I'll take it back now."

"Yes, sir." He returns control of the plane back to Mikulin. "Man, that side blast of wind is deadly."

"Roger, Nikie." Mikulin can feel it in the control surfaces. He keys his mike. "Kosa, when do we get a break from this storm?"

"Sir, we should get clear just south of the Chandeleur islands. They're about thirty kilometers due west of us now. Over."

"Good. I'll be glad to get out of this stuff."

Kosa looks back down into his scope, looking ahead into the night. As he is looking into the hood, the plane hits a pocket of major turbulence. It shakes the whole length of the bomber. In the black box, it moves the quartz clock over the capacitor. The solder joint on the clock hits a pin on the board and the wire on the end of the capacitor. A bridge is formed between the two. The sudden power source begins loading it up. As it begins loading, it starts a low shrill whistle. The more it loads, the higher the pitch of the whistle becomes.

Kosa looks up from his scope and can just make out a high pitched tone near him. He notices that the radio operator is looking around also. "What the hell is that?" The radio operator shrugs his shoulders, and starts looking over his equipment. Kosa looks his station over.

"What's the matter?" Nikie looks back towards Kosa and the radio operator.

"I don't know."

"Kosa, what's that high pitched tone?"

Kosa shakes his head. "I don't know, but it almost sounds like a capacitor about to blow up."

"It sounds like it's coming from under my console." Kosa unbuckles and slides out of his chair.

"Well, check it out."

"Yes, sir." Nikie turns to watch as Kosa bends down to look under the console. He runs a small flashlight over the rows of equipment. The capacitor reaches its maximum load and discharges through the timer.

Mikulin has both hands on the yoke as an unbelievable pressure slams into him from behind. He is slammed into his harnesses as a red-orange ball of fire engulfs the cockpit. He blacks out as the bomber begins a slow right descending turn.

Ski, in his position out beyond the left wing of the bomber, is startled to see a bright orange and yellow flash explode from the side of the bomber. Before he can react, the tongue of flame carries shards of torn metal into the side of the Mig, just in front of his intake. He yells in pain and grabs his leg where the metal has ripped into his flesh. His right arm has gone dead, and his canopy is breached in two slashing rips. The wind tears into the cockpit with a frozen blast. His plane rolls to the left, and into a steep diving turn. Smoke begins billowing out of his right engine.

"Shit!" Shark 1 sees the explosion and the sudden maneuvers of the two aircraft. "Lobo, we have a major problem here."

As the bomber turns towards him, Norba pulls his Mig up out of its way. Shark 2 stays right with him; they both roll up into the night. "Bingo, what the hell is going on?"

"There was an explosion on the bomber, and the shrapnel ripped into the Mig on this side."

"I'm with Mig number two' he has gone weapons up. This could get touchy."

"Roger that. Stay with him. I'm going after the other Mig. Heat everything up until we find out what is going on." Both Tomcats arm all weapons systems.

"I roger that. Over." Their targeting radars begin picking up the Migs as they maneuver through the sky. Shark 2 rolls over and dives to join up with Ski's Mig. As he nears it, he can tell the pilot is trying to regain control.

"Bear, this is Raven leader. Over." He pauses. "Bear, this is Raven leader. Over." Norba's calls go unanswered, as the bomber continues to descend.

The refueling plane south of them hears the calls and joins in the net.

"Raven, this is Badger 1, receiving you 5/5. Over."

"Badger, the bomber and Raven 2 have been hit. Both have fallen out of formation. We have a mayday situation. I cannot raise Bear leader. I'm going hot; the American escort may have fired on us. They are arms up. I'm getting tone from the fighter behind me. We are in trouble. Mayday."

The circling Badger aerial tanker acknowledges the call and radios back to the command center outside of Havana. They pass on the mayday message from the fighter.

CUBA

A call is made to General Morales at his home. He is woken by an aide.

"What is the matter? What has happened?"

"Sir, the Russians have been fired on by American fighters. We have a mayday message from the escort fighter. The other one has been hit also."

"I told them." He slams his hand into the bed. "The Americans have given us an opportunity to teach them a long overdue lesson." He picks up the phone next to him. "Give me the duty officer."

"Yes, sir, General."

"Sir, this is the captain." His words are cut short.

"Send fighters to assist the Russians. They are to assume that any other aircraft in the air are hostile. Put all forces on condition red."

"Yes, sir." The phone goes dead. The duty officer reaches over the operator and pushes a red switch forward. "Everyone, General Morales has ordered all forces to condition red. Controllers are to dispatch fighters to assist the Russian bomber and to take up defensive positions around the island."

Alarms sound at air bases along the north coast of Cuba. Missile batteries are brought on-line as the Cuban military goes to full alert. Fighters are being armed with missiles and sent towards the north.

THE GULF

"Bear, this is Raven. Over." Still no reply.

"Norba, this is Ski." He fights the pain in his leg, and pulls the nose of the Mig up. "There was an explosion on the Topolov. I've been hit by shrapnel. I have shut down one engine, will need to land."

"Ski, were you fired on? Over."

"No, I repeat, no. The explosion came from the bomber."

"Raven, this is Shark. There was an explosion on the bomber. Over."

"Roger, Shark. My English is not so good. I am hit and losing power in my right engine. I have shut it down. Over."

"I will stay on this frequency. Hold one." He switches his radio to the TAC net. "Top Hat, Top Hat, this is Shark. Over."

"Roger, Shark. We see dispersal of aircraft. What is your situation?"

"We have a mayday situation. There has been an explosion on the bomber, and one of the Migs has been hit with shrapnel. Over."

"Roger, Shark leader. We saw the bomber suddenly make a diving turn and the Migs rolling out."

"Top Hat, we have gone weapons up status. The other Mig does not know what has happened and it could get dicey. Over."

"Roger, Shark." An officer joins the chief at his console on the AWACS.

"Damn, we had better get some help up there with the Shark flight. And contact the Coast Guard."

"Yes, sir."

"Coast Guard, this is Top Hat. We have a mayday situation. Over."

"Roger, Top Hat." The Coast Guard communication center takes the call and gets locations from them. He hits an alarm. At the docks at Breton Sound, the cutter *Southwind* begins to prepare for a possible water landing. The helicopter base is informed and two crews are woken. They dress for their briefing.

"Raven 2. Over." Norba has rolled his Mig in behind the lead Tomcat. Shark 2 has a loud buzz in his threat indicator, his cockpit is full of the tone. Shark 1 lines up behind the Mig. Norba hears his tone indicator register a lock on him.

"Raven 1, I've been hit. There was an explosion on the bomber. It came from inside the bomber."

"Ski, what are you saying?"

"Norba, the explosion came from the bomber. I've been hit by pieces of the plane."

The piper on the heads up display in front of Norba blinks red on the back of the Tomcat before him. At his rear another HUD blinks red with the piper lined up on his rear. Fingers rest lightly on triggers, a hair's breath from firing.

"Norba, the American has called a mayday to the Coast Guard. I've shut down power in my starboard engine. I've been hit in the leg, and the canopy has a couple of holes in it. Over."

"Roger, Ski. The Topolov has dived below us."

"Raven flight, this is Top Hat. Do you need an interpreter. Over."

"Roger, Top Hat. This is Raven; our English is not so good."

"Roger. Hold Raven." The next voice on the radio comes in Russian. He talks with the two Mig pilots and gets their status.

"Shark, this is Top Hat."

"Roger."

"The Migs know that the explosion came from the bomber. The Mig leader is going weapons down. He will be pulling out and going after the bomber. Over."

"Roger, Top Hat."

"Shark flight going weapons down. Over."

In the lead Tomcat, his missile tone goes quiet, and he switches his system to stand by. Norba lifts above the two fighters as his tone goes silent. Shark leader tells his wingman to form on the crippled Mig and escort him back to the base. He will join the second Mig and go after the bomber.

"Shark leader, there are aircraft taking up position all around the Gulf. You will have a flight of Cats with you soon. They're scrambling now. Over."

"Roger, Top Hat. I'm joining on the Mig. Over."

"We will have an open line to the Mig. If you have a question, the interpreter will pass it on. We have the bomber at 10,000 feet, at five miles. It seems to have leveled off. Over."

The search radars on both the fighters find the bomber. They dive away from the others; their wings pull back as they both go to afterburners. The dart-like shapes dive from 30,000 feet into the darkness below. Ski looks out the right side of his plane and levels the Mig off. Some of his instruments have been shattered. The cold wind rips in at him through the two holes in the canopy and the hole near his right leg. He puts a cord around his leg and pulls it tight. The pain almost causes him to black out. The sky has lightened up, but it is still too dark to see down below him. He looks to the right and sees the Tomcat; it has its running lights on. The Russian voice comes back into his headphones. "Raven 2, this is Top Hat."

"Roger, Comrade."

The interpreter conveys the headings to the base. He says that a Russian-speaking controller will bring him in. At the same time, Shark 2 is told of the Mig's situation. "Shark, the Mig will stay with you back to the base. He has enough fuel and power to make it. He is hurt pretty bad, but says he can get it down. You will be coming in almost due east of the base. They're getting ready with medical units and crash equipment. We will be handing you over to them. Over."

"Roger, Top Hat. We're heading in. Thanks. Over."

"Roger, Shark 2. It's our job, sir. Good luck. Over."

As Shark 1 and Norba's Mig catch up with the bomber, they are surprised to see it in almost level flight. Norba eases his Mig up off the left wing of the bomber. Both fighters have their running lights on. "Bear, this is Raven. Over."

The call is repeated over and over. Mikulin can hear the call, but it's like it's coming from a long way off. He moves his head and immediately gets a sharp pain in his shoulders. His left hand grasps the yoke. The still-smoldering glove on his right hand seems to be burned into his flesh. The instruments are a shamble. He tightens his grip on the yoke and rolls his radio with his left hand. His movements are from years as a pilot because the pain in his head will not let him concentrate. "Bear, this is Raven.

Over." The voice suddenly booms into his earphones. His left hand toggles his mike switch.

"This is Bear. Over." His voice seems foreign to him as he tries to move his jaw. Pain answers his attempt.

"Comrade, we thought we had lost you. What is your situation?"

Mikulin tries to clear his thoughts. "I'm hurt badly. I think I'm the only one alive. There was an explosion at the radar position. Cockpit is a mess." His voice just drifts away on the radio.

"Bear, the Americans have called a mayday in for both you and Raven 2. He was hit by shrapnel and is trying to make it to an airfield. Bear, can you turn on your landing lights?"

"Roger." Mikulins hand reaches for a panel nearby and flips a switch. The landing lights shine along the front of the bomber. Norba looks over the side of the plane. The light shines on a huge smoldering hole on the side of the bomber.

"Bear, you have a two meter hole just behind you. The metal is peeled out; there are also tears in the wing. What caused the explosion?"

Mikulin looks back as far as he can. The right side of his face burns from the effort. His good eye shuts in sympathy with his swollen right eye. "I think we have been sabotaged." Again Mikulin fights the pain to look around the cockpit. He finally sees the horror of the scene. Nikie was looking back at the radar station, when the blast hit him. His torso is strapped in his seat, with no arms or head. The windows next to him are blown out. The instrument panel is full of holes and blood covers the floor. He turns to look back at the radio position. The operator was gone; a shredded heap of smoldering flesh remains. It looked like a shot gun had been fired into the area. There was no need to look at the radar position; all that was left is a gaping hole. Kosa was completely gone. The jerking of the plane brings his attention back to the front.

"Raven, this is really bad."

"Roger, Comrade Mikulin. I will be with you all the way."

"Raven, contact the base and let them know what has happened. Tell them to get Val in on this."

At NAS New Orleans, four Tomcats race down the runway and rocket into the morning sky. As they rise out of sight, four more take their place. They also race down the runway and into the sky.

"Top Hat, this is navy flight 108."

"Roger, 108."

"We are going to afterburners. We're on your heading to target area. Over."

"Roger, Mig 1 is at 20,000 feet heading into base. The bomber and Mig 2 are sixty miles out. Over."

"Roger. We'll be on the scene in just a few minutes. Over."

In the control room at Ironman, the sergeant at the console panel has seen the Gulf flight suddenly go flying in all directions. "Holy shit, sir."

The young captain looks up at the screen. The once placid "V" formation has broken apart. "Sir, the call in from Top Hat is that all planes have gone hot. And they're scrambling jets out of NAS New Orleans."

"What the hell happened?"

"Now were getting a mayday about explosions on two of the aircraft."

As they watch the screen, two fighters join the bomber. The other two start for the coast. The officer picks up a red phone next to the console.

"Ultima, we have a blue flash message. We have a situation in the Gulf."

At the war room in Washington, an officer picks up the phone. "Stand by, Ironman."

As the line sits silent, other officers and men at other consoles join the men at Ironman. At a nearby position, another officer looks at the screen and picks up a phone. "To all commands in the Gulf area, a yellow condition is in effect."

All military bases on the Gulf come to life. Men pour out to assigned areas and prepare their planes for immediate take off.

In Washington, Ultima comes back on the line. "Ironman, the Secretary is being informed now on what seems to be the situation in the Gulf. AWACS aircraft are getting airborne now. You are in tactical command until we can get into position. We will remain at condition yellow to see where events go. We will get back to you. Ultima out."

As the E-3 Sentry orbits its station, eight blips appear in the southwest quadrant. "We have company, sir. Eight bogies inbound from Cuba, heading towards the bomber." The officer leans over his shoulder and looks at the scope. He keys his mike. "Ironman, we have eight bogies inbound. Over."

"Roger, Top Hat. We are tracking the bogies. Over."

Another AWACS aircraft comes on station. "Ironman, this is Sky 1. We are on station. We confirm Top Hats bogies. Over."

"Roger, Sky 1."

The screens at Ironman are revised to show the eight new aircraft heading towards the scene. "Sir, we have confirmed they are fighters. They must think we shot the bomber down." The officer next to him picks up the phone again.

"Gulf command, this is a flash message from Ironman. Get Gulf air caps up. And have southern Florida send air cap to cover AWACSs. We have Sky 1 on net. Over."

Jets begin lifting off from bases all around the Gulf. They proceed to prearranged areas. "Ironman, this is Sky 1. Over."

"Roger, Sky 1."

"Ironman, we are getting a full alert situation from Cuba. We assume that fighters inbound are coming in hot. Repeat, inbound presumed hot."

"Hound, this is Raven. Over. Hound, this is Raven. Over." Norba resets his frequency. "Hound, this is Raven. Over." The operators at the Cuban control center try to find the right frequency of the Mig. "Roger, Raven, ssssssiiiiiiiier."

"Hound, you're breaking up. Over."

"Raven, siiissiiii storm is siisiii over base. You are breaking up."

"Badger, this is Raven. Over."

"Roger, Raven. We are receiving you 5/5. Over."

"Badger, can you reach Hound from your location?"

"Roger. We'll pass your message on." Raven tells them what has happened. It is passed on to ground control at the airfield in Cuba."

"Ironman, this is Sky 1. We have an additional aircraft which are moving into position due south of our position. We ID as Badger type aerial tanker. Over."

"Roger, Sky 1. We confirm tanker location."

MATANZAS AIR BASE
CUBA

The door suddenly flies open and the Russian runs into the room, soaking wet. "Comrade Val! Comrade, the bomber has been fired on." He turns the light on as the sleeping forms of Val and Brock sit up in their beds.

"What? What the hell are you talking about?"

The man sticks a wet piece of paper into Val's hand. "I'm going back over to the communications shack. The shit is hitting the fan."

The man rushes back out the door as quickly as he had come. Val reads the typed text over. "Shit, Brock. We need to get to the communications room now. The bomber and one of the fighters have been fired on and are going down." The two men dress hurriedly and race out the door to the communications room. They step out into the blast of the passing storm. Rain and wind tear at them all the way to the hangar. As they enter the communications room, the sound of the radio fills the room.

"What the hell has happened?" Val looks around.

"We're getting more info from the Badger. He used the word sabotage, but were not sure." Val shakes the water off his head.

"Shit. Get me the Badger. He can patch me through to Raven leader. What are the Cubans doing?"

"They sent out a flight of 21s. They're outbound now."

"What the hell? Get me the commander over at the tower." One of the men at the radios waves Val over. "I have the Badger." Val takes the headset and mike and begins talking to the air tanker. "Can you patch me through to Raven? Over."

"Roger."

Val is soon speaking with the Mig. "Norba, what the hell happened?"

"There was an explosion on the Topolov. I can see a hole behind the pilot of about two meters. It came from the inside. Mikulin used the word sabotage. Over."

The word rings in Val's mind as he looks around the room. "Roger, Raven. Keep us informed of the situation."

"Roger. Raven out."

Val takes off the headset and sets it down. "Do we have any coffee?"

"Yes, sir. I'll get a couple of cups."

"Thanks." He motions to Brock. "I think we have a real problem going." They each get a cup of coffee and drink a large swallow. "Sir, the base commander is on the line." Val takes the phone and explains the situation to the commander. "So you see. You need to recall the fighters or were going to have a goddamn war on our hands."

"Val, the response is a direct order from General Morales. The fighters will have to refuel at the tanker. Maybe by that time we will have gotten a better picture of the situation. From our radar picture, the entire Gulf area is at least on alert level yellow. There are more planes in the sky than I have ever seen."

"Thank you, commander. We will get back to you, as soon as we have more information." Val hangs up the phone.

OVER THE GULF

"Shark 1, this is NAV 108. We are at your twelve o'clock. Do you need assistance?"

"We're all right, 108." The pilot looks up and sees the running lights of the other Tomcats.

"Good, we have eight inbound from Cuba. We'll proceed to intercept. Sky 1, give us a vector to incoming bogies. Over."

"Roger, 108. Bogies are on heading. Hold one."

"108, we are receiving traffic. Inbound are being ordered to join up with their tanker and hold for further orders. You are directed to proceed due south and establish no fly zone at 100 miles. Over."

"Roger, Sky 1." The eight Tomcats turn to their right and proceed to their holding area.

"Top Hat and Sky 1, this is Ironman. Over." A "roger" is received from the two aircraft. "Sky 1 will assume tactical control of the southwest group. Top Hat will assume tactical control of the central area. Tactical control of the eastern area will be taken by south Florida. Over." Both acknowledge the message and watch as groups of fighters begin orbiting at pre-arranged positions.

"NAV 108, this is Sky 1. Over."

"Roger."

"You are being assigned as Hawk flight. Over."

"Roger, Hawk flight."

"Hawk leader, hold at your station. We have Fox flight moving in ten miles due east of your position. Tankers are being sent to each of your locations. Over."

"Roger, Sky 1."

"Sky 1, this is Fox leader. We are going into position. Over."

The operator on the Hawkeye watches his screen as the second flight of fighters moves into position. "What's our status, Chief?"

"Well, sir," he points to the screen, "we have the eight Tomcats holding here. And we have the second group of F-18s at this position. We also have a group of S-3 Vikings running ASW sweeps just behind the fighters. The tankers are just coming up on the screen. They will be on station in just a few minutes."

"Thanks, Chief." He reaches over and picks up a mike. "Ironman, this is Sky 1. Over."

"Roger."

"Ironman, we suggest all commercial flights be diverted out of this area. The Cubans are still running hot. Over."

The men in Ironman look at their screens. "Roger, Sky 1. We agree with your assessment."

Top Hat orbits and watches as other blips begin appearing on their screen. "Sir, we now have two additional flights out from Cuba. From radar and voice traffic, they are on full alert. We are also picking up high speed surface craft moving into positions off southern Florida and into the Gulf area." The information is sent to Ironman, as two air force groups move into position off southern Florida.

ULTIMA
WASHINGTON, D.C.

In the war room in Washington, the men and women watch as more and more blips appear on the screen. "Holy shit! The Cubans have sent out their *OSA* and *Komar* class boats. We are now getting word that their *Kotlin* class destroyers, and their

Riga class frigates are putting to sea. They have definitely gone full alert."

"Get Captain Van Nar. She is the duty officer tonight."

One of the men runs down a semi-dark hall to the duty officer's room. He knocks on the door. She is told of the problem and begins getting ready. Soon she is in the hall and walks back to the war room. As she enters, her attention is drawn to the screens. In her eighteen years in the navy, she had only seen this condition during Operation Desert Storm. Her training at the naval academy and the war college was going to be put to the test today.

OVER THE GULF

The cold wind brings some relief to the burns on Mikulin's body, but he is still being racked with pain trying to keep the bomber level. He looks out the window towards the Mig and feels some comfort in not being alone. He is cruising in at 10,000 feet and seems to be losing height. Scanning the panel, he notices that his hydraulic pressure is dropping. A blinking light next to him catches his eye. The fail-safe screen seems to be active. The side of the box is ripped open, and the screen is tilted away from him. With extreme pain he raises his right arm and reaches for the top of the box. He is unable to grab the top so he slides his claw-like hand over it and pulls it back to face him. His fingers leave a track across the face; blood or oil seems to cover most of it. In the track marks, he can see orange hue letters and numbers activating across the face. His mind pushes the pain out to grasp what seems to be happening. Taking a piece of torn cloth, he drags it across the face of the screen; it smears the thick ooze. The bomber shudders in its wounded state, causing him to direct his attention back to the front.

Once he gets the plane back on course, he raises his right hand and looks at the rag. Its rich red color explains the oily covering on the screen. He rolls it on his leg, trying to find a clean spot. Reaching over, he again wipes the face of the screen. It clears most of the blood off. The numbers and letters are forming into eight individual boxes. A flash of an electrical short pops behind the top of the box. The screen flashes and all of the activity on the screen stops. Each box is complete.

"Sky 1, this is Shark 1. Over."

"Roger, Shark 1. We have you on a straight line to NAS New Orleans. Can the bomber be landed? Over."

"Roger, Sky 1. Captain Mikulin believes he can get the bomber down. It's in bad shape but seems to be holding together. Over."

"Roger, Shark 1. We have now declared an Echo 1 Intrusion to Ultima, as of 0400 hours on the Backfire. You will now deal directly with NAS New Orleans. Call sign Touchdown. They have a Russian speaker in the tower for your assistance. Good luck. Over."

"Roger."

"Shark 1, this is Touchdown. Over."

"Roger, Touchdown."

"We have you at fifty miles due east of base. We will be landing Shark 2 and the Mig in a few minutes. Preparation for your landing are set. Over."

"Roger, Touchdown. We will go feet dry in twelve minutes. Over."

At the naval station, emergency crews are assembled to move as soon as the Mig is down. The bundled up figures wait by their equipment, searching the dark morning sky for the two planes.

"Shark 2, we have you at five miles. You're on the glide path; you will be coming in on runway fifteen eastwest. All ground lights are up. Radar has you inbound three miles. Over."

"Roger, Touchdown. We can see the field."

Ski moves his hand. It feels like it is frozen. The air still rushes into the cockpit of the Mig. He pushes the landing gear lever and feels the thump of the wheels going down. A Russian voice comes over the radio. "Raven, this is Touchdown. Over."

"Roger, Touchdown."

"Good, you're on the flight path. If you have any questions just speak up. Over."

"Thank you, tower. We should be down in just a minute."

Ski sets his flaps and tilts the Mig up a few degrees, and begins the descent to the runway.

"There it is." The fireman points east into the morning sky. The lights on the two aircraft can just be seen. The men mount their machines and prepare for action. As his Mig crosses the outer markers, Ski can see the lights on the emergency equipment flashing red and yellow. The emergency crews watch in awe as the Mig touches down. The Tomcat does a fly-by across the field and turns to land. Ski watches the field rise up to him and a hard thump as the Mig sets down. The tower tells him which exit to use and directs him to a hangar off the side of the field. He passes a couple of rows of F-18 fighters and rolls to a stop with the emergency vehicles all around him. Cutting the engines, his hands go limp. He can see men running up to the plane.

As he opens the canopy, a hand reaches in to unbuckle his harness. "You're going to be all right, sir. We'll have you on your way to the hospital in just a few minutes."

Not understanding all the words, he can tell from their tone that they understand his plight. A corpsman climbs up to give him a quick check. "The metal from the bomber hit here." He points to the side of the aircraft. "We'll need to bend it back so we can get him out." The corpsman applies some quick bandages and removes his helmet. He climbs down as a fire rescue man climbs up to look at the problem.

A second rolling ladder is placed on the other side of the plane, and another fireman climbs up to the cockpit. "Bob," he yells back over his shoulder. "I think I can get it with a hammer." A man runs to the side of a fire truck and opens one of the bends. He grabs a hammer and runs back to the plane. He hands it up to the man on the ladder.

He puts his hand on Ski's shoulder. "OK, just sit still." He aims the hammer and strikes the ragged metal piece. "All right." Dropping the hammer, he reaches in to help lift the Russian pilot out. As Ski tries to help, the two men gently lift him out of the seat. Another fireman locks hands with him, and Ski is carried down the stairs in a seated position. "Watch his leg." Hands reach out to guide him to the waiting gurney.

"You're going to be all right." Hands resting on each shoulder gently pat him. As the gurney reaches the back of the ambulance, Ski grabs the hand of the doctor and sits part way up.

"Gentlemen, thank you." His head rests back on the pillow. A rousing cheer goes up from the rescue teams.

"Captain Mikulin, this is Shark 1. We're fifty miles from touch down. Can you hang in there?"

Mikulin shakes his head to try and clear it. His body is being racked in waves of pain. Out of the front of the plane, lights are beginning to appear. A gust of wind slams into the plane. "My hands...." The cold has done its task; his right hand slips from the yoke.

"Mikulin, Mikulin, you're drifting left." The bomber slowly slides to the left in a gradual turn.

"Bear, this is the tower. Over." There is a pause. "Bear, you are leaving the flight path. Over." The Russian words ring in his ears.

Trying as hard as he can, nothing seems to want to move. His head rolls back towards the center console. His half-dead eyes play across the cockpit. He can feel the movement in the plane, as the bomb bay doors open. His mind now trapped inside a non-functioning frame registers the change on the face of the fail-safe box. The eight squares are framed in red, and a number half covered with blood blinks. The two fighters next to him call over the radio trying to reach him. The bomber levels off and begins running southwest.

"Bear, this is the tower. You're five miles off the glide path. Over."

"Rescue, this is Touchdown. Over."

"Roger."

"Vector all rescue helicopters to the southwest towards Carlisle and Myrtle Grove. Over."

"Roger, tower. We are in pursuit now." The helicopters turn towards the south and chase the three jets.

The two jets position themselves above the turning bomber, and continue to vainly call to Mikulin. His head is frozen to the right, his eyes stare flatly at the fail-safe read out. The flashing lights repeat the same message: Death Mode. The flashing lights seem to draw him into the machine. Death Mode 24. As the plane aligns itself with the lights to its front, the whine of the cylinder cannot be heard above the roar of the wind. As he watches, the number one square is crossed by a red line and the number goes out. The cylinder rotates to the next position. Under the bomber, hidden from the two fighters, a white cylinder falls into the morning darkness.

As Mikulin forces his head forward, the lights of a town pass to the right of the bomber. "Something is wrong," his brain cries inside his scull. "We're on auto-pilot. I'm not flying the plane." The voices on the radio continue to call for him. His head is slung back to the right, his eyes once more on the read-out. The number two is highlighted, and a red line crosses it. The square goes out. The cylinder whines into the next position. The number three is highlighted; his mind flashes awake.

"No, my God, no!" He stares at the dial as it continues to advance. With all his strength, he lifts his hand and brings it down on top of the screen. The pain blasts up his arm and into the rest of his body. "Bear, this is Raven. Answer, Mikulin."

As the pain subsides, he tries to grasp any energy left in him. His hand keys his mike switch. "Raven, it's in Death Mode. God stop it." He takes a deep breath. "Raven, shoot me down now! That's an order! Shoot me down!"

"Captain, what are you saying? You have turned away from the airfield. Can you fly it back?"

"Raven, the bombs. My God, the bombs. They're being dropped."

"Mikulin, what bombs?" As the last bomb leaves, the doors slowly close.

"Hold one, Bear." Norba moves the Mig to the side and drops below the bomber. "Bear, I see bay doors closed. I repeat, you have bay doors closed."

"What? They're closed?" His mind screams for answers. Looking back at the screen, the number twenty-four rests there. As he watches, the screen goes blank. The Death Mode is removed and the plane drops into a dive for the earth. Mikulin's hands grab the yoke and attempts to pull the nose up. The nose comes up a few degrees, just as the first trees begin striking the under body of the plane.

"I love you, Nicole." The words freeze in Mikulin's mind as the bomber slams into the sand and mud. As it slides, it strikes some rocks on the beach which tear the cabin away from the body of the plane at the point of the explosion. The world spins as the cabin is tossed aside. The headless fuselage skids to a stop as fuel from a ruptured tank finds an ignition point. The fire illuminates the area around the plane.

"Touchdown, this is Shark 1. The bomber has crashed 0500 Zulu hours. The choppers should be able to see the fire. We will circle until they arrive. Over."

"Roger, Shark. They should be there in just a few minutes. Touchdown out."

"Ironman, this is Touchdown."

"Roger."

"Ironman, the bomber has crashed at 0500 Zulu in southern Louisiana."

"Roger, Touchdown. We'll advise Ultima. Ironman out."

ULTIMA
WASHINGTON, D.C.

"Ma'am." The chief turns to Captain Van Nar. "We are receiving a call from Ironman. The Russian bomber has crashed in Louisiana."

"All right, Chief." She picks up a phone and lays a call-out list on the table. She hits a speed calling button and looks up at the screens.

The phone rings twice and a groggy voice comes on the line. "This is Brant."

"Mr. Secretary, this is Captain Van Nar. We have a blue flash message from Ironman. A Russian bomber has crashed in southern Louisiana, and the Cubans have gone to full alert in the Gulf."

"Good God. I'll be in as soon as I can. Have you called the Joint Chiefs?"

"They're being called now, sir. Ironman is in tactical command of the area, and we have response units in the air around the Gulf. I have ordered a car to pick you up."

Brant looks at his clock; the numbers glow red. It's 5:05 A.M. "Very good, Captain. I'll be there shortly." He slowly hangs up the phone.

"Is everything all right, dear?" His wife's hand rubs his back as he sits on the side of the bed.

"There's some trouble in the Gulf area. They have a car on the way. I have a feeling you will be eating alone tonight, dear." His hand finds hers in the dark and applies a soft squeeze.

"Should I get you something, dear?"

"No, go back to sleep. I'll call you later."

He goes into the bathroom and turns on the light. His fifty-five years have chosen to age him gracefully. He blinks his eyes, and he gets his razor out.

MATANZAS AIR BASE
CUBA

Val looks out the window as the rain lashes the walkway outside. It passes through the light like a solid sheet. He looks back at the radio operator. "Get me the air marshal now! I don't care about the weather. Get me through."

He leans over to Brock. "Are you thinking the same thing I am?"

Brock looks him in the eyes. "Those two Cuban techs that got on the plane, right?"

"Right. I want them. I'll be going to the crash site. I want you to catch them."

"Right." Brock moves away from the table and signals two of the Russian guards to follow him. "I'll be on the radio. This damn storm is not going to help things." As Brock opens the door, a gust of wind and rain blows into the room. Val watches as they leave.

"Sir, Moscow is on the line."

BUS, TRAVELING EAST OF HAVANA

The rain howls outside as the bus moves around another mudslide on the road. Luís checks his watch: five o'clock. His mind envisions the explosion. "Just forty-five more minutes." The bus stops to let another group of army trucks pass by. He watches them out the window. "It must be the storm." His mind searches for an answer. He checks his map. "Damn it," he mumbles to himself. "We have only gone 100 miles in three and a half hours. Only thirty miles more and I'll be in the village." The clanking of the bus echoes as the bus moves forward again. Others around him stir. He pulls his arms up and crosses them on his chest for warmth. His head slowly settles against the cool window glass.

CHAPTER 3

MATANZAS AIR BASE
CUBA

The Russian radio operator turns more dials at the console, trying to clear the static from the speaker. "Sir, I'll have to go through Sierra Vista to clear this storm."

"All right, just do what you have to." Val's eyes blink as another bolt of lightning burns a path through the sky. His mind rolls as he looks out the window. "How could this happen? Those idiots had to pick that particular plane." The rain finally brings some relief from the hot dry air of the last couple of weeks.

His call is run on landlines a hundred miles north to Sierra Vista to clear the storm. High on the mountain, the transmitter sits in the clear sky. "Sir, I have them on the line."

Val reaches over and picks up the telephone. "Is this a secure line to Moscow?"

"They're putting a scrambler in the system at their end. Go ahead, sir. Moscow is ready."

The call is transferred to the office of the air marshal. "This is Shagan. Val, is that you?"

"Yes, sir. I have bad news about flight 117."

"Yes, I know. We have been picking up radio traffic and the fact that the Cubans have gone to full alert."

"Yes, sir. It looks like some type of bomb was placed on board by the Cuban technicians. Comrade Brock is now tracking down our suspects. We have not heard anything about the bombs. We did receive Mikulin's request to his escorts to shoot him down; we have no idea what he wanted. The weather here at the base has gone to hell. The storm has passed out to sea, but we're getting the tail of it. There's lots of lightning, so we are just now getting information in on the radios."

"Val, I have already called the information I had to Secretary Sholenska. We are making a point to stand down all military units at other areas around the world. We will be contacting the Americans shortly. And we wish to show this was exactly what it seems to be: a major accident. We will be clearing a flight into the crash site for you. We will get our embassy people on to NAS New Orleans. How soon could you be ready to fly?"

"Sir, nothing is going to leave this field for a while. We're getting forty to fifty mile per hour winds. I'll have to wait for the weather to calm down. And with the crazy Cubans on full alert, they would probably shoot us down."

"All right Val. We'll be diverting the *Moskva* sea group to the crash site. They will take charge of transporting the weapons back. They are securing from their training exercise and awaiting further orders."

"Yes, sir. I'll have a plane prepared and ready to fly as soon as the weather clears. I'll contact you again as soon as I get on site."

"I'll give the secretary another call. Good luck."

"Thank you, sir." The line goes dead. Val holds the receiver to his ear, listening to the static.

"Sir, we will be breaking the lines down."

"OK, right." Val puts the phone back on the cradle. The howl of the wind outside overpowers the noise in the room. Walking to the window, he looks out on the field. The rain swirls and lashes at the ground ,and rivulets of water run in all directions. "Get me the air chief. I need to see him now!"

The radio operator calls to the flight shack and summons the air chief to the radio room. "Sir, he is on his way. But he is not to happy."

Val watches a lone figure lean into the wind and head to his location. The elements seem to be attacking him from every angle as he fights to keep his footing. The door flies open with a great rush of wind and rain. "Holy shit, sir. This had better be important. I don't want to seem ungrateful, Comrade, but there is a full blown storm outside."

Val watches as the man shakes like a wet dog to clear some of the water off him. "Over here, Comrade Chief."

"Yes, sir." He removes his raincoat as he walks over. One of the other men in the room hands him a cup of tea. "Thanks Comrade. What do you need, sir?"

"Chief, I need to be able to fly out of here as soon as possible."

"Sir, there is no way of getting anything out of here until this weather clears up. If we had some more of the Mig-29s, like the ones that left last night, they could pull this storm easy. But someone could get killed trying to fly out of here now."

"I understand, Chief. But a grave situation has occurred. Flight 117 is down. We believe it was sabotaged and has crashed on the American mainland."

The chief's face shows a sign of disbelief. "The Tupolev went down? Shit!" His hand rises to his mouth as he ponders his next move. Val can see him thinking of his choices of aircraft.

"Well, sir. Helicopters are out of the question. And the bigger planes are all Cuban. I would suggest a Yak-36. We have been getting them set up to transfer to the *Moskva*. It's fast and VTOL, and we have a couple of two-seaters. We could have one prepared and ready in about thirty minutes."

"Good, Comrade Chief. I'll get my stuff together and meet you in the hangar."

The chief stands and puts his raincoat back on. He drinks the last of his tea. He heads for the door, then turns back to Val. "Also, Comrade, do you want it armed?"

Val looks the chief in the face, then out the window, and back to the chief. "I think it best to go with a full combat load."

"Yes, sir. It will be ready for you." He opens the door and moves back into the storm. Val gets his raincoat and puts it on. "Is there anything else I need from here?"

"No, sir. Your handheld will work using the Yak's transmitter." Val opens the door and heads for his quarters.

As Brock and his two guards approach the tech shop, they spread out. One of the guards looks through the window as Brock checks the door. "Damn." He steps back a pace and kicks his foot into the door near the handle. As it flies open, they rush inside with their guns drawn. One of the guards almost trips over the case on the floor. Brock looks over the room as the other two check the back rooms. "All clear!"

"Right. I figured they wouldn't be here. It looks like they just tossed the case into the room." He checks the workbench, and opens the case. "Nothing. Let's head for the main gate." Going back in the rain, the wind whips around them. They start jogging to clear the distance faster. As they reach the gate, the guard opens the door to the guard shack for them. Brock hits his hat on his leg to knock the water off it as the others move off to the side.

"I saw you coming down the path. What is wrong, señor?"

"Comrade, have you been on duty all night?"

"No, sir. I came on at 0400. Juan was on duty last night. He is over in the barracks sleeping."

"All right, I want you to close down the gates. No one leaves."

"Sí, señor."

"We have been ordered to full alert status." He leaves to close the front gates as Brock grabs a phone and calls the duty officer.

"Captain, this is Brock. Yes, good morning to you also. I need to talk to the guards who were at the plane last night, as well as the main gate guard. Also, I need the records of the two techs that were on duty last night. I understand that the base is under full alert. I'll be with you in just a minute to explain what has happened."

Putting the phone down, Brock can see soldiers coming onto the base. Through the rain he sees two armored cars pull in and park just outside the guard shack. Their weapons point out into the town.

"Let's go." The two men follow Brock back into the rain. They run up the path to the duty office.

The captain stands as they enter the duty office. "Comrade Brock, does this have something to do with the alert?"

"Yes, Captain Urebe. May I speak to you in private?"

"Sí, this way." They walk into a side room and close the door. Brock explains the situation.

"But Señor Brock, we were told that the Americans shot the bomber down. No one said anything about sabotage."

"I know. We're just getting the information in ourselves. Let's talk to the guards and see what they know."

"Sí." The two move back into the main office, as four men enter from a back door.

"Sir, the people you requested to speak to."

"Thank you, Sergeant. Señor Brock, here are the guards."

He looks over the two plane guards. "Last night, did the two techs tell you what they were doing on the plane?"

"Sí, señor. They had a black box about this big." He spreads his hands to show the size. "They said it was broken and they needed to fix it. Is something wrong, señor? It was just Miguel and Luís. They are always working on the airplanes."

"Yeah, except last night we think they put a bomb on the bomber. It crashed in the United States, and we have a hell of a problem."

The gate guard speaks up. "Señor, I checked them out at 0145 last night. They were going home."

"Did they do anything different after they left?"

"No. Wait, they shook hands in the street, and said goodbye. Then they left to go home."

Brock turns back to the captain. "I need the files on the two men."

"Here they are." Opening them both, he lays them on the desk. He looks over their pictures and reads some of the files. "These are the two. I would like some men to go to these addresses and see if we can pick them up."

"Sí. I'll have two trucks brought around and we will go after them." He makes a call to the barracks and tells them what he wants. "They will be here in a few minutes." The captain gets his helmet and checks his side arm. A sergeant moves over to him and hands him a machine pistol. "Thank you, Sergeant."

They get their jackets on and prepare to leave. "Here, Señor Brock. This is the picture of Luís. I'll take Miguel and we will move on both addresses."

"Good, Captain." He looks at the picture of the young man. He tries to read the whys and hows in the silent face. The sound of trucks pulling up diverts his attention.

AIR RESCUE
SOUTHERN LOUISIANA

"Air-sea, this is Shark." The Tomcat and the Mig pass back over the crash.

"Roger, Shark. I think we can see the fire, southwest of our position."

"Air-sea, we will make a pass south of the crash site, over the water. We will push flares. Over."

"Roger, Shark. We'll look for flares."

The Tomcat and Mig do a sweeping turn north of the crash site. Then pull around and fly parallel to the beach over the water. As they come abreast of the crash, they each fire flares behind them. They form straight lines in the morning sky.

"Shark, we have you dead on. We'll arrive over site in five minutes. Out."

"Roger, Air-sea. We will hold air cap. Out."

"Touchdown, this is Coast Guard. Over."

"Roger, Coast Guard."

"We are just arriving at the crash site. It is at the north end of Barataria Bay. I can see some fire on the beach around the main fuselage. The cockpit area has broken off and is about sixty feet from the fuselage. It is 0520 local. Over."

"Roger, Air-sea. We show you at crash site. Are there any signs of survivors? Over."

"It doesn't look like it. Over."

The co-pilot has a camcorder, and films the site as they fly over it. "We will be landing just behind the crash. We'll search for survivors and recontract you. Over."

"Roger, rescue. We'll stand by."

They maneuver the two helicopters into position and set down. A squall is passing over them as the wheels touch the wet sand. The rain is putting out some of the flames. From both helicopters, men jump out with extinguishers and run up to the flames. They soon begin knocking down the rest of the fire.

"Sir, the fire is going down. But there is a lot of gas around. This thing could go up in one big boom. I suggest no flares be put out at this point."

"Right, no flares. Pass it on to the others."

More men are out and begin searching the crash for life. The beams from their lanterns cut through the morning darkness like lasers. After a quick check of the main fuselage, they start heading for the broken front portion in the surf line.

Mikulin's brain feels no pain. But he can hear the lapping of waves running up against the side of the plane. His head rests against the left side of the cabin; he can see water splashing on the window. A fierce cold seems to have invaded his body; nothing seems to work. He can hear rain hitting the top of the cabin. His disorientation makes him think he is hearing voices. Suddenly two jets roar over head. The noise stabs into his body, and he realizes that he is hanging upside down.

"Touchdown, this is Shark. We are completing a pass over the crash site. Both choppers are down. Fires are out. Over."

"Roger, Shark. So far no survivors. Over."

"Roger, Touchdown. We will remain air cap for a little longer. Shark out."

The co-pilot is filming the fuselage. He joins up with the men in the water getting to the front cabin. The rising sun throws a lightening shade of gray over the area. The sun must fight the clouds and rain for space.

The waves lap over their boots as they approach the cabin. The crew chief sticks his head in and tries to see up into the front seats. "Holy shit. There is blood everywhere. Hand me a light. I'll have to climb up inside to check on the two people in front."

One of the men hands him a flashlight. "Here you go, Chief."

He shines it into the interior. "I can tell one didn't make it; his torso is hanging from his seat. He was decapitated."

He climbs in and moves to the back of the seats, holding on to the consoles above him. He pushes the hanging torso aside so he can check the man in the pilot's seat. He pushes under the hanging body, and can feel the weight against his back. As he reaches over the pilot, to check for a pulse. The head turns and looks at him.

Startled he pulls back, the torso pining him into the seat. "Goddamn, we may have a live one."

"Sir, the chief said he may have a live one." The commander grabs the mike. "Chief, is there someone alive?"

"Sir, the pilot just moved. He is in bad shape. We'll need to get him out and back to the hospital."

"Roger, chief. The packs are on their way."

"Let's get some men to grab the medical equipment. The chief has a live one in the cabin. Let's move."

As crewmen grab emergency medical equipment and back boards, they all run along the surf to the forward cabin. The chief runs his hand along the man's neck and tries to take his pulse. He rests his hand for a minute and then climbs back out of the cabin.

The commander runs up to him. "What have we got, Chief?"

"Sir, the pilot is in bad shape. He has a real weak pulse. We'll need to remove the other body first in order to get him out. It's going to be rough; he's pinned in there on his side."

The man with the camera moves into the shell of the cabin and films the interior. He backs out to let the others in to remove the co-pilot's body.

The rain helps wash the blood off the chief's jacket as the men inside try and figure out how to pull the body out. A body bag is unfolded and set out to receive the body. Someone yells from the inside. "Can we get someone up on top to release his harness through the window?"

Another crewman climbs up on the fuselage and crawls to the blown out window. The two men inside try and push the body back into the seat; one crawls up onto the instrument panel to keep the body from falling onto the pilot.

"All right, hit the harness lock." As the hand reaches into the window, and hits the lock the body suddenly falls full weight onto the man on the instrument panel.

"Oh! Goddammit. Get him off." The headless torso lies on his chest. The other men pull the body back into the cabin and others grasp it, moving it out onto the sand. The chief opens the body bag as they lift the body into position. The sound of the zipper cannot be heard as one of the crewmen vomits into the tide.

"Damn, what do you think happened, Chief?"

"I'd say some type of explosion. It just tore these guys up."

"Chief."

"Yeah." He turns back towards the main fuselage. "What is it?"

A crewmen from the other helicopter points to a shoe in the sand. "There's a foot still in it. I think there are other body parts from the cabin back to the main part of the plane."

The chief throws him another body bag. "All right, your team will work from here back."

He takes the bag. "Thanks, Chief."

The cabin moves a little as the waves outside continue to hit up against it. The drizzling rain stops, replaced by hot humidity in the air. One of the crewmen crawls in next to the pilot and moves up with his back on the instrument panel.

"All right, I'll release his harness. Try and get him from the back of his collar." The other man moves into position.

"Sir, I hope you understand English. We're going to move you out. You're hurt. This is not going to be pleasant."

A raspy sound comes from the swollen face. "Do it."

The men are surprised at the words. "Yes, sir. Bear with us." His hand undoes the clasp and Mikulin slumps forward. A hand grabs the back of his collar and pulls him towards the aisle. The pain sears through his body; a black curtain drops on any cohesive thought. "He's out, Chief."

"Right, let's move before he wakes up."

They lift him up and out. Others grab handfuls of clothing and lift him out of the plane. A support board is slipped under him, and he is strapped to it. The corpsman runs an IV into his arm, and a syringe of morphine is injected into his arm. A splint and wrap is put on his right leg to support it. His helmet is removed, and a compress bandage is put on his right eye.

"Let's get him on the helicopter and out of here." They lift together and race up the beach to the waiting chopper. They lift him in and continue to work on him as the main rotors begin spinning in the thick air. Small swirls of vapor are formed and pushed down to the ground. "Sir, we're loaded."

"Right, Chief." The whine of the engines increases, and it begins lifting into the sky.

"Touchdown, this is Coast Guard 15. Over."

"Roger, 15."

"We have the pilot, and we'll be coming in hot. Have an emergency team at the door. We'll set down in the parking lot right outside. Over."

"Roger, alerting team. We'll clear everything out of your way."

The Dauphin helicopter rises up into the sky and takes a sharp left turn and heads directly for the base. His path retraces the flight of the bomber.

Mikulin's eye slowly opens; some of the killing pain is gone. He can hear the men working on him. "Here get a bandage on that, and I'll put a compress on this one." The corpsman looks at his face. "All right. Welcome back, sir. We're on our way to the hospital. Just stay with us, sir."

Mikulin doesn't understand every word, but he understands their kindness. His mind recognizes the Coast Guard insignia on the men's uniforms. His hand opens and he feels a strong hand close on his. His eye looks directly into the face of a seasoned sailor. A smile breaks across his face. The chief leans forward. "Hang in there, sir." He looks into the torn face. "We have never lost a pilot yet, and we're not starting now." The unique sound of the Dauphin whines in the air. They pass over houses along the route, but the noise doesn't bother the women lying on the floor of her kitchen. Nor does the rain and wind coming in through the hole ripped in the outside wall. Nor the large white cylinder sticking in the wall between the kitchen and the living room, with the husband beside it.

"Touchdown, this is Shark. Over."

"Roger, Shark."

"They have picked up the pilot. I'm requesting permission to bring the Mig back to base. Over."

"Roger, Shark. He has requested to be with the others in his group. You have a vector of thirty degrees northeast, at 5,000. Over."

"Roger. We're leaving the crash scene. Out."

ULTIMA
WASHINGTON, D.C.

"Mr. Secretary, we have confirmation that the Russian pilot is being air lifted to the naval hospital at NAS New Orleans by the Coast Guard."

"Thank you, Captain Van Nar. Has anyone been able to figure out what the pilot was talking about? A bomb?"

"No, sir. We have Coast Guard on site; they're doing a preliminary site check. We're in contact with them. So far, everything is negative."

"Thank you, Captain. We're just passing the Jefferson Memorial. I'll be there in about fifteen minutes." He hangs up the car phone and leans back in the soft leather seat. He lowers the window and lets the cool morning air blow over his hand as it rests on the window sill. The sun's rays color random clouds with pink and orange tints, and bathes the area in fresh, new light. He remembers back to his days in college at ASU, when he and his friends would climb South Mountain in the early morning. The physical exertion and the fresh desert air seemed to rejuvenate them all. A slight smile crosses his lips.

Since then, his advanced degrees from Rice in business, and his tutorship of both oil and electronic companies, had trained him to deal with adverse situations and to focus on the main problem. He was best known for keeping a clear head in the most heated situation, and getting all parties to work for a positive end. His successes in business and his long relationship with President Wayne had led to his present position as the Secretary of Defense.

In his last two years, he had come to appreciate the officers of the Joint Chiefs. Their commitment to duty and their personal integrity had brought them together to reduce spending, yet also to continue to improve the separate armed forces into more efficient forces for their roles in American policy.

His attention is brought back to the present as they pull in to the guard booth. They are checked and then waved through the heavy iron gates. As he gets out, two others are alighting from their vehicles. They walk up to the entry door, and wait for the secretary. The marine guards are at attention.

"Good morning, Mr. Secretary," both men call to him as he climbs the few steps up to the landing.

"Good morning, General Becker. How is the army doing this morning?"

"We're on stand by, sir."

"Good. Good morning General Lane. And how is the air force doing?"

"Fine, sir. We have taken up positions around the Gulf, and are at condition yellow."

They walk in, and head up the long hall to the elevator. They speak softly in the empty hall. Guards at the elevator present arms as they enter the elevator with the armed marine captain. The doors open several floors down. Other guards come to attention as they pass. The doors to the war room are opened as they come near, and they join the others around the large oval table. Brant looks around and smiles. "Good morning, Mr. Secretary."

"Good morning, Admiral."

"You know Admiral Hilling. I believe that both you and General Swane must sleep here. I have yet to beat either of you here, no matter what."

"We were both staying in town last night. We had gone to a reception over at the marine barracks."

"Well, everyone. We need to get up to speed on this issue."

"Well, Mr. Brant. With all the activity going on in the Gulf, the only thing we're missing are ground troops."

"I believe you're right, General Becker. We still have not seen any overt action in any other parts of the world. I believe that just the Cubans and us are up to alert status."

"Sir." The secretary turns to Van Nar at one of the big screens. "We have a new projection." The picture from the satellite moves west of Cuba. "The Russians have a cruiser group in the Gulf that has been running some anti-submarine drills. They were to return to Havana and pick up some aircraft. When this started they were ordered to remain in international waters and to prepare to steam towards the Louisiana coast."

The formation of ships comes up on the screen. "Sir, we have a Los Angeles class submarine that has been trailing this group since it left the Mediterranean."

"Well, what are we looking at?" Brant and the others watch as the camera on the satellite zooms down on the five shapes.

"Well, sir." Captain Van Nar takes out her laser pointer. "We have the helicopter cruiser *Moskva*, one *Kresta 2* cruiser, and three *Sovremennyy* class destroyers. There are also two *Victor* class submarines attached to the group. They are at a non-belligerent state."

Brant looks back at the others around the table. "The president sees this as an accident, and will be dealing with the parties involved. He request that any change in the situation with the Cubans be called to him immediately."

Admiral Hillings looks up at the screen. "Mr. Brant, we would be in a hell of a lot better position if the Cubans would back their stuff down. We're concerned that something we're unaware of may heat this thing up."

"I agree, Admiral. The Russians are trying now to get them back to their bases. But they have to deal with General Morales. And he is still unhappy with the Russian pull out, anyway."

The red phone next to Brant comes alive. Everyone in the room watches as he answers. "Yes, Mr. President."

Brant listens intently and writes down a few notes. "Yes, sir. We'll expect Air Marshal Shagan's call. We can advise him of the status of their injured people and work with him on the salvage of the aircraft by the *Moskva*. Yes, sir. We will keep you informed." Hanging up the phone, the room waits for his directions. He stands up and stretches.

"Gentlemen, the president has requested that we provide all assistance to the Russians. He had just gotten off the phone with the Soviet secretary. He apologized for this situation. He has assured the president that they were in direct contact with the Cubans, and were requesting them to stand down their combat groups. But they have run into some difficulty dealing with General Morales. So they are also dealing with the Cuban ambassador in Havana." He takes a drink from his glass of water.

"They have requested clearance to bring the *Moskva* cruiser group up to recover the aircraft and injured pilots. Also, a request was made to put a Soviet investigator at the scene. He will fly in directly from Cuba. The president also felt that there was more to what has happened. He requests that when we talk with Air Marshal Shagan, we see if there are any other problems."

RUSSIAN WAR ROOM
MOSCOW

"Yes, sir, Comrade Secretary. You're saying that President Wayne did not say anything about the bombs?" He pauses. "Yes, sir. I agree. We can salvage the plane, and avert any international incident. The *Moskva* is picking up a Mila-10; it will do the retrieving of the plane from the beach. The weapons will be stored on board and returned. I'll be in contact with Commander Val; he should be at the site soon. The weather in the area is really bad; the tropical storm that hit them is still trailing through the area." He pauses again. "Yes, sir. I'll call Secretary Brant and arrange for the ships and airplane passage. Yes, Comrade Secretary. I will call as soon as we get Val on site."

Shagan replaces the phone and goes to the radio room, off to the side of the main room. "Get me Comrade Val."

"Yes, sir." In seconds the radio link to the air base in Cuba is reestablished.

The chief in the hangar answers the phone and motions for Val. "Comrade Val. It's for you—it's Air Marshal Shagan."

He completes adjusting his flight suit as he walks over to the chief. "This is Val."

"Comrade, this is Shagan. We need to get you on site as soon as possible. The secretary has talked to the president, and no mention of the payload was made. The Americans have agreed to give all possible assistance to us. We believe that we may still salvage this situation. But we have to know what is going on over there. How soon can you leave?"

"We will be taking off shortly. The storm is moving just west of us; the big winds seem to be falling off." He looks over his shoulder as the last of the missiles is slid onto its rack. "They should be done in just a few minutes, Comrade Shagan." Val checks his watch. "It's about 6:00 A.M. here, we should be on site in about two hours. Where are the ships?"

"From their last transmission, we show them about 200 miles west of Havana. Their waiting for the Mila-10; it left about fifteen minutes ago. When it is aboard the *Moskva*, they will start north. But you won't see them until sometime late tonight. As soon as I hang up, I'll be calling Secretary Brant to get the final clearances. So tell the pilot to keep the radio clear in case their are any last minute changes."

"Yes, sir. I'll call you from the site."

Val hangs up the phone and turns to the plane as a gun pod is put in place. The crew chief is pushing the men to finish up. The pilot stands off to the side waiting, for the men to finish.

"Comrade Val." The chief comes over. "You need to get the rest of your gear. Everything is ready to go."

"Right, Chief."

The hangar doors begin sliding open and Val can see the tanker truck outside ready to fuel them up. "I wonder what's going on over at the site, Comrade."

"I don't know, Chief."

Val ponders the way things are working out. Picking up his helmet and gloves, he leaves the ready room and joins the pilot near the hangar door. "We will have a good flight, Comrade Val." The Russian pilot nods his head, and begins walking to the plane.

Val blows a breath out and looks over at the chief. "Do they all have to be that young?"

The chief smiles. "Yes, sir. They're young, but good."

He pats Val on the shoulder. "Have a good flight, sir."

"Thanks, Chief."

He slips the helmet on and walks to the plane.

His hands grip the side of his seat as the Yak's engine howls. It seems to shudder and then rises above the ground. Val watches as the crew chief waves them away. They rise and begin forward flight, their speed accelerating by the second. He can see lightning flashes out the side of the canopy.

"Sir."

Val responds to the voice over the plane's intercom. "Yes."

"We'll be climbing to cruise altitude to bypass the storm. My understanding is that we will be picking up two Mig-21s as escort about fifty miles out. With no problems we should be there in about two hours."

"Thank you, Lieutenant." He can't help but think of the Cuban fighters out in the void in front of them. As they pass over the Cuban coastline, Val can see missile batteries with their launchers pointing out to sea. He can hear the high pitched tone go off in the cockpit.

"Sir, those missile batteries we just passed over are tracking us." The push in Val's back tells him the young lieutenant has applied more power as they move out over the Gulf.

STEVE SIMMONS

THE BUS TO MATANZAS
CUBA

A bump in the road, and a jerky motion of the bus brings Luís out of his sleep. He thinks to himself, "Next stop Arccos de Canasi, for about ten minutes, and then on to Matanzas." He checks his watch: six A.M. "It's done."

Others on the bus are getting ready to get off the bus to stretch. They move into the small fishing town. The ocean is gray from the overhead clouds as the bus winds its way into the town. Luís stretches his back, neck, and legs. There is stiffness in his legs from sitting in a tucked position for a while. The bus comes to a stop in front of a cantina, and people begin filing off. Getting his bag from a rack over his head, he walks to the exit door. "You getting off, señor?" The driver looks at his bag.

"Sí, a little vacation. A few days off."

"Sí, well, you should get relaxed here. All they do is fish and sleep. It's too quiet for me." Luís climbs off the bus. "Señor." He looks back at the driver. "Good luck."

As Luís moves away from the bus, he knows the driver senses why he is here. Still stiff from the ride, he stumbles along the dirt path towards some run-down houses near the beach. Moving around some boats that have been pulled up out of the water, he feels the sand under his feet. The surf pounds the shore and makes a loud hissing noise as it recedes. He takes out a piece of paper and checks the location of the shack he needs to go to. Looking up from the paper, he sees the blue shutters and heads for them. As he walks up the path towards the shack, a man appears at the door and motions him to hurry.

"Señor, quickly. Come in." He looks around as he enters the door. "There has been a lot of military activity on the road today. We must take care. Here is some coffee; drink it to cut the chill. Then we must be leaving."

He takes a long drink and feels the warmth burn into his body. The other man gets a bag, and slides the strap over his shoulder.

"We will leave soon."

CHAPTER 4

General Morales puts the finishing touches on his dress uniform. He looks once more into the mirror and smoothes his mustache to the sides. As he moves down the hall on the second floor, he looks out the windows along the outside wall. Out over the bay, the rising sun throws bands of red and yellow across the blue-gray waters. He reaches the stairs and heads down to the kitchen; his boots sink in the rich red carpet. As he reaches the landing, he can hear his wife talking to one of the maids. The smell of spiced coffee fills the kitchen and the adjoining rooms.

The large kitchen, crafted in ceramic tile and adobe brick, is filled with the cook and others getting his breakfast and preparing for the afternoon meal. His wife finishes with the maid and turns back to greet him. "Good morning, my general."

"Good morning, my dear." He kisses her on the cheek as they pass, and he heads for the table out on the verandah. Raindrops seem frozen on the window panes, and the wet tile beyond the door still shows the passing of the storm. He takes his seat looking out over the bay, as the maid pours him a cup of coffee. "Thank you, Maria."

"Sí, señor."

His wife joins him. "You look grand today, dear."

"Thank you, Percilla. This may turn out to be the first day of a new time in our lives. Fidel is in Bolivia, and we are at full alert in the Gulf. I will be going to the command center to deal with the Russians."

"Please have a good meal, so that you will be able to deal strongly with them."

Their meals are brought and they eat and watch the gathering clouds out over the Gulf. As he finishes his meal it is taken away, and he is poured another cup of coffee. He walks to the edge of the verandah, and puts his foot up on the rail. "My dear, I would like you to stay close to the house today. It will only be for a short while. I want to be sure that you are safe."

"Are you sure it is the time, dear?"

"Yes, tomorrow there will be a new Cuba." His eyes are drawn to a black Mercedes coming up the road below the villa. "I must leave."

"I will do as you requested, dear."

He kisses her and picks up his hat. "Be ready to become Cuba's first lady."

A knock at the front door draws his attention. The maid calls out, "General, your car is here." He walks out to the car, and his aide closes the door.

The car pulls down the driveway to the iron gates and turns to go down the hill.

As they move along the road, he sees some of the damage done by the passing storm. As they drive by some missile batteries outside of Havana, he can see that they are pointed into the morning sky. Armed men patrol the compound.

"Sir." The aide next to the driver leans back from the front seat. "We are getting a call from the command center, General."

He picks up his car phone, and talks to the other person. He assures him that they will soon be at the center. "Tell Marshal Shagan that I will call him as soon as I get to my office." He listens to the other person. "Yes, send General Quintano to meet with the Russian investigator."

"Very good." He hangs up to phone. He goes back to the window and watches as they pass through a small cluster of houses. He can see trucks from the power company working to restore power. They splash through some potholes and turn on the road heading for the command center.

As they pass through the gates, two armed guards salute the car. Pulling up to the entrance, officers from his personal guard are waiting. Their black berets set them apart from the regular troops. One opens the door. "Good morning, sir."

"Good Morning, Captain. Is the area secured?"

"Yes, sir. The building is in our control." They both walk up the stairs and enter the building. He passes through the communications room to his office. A steaming cup of coffee is placed on his desk. He hangs his jacket up, and goes to the desk and sits down. "Bring me up to date on what is going on."

A captain comes into the office. "Sir, the Americans have put up a 100-mile no-fly zone south of the crash site. The Russians are in contact with the *Moskva* group; they are getting ready to move north. One of the Russian investigators is en route to the site."

"Do we know for sure what has happened?"

"General, all we know is that the aircraft are down. There has been no contact with the pilots since earlier this morning. We have moved some of the forces in the east to help in the flood-damaged areas."

"Do we still have forces around Guantánamo?"

"Yes, sir. They have not been pulled back."

"Thank you, Captain. I will now be talking with the Russians. Please excuse me."

"Yes, sir." He leaves and Morales's aide puts through a call to Moscow.

"Sir, your call is through to Moscow. They are getting Marshal Shagan. It is on line four."

"Thank you." Morales reaches over and pushes down on the blinking button.

"General Morales."

"Yes, good morning, Marshal Shagan."

"Good morning, General." In Moscow, Shagan squeezes the handle of the phone in his grip. "General, we have asked you to back down your response in the Gulf. We have naval and air elements en route to the scene. Your fighters running hot all over the Gulf are causing a situation that could explode into armed conflict with the slightest provocation."

"Sí, ex-Comrade Shagan. We have yet to receive confirmation on what happened on the Tupolev. Until then, we will continue to protect our sovereignty in the way we see fit. We are adhering to the boundary lines that the Americans have put in place. But we are not so gullible as you in believing every word that your new comrades say."

"General, could you hold for just a minute?"

"Why yes, Air Marshal."

Shagan places his phone on hold. "That arrogant asshole." The other officers in the room silently watch as their commander regains his composure. An orderly pours more tea into Shagan's cup. He flexes his jaw and stretches his shoulders. He reaches over and his finger pushes the button down.

"Comrade General, again. We are in direct contact with the Americans. We will also request that we have a direct line open to you. Do you agree?"

"Sí, Comrade. We will consider any open dialogue with our two democratic participants. Perhaps we should deal directly with the Americans so they don't take advantage of our new democratic comrades."

"General, your volunteering to deal in our behalf is very cavalier. But we will continue to deal with the Americans on this issue until we have all the information we need to get to the bottom of this mishap."

"Very well, Marshal Shagan. I will continue to direct the forces of Cuba in this situation. Any assistance from your staff or yourself will be helpful in maintaining the security of the Gulf region."

"Thank you, General. We will get back to you shortly." The line goes dead in Shagan's ear.

"Son of a bitch! That arrogant shit is going to start something that is way over his head."

Shagan motions for the others to follow him into the next room. They pass through large wooden doors which are embossed with carving from the czars' period.

They enter the war room. Its rich marble floors and wood panels seem out of touch with the screens on the wall projecting parts of the world. The center screen is the focus of their attention as the ten officers take seats around a large oval table. Shagan walks to the head of the table and grabs the back of his chair. The red velvet slides under his hands. "Gentlemen, we have a situation here that will require quick and informative answers. The Americans continue to give us their full support, and our people are moving to the site as we speak. As I explained earlier, the weapons are not an issue at this point. The secretary believes and I agree that after talking with President Wayne, there is no reason at this point to cause any panic about the weapons."

Looking at his watch, he checks the board. The others watch it also. "This screen is coming off the radar tract of the *Moskva*. "It looks good; we will be able to track that idiot's deployment."

Walking around the ornate chair, he sits and takes a bottle of vodka and pours himself a glass. The others also pour a glass. "Gentlemen, to our success."

"To our success," they all choir as they drink.

CRASH SITE
LOUISIANA

"The crash site is just ahead, Captain."

"Roger." A rain squall is sweeping the area as they approach. The two navy Sea Kings sweep in over the men on the ground. They pass by and then turn left to approach the area from front and back.

"I'll drop in beside the Coast Guard chopper."

"Roger. We're landing about twenty yards in front."

They settle to the ground, blowing sand and rain in all directions. Once down, the engines whine to a stop, and the men begin walking up the beach to join the guardsmen. They meet with the Coast Guard commander and discuss where they can be of assistance.

"Captain, we need to seal off the area around the bomber. I think we have removed all of the remains. But it was a bit messy earlier."

"Right, Commander. We'll disperse our people around the area." Each helicopter had brought six seamen with them; they fanned out around the wreck.

The captain and the Coast Guard commander walk up the beach to the main section of the bomber. "We don't expect to see anyone out here. It's pretty desolate. And with that hurricane coming in, things could get pretty bad along the shore here."

"I agree with that."

The men around the perimeter of the plane set more beacons as another squall sweeps in on top of them. The captain looks around the front of the bomber. "Damn this rain. Have your guys found anything out of the ordinary?"

"No, but we haven't been able to open the hatchway to the back of the plane. When it crashed, it tweaked the door." The captain looks at the hatchway door and the twisted metal around it.

"Let's move over here under the wing. We are to wait for a Russian investigator who is flying in from Cuba."

The commander looks around. "Well, sir. If this weather gets any worse, we're all going to be leaving here." They both watch as the navy pilots walk down to the cabin of the plane with the Coast Guard pilots.

"Man, this thing is history."

"You're right." The Coast Guard pilot points up into the cabin. "We pulled the pilot out and sent him back to your facility."

As the navy pilots climb up into the cabin, the sound of a helicopter reaches them through the wind. The pilots look back towards the east. "Who's that?"

They squint their eyes looking into the gray sky. "There he is." The Coast Guard pilot points into the sky. "He's coming straight in." They watch the black dot against the gray clouds grow in size.

"It's not Coast Guard." The others look harder. "It's not navy either; it looks like a Bell Ranger."

"He's doing all right, with this weather and everything." As they watch, the red and white helicopter flies over their heads. The large letters on its side answer their questions.

"Coast Guard, this is KNLT news helicopter. We are requesting permission to land at the crash site."

The captain raises a hand radio. "Wait one. We have no authority to allow a landing at this time."

"Roger, Coast Guard. Could you check with your command? Over."

"Roger, KNLT. Hold one." The captain calls the helicopter, and has them contact the base. "Touchdown, this is 11 at the crash site. Over."

"Roger, 11."

"We have a news helicopter at the crash site. They are requesting permission to land. Over."

"Roger. Wait one."

BACKFIRE

The news helicopter circles the area, filming the crash site. "We're over the crash site; can you take us live?"

"Roger. We're trying to align your signal now."

At the news station in New Orleans. a rolling static picture begins to appear. "We're getting something, News 1." Suddenly the picture clears up and the site of the wreck moves slowly across the screen. "We got you, News 1. Good picture. We're setting up to go live. Stand by."

The pilot at the helicopter gets a call back from Touchdown. He ends the conversation and calls the captain.

"Sir."

He lifts the radio up. "Yes."

"Sir, they have no restrictions applied to news helicopters, if area is secured. You are to make the decision using your own discretion in matter."

"Roger." He looks up at the circling helicopter. "News 1. Over."

"Roger, Coast Guard."

"You can land west of the navy helicopters. I'll meet you there."

"Roger. West of navy helicopters."

They land just outside the perimeter and climb out, getting their equipment ready. The two seamen near them direct them to the rear of the Sea King. The cameraman and sound assistant trudge through the wet sand, trying to keep up with Marcey Lane. As one of KNLT's top news reporters, she senses a good story here. As she rounds the Sea King, she gets a full view of the front of the bomber. "I'd say right here for our opening shot. Then over there beside the main part of the plane."

"Miss Lane, I'm Captain McFarland, with the navy."

"How do you do, Captain McFarland?" She shakes his hand. "Can we get up near the plane?"

"Yes, but you will have to remain about fifteen feet out. We're still checking this thing out." Whiffs of gas float in the air as the TV crew set up at the front of the torn cabin.

She grabs the captain by the arm and brings him up next to her. "There. We'll tape the interview here. Is that OK, Captain?"

"Yes, that's fine. You do understand that we still do not have all the information regarding what happened."

"That's fine. We'll just get what we can. My pilot said we only have a short time on the ground. We'll need to head back to the station because of these squalls and the storm building in the Gulf."

"Right, we're going to have to get going ourselves soon."

"OK. Stand by. We'll start taping."

KNLT
NEW ORLEANS

"I think we have everything ready." The producer looks at the others in the control room. He looks out at the announcer. "Let Bob know. We're going with the stuff that Darin sent from the naval base, showing the two Migs landing. Then we'll go with the aerial shots that Marcey got in. As soon as they're airborne again, we'll pick up her interview with the Coast Guard."

On the studio floor the morning news is going out over the air, the anchorman is given a signal that they're ready to go in the control room. The director raises his finger and points to Bob.

"This just in—a Russian bomber has crashed near Barataria Bay. We have Marcey Lane on site with the Coast Guard. We'll have her live in just a moment. But first we will go live to Darin Bodine at the naval base."

The picture of Darin along the perimeter fence comes up on the screen. "We'll show you the first pictures we have of the trouble out over the Gulf." The first pictures show a crippled Mig-29 coming in for a landing with an F-14 Tomcat flying next to it. They follow it in as the lights of the emergency vehicles block out the picture. The camera is back on Darin live. Darin appears on the screen with the parked jets as a backdrop.

"We have just finished a news conference with the base press officer. He has verified that a Mig-29 Russian fighter has landed at the base. You can see it behind me." The camera pans the scene and zooms in on the Mig sitting in front of the hangar with emergency vehicles around it. "We have been told that they are treating two of the Russians at the base hospital. Apparently one is a fighter pilot and the other is the pilot of the bomber. The Coast Guard and the navy have helicopters on the site. There is a strong suspicion that the bomber was sabotaged, possibly by the group that calls itself Libertal in Cuba. Also, what we understand is that an alert is in·effect in the Gulf region from the coast of Texas to the coast of Florida. We'll stay on this story. This is Darin Bodine at NAS New Orleans. Back to you, Bob."

"Thank you, Darin. We'll get back to him if there are any new developments. Now we're going to shift over to film from Marcey Lane as she flew into the crash site."

The pictures of the crash appear on the screen, with Marcey's comments describing it. "This is our first sight of the crash. The bomber hit the tops of the trees and then slid along the beach. The forward cabin broke off and rolled down to the water's edge." The helicopter circles the bomber one more time. "We are in contact with the Coast Guard at the site. We are going to try and get permission to land. This is Marcey Lane on Barataria Bay."

The picture comes back to Bob. "These pictures are a KNLT exclusive. We have since learned that the KNLT helicopter is on the ground. We'll go back to them as soon as they get airborne again. Now for the weather."

ULTIMA
WASHINGTON, D.C.

"Mr. Secretary, we now have all players in place." Admiral Hillings looks up at the screen with the others. "I would like to have Captain Van Nar explain what we will be seeing."

She grabs some papers and walks to the lectern just below the screens, her rows of ribbons showing years of dedicated service. "Mr. Secretary, gentlemen. Screen number two will be reconfigured using the satellite now in place above the Gulf region." The screen goes completely blue and then returns with a green hue. On the screen the outlines of ships appear. "We now have the thermal imaging cameras looking down at the *Moskva* squadron. As you can see, we will literally be able to watch the progress of any ship, plane, or whatever in the region."

The camera pulls back and the field of vision expands to a 100-mile radius. Brant moves up beside Captain Van Nar. He looks up at the screen. "My God, this always amazes me. It's like watching some kind of video game."

"Yes, sir." Van Nar turns to him. "Except the players are real and running hot. Screen two is showing the radar track of the hurricane Evita. The third screen is showing a map of the Gulf area, and screen four is showing the passage of the bomber over southern Louisiana."

"Thank you, Captain. The call from Air Marshal Shagan will be coming in soon. Please keep us informed of any changes per your interpretation."

"Yes, sir."

An aide gives Van Nar a note as Brant goes back to his seat. "Gentlemen, screen one is being set up to show a news presentation from CNN." The screen changes from blue to CNN news. As they watch, the anchorwoman describes the film as coming from their affiliate KNLT in New Orleans. "These are the first news pictures of the crash site." They all stare at the bomber on the beach as the voice of a woman reporter describes it.

"Gentlemen, they picked this up from station KNLT in New Orleans. This next segment is from the Naval Base. We will freeze frame the Mig-29 in front to let you see where the damage is." The picture is zoomed in. "This is where the explosion on the bomber blew metal fragments into the cockpit." She uses her light pointer to show the area. An aide walks over and bends down to talk to Brant. He nods his head.

"Thank you, everyone. Air Marshal Shagan is on the phone, from Moscow." He reaches over and picks up the yellow phone, after exchanging pleasantries, they begin to discuss the crash situation and the alert conditions in the Gulf. Brant puts his hand over the mouthpiece. "Everyone, Marshal Shagan feels we should leave the line open until the Cuban situation has calmed down. They are having problems dealing with General Morales, and they see the situation as potentially dangerous. His staff is with him in their situation room and will respond to inquires if necessary." Brant looks around the table, and each man nods his head. "We are in total agreement, Air Marshal, we will have the line left open."

"Sir." Brant looks up at the screen, where Van Nar has highlighted three aircraft.

"Bring in the range." The picture grows larger.

"Two fighters have joined on the Russian plane flying out of Cuba." As they watch, two planes move up to the sides of the Yak.

Brant turns back to the men at the table. "Shagan, what are those two fighters doing? They look like they're joining up with your flight out of Cuba. You requested clearance for one plane, not three."

"Mr. Secretary, we don't know what they're doing. We believe it is Comrade Morales's doing. We'll check and get right back to you."

"Thank you, Air Marshal."

Brant hangs up the phone. "Gentlemen, what is our recourse?"

"Sir." Admiral Hillings looks at him and then up at the screen. "We have Tomcats in that area. They're carrying Phoenix missiles. We were to meet the Russian jet at 100 miles. If the fighters continue to fly in with the Russian, we will dump them all at ninety-five miles. Or all three planes will turn back to Cuba."

"Very good, Admiral."

CONTROL CENTER, GENERAL MORALES'S OFFICE

Morales leans back in his chair as he listens to Shagan. "Comrade General, for some reason two Mig-21 fighters have joined up with the Yak. We requested permission for one aircraft to enter American air space. We are in contact with them now. You must turn your planes around."

"Marshal Shagan, we believe that this may be a trap like the one that got your bomber shot down. So we decided to make sure and escort our Russian friends."

"General, can I assure the Americans that the planes will break away and go back to there holding area?"

"I will have to think about that, ex-Comrade Shagan."

"I'll be talking with the Americans. I will get back to you General."

"Certainly, Comrade." Morales hangs the phone up.

ULTIMA
WASHINGTON, D.C.

Brant picks up the yellow phone. "Yes, Marshal Shagan."

"Mr. Secretary, it is as we thought. General Morales sent the two fighters to escort the Yak. We have requested them to disengage and return to their stand-by positions."

"Air Marshal Shagan, you must understand that with the level of alert now in the Gulf, I must give you two alternatives. At the rate of closure, a decision must be made soon. The choices are: the two fighters return to their previous position, or all three aircraft turn back before 100 miles. Any incursion within the 100-mile zone will be considered an armed provocation. At that time our fighters will assume an attack mode and will fire. We will hold for your reply."

"Thank you, Mr. Secretary. We understand your position. I will speak again to General Morales and get back to you." They both hang up.

WAR ROOM
MOSCOW

As Shagan puts the line on hold, he looks at the other blinking light. He slams the table with his fist, and half raises out of his chair. "That arrogant bastard is bound and determined to get someone killed. I think we should launch some fighters off the *Moskva* and blow these assholes out of the sky. Damn, he makes me angry." The others in the room can feel and taste the hate in the air.

"Sir."

Shagan looks at the commander down the table. "Yes, Comrade."

"At the present closing speed, a decision will be necessary in about thirty minutes. If we were able to launch aircraft from the *Moskva*, you must remember that they were unloaded in Havana. It would also add to the turmoil in the Gulf. They would intercept within the 100-mile zone and add to the tension. With a refusal from General Morales to disengage, we could have the Yak fly to the *Moskva*. Once there and out of harm's way, the *Kresta* cruiser could shoot them down."

"I like that." A smile crosses Shagan face, and he returns to his chair. He reaches over and pushes down the button. The ring is far off in the handset.

"General, the Americans will not allow your fighters within 100 miles. If they continue to push the situation, the Americans will attack. You have to withdraw your fighters now."

"Ex-Comrade Shagan, is that an order? Perhaps you forgot that you are in Moscow, and I sit in the battle area."

"General, there is no battle area other than what you are causing. The Americans know that we have remained in a non-aggressive profile both in the Gulf and around the world. This saber rattling you are doing could have major implications. A wrong move now could start a shooting conflict."

"Comrade, we are fully prepared to deal with the American forces in the Gulf."

"Excuse me, General, but do you really believe that? I find it hard to believe that Fidel wishes to start a war with the Americans."

"Shagan, the island is now under military law. And as to Fidel's position on this matter, he is in Bolivia. I am in control of Cuba."

"General, let me enlighten you on some facts. The two Mig-21 fighters are prepared to engage others at ten miles. The Tomcats they are flying into can engage them at 100 miles with Phoenix missiles, and then follow up with Sidewinders and Sparrow missiles. At least we know our weapons capabilities. Again we are requesting you to withdraw your fighters now."

"I thank you for the weapons lesson, Comrade Shagan. Again, I feel I am being told what to do, and not requested in a proper manner to redeploy my forces. Ask me properly and I will consider your proposals."

Red washes over the face of the Air Marshal, as his hand grips the phone handle. "Very well, Comrade General. Would you please withdraw your fighters? We do gratefully appreciate your concern for our people. But we can deal with this situation by ourselves."

"Better, Shagan. I will consider your appeal and get back to you." The line goes dead in Shagan's ear. He slams the receiver down so hard it breaks in half. "Son of a bitch!" He throws the handle aside. "Get this fixed now!"

Without getting a glass, he drinks directly from the bottle of vodka. His eyes seethe with hate towards the general so far off. An aide replaces the phone handle and puts it back on the cradle. "Thank you." He reaches over and pushes another button. The line rings.

"Secretary Brant, we believe that General Morales will break off his fighters prior to the 100-mile demarcation. It is hard to deal with him sometimes."

"We understand Air Marshal. Some of the officers here have had to deal with his arrogance. We will wait and see what happens." They both hang up.

YAK FIGHTER
THE GULF

As Val looks out the side of the Yak, breaks in the clouds let him see quick glimpse of the water below. It seems like a moving gray mass.

"Sir."

Val concentrates on the voice in his ears. "Yes, Lieutenant." As he goes to speak, the noise of the missile lock indicator comes to life. "What the hell?"

"That, sir, was what I wanted to let you know. We are being joined by two Cuban fighters. They will be beside us in a minute or so."

"What the hell are they doing targeting us?" As he speaks, the Mig-21s slide in next to them. Val looks from one to the other. "Can you contact them, Lieutenant?"

"Yes, sir."

Val continues to watch the fighters as they talk to the pilot.

"Sir, they were ordered by Havana control under General Morales to escort us into the crash site."

"What the hell! Get me the *Moskva*, Lieutenant."

"Yes, sir."

Val looks past the pilot at the bank of clouds they are flying at. He knows that somewhere ahead death hangs from the wings of the American interceptors.

"Tiger one, this is Top Hat. Over." Four Tomcats fly their area at 40,000 feet. "Roger, Top Hat."

"We have inbound aircraft joined by two Cuban fighters. Middle aircraft still running cold, two escorts are at present hot. Proceed to intercept. If all three aircraft pass the 100-mile demarked zone, they are presumed to be hostile, and appropriate action will be taken. Per Ultima, you are free to fire. I say again, you are free to fire."

"Roger, Top Hat. Tiger flight hot, we are receiving intercept vectoring. Over."

"Roger. Good hunting. Top Hat out." The four F-14 fighters turn in unison, and go to afterburners and accelerate into the clouds.

"Sir, we have the *Moskva*."

"Thank you." Val talks with the cruiser, and a patch is established through to Moscow.

"This is Shagan."

"Marshal Shagan, this is Val. We have a situation. There are two—" His words are interrupted as Shagan cuts him off.

"I know Val. We have talked with General Morales to have the fighters disengage and go back to their orbiting position."

"Well," Val looks at the two fighters off their wing, "we're right here together. And I would be guessing the Americans will shoot us down if they continue."

"I couldn't have said it better. You have to the 100-mile demarked zone. If they're still with you at that time, the Americans will assume that this is a hostile attack."

"Well, shit. They don't seem to be breaking off."

"From our calculations, you have fifteen minutes. If they're still with you, bank and fly back to the *Moskva*. If they follow you there, land on deck and refuel. The ships have been given orders to fire on the two Cubans."

Val keys the intercom. "Lieutenant, if the fighters are still with us in fifteen minutes, we are to fly back to the *Moskva*. All right?"

"Yes, sir. We are receiving a call from the American fighters. If we cross the 100-mile demark line, they will shoot us down."

"Oh, great."

"Sir, a suggestion. We could reduce power, allowing the two Migs to jump in front of us. I would then be in a firing position. I'm picking up the scans from the fighters in front of us; they have a lock on us. They are moving forward to the demark line, and are positioned for the attack."

Val passes the information on to Shagan. "Sir, I'm starting to feel real bad about this mission. We're going to have to turn back to the *Moskva* and—" The words stop as the two Migs have suddenly gone strait up into the air and rolled back from the line.

"Val, what happened?"

"Well, sir, the two fighters broke off at five miles from the demark. I'm going to have to change clothes when we land. We're about to enter the 100-mile zone and the Americans did not fire."

The pilot points at his ears. "Just a minute, sir."

Val changes over to the intercom. "Yeah."

"Sir, the Americans have gone to a passive mode. You will be able to see them in a few seconds." As Val looks out the canopy, two Tomcats sweep by them on each side.

"Comrade Air Marshal, we now have our American escorts. I will contact you from the beach."

"Very good, Comrade." The line goes dead. Val rests his head on the back of the seat as the Tomcats come up beside them, two on each side. He listens as the pilot talks with them and can feel the plane make some course corrections. Val's head moves from side to side. He thinks to himself, "I'm too old for this kind of shit."

ULTIMA
WASHINGTON, D.C.

Everyone watches the blue and red colored triangles converging at the white demark line. Suddenly two of the red triangles separate and begin flying away from the line.

"They have turned back, Mr. Secretary."

"Thank, God." A round of applause goes up.

"Sir, the Yak should arrive at about 0710 at the crash site." He nods at Van Nar. "Thank you, Captain." Brant rubs the back of his neck. "That was too close. I believe Shagan was right. General Morales is playing games."

Brant reaches over and picks up the yellow phone. "Well Marshal Shagan, it looks like disaster has been avoided for now."

"Yes, sir. We will continue to work with that fool Morales. As for now, we can breath a little easier. We will wait for the arrival of Comrade Val at the crash site and get back to you at that time."

"Very good." They both hang up. In Moscow, Shagan and his staff watch CNN. It flashes the first pictures of the crash. They await the interview with the Coast Guard on the site. In Washington, Brant is handed a computer read out. He looks it over and turns to the others at the table. "Well, gentlemen, please read this over and tell me what you make of it."

They all read over the intercepted conversation between Morales and Shagan. Some things are highlighted. "Mr. Secretary." Brant looks up at Admiral Hillings. "Shagan has his hands full dealing with this arrogant bastard. And we know that Fidel is in Bolivia. But from his statement that he is in charge of Cuba and his mannerisms, I believe that we could be seeing the beginning of a coup. I wouldn't put it past General Morales. And right now, he is in full control."

"I agree, Admiral. That statement of being in total control could lead to trouble. I would like a profile done on the general and his senior subordinates. Also, I want to know where President Castro is at all times, until this thing settles down. I need to update President Wayne on this situation. We'll review this other material when I get back. Thank you, everyone." Brant gets up and leaves the room. As he moves down the corridor, his two marine guards walk beside him.

HAVANA CITY, CUBA

The rain falls in blowing showers as the two vehicles pull up in front of an apartment building and cut their motors. "I think this is the one." Captain Vargas points to the apartment building down the street. Brock looks at his watch. "We'll unload here and proceed with caution. This guy could choose to go out fighting."

"Sí, señor." He waves his hand and men climb out of the truck. "Señor, we are moving the other truck down the street to block off both sides. We also have men positioned around the back of the apartment."

"Sounds good." Brock watches as the rear truck pulls down the street and men begin pouring out. The wind-driven rain continues to pelt the men as they assume their positions.

"We are ready, señor." Vargas brings his pistol up into the ready position. Brock moves along the men crouched on each side of the apartment stoop.

Checking the street one more time, he watches a vehicle move around the men at the roadblock. An armored personnel carrier moves down the street and pulls up facing the front door of the apartment. The back doors open and soldiers climb out and move to a position on each side of the BTR-60. An officer moves up to Brock and Vargas.

"Sir, General Quintano asked us to join you. He feared that there may be a tendency for these men to fight back."

"Right, we thank the general. Hold your men here. We'll call if we need more help."

"Sí, señor." He moves back with his men.

Two soldiers signal them from the hallway and they begin entering the building. Without a word the captain signals the men up the stairs to the second floor. They check the hallway in both directions and take up positions on each side of the apartment labeled 216. People look out their doors at the troops in the hall. Holding their fingers to their lips, a soldier moves in each direction motioning them back into their apartments. Brock moves to one side of the door, and Vargas on the other. He nods at Brock.

"Luís, this is Captain Vargas. Open the door and put your hands on your head. We need to talk to you about last night."

They sit and wait. No response is forth coming from the apartment. Another nod. "Luís, open the door, now!" Again no response. Vargas signals two men forward. They take a position directly in front of the door. The captain's eyes look from the men to the door. "NOW!"

They hit the door, causing it to fly open, and continue into the room. Men pour into the room behind them, their weapons at the ready. Brock follows the others in. "It's all clear, señor."

Brock looks around the apartment. "Search every thing." The men begin looking through the contents of drawers and pulling cushions off the sofa. A man appears at the door, talking to the guard. "Señor, my door. I have a key."

"Over here." Vargas signals the landlord over.

"Señor, my door."

"Sí, it will be fixed. Do you know this man?" He shows him the picture of Luís.

"Sí, señor. It is Luís; he is a good renter. He pays on time and does not cause any trouble. What has he done?"

"I can't discuses that with you, but it is important that we talk to him. Do you know where he is?"

"No, señor. But last night I saw him come home, and then leave a short time later."

"You saw him last night?"

"Sí, señor."

"Was he with anyone?"

"No, señor. I saw no one with him."

The older man looks into Brock's eyes and nods his head. "I think he is in bad trouble."

"What time was it when you saw him?"

"I must think." He runs his hand back through his hair. "I could not get to sleep and was watching a late movie. When I heard him come in, it was a little before 2:00 A.M. He did not stay long. I saw him leave and watched him out the window. He walked to the bottom of the steps and then headed up the street towards the market."

"Thank you, señor. If we need anymore information we will get back to you."

"Sí, Captain. If you have anymore apartments to enter, please call me. I have a key."

Vargas nods his head. "All right." The landlord moves into the hall to calm the other renters on the floor.

"Sir, you have a call from the armored car." Brock watches as the captain talks to the men outside. His hands run over some cards at the small desk. A blank note pad on the desk catches his eye. Holding it under the lamp, he sees impressions on the paper. Taking a pencil, he rubs it over the paper. The name Mary appears, in addition to the word Libertal and the time 2:10.

"Sir, they have a police officer who patrols this area downstairs. He may have questioned Luís last night."

Brock holds the paper up. "Do you make anything of this?"

Vargas looks it over. "No."

"Well let's go talk to this officer." Brock and Vargas go downstairs as the others continue to search the room.

Two men in raincoats wait by the front door, water still dripping from their cloths.

"This is the officer I called about, sir. He may be of some help."

"Have you seen this man?" Brock hands him the picture.

"Sí, señor. I stopped him last night and checked him. Everything looked in order, so I let him proceed."

"What did you stop him for?"

"Nothing really. Him and some other men seemed to be arguing with some ladies."

"Where was this?"

"About 2 blocks from here."

"Patrolman, if you would get into the armored car, we'll drive back to where you stopped him."

"Sí, Captain."

They all move back to the armored car and get in. "I'm going to leave a few soldiers here at the apartment. The others will move with us."

"Good. These people may have been contacts. He may have let them know that he had placed the bomb."

"Bomb?" The policeman looks at both men. "What bomb?

As the armored car moves up the street, they are jolted around. "We believe that this Luís was involved in the sabotage of a Russian bomber. And officer, that information, for the present, is not to be put out."

"Sí, señor." He moves to the front to direct the driver.

Vargas leans across towards Brock. "The name Mary is in his file. It would appear that she is his girlfriend."

"Well, where does she live?"

"It seems she lives in Miami, according to the files."

"Shit." Brock hits the side of the vehicle with his closed fist. "He is going to make a run for the American mainland; I feel it."

Vargas looks out the front. "It could be, but with this weather it can't have happened yet." The armored car stops in front of another apartment building.

"We'll go get these people, and bring them back down." Vargas opens the rear door, and climbs out.

"All right, Captain. I'll wait here." Brock runs the paper through his fingers, thinking of the meaning of the time on the note. He leans back against the side of the vehicle and looks out the back at the misting rain. He hears something out of the ordinary, and leans his head out the back.

BAM! BAM! Shots ring out into the street, followed by an explosion.

"What the hell?" Brock jumps out of the back of the armored car and looks around the side towards the front of the building. Machine gun fire comes from the building. Troops outside are on the ground and up close to the walls. The front doors fly open as a soldier carrying another man bolts out and down the steps. He carries the wounded man to the back of the truck; a medic begins working on him.

Brock moves up the side of the BTR, using its armor for protection. As he gets ready to run for the front steps, the sound of breaking glass reaches him. He moves to the front of the vehicle, and looks around the side. The staccato of automatic fire fills the street. Bullets bounce off the street and the armor around him. Pulling back, he tries to squeeze as close as possibly to the cold steel. The bullets ricochet around him, and then their vengeance is turned on the troops around the trucks. Brock sees two men go down near the truck and watches as the fire falls onto the men near the wall. Someone near the truck is firing up towards the window that is racking his position.

Again he tries to look around the front. The men at the truck now see the shooter. He watches as the rounds begin hitting the brick around the windows on the third floor.

"Grenade! Grenade!" Men run from the front of the building directly under the window. The shooter fires into their midst. Two men fall as they run for the cover of the truck.

BOOM! The blast from the grenade rocks the street. Weapons are being fired from both trucks at the windows. As Brock looks around the front of the armored car, the turret gun joins the assault. He covers his ears as the machine gun rakes the windows on the third floor. Spent cartridges fly everywhere as the turret moves back and forth, they begin falling on and around him. He covers his head with his hands; the hot brass burns as it hits them. "Goddammit!" he yells into the wind. His screams are lost in the blast of the gun.

An explosion from the building blows out some more windows. Gunfire from inside the apartment erupts. The turret on the armored car pops open. "Cease fire, cease fire! Our people are inside the apartment!" The firing stops and the men on the street wait silently with their weapons at the ready. They continue to aim up at the apartment windows. Shots continue to come from the apartment, then there is just silence. The man in the turret yells to the others.

"The captain is coming to the window. The apartment is secure. Tend to any wounded. All clear." He repeats the message twice before the men at the truck lower their weapons. Brock stands up and brass cases fall to the ground. He looks up at the shattered windows and sees Captain Vargas.

"Damn it." He walks across the spent casings all around him, and heads for the front door. Men are helping wounded and checking the vehicles.

Vargas comes out of the building with the patrolman. "Señor Brock." As he walks up, there is blood all over the left side of his uniform.

"Are you OK?"

"Sí, when we got ready to go in, they fired through the door and hit one of my men. He fell on me, and then the whole thing went up in smoke. Someone in the apartment next to him opened his door and rolled a grenade down on us. So we had to assault both apartments. I'm afraid we have no suspects that can talk; there are two men and a woman in the front apartment. And one man and another women dead in the second apartment. We also have some injured bystanders. We had three killed and four wounded in the assault.

"Why the hell did they open up on you?"

"They were drug dealers. I guess they thought that we were a narcotics raid."

They walk over to the armored car. Vargas pats the front steel. "When this baby opened up, it really got their attention and gave us a chance to get in. I got a call from General Quintano. He wants to talk to you." Vargas hands him his radio.

"Señor Brock, I've been waiting for your call."

"Good morning, General Quintano."

"I talked with Captain Vargas. It seems we are all having a bad day. When we went into Miguel's apartment, his roommate drew a gun. Well, he wasn't as fast as my sergeant was. It looks like all of our suspects are getting themselves killed. We searched his apartment but found nothing. However, his roommate's car is missing. And a neighbor said they heard someone drive out this morning about 2:30. I've called the police to be on the lookout for that car and both of our suspects."

"Good, General. We are not doing to great either. I did find a note with the name of his girlfriend on it and the name Libertal, also the time 2:10. We wondered if Miguel was to pick Luís up at that time or what. But if Miguel didn't leave until 2:30, then I don't know. But I now believe, Comrade General, that their intent is to leave the island and get to America."

"I would agree with you, Comrade Brock. But with the hurricane and the military alert, I think we still have a chance to catch them."

"Brock, I'll meet you back at my office, after we turn this over to the police. It's 6:50 now. We'll see you in about ten minutes."

"OK, General."

A gentle rain falls as bodies are removed from the apartment building. Two ambulances are loading injured people and getting ready to leave. Brock rejoins Vargas. "Captain, will be meeting General Quintano back at his office."

"Sí, señor." He moves to the trucks on the right and tells them to return to base. Brock leans on the armored car, and gets ready to climb in.

"Sir, pardon me."

Brock turns to the officer. "Yes, officer." He steps back from the rear door.

"Señor, I was not eavesdropping on your conversation, but I heard you say 2:10."

"Yes, that's right, the note said 2:10. But it didn't match up with his partner leaving at 2:30."

"Sí, but what if they each took a different mode of transportation, so that both would not be caught at the same time."

"All right, so what's your thought?"

"Señor, at the market I patrol, there is a bus to Matanzas."

"Yes."

"Señor, it leaves here at 2:10. When he left his apartment, he was headed for the bus stop."

Brock considers the words of the policeman. "I think you're right, Officer. You have been a great help." Brock shakes his hand and climbs up into the armored car. Vargas gets in with him. "Let's go back to base." The motor revs up and they begin the ride back with Brock letting Vargas know what the patrolman had told him.

CONTROL CENTER
HAVANA

The lieutenant adjusts the papers in his hand and knocks at the generals door. "Excuse me, sir." He waits for Morales to acknowledge him.

"Yes, what is it?"

"Sir, the civilian authorities are requesting aid from us. The storm has closed some main roads going east of Havana. With the alert on, we cannot release any troops." The general walks to the window and looks out on the rain still falling.

"Sir, we are also getting reports from our surface craft. They are experiencing heavy seas. And some of the *Komar* boats are having a hard time with the storm waves."

Turning from the window, he looks his aide over and walks back to his desk.

"Very well, Lieutenant. Order the army groups in the east to send reserves to help with the storm damage. But I want the units along the northern coast to remain at full alert. And I want all missile batteries to remain on full alert in that sector until we have confirmation from the crash site."

"Yes, sir." He moves to the door as another officer comes in.

"Sir, we have General Quintano on the phone. He and the Russian Brock are following up on the two men thought to have sabotaged the bomber."

"Thank you." Morales pushes down the blinking line on his phone. "This is General Morales."

Quintano smiles at Brock. "Good morning, General. This is General Quintano. I have an update on the two suspects."

Morales listens as Quintano tells him of the mornings events and where the investigation stands.

"Very good, General. I would like you to pursue every lead, and not bother yourself with the alert. I want to know any changes in the investigation. Please keep me informed." The line goes dead.

Quintano rolls the phone handle in his hand. Brock sits across the desk and looks at his face. "Let me guess, General. Stay with the investigation, and stay out of my way. How's that for a guess, General?"

"Is it that obvious, Comrade Brock?"

"No, Comrade Quintano. General Morales's hate for you is kept just below the surface. It takes a trained observer to see it when you're both in the same room. He fears you, my friend. And from that fear, he will not miss any opportunity to help you meet your maker."

"I have to agree. We have been told to stay out of the mainstream and to not bother him. How about some coffee, my astute friend?"

"It sound great."

ULTIMA
WASHINGTON, D.C.

"Mr. Secretary."

"Yes, Captain Van Nar." She walks up to the lectern and uses her pointer on the screen. "We are receiving a Cuban order for air and surface vessels to move out of the path of the storm. They have downgraded the alert in the eastern half of the island south of Florida, but seem to be maintaining the western alert. We believe that the civilian authorities have requested assistance to combat the storm damage."

As they all look at the screen, the satellite refocuses towards the eastern part of the Gulf and moves down. The planes and ships can be seen turning back towards Cuba.

"Mr. Secretary." Brant turns from the screens and looks down the table to General Lane. The air force general leans forward on the table.

"Sir, I believe we can assume that General Morales has come to his senses. We could begin returning some of our planes back to their bases. The hurricane is moving out into the Gulf, and we are getting some foul weather out there. So we could leave the Coast Guard cutters on picket duty, and the naval ships at sea. We could reduce the air cap in the eastern region to air patrols of minimal size."

Brant looks over at Admiral Hillings. "I agree with General Lane. We can match their reduction, as a show of good faith. But still keep response groups on station."

The secretary checks the others. The Joint Chiefs all agree on the course of action.

"I agree, gentlemen. Give the order, please."

General Lane makes a call, and the screen soon shows aircraft turning towards the Florida coast. Secretary Brant picks up the red phone. "Mr. President, we believe that the tension in the Gulf is subsiding. The Cubans have begun to lessen their alert in the eastern portion of the Gulf, and begun to reposition units to assist the civilian authorities with storm damage."

Brant listens and looks up at the screens. "Yes, sir. We are reciprocating in the same area. If there are any changes, I will call immediately."

After hanging up the phone, he looks over the others in the room. "Well, gentlemen. I believe we have seen the worst of it. President Wayne seems satisfied. May I suggest we have breakfast, and then continue to deal with the situation."

All heads nod. "That sounds good, sir."

Side doors open and stewards begin taking orders from those in the room. As the men around the table are being served, Captain Van Nar continues to watch the screen. "Excuse me Captain. What would you like?"

She looks back at the orderly and then down at the menu. "Ah, just some fruit and juice, please. Oh, and also a bagel."

"Yes, ma'am."

The orderly returns with her order, and puts it on the desk in front of her. As she takes a bite from the bagel, she continues to watch the screen. Picking up a phone behind her she talks to someone and hangs up. Putting down the bagel she walks up to the lectern.

"Mr. Secretary." Brant and the others look up from their breakfast. "Sir, I just talked with Top Hat. I had noticed that this particular boat had made the turn and then began drifting to the northwest. It seems that this is a *Komar* boat, and it has lost power in one engine. The others are overheating. That's what Top Hat is getting from their calls."

The screen pulls down over the scene. The shape of the hull sits at the center of the screen. Waves seem to be breaking over the side.

"From appearances, the boat is floundering in the troughs." She calls on a phone at the podium and the picture pulls back.

"We have the two destroyers here." She points with her laser. "They're running in front of the others. My guess is two *OSA* and four *Komar* boats, and the group on the left is short one boat. But it is continuing to try and join the others. We have not received a mayday call from the boat. Our estimate is that the closest ship to assist has now become a Coast Guard cutter." She looks at her notes. "The *Eastwind*."

"Thank you, we will continue to watch this event."

As Brant drinks some juice, he turns to the Coast Guard captain down the table. He picks up a phone. "Sir, I'm in contact with the *Eastwind*. They are tracking the boat. The weather is bad, but they think that they can launch a chopper and retrieve the crew. But it will be close."

Brant nods his head and looks back at the screens. "Thank you, Captain Stedman. Can they move closer just in case?"

"Yes, sir. They are moving at an oblique that will bring them closer. One moment, sir." The captain looks at the screen as he listens.

"Well, that's it." The captain holds his hand over the receiver. "They have just received an SOS mayday call on the *Eastwind*. They are requesting permission to proceed."

Captain Van Nar cuts into the conversation. "Sir, we have confirmation from Top Hat. The missile boat has lost all four engines and declared an emergency condition."

Brant looks at the screen. "We will hold until we see the reaction of the Cubans."

CONTROL CENTER
HAVANA

"Sir." An aide runs into Morales's office. "Sir, we have a missile boat sinking. They have sent a SOS."

"Well, who do we have near them?"

"That's it, sir. The closest ship to them is an American cutter. They have requested permission to render assistance."

"Damn!" His fist hits the desk top. Morales jumps to his feet. "We must ask the Americans for help. We should let the stupid bastards sink."

"Sir, the *Komar* boats were over-committed in this weather."

A red flush passes over Morales face. "Very well, have them request assistance from the Americans. But destroy the boat as they leave. Do you understand?"

"Yes, sir. It will be relayed to the captain."

Morales paces the floor as the aide leaves the room.

ULTIMA
WASHINGTON, D.C.

"Sir." The Coast Guard captain covers the receiver. "The *Eastwind* is now moving in to assist the missile boat. They have received an OK from the Cubans."

"Thank you, Mr. Stedman."

"Sir." Van Nar walks up to the podium. "Top Hat has intercepted orders from General Morales that the boat is to be scuttled when they leave." The screen moves in closer; the boat is being tossed about. Debris is floating away from it. "Top Hat has the helicopter from the *Eastwind* inbound now. They should be there in a short time." She sits down and they all watch the screen as the small boat fights for its life.

RESCUE HELICOPTER
THE GULF

"Sir, we should be over the boat in about ten minutes. It will come into view off our port side."

"Roger." The pilot fights the stick as the wind and rain outside push and pull at the helicopter. "There she is, sir." They see the missile boat rolling violently from side to side as it rises and falls in the running sea. "We see you! We see you!" the boat captain yells into the mike to counter the howl of the wind. He watches as the Seahawk maneuvers to begin picking up his men.

"Roger, Captain. We'll have to reel you in one at a time. Over."

He turns the helicopter so that the open door is away from the wind. The crew chief begins lowering the harness. As it nears the deck, a crewman moves out and grabs it. They put it on an injured comrade and signal to retrieve him. He is lifted away from the boat and the wind blows him about like a pendulum. The helicopter moves away as they pick up each crewman, and then it moves back for the next.

"Sir, I believe that the captain is the only one left on the boat."

"Roger, Chief. We have got to get out of here."

The captain sets the timer on the satchel charge for ten minutes and pushes the button. A red light comes on and the timer begins counting down. He runs to the hatch to get on deck, but the boat almost rolls and slams him into the door jam. His body is half in and half out of the hatch. The crew chief looks down from the open side door of the helicopter. "Sir, we have a problem."

From his position the pilot can't see the deck. "What is it, Chief?"

"Sir, that last wave about rolled that thing. I can see the captain lying across the threshold of the hatch. I think he is unconscious."

"Roger, Chief." The helicopter backs off to get a better look. "Shit, he's down."

"Sir, the Cuban chief says he will put on a harness and go down for the captain."

"Roger. Get him ready." They watch as water splashes over the deck and the limp body of the captain sways with the motion.

The counter continues to move, passing five minutes. The Cuban chief descends from the helicopter; he swings in the air as he is lowered to the boat. When his feet touch the rolling deck he crawls to the hatch. "Captain, Captain." His words are pulled away by the wind. He yells to him and slaps his face. The hand holding his head up has blood on it. The captain's eyes slowly open and he come awake.

"Chief, what happened?"

"Sir, you hit your head."

"How long have I been out?"

"Just a couple of minutes."

"We have to get going. I set the charge to blow in ten minutes." The Cuban chief calls up to the Americans and tells them the situation.

"Sir, we have another problem."

"What now, Chief?"

"According to the Cuban chief, the captain set a scuttling charge. He has him laced to the rig with the second harness. He suggests that we haul ass, sir."

"I roger that, Chief. Stand by." The helicopter rises with the two men in tow and takes a sharp turn to the right. They move away from the boat to a safer area. The counter reaches zero. The blast blossoms from the boat. Then the two STYX missile warheads join in the explosion.

"Holy shit." The helicopter is slammed by the concussion of the blast. Where the boat had been was now a cloud of fire and smoke. Something had slammed into the back of the helicopter. A warning alarm begins to go off. The helicopter begins to waver in the air as the pilot fights to regain control. The chief looks down the line at the two men still hanging outside the door. Neither is moving and the gyrations of the helicopter prevent him from pulling them up.

The pilot yells over the intercom, "We're losing oil pressure on the starboard engine." He looks over at his co-pilot. "Tell the ship we're coming in. Declare an emergency. I think we can get back."

"Yes, sir."

The captain on the *Eastwind* lowers his binoculars. The fireball in the sky off the bow slowly melted away. "Sir, that explosion was the missile boat. Our helicopter has taken some hits, and is returning in an emergency condition. They got the last two onboard. One was dead."

"All right, I want full speed in a direct line with the helicopter."

"Yes, sir." The helmsman makes a small correction at the wheel and the engine room gets the order for full speed ahead. The bow of the cutter sinks into the oncoming waves and emerges, reaching for the sky.

ULTIMA
WASHINGTON, D.C.

Brant and the others watch the screen as the Coast Guard helicopter picks up men in the blowing spray. As they watch, two men are lifted at one time. The helicopter suddenly veers off the boat, with the men swinging beneath. As the field of view is widened, the boat vanishes in a yellow and red ball of fire. The first blast is joined in a heartbeat by the exploding warheads.

"Sir, the missile boat just exploded." They all look at the screen in disbelief. "They must have left a scuttling charge. The exploding warheads on the missiles caused the second blast."

As they watch the screen, Captain Van Nar picks up a phone and listens for a minute. " Gentlemen, Top Hat has received traffic from the helicopter. They were hit by debris and are coming in on one engine."

The satellite zooms in on the helicopter as the last two men are reeled on board. It moves back to show the cutter and the helicopter on a race against time.

COAST GUARD CUTTER
THE GULF

"Sir, we have the chopper at eight miles dead ahead."

Very good", he looks out through the squall with his binoculars. "All right, there she is. Reduce speed to one third, and hold it in the wind."

"Aye, aye, sir. Recovery team is ready."

"Fire a flare off the starboard side."

"Roger."

A flare is fired off the ship into the rain and wind; it deploys about 500 feet in the air. The red glow dances in the sky, casting an odd color in the rain.

"There she is, sir." The co-pilot points to the rising flare off to the right. He calls forward to the ship. "Sir, she is holding into the wind and reducing speed." A yellow smoke canister is popped on the rear flight deck.

The helicopter turns and lines up with the back of the ship, and moves in to land. The hangar doors are opened on the ship, and lights direct them onto the pad. The ship comes up with a jolt, and the helicopter is down. After cutting the engine, a quick check is made by the ground crew. The blades are refolded. The helicopter is pulled into the hangar. The men inside are helped out of the helicopter, and it is tethered to the floor.

"Sir, we have recovery."

"Very good. Give me a course back to our patrol area, and three-quarters speed." The *Eastwind* turns about and moves back to its patrol area.

ULTIMA
WASHINGTON, D.C.

Admiral Hillings pushes back from the table and stands. "That, Mr. Secretary, was spectacular. My compliments to the Coast Guard." He walks over to get some coffee.

Brant stands up and stretches. "I agree, Admiral. Please pass on our compliments to the captain aboard the *Eastwind*. It was a job well done."

BACKFIRE

The Coast Guard captain smiles. "Yes, sir, thank you. I will send a telex off to their command also."

CONTROL CENTER
HAVANA

"General."

Morales looks up at his aide. "Yes."

"We have confirmation that the men were rescued off the missile boat, apparently with the loss of the captain in the process. All others are safe and will be flown back to Cuba on a commercial flight. Some of the fighters in the area saw the flash of the explosion."

"Very good, that will be all."

"Yes, sir."

CHAPTER 5

YAK
THE GULF, 7:00 A.M.

"Sir, we'll be over the crash site in about fifteen minutes. The navy has flares around the area to highlight it. We'll be flying straight in."

"Roger, Comrade." Val's eyes look forward of the plane at the wall of dark gray clouds which burst with sudden flashes of lightning. He watches the pilot nod his head as he talks to the Tomcat on the right. He can feel the plane shudder as they begin to lose altitude. Soon they pass through the overcast, and begin flying over some of the outlying islands. They continue to drop in altitude, as rains rage close in around them.

Val catches his first look at the crash site; the flares around it form a crescent. Coming in from the south, they fly over the site. The lines of the bomber seem like some type of space ship crumpled on the beach. He counts four helicopters on the ground with men moving around the wreckage. A sudden turn by the pilot brings his vision back to the front. The two Tomcats have risen up in front of the Yak. The pilot turns the plane back and brings it around over the water. He lines up on the beach. The vectoring engines cut in with a screaming whine. The Yak begins to slow its forward movement, and it hangs in mid air.

"Captain McFarland, our guests are here."

"All right, Chief. Assemble the men over by the helicopter."

The men around the wreck had watched as the three jets flew over their position, the news camera filming their arrival. "Miss Lane, you and your people need to move over by the others. We're going to bring the jet in on the beach."

"Thanks, Captain. Smoky, are you getting all of this?"

"We're on it. I didn't know they had this type of plane." The camera sights on the hovering jet out over the water as its landing gear is lowered.

One of the navy crewmen walks out into the center space and turns on two signaling flashlights, and he begins to bring the Yak in. Everyone is watching as the Yak makes precise adjustments and moves forward about twenty feet above the water. It slides forward on the down blast, as everyone covers their ears and looks away. It moves up the beach, stops and gently descends to earth. As the pilot checks everything and cuts the engine, the canopy begins opening.

McFarland walks up to the man climbing down from the back seat. "I'm Captain McFarland. We have been expecting you."

"Thank you, sir. I'm Commander Val." They shake hands.

Marcey Lane leads her film crew up towards the plane. "Sir, could we speak to you?"

Val is a little surprised to see a camera crew there. "Me? I don't have much to say at this point, having just gotten here."

"The rumor here is that someone sabotaged the bomber. Is that true?"

As they are filming the pilot climbs down behind them and walks up to Val.

"Sir." He salutes Captain McFarland. "I'm in touch with the *Moskva* group. They are ready when you are."

"Thank you, Lieutenant." Val removes a hand held radio from his flight suit. "Please excuse the lieutenant and myself. Our English is limited, and we are here to investigate the explosion and either confirm or deny your rumor. So please excuse us for now."

The camera crew sets up to film Marcey's commentary with the Yak in the background. The camera turns from her as she is finishing and follows the two Russians and the captain up the beach to the main fuselage.

"OK, Marcey, we need to get going. The pilot said the weather is getting bad."

"Damn, I wish I understood Russian." They move back out of the rain into the helicopter.

McFarland leads them up to the main fuselage. "Everything is exactly like we found it. We tried to open the hatch door here, but it's jammed."

"Thank you, Captain. Your efforts to this point are greatly appreciated. I would ask that a total effort be made to open the hatch. We need to check that area for some equipment that was loaded in Cuba."

"Very good, Val. We'll check with the base to see if they can send us some cutting equipment."

Val checks his watch. It's 7:25. He and the pilot walk down to the forward compartment. As they walk up, they can see small rivulets of red seeping from the cabin.

"Sir, I'll climb up and check the flight controls."

"Good, Lieutenant. From the look of the rip here," his hand rests on the peeled metal pushed out from the explosion, "this was sabotage. There was nothing on the plane that would cause this."

"I agree." The lieutenant climbs in and moves forward. The waves have gotten bigger, and they rock the cabin with each incoming break. "Damn." He grabs a panel near him to steady himself. Water rushes around the base of the cabin.

"This was bad." The lieutenant shakes his head as he squats between the two seats. He puts his gloved hand down on some instruments under his feet to steady himself. The drying blood is like burnt amber on the instruments. He tries to read them, but being upside down makes it difficult.

"See if you can find the fail-safe box, Lieutenant."

"Sir," the lieutenant lifts the sheared half of the box, "it looks like it was destroyed in the explosion."

"Hell, Mikulin said the fail-safe came on."

"I don't know how; it's in pieces. Perhaps his injuries were so severe that they caused him to think it was on. Even if it did come on, there were no weapons on board, right?"

Val doesn't answer; instead he backs out of the cabin and moves up the beach out of the water. He walks by some men working on the hatch cover; they strain at crowbars wedged in at different angles. As he walks along the fuselage, he reaches into his front pocket and takes out a small round device. He holds it cupped in his hand and runs it along the side of the plane. He stops at the tail section, and checks the read out. Looking at the dial, he thinks to himself. "Damn." There's nothing out of the ordinary. "Shit." He puts the small Geiger counter away and hits his hand flat on the skin of the plane. "They're not here." He looks around.

McFarland walks under the wing. "Val, they got the crank on the hatch to move. The chief believes he'll have it open in just a few minutes."

"Thank you, Captain. That is good news." He joins him under the wing as a gentle rain begins to fall.

"There are some major squalls coming in. We'll have to move some of these aircraft back to base."

"Yes, the weather is looking bad." Val watches as the film crew huddles under an umbrella while they film the men working on the hatch.

A ripping sound carries in the air as the hatch crank slowly turns. They reposition the bars and push again with the same ripping sound. Then the hatch pops slightly open. "We have it, sir." The chief waves his men away from the opening.

"Thank you, men." McFarland climbs up into the fuselage with Val following. He reaches a spot next to the chief. "Here's a light, sir."

The chief and McFarland pull the hatch open and he shines the light into the void. Val gets ready for his words. He thinks, "Please, let the bombs be there."

McFarland looks around and hands the light back to Val. "It looks empty to me. I hope you find what it is you're after." Val climbs to the hatch and shines the light into the space. His teeth clinch. Sticking his head into the hole with the light extended, he checks the bay. The light shines off the rotary holder, but it is empty. Resting his weight on the edge of the hatch, he allows his mind to gather all that this represents.

The light shines one more time into the void; he hopes that the bombs would appear. He pulls back and climbs down. "Captain McFarland, we need to talk alone. Is that all right?"

"Certainly Val. Let's walk over by my helicopter."

"Sir, this area needs to be secured. I would advise you that it would be best to get the news crew out of here. I can only tell you that this situation is about to become the focal point of your government. I will need to go to your base and talk to Captain Mikulin and then to Air Marshal Shagan."

"Val, the crash and the loss of life were bad, but there is nothing here to cause an international incident."

"I agree, Captain. It's what isn't here that is the problem. At this point I am requesting a ride to your base to confirm what has happened. I'll send the Yak back to the *Moskva*, and I need to meet with the Russian consulate chief in New Orleans. That is all I can tell you now. Your Secretary Brant will be forthcoming with what ever procedures will be followed."

"Very well, Commander. I'll fly you back to the base in my ship. I'll have Commander Hicks keep some men here to secure the site."

"That sounds good, Captain." Val waits to the side as McFarland gets the other officers together and tells them the situation. As they finish, the Coast Guard units go to their helicopters and are the first to begin warming up their engines. Commander Hicks and his men set up around the crash site. McFarland walks back by Val. "I'll let the TV people know it's time to leave. We'll be pulling out in just a few minutes, Commander."

"I need to talk to the pilot, and then I'll join you."

Val watches as McFarland tells the news crew that it's time to leave. Marcey Lane shakes his hand and her film crew starts back to their helicopter. She waves at Val and runs down the beach to him. "Sir, one last question?

"Yes, Miss Lane."

"Was it sabotage?"

Val smiles at her. "Your rumor was right this time. There is an investigation going on in Cuba as we speak." They shake hands.

"Thank you." She spins and runs to the waiting helicopter. As soon as she is on board, it lifts into the morning sky. The Coast Guard units follow it; they lift off and head to the east. The chief has his men back on the helicopter and the engines begin to warm up. McFarland waves to Val and heads up the beach towards his ship.

The lieutenant walks around checking his plane, and joins Val at the front.

"Everything is OK. I'll be heading back to the *Moskva*, Comrade."

"Very good, Lieutenant. When you're en route. I want you to send a message through the *Moskva* to Air Marshal Shagan. Tell him that the package is missing, and that I will be contacting him from the naval station in New Orleans. And to have the Russian consul meet me on the base with a scrambler."

"Yes, sir. What package?"

"You'll know soon enough. I should be at the base in a short while."

"Yes, sir." He climbs up into the Yak and begins preparing for lift off.

Val calls up to him. "Lieutenant, thanks for the lift. And have a good flight back."

The lieutenant throws him a salute. "Good luck to you, sir."

Val waves to the Yak as he runs to the waiting helicopter. The whine of the jet can be heard above the spinning blades of the helicopter. It lifts off and turns southeast, then slowly begins moving away from the beach.

"Sir." A hand reaches out to help Val up. He sits down next to McFarland.

"I want to let you know that I called the Tomcats for an escort of the Yak back to the demark."

"That's great, Captain."

As the helicopter lifts off and begins to turn northeast, he looks out the window as two fighters drop from the overcast and race forward to join with the Yak.

ULTIMA
WASHINGTON, D.C.

Van Nar hangs up the phone at the side of the podium. Her job of presenting the mass of incoming information to the Joint Chiefs puts her at the hub of the operation. "Gentlemen, on screen two, we are showing the Gulf area west of Cuba. We have two inbound. They are flying in the squalls at low altitudes. We believe they are drug runners."

"Aren't they aware that they are flying into an excluded area?" The secretary looks around the table. The screen moves in closer; they see the Cuban fighters circling. The two new blips on the screen move just west of the group.

"Top Hat has confirmed: two inbound. There both prop-driven and are definitely staying in the squalls. They have alerted the closest air cap to vector two fighters to intercept at the 100-mile boundary."

The screen pulls back. "We also have the escort fighters with the Yak that left the crash site. They will drop off at 100 miles and rejoin their group. Sky 1 has picked up radio traffic that one of the Cuban fighters is having electrical problems and is requesting to return to base. We still see the western portion of Cuba on full alert." Captain Van Nar sits down behind the podium and continues to watch the screen.

"Mr. Secretary."

"Yes, Admiral."

"Sir, according to Captain McFarland, the Russian was very interested in what was in the bomb bays. And when he left in the navy helicopter, he asked that the area be secured. Mr. Secretary, your name was mentioned — about some procedure that will be put into effect?"

"I don't know what he is talking about, as to some procedure."

"I know, sir. We at this point have no idea of what is going on, but from the earlier message from the pilot mentioning bombs, I'm getting a funny feeling."

"I agree, Admiral. I would think that the Cubans would drop their alert with the confirmation of the sabotage on the bomber. I would like the base commander to meet and remain with the Russian when he arrives."

"Yes, sir. We have taken the liberty of already contacting Captain Nelson. He is standing by for further orders."

"Very good." Brant gets up to stretch his legs. "Gentlemen, I will wait about ten minutes before I call the Air Marshal." He looks at his watch. "That should be about 7:30 our time."

Admiral Hollings looks up at the screens and back to Brant. "Sir, I have been talking with General Swane. We believe that we should send in a group of marines to secure the area. The naval personnel were sent out to assist the Coast Guard. They are unarmed, and from the messages and other events going on, we believe that it would be prudent to dispatch them to the scene."

Brant looks over to the marine commandant. "General Swane, how long will it take to get some of your people out to the site?"

"We have a Recon platoon at the base. The storm broke up a training exercise. They could be in the air in a short time and release the seamen at the crash site."

"I have to agree, gentlemen. There seems to be more going on than we are aware of. Just a second." Brant reaches over and picks up the red phone.

"Mr. President, we are feeling uneasy about the actions of the Russian investigator at the crash site. He requested that the area be secured, and was very interested in the bomb bay area. No, sir, we don't know why."

Brant listens and looks up at the screens. "Sir, Admiral Hollings and Commandant Swane have requested putting marines on the crash site to secure it, until we know what is going on." Brant looks around the table. "Yes, sir. I'm sure that Secretary Sholenska is requesting the call to tell you about the crash. Yes," he nods his head, "I'll wait for your call. Yes, sir. It does look like the Cubans are finally backing off their alert." As he talks he scribbles a note down and shows it to Hollings. He slowly reads it, "It's a go with the marines, NOW!"

The admiral nods and the commandant gets on a phone to talk to his commander in the field.

"Yes, sir. We'll talk soon." Brant hangs the phone up.

"Sir, the marines are being issued combat loads, and two super Stallions are prepping now to take them out. One will transport the men, and the other will provide additional supplies."

"Very good, General. I think we are making a good move. Something is definitely wrong. President Wayne will be speaking to Secretary Sholenska in Moscow. He will give us a call as soon as he finds out what is going on."

Van Nar moves back to the podium. "Gentlemen, if I could draw your attention to the two bogies reported earlier. They are continuing to fly in the squall front, and have remained low to evade radar." Backtracking doted lines appear behind the blips, one to Mexico and the other to Columbia. "We ran a check with DEA and the Coast Guard. They are verifying drugs being flown into the United States. The reason I bring this to your attention is that the Cubans have apparently also picked them up and have dispatched two fighters each to intercept." As they watch the screen, two fighters drop and begin flying due west, and two drop out heading southwest.

"We predict interception in about twenty minutes. There are also two Cuban jets flying to meet the Yak from the crash site. They will probably escort him back to the *Moskva*."

"It doesn't look like the Cubans are backing down much." Brant shakes his head and looks at the air force general. "I agree, General Lane, and the tropical storm is getting worse."

The third screen shows the radar picture of the storm. The center has moved off the coast of Cuba. "Yes, sir. It looks like Evita is working its way up to a hurricane. It's moving north at twenty-five miles per hour. The storm area is about 100 miles wide. We are receiving reports from Havana of winds in excess of seventy-five miles per hour. Their coast is being hit by twelve to fifteen foot tidal surges. The leading edge is beginning to pick up additional support from the storm coming out of Texas. At present, its path is predicted northwest. Louisiana is in its path."

CONTROL CENTER
HAVANA

"Sir." The lieutenant knocks on the open door.

"Yes." Morales looks up from his desk.

"Troops are now moving towards Havana. We are still having difficulty; most roads are blocked by fallen trees or mudslides. And anything near the water is being battered by the high winds and waves."

The winds outside the office howl, and small pieces of debris bounce off the shudders. Morales sits back in his chair and puts his feet up on the desk, a cup of coffee in one hand.

"And what of our brave comrades—any new developments?"

"We have detected two unknown aircraft coming in from the south and the southwest. Fighters have been dispatched to intercept. The storm is causing a lot of problems with the radios and damage to our landlines. We have towers down, and telephone lines are down everywhere. The smaller boats have moved in close to the larger ships. But they are still having a great deal of trouble, General."

Morales takes a drink of his coffee. "Have the smaller boats return to port, but I want the *OSA* boats to stay with the frigates. We may need their fire power."

"Yes, sir. We are having problems in contacting the eastern flight. We believe there is a damaged aircraft returning to its base."

"Have we heard anymore from General Quintano?"

"No, sir. Do you want me to contact him?"

"No, that is all. I expect that bloated Russian to be calling soon."

ULTIMA
WASHINGTON, D.C.

"Gentlemen." Van Nar points up to the screen. "The *Komar* boats are being sent back to port. The *OSA* boats are being brought in closer to the frigates. The ships are now basically on a course east but parallel with the *Moskva* squadron. We now have word on whether they sent their submarines into the area. It is possible that there are two to three in the Gulf area."

Brant looks over to Hollings. "Admiral, how much of a threat do they pose?"

"Well, sir. They're always a threat. They have Kilo class subs. They're diesel and armed with either torpedoes or mines. They have the potential of being very dangerous. But they need to be close to their target. Against a Los Angeles class boat, they won't have a chance."

"Good."

"Well, let's hope they're out of the area. We don't need another player in this scenario."

A marine orderly moves over next to Brant's chair. "Sir."

Brant looks up at the sergeant in dress blues. "Yes."

He leans down to talk to him. "We have been informed that the president is on his way to the situation room. After his talk with Secretary Sholenska, he dropped the phone and ordered his people to go to the situation room on the double. He then left in a hurry, sir."

"Thank you, Sergeant." Brant stands at the end of the table. "Gentlemen, I have been informed that President Wayne will join us in a few minutes. He talked with Secretary Sholenska and immediately left to join us here. I believe that the questions we have been sharing are about to be answered."

The officers around the table move over to their aides and discuss the situation and prepare for any questions. Communications are checked as they return to their seats and arrange their paperwork in an orderly manner. They become aware of a commotion in the hallway leading to the situation room. Someone is shouting orders and the sound of fast-moving feet arrive at the door. The marine guards open the door, and the president enters the room.

"My God! My God!" The president looks up at the situation screens. The men with him move to seats around the room. With his open palm, he shields his eyes and silently stands for a minute to compose his thoughts. He walks over next to Brant.

"Mr. Brant, has Marshal Shagan called you yet?"

"No, sir. I was going to call him about the situation at the site."

"I asked them to wait until I arrived to make the call."

"Sir, what is the situation?"

"We believed that there was more to this crash than we were being led to believe."

The president walks over to a chair next to Brant. He slumps into it. He closes his eyes and shakes his head. "I've canceled all my appointments for today, and I would advise you gentlemen to do the same. I also want no one in this room to leave, until we resolve the situation. I will call Marshal Shagan and then let you speak to him. I want the conversation put on the speakers so everyone can hear."

"Yes, sir." Brant nods to Van Nar. She calls to the control room to get the call put up on the speakers. Brant reaches for the phone.

"Just a minute." He puts his hand on the secretary's forearm. "Gentlemen, the news given to me by Secretary Sholenska is unbelievable. I think it best that Marshal Shagan explain it. But know this, it is believed that eight nuclear weapons have been dropped on U.S. soil."

"My God." The words slip from Brant's lips. Everyone in the room seems to have sucked in a breath at the same time.

"The secretary is saying it was a major mistake, caused by the sabotaged bomber. The weapons were being returned to Russia."

Brant turns to the president. "What the hell were they doing in Cuba?"

The president nods towards the phone. Brant picks it up. "Mr. Secretary, this is Air Marshal Shagan." The voice assails the silent room. "Is President Wayne with you?"

"Yes."

"I have been asked to answer your questions regarding this incident. And I must emphasize that no overt act or premeditated action was taken to endanger the good relations between our countries. We had hoped to remove the weapons with no one knowing about their existence at the Cuban location. After the crash, our hope was to recover the main fuselage and have the *Moskva* bring them back. We are now aware that the weapons are not on the aircraft. So Commander Val is en route to the naval station to get more information from the pilot."

"Marshal Shagan, this is Secretary Brant."

"Yes, sir."

"Under the pack signed in 1963, no offensive nuclear weapons were to be brought into the lands of the Western Hemisphere."

"Yes, I am aware of that. I must explain that the decision to deploy these weapons came about with the change from the old regime to where we are now. Certain groups in the system, not knowing which direction the government was going and sensing a loss of potential power, ordered the placement of weapons at six locations. They were to be, as you would say, an ace in the hole. With the transition going the way it has, their fears were found to be unwarranted. The weapons were returned from five of the locations and are now being disarmed. The sixth and last was to meet the same fate, but the sabotage of the bomber has changed this."

"Air Marshal, this is General Lane."

"Yes, General."

"Sir, we have dealt with missing nuclear weapons before, like off the coast of Spain. I see this as clearing the area and retrieving the bombs. We can get them aboard the *Moskva* and that's the end of it."

The voice coming back over the speakers fills the room. "I understand, General, but we believe there is one more problem. It is thought that the bombs are armed."

"Holy shit, Mr. President, armed!" The room is suddenly full of voices echoing General Lane.

"Gentlemen, gentlemen. We need order." The secretary slaps his hand on the table. "We need to maintain an orderly response for the president."

"We have no reports of explosions in the area, so they must be on some type of time delay."

"Whoever that was, he is correct."

"That was Admiral Hollings, Air Marshal."

"Yes, the admiral is correct, but the bombs can be set for detonation up to twenty-four hours."

"This is General Lane. What is the time setting for these bombs?"

"We don't know at this time; the pilot is the only one who saw the read-out. Commander Val is going to talk to him to get the answer."

The president stands up. "Marshal Shagan, if you would please stay on the line, I would like a few moments to talk to the others here."

"I understand, Mr. President. I will be standing by."

Brant pushes the hold button, and the light begins flashing. The president rubs the back of his head. "Good God! If I understand this, we have eight nuclear weapons on the ground that could go off at any moment. They're just south of New Orleans. Gentlemen and ladies, we need a plan of action, and we need it now. If this disaster were to occur, only God would forgive any of us." The strain on the president's face seems to age him beyond his fifty-seven years.

"Sir."

The president looks at General Lane. "Yes, General."

An aide puts a paper in front of the general. He holds it up. "Sir, if these assumptions are correct, this is what we are facing. They must have used the standard rotary of bombs. We have eight five-kiloton weapons, if they used the standard MK-5 nukes."

"Mr. President."

"Yes, Admiral."

"Sir, we are now having the computers draw a flight path from the explosion to the crash. We can use that as a base line and attempt to move civilians back at least twenty-five miles or more. The marines will be on site soon, so we can use them as search teams. We can have air reconnaissance from NAS New Orleans, but the whole key is this—how much time do we have?" As they watch the screen, a red line begins drawing itself from the explosion on the bomber to the crash site.

Brant looks back to the president. "Sir, we can, I believe, use the on-coming storm to order people out of the area. That would give us time to get in and disarm the bombs without the press all over us."

"Good, good, Brant. We need to keep this totally under wraps at this point. That report on CNN from the station in New Orleans is out, and I have a news conference called for nine o'clock. At that time, I will announce the evacuation of the area in southern Louisiana. We can have the national guard standing by to assist and block the area from the north. I want the entire area around there secured. No more news helicopters."

"Yes, sir. We'll seal off the area and begin a search as fast as we can get men into the area."

"Jesus, we're going to send our young men into a situation that we know can turn into a disaster in a second. I don't feel good about that." The president shakes his head.

"We understand, Mr. President; we feel the same. But we are left with such a short fuse, we have no choice."

Brant looks back at the phone. "Sir, we need to work with Marshal Shagan and his people to get as much information as we can."

"You're right, Mr. Brant." He looks at his watch. "It's about five minutes to eight. I need to get back and get ready for the news conference. I want up-to-the-minute info on this. Any changes I want to know immediately."

"Yes, sir." The secretary gets up, and so do the others in the room. As the president is walking to the door, he turns to the group. "May God bless us in the coming hours." A marine guard opens the door, and the president and his group leaves.

Brant sits down and pushes the blinking light down. "Marshal Shagan."

"Yes, Mr. Secretary."

"The president has left, and we need as much information as we can get about the bombs and their dispersal."

"Yes, we are ready to give any information we can to expedite the removal of the weapons."

"This is General Lane. Are these MK-5s?"

"Yes, General."

"We have a line drawn on the map from the explosion to the crash. Can we assume that the weapons were dropped at some specific interval?"

"Yes, I believe we can. Just a minute General." Shagan speaks with someone off the line. "I have been reminded by my aide that we may have a problem. When the death mode is enacted, it realizes that it is to attack ground targets. When the aircraft passes over water, it uses an infrared sight at the front of the plane and will adjust the aircraft to fly over a landmass. So the line across the area you're in may have been adjusted for water."

"Great, half of the flight path is over swamps. How do we disarm the weapons?"

"That may present another problem. The triggering mechanism has some anti-tampering devices associated with it."

"Well, Christ, Shagan. Is there anything that will be easy in dealing with these things?"

"I'm sorry, General Lane. But like your weapons, they were made to be used once. The thought of disabling one after delivery is something new for us also. And because of the special use of these weapons, they are especially difficult. We have personnel on the two SSMs, or *Victor* submarines, as you call them. They are trained in dealing with nuclear weapons. We assume that there has been a Los Angeles submarine in escort with the *Moskva* group, so you have been aware of the subs."

"Yes, we are aware of the two subs with the group." Admiral Hollings looks up at the screen. "Air Marshal, how soon will Commander Val get back to you?"

"It is a little after eight A.M. in New Orleans, we should hear from him in a very short time. I will also be in contact with General Morales, to get him to drop his alert in the western area. I will be talking with him in a short time; as your officers know, he is a bit belligerent. The secretary tried to contact Comrade Castro, but he is on a good will trip to Bolivia. So until we hear from Val, we will remain near the phone. If your officers have any questions, we will respond immediately. Our hope is that the weapons are at the extreme end of the timer at twenty-four hours. If this is so, we will have only lost four hours. I will contact the SSMs and talk with Morales. Mr. Brant, I will get back to you as soon as I can."

Brant pushes the button on the phone. "Gentlemen, using the information from Shagan, we need a plan of action."

The others in the room begin working with their aides and writing notes. Brant watches the screen; the red line stands out boldly. Even though he closes his eyes, he can still see the red line and hear the muted conversations around the room. Easing back, his head rests on the leather of the chair.

CUBA, ON THE NORTHERN COAST

"This way, señor." The man in front leads Luís up the side of a cliff on a narrow path. The surf slams into the beach below with a loud hissing sound. The trail cuts back up a narrow gorge and the man walks to some bushes and stops. He waves Luís up to him, and then slowly looks both ways. His hand pushes the foliage apart.

"In here, señor."

As he follows him into the bush, a cave mouth is just inside. They walk through a dark tunnel for about sixty feet; it opens to a cavern about eighty feet wide with a high ceiling. A small fire burns towards the back and two people sit on blankets; their eyes follow the two men.

"Señor, you will have to wait here until we are ready to leave. There is coffee and some food. I must go back to the beach to find your friend who will be going today. You must remain in the cave; there are aerial patrols at different times. This man and this woman will also be going; they have been here since early this morning. As soon as I locate your friend, I'll be back."

As he reaches the mouth of the tunnel, he turns back. "You can have the fire but be sure you do not have a lot of smoke. It will drift up through the cracks in the rocks and can be seen. I will be back soon." He turns and disappears. Luís greets the others and then arranges his bag with a blanket, and he lies down to rest.

MIGUEL, ON THE ROAD

The cars in front of him move slowly around the stalled truck; the rain comes in bursts pushed by the high winds. Miguel checks his watch. "Damn, it's almost eight o'clock, and I still haven't made it to San José."

The windows are partly clouded; the small heater tries to combat the chill and the moisture in the car. The movement of military vehicles and the washed out roads has cost him dearly. A man in the rain waves him forward, and points to a side road to detour on. Up the road, water and mud stream across the pavement. They move through run-down neighborhoods, the people stand outside on rocks and boards. The wind cuts through the shanties unmercifully; canvas and cardboard strain under the pull. Cook fires are visible up the muddy streets.

"This is why I did what I did." In his mind, this site justifies their actions. "The government has lost the thought of the people; it serves no one but itself. But one day the people will rise up and be free again. On that day Luís and I will return as heroes."

"Señor." Someone taps on the window. "Señor." He rolls the window down halfway. "Señor, you will have to remain here for a while. The road is washed out about a mile ahead; they are working on it now. You can turn off your motor; no one will be moving for about an hour."

"Sí, is there a coffee shop around here?"

"No, señor. You must be from the city."

Miguel nods his head.

"There is a small canteen just up the road. I know they have coffee there."

"Will you watch the car if I go get something to drink?"

"Sí, señor. This is my place to work. I will watch it."

As Miguel gets out of the car, a truck of army troops passes by. The tires throw mud into the air. Miguel and the man cover their heads.

"Damn, can't they slow down?" He brushes the mud off his cloths.

"It has been like this. They are rushing to Havana."

"Yes, I've seen them all morning on the roads."

"The canteen is there." The man points to a brightly painted section of wall about halfway up the block. Others are getting out to go to the canteen as Miguel walks by. Pulling his collar up, he trots to the door and goes inside.

QUINTANO'S OFFICE
MATANZAS AIR BASE

"Brock, they're still having trouble getting through to the control center in Havana. They're hoping to get it fixed soon. Our problem is in Havana; there is a lot of damage from the storm. General Morales has ordered the alert canceled in the eastern provinces."

"How soon do they think we can get out of here?"

"The main part of the storm is moving out to sea. It should be soon. The manager at the bus terminal said he believes that the 2:10 bus got through."

The phone rings next to Quintano. "Sí, just a minute."

"Brock, it's for you. It's your radio room." He hands him the phone.

"Thanks, General. This is Brock. All right, I'll be there in just a minute." He hangs the phone up.

"I have to go over to the radio room; there is a message coming in."

"All right, I'll keep checking with the phone people."

As he goes out the door, he sees that the rain has stopped. But the wind still whips around. Running to the end of the path, he crosses over a corner of the tarmac to the radio room. The storm seems to be breaking up. He opens the door.

"So, what's the news?"

"Well, Comrade Val saw the crash site, and it is definitely sabotage."

"Well, we pretty well figured that. And the payload?"

"It's not on the plane."

"Not on the plane! What the hell?"

"Apparently, the fail-safe system went into death mode and dropped the bombs."

"Holy shit! Where is Val?"

"He has gone to the air station to talk to Captain Mikulin and the other pilots. It is believed that the timers on the bombs are set for twenty-four hours. But that is just speculation. Also Commander, there seems to be some strained relations between Air Marshal Shagan and General Morales."

Brock sits in a chair looking out over the field. "Shit, I can believe that." He pours himself a cup of coffee.

"They suggest that we remain on base and not to go into town."

"Very good, Comrade. Pass the word on to the others to stay on the base."

"Yes, sir." The operator gives Brock the printed message.

He takes the paper and reads. "All right, I'll be with General Quintano. If the chief has any questions, have him call me there. And stay on that radio. I feel we're going to be getting more orders soon."

"Yes, sir."

Quintano looks up as Brock pushes the door closed behind him. "Good news I hope?" He goes back to some paperwork.

Brock pulls the message out of his pocket, and hands it to Quintano. "Take a look at this, General." Quintano takes the wrinkled paper and reads the message.

Quintano looks back at Brock. "Come with me." They walk back to his office.

"Comrade Brock, this message is top secret, addressed to you."

Brock slides into a chair. "Yeah, but I wanted to see your reaction to the last part."

"I see that there are some parts missing."

"I took some things out."

Quintano nods his head. "I can believe that Marshal Shagan is having problems with General Morales. Every time Fidel leaves the island, we all get nervous. He has declared a state of emergency, and martial law is in effect. And the western sections of the country are still on full alert. I would have thought that he would drop the alert. I have no orders to the contrary, so we will continue to work together to find these men."

"Thanks, General. I was hoping that you would say that. The others on the base will remain near their work areas."

"That's a good idea, if you have received that message. I am sure that I will be getting something soon. By the way, I have had a bulletin looking for the car sent. I don't know when it will get out to everyone. So for now we will just have to wait until something breaks." Quintano goes back to his paperwork.

"Well, I hope it's soon." Brock closes his eyes and folds his hands behind his neck.

CHAPTER 6

GULF REGION, 8:00 A.M.

The wind buffets the Mig as the young Cuban lieutenant trims the aircraft. It's like flying in a vacuum with no radio and radar lost. He hopes the rugged Mig-21 can get him home. Not able to return to his base in the eastern sector, he heads for an alternative field in the western area. Coming in at 3,000 feet and using what's left of his gauges, he hopes soon to be able to see some reference points. Sluggishly, the fighter pushes through the storm clouds, its wing tips lost in the mist.

"Sir." The radar operator calls the lieutenant over to his scope. He leans over to look at the screen. "Is that the bogie that was going east?"

"Yes, sir." The men in the Cuban missile battery watch as the blip suddenly turns south and heads directly for them. "We still have no IFF."

"All right, just a minute." He picks up a phone and calls the other battery in their group.

"This is Battery 2."

"Are you tracking an incoming bogie?"

"Sí, sir. We have the inbound with no ID."

"We have not been able to get through to the control center. We believe that they lost their radio towers in the storm. Our landlines are not working either."

"Sí, sir. I'll stay on the phone."

Covering the mouthpiece, he looks back at the operator. "Sergeant, put a lock on the bogie."

"Sí, sir." The designator on the scope locks on to the inbound. Others in the van gather around the scope, and silently watch the glowing dot move towards them.

In the rain, rivulets of water run down the length of the three missiles pointed into the sky. Their tracked chassis backed up against sandbags, their pointed noses stuck defiantly into the wind, they wait.

An officer comes on the line at the second battery. "Sir, we have tried to contact the aircraft, and we also have missile lock." He looks at the scope and listens.

"Do you think it could be an American reconnaissance aircraft?"

"It could be, sir. That decision is yours. With no communications with sector command, yours is the final call."

"Unless he changes course, we will both engage at twenty-five miles."

"Sí, sir."

Hanging up the field phone, he walks back to the console. The others in the van step back. Removing a key from around his neck, he put it into the weapons safety release. He turns it and the firing board lights up. "Sergeant, at twenty-five miles, we will engage the bogie."

"Roger, sir." He throws some switches on the console and lights begin flashing on the panel. The others in the van move to armored windows in the van to watch the missiles.

"Sir, we have thirty miles now." Both batteries are connected; the officer at Battery 2 turns his key and waits for the command to fire.

"On my count from five." He looks up at a running clock on the console. "Five, four, three, two, FIRE!" Both officers press down the buttons on number one. The green lights under it go out, and red lights above them come on.

The steel dart on the launcher feels the sparks of life suddenly touch its heart, and the modern arrow is boosted into the sky. Flames and mist are blown back by the igniting rocket motors. At the same instant on another tracked launcher, a second missile vaults into the air. As the ramjets cut in, the missiles correct their courses. The men in the vans are cheering as their messengers race through the sky.

The Mig-21 breaks out into a patch of clear sky, the young pilot looks up into the blue sun-drenched sky. As he looks forward two black darts emerge from the clouds in front of him. Too late he senses his fate. The two missiles hit the Mig in a thunder's blast. The shredded remains fall into the sea below.

The blip on the screen goes out. "Sir, we have a kill." The men in the van cheer again, and pat each other on the back.

ULTIMA
WASHINGTON, D.C.

"Sir, we have a missile lock from two of the Cuban batteries near Bauta."

As the men turn to look, two streaks flash from the Cuban coast.

"My God." Captain Van Nar catches herself. A sudden bright flash and the radar blip is gone.

"What the hell was that?" Brant continues to look at the screen.

Van Nar picks up a phone; she talks for a second and hangs up the phone.

"Mr. Secretary, Sky 1 has confirmed the downing of a Mig-21 fighter by SA-6 Gainful missiles fired from Bauta. Our assessment is that they shot down the aircraft reported earlier having trouble from the flight north west of Havana."

"But why did they shoot down their own fighter?" Brant looks around the table.

"Sir, we might assume that the fighter had lost IFF, and they assumed it was hostile." Brant shakes his head. "I believe that Marshal Shagan was correct. The Cubans are dangerous."

OVER THE GULF, WEST OF CUBA

Two camouflaged Mig-23 fighters break from the clouds, and with wings folded back, they knife through the sky. The lead ship calls back to the tanker.

"We are on track, beginning right turn."

"Roger, Tango flight. Bogie is at ten miles and below you 3,000 feet."

"Roger. Ten miles and 3,000 feet."

"Tango, you are cleared to fire. Over."

"Roger. Tango out."

As the Migs turn, their wings move forward and lock into the extended configuration. They slide to the right and begin to drop in altitude. Their radars pick up the unknown blip in front of them. They pass into a moving front and continue to drop. A drizzling rain is flung from their canopies. They line up on the blip from behind and begin advancing forward; they soon see a dark shape looming in front of them.

"This is Cuban Air Defense. Identify yourself. Over."

The message is repeated several times. Only silence fills their headphones. They move up on each side and get a better look at the plane. The sleek outline of the Beech Queen Air comes into focus. The aircraft has no markings, and the ID numbers are covered. As they move up to signal the pilot, the plane dives into the storm below. Both fighters fall in behind the fleeing plane; again it does not answer radio calls. Again it rolls into a new heading, this time to the northeast. They demand that the plane turn towards Cuba. It dives for the surface of the water and skims along at fifty feet off the waves. The two fighters drop in behind the fleeing plane; the lead pilot arms his Aphid missiles. They watch as the plane veers left and then right to avoid them getting any kind of lock on him. He heads into a squall and continues his evasive action.

The pilot pushes the button on his stick, and the missile slides off the underbelly pylon and races into the on-coming rain. A bright orange ball appears in the clouds, and the radar blip disappears. They lift their noses and go to afterburners; their wings automatically move back into their delta configuration. They get back up to altitude and call forward to the tanker.

"This is Tango 1. We have splashed one. I repeat, splashed one. Over."

"Roger, Tango 1. Confirmed one down. Well done. Out."

ULTIMA
WASHINGTON, D.C.

"Sir, the Cuban fighters, which were sent to intercept the bogie out of Mexico, have shot it down. We'll replay the event on screen one." Those in the room watch the screen as the two fighters move in behind the plane. They see the sudden dive to escape the threat and the fiery demise of the plane.

"What the hell are they doing? That plane is a good 200 miles off their coast. I'm sure the DEA is glad they're out there."

"Sir, the second group will make contact with the other bogie in about five minutes. Sky 1 is reporting that the Cubans have begun to reestablish their radio net, which the storm knocked down. Sources on the island are saying that the ground communications are out and are being worked on to get through to Havana."

Brant turns back to the others. "Well, let's hope that Marshal Shagan gets through to General Morales soon. Well, gentlemen. Where are we now?"

"Sir." Commandant Swane moves up to the podium. A screen is shown of the crash site and the area twenty miles around it. "We will have marines on the site in just a short time. They will secure the area here." A line begins drawing itself around the crash site. "The naval personnel will move back to the center of the perimeter. They will be ready to assist the marines or the Russians at the site. We will break the platoon into two search teams. Each will have a sector of the supposed drop line. We have asked the DEA to send three people to the site. These men will assist in moving through the areas. Some are swamp and savanna areas. The DEA have been in and out of these areas. We are waiting to hear back from their field personnel in the area."

"I like the site plan and the evacuation plan, also, Commandant."

"Mr. Secretary, I would like to turn this over to Admiral Hollings." They exchange places.

"Sir, we have ships south of the delta on picket duty. Over the last few hours, the crescent around the crash site has expanded out to fifty miles. Captain Thorp and his command have taken over the inshore waters, and they will be diverting any surface craft from the area." The admiral points up to a screen showing the area of the crash. Different shape squares and circles begin appearing on the screen. The names of the ships are placed beside each one. Four triangles are moving towards the crash site. "As you can see, all the players are getting into place."

"I would like to point out that the FBI is also working with them, and we'll be working with the local law enforcement to evacuate the area. As soon as the weapons techs arrive, we'll be able to begin the dismantling of the bombs. Also, General Becker has the army quick response group out of Alabama. They are loading in vehicles and will move to the blocking sites twenty miles north and south of the center line. The naval forces will put an air cap over the evacuation area. General Lane's air groups will take over the extended patrols into the Gulf in the east to maintain the 100-mile exclusion zone."

"Thank you, Admiral Hollings and also everyone else. This plan looks good. Let's put everything we can in place, so that when we hear from Marshal Shagan, we're ready to go." Brant makes a call as others around the room also get on phones to dispatch their units to their designated areas of responsibility. The secretary uses the time to call the president and fill him in on events as they stand.

As he talks, the screen on the left draws in to show two fighters beginning to turn to their right. Captain Van Nar regains the podium and points out the next confrontation. Brant completes his call and hangs the phone up.

"Gentlemen, we believe that the two Mig-23s sent to the south have now acquired the second bogie, and are at this minute maneuvering in for the kill." The words seem strange as they watch the forms coming closer together.

"Let's hope that this time they use a little discretion in their tactics."

"Yes, sir, Mr. Secretary."

As Van Nar turns to the screen, again two bright tails flash from the lead fighter. In seconds the bogie blip is gone from the screen. Van Nar is on a phone and nods her head. "Gentlemen, we have confirmation; the second bogie has been shot down."

"I don't believe these guys." General Lane leans forward. "I think that General Morales has lost control of his forces."

"I agree with General Lane." Brant shakes his head.

The yellow phone next to Brant rings. He picks it up, "This is Brant."

"This is Shagan, Mr. Secretary. We are getting word from the Badger that the Cubans are reporting American fighters downed in the Gulf. They are also reporting a reconnaissance plane shot down by coastal missiles."

"Air Marshal, they have shot down three aircraft in the last thirty minutes, but none are ours. We believe that two drug runners were shot down in the Gulf, and that their missiles at Bauta shot down one of their own fighters."

"Damn, this is getting out of hand. That damn Morales is running berserk. We have not been able to get through to him for a while because of the damage done to his communications. We're hoping to reach him soon. But I must say my personal feelings are that he is too far into this event to back down. We're hoping to reason with him, and then be able to concentrate on the weapons. I should also be hearing from Commander Val soon. Good luck, Mr. Secretary."

"Good luck dealing with Morales." He hangs the phone up.

CONTROL CENTER
HAVANA

"Sir, we have the radios back up."

"It's about time!" Morales waves the man into his office. "Well, where do we stand now?"

"We have good news, sir. One of the missile batteries at Bauta shot down an American reconnaissance plane."

"What?" Morales jumps to his feet. "We got one?"

"Yes, sir. About fifteen minutes ago."

"Good. I knew something was up."

"Also, sir, we have confirmation by the fighter group that they have shot down two American fighters over the Gulf with no losses to us."

"Yes!" Morales dances around the room. "Yes! Have any other responses come from the Americans?"

"No, sir. It's strange. They have still continued to remain in a passive mode, and they have relaxed their air coverage in the eastern Gulf. They remain within the 100-mile zone around the crash site. We have picked up no verbal response to the loss of the three planes."

"Of course. They can't admit they lost the aircraft. They would be held up for ridicule, and their top-secret missions over Cuba would be out for everyone to see. But we don't have to wait for them. We can get it out to the people around the world that we have stood up to the great American forces and have driven them back. Call the radio and TV stations and have them come here. I'll have a news conference."

"Yes, sir."

"Also, send out messages to the fighters and the missile battery from me. It was a job well done."

NAVAL AIR STATION
NEW ORLEANS

As Val looks out the window, the base slips under the helicopter. Oddly, it strikes him how similar all military bases look, here in America and in Russia. His flight suit is damp from the rain at the crash site. The smell of wet military clothing fills the interior of the helicopter.

"Commander, we'll be landing near the control tower in just a minute. They will have a car waiting to take us over to the hospital."

"Thank you, Captain. That is good." The Sea King banks slightly and comes in facing the tower. As it rolls to a stop, a car pulls up near it and two guards get out. Val hands his helmet to the crewmen and climbs down to the ground. The men by the car wave him over. The guards open the door, and Val gets in beside another man.

"Commander Val, I'm Captain Nelson, the base commander." They shake hands and the captain explains the situation as it stands.

"I must speak to Mikulin as soon as possible." Val can see marines loading on two huge helicopters and two slim Cobra gunships off to the side.

"They're on their way to the crash site. Your two fighters are in the hangar over there." The captain points out the window as they pass.

"I'll need to see the planes later."

"All right, the hospital is coming up on the right. I have been instructed to remain with you to facilitate you getting around. I'm in contact with my XO, so we can keep abreast of what is happening." The car pulls up into the emergency zone. Captain Nelson leads him into the corridors and to the elevator. "We need to go up to the third floor. An area has been closed off for your pilots."

As the door opens to the hallway on the third floor, two armed guards come to attention. They salute the captain as they pass.

"This way, Commander. His room is right here. I'll go get the doctor in charge."

"Thank you, Captain." Val looks in through the window. Mikulin has bandages over most of his body, and he lies sleeping. Moving on to the next room, he finds the fighter pilots in the room. They see him in the doorway.

"Comrade Val! Welcome." He walks into the room over to Ski's bed.

"How are you feeling, Comrade Ski?"

"Fine. The doctors sewed me back up, but it still hurts."

"Yes, Comrade. He likes the nurses here." Norba calls over from the bed next to him.

"I can see that, Comrade Norba. I must ask you some questions about what you saw out there. We know now that the weapons on the bomber were dropped. They were not at the crash site." Norba jumps down from his bed.

"Weapons, Comrade Val? There were cameras loaded on the bomber."

"I'm sorry, Comrades. I forgot that you were not told of the true load on the bomber. It was carrying a rotary of nuclear weapons."

"Shit, Comrade. You're saying that we have bombed the Americans? With nuclear weapons?"

"Yes, Comrades. They were being moved back to Russia to be disarmed. The saboteurs changed all of that. They were not at the crash site."

"We saw no explosions. Are the Americans aware of all this?"

"They have been told. They are working with us to recover them. Did you see anything that would help in the search to recover them?"

"No, Comrade. The American Tomcat and myself were above and just behind the wings of the bomber. We saw nothing. Ski had dropped out of the flight."

"All right, I must talk to Captain Mikulin to find out what the timers were set for."

Ski shakes his head. "He is in a bad way. They removed his leg from the knee down on his right side. And he had some bad head injuries."

Their attention is drawn towards the hall. "I'll be back in a little while. So relax."

"Yes, sir."

As Val walks out into the hall, he can see Captain Nelson talking with a man in scrubs and another man. The man with Nelson walks up to Val. "Comrade Val, I came as soon as I was called. I am an assistant to Comrade Menaul, our minister here in New Orleans. I am Comrade Sozinov; I have brought the communications equipment you requested. They have set aside a room down the hall to use."

"Very good, Comrade Sozinov. I'll get with you in a few minutes."

Captain Nelson brings the man in scrubs over to Val. "Val, this is Captain Rollens. He is the doctor in charge."

"How do you do, Doctor." They shake hands.

"Doctor, it is imperative that I talk to Captain Mikulin."

"I'm sorry, Commander, but he is under heavy sedation. He may not make it as it is. To attempt to wake him could mean his life."

"I understand, Doctor. But I must insist that it be done."

Rollens turns to Nelson. "I can't do this. The man will die. I'm sorry, Commander, but no way." He turns back to Val. "Commander, is the knowledge you need worth this man's life?"

"Yes, Doctor. I must insist. If we do not get the information that only Captain Mikulin has, the deaths of thousands may be involved."

Rollens looks deeply into Val's eyes and sees the cold truth. Nelson takes Rollens aside. "Captain, the order is to awaken the patient. If my authorization is not enough, I can get a direct order from the president."

Rollens looks at Nelson and shakes his head. "That will not be necessary, Captain. Your involvement denotes the urgency. Besides, I think we could do a better job than having our guest stick an electrical cord up his ass. I just hope this situation is worth the life of this man."

Val steps over. "He is a soldier, Comrade Doctor. And he may have to pay the final debt. But he knows that I would not do this unless I had to. And sir, I would ground his foot and touch his tongue with the electrical lead. We quit sticking things up peoples asses a while back."

Rollens shakes his head and calls the nurse. He instructs her to get the equipment to wake up the patient. He walks to Mikulin's door and waits.

"I need this information to determine how much time we have left."

"I understand, Commander. I also sense that the pilot is more than just a pilot you met."

Val smiles. "Doctor, we have served together for many years; he is a man I can truly call a friend."

"Val." Nelson points down the hall. "We have set up your equipment on the phone in the room down there. Your consulate is trying it out to be ready for you."

"Good." They both watch as the doctor gets his people together and an emergency cart is placed by the door. The medic group, dressed in green scrubs and masks, enters the room. A nurse gives Val and Rollens surgical masks to wear. They follow them into the room, and Val stands at the foot of the bed.

Rollens looks over the others, and clears a syringe. "Everyone ready? I'm going to give him ten cc's of Narvon; this will clear the drugs out of his system. It's pretty drastic, and the response will be sudden." He positions the needle and looks up at the monitor above the bed; the needle is plunged into Mikulin's neck. The lifeline performs some erratic jumps, and a muscle jerks in Mikulin's body. He takes a deep breath and suddenly opens his eyes; a noise of pain sweeps through the room.

"Captain, can you hear me?" Rollens leans down near his ear. "Captain, can you hear me?"

Mikulin's mouth moves slowly. At first nothing can be heard. Then he whispers, "Yes."

"This man needs to talk to you. He is looking for an answer to an emergency situation." His eyes sweep around the room and alight on Val.

"Comrade." He tries to raise his hand. Val moves to the side of the bed and takes his hand. "Mikulin, I must ask you some questions." Rollens moves to the head of the bed. Mikulin's hand tightens on Val's. "Val, the bombs! The bombs!

"Yes, I know, Mikulin. But quickly, what was the timer reading on the panel when the bombs were dropped?"

"The timer." Mikulins eyes water and seem to fade.

Val shakes him. "Mikulin, the timer. What was it?"

"It was bad. The timer was logged in at twenty-four hours. All weapons were dropped. I couldn't stop them."

"I know, Mikulin."

He grabs hard on Val's hand. "You must stop them."

"We will, Comrade. You have given us the final link. Now rest easy, and get well." Mikulin's head slips to the side, and his grip goes limp.

"Out of the way, Commander. This man is dying."

Val moves so that Rollens can get to Mikulin. The machines around the room begin to beep and wail.

"We have cardiac arrest." The cart at the door is wheeled into the room. Val and Nelson leave as Rollens and the others work to bring Mikulin back. Val meets the consulate in the hall and follows him into the next room.

"Here you are, Comrade Val. The equipment is connected to the telephone. I made a call to Moscow. The line is open for you."

Val picks up the phone and turns to Nelson. "Captain Nelson, you should tell your people that the time frame is twenty-four hours. And we will all have to work fast."

"Very good." Nelson leaves and goes down the hall to the doctor's office.

Val talks to Shagan and verifies the situation. "One last time Val, our talks with General Morales are not going well. He has ordered all Russians put under guard. Their aircraft have shot down two planes and a missile battery knocked down another."

"Three planes? Whose were they?"

"It is believed that they were two drug runners and one of their own fighters. I will be talking with General Morales soon, to get him to call off his alert."

"I wish you luck, Air Marshal. He is a hard man to reach sometimes. I'll remain here for a while, and then meet the others at the crash site."

"Good, Val. I'm going to call the *Moskva* to pick up the weapons techs off the submarines and fly them to the site. You can then take charge of them and hopefully get this situation taken care of."

"Yes, sir. Let's hope for the best. I will call you from the site." He places the phone down and walks back out to talk to the other pilots. He sees Captain Nelson talking over his radio; the noise of people talking fast comes out of Mikulin's room. As he reaches the door, figures in green begin to leave the room. The noise of the buzzers is now quiet; two people push the cardiac cart out the door. He looks into the room, expecting the worst. Dr. Rollens is leaning over Mikulin, and two nurses are moving things off the bed. His eyes look up at the monitors, the line pulses into sharp peaks. Rollens takes the stethoscope out of his ears and sees Val in the doorway.

"Continue the fluids, and call me if there is any change."

"Yes, sir." The nurse nods and continues to clean up the area.

Removing his mask, Dr. Rollens walks into the hall. "I hope you got what you needed." Val nods. "This little wake up call could still cost him his life. We have him stabilized; he had a heart seizure. But we're not out of the woods yet."

"Thank you, Doctor. I would not have done this if it were not such an extreme emergency. Mikulin and I have worked together over the past few years, and I call him my friend. This decision did not come easy for me."

Rollens nods his head. "We, I think, with some help from above, have gotten Captain Mikulin stabilized. He should make it." Val smiles as the doctor moves down the ward to check on other patients.

CRASH SITE
BARATARIA BAY

"Sir." The radio at the lieutenant's side comes alive. He keys the mike.

"Roger."

"Sir, we have just made contact with the ready force. They will be on site in just a few minutes."

"Roger—" As he goes to say his next words, a new sound is blown into the crash site. At first it is muffled, but it grows in intensity.

Whomp, whomp. They all look to the tree line northeast of the site. Two marine Sea Cobras move towards them and circle the crash site. Just behind them, two H-53 Super Stallions fly in under the cover of the gunships. They circle the site and are directed to the north end of the crash by a red smoke grenade. They move out over the water and then in to the beach. Both touch down at the same time; the large helicopters block out the view west of the site. The ramp on the closest one lowers, and the marines begin to disembark. As the engines on the helicopters slow down, they form into three files, and a single man walks towards the lieutenant. He watches the figures in camouflage work their way up the slope of the beach.

"Lieutenant Thorp?"

"Welcome, Captain. We have been expecting you; it's nice to have some company out here." They shake hands. "I'm Captain Johnson. We were briefed to secure the perimeter and relieve your people."

Thorp looks at the name above his pocket, and back into the face of the black officer. "This way, Mr. Johnson."

"Excuse me, Mr. Johnson. But weren't you the all-American end at the academy?"

"That was a few years ago, Mr. Thorp."

"I knew it. I was a year behind you. You were one hell of a player."

"Thank you. Those were good days."

"I hear that, Mr. Johnson." He adjusts his collar against the drizzling rain. Moving up a small knoll behind the wreck, they reach the top and look out over spreading wet lands. "From here you can get a little better view of the area."

"Right." Johnson had reckoned the site from the air on the way in, and he makes a final adjustment in his mind as he looks over the area. He looks back at the crash. "I knew there was a reason why I didn't want to be a pilot."

"I agree." Thorp chuckles, and pats Johnson on the back. "It's all yours, Mr. Johnson. I'll pull my men back to the helicopters."

"Very good, Mr. Thorp." Johnson's hand raises into the air and closes into a fist with his index finger pointed into the air. He circles his hand. Without a word, the first ranks of marines move out and gather around Johnson. "Sergeant, I want one gun over their and the other two along the knoll here."

"Yes, sir." They split into three squads, and each machine gun and its fire team move to their assigned positions. They begin to set the guns, to cover all land access to the site. As Johnson watches the guns being placed, the second line of men moves up to him and kneels in the sand. Without looking around, he begins speaking. "Second squad, position from the helicopters to here." He points to his direct front.

"Aye, aye, sir." They move out and fan out to begin digging in. The next rank of men moves up to him.

"Sergeant, from the back of the site to our forward front."

"Aye, aye, sir." They move out, leaving Johnson with his two gunnery sergeants. They kneel in the damp sand and watch the men digging in. Soon there is a crescent formed around the crash by the marines.

"It looks good, sir."

"Yeah, Gunny. We'll hold here until we get more directives." As the marines settle in, the sailors make their way back to the beach. Johnson's radio operator joins up with the men on the knoll.

"Sir." He hands Johnson the handset. "It's Touchdown." He talks with Captain Nelson at the base, and is briefed on the latest developments. "Aye, aye, sir. Bulldog 2 out."

He turns to his men. "Gentlemen, we are at full alert, and we are locked and loaded. No one gets into this position without clearance. If anyone wants to push the situation, we will fire. After we get set in, I want two people from each squad to get back to the beach and get rations for their group."

"Aye, aye, Skipper." The two gunnies move to the men digging in and tell them the captain's message. As the machine guns are set up, a belt of ammo is laid in and loaded. Soon men begin moving back to the beach to get the rations; a mule from the second helicopter pulls out and begin moving up the beach towards the knoll. As it gets to the seaward face, the marines start unloading the supplies.

The two gunnies watch the rations being distributed to the men, and have a talk with the other sergeants. They walk back to Johnson on the knoll.

"Everything looks good, Skipper."

"Very good, let's go look at the plane."

"Yes, sir." They walk down to the crumpled fuselage, and look it over. "Damn, this thing is big, sir."

"You're right, Gunny. And apparently worth something, or we wouldn't be out here on full combat alert." They climb up on the torn front and look back into the open access door.

"This thing looks like it could deliver a pretty good punch."

Johnson nods. "Yeah, I'd make a bet it would be all nuclear, too."

The radio operator moves up with them. "Sir, one of the Cobras is coming in south of the navy helicopter."

Johnson talks to the pilot of the Stallion helicopter, then hands the handset back to the operator. "They're leaving one of the gunships up, and one in reserve. One of the Jolly Greens will be flying back to base to pick up more supplies and get our Russian guest out here also."

"I think you're right, Skipper. There is something definitely going down."

They move down the beach to the water's edge, and look over the forward cabin. Johnson walks around and looks into the cockpit. "What a mess. I'd say this was a real bad crash. There is blood everywhere."

"The pilot actually made it; he's in the hospital back at base." Johnson turns as Lieutenant Thorp walks up. The two gunnies come to attention.

"At ease, gentlemen. The pilot survived, but there was something on the plane that is missing. The Russian got real concerned and flew back to the base. We haven't heard anything since."

"I would like to ask you, Captain, if we could get some rations from you. We flew out pretty quickly and didn't bring anything with us."

"Sure, Mr. Thorp. We brought extra rations for your group. We'll get the sergeant to run a load over to your men."

"Thank you. My chief was watching your unloading and asked if they could help. Until we get other orders, we're just sitting around."

"I'm sure they would appreciate the help. Gunny Caballero, would you get with the chief and see where they can help."

"Yes, sir." He moves over to the chief and they shake hands. He takes them down the beach to the helicopter.

"Also, Captain, we were told they're sending a reconnaissance flight over us in a little while; you may want to let your people know."

Their attention is drawn to the east as the Cobra gunship settles to the sand east of the navy helicopter.

"Gunny Marshall, let everyone know we have an over flight coming in."

"Yes, sir." Marshall gets the handset from the radio operator and talks to the sergeants with their groups.

Johnson and Thorp begin walking up the beach. "As soon as we get situated we're going to send out some recon patrols to see what's in front of us."

"That sounds good, Captain." Thorp turns back towards the beach. "I'm going to grab some of those rations before they're all gone, and I need to call the base for our orders."

Johnson continues up the knoll as Thorp turns towards the helicopters.

Johnson looks back. "Mr. Thorp, do you eat many c-rations?"

"No."

"Stay away from the beans and mothers."

"Thanks, I'll take your word for it." He waves back over his shoulder, and trots over to the cases of rations.

Johnson and the radio operator reach the top of the knoll and kneel down. Johnson sweeps the area to their front with his binoculars. The sound of a jet coming in from the east makes them turn their heads as it streaks across the crash site. As the Phantom gets out over the water, it does a rolling turn and disappears.

"Damn." The radio operator looks both ways.

"Yeah, quick. Right, Gleason?"

"Yes, sir."

ULTIMA
WASHINGTON, D.C.

"Mr. Secretary, if I could draw your attention to the screen." Brant and the others watch as Van Nar gets to the podium. "We have confirmation from Captain Nelson at NAS New Orleans; the marines are down and have established a secured perimeter around the site. Also, a Phantom photo reconnaissance flight is now on its way back to base. They hope to see if they can spot any of the bombs." As they watch the screen, a yellow line appears alongside the red line on the screen. "It flew the bomber path, as you can see."

"Thank you, Captain. We seem to be getting all the pieces into place." Brant looks at his watch; it's 8:45. "The president's press conference is coming up shortly, so I'll call him and bring him up to speed. It looks like everything else in the Gulf is holding."

"Sir."

"Yes, Mr. Sturn."

"Our people from the FBI office in New Orleans are now talking with the local law enforcement people, and the hurricane cover story is holding its own after the reports from Cuba and the damage they received."

"Good." Brant nods his head. "We'll continue to move in support personnel behind them."

"Also, Mr. Secretary, the DEA has some of their local people on their way to the base. They will join the second group going out to the site. Apparently, the DEA would consider sending the Cubans a Christmas card for the two drug runners shot down by their fighters."

The others around the table smile, and Brant nods. "I don't doubt it."

CONTROL CENTER
CUBA

"Sir, the news people are here." He knocks again, and slowly begins to open the door. It suddenly is pulled open by General Morales. "Very good, are they in the conference room?"

BACKFIRE

The startled aide stammers. "Yes, sir. This way." Morales has changed his outfit to military camouflaged fatigues. His stars and ribbons festoon his collars and chest. His pistol rides high on his right hip; it has a chrome finish with black horn grips. He pushes the door to the conference room open. All eyes are on him as his aide steps forward to the podium.

"Ladies and gentlemen, the general will answer your questions after he delivers a short message on the events of the day." As he steps to the podium, he looks around the room at the TV cameras and the photographers. He clears his throat to silence the room.

"The news I will be presenting will come as a shock to many people here in Cuba. At approximately 4:00 A.M. this morning, a Russian bomber flying in international waters was possibly attacked by American air forces and shot down."

The news crowd suddenly comes alive. "General, where did this happen?"

Morales raises his hand. "Please, in just a moment I will answer specific questions. This action by imperialist America has forced us to go to a full alert situation. This, at a time when our efforts were being focused on assisting the injured here in Havana and moving in emergency supplies. We have been asked by the Russians to help protect a squadron of ships now operating in the Gulf. In this capacity, our military air and missiles batteries have shot down three American aircraft."

The room explodes in yelling voices and questions. Again Morales raises his hand to wait for the news people to settle down. He turns back to his aide and a cynical smile paints across his lips. He quickly turns back. "Please, again. All your questions will be answered."

He takes a drink of water. "Our fighters shot down two American fighters that had defied the air restrictions around our homeland. The third aircraft, an American reconnaissance jet, was attempting to fly over the air base at Bauta. It was engaged by the missile battery there and shot down. We continue to maintain air response groups around our Russian comrades and the western sections of the Gulf. We are on limited alert in the eastern areas in order to get more military personnel to assist in the aftermath of Evita."

"I would like to end with a statement from both Fidel and myself. We would like it to be known that we find it abhorrent that we were put into a position to shoot down these young American pilots. We know that they were following the orders of both President Wayne and his co-conspirator Secretary Brant, in their defiant manner of assuming that there is no penalty for their attempts to bully small countries around the world. Our regrets go out to the mothers and wives of the fallen airmen. But they must understand that Cuba will defend its territories. Thank you."

The reporters are on their feet trying to get their questions answered. The general works the crowd, answering their questions and allowing his picture to be taken as often as he can. His aides help in answering and directing people to now-working phones. Morales raises both his arms over his head. "Ladies and gentlemen, I must get back to work. We are still in a dangerous situation in the Gulf. We must be prepared for whatever the Americans will try, although we believe they have learned their lesson."

As he leaves, the group applauds and pats him on the back. Once back in the hallway, he relaxes his demeanor. "Well, that should get the Americans' goat."

"Sí, General. Again you work with the press in a most gracious manner."

"Thank you." He looks at the aide. "We should always nurture our friends in the press."

CANTEEN, OUTSIDE OF SAN JOSE

In the canteen the smell of stale beer hangs heavy in the air. The coffee that Miguel drinks is strong and hot; it cuts the chill. "More coffee, señor?"

He looks at his watch; the hands show nine o'clock. "No thank you, this is fine."

"Sí." The bartender moves to others that have been trapped in the wake of the storm. Two men with guitars play old songs in the corner. The music has the feel of working people; their lyrics speak of work and love. Miguel finishes his coffee and throws some coins on the counter. He pushes aside the serape over the door opening, and steps outside. It was still gray and chilly; he pulls his jacket closed and begins to walk back to his car. As he looks up the street, two military policemen are talking to the old man with the road sign. Pulling his cap down, he turns and crosses the street. He passes by a building and stops. He moves back to the corner and looks around the edge back at his car. The men are walking around it and talking to each other; one writes down the license number. They talk with the old man again and he points to the canteen down the street. They move away from him, and head in that direction.

"What will I do?" Miguel rubs the back of his neck. His car is still stuck in the traffic. "Shit." He watches as the two policeman go into the canteen. "My stuff." He looks back to the car. "I need my duffel bag."

The man with the sign heads up the road to new cars coming on the scene. Miguel's mind races. "Now, go for the bag." He leaves the corner and runs to the passenger side of the car. He slips the key in and turns the lock; the door cracks open. Reaching in, he grabs the handle on the bag and drags it out. He looks both ways; the man with the sign is walking back. The two policemen appear outside the canteen and are looking in all directions. He ducks down and begins to creep along the side of the car and around behind the car next to him. He moves across the sidewalk and to the side of a building.

"Señor." He looks around. "Señor, your car." The old man has seen him and waves for him to come over. Looking around the corner he sees that the two policeman have seen the old man waving to someone and are heading back to the car. Miguel bolts and runs up the muddy alley, his feet sliding under him. Suddenly, he falls forward into the mud but scrambles back to his feet. "Shit." He brushes off his legs. When he looks back, the policeman are talking to the old man, and the man points up the alley. They both look up, and see Miguel at the end of the dirt road. Moving through the cars, they head up the alley, their whistles blowing.

"Shit." Miguel runs around the corner and blindly races up the street. He can hear the whistles as he turns up a muddy path and runs around some shanties. He darts through open fences and around corners. His heart pounds from sudden exertion, running and sliding, using his hand to catch his falls. He runs around a corner and is on another main street; a cab is rolling by. "Cab," he yells as he runs. "Cab, cab!" The vehicle comes to a stop. He rips the door open and jumps inside.

"Where to?" the cabby starts to say.

"Get the fuck out of here, anywhere, just go, go!" He can feel the cab move forward, and he looks out the back window. The two officers have emerged from the alley and are looking up and down the street. They turn and point back up the alley and disappear.

"Holy shit." There are almost tears in his eyes. "Holy shit." The scene at the alley was not missed by the cabby.

"Police trouble, señor?" His eyes stare at him in the rearview mirror.

"No, I just need to get somewhere in a hurry."

"Sí, I saw them in the alley, and with the mud all over you, my guess is you're who they're looking for."

"Just drive. It's none of your business."

"Sí, señor. I will drive. But you will pay double the fare, OK?"

"Fine, I need to get to Cardenas."

"Sí, I know a back way, but it will still take some time. The roads are real bad."

"Just get me to Matanzas."

"Sí, señor." Miguel can feel his eyes on him.

The cab moves up the road and around mudflows and slides. Miguel gets out some new clothes, and he changes. He wipes his face and throws the soiled garments out the window. From his bag he takes out a pint of rum and takes a drink, and he shakes his head. He watches the cabby in the rearview mirror. His mind races. "That was too close, and now they know where the car is." He closes his eyes to focus his mind. "I still have time; I must be more careful from here on." His head rests back on the seat, and he lets out a slow breath.

ULTIMA
WASHINGTON, D.C.

"Sir." Secretary Brant continues to read a paper in front of him. "Mr. Brant, we have a contact from the listening stations in south Florida and verification from the base at Guantánamo. General Morales has gone on TV and radio, saying that they have shot down three American aircraft."

"What?" Brant now focuses his full attention on the air force general. "Shit! What were the contents of the speech, General Lane?"

It is just coming up on the main screen. Brant and the others watch and listen to General Morales's speech on the day's events. The text of the speech is printed at the bottom of the screen. Brant looks at his watch.

"Damn, the president's press conference goes on in five minutes. If we have it, you can bet that some of the news groups are filing the story also. This thing would catch the president out in left field. Who do we have with him?" Brant is on the phone.

The voice on the other end explains. "He left a few minutes ago; try him in the press room."

Admiral Hillings leans over. "I'll send one of the guards down to tell him to call you, Mr. Brant."

Brant nods. "Thanks, Admiral." He hangs up and dials another number, but the line is busy. "Sam." He motions his hand to a man working on some figures at a side desk.

He looks up. "Yes, sir."

"Try and get hold of Gordon, and have the president call me before he goes out."

"Right." Sam moves to a phone and calls the radio room. "Try and reach Gordon on his radio; have him call Secretary Brant ASAP."

As the president walks out, the news reporters stand and applaud. He looks over the men and women gathered. "Thank you, everyone. I appreciate your coming on such quick notice; we will have a few issues to cover."

The radio in Gordon's ear buzzes and asks him to call Brant—now! He signals the other secret service agent and moves out of the room to a group of phones in the adjoining room. "Mr. Secretary, this is Gordon."

"Great. Gordon, we need to get a message to the president. We have one of the marines on his way down; you should see him in just a few minutes."

"I'll keep an eye out for him. President Wayne is already at the podium. I'll get with the vice president and have him give him a note, or I'll have the vice president call."

"That sounds good, Gordon. If the subject comes up, he can deal with it."

"Right, I'll go inform him." As Gordon moves into the hall, he can see a marine moving quickly towards him. "Sergeant, did Mr. Brant send you?"

"Yes, sir. I have a note for the president."

"Very good. I talked with Mr. Brant, and I would like you to deliver it to the vice president."

"Yes, sir." The marine guard moves out into the pressroom and walks behind the president to the vice president and hands him the message. Nodding his head, he opens the paper and reads it. Looking back to the marine, he motions him into the other room. The passage of the vice president is not missed by those in the room; their eyes follow him leaving. As he closes the door, Gordon has a phone line open to Brant. He hands him the phone and goes back out to the meeting.

"Mr. Secretary."

"Vice President Cooper, thank you for responding so quickly."

"So, what have the Cubans done now?"

Brant explains the new situation with the TV report from Cuba, and says that probably some of the news groups have the story.

"I would agree, Mr. Secretary. I'll tell the president as soon as I can. If the subject comes up, I'll answer any questions." Hanging up, he goes back to the press room and stands behind the president.

MATANZAS SECURITY OFFICE
CUBA

"Sir." Quintano and Brock look up at the corporal. "Yes."

"That bulletin on the car we sent out a while ago."

"Yes."

"We have a call from a village about eighty miles east of Matanzas. The police there have impounded it. They gave chase to the driver, but he got away. They think he may still be on foot, or he may have caught a cab to drive him the rest of the way."

"Great, we need to get up there now. Corporal, call over to the hangar and get a request in for a helicopter. We will be leaving as soon as they're ready."

"Yes, sir."

"Well, we might have gotten a break." Quintano stands up and stretches. "The bus was going to Cardenas also."

"Yeah." Brock gets up and puts his cup on the desk. "We have two guys heading east." His finger slides along a map of Cuba. "You think, General, that they might be heading to Guantánamo or trying to get to a boat and run for Miami?"

"Could be either one, so we'll cover both cases. I'll call the area commander around Guantánamo and have them put up road blocks and check the buses coming into town." He opens the door and calls to the corporal. "Fax a picture of both of them up to sector five headquarters. I'll be talking with the commander."

"Yes, sir."

"Brock, you need to go get a flight suit."

"All right, I'll meet you at the hangar."

"I'll change now. And let General Morales know where we stand." He looks at his watch. "It's nine o'clock now; we'll meet in ten minutes."

"Right." Brock leaves and heads for the Russian ready room. Cuban guards stand around the perimeter of the buildings occupied by the Russians. They watch as Brock walks to the building. When he enters the radio room, the operator looks back. "Welcome back, Comrade Brock. We are being told not to leave the building."

Brock looks out the window at the guards standing around. "Who gave that order?"

"They said it came down from General Morales's headquarters. Some of his black suits were driving around with the base commander. They have just been standing around out there."

"All right, get someone to bring me a flight suit and a helmet. Also, I need to get a call through to Marshal Shagan, so that he is aware of our status here."

"That might be a little hard. The Cubans have cut out our power to the main radios."

"Shit, can we reach anything?"

"Only on land lines. They said that they will have the suit and helmet over to you in just a minute."

"Great." Brock continues to look out the window, and he throws his coat on a chair.

ULTIMA
WASHINGTON, D. C.

"Captain Van Nar."

"Yes, Admiral."

"Am I mistaken, or are the Cuban ships closing on the *Moskva* group?"

"You're correct, sir. They have been closing at about one degree per hour on the Russian squadron."

"Yeah." The admiral bites his lip and stares at the screen. "Do me a favor, and work up a scenario that would have the Cubans intercept the Russians. I also would like an analysis of the capacities of both groups."

"Yes, sir. We'll get started immediately."

"Good. I just have a feeling we're not done with the Cubans yet."

"Really, Admiral? Do you think that they would attempt such a thing?"

"Mr. Secretary, General Morales has given momentum to his actions. It is possible that he has far greater ambitions than we are aware of at this time. He is playing with wild cards, and we may soon see the joker."

"Well, let's hope he comes to his senses."

"Yes, Mr. Secretary." The admiral sits and stares at the screen.

THE BRIDGE OF THE *MOSKVA*
THE GULF

Admiral Kirsanov stares out the side windows of the bridge. The spray over the bow of the *Sovremennyy* destroyers settles gently back on their decks.

"Sir, the Cubans have moved one degree closer; they are still parallel and just ahead of us." He looks over at the young lieutenant.

"Thank you."

The junior officer nods his head.

"Captain." The ship commander moves up to him. "Sir."

"Signal the others that we will be launching four Kamovs for ASW searches to all four points around the force. And also one out between the Cuban forces and us, to keep an eye on them."

"Yes, sir. This weather will continue to get worse as we head north."

"Correct, Comrade Captain. Also, hold all the guidance radars on passive, but I want all systems loaded and ready for an instant response."

"Yes, sir. Do you feel they might try and intercept us, Admiral?"

"I hope not. But if they do, they will pay dearly for their efforts. Until we cross into the 100-mile zone, we will continue on full alert."

"Yes, sir." His commands are put into action as Admiral Kirsanov moves out onto the flying bridge. The cool wind, heavy with moisture, blows over his heavy coat and fur-lined cap. A look-out scans the sea around them as the elevators on the main deck raise two Kamov KA-25 helicopters onto the windy deck. Kirsanov watches through his binoculars as missiles begin sliding onto their launchers on the ships. They move into place and lock; the turrets slowly turn towards the northeast. The captain joins him as they move to the back of the bridge. They watch as men move about, preparing the helicopters for their flight. After a short period of preparation, the engines on the two helicopters begin to howl, and the dual rotors began to spin. Gusts of water vapor are sent swirling from the spinning blades. The blunt looking little bugs with the big noses rise up from the deck and leave to their assigned search areas. As they depart, two more are brought up from below and prepared for launching.

"So far everything is going good, Comrade Admiral."

"Yes, Captain. Let's hope it stays that way." They walk back to the bridge and move back into the warmth. They can hear the pilots of the helicopters registering their positions with the bridge. Kirsanov watches through the window as the last Kamov flies past the bridge and crosses over one of the destroyers. It moves northeast of the force. In Kirsanov's mind, he knows if anything happens, this one will not be coming back. Its main role is to guide missiles over the horizon, and the Cubans know its purpose, also.

"Sir, we have checked with the submarines. We are showing no other contacts beside ourselves. The sea directly ahead is clear."

"Thank you, Captain. I'll be down in the combat center. I want to look at a few possibilities."

"Yes, sir."

He moves to the back of the room and down a stairwell to the nerve center of the ship. As he enters the room, the dim lighting makes him blink his eyes. They slowly begin to get used to the glow of orange and green screens all around the room. Men move to different locations and check on the returning signals. Moving to the plotting tables and the screen, he checks their location and the Cuban forces.

"Good morning, sir."

"Good morning, Pstygo. How are we doing?"

"Fine, sir. We are continuing to monitor all movement in the area, as well as the conversations from the ships and aircraft back to Havana. The movement of the Cuban surface forces, however, still remains a mystery."

As they both look up at the display board showing the radar positions of the different groups, the blips of the five launched helicopters move into positions around the squadron.

"It looks good, Pstygo."

"Thank you, sir. The analysis of the Cuban force is finished and on your desk."

Nodding his head, Kirsanov walks over to his desk and removes his coat and hat. A fresh cup of tea is placed on the desk as he settles into his chair. His eyes begin reading the information on the Cuban group. His gaze is moved up to the main screen from time to time as he looks through the information.

CUBAN FRIGATE
THE GULF

"Captain."

"Sí, lieutenant."

"Sir, we continue to move closer to the Russian squadron as you ordered."

"Good, hold this course for thirty more minutes and again move over. We need to keep moving west of the storm path."

"Yes, sir."

The captain steps out the side door and looks back at the *OSA* boats following the frigates. They move in the sea, bobbing between the mounting rollers. A young officer moves up to him.

"Sir, we have new contacts from the Russian group. There are four aircraft presumed to be ASW helicopters, and one has taken up a position halfway between our position and theirs."

The captain's hands grip the rail and then release it. Staring out over the sea, he can picture the pilot of the helicopter. If missile strikes were launched, this would be the control.

"Sir." His executive officer joins him.

"Yes."

"Do you think it strange that our good comrades have placed a Kamov in such an odd position?"

"I believe our comrades are acting a little strange. Perhaps it is just a precaution as they move towards American waters."

"Or maybe, Captain, they are running some kind of drill, using us as an aggressor force."

"Well, within the next few hours, we will be turning farther west to clear as much of the storm as we can. This area is going to get some rough seas."

"Yes, sir. It continues to follow us at a steady twenty-five miles per hour. It would not do well to be in its path when it hits."

They move back into the bridge and have a cup of coffee to cut the chill of the morning.

KAMOV HELICOPTER
THE GULF

The lone Kamov holds his position, and his scans bounce off the Cuban ships. They know their purpose, and continuously up date the targeting information. "Sir, do we have some reason to expect the Cubans to attack?"

The pilot looks around and shakes his head. "Not that I know. I think we're doing some kind of drill, using them as aggressor forces."

"Yes, sir. But isn't this kind of shitty weather to launch five of us out for an exercise?"

"It does seem a little strange. But just keep tracking, and sending your updates to the *Moskva*." The pilot moves down closer to the sea; the rolling gray-black water is broken by the windblown tops of the swells. And as he swings around, he stares directly into the oncoming hurricane.

"I know this: we had better be back on board before that thing hits us."

"Yes, sir. It covers about half the long range scope on regular mode."

"Roger." The pilot turns the helicopter around and rises up from the surface. A gentle rain brushes over them.

CHAPTER 7

PRESS CONFERENCE
WASHINGTON, D.C., 9:00 A.M.

The president takes a sip of water as his eyes look around the room. A prepared text has been handed out to the press; they are scanning it as he puts his water down.

"Ladies and gentlemen, I would like to cover the main issues in the press release that you have all gotten. The primary focus of our resources in the coming hours is the people of southern Louisiana. As far as the Gulf area is concerned, it is secured by our military. I have been informed that we can counter any and all aggressive moves by Cuban forces. Our hope is that General Morales will soon relax his posture in the region. Air Marshal Shagan is in contact with him and is continuing to urge a downgrade in his response. He is aware that the crash of the Russian bomber was precipitated by the saboteurs in Cuba, and he has an investigative team tracking them now. We're just not sure of the general's motives at this time."

"Mr. President." Wayne nods at the reporter from the *Post*.

"Sir, our reports say that the area around the bomber has been ordered secured by marines, and that a Russian officer is now at NAS New Orleans. Was the bomber carrying nuclear weapons?"

Wayne smiles. "No to the question. But you're correct, Paul. The area around the crash has been ordered secured, and marines are on the site as we speak. This is so a full investigation of the site can be carried out. An investigator from Cuba, at the request of Air Marshal Shagan, has joined our forces at the site. He has gone to the naval base to talk to the pilots. But again on the last issue of nuclear weapons, there are no weapons at the crash site."

"Mr. President, have we had any contact with the Cuban forces?"

"Yes, earlier a Coast Guard cutter was sent beyond the exclusion zone to rescue a crew of Cubans off a sinking patrol boat. Both the Cubans and us are flying in holding areas in the western Gulf area. Areas in the eastern portion of Cuba have been reduced to low response levels. We have received word from Guantánamo Bay that the Cuban forces have moved away from the base perimeter. But because we are not aware of their future actions, all non-essential personnel are being flown out as I speak."

"Sir, Lynn Nash from CNN."

"Yes, Lynn."

"Sir, I have received a report from our southern bureau stating that General Morales has gone on Cuban TV and radio. He is claiming that Cuban forces have shot down three American aircraft. Do you have a response to this?"

Wayne is caught off guard. "I'm unaware of...." He looks back at the others behind him.

The vice president steps forward. "Sir, if I could respond to this question?"

"Certainly. Vice-president Cooper will field the question." Cooper steps up to the mike as Wayne moves over.

"We are aware of General Morales claims that the Cubans downed American aircraft. It is not true. I reiterate that no American aircraft have been lost. I just talked with Secretary Brant. The aircraft in question are believed to be two drug-running planes out of Columbia and Mexico. The third aircraft is believed to have been one of his own. I again stress that no American aircraft have been involved with Cuban forces." He turns towards Wayne. "Thank you, Mr. President."

"Thank you, Glen." Wayne takes another sip of water. "The actions of General Morales have caused us to divert all flights over the central Gulf. His reckless use of force in the area continues to be of grave concern. But believe me that Secretary Brant and the Joint Chiefs are on top of this issue, so that we can continue to focus our efforts on the evacuation of southern Louisiana. At this time, the hurricane Evita poses the greatest threat to the United States."

"Mr. President, Mr. President." The room is full of the cries of the news people.

Wayne raises his arms to quell them. "I must get back to the situation, but I will have Secretary Brant and his staff give a status report around," he looks at his watch, "let's make it around ten o'clock or a little after. They will bring everyone up to speed on the events so far. Thank you." He picks up his papers and leaves through a side door, accompanied by the others at the podium. As they get into the hallway, he stops the entourage. "I need to take care of some business in the office, but let Brant know about the press conference at 10:00. And tell him that I will be joining him in the center in about thirty minutes."

"Yes, sir."

AIRFIELD AT MOA
NORTHEAST COAST OF CUBA

A Cuban EMB-111 Bandeirante coastal patrol plane races down the runway and lifts into the gray sky as rain squalls work their way through the area. The men on board begin watching their scopes and testing out their positions. They fly out over the Gulf about twenty miles, then turn west towards Punta Mangle. A Cuban *Komar* class missile patrol boat rounds the headlands near Cabo Lucreca outside the reef. Its crew watches out the windows looking for foreign surface craft as they are raked by another squall.

ULTIMA COMMAND CENTER
WASHINGTON, D.C.

Captain Van Nar steps up to the podium. "Gentlemen, we are receiving traffic from the Russian force. They have stationed four of their Kamov ASW helicopters around the force. The one facing the Cuban force is transmitting target data back to the *Moskva*. We believe that the Russian commander Admiral Kirsanov is not taking the posturing of the Cubans lightly."

As they watch the helicopters get on station, the cloud layer from Evita continues to fill screen four. Brant continues to look at the screen as he picks up the phone ringing near him. "This is Brant."

"Yes, Mr. Vice President." He turns back to the table and gets his pen and scribbles down a couple of notes. "Yes, sir. We'll expect him in about twenty-five minutes. We'll get prepared for the news conference." He hangs up the phone and looks up at the others around the table.

"Gentlemen, that was the vice president. He wants us to prepare for a news conference at ten o'clock, and the president will be joining us in about twenty minutes. He wants to be updated on the situation."

An aide moves up to Admiral Hillings and hands him a message.

"Mr. Secretary, we may have some good news."

Brant looks over at him. "That would be a change, Admiral."

"Sir, I had my staff run a check on possible people we could get to assist with the bomb disposal. They contacted PENTEX and the staff at Los Alamos. It seems that fate may have worked on our side in this situation. Los Alamos has their two top people in New Orleans. They had gone to a conference in Atlanta and took a few days off to visit friends in New Orleans. It's Dr. Susie Davies and Dr. Emanuel Reddeer; we couldn't find two more qualified people. They could assist the Russians in dealing with these things."

"Excellent. Have they been contacted?"

"Not yet. I'll call Captain Nelson to have someone sent to pick them up."

"That sounds good, Admiral. It's been a while since I locked horns with Dr. Davies. This incident will fire up her dislike of the way the military handles these nuclear devices."

"Yes, sir. But I would say, we're lucky as hell to have them so close."

"You're right. Let's get them in and appraise them of our situation. They can contact Los Alamos from the naval base."

"Yes, sir." The admiral nods to an aide, who gets on the phone to Captain Nelson.

"Also, Mr. Secretary. I have a profile of all the main players being compiled, and a description of the type of weapon we'll be dealing with. We will present it when the president gets here."

"Excellent, Admiral." Brant stands up at the head of the table. "I would like to commend everyone here in dealing with this situation. I believe that in the coming hours we will face new and unknown obstacles. But if your work and planing up to this point is the benchmark, our success is guaranteed. Thank you, everyone."

NAVAL BASE
NEW ORLEANS

Four Humvees pull out of the front gate and drive through the gentle rain. When they reach highway 23 north, they pull on and head into the city. A navy Blackhawk warms up on the field near the tower, waiting for the security group going to the Radisson. At base headquarters, Captain Nelson briefs the commander of base security on whom he is after, and tells him that it is imperative they be brought back to the base. When he is done, the three men head for the cars waiting outside. The wind and rain buffets them, and their flight suits begin to darken from the moisture. As soon as they reach the tarmac, they run from the cars to the waiting helicopter. When they are on board, it begins to taxi as the crew chief slides the door closed.

In the basement of the Radisson, the men riding life cycles look up from their papers. The sound of women yelling in the racquet ball court cuts through the room. As they go back to their papers, the sound of the ball hitting the walls again takes precedence.

As Susie hits a kill shot into the corner, she and her partner Patti burst into a loud Indian cry. They jump into the air and high-five. Susie moves to the backcourt as her partner steps up to serve. "We have them, Patty."

She bends her knees slightly to await the coming volley. After forty-seven years, her love of sports and the outdoors has served her well. At five feet, one inch, in height and 115 pounds in weight, she is only ten pounds over what she weighed in high school. At Stanford, she had always integrated academics and athletics. At her ranch in New Mexico, both she and her husband enjoy the great outdoors. From hiking to biking, they both enjoy a healthy life style. Lately horseback riding has become her passion; she would become as one with her Morgan mare Mia. As in all things, Susie demanded more of herself and those around her.

Mia answered the call, whether it was her head held high, strutting for the stallions, or racing pell-mell up a forest trail. They both displayed the belief that there were no obstacles they couldn't overcome. The area around Los Alamos lent itself to active people. From the park at Bandolier, to the fun of hiking Bear Trap, she and her husband relish their time with nature. And their runs into Santa Fe take care of their need to visit a larger city and indulge in their collecting of Indian jewelry and pottery.

"All right, Patty, three more points and we have the game."

Marsha moves over and gives Susie a bump with her hip. "We won't quit without a fight, Susie girl."

"Just like back in college, Marsha." She looks over and smiles. "It's time to die and be humiliated by the women's racquet ball wonders." She runs the edge of her racquet up the back of her friend.

Patty's serve is strong and she heads for the back of the court. Marsha sets herself and sends the ball sizzling high into the corners. It hits the sidewall and then the front wall; its speed seems to increase as it is hurled at the sidewall in the back of the court. It is coming in high on the wall. Susie sprints for the ball; she plants her foot on the wall and leaps into the air. Her racquet catches the ball, and its edge burns along the smooth wood. Like a cat she drops back to the floor. The ball hits with a pop into the forward wall, and rockets to the floor. Nancy sets and sends it screaming for the high corner. The back wall stops its long arc to the back of the court, and it bounces to the floor. Susie spins her racquet and catches it two feet off the floor. She follows through to one knee as the ball rockets into the front corner and dies without a chance of return.

"Oh, yes." Patty struts back to her partner. "Oh, yes, the kill shot queen is still alive." She and Susie both scream with delight. The men on the life cycles again look up from their papers as the yelling subsides.

The four Humvees turn up the main street, and move towards the Radisson. The streets are almost void of traffic as all businesses have been ordered to close and keep only essential personnel. A bolt of lightning rips across the sky as a beating rain sweeps over the vehicles. They pull into the entrance of the hotel and move into the valet parking. Armed marines climb out and set up a perimeter. Their lieutenant talks with the lot manager.

"Sir, we'll need to get these cars out of the lot. We're going to bring in a helicopter."

"All right, lieutenant." He gets his crew together and they begin moving the six cars still parked in the rain. Some of the marines move under the canopy and wait with the lieutenant.

As the last car is moved into the parking structure, the sound of the helicopter begins echoing off the surrounding buildings. One of the marines walks to the center of the parking lot and pulls the pin on a smoke grenade. He shakes the canister, and sets it on the ground. As he walks to the side, the yellow plum of smoke lifts into the gentle rain; soon half the lot is shrouded in yellow smoke. As the Blackhawk comes in for a landing, the wash from the rotors blows the smoke in all directions.

As soon as they're down, the navy commander climbs out and joins the marines at the steps near the entrance. "It looks good, Lieutenant. Let's go see if we can find our two doctors."

With two armed marines leading the way, they cross the lobby to the front desk. The manager has come out of his office, and he greets them. "Can I help you," he looks at the badge on the uniform, "Commander?"

"Yes, I need to locate Dr. Susie Davies and Dr. Emanuel Reddeer. We were told that they were staying here."

"Yes, they are here. I believe that Dr. Reddeer is in the dining room with his family. I'll escort you in, gentlemen."

The manager leads them down a side hallway to the dining room. The door is opened by the head waiter. "Thank you, Ken." He walks up to the seating chart and takes a quick look. "This way, gentlemen." He leads them by people eating their breakfast and around some pillars. He walks up to a man eating some eggs with his wife and two children. "Dr. Reddeer, I don't mean to disturb you, but these gentlemen say it is imperative that they talk with you."

Emanuel looks past the manager and can see the naval officer and the two armed marines. "Nan, finish your breakfast. I'll find out what the problem is." Her eyes follow her husband and the others as they walk out into the hallway.

"Sir, if you could excuse us. Thank you for your help." The manager nods as he is lead away by one of the marines. The hallway is then sealed off, leaving Reddeer with the commander.

"Sir, I'm Commander Linden. I have been sent by the base commander, Captain Nelson, on orders from the president. I am requesting you accompany us back to the base. I can only say that it is of grave national security."

Emanuel sort of pulls back and stares into the face of the commander with a puzzled look on his face. "Have you contacted Dr. Davies?"

"Not yet. We'll go back to the main desk and call her room."

"She is an early riser. She told me last night that she was meeting some of her college friends for a game of racquetball and then some breakfast. They are not in the dining room, so they are probably still down in the gym."

"We'll go down to the gym and make contact with her. Please finish your breakfast with your family while we find Dr. Davies."

Reddeer goes back to his family as the commander and the marines head for the stairs to the lower levels. When they reach the bottom of the stairs, they walk down a hallway to the gym. As he enters, the yelling from the racketball courts fills the room. Linden goes to the door and looks through the window; the four women inside are yelling and laughing. He slowly opens the door. "Ladies."

The court goes quiet. The woman about to serve turns around and looks him over. "What's the problem? We're making too much noise?" The women all snicker.

"No, ma'am, I'm trying to locate Dr. Susie Davies."

"Well, Commander, you have found her. But I must ask you to please wait a minute. We're on the last point, and it is my serve. I'll talk to you after that."

"Doctor, I'm under the highest orders to contact you."

"Unless we're in imminent danger this second, I again ask that you wait outside for a minute."

"Yes, ma'am." Linden closes the door.

"It sounds important, Susie."

"It always is, but we can finish our game." The others all yell in unison, "Go girlfriend!"

Susie launches the ball against the front wall; it takes an angle about a foot off the center of the court. Marsha catches it and sends it back. Patty yells out and fields the ball off the back wall. It compresses and is jettisoned straight back. As it crosses the serve line, Susie's racquet collects it up and sends it into the corner. It hits the side, then the front, and dives into the floor. Both her and Patty leap and yell; their war hoops migrate out into the gym.

"Damn, you haven't lost a step, Susie."

"Thanks, you guys. It's always so much fun to get together with all of you." They put their racquets away and begin picking up their coats and bags.

"Well, our next opportunity to beat you guys is going to be in New Mexico. By that time, you two girls are dead meat." They all yell and high-five. Marsha opens the door out into the gym; the two marine guards are waiting outside. "Susie, your escorts are waiting."

She slips on her jogging suit and walks out with the others. "Wait just a minute, girls. I'll be right back."

The marines clear the gym so that Susie and the commander are alone. He tells her the situation and they talk for a few minutes. They both walk out into the hallway together.

She talks with Linden and nods her head, then rejoins her girlfriends. "Girls, I have to go with these gentlemen. So I won't be able to have breakfast with you. I'll call you as soon as I get back to the ranch."

"Is everything all right?"

"Yes, they just need some advice. Don't worry." They all hug and kiss and say quick good-byes. They take the elevator as Susie joins Linden and the others at the stairs.

As they get to the top of the stairs, Linden leads her into the manager's office.

Emanuel is sitting having a cup of coffee. Linden closes the door behind them. "We have been allowed to use the manager's office. Is their anything we can get you, Dr. Davies?"

"No, thank you, I have some water in my bag." She looks over at Emanuel.

He shrugs his shoulders. "I don't have a clue, Susie." Susie sits down next to him on the couch.

"Dr. Davies and Dr. Reddeer, I have been asked to locate you and request that you return with me to NAS New Orleans. This is coming from the president of the United States, and the secretary of defense, Mr. Brant. It is of grave importance. I cannot explain the overall situation. Captain Nelson, the base commander, will explain that to you."

Susie looks over at Emanuel, then back to Linden. "We'll need a few minutes to get our things together."

"Good, shall we say fifteen minutes in the main lobby? We will make sure that Dr. Reddeer's wife and children get to the airport and that your luggage is taken care of."

"Thank you, Commander. My wife has already packed most of our things. We'll meet you in the lobby."

"Right." Susie and Emanuel get up to go.

"I'll contact the base to let them know we will be on our way soon. Thank you, both."

Susie and Emanuel head for the elevator. After they're inside, he punches the button for the twelfth floor. The doors close and they begin to rise. Emanuel looks over at Susie.

"So what do you think it is, boss?"

"I don't know. I'm just wondering if it has anything to do with that Russian bomber that crashed south of here."

"Susie, you think there may have been nuclear weapons on it?"

"I don't know Emanuel. Could be."

"Isn't that against international treaties?"

Susie chuckles. "Emanuel, your twenty-seven years are showing. Where the military is involved, they always have some stupid excuse for being extremely stupid about nuclear weapons. So I'm sure that the Russians would have the same lame excuses for carrying a lethal load of weapons, against all logic." The door slowly opens on the twelfth floor.

Susie steps out. "We'll meet back here in fifteen minutes." They both check their watches. "All right, Susie." They head for their rooms.

In the office of the hotel kitchen, one of the waiters dials out on the phone. He looks around the kitchen as someone at the other end picks up the phone. "This is KNLT. May I help you?"

"Yeah, this is Joe Burger over at the Radisson. There is something going on. We have navy and armed marines all over the place. They're here to pick up two of the guests. That's why I called in on the tip line."

"Please hang on."

The secretary takes the note over to the dispatch supervisor. "Thanks." He reads the note and checks his board. He picks up the phone and calls upstairs.

"Bob, this is Larry. We just got a call from a guy at the Radisson downtown. It seems that there are armed military all over the place, with some naval officers and a helicopter. They're apparently there to pick up two people staying at the hotel."

"What the hell? Thanks Larry. I'll see who we have to check on it."

Marcey had gotten back a while earlier from the crash site, and she is getting her copy ready for the noon news. Bob makes his way down the hall to her office.

"Hey, Marcey. I just got an interesting call on the tip line. It seems that a helicopter has landed down at the midtown Radisson, with armed marines and naval officers. They're picking up two people staying there."

She looks up at Bob. "What two people?"

"The guy said he didn't know, but that these guys mean business."

She looks at her watch. "Let me have it. We can get over there in about twenty minutes. Today is turning out to be one of those odd days, when stories seem to just fall out of the sky. I'll get my crew ready."

Bob puts the note down on her desk. "It's all yours. Keep us informed."

OFF NORTHEASTERN CUBA, OVER THE ATLANTIC

The Cuban patrol plane contacts the radio station at Banes and turns northeast out over the ocean. As they leave land behind, they pick up the patrol boat to the west. As they move out, the clouds begin breaking up and soon the deep blue of the water can be seen in shafts of sunlight.

From a cove near Punta Mangles, a sixty-foot sailboat puts out to sea under the low lying clouds. The mains are set on the old girl. As they head northeast, they all hope that they will be able to elude the patrol boats. The people packed on the deck huddle in the morning chill. Whiffs of fog pass over them as the boat clears the reef and makes for the open sea.

ULTIMA COMMAND CENTER
WASHINGTON, D.C.

Everyone stands as the president enters the room. "Thank you, everyone." He takes a seat next to Brant. "Could I get a 7-Up or something? My stomach isn't what it should be." A steward brings him his drink. "Thank you." He sips the drink and looks up at the screens. "Well, where are we now in this tragedy?"

Brant turns towards him. "Sir, we may have some good news. We have made contact with Dr. Davies and her assistant Dr. Reddeer. They will be arriving at the naval base within the hour. We have the impact area totally secured with the marine force, and scout teams are being formed to go out to the first two suspected sites. Also, we have had no new incidents in the Gulf."

"What about them shooting down those three planes?"

"We have contacted their envoy at the United Nations. He has been informed that we will respond to any attacks in international waters by Cuban forces. Also, a meeting of the security council has been called for eleven o'clock. The Russian envoy has talked with Vice President Gutaras in Cuba about the situation. He told them that he is going to go to the command center and demand that the alert be canceled.

"Very good. I wish him luck with General Morales." The president sort of gazes off for a second. "Dr. Davies.... Brant, isn't she the one who accused us of not having any balls?"

"Yes, sir. She holds to her convictions." They both smile and the president slowly shakes his head.

Brant turns back to Admiral Hillings. "Do we have that players presentation ready?"

"Yes, sir." He nods to Van Nar.

She moves up to the podium. "Mr. President, gentlemen. We have put together a collage of the primary players in this situation. We will begin with the Russians." On screen one, a chain of command comes on with the names and pictures of the men they will be dealing with, from Secretary Sholenska to Shagan and his war council, down to Admiral Kirsanov and Captain Sokolov on the *Moskva*. Their pictures sit next to their names.

"We would like to highlight General Kuznetsov." His picture is circled by a white ring. "He is the one who is working with our weapons people on the devices down in Louisiana."

The screen changes to two men. "These are the two officers the Russians moved to Cuba to load and move the weapons. We have Commander Valeski at the naval base; his next in command is Lieutenant Commander Brock. Both are seasoned veterans and officers in the Soviet Spetsnaz special forces. Commander Brock is leading the Russian investigation in Cuba with General Quintano. As you can see, both men have been involved in almost all of the Soviet military actions in the last twenty years, either as trainers or as direct participants in the fighting. Both are highly decorated soldiers." A new group of three photos appear on the screen, each shows both men at different locations in the last six months. "The photos show both men at different sites where a platoon of Spetsnaz troops were left with a special assignment to guard a single bunker at an outlying base in either Russia or one of the new countries since the break-up of the Soviet Union. This seems to be the same scenario at the Cuban site. All sites except Cuba have been recalled. Cuba seems to be the last one."

The president smiles and turns to Brant. "Now there are a couple of guys who look like the classic Russian agents." They all laugh around the table.

"Next we have the Cuban chain of command." The screen changes and a picture of Fidel is at the top. "We would like to highlight General Morales." His picture is circled. "We believe he is operating totally on his own at this time, disregarding all civilian authority." The highlight moves to four pictures under his. "These are his security commanders. They are now in control of the four major districts around Havana."

The highlight moves to the next picture. "This is General Quintano. He is Fidel's only hope if General Morales attempts to pull off a coup. His father is Judge Carlos Quintano, a close friend of Fidel's and a man with a distinguished career on the bench. He was once asked to sit on the World Court, but he was not allowed by Fidel for political reasons. His wealth and fame have made General Quintano the prime target of General Morales's hate. If his course of action is to try and take over the island, he will have Quintano killed."

"I have met General Quintano, Mr. President."

"What was your impression, General Becker?"

"I found him to be a very astute officer, who believes that Cuba will one day join others in the hemisphere in peace. Both he and General Morales come from wealthy and influential families. Fidel's advisers have moderated his military movement because of his father's views. Morales's supporters played this off on Fidel. That is why Morales is the commanding general. If Morales is contemplating a takeover, then General Quintano is his biggest enemy."

"Thank you, General. This day may prove you right. And General Quintano may become the only hope for peace in the Western Hemisphere."

Van Nar looks up at the screen as it changes to a depiction of a bomb. "At this time, Colonel Zane from the army weapons college will give an overview on the weapons that are on the ground in Louisiana. He and others under General Becker have been working with General Kuznetsov and his staff in Moscow."

Zane takes the podium. "Thank you, Captain Van Nar. Mr. President, gentlemen, what I'm about to describe is something we did not know they had, and this thing will be a nightmare to disarm. But first I'll give you the background of the weapon and its proposed tactical use." He takes a sip of water. "The basic concept for this weapons development was for a preemptive strike, either in the west or along the Chinese border. Or basically, a winable first strike scenario."

"What the hell? We would retaliate if nuclear weapons were used." Wayne looks back at Brant. "They had to know that, right, Brant?"

"Yes, sir. We would destroy their ability to fight by tearing out their infrastructure. But I must add, Mr. President, that we, too, have had contingency plans for a first strike winable nuclear exchange."

"I've never seen those." He looks at Brant.

"The studies are in files, sir. They were conducted by some earlier administrations; the change in the world situation has put the idea to bed forever. I think the Russians got caught in the same problem and were trying to get rid of the evidence."

Zane breaks in. "You're completely right, Mr. Secretary. With the changes in the political world, these weapons became a liability. The eight that ended up here are the last of the eighty actually produced. But before I get into the actual weapons themselves, I would like to show you the attack scenario that was planned during the cold war." On the screen, a map of West Germany is brought up. The pertinent military units are shown on the map.

"We will now add the flight paths of the ten Russian bombers. As you can see, they would fly north over the Baltic Sea and then turn south at speed to deliver the weapons. They would be going over 800 miles per hour, and right on the deck, the planes are fifteen miles apart. The bombs are dropped at ten-mile intervals, forming a box eighty miles wide and 150 miles deep. Each row is programmed to detonate at a pre-set time. As you see, most of our forward elements are inside the box. They would close with the forward elements as the weapons destroyed our supply, command and reserves in the rear." Yellow lines from the boarder cross the map of West Germany forward.

"We have made the M1 Abrams NBC proof, but any other weapons system, whether in the air or on the ground, would be destroyed."

He takes a drink. "The system mentioned by Captain Mikulin, which he called the death mode, is an enhancement to the fail-safe system. What it does is take command of the aircraft; it senses a loss of control by the aircrew. It uses a special set of sensors to ensure the bombs are hitting hard ground. It would hold a drop if it senses water."

He stops and looks around the room. "Are there any questions, gentlemen?"

"Would this plan have really worked, Colonel?" The president looks from him to the map.

"Probability is very high, though it would depend on the time of day and the situation at the time of the strike. We'll cover the rest of the plan so you will be able to see how all this fits together, Mr. President.

"One has to understand that this attack would not occur as an isolated event. All over the world, stockpiles of nuclear weapons would be attacked at the same time. You might picture Russian submarines off the West Coast; they tilt in towards the shore to fire. Their primary targets are missile and military bases.

"Now, gentlemen, on the screen we will activate the scenario in West Germany. Prior to the attack by ground forces, the bombers have made their pass. The forward elements open with a massive missile and artillery attack. Aircraft such as the Sukhoi 25 would stream forward looking for tanks and other targets. The Russian tanks would move forward to engage. Very shortly, they would unify their front, and all aircraft would then be moved back behind the lines."

The Colonel looks up at the screen. The eight dots representing the weapons along the first line explode into white circles. "These are five kiloton neutron weapons. Their payload is fired 1,000 feet into the air. As you see, they overlap. The blast effects of the bombs are secondary to their neutron effects and their electromagnetic pulse. The EMP will knock out the computers and all electronics in the blast area and beyond. All living things, whether in tanks, personal carriers or houses, are killed by the neutron concentration. The Soviet armor is NBC protected. They would immediately attack with their forward elements.

"The friendly forward forces are now effectively cut off from their supplies and reserves. Because they are locked in combat with the forward elements, our ability to fire into the initial onslaught is tempered by the fact we would have to destroy our own troops."

The battle line on the screen moves forward. As they push the forward elements back through the dead zone, they again consolidate. The second line of bombs is detonated. Again a white circle is drawn on the screen at the next line of weapons. "This scenario would continue as they push their way into Germany." Each of the lines is detonated as the attack line moves across the screen. Brant looks back from the screen. "So, Colonel, what your describing is some type of nuclear mine?"

"Yes, Mr. Secretary. These are the world's biggest bouncing Betties. If there are no more questions?" The colonel looks around the room. "We will now turn to the weapon itself." The screen changes to a single bomb. "This weapon is a modified version of their Mark 81 series. It has a hardened case and large retard fins. The biggest change is in the payload with its rocket booster. Marshal Shagan's group sent us this drawing of the weapon." The screen pulls in to the side of the casing. "When the bomb hits, it is in a vertical position. If not, just after firing the payload will bring itself to the vertical. Once down, the weapon activates two anti-tampering systems. If the weapon is moved more than ten degrees from its axis, it detonates. The timer is activated at the time of the drop; also you can see this panel at the side of the casing. It has eight screws holding it on. Each bomb has a different sequence of removal of these screws. If you remove one out of sequence, the weapon will explode. The bomb sequences are held in Moscow at the ministry. They will relay them to each site."

Zane takes a drink of water and turns back to the screen. He points the laser pen at the screen; the red dot appears at the back of the bomb. "Just before detonation, these retard fins are blown off the casing. The weapons payload is then fired 1,000 feet into the air for maximum dispersal. I would like to add that of the eighty weapons built, only twelve were kept in East Germany. The majority of the weapons were kept along the border with China. The Chinese tactic of using mass formations in their assaults would have been devastated by these weapons."

"Good God." Brant looks around the table at the others. "We have a major problem, here. Refresh my memory—none of the weapons people off the submarines have dealt with this type of weapon?"

"You're correct, Mr. Secretary."

"Well, Colonel, can they be stopped?" The president searches his face for a clue.

"Mr. President, basically these things were made as a one-way weapon. No one trained on them; the added anti-tamper proof devises are there to kill anyone trying to mess with these things. But with everyone committed to the effort and a little break from the weather, I believe our people could do it. But it is going to be a slow and dangerous process."

"Thank you, Colonel." Everyone sits for a moment and silently lets the information sink in.

"Mr. Secretary?"

"Yes, Admiral."

"Sir, we'll send a copy of Colonel Zanes report to Captain Nelson so he can get it in the hands of Dr. Davies and Dr. Reddeer as soon as they get to the base. And I would suggest that we get one of the Russian-speaking staff in here to monitor the link with the field."

"I agree, Admiral. Also, I would like you to accompany me to the news conference. We'll leave in about twenty minutes." The admiral nods his head and goes back to his staff.

Van Nar goes back to the podium and looks up at the second screen. She picks up a phone and talks to Sky 1 and then hangs it up.

"Gentlemen, we may have another situation developing. Sky 1 has traffic from the patrol plane here off the eastern sector." With her pointer, she positions the red dot just off the coast of Cuba. The screen moves to the northeastern side of Cuba and zooms in. The plane is a yellow circle, and the patrol boat is a yellow square. South of the aircraft, a blue square moves north.

"Apparently the patrol plane has acquired a boat trying to head north under a fog bank. It has contacted the control center; their standing order is to force it back to the coast."

"What if it doesn't turn back, Captain Van Nar?" The president looks back from the screen to Brant. "What would they do?"

"Mr. President." He looks back to Van Nar. "Our understanding is that General Morales has ordered that if they don't turn back, they will be sunk."

The satellite picture is shifted and zooms down on the boat. In the green and white image, people can be seen packed on the deck. They look up as the patrol plane flies over.

"We're going to have the transmissions from the patrol plane and the command center shown on the screen." The translation in English is typed at the bottom of the screen.

RADISSON HOTEL
NEW ORLEANS

Susie quickly runs the hair blower around her head as she runs her comb through it. She looks in the mirror at an errant tuff of hair. "Why is it that every time there is a national emergency, I have a weird hair day." The shower felt great, and now she quickly applies some foundation. Fortunately, her packing was all done, and she had laid out some casual clothes for lunch with the girls and her flight home later.

As she puts the make-up on in stripes, her face looks made up for some kind of tribal dance. As she blends the color in, she squints her eyes. The small lines at the corners of her eyes seem to be growing. She runs her comb through her hair, and teases it a little. A slight frown crosses her face; not all the color was from natural growth. "Damn it." She rubs a spot at the back of her head where the blower got to close.

After applying eyebrow pencil and blush, she steps back to admire her work. She cocks her head. "You're getting older." Her hands push her breast up under the towel. "It's simple gravity; you can't fight the laws of nature." Quickly she dresses and goes back to the mirror to put on her lipstick. She walks back out into the main room and looks at herself in the tall door mirror. "All right." She adjusts her slacks. Just as she picks up her raincoat, a knock comes to the door.

"Dr. Davies." A second knock.

"Yes."

"This is Sergeant Whitehead. If your ready, ma'am."

She opens the door; the sergeant and two armed marines stand in the hall. "I'm all set." She puts on her raincoat and steps out into the hall. "I'll have one of the men get your bags."

"Thank you, Sergeant." Down the hall, marines have also herded Emanuel and his family into the hallway. Susie joins them at the elevator, and they all get on. Two of the marines join them; the others wait for the other elevator.

"Susie, I'm scared." Susie puts her arm around Mary's shoulders. "Don't worry. This is probably some sort of situation they just want to pass by us."

"God, I hope so." A tear tracks down the side of her face, and her daughter holds tightly to her dad. Her son holds on tightly to her hand.

Emanuel puts his arm over Susie's around his wife. They all hug. He whispers in her ear, "Everything is going to be fine. Remember I'm with the best in the business."

"I know, but both of you are in a very dangerous business."

As the door slides open, Commander Linden and the other marines are waiting; a box of armed men surrounds them. The hotel staff and other guests stand off to the side and silently watch the proceedings.

Linden steps forward. "Doctors, we need to be on our way. I'm sorry, but we have to leave now."

"All right, Commander." Susie kisses Mary on the cheek. "Give that to Steve when you see him. And don't worry, I'll look after Emanuel."

"Thanks, Susie. Thank God you're with him." Mary hugs Emanuel and kisses him. "I'll see you back at home. Just be careful."

"I will; remember, I'm the less adventures one." He puts his daughter down and kisses each of the kids. His hand slowly slides out of Mary's till only their fingertips touch; she quickly catches his and squeezes them. He smiles and walks over to Susie and the commander.

"Your wife and children will be escorted to the airport by Lieutenant Carroll and three of his men. All your bags will be loaded and sent along." Emanuel looks back at his wife.

"Sir." Commander Linden leans over to Emanuel. "Let me assure you Dr. Reddeer, as tough as the marines are in combat, they handle these situations with professional velvet gloves. You will be able to call her from the base later."

As they move outside, a drizzling rain is falling. Quickly they cross the parking lot to the waiting helicopter. The down draft from the rotors throws swirling spray over the group. Susie lowers her head and pulls the hood tighter over her face.

"I hate this part," she yells over the noise of the rotors as they are helped up into the helicopter. They take their seats. They are drenched from the down draft.

Susie looks around. "I hope the situation is better than the weather. God, I'm soaked."

Emanuel brushes off his jacket. "Boy, you aren't kidding."

The crew chief moves over to them. "Please buckle your seat belts. This weather is causing us to bounce around a little." They snap the buckles shut as the others take their seats. The crew chief makes one final look out the door and slides it shut. "Sir, our passengers are snapped in."

"Roger, Chief." The pilot looks out the front as the rain increases. A marine with a flash light signals clear, and moves back from the down draft. The pilot brings the engines up and the Blackhawk shimmies. He checks both ways and slowly lifts the helicopter off the lot. After rising about fifty feet, he tilts the nose down and begins to work his way down the canyon formed by the surrounding buildings. The Humvees are loaded, and the marines take Mrs. Reddeer to the airport.

As the helicopter moves down the street, its noise echoes off the surrounding buildings. As it flies over a news van stopped at a light, Marcey leans forward to see it pass overhead. "Damn it, I'll bet that was the one at the Radisson. Let's get over there."

"Hang on, this rain isn't helping us." The driver gets the green light and pulls through the intersection. When they reach the turn in for the Radisson, a group of four Humvees pulls out, heading the way they came from.

"Shit!" Marcey beats her hand on the dash. "The story is driving away from us. Let's get in there."

"Hang on, we'll be there in just a second." He pulls the van in and drives up under the canopy, parking to the side. Marcey jumps out and heads for the front door.

CONTROL CENTER
CUBA

"Roger, Search 4. Boat continuing north. Out." The man at the console looks around and catches the lieutenant's eye.

"Sir, the flight out of Moa cannot make contact with the boat. They are tracking it under the fog bank. They have made passes over it and dropped flares. It is continuing north."

"Damn, what do we have in the area?"

"We have a missile boat about twenty-five miles west. It's the only thing in the area. The plane has contacted them, but they are too far away."

"Contact the plane, and have them start sending targeting information to the missile boat."

"Yes, sir."

"Search 4, this is Hound over."

"Roger, Hound. We still have the boat continuing north. Over."

"Search 4, you are to begin sending targeting information to the missile boat. Over."

"Say again, Hound." The pilot and the co-pilot look at each other and shake their heads.

"I repeat, Search 4, begin sending targeting information to missile boat. Over."

"Roger, Hound. Search 4 out." The pilot shakes his head. "Contact the missile boat and inform them we will begin sending targeting information." The co-pilot shakes his head and calls to the boat.

In the Gulf the missile boat plows through the choppy sea as another rain shower starts. In the main cabin, the radio comes alive as the voice blares from the speaker into the cabin. "Alpha patrol, this is Hound. Over."

The radio operator holds on with one hand and keys his mike as the boat rolls to one side. "Hound, this is Alpha. Over."

"Alpha, you are ordered to intercept target from Search 4. They will begin sending targeting information. You are to assume firing imminent. Over."

"Hound, you want us to fire on a refugee boat? Over."

" Alpha, you have been ordered to prepare for a possible firing. Over."

"Roger"

Five other men in the cabin stand silently as the operator lifts the phone to the bridge from its cradle. The boat commander lifts the handle up on the flying bridge. "Yeah." The operator passes him the message; he ducks down behind the windscreen as another blast of spray from the bow passes. "Are you sure that's what they said? All right, I'll be down in a minute." He hangs the phone back in its holder as his eyes look over to the two huge missile containers on the port side. The rain and spray have painted them dark gray. He tells the others on the bridge their orders. The young lieutenant looks into the face of the more experienced chief. "Sir, we have never fired on a refugee boat."

They both cross over to the port side; he puts his hand on the huge launcher. "Especially with one of these." The radioman comes up from below. "Sir, we're getting targeting from the patrol plane. It's being fed into the missile control unit now."

"Chief, take over. I'm going down to call the commander back at base. This order can't be true!" He works his way down the ladder to the main deck and into the cabin. "All right, get me the base. I want to talk to the commander."

As the operator resets his dials, he hands a mike to the lieutenant. The operator keys his set. "Blue 1, this is Alpha 4. Over."

"Alpha 4, this is Blue 1."

The operator looks up to the lieutenant. "Just key your mike when you want to send, the response will come over the speaker."

"Blue 1, this is the commander of Alpha 4. I need to talk to the base commander *now*. Over."

"Roger, sir. We'll get him. Hold one."

"Get the base commander. Alpha 4 has a problem." The man runs to the end of a long hall to the commander's office. "Sir, Alpha 4 needs to talk to you."

Commander Lunas puts his pen down. "Do you know what the problem is?"

"The control center wants him to fire on a refugee boat, sir."

"What the hell?" They pass into the radio room. "They're on the net now, sir." Picking up the handle, he pushes the button. "Lieutenant, what the hell is going on?" The boat commander goes over the order from control. "Hold Alpha, I will contact control." He turns to the operator. "Get me Captain Ruiz, now!"

Ruiz is called to the board at the control center. He quickly talks with the base commander and has him hold. Putting down the mike, he walks to Morales's door and knocks.

"Come in." The general is sitting behind the desk, looking over some papers.

"Sir, I have been talking with the base commander at Gibara; one of his boats is being given targeting information to fire on a refugee boat."

Morales looks up. "So."

"General, we're talking about a 2,000-pound missile with an 800-pound warhead against a unarmed boat. If this happens, the Americans may decide to intervene directly."

"What is the order that I issued earlier, Captain?"

"That if the boat does not turn back, it is to be sunk."
"Is there something in that order you do not understand?"
"No, sir. The base commander just wanted verification."
"So he wants verification. Is he on the radio?"
"Yes, sir."

Morales gets up and motions for him to follow. He walks out to the console and picks up the mike. He tells the operator to put it on the loud speaker.

"Commander, this is General Morales."

"Yes, sir." The voices blare into the room from the speakers.

"Apparently there is some confusion about an order I gave earlier. Well, let me repeat that order for you. Your boats are to fire if they are contacted by this command center. If there is any departure from that order, I will have the boat commander shot for treason. This also applies to you. So I would suggest that you do what you have been ordered to do and keep the radio waves open for important traffic. We'll monitor your progress from Search 4. Do I need to say anything else?"

"No, sir. I understand and will pass the message on to the boat commander. Out."

"Captain Ruiz." Morales looks into his eyes. "If the pressure of command is to much for you, I suggest that you step down now. If this happens again," he moves closer to Ruiz, "I may be forced to do something I don't want to. And it would not be healthy for your career, or your life." With a small smile, he turns and walks back into his office and closes the door. The control center personnel go back to their work.

Back on the boat, the lieutenant and the others listen to the orders of the base commander. "I understand, sir. The missile is prepped for firing. We will stand by for orders. Alpha out." The sound of the wind and the crackling of the radio fills the main compartment as the lieutenant hands the mike back to the radio operator.

"Get the missiles ready to fire. We will launch on command!"

ULTIMA
WASHINGTON, D.C.

The president watches the translation of the message from Morales to the base commander pass by on the screen.

"My God. He wouldn't actually fire, would he?" He looks from Van Nar to the others around the table.

"Sir." General Lane moves towards the podium. "With the message directly from Morales, it's not if but when."

"Can't we do anything?" Wayne looks around. "Shoot it down or something?"

"Mr. President, the closet thing we have are the fighters on air cap around southern Florida and the marines out of Guantánamo. They're loading the C-130s with all nonessential personnel to fly them out. If they go to the assistance of the boat, it leaves the C-130s flying into harms way. You must understand, there are Mig-23 fighters flying air cap over these guys. We attack the missile boat; they attack the C-130s. We have to hope that they will come to their senses and let the boat go."

"Sir." The president looks over at Captain Van Nar. "Things may be getting worse. One of the other Cuban patrol planes has a contact further east, between Cuba and Haiti. They also have been ordered to send targeting information to a patrol boat." A second set of squares and circles appears further east.

Brant walks up next to Wayne who is fixated on the screen. "Sir, Admiral Hillings and myself are leaving for the news conference."

"Good, Brant. I'm going to stay here to see where this thing is going."

Brant looks up at the screen. "Yes, sir."

Wayne closes his eyes and can visualize the up turned faces of the people on the boat as the plane flies over it. They seem to be looking through the screen into his soul. His heart screams for an answer to their dilemma, but his mind knows that there is nothing he can do. He mumbles a prayer under his breath, as Brant and Hollings leave for the press conference with two marine guards.

RADISSON HOTEL
NEW ORLEANS

Marcey talks to the bus boy that called in the tip to get all the information he had. "Did you, by chance, get the names of the two people picked up?"

"Yeah, I thought you might need them. It was a Dr. Susie Davies and Dr. Emanuel Reddeer. They just got in a few days ago. I think it was Friday. They flew off in the helicopter, and the guy's wife left with the marines in one of the Humvees."

"Great. I've got your address, Mike. You'll be getting a check for 100 dollars in the mail, all right?"

"Hey, it sounds good to me."

"Thanks again, Mike." She shakes his hand and heads back into the lobby to talk with others who saw the helicopter come in. She then heads towards the manager's office while the cameras are being set up.

CUBAN MISSILE BOAT ALPHA 4

The radio operator sticks his head out of the cabin door. "Sir, it's for you. It's the command center."

"All right." The lieutenant looks around the bridge. "Shit, is everything ready, Chief?"

"Yes, sir." He has to yell over the sound of the wind.

"Very good, Chief. Let's get everyone inside."

"Yes, sir." As the chief herds the last of the men into the cabin, the lieutenant takes one more look over the deck and out over the open water, then turns and goes inside.

He grabs the mike. "This is Alpha 4. Over."

"Alpha 4, this is Hound. You are cleared to fire. I repeat, you are cleared to fire. Over."

He looks around the cabin at the others. "Roger, Hound. Hold one."

He crosses his chest. "God help them." His finger pushes down the firing button on the control panel. A loud boom is heard as the covering over the starboard missile tube is blown off. Instantly, the missile is launched into the air. The ship is rocked from the blast and shrouded in smoke. The wings on the missile deploy as it accelerates into the sky.

"Hound, this is Alpha 4. We have a launch, I repeat, we have a launch. The crew on Search 4 will assume command on final leg. Over."

"Roger, Alpha 4. Hound out."

ULTIMA
WASHINGTON, D.C.

The president sits up in his chair as the text of the order to fire passes at the bottom of the screen. He jumps to his feet. "My, God. They're going to launch."

Everyone looks up at the screen. From the yellow square of the missile boat, a red triangle is tracked towards the refugee boat.

Van Nar picks up a phone, then cups the mouthpiece with her hand. "Mr. President, Sky 1 is confirming the launch of a SS-N-2B Styx missile. It was fired from thirty-one miles. The patrol plane will correct its flight in its final stage."

A ghostly image comes up on screen four. In shades of green and white, the image of the boat fills the screen. It pulls back to show the whole boat and the water around it.

"Sir, screen four is a thermal image from the satellite over the area."

Wayne watches as the track on the screen closes the distance to the boat. Finally, the two symbols merge. Everyone in the room watches in disbelief as the people on the boat rise their arms into the air. A dark form slams into the side of the boat. A blinding light fills the screen; where the boat was, there is now only a huge depression in the water. It is shrouded in a coating of smoke.

Wayne's mouth falls open, and he raises to his feet. "Oh, my God! My God, those people." As the smoke clears, there seem to be bodies floating everywhere in the water.

Van Nar steps forward. "Cut the image on screen four *now!*" She takes the president by the arm. "Sir, you need to sit down. It was a horrible thing to do."

"God, Captain. They were looking right at me. And I could do nothing, nothing."

"Yes, sir. I'll get a message sent to Mr. Brant."

"Yes, that will be good, Captain. I need to go back to my quarters for a while." His aides help him to his feet. "Thank you, I'll be all right." Two armed marines fall in line with the group, and they head up the hall to his quarters.

As Van Nar gets back to the podium, the number four screen comes back on. The scenario is being repeated at the second contact. She talks with Sky 1, who verifies the second launch. Again the symbols merge as the boat disappears in a blinding flash.

General Becker writes a note down and gives it to his aide. "Captain Van Nar, I am sending a note up to Secretary Brant on the latest situation."

"Yes, sir." She hangs up the phone.

CUBA, THE BACK ROADS

Miguel is thrown again into the side of the cab as it rounds a corner and slides in the soft mud. "Goddammit, how much longer?"

"I'm sorry, señor, but the storm has flooded this whole area. It is very dangerous."

The cab once again comes to a stop as a torrent of water washes over the road. The driver shakes his head. "We have to wait until it slows down, or we will get washed over into the canyon."

"Shit, we have been stopping every half mile or so." Miguel rolls down the window and lights a cigarette. His hand picks up his pint of rum, and he takes another drink. The hot liquid boils down his throat as he rests his head on the back of the seat. His mind races. "Will this ever end?" The words fill the inside of the cab.

HELICOPTER
MATANZAS AIR BASE

Brock crosses the field to the hangar as guards in black watch his every move. Reaching the hangar, he goes into the office.

"You made it?" Quintano looks up from the desk.

Brock looks out of the office door at two guards at the hangar doors. "They have cut the power to the radios, and guards are watching our men. What the hell is Morales up to?"

Quintano glances up at Brock. "I don't know yet. But I want you to get on the helicopter in the hangar; they have ordered all Russians under guard. And I don't want to provoke the commander of the special guard. We'll leave in just a minute."

Brock puts his helmet on. "I'll meet you on the helo." Quintano nods his head as Brock works his way to the helicopter and climbs aboard. The ground crew hooks a mule up and slowly begins pulling it out onto the tarmac. The rest of the crew comes out and climbs on board; they wait for Quintano as the engines warm up. Quintano hangs up the phone; he picks up some papers and heads for the waiting helicopter. As he passes the men at the hangar doors, they give him a salute. He returns it and looks over at the hangar with the Russian crews in it. Two armored cars sit at angles at each side of the huge closed doors. He climbs aboard. They begin to taxi as he fastens his seat belt. They move out to the edge of the runway, the craft shakes as the engines are run up. The helo begins to lift up into the air. The co-pilot looks back at Quintano. "Sir, we are heading east, correct?"

"Yes." He looks at the map in his hand. "Along the coast to Santa Cruz Del Norte. It's about fifty miles out."

The co-pilot nods. "Yes, sir."

They move away from the base as a gentle rain falls. They can see roads washed out and water running wildly into the sea. Brock looks back from the window. "That storm really dumped on this area."

"You're right, but it may help us catch these guys. It's got to have slowed them down, too."

"You're right." Brock looks out the window and back at Quintano. "I just wonder what's going on at the crash site, and what Morales may do with the men at the field."

"I share your concern, my friend. Let's hope things are returning to normal, but it's odd. I couldn't get through to Captain Ruiz at control."

Brock and Quintano's eyes meet. "I hope things do return to normal, General. But I have a bad feeling in my gut." Quintano nods his head.

CHAPTER 8

WEATHER OFFICE
WASHINGTON, D.C.

The people moving about the weather office step aside as the captain and his aide walk to the large circular table at the center of the room. "Ladies and gentlemen, we need final status on the Gulf area. I'll be presenting it to Secretary Brant as soon as he returns from his news conference. We need to get the latest satellite photos of Evita and to print up the hand-outs for the Joint Chiefs."

The latest pictures of the hurricane come up on the main screen. "Sir, it hit Cuba at a number two, and now it's working it self up to a number four."

"I see that." They lean over the table to look over read-outs from different locations. As they talk, the huge swirling mass of the storm moves on the screen behind them. The captain looks back at the screen and sees others looking up at the massive cloud formation. "I don't know what their problem is on the ground, but anything in the path of Evita will be in a world of hurt."

In another part of the building, Brant checks his watch and continues to talk to one of the naval aides. "Very well, thank you. Gentlemen, let's get in and get this thing over with." They enter the room and walk through the crowd of news reporters to the tables at the front of the room. As they take their seats, an aide moves to the podium.

"Ladies and gentlemen, we have hand-outs that will be available to everyone. They are passing them out. Mr. Brant will give an up-to-date summary of events." The aide moves back to his seat as the Secretary gets to the podium. Taking a long slow drink, he looks over the faces of the assembled group.

"Ladies and gentlemen, I'm sorry about the tardy arrival; we will only have a short time here, so I would like to cover the events from early this morning." Brant arranges his papers; the reporters know him as a man who can work the crowd. But now he seems preoccupied with the events of the day. They know this will be hard and fast; it sizzles their collective juices. Anyone could smell the blood trail of a big story, and the pack waits for the right moment to go for the throat.

"We would like to cover three main events: one, the crash of the Russian bomber; two, the level of response from Cuba; three, the arrival of Evita in the Gulf. I'll have Admiral Hillings cover you on the Cuban issue, with regards to the reports coming out of Cuba." Brant picks up his drink and takes another slow drink. The reporter from the *Times* stands up; a surge of tension rushes through the room. The aide rises and moves forward. "We said that there will be no questions during the presentation." Brant raises his free hand, and the aide goes back to his seat. He nods at the man over the rim of his glass.

"Sir, I'm sorry, but events of today continue to confuse us. We have received reports from our southern bureaus along the Gulf that huge explosions have been monitored. Disregarding the reports from Cuba, have any American lives been lost to this point?"

Brant puts the glass down. "Bob." The reporter sits back down. "And this is for all of you. Bob's question is answered in the negative. Absolutely no American lives have been lost, and our forces are at an alert condition in the Gulf. If that answers the primary question, we must move on."

"On item one, a Russian Backfire bomber was sabotaged off the coast of Louisiana, and it subsequently crashed on the beaches of Barataria bay." A large screen behind him shows a map of the area. A red line shows the path of the bomber. "The pilot, Captain Mikulin, survived the crash and has been transported to NAS New Orleans. The two escort fighters are also at the naval base. One of them was hit by debris from the bomber, and the pilot and the plane are being patched up. The captain is in critical condition, and we hope for a speedy recovery. The president has been on the phone with Secretary Sholenska, and we have been working directly with Air Marshal Shagan. We are giving the Russians any and all support on this issue. It is believed that the Cuban group Libertal is responsible for the explosion. A Russian investigator has been flown in to the crash site, and our understanding is that they are in pursuit of the persons involved in Cuba.

"On the second issue, I'll have Admiral Hillings expand on our deployment. But suffice to say, the Cubans have overreacted to the situation. They went to a full alert status, which has subsequently been downgraded in the eastern sector. As you know, we do not have direct links with the Cuban command, so Marshal Shagan's group has been dealing with General Morales." A murmur runs through the crowd. Brant notices the tone.

"And those of you who have had the pleasure of dealing with General Morales will appreciate the situation in which Marshal Shagan finds himself. Again, the admiral will cover the specifics of the situation."

"As for item three, we will be getting an update on the path and intensity of Evita. The president's order to evacuate the southern peninsula in anticipation of the hurricane is in progress. Our last report would indicate a force four storm which will hit the area early tomorrow morning. You will be receiving updates from the hurricane center in Florida and the national weather service. I'll bring Admiral Hillings up, so if there are any other questions?"

"Sir." Brant nods to the lady from the *Post*. "We have received reports of a strong military force at the site, and have been told that no one is allowed near the crash. Is that true?"

"Yes, a marine group is on site, and they have secured the area. This was done to facilitate the investigation. Nothing has changed since this morning when the news team took their pictures of the crash."

"Sir, sir." Brant picks another reporter. "Mr. Secretary, we are also told that the response force from Georgia is being activated and sent to the scene, and that there is a high volume of air activity around the area."

"Yes, we have the alert group coming in to help because of the approaching hurricane. The president's thoughts are to put resources on the ground prior to the storm. That way we can move in supplies of food and medicine immediately."

"Sir, sir." Brant points to a reporter. "This will be the last. I'll have the admiral cover the situation in the Gulf."

The man stands. "Sir, in our dealing with General Morales, we found him to be quite ego-driven and that he liked to show his power. Are his dealings with Marshal Shagan progressing smoothly, or is he as arrogant as usual?"

"I can only say that Marshal Shagan is trying to deal with him in a very calm manner. They have run into some resistance, but we believe that with his relaxing the alert in the eastern areas, progress will be made.

"All right, let me get the admiral up here to cover you on the other items. Thank you."

Brant goes back to his seat as the admiral begins his presentation. "Ladies and gentlemen, I again reiterate that no American forces have been involved with Cuban forces. We established a 100-mile no-fly zone at the time of the crash; this is still in effect throughout the Gulf area. I might add that there are more than enough surface vessels and aircraft in the area to handle any situation from the Cuban forces. They are respecting the no-fly zone, and we have been monitoring them from the very start of the situation.

"In regards to the three aircraft shot down, none were military or commercial craft. After speaking with the DEA, we believe that two of the planes were possible drug runners trying to enter the United States, using the storms as cover. The third aircraft we believe was, in fact, a Cuban fighter that was experiencing electrical failure. It was shot down by the missile battery at Bauta.

"A request from the Russian government to allow a surface group in to pick up the bomber was agreed upon by President Wayne and Secretary Brant; they are in route to the scene and should arrive early tomorrow morning.

"I would like to draw your attention to the map on the screen; the red stars are the locations of the planes shot down by the Cubans. Also, earlier today, the Coast Guard cutter *Eastwind* gave assistance to a Cuban missile boat caught in the storm. This was one of the early explosions that was picked up along the Gulf. The captain died in the rescue, but the crew is being held in south Florida and will be flown back to Cuba on a commercial flight." As the admiral is pointing to the spot on the map where the rescue took place, one of his aides enters the room and walks up to the podium. He hands the admiral a message and leaves. After reading it, Hillings walks back to Brant and hands him the message. The secretary shakes his head and nods to Hillings.

Regaining the podium, he puts the message down. "In regards to the large explosion south of the Keys, we have confirmation that a Cuban patrol boat fired a missile on a refugee boat out of Cuba. The message we just received confirms that a second missile has been fired. This has occurred at approximately this location." The admiral's pointer moves to the eastern portions of the map. "In the straits between Cuba and Haiti, a Haitian refugee boat was sunk. We have verified an order issued by General Morales that any surface craft in Cuban waters will be returned to the island or sunk."

"Sir, sir." The admiral points to a reporter. "Sir, you're saying that the Cuban forces are firing some type of missiles into refugee boats?" The admiral nods.

"Sir, what are we doing to stop this?"

"At this point, we can only rely on the negotiation going on at the highest levels between Air Marshal Shagan and General Morales. The president has called for a UN security meeting and is in direct contact with the Cuban ambassador. He is doing all he can to stop the situation. One problem is that Castro is in Bolivia, and the island is under martial law, which puts General Morales in direct control. Our understanding is that President Gutaras is en route to talk directly to the general. Any incursion by U.S. forces in the area would only add to the mass confusion in dealing with General Morales."

"Sir." A newsman stands in the front row. "Your intimating that General Morales has lost control of the situation and has gone amuck. Is that what you're saying?"

"I will say that the general has chosen to use any and all weapons at his disposal. It seems that deadly force is the byword in the Cuban area of control. Our intervention at this point would, in all probability, put the Russian surface forces and their personnel in grave danger."

"Sir, so what you're saying is that the negotiations between him and the Russians are not going very well?"

"I can only say that they're making progress and that we hope for a halt to the aggressive actions by the Cuban military."

Brant moves up next to the admiral. "Ladies and gentlemen, we must excuse ourselves. The situation in the Gulf requires us to get back to the situation room. Thank you all."

They leave the room and move down the hallway, passing marine guards in camouflage uniforms who are armed with rifles.

A newsman talks on the phone with his producer. "Greg, the president has canceled all his meetings for the rest of the day. I think we should get with the people at KNLT and have them try and find out more. Something is definitely wrong here, and I think that the crash site is the focal point. We should see if they could get back out there. I know, but some rules were made to be broken. I'll call you from the office. All right." Hanging up, he and his camera crew walk past the guards in the hall and leave the building.

Brant looks at his watch. "It's twelve after. I need to make a couple of calls. I'll meet you and the others back in the room in about fifteen minutes."

"Yes, sir." The secretary turns down the hall to his office as the admiral continues towards the situation room.

QUINTANO'S HELICOPTER
CUBA

As the helicopter lands, the wind from the blades throws mud and standing water in all directions. A misty fog seems to engulf it as the wheels touch down. Those nearby shield themselves from the flying water and debris. As the rotors spin to a stop, a figure moves to the side of the copter.

"General Quintano." The man salutes the figure climbing out of the side door.

"Sí." He returns the salute.

"We have been expecting you; the car is over here." He points to the vehicle parked off the side of the road.

"Very good." Brock gets out with him. The crewmen move around the helicopter and make sure all is right with the landing gear. They throw their helmets back into the helicopter and walk through the mud to the car. "It looks like they got a lot of flooding in this area."

Quintano looks around. "Yeah, the rivers overflowed and they have had a lot of mud slides. Watch your step, this stuff is slippery."

"Right." Brock nods as his boot slides on the underlining clay. "It's like being on ice."

The policemen around the car come to attention as Quintano walks up. "Carry on, men. We need to see what was left in the car."

A guard opens the door. "Sir, we put anything in the car on the rear seat. This is all that we found."

"Thank you." Quintano leans in and looks at the small amount of materials left. He runs his hand over the objects: the car registration, a couple of matchbooks, two foam coffee cups, a day-old newspaper, and a pint of rum. He picks up the bottle, it is half full. He puts it back down and picks up the matchbooks and the registration as he backs out of the car.

"It's his roommate's car, all right." He hands the registration card to Brock. "Not much left." He turns the matchbooks in his hand. "Sergeant." The man near the front of the car moves back.

"Yes, sir."

"You were one of the men who chased this suspect into the alley?"

"Sí, Señor General. He ran through the back streets and jumped into a cab two blocks over. The cab took off to the east. We called and alerted the checkpoints on the roads to be on the look out for him."

"Very good, Sergeant. And the other man who spoke to him?"

"This way, sir." Brock follows the two men across the congested road, to an old man directing people to remain in their cars.

"Please remain with your cars. They hope to have the road open in just a few minutes."

"Señor." The sergeant waves the man over. "This is General Quintano; he has some questions for you."

"Sí, señor, whatever you wish."

"Sir, you spoke to the man who was driving that car?"

"Sí, señor."

"Did he say anything to you about where he was going?"

"Sí, he said he was going over to Cardenas to do some fishing or something. But the road is blocked and I told him I would watch his car if he wanted to get some coffee at the canteen." The old man points to the canteen just down the street. "The wait was about an hour, so he got out and went to have some coffee. Perhaps they can tell you more, señor."

"Thank you. We'll check with them. We'll be back in just a minute, Sergeant."

"Yes, sir." He and Brock walk to the canteen and go in through the hanging curtain. Their eyes have to adjust to the darkness as they walk up to the bar. "Would you like a drink, señores?"

"Sí, two cervezas, please."

The bartender gets the bottles and opens them. "Glasses, señores?"

"No, this will be fine. Señor, earlier there was a young man in here for some coffee. Did you talk to him?"

"Ah, the young man from Havana. Sí, he had coffee and rum."

"What did he say to you?"

"I could tell he was educated from the way he talked. We talked about the storm and the closed roads because he had to get to Segva la Grande."

"To Segva la Grande, for what purpose?"

"To meet someone, but that is all he said. He seemed disturbed by something and kept walking to the door and looking out at his car. I guess that is when he saw the police around his car. He threw money on the bar and moved carefully out the door to the other side of the street. Soon after that, the police came in and asked who owned the car. When I told them he had just left, they ran out, and I guess they chased him. What did he do, señor? He seemed like a nice young man, but I could tell he was troubled."

"What makes you think that?"

"While I was getting beer for others, I heard him talking to himself. He said he had done the right thing, and he hoped that God would forgive him. That was all, señor."

"Thank you, señor."

They finish their beers and walk back outside. Quintano shakes his head. "Well, that pretty much tells me our man was here."

"Yeah, but now we have two places he seems to be going. In my experience," Brock looks at Quintano, "a man will tell his bartender what he will not tell his priest." Quintano smiles.

"Sí, I agree, my friend." His eyes look over the two matchbooks. "Hmm." He opens one of the books. The time four o'clock is written on the inside cover. "Well," he hands it to Brock, "what do you make of this?"

"Well, four o'clock. The same as the note in Luís's apartment."

"Sí, and it could not be four this morning. It has to be this afternoon or tomorrow morning. The clock is running on our two saboteurs, so will have to get moving."

"Right." Brock hands the matchbook back as they walk back to the car.

The old man asks, "Did they help you, señor?"

"Sí, you told the police that you saw the young man back at the car?"

"Sí, they walked down to the canteen and were told that he had just left. They wanted me to tell them if I saw him. When I looked around, he must have come from behind that building. When they walked to the canteen, I saw him at the car. I called to the police that it was him. He grabbed a bag and ran up the alley with the police after him. Then later we helped the police push the car over to the side of the road."

"Thank you, señor." Quintano shakes his hand. Looking up the road, cars and buses are at a dead stop. Horns beep as people grow tired of the wait.

"Get the road open!" they shout.

The old man waves to the people. "These mud slides have really caused a problem. I must get back to work. Goodbye, señor." The old man works his way up the cars, trying to settle down the drivers yelling and honking.

"Brock, we will fly east towards Cardenas. The sergeant said that even though there are roadblocks up on the main roads, the cab drivers know a hundred ways of getting over the hills to

Cardenas." They thank the police and walk back to the helicopter.

"I'm going to report in to Morales and find out what's been going on." Brock takes out a cigarette and walks around the front of the helicopter to watch the cars on the road.

CUBAN CONTROL CENTER

The aide knocks on the door to Morales's office. "Yes, enter."

The man comes to attention in front of the desk. "Sir, Marshal Shagan has called again and demanded to speak to you."

Morales waves his hand in the air. "What else?"

"General, Vice President Gutaras is on his way here from the palace to see you."

"Show him in as soon as he arrives."

"Yes, sir." He turns and leaves.

"Captain Ruiz, the operation that I asked you to look at, are you done?"

"Sir, I need to get in contact with Admiral Rivera, General Quintano and Colonel Vasquez at the air base."

"Very well, but get going. I want the information as soon as possible. And don't worry about Quintano. I'll be talking with him."

"Yes, sir." Armed men from Morales's personal guard move into the command center, and take up positions around the room. Two men walk into Morales's office as the captain is stepping out.

"General, I need to get some papers from my office and make a few calls. I'll be back in a few minutes." Morales watches as the captain walks through the outer office. He motions one of the guards over and whispers into his ear. The man salutes and leaves the office. As Ruiz walks to his office, he sees more of Morales's men around the command center. Two armored vehicles have pulled up in front of the building, and they form a barricade across the front.

As Vice President Gutaras's car pulls up to the front gate of the command center, he is stopped by the guards and checked. The driver rolls down his window. "This is the vice president's car; why have you stopped us?"

"I'm sorry, but we need to make positive identification of all personnel entering the compound. Those are our orders."

"Your superiors will hear about this."

"Yes, sir." The guard checks their papers. "Thank you, sir." He salutes the vice president as the car is waved through. Gutaras looks out the window at the men around the compound. "Luís, aren't these Morales's personal guards?"

"Yes, sir. I was just going to comment on that. They have moved the normal guards out of the compound. I would suggest that you be extremely cautious around Morales. I don't like the look of this."

"Sí, it seems our general has his own agenda. We need to put a stop to this immediately." The car pulls up to the front of the building. "Luís, are you armed?"

"Yes, Mr. Vice President."

"Good. Stay close."

Luís opens the back door slowly after looking around the area. The vice president gets out and begins the walk up the stairs. As they pass, the men on guard stand at attention and salute with their rifles. "Gentlemen." Gutaras nods as he passes. They enter the building; there are more guards in the halls. A lieutenant walks up to him.

"Sir, may I escort you to the command center. General Morales is pleased to welcome you, and he asks if there is some refreshment I can get you." Gutaras looks around the outer offices and sees the guards at the side of the room.

"Some coffee would be fine, Lieutenant."

"Yes, sir."

Gutaras walks into Morales's office. He is standing in front of his desk and salutes as the vice president enters. "Sir, it is a pleasure to welcome you to the command center." He directs him to a chair in front of the desk and walks around to his seat.

"Sir." The lieutenant enters the room. "Vice President Gutaras's coffee, sir."

"Gentlemen, I would like to talk to the vice president alone." The two guards leave the room, and Luís waits in the outer room.

Gutaras waits until the door is closed, and sets his coffee down on the desk. "General, you must recall all forces operating in the Gulf. The situation is getting out of hand. I talked with the ambassador at the UN and with Secretary Sholenska. Apparently, Air Marshal Shagan has been trying to contact you, and you are not returning his calls. The United States is gravely concerned about this situation accelerating into some type of mini war. The Americans are working with the Russians. We know that the plane was sabotaged by someone here in Cuba. A full alert of our military is unwanted and foolhardy. So as acting head of state while Fidel is in Bolivia, I now order you to recall all military units operating in the Gulf." Gutaras looks into the dark eyes of the general. "Do you understand that order, General?"

Morales's expression does not change.

"I want this done now; this is madness. We are being accused of firing missiles into unarmed refugee boats. My God, have you lost your mind? Well, General?"

Gutaras watches as Morales takes a long, slow drink from his glass of rum. His eyes never leave Gutaras's eyes.

"Mr. Vice President, the nation is under martial law. Which, I must remind you, puts me in command, not you. The Russians are working with the Americans on some other purpose besides the crash. I know the Americans are concerned because we have shown them up as paper tigers. The orders in effect will stand until I feel they need to be recalled. I would suggest that you may want to remain here at the command center for the duration of the situation."

"General, is that a threat?" He looks deep into the dark eyes. "You have my orders, General. I suggest you follow them to the letter. You have us in an untenable position in the Gulf; our allies the Russians see your actions as a threat to their safety. And the Americans are not going to tolerate a loose cannon in the Gulf. I want you to leave with me after you give the order to recall. You will join me at the judicial palace and wait for the return of Fidel. If you refuse to follow these orders, I will have you arrested and put under guard." Gutaras gets up turns and takes a couple of steps. "General, I'm waiting."

"Sir, you won't have to wait any longer." When Gutaras turns back to the general, he is staring down the barrel of a Russian 10 mm automatic.

"How dare you pull a weapon on me."

The report from the shot resounds in the outside office. The look on Gutaras's face is total disbelief; his hands clutch the hole in the center of his chest. Morales watches as the light of life drains from the vice president's eyes, and Gutaras crumples to the floor. The door flies open and two armed guards burst into the room. "Sir, are you all right?"

"Yes, but the president has been killed."

Luís comes in behind them. "Mr. Vice President, what has happened?" Luís rolls the vice president over. Seeing the hole in his chest, he reaches for his gun. "You son of a bitch!"

As the gun begins to move out of his jacket, the cold steel of a machine gun barrel touches his forehead. "Drop the gun on the floor, and step back."

Luís follows the command and stands up. Morales comes around the desk. "Sergeant, it is horrible when an honorable man like Vice President Gutaras is gunned down by his own bodyguard and driver. This act will not go unpunished. Take this man outside, and have the vice president's body removed. I will contact his family and the palace of justice to tell them the bad news. Now let's deal with this animal."

Luís shouts into the room. "He has killed the vice president! Do something! He has gone insane!"

His calls fall on deaf ears as they drag him through the outer office. Ruiz runs up from his office. "What was that shot? What happened?"

The guards push Luís by; he yells back at Ruiz. "Morales has killed the vice president! Stop him! He is insane!"

Morales emerges from the office. "That traitor of a driver just assassinated the vice president. He is going to pay for the deed."

Ruiz steppes back as four men carry the body of the vice president into the hallway and down to the dispensary. "My God!" Ruiz mind reels.

Still yelling, the driver is walked near the armored cars and told to run to the car.

"Move asshole. Get in and get out of here, or you will be shot in place."

Luís knows his fate, but there is another gun in the car. He looks at the men around him. He lashes out with an elbow into the face of the guard next to him and kicks the other guard. They both go to the ground, and Luís sprints for the car. The armor in the door will protect him, and the rest of the armor thorough out the car is almost foolproof. He can get out and spread the news. The rush of adrenaline pushes him up to the car. His hand grabs the door handle as the first few 23 mm rounds from the machine gun on the top of the armored car strike him. The impact throws him along the side of the car and onto the ground. Additional rounds chew into the lifeless form on the ground, and then all is quiet. Morales swings the gun back to the side, and climbs down from the vehicle. "I thought he might run."

As he walks up to the body, he places a pistol nearby. "Call the news people and have them get over here to get a picture of this traitor to Cuba." He struts back into the building and goes back to his office. Ruiz runs to his office and calls the commander at the patrol boat station.

"This is Ruiz. God help us. Morales has killed Vice President Gutaras. He has lost control; he has gone mad. Get hold of Quintano; if I call from here, I'll be shot. OK, bring some men and we will put him under arrest. But watch out for his guards. They're all over the place. I'll have two men with me. We'll wait for you." Ruiz hangs up the phone, but the commander at the base hears a second click.

"Shit." He throws the phone down. "Chief, get me twenty good men and get them armed. We're going to the command center. Morales has gone berserk."

"Yes, sir."

The chief runs to a nearby barracks and gets his men, and they head for the armory.

Ruiz gathers some papers and goes back to the command center. He walks by a man cleaning up some blood on the rug in Morales's office. "Sir, I have some other papers to get, and we'll discuss the ships. It was terrible to see what happened to Vice President Gutaras."

"You're right. If only I could have known what that madman was going to do, I could have spared our country the loss of such a great man."

"Yes, sir. I'll be right back."

"Fine, Captain. I'll be waiting."

Ruiz moves to the men working on the radios and screens around the room and tells two of them to follow him. They go down the hall to his office, and he closes the door. The base commander tries to call Ruiz back, but the line is busy. After three or four calls, he gives up.

Morales walks back into his office and yells at his aide. "Get me General Quintano on the line; he is in his helicopter somewhere."

The radio call is placed and transferred to Morales's phone. His aide comes to the door. "Sir, General Quintano is on line two." Morales nods and pushes down the button.

"Yes, General Quintano. Where are you now?"

"General, we're outside of Cardenas. We have tracked one of the saboteurs to his car here. He escaped the police, but we think he is headed for Segva La Grande. We're going to go search the area east of town. Over."

"Very good, General. You're doing a fine job. Please keep me informed of your progress."

"Yes, sir. Quintano out."

Morales slowly hangs up the phone. "I want a close watch on his movements in the next few hours."

"Yes, sir."

After twenty minutes, news crews begin arriving at the command center. One of the guards calls into Morales's office. "Sir, the reporters are here. They're taking pictures of the driver out front."

"Very good, I'll come out to talk to them. Get me the secretary to the president, so I can pass on the news of the assassination." Morales straightens his jacket and puts on a beret. He moves with two of his guards out to the two armored vehicles. The cameras are rolling as he walks out to them.

"Ladies and gentlemen, it is my unfortunate responsibility to tell the people of Cuba that Vice President Gutaras was assassinated by his driver. The madman then attempted to escape and was killed where you see him. I was inspecting the vehicle here when it occurred, and I was able to terminate the traitor before he could get away. I do not like to kill, but in this case it was a pleasure to be the angel of death to this coward." With that, Morales spits on the corpse of the driver.

ULTIMA
WASHINGTON, D.C.

"Sir, the Cuban ambassador to the UN is on the phone. The secretary believed that you should hear this direct."

"Sir, this is the president."

"President Wayne, we have received grave news from the palace of justice. Vice President Gutaras has been assassinated at the command center in Havana."

"What?"

"It was reported by General Morales, who ended up killing the gunman. My personal view on this is that we have a renegade general in control."

"Thank you, Mr. Ambassador. Your cooperation is greatly appreciated."

"Get me Brant, now!"

The red phone rings at the secretary's side. "Mr. President." He listens and shakes his head. "Yes, sir. We will see you in about thirty minutes, correct? At eleven o'clock. Yes, sir." He hangs the phone up.

"Gentlemen, that was President Wayne. He was just informed that Vice President Gutaras has been assassinated. We now have General Morales as the top figure in Cuba."

"Holy shit! He killed the vice president?"

"It looks that way, although they are blaming his driver."

"Shit. I'll bet they're blaming the driver."

"Please get me Marshal Shagan."

Shagan lifts the phone to his ear. "Secretary Brant, we just received the news from our ambassador in Havana. Yes, we believe that idiot Morales killed him. That bastard won't answer my calls. He has, in our opinion, gone mad. He has all Russian personnel on the island under guard, and no communications are allowed. We now can only communicate with the *Moskva* force. We will continue to call. I will contact you as soon as we get through."

HELICOPTER
APPROACHING NAS, NEW ORLEANS

"Dr. Davies, we will be landing in just a few minutes."

"Thank you, Commander."

The noise in the compartment is loud. She leans over to look out the window. She can just make out the airfield as they make a sweeping turn to the right. She can see other aircraft on the ground being prepped for flight as a group of fighters race down the runway.

The helicopter moves across some open grass area and moves up near the main tower. It turns, facing the tower, and slowly lowers to the ground. As the whine of the engines begins to slow down, the crew chief opens the door and jumps down to the tarmac.

"Ma'am." The chief extends his hand to help her and Dr. Reddeer out of the helicopter.

"Right that way." He points to the car in front of the tower. As they approach the car, a naval commander gets out to meet them.

"Dr. Davies and Dr. Reddeer, I presume?"

"Yes." They shake hands.

"I'm Commander Marino."

Susie looks down the apron at the Russian Mig in front of the hangar, and at the two Cobra gunships, which are loading rockets farther down the field. Two other gunships fly over the landing area and turn towards the west. Fighters are lined up on the approach lanes to take off; they are all loaded with rockets.

"There seems to be a lot of fire power out here, Commander."

"It's because of the alert in the Gulf. But that will all be covered for you at the briefing. If you would, we need to get to the command center."

The car moves along the road with an armed escort. This did not go unnoticed by the two doctors. As they pass close to the hangars, the Mig stands boldly out of place. Commander Marino leans over the front seat towards the two scientists.

"I see you are wondering about the Migs?"

Susie looks back at the commander. "Yes, was it with the bomber?"

"Yes, there are actually two on base; the other one is in the hangar. They have been checking it out, and I believe they are trying to repair the damage so the plane can fly out under its own power."

Armed men move along the road next to them as they drive to the base commander's office. They can see the F-18s lifting off the runway and going to afterburners. A large helicopter flies low over them and heads down the airfield.

"That's the Jolly Green Giant; it will be carrying supplies out to the crash site. You will probably go out with them and the Russian commander. His name is Val; he will be at the briefing."

"So why are we here, Commander?"

"That will be answered by the base commander, Captain Nelson. Other personnel have been flown in, also. We should be there in just a moment."

The car takes a turn around a large, circular, grassy area, home to the base flags and two cannons. It stops in front of a large brick building. A large brass plaque reads "Headquarters Building, NAS New Orleans."

The commander gets out and opens the door. "Here we are; please follow me."

As they walk up the steps, the two armed marines at the door salute the commander as they go into the building. "This way." He leads them up a flight of stairs to the second floor and down a corridor to the offices at the end. Two marines stand at the entrance to Captain Nelson's office.

The commander opens the door to Captains Nelson's outer office. There are a lot of people in the office. They are working on computers and maps. There are aerial photos on the tables, and people scurry back and forth. As they walk in, a chief walks up to them.

"So you found them, Commander Marino?"

"Yes, Chief."

"Dr. Davies and Dr. Reddeer, this is Chief Lang. She will be seeing to your needs. I'll rejoin you in the captain's office in just a few minutes." He goes back out the door and disappears down the hall.

"Well, I know this is a little unnerving; it's not normally like this. Please follow me. Can I get you something to eat or drink?"

"Yes, I'd like some coffee."

"And you, Dr. Davies?"

"Do you have some orange juice?"

"We sure do. I'll have it brought in to you in just a minute." She opens the door to a small waiting room just off the captain's office.

"Please wait in here and make yourself comfortable. I believe the briefing will get started in about ten minutes. They're trying to get all the information together, and we have some late arrivals still on their way."

"Thank you, chief." They both go in and sit in two leather chairs near a window.

"Susie, something is really going on." Emanuel leans forward. "Susie, you may have been right. Whatever we're here for must concern that bomber out there."

"Yeah, Emanuel. Because it's an airplane, I believe we're talking weapons here."

"You're right, Dr. Davies." The voice startles the two; they had not heard the door to the captain's office open. The man walks over to them. "I'm Captain Nelson." He shakes hands with them both.

"The chief called me, and let me know you were here. We'll have the main briefing in just a few minutes. We have a plane in orbit around the base while the jets take off. Soon it will be clear if they will be landing. I need to get some other information, so you must excuse me."

As he gets to the door to leave, he turns back to them. "You know Dr. Davies, I was told that you would probably figure this situation out: Your reputation regarding your powers of perception has preceded you. Please make yourselves comfortable. I'll be back in just a minute."

As the captain opens the door, the chief is just coming in.

"Good, Chief. I needed to talk to you." They move over to the other side of the room. A steward puts a sterling silver pot of coffee and a pitcher of orange juice down on the coffee table in front of them. The captain talks to the chief in hushed tone, and he then goes back into his office.

"I need to get some work done for the captain, so if you need anything, please just open the door and call me over."
"Thank you, Chief; this really hits the spot."
She closes the door, and they both sit in silence.

TAXI IN THE MOUNTAINS
CUBA

"For God's sake, can you slow this thing down?"
"I'm sorry, señor. But I must move quickly on these back roads. If we are stopped, I will be in as much trouble as you are, for having you in my cab."
The taxi slams the frame down into another deep hole in the road; Miguel is lifted from the seat and slammed back down. "Shit. It's not worth it if my back is broken trying to get there." He drinks from his bottle of rum; the last of it flows down his throat.
"Shit." He throws it out the window. "Do you have air-conditioning?"
The driver laughs. "You are from the city, señor." His eyes look into the rearview mirror at his passenger. "I have a pint of rum, if you want some more."
"Fine, I'll take it."
"Sí, it will cost 200 pesos."
"Bullshit, keep the son of a bitch."
"Sí, señor." The cab careens around a corner, just missing a large tree trunk. It slides as it cuts through the mud on the trail. But so far no police or military are on the roads. As he concentrates on his driving, the cabby is tapped on the shoulder. A hand holding 200 pesos moves into view, and drops it onto the seat next to him. The cabby reaches under the front seat and removes a pint bottle of rum and puts it into the hand. It moves back and he hears the sound of the cap twisting off.

COMMAND CENTER
CUBA

As Captain Ruiz opens the door to his office, General Morales confronts him with a pistol aimed directly at him.
"Please step out, Captain, and the other two, also."

"Sir, what is the meaning of this?"

"Against the wall, now!"

The two soldiers with him disarm the captain and pat down the other two. Then they step back and bring their automatic weapons up to cover the men.

"So I have gone insane. Right, Captain?"

"I don't know what you're talking about, General."

"Your call to the patrol base. Let me enlighten you. You and that situation are being taken care of *now*!"

"Sir, I only ask that we reevaluate the situation."

"Well, there's an interesting new term for mutiny. Move the captain out to the front of the building."

As they walk outside, they are instructed to move over to the wall near the entrance of the building. They put their hands on their heads as two other soldiers, who have their weapons aimed, join the general.

"Sir." Ruiz lowers his hands. "These two men are innocent of what ever you think I have done. Please let them go."

"They will remain, Captain." The general holsters his pistol.

"Sir, my actions were to bring some sanity to a situation that is going out of control. With what has happened up to this point, and the plans you wanted me to work on, my assessment is that you have lost sight of the situation. You are gorging yourself on pure power and it is corrupting you at the same rate. We must contact Fidel, before you bring total annihilation to Cuba."

"The sentence for your mutinous actions must be dealt with now and harshly. The sentence is death. Sergeant, you may carry out the sentence of the court martial."

"Sí, my general."

Morales moves back inside the building, and turns to watch out the windows.

"Stop him!" Ruiz takes a step forward. "For Cuba's sake, you have—" The words are cut short by the staccato of the automatic weapons. The rounds rip through the three men as long red smears on the wall follow their bodies to the ground.

The general continues to watch as the three guards rejoin him in the hall. As he walks into the office, the men working are quiet. He walks up to his door and stops. "For everyone, when I give an order, it is to be followed immediately. Any hesitation will be considered insubordination. The penalty will be death. I do hope that we will be able to work efficiently together."

"Now, put through a call to Air Marshal Shagan." He looks at his watch; it's 10:50. A smile crosses his face. He closes the door behind him, and the others go back to work. The phone next to Morales rings as Admiral Rivera knocks on the door and lets himself in. The phone continues to ring as Rivera walks up to his desk.

Morales raises his hand and picks up the phone. "Ah, Air Marshal Shagan, I'm glad we can finally talk. If you could please hold on." Morales pushes the button before Shagan can speak.

"You called me, General?"

"Yes, Admiral Rivera. Your subordinate choose to try mutiny."

"Sir, I have known Captain Ruiz as a competent officer and a patriot of Cuba."

"Well, we have both learned a lesson here. I want you to formulate a plan for our surface forces in the chance that the Russians attempt to take offensive action against them."

"Offensive action, General? I don't understand."

"Coordination will be with Colonel Vasquez at the air base at Matanzas. Whether you understand or not, have a tentative plan with in the hour. You can use Ruiz's old office. Don't disappoint me Admiral."

"Yes, General. I'll begin working on it with my staff."

"Very good, Admiral."

"Now I must get back to my call."

The admiral leaves the room, and Morales pushes the button back down. "I'm so sorry about that delay, but Admiral Rivera had to ask my opinion on another matter."

"Why, of course, with the multiple activities going on there, we appreciate your tight schedule." Shagan's hand squeezes the phone handle. "General, we have received word of Vice President Gutaras's death. We grieve with the people of Cuba over his sudden demise."

"Yes, the loss of him to the continuing growth of Cuba will be sorely felt. If only we could have prevented it. I blame myself for not having his driver searched when he arrived. And to have it occur in my own office. I abhor senseless violence."

"Right, General. We again request that your forces be brought back to a state of normalcy. The Americans are claiming that your forces are firing rockets on unarmed boats, and they find themselves in a threat posture.

"Also your forces have been moving closer to the *Moskva* squadron. We have safe passage to the crash site. Your posturing near us puts the group in a compromising situation. Again, we request that you remove your forces from the area."

Silence sits on the line for a minute.

"Shagan, Shagan. Again the American dog wags the Russian tail. My understanding is that the rockets fired were against covert high-speed craft operating in Cuban waters. Again, the Americans squeak when they get their hands slapped. And with the continued aggression of the American forces, we must continue to remain on alert for any surprise moves they make.

"Our intention as to the *Moskva* group is to provide air cover for them, and to put our surface forces between you and the sneaky Americans, until we can figure out their purpose."

"General." The sternness of the word is not missed by Morales. "We seek to cooperate fully with the Americans. Secretary Sholenska spoke to Vice President Gutaras before he came to see you. We were assured that the alert status in the Gulf would be called off. Did he convey that message to you before he was assassinated?"

"I believe he was trying to tell me something, but he forgot that martial law is in effect. Your secretary was dealing with the wrong man."

"Morales, let's be honest here. Neither we nor the Americans are going to continue to tolerate your actions in the Gulf.

"I don't know what the hell is going on in your mind, but listen well. If there is any attempt to intercept the *Moskva* squadron, the gravest of actions will be taken. Your actions so far have resulted in the deaths of innocent bystanders whose only crime was that they were in the path of your outragous behavior in the Gulf. Now recall your forces before someone steps on your illusions."

"My goodness, Shagan. I thought my father had gotten on the line. But he, like you, has grown old and lost the taste of the fight. And you sit in Moscow with the blood of Afghanistan on your hands and preach to me of morals."

"I think not!"

"How dare you presume to sit piously in your war room. You fought rocks with machine guns, you put down revolts with tanks, you shot down commercial airplanes. The blood from your actions runs in rivulets from your feet. And now like some dog bitch in heat, you hang your heads and let the others in the great pack do as they will with you. You have used the forces of Cuba to fight your wars for you in Africa and in South America. Well, we are no longer your mercenaries; we now stand alone. But we learned a great lesson from you: if you bend, you break. Your training over the years has honed us to a very good fighting force. It may be time for the pupil to teach the master some new tricks. So don't presume to speak to me as some kind of patronizing father, or the stern world power. Fuck you, Shagan. And fuck Mother Russia."

"You asshole, Morales. Fuck you, and Cuba too. Well, now that we have cleared the air, let me be up front. If any of your shit forces make any attempt to impede the *Moskva* squadron, the fucking Gulf will run red with Cuban blood."

"So finally we can get direct, you bloated bastard."

"Also, Morales, we have not been able to communicate with our personnel at the bases. If any harm befalls them, you will be held personally responsible."

"Oh, Shagan, you have caused me to soil my uniform with your frightening threats. Why is it that the dog who barks the loudest is the one who was neutered? From the distance you are from the scene, by the time anything might happen, it will be old news to you.

"Here we offer poor, democratic, imperialist swine our help. And all we get back is the poor whimpering of a beaten people."

"Goddammit, Morales, you've gone insane. Good men and women will suffer from this power mania. Start acting like the officer you should be, instead of some stupid little shit from the streets. Call off the alert!"

"Well, Shagan, it's been nice talking to you. I have a tense situation going on in the area around me, which I must address, while you and your staff, like eunuchs, sit in the dark. I will leave you with this parting thought, because there will be no more communications between us. So listen well. If any actions by the *Moskva* fleet are taken towards our forces, blood will run in the Gulf. But it will not be Cuban.

"So goodbye, my friend. I'll see you in hell."

The line goes dead in Shagan's ear. The scream of a wild animal erupts from his throat as he picks up the phone and throws it across the room. The blood vessels on his neck and face push the skin out. His behavior has caught the others off guard, and they cower from this man who is bellowing like a bear.

"Shit! Get me the commander of the *Moskva* squadron *now!*"

NAVAL BASE
CUBA

The jeep pulls away from the front of the building at the naval station. The two trucks behind follow its movement through the base to the front gate. The guards salute as they pass by, yelling for freedom.

"Keep the men quiet. We'll have to get through the guards at the command center."

"Roger."

The captain puts the walkie-talkie down and looks out at the passing scenery. "Damn, I wish I could have talked to Quintano before we left." He repositions the assault rifle on his lap. They pick up speed when they hit the open road. People along the road wave as they pass.

"Once we get around the bend up here, take the turn off to the southwest. It will get us there faster. I'm afraid for Captain Ruiz; when I called back, his line was busy. We have to stop Morales before he gets us all killed. But I think we can pull it off...." His words drain away.

The jeep comes to a full stop with the trucks behind it. They all stare up the road about 200 yards; two T-72 heavy tanks block the road. At each side are BMP troop carriers with men in position around them. The barrels on the two tanks move around and lower directly at the lead vehicle.

"Captain, you and your men will get out of your vehicles and move to the side of the road," the loud speaker blares at the captain. "Blink your lights to show confirmation. Blink the lights. Keep the motor running.

"Very good, now leave your weapons on the vehicles and move to the side of the road." The BMP on the right starts to move forward, its gun trained on the jeep.

"Out of the vehicles, now!"

Three RPG rockets scream from the first truck, hitting the personnel carrier. The explosions bring the vehicles to life, and they try to turn around behind the burning BMP. The air fills with machine gun fire as both sides open up. The drivers try to turn the vehicles around. More RPGs fly towards the two tanks; one hits short and the other glances off the side of the turret, exploding near the other armored car. The boom of the tank main gun fills the air, as the second truck explodes in a ball of fire. A burning skeleton is left crumpled on the side of the road. The second tank fires long; the round shrieks by the first truck and explodes on the road behind them. An RPG hits just in front of the jeep, throwing it into the air. The driver is killed instantly. The captain lies on the road, his leg broken. Firing from the truck continues, and two shells from the tanks smash into the vehicle. The captain watches as one of the tanks moves forward, its machine gun still spraying the burning wrecks. It stops and picks up the commander from the burning BMP, then moves forward. Like flailing chains, its treads cleat into the roadway, pushing the monster closer. It stops twenty feet from the captain. The commander looks down at him.

He lies on his back, and rolls his head to the side to see the commander. Slowly he raises his hand, and gives him the finger. "Fuck you!"

"Forward." The commander's voice is lost to the captain as the treads of the tank roll over him. They move down the road towards the base to secure it.

"General." The commander speaks into the mike. "We have stopped the mutineers on the road. We'll now neutralize the naval base."

"Thank you, sir. I will pass that on to the men. Out."

The general pushes down a button on his phone to signal his aide. The door opens. "Sir, you called."

"Yes, we will take no more calls from the Russians. Do you understand?"

"Yes, sir."

Morales gets up and walks to a side table. He pours a small glass of vodka. Rising the glass to eye level, he peers into the clear liquid. "This was the best thing you bastards brought us." He quickly downs the shot and puts the glass back down. Slowly he stretches his back with his arms over his head. Walking to the door, he checks his watch; it's 10:58. He flings the door open and steps into the outer office.

"Everyone listen up. I have just spoken to Air Marshal Shagan in Moscow. He has requested us to assist our Russian allies, and I have confirmed our solid support for our comrades. I was just informed that the downing of the Backfire bomber is linked to the *Moskva* surface group. Under a direct order from Secretary Sholenska to the task force commander, they were ordered to return to Cuba. The commander refused and stated that they are going to request political asylum when they reach American waters. We, the forces of Cuba, have been asked to intercept the squadron and force it back to Cuba. We will pursue this mission for our comrades, who have given so much to Cuba. Our priority from this moment on will be the interception of the *Moskva* squadron. This mutiny by this group will not go unpunished. Both air and surface units in the western sector are to be alerted of the situation and to await operational plans for offensive action against the *Moskva* group. This is not to go out on open channels; it is imperative that a high profile of secrecy be maintained.

"To our comrades," Morales yells into the room. The men and women echo it as they prepare to transmit to their operational units.

Morales walks back into his office and closes the door. A smile crosses his face. It is the smile of the crocodile as it positions for an attack.

ULTIMA
WASHINGTON, D.C.

Brant looks at his watch, eleven o'clock. The marine at the door moves over to his side. "Sir, the president is on his way."

"Thank you, Corporal."

"Everyone, President Wayne will be joining us shortly. I've been informed that he is on his way. As soon as he arrives, we'll have the report on hurricane Evita."

The others in the room straighten up their papers. The center screen is focused on the western Gulf; another screen is set on Evita. Its swirling mass covers half of the screen; numbers fluctuate up and down along the sides of the screen. Captain Emmett from the weather group arranges his papers at the podium.

His aides pass out the prepared report to the Joint Chiefs and the secretary as Captain Van Nar puts a clip mike on Emmett's lapel so that he can talk to the person operating the screens. Van Nar leans forward.

"Chief, is everything working all right?"

"Yes, ma'am. We're ready when you are, Captain."

Brant gets to his feet as the guard at the door signals the president's arrival. "Sir, attention on deck."

The president walks into the room with four of his aides. "Please, everyone as you were. Mr. Secretary," they shake hands, "I liked your news conference."

"Thank you, sir. We have a desk set up for you here. All communications are available. We were about to have Captain Emmett bring us up to speed on the hurricane. On its present course, it could prove to be very detrimental to our operation."

"Right." He turns to the room. "Please, everyone, do be very candid with your opinions and observations. I do not want my presence to disrupt the operation we're about to undertake. My presence is more in the role of authority back-up for your committee and your joint decisions. My understanding is that Secretary Sholenska has also joined Marshal Shagan's group in Moscow. Our intent is to defuse this whole situation and work jointly in its resolution." He moves back to the seat behind the desk and looks up at the screens.

"Thank you, Mr. President. We will now have Captain Emmett's report on Evita's threat to the operation."

"Thank you, Mr. Secretary. I would like to cover the storm, which has been named Evita. Basically when she hit Cuba, it was ranked as a class two hurricane. Although it did cause a good deal of flooding and structural damage on the island, it spared the island its full fury. It was hoped that once it had passed over Cuba, it would degenerate back to a tropical storm, in that the landmass would break up the winds." A map appears on the screen of the area from South America to the United States. "The storm developed south of the Antilles and has been following this course." A red dotted line begins to appear on the map. "As you can see, it just skirted the west side of Jamaica, and it went just north of the Isle of Pines. When it hit the western area of Cuba, it crossed about fifty miles southeast of Havana. The eye, when it crossed, was approximately seventy-five miles wide, with winds gusting to perhaps sixty to eighty miles per hour. At one point, the storm straddled the island, drawing strength from both sides. It stalled for a short time after leaving the island, but once in the Gulf, it's gotten its second wind."

The screen changes again, showing the satellite picture. The swirling mass appears on the screen. "At present, Evita is sitting almost dead center at twenty-five degrees north longitude and eighty-five degrees west latitude. The eye is now forty miles across. This is a reduction of thirty-five miles, since leaving Cuba. This is a bad sign; as the storm reduces, it gains in strength. Its progress is between twenty and twenty-five miles per hour. Our projection for its path is as follows. It will, if it continues on its present course, hit New Orleans at approximately 4:00 A.M., at a level four plus. The recent above average temperatures in the Gulf region, which have raised the water temperatures, are feeding Evita's insatiable appetite."

The others in the room watch the swirling mass; at its center a dark hole forms the core of the pinwheel.

"Then you're saying we have another Andrew on our hands?"

Emmett looks back at Secretary Brant. "Yes, sir. But maybe with a more terrible punch. I would like to point out a couple of other features on the expanded map." The area on the screen changes back to the entire Gulf region. "We will now add the other weather patterns in the area."

A yellow line snakes across the screen, passing over the red predicted path of the hurricane. "This is a plot of the jet stream. It has dropped to a location south of Galveston, and it swings back north through Apalachicola, Florida. If it remains at this location, it, too, will become a feeder to the storm. And now, the final ingredient. This large chain of thunderstorms running from Brownsville, Texas, to Mobile, Alabama." The arc of the thunderstorms appears green across the map. "These storms have been drenching the areas they're crossing over. It was believed that the storms would move into the Gulf and dissipate most of their fury at sea. But in the last few hours, we have seen a definite movement to the southeast. If this continues over the next few hours, we will see the results of three major weather forces combining into what we have named the Sango effect. The name is taken from the thunder and lightning god of southwestern Nigeria.

"The result of the Sango effect will be that the jet stream will pour energy in from the top, and the chain of thunderstorms, like a machine gun belt, will feed the storm from the side." The screen changes, and the lines on the screen converge.

"This convergence could spawn the worst hurricane ever recorded. Along with this is the probability of a storm surge, estimated at forty to fifty feet. It will decimate the Gulf-facing areas and cause a great deal of property damage.

"Bottom line, we may be witnessing the creation of the ultimate killer storm. Anything in its path will face forces that we have never recorded. Because of the situation with the Cubans, we will not be able to have one of the C-130 hurricane chasers get near this thing until it gets deeper into international waters. It will enter the storm from the northeast and exit due east. It will then return to its base in southern Florida. That will give us the final pieces of the puzzle in regards to wind speed and force level. Are there any questions?"

"Well, Captain Emmett, I believe we were probably hoping for a little grace from the weather. This Sango effect—what's the probability of it happening?"

"Best guess at this time, Mr. Secretary, is fifty percent. A lot can happen in the weather in the next sixteen hours."

"Well, I'm beginning to feel good about ordering the evacuation of that area." The president leans forward on the desk. "It should save many lives."

"Yes, sir, Mr. President. If there are no more questions for Captain Emmett...." He looks around the room. "I'd like to thank you and your staff for a very graphic presentation. And I'd like to request a follow up briefing at four o'clock. In those five hours, we may see the Sango effect."

"With that gentlemen, we need to discuss the placement of our forces in the area, as well as the disposition of the search teams in the drop zone."

"Mr. Secretary."

"Yes, Commandant Swane."

"Sir, the meeting at NAS New Orleans should be commencing about now, and the move to the crash site will directly follow it. So we should have the particulars in a short time."

"Thank you. I need to discuss a couple of items with the president, so let's take five and then resume."

CAPTAIN NELSON'S OFFICE
LOUISIANA

Chief Lang comes into the room. "Well, it's show time. This way please." She opens the door to the captain's office and lets the two scientists enter. "Sir, here are the reports you wanted. Could I get anyone something to drink?"

"Just keep the coffee hot, Chief."

"Yes, sir." She closes the door behind her as she leaves.

The two scientists sit at two vacant chairs at the end of a long table. In front of them are two folders with their names on them. "Good, let's get started. The military people here know each other, so I would like to introduce our two new members of the group, Dr. Susie Davies and Dr. Emanuel Reddeer.

"We met earlier, and you know Commander Marino." The captain moves around the table. "This is Mr. Sandovol, from the DEA." He moves along. "And this is Marine Colonel Knight, from Camp Lejeune. He is the commander of the recon group now at the crash site." The captain moves back to the front of the table to a map of southern Louisiana.

"At approximately 4:00 A.M. this morning, a bomb exploded on a Russian TU-26 Backfire bomber. This act of sabotage set in motion the series of events that has now brought us together. On board the bomber was a secret cache of nuclear weapons. They were being moved back to Russia for disposal. The explosion killed most of the crew and gravely injured its pilot. It also activated the craft's on-board fail-safe system. In the system was a sub-program called automated weapons delivery. Or as the crews called it, the death mode. When the captain became unable to fly the aircraft, the computer took over."

He turns to the map. "At approximately this point, the aircraft turned southwest. Its final resting-place is on the shore of Barataria bay. From the point of the turn to the crash, the computer deposited eight one-megaton bombs on Louisiana."

"My God." Emanuel looks at Susie. "You were right, Susie."

"What we need of you and Dr. Reddeer is your expertise from working at Pentex to oversee the neutralizing of these weapons."

At that time, all eyes turn to the side door. Val enters and takes a seat next to the captain. "Well, our final member. Commander Val, this is Dr. Davies and Dr. Reddeer."

Val gets up and walks down the table to where they are sitting. "It is an honor to meet you both." They shake hands. "I see myself fortunate to meet the lady who helped my countrymen at the Chernobyl site. I'm sorry we meet under such adverse circumstances."

He moves back up with the captain. "Commander Val will now give us a briefing on what to expect when we find the bombs. Commander Val."

"Thank you, Captain Nelson. I will try and give you the information I have received from our people in Moscow. The bombs are approximately fifteen feet long; they are five kilotons each. These bombs were designed to be dropped at low altitudes on high-speed runs. The timer involved was brought into play depending on the tactics being employed.

"They could be dropped with minimal detonation time; while others are set to explode, the enemy believes it is clear in the area. Also, if it were necessary to move troops back, an area could be salted with the weapons. A delaying action brings the enemy force on top of the bombs at a predesignated time. This particular type of weapons pose a real threat as far as disarming them are involved. There are two anti-tampering devices in place. Once the bomb is dropped, a set of retarding fins are deployed. The bomb is positioned to hit like a durnal anti-runway bomb. At its point of impact, it buries into the ground. An anti-movement booby trap inside is triggered if the weapon is moved beyond ten degrees in any direction. So they must be secured into a position that will not allow the bomb to move.

"There is an access plate on the side of the bomb. There are eight star tap screws in the plate; they must be removed in a particular sequence. If they are removed at random, a circuit is activated and the bomb detonates.

"Once inside the access plate, the triggering device is accessible. It has two hold-down collars that should be unscrewed and a pin should be removed. At that point, the device can be taken out, and the bomb is neutralized.

"Each bomb is numbered, and that number coincides with top secret cards stored in the war room in Moscow. When a weapon is located, its number will be passed on to Marshal Shagan's group. They will open the corresponding envelope. The sequence number for the screws will be passed on and the access plate opened." Val looks around the room. "There are two nuclear weapons people on each of the *Victor* submarines with the *Moskva* squadron. They will be airlifted out and flown to the crash site. Those going out with me will meet them at that time."

"Commander?"

"Yes, Dr. Davies."

"We had heard rumors of this type of weapon, but none were ever documented. This type of tactical nuclear weapon is usually kept in the kiloton range."

"Correct, Doctor. These were specially built for an assault on Russia from the western forces in Germany or an assault from the Chinese in the eastern regions, where a large massing of armor and infantry would be dealt a devastating blow in the initial contact."

"Have the men on the submarines disarmed this particular type of weapon?"

"I'm sorry to say, Dr. Reddeer, but no. As far as I can determine, the thought was, once delivered, we would never have to disarm them anyway. So with these particular weapons, we learn as we go."

"Excuse me, Val." Captain Nelson joins him. "I must stress that your assistance in this matter will be your personal choice. It is stressed from the Joint Chiefs, by way of the president, that this is strictly volunteer. We would more than understand anyone's reasons for not going on this particular mission.

"Also, I would like to lay out our deployment plan. Colonel Knight will assume command at the beach site. Commander Marino will be the beach master. He will coordinate the naval activities of our forces, as well as those of the Russian squadron, when it arrives. I'll be here at the base, directing air cap and support for all in the field. Mr. Sandovol will be one of two DEA agents on site to help in the search. His group is relatively familiar with the field areas that need to be searched. Each of the teams will have two of the Russian weapons people with them. Commander Val will be at the crash site to assist both Colonel Knight and Commander Marino. So basically, that's it in a nut shell. We'll take a short break to allow our two guests to consider if they want to ride with us Don Quixotes."

"Thank you, Captain." Susie and Emanuel go back into the waiting room to discuss the situation.

"What a mess." Emanuel puts his hands on his hips. "God, you've been through this kind of thing before, Susie. Hell, this thing scares me shitless."

She looks up at her associate. "I feel the same way; it's the same each time this has happened before. But these guys are pros, and there is time to disarm the bombs."

"My God, they talk about them like they're sticks of dynamite, instead of five thousand tons."

"They understand. It's just they get volunteered automatically."

He sits down across from Susie, and looks her in the eyes. "Shit." He shakes his head. "I don't have to be a medicine man to see where you're going." A shy smile crosses her mouth. "OK, I know how ballsy you are. But this is like major chahonas. I take it that you think we can pull this off."

"Yes. But Emanuel, this is your choice, too. Make it from your heart, not just your mind. It deals with your family and your future. Make sure this is something you would do."

"Shit, I know we could do it, too. Hell, we have knocked out these bad boys before, back at Pentex."

Susie smiles. "Besides, I'm feeling invincible today."

"Yeah, right." They both stand and their hands meet in the air above them. As they come back into the office, aerial maps are being laid out on the table. The others in the room watch them as they walk up to Captain Nelson.

"Well, Captain, you've recruited your two new members."

"Excellent, I need to make a call to Admiral Hillings."

"Commander Marino, please show the doctors the two sites we have confirmed. These will be where we start."

As they lean over the table looking at the two photos, Chief Lang comes into the room. She is carrying two naval flight suits. "Excuse me, Doctors. I think these should fit. I had to eyeball your sizes when you walked in. We don't have any quite your size, Dr. Davies. You may have to roll up the cuffs."

"Thank you, Chief. Every pair of pants I buy has to be shortened."

"OK, I guessed at your boot size. Dr. Reddeer, an eleven and a half, and you, Dr. Davies, I had them get you a seven, to give you a little room."

"Right again, Chief."

Another sailor enters and puts the boots on the table next to them.

"Thank you, Chief. Everything looks good."

"Sir, did you want them issued side arms?"

"No, I don't think so. They will have the marine squads with them."

"Aye, aye, sir."

Susie picks up her boots. "Pretty confident that we would go, Commander."

"Your reputation again proceeds you, Dr. Davies. The smart money was on your taking the assignment. And that came out of Washington."

They sat down to put on their gear. They had noticed that the others had flight gear on when they came in. They finished getting dressed and went back to the photos. In what looked like a grassy field, the photo revealed a slight scar in the ground. "Here's the enlargement of that photo."

The scar was a slight trench maybe eight inches deep and four feet long. At the end of the trench, four black bars seemed to be lying on the ground.

"They believe that the bomb was oscillating when it came down, and that caused the trench. These are the retard fins. From the estimates, it is believed that this is bomb number seven. And this one," a new set of photos is put in front of them, "is number eight. Again, like the other photo, the black plus sign shows in the photo."

"Once we have verified and neutralized these weapons, we'll be better able to determine the locations of the others. We will airlift the teams in as close as possible. But after talking with Mr. Sandovol, our best guess is that you'll have to hike into over half of the sites. As soon as we have a sighting, Captain Nelson will relay it on to the field.

"Ladies and gentlemen, I have just talked with Admiral Hillings. The president is now in the war room with the Joint Chiefs. Mr. Brant passed on the acceptance of our two doctors, and it was greeted with great enthusiasm. Also, Admiral Hillings is sending down the latest weather reports. I must be honest with everyone; it does not look good. Hurricane Evita is apparently stacking up to be one of the worst they have ever seen.

"Also, relations have broken off between Marshal Shagan, and General Morales. A warning was issued to Cuba to stay away from the *Moskva* squadron. The forces are now within range of each other. The unthinkable would be an attempt by Cuban surface forces to intercept."

"I had heard that there was some military actions in the Gulf by Cuba, that sounds serious," Reddeer says.

"It is, Dr. Reddeer, but be assured that your area of operation is completely covered. We have air groups at the 100-mile zone, and I assure you nothing will get through. We also have surface forces at the zones, which are more than adequate to deal with the situation. So, basically, all you have to worry about are the bombs themselves."

"Gee, we all feel a lot better now." Susie laughs. "Let's see what we're up against. A killer hurricane, eight five-kiloton bombs, and a possible mini sea battle off the coast. All things being equal, I don't see any problems." It is the first time any laughter has shown itself in the office.

"You're right, Dr. Davies. You couldn't make up a weirder scenario."

"Well, unless there are any other questions? I'm waiting for the weather report from Admiral Hillings, so the rest of you can looks over the sites and the other reports we have. And Commander Val, the admiral said that Marshal Shagan wished to speak to you as soon as possible." As the others read over the material in the folders, Val steps out to call from another office.

KNLT NEWSROOM

The phone on Sam's desk rings to life; the two men look up from the table and see the light blinking. "I'll get it." His secretary picks it up.

"KNLT news. OK, Marcey. They're going over the stuff for the noon news. Hold on." Her hand covers the phone receiver. "Sam, it's Marcey. She wants to talk to you."

"All right." He reaches over to a phone near him and pushes down the button. "Hi, Marcey. What's going on?"

"I don't know, Sam, but I'm over here at the Radisson. It seems that two guests were airlifted out of here by the military and taken to the naval station."

"So do you know who they were?"

"Yeah, I did some real reporter type work. One was Dr. Susie Davies, and the other was Dr. Emanuel Reddeer. Do the names ring a bell, Sam?"

"Yeah, Dr. Davies sure rings something."

"It should; she lead a NATO team into Iraq after the Gulf War. I had a chance to talk to her after that; remember that interview?"

"Right, just a minute. Nancy, run a profile on Dr. Susie Davies and Dr. Emanuel Reddeer."

"Right, Sam." She gets on the computer at his desk and begins typing in the information.

"All the military personnel are gone. But I talked to a couple of the porters here. Apparently, Reddeer's wife was taken to the airport, along with Dr. Davies' luggage. And it seemed that the military disappeared as fast as they arrived."

"Hold on, Nancy has the print-out." Sam quickly reads down the profile of the two scientists. "Marcey, both of them are weapons experts out of Los Alamos."

"I knew it. There is something going on out at the base."

"But it's no good. I just spoke to Darin out at the base. It's been locked down tight. He is still trying to get on base and talk to Captain Nelson."

"So why would they need weapons people on the base? And why did they restrict any attempt to get near the bomber crash? Hell, we flew in without any problem. And we were able to get shots of the crash scene."

"Well, maybe they found out something after you left. From the Russian pilots or that other Russian who flew in."

"Damn, you may be right, Sam."

"Well, let's test the water. You have your crew with you, right?"

"Yeah, we could be set up in a few minutes."

"Good, we'll go live with you during the noon news. Get all you can. Then we'll wait to see if we get a response from someone."

"Right."

"I'll call over to the control room to have them stand by for your set up, and we'll go from there. "

OK, Sam. See you in a while."

"Right, Marcey. Head back in when you're done."

ULTIMA CONTROL ROOM

"Excuse me, everyone." Captain Van Nar walks up to the podium. The first screen narrows down its focus. "We are receiving word from Sky 1 that four aircraft have just left the airfield at Matanzas." Four new triangles appear on the screen. "Two are jet, and two are prop-powered. They are proceeding north northwest. Their only transmissions were with the tower on takeoff. They are moving under radio silence." She listens to her headset for a second. "We have just confirmed that they are not fighters. Possibly ASW and ECM aircraft, from radar profiles so far received. Knowing what is stationed at Matanzas, we would assume these are two Ilyushin Il-38 ASW aircraft, and two Tupolev Tu-16-J series, code name Badger."

She again holds her hand over her ear. "Sky 1 is now reporting the lift off of two aircraft from the air base at Segva La Grande. We match two Ilyushin Il-76 air-refueling tankers. They too are now flying in a north northwest direction." They watch the screen as two additional triangles appear on the screen.

Brant turns back to the people at the table. "Admiral Hillings, what do you make of this latest move?"

"I'd say something is in the wind; they're setting up for something. If I were Marshal Shagan, I would advise the squadron commander to be at full alert."

The president walks up next to Brant's chair. "Excuse me, Admiral Hillings, but what would be the outcome of a battle like this?"

"Well, Mr. President, the Russians have the advantage in surface ships. Both in type and fire power. However, you cannot discount the Cuban forces; there is a lot of fire power in a small package there. But the real disadvantage is in air power. The Cubans control the air; the only air defense for the Russians is a single Yak-38, which is not the most agile plane out there. Plus, they would be totally outnumbered. I earlier asked Captain Van Nar to work up a scenario of a possible action against the Russians. Some additional players have been added with the ECM aircraft and the others. Please run the scenario." Van Nar calls to the chief to run the scenario on screen one. Like models on a table, the ships in the scenario begin moving and firing. In a short period of time, the scenario ends. The losses to the Cubans are acute, but the Russians have not escaped unscathed. The saving grace for the Russians is the two *Victor* class submarines which could carry the day.

"My God, I hope it doesn't come to that."

"We agree, Mr. President, but I can assure you that the squadron commander out there is on full alert."

"Thank you, Admiral. We need to get a review of the evacuation now in progress on the peninsula."

General Becker gets up and goes to the podium. The screen behind him displays the southern portion of Louisiana.

"All traffic south of Gretna, on both the 23 and the 39, is controlled. All lanes are one-way north; we have allowed one southbound lane until four o'clock P.M. This is only for troop movements and for civilians who live in the towns to retrieve family members, pets, etc. We moved National Guard troops down to Venice, on the most southern portion. With both local police and the guard, a push has started from there up. We must say that everything seems to be going along great. We have the alert group airborne, and they will be flown by helicopter into the area to assist in the evacuation. We have navy, army and Coast Guard helos flying out patterns from the roads, looking for anyone not contacted on shore. Any boats in the area are being directed to proceed north or to get to shore to be moved by the military. Again, it seems to be going quite well.

"Once in the city, people are being directed to the Super Dome. It can seat 70,000; we're looking at about twenty-five to thirty thousand. There is sufficient parking to facilitate everyone, and the National Guard has set up food distribution. There are sufficient toilet facilities, and the young folks are free to play on the field. The navy has sent over some balls and frisbees for the kids. The main screen is being hooked up to play movies and show the local news.

"The city fathers are cooperating completely with us; traffic coming from the south is directed to one-way streets leading to the dome. There will be medical teams moving to the dome by two o'clock. And the disaster control office is at full operation. I'll update this report as the day progresses. We are estimating a fully cleared area by six o'clock tonight."

"Thank you, General Becker; at least something is going along great."

ON THE BRIDGE OF THE *MOSKVA*
THE GULF

"Sir, we have a call coming through from Moscow." Admiral Kirsanov looks over the plotting of the Cuban forces and walks back to the bridge.

"This is Admiral Kirsanov."

"This is Air Marshal Shagan, Admiral."

"Yes, sir."

"Admiral, talks with the Cubans, especially General Morales, have broken off. We fear that a possible attempt may be made by the Cubans to intercept your squadron."

"Sir, preparations have been taken since our last talk. We are at full readiness; any move by their forces to interfere in our objective will be dealt with in a most harsh manner. We are about to reposition the *Sovremennyy* destroyers; Mr. Pstygo has plotted our missile positions on the Cuban squadron. Although we lack air cover, we will make up for it in sheer firepower. Our two escorts are well aware of our situation and will add greatly to our cause."

"Admiral, I would like to pass on from the war committee our highest regards for the disposition of your forces. Our thought is that this battle group could not be in better hands. And we regret that you may have been sent into harm's way."

"Sir, I will pass on the words of confidence, as well as your concern for the brave officers and seamen of the group. And I pass back to you our oath of honor: to distinguish ourselves in the great tradition of our comrades who faced dire straits before us. We hope for the best, but if they slip the dogs of war, every drop of Russian blood will be extracted ten-fold on our adversaries."

"We again wish you the greatest luck. From now on, we will be updating you on any information we have. Our confidence sits with you in the coming hours, Admiral. Fleet Admiral Gorshkov extends his best wishes and would like to stand with you on the bridge."

"Thank the Fleet Admiral for me, sir. And please pass on that if he were with me on the bridge, it would be too great of a Russian advantage for the Cubans to overcome. Goodbye, sir."

The ships around the *Moskva* form a box with the cruiser in the middle. All guns and launchers are loaded and ready for immediate action.

"Lieutenant Pstygo."

"Yes, sir."

"What is our position, and where are the two submarines?"

"Sir, were at eighty-seven degrees west latitude, and twenty-five degrees north longitude. Right here, sir." He puts his finger down on the map. "The two submarines are at right angles to the bow, and fifteen and seventeen miles out."

The air officer walks up to the two. "Sir, we're on the second rotation of the Kamovs. We're bringing the anti-ship helicopters in and have launched the replacement. The *Sovremennyy* has launched its helicopter as the replacement. The *Otlichnyy* has also launched its helicopter; it will be on station in just a few minutes."

"Thank you, Air Captain. Is the Yak ready to fly?"

"Yes, sir. We have fueled it and checked its weapons; all is ready."

"How soon can we launch the helicopters to fly the weapons techs off the submarines?"

"We have two down below from which all weapons are being removed, in order to lighten them up. Normal combat range is 350 miles; even lightened it's a long haul for them." Pstygo points to a place on the map. "In another hour we should be here. Just within the range of the Kamovs."

"All right, Air Captain. Please come with me." They go up the stairs to the bridge; as they walk in a seaman calls out, "Admiral on the bridge."

He sees the captain looking out over the stern of the ship.

"Captain." They join him at the windows.

"Sir, we're recovering the last of our helicopters. The weather continues to get bad, and the storm is running parallel to us."

"I know, Captain. We need to arrange a pick up from the two submarines."

"We could attempt it in about forty-five minutes. I know they're working on the two Kamovs below; we need to have them over the subs when they come up so they're not on the surface long."

"Right, Captain. Contact the subs...." He looks at his watch. "Let's make it 11:50. It looks like the sea is working itself up. The swells are getting bigger all the time, and this on-and-off rain won't help."

CUBA, IN THE TAXI

"Señor, the road is just ahead." The driver can see the "T" in the road, but there is also a car parked to one side.

"We may have company up ahead." Miguel looks out the front window and reaches for his bag.

As they approach, two men get out, and one raises his hand for them to stop. The other man leans on the front fender of the car.

"Señor, they are from the local police. It's a checkpoint. I must stop."

As they approach, the green uniforms of the officers are easy to see. They stop in front of the officer in the road, and he walks up to the driver's side. Both Miguel and the driver roll down their windows as he approaches. The other officer leans on the fender, looking at the two men.

"Señores, your papers please? And may I ask what you are doing out here? We are away from the main highway."

The driver pulls his papers down from the sun visor. "Sí, but the main road is closed, and this señor has to get to Cardenas as soon as possible." The officer checks the picture with the driver and his cab number. He hands his papers back.

"And your papers, señor?" The officer leans down at the back window.

"Yes, officer, let me get them." His hand moves from his bag to the window. A loud boom goes off just behind the driver's head, and blood splatters his left arm and shoulder. The officer falls past his window, his hands clutching his chest. Two more shoots ring out as the other officer tries to draw his gun. The bullets throw him back onto the hood of the police car. A pool of red begins forming on the hood. The cab driver covers his ears. The shots are still ringing in his head.

"Holy Mother. What have you done, señor? Please don't kill me."

"Shut up, you fool." Miguel opens the door and gets out.

"Get out of the cab." The driver opens his door and steps over the legs of the officer on the ground. Miguel checks both men.

"Help me get them of the road." Miguel puts the 9 mm automatic in his waistband. They each grab an arm and drag the officer to the side of the road. They push him down a slight embankment. The body limply rolls to the bottom. They grab the second officer and throw him next to his companion.

"My God, señor. They will kill us both for this. Please take your money back, but don't kill me. I will not talk to anyone. I will say my cab was stolen in Cardenas. But please let me live."

"Shut up, you asshole. I'm not going to kill you. Get back in the cab, and let's get going." As Miguel closes his door, the cab begins moving forward.

"Just get me into town, then you can leave."

"Sí, señor, just to town." The driver looks into the rearview mirror. Miguel's two eyes are fixed on his. The cab moves swiftly down the black top road. The driver can feel Miguel's eyes in the back of his head. They are alone on the road as they move from the foothills and begin driving along fields of sugar cane.

"Pull the cab over." The driver's mind races; he hopes he can say the right thing. He pulls over on the side of the road and turns off the engine.

"Please, señor, I have a wife and family, and these are hard times. I will give you the money back." He reaches into his pocket. "Please, do not kill me."

"Keep the money. Give me the keys to the car. Now I just stay on this road, right?"

"Sí, señor. You will get there in about thirty minutes. Also, if they are this far out, there will probably be no more checkpoints."

Miguel gets in and starts the engine. "I didn't plan to have to kill anyone, but I cannot be stopped. What I have done is for you, and the rest of the people of Cuba. I'll leave the cab in the city; you can find it there."

He revs up the engine, and moves away from the driver. He watches in the rearview mirror, as the figure in the road gets smaller and smaller.

HELICOPTER OVER THE COAST

The sound of the copter's engines seem to drone on and on as those aboard look out the window. "Sir, we have a call from the base. They say that the captain at the naval base was trying to reach you. And he requested you call as soon as possible."

"Roger." Quintano reaches down and adjusts his radio.

"Control, this is General Quintano."

"Roger, sir."

"Patch me through to the naval base. To the base commander."

"Yes, sir." A connection is made, and the base operator answers.

"Naval base, may I help you."

"Yes, this is General Quintano. I would like to speak to the base commander."

"Wait one, sir."

"General Quintano. This is Major Perez, may I help you?"

Quintano looks over at Brock and signals him to key in his headset, on his channel.

"Yes, Major. I was trying to reach the base commander. I'm surprised to speak to you at that location."

"Sir, the base commander has been relieved of duty. I am in command of the base at this time."

"Do you know why the commander was trying to reach me?"

"No, sir. But we are under a full alert at this time. My orders from General Morales are to secure the base and assume command of the facility. Any additional information will have to be gotten from the control center."

"Roger, Major. Thank you for the assistance."

"Yes, sir."

"Quintano out." He glances at Brock. "Brock, something is very wrong."

"Yeah, isn't Perez one of Morales's special forces guys?"

"Yes, and he would never be given the command of the naval base."

"I'll call Ruiz at the command center, and find out what's going on. Remember we heard that missiles had been fired. And you have not been able to get through to any of the Russian groups on the island."

Again he adjusts his radio. "Control, this is General Quintano."

"Yes, sir."

"I would like to speak to Captain Ruiz."

"Yes, sir. Please wait." The sailor patches the call through to Ruiz's office.

"This is Admiral Rivera." The answer again catches Quintano off guard.

"Admiral, this is General Quintano. I was trying to reach Captain Ruiz."

"Quintano, I will speak quickly. All hell is breaking out everywhere. Ruiz is dead, shot by order of Morales. The vice president is dead. Gutaras was killed in Morales's office, they say by his driver. And the commander at the naval base is also dead. Morales has no great liking for you. Do not call back."

"Admiral, what the hell is going on?"

"Quintano, Morales has gone insane. I am at this time preparing a plan to attack the Russian squadron. Colonel Vasquez is launching aircraft for a strike. It's insane. Morales is saying that Air Marshal Shagan has requested the Cuban forces to stop the *Moskva* squadron because they are going to defect to the United States."

"That's insane."

"Ruiz tried to move against him, and he was shot for treason. He has his guards everywhere. My advice to you is stay out of his way. Your family and position can only protect you so far. I wish you good luck, my friend."

"Good luck to you, Admiral."

The headphones go dead. Quintano looks straight out the window and then back to Brock.

"Holy shit, General. We have to try and warn the squadron. And that is why I can't get through to any of the Russian groups."

"I know, my friend, I'm trying to think where we can get to a transmitter." Quintano turns back to the front. "I have lost some good friends. And the vice president was a personal friend of my family."

"Quintano, even I know that Morales hates you. I agree with Admiral Rivera. Keep away from him."

"Sí." Quintano looks out over the land running down to the beach, and he thinks of his friends. He switches his headset to intercom. "Let's turn inland and try the roads up near the hills."

"Roger, sir." The pilot brings the helicopter around and starts inland.

"Sir, there is a call coming in for you."

Quintano nods his head and turns his head back to the radio. "This is Quintano."

"This is General Morales."

"Yes, sir. How can I help you?"

"How is your hunt for our saboteurs going?"

"We have been flying along the coast, and we're going to turn inland to see if we can catch sight of the cab that one of the fugitives is in. There has been some major flooding on the main roads."

"Very good, General. And by the way, Major Perez called to inform me that you had called the naval base."

"Yes, sir. The base commander had left a call at headquarters, to call him. I don't know what it's about, but Perez said that he is in command of the base."

"That is correct. Concern yourself with your manhunt, Quintano. And keep me informed of your progress. I would be very selective of who you try and call, General."

"Yes, sir."

"Good hunting, Quintano."

The headset buzzes with static. He looks back at Brock.

"Shit, Quintano. I do believe you have been told to stay the hell away."

"I think I kind of picked that up myself."

The chopper moves inland, following a major road to Cardenas. To the south, the high mountains rise into the sky.

"Everyone, keep an eye out for that cab."

The radio bursts to life. "General Quintano, this is Police Captain Bodus."

"Yes, Captain."

"Sir, we would like to know if you could check one of our checkpoints. It is on the inland road. We have not heard from them, and they are pretty far out."

"Roger, Captain. We're now flying back towards you, along the hills. We'll check and see what their problem is."

"Thank you, General. We would appreciate it. Bodus out."

"OK, everyone. Let's see if we can find their missing checkpoint."

As they fly, the helicopter passes over patches of jungle and open stretches of sugar cane. The storm had not caused much damage to this region. They had received more of a heavy rain and some wind. The green jungle areas glisten vividly, with small diamonds on their surface. Creeks run down from the hills, racing over rocks and droping off small waterfalls. Children on isolated farms play along their banks, and they wave at the helicopter as it passes. They watch as cars and trucks move along this inland route. The cane fields run across the flat farms and stop at the rolling foothills. The hills run south of them and collide with the higher mountains.

Brock keys the intercom. "We're going to have a problem spotting that cab with all this traffic."

"You're right." Quintano looks down at his map.

"We'll follow this road until it hits route five into the mountains. Then will go up route five to this location; it's one of the last roads out of the hills. And I believe the police checkpoint is some where around there."

The pilot looks over the map and nods at Quintano. "Roger, sir."

ULTIMA
WASHINGTON, D.C.

"Gentlemen, if I could bring your attention to the main screen." Those around the table look up at Van Nar. Their eyes are drawn to eight triangles leaving the coast of Cuba, just east of Havana.

"Sir, Sky 1 has confirmed eight jets leaving Matanzas, and heading north northwest. As soon as they cleared the coast, they went to afterburners. From radio conversations between the group leader and the tower, we are assuming that these are Mig-27 attack bombers. Their call signs and their radar signatures would indicate that."

They watch as the triangles form two diamond shapes and move away from the coast.

"Get me Marshal Shagan."

"This is Air Marshal Shagan. Yes, Secretary Brant."

Brant describes the latest additions to the air marshal.

"Yes, sir, Mr. Brant. We inventoried the available weapons left to Morales. We now have no doubt about his intentions. It seems we have ended up not helping either of us by allowing them to purchase advanced weapons. I will pass on this latest information to the squadron."

"Mr. Brant, have the people left the air base for the crash site?"

"My information is that they will be leaving very soon. Also, we have identified possibly four of the weapons on the ground, Marshal Shagan."

"Admiral Kirsanov must move the techs off the submarines as soon as possible, so that all of the players are at the scene."

"Thank you, Marshal Shagan. We will be getting back to you shortly." Brant hangs the phone up. "Get me Captain Nelson at the naval base."

CONFERENCE ROOM
NAS, NEW ORLEANS

"This is Captain Nelson." He pauses. "Yes, Mr. Secretary." The others in the room look up at Nelson.

"Sir, the group going to the site is preparing to leave as we speak."

"Yes, sir. I understand." The captain nods as he listens to Brant describe the latest events in the Gulf. "Yes, sir. Just a minute." He puts his hand over the receiver. "Commander Val, Marshal Shagan has requested you to call him immediately. And Dr. Davies, Secretary Brant would like to talk to you."

"Here, I'll finish this up." Emanuel takes some papers from her and continues putting them in a waterproof bag. Susie walks up to Nelson to get the phone.

"This is Dr. Davies."

"Hello, Dr. Davies, this is Secretary Brant."

"Mr. Brant, it seems you have a bit of a situation."

"You're right, Susie. Is it all right to call you Susie?"

"Certainly."

"Good. I thought that since we have worked together on other projects, we could deal with this on a friendlier basis."

"It's OK, in that this is the first time we're both on the same side of the fence."

"You're right, Susie. I have just been speaking with the president, and we both feel that we are putting our best personnel forward in this crisis. We sent forward an agreement that you will make the calls from the field. If the situation becomes too dangerous, a full-scale evacuation will immediately go into effect.

"You will have access to any and all resources that you need. Admiral Hillings has diverted a naval supply ship to an area just off the crash site. It will be able to provide Commander Marino with supplies. We'll be talking to you in the field, and from all of us, we wish you the very best."

"Thank you, Mr. Secretary. We also hope for the very best."

She hangs up the phone as Val comes back into the room. "We're ready, Commander, when you are."

"I must ask that on the way to the field, we stop by the base hospital. It will only take a minute."

"Very well, let's go."

Captain Nelson leads the others out of the office and down to the waiting cars. "Commander Val, you will ride with me. The others will be taken to the field to load up. We will join you shortly."

They get into the Hummers and begin their ride to the field. As they pass an intersection, the captain's vehicle turns to the right and heads for the base hospital.

The other vehicles continue on to the field. As they drive on to the tarmac, they turn and drive down the line of hangars. Men are working on jets and helicopters along their path. They pass just behind the Mig-29 parked outside. In the hangar, men are working on the other jet.

"The sheer size of fighter aircraft always amazes me."

Commander Marino turns around in his seat. "We have rotations going out to the edge of the zone. And those on the ground are being prepared for immediate take off."

At the front of the Hummer, a large Super Stallion with its back door open waits for the convoy. They pull in behind the huge helicopter, and they all get out. Colonel Knight walks up to them.

"Dr. Davies and Dr. Reddeer, Mr. Sandovol and I will meet you out at the crash site. We'll set up a command post out of the back of the Stallion. Commander, we'll have your equipment set up also."

"Thank you, sir." The two men salute and Knight and Sandovol head for the back of the helicopter. They wait by the ramp. The engines of the helicopter come to life and begin a slow spin, which accelerates to a withering blur.

"Let's step over here." Marino leads them to the other side of the vehicles. Two lines of men emerge from a nearby hangar, and double time to the rear of the helicopter.

"Sir." The lieutenant runs up to Colonel Knight. "We're ready to load, sir."

"Carry on, lieutenant." The lieutenant steps down the ramp and signals the men aboard. They carry packs and their weapons are at port arms. They form a single line and disappear into the gapping maw of the helicopter.

"Mr. Sandovol, let's get aboard."

They walk up the ramp, and the big door begins to close. The big green helicopter begins to move forward and then turns to go out onto the taxiway. In the air above them, a slim Cobra gunship waits patiently for its big brother. The word "Marines" stands out on the side of the Stallion as it raises into the air.

"Doctors, we'll be going out to the site in a Seahawk as soon as Commander Val gets here."

"All right." Susie pulls the hood of her jacket tighter around her face. As they look around, another helicopter begins taxing up to their position.

"Here comes our ride now." It moves up next to them and sits idling, waiting.

Captain Nelson and Val get out and go into the hospital. They move to the room where the fighter pilots are. As they walk down the hall, Captain Rollens comes out of a room and sees them.

"No way! I will not wake up my patient a second time!"

"Comrade Doctor, we are not here to wake Comrade Mikulin."

He puts his hand on his shoulder. "We wish him a fast and speedy recovery. But I do have a question. Can Ski fly?"

"You have got to be kidding me! My second patient with two shrapnel wounds? And now you want to have him fly?"

"It is just a question, Comrade Doctor."

"I understand, Commander. But I have a feeling that my patient is about to be asked to commit to something."

"You should be a physiologist, Comrade Doctor."

"It would be possible to fly, but he would be in a lot of pain."

"Very good, Doctor. Thank you."

Val moves down the hall to the room. Norba is watching at TV, and Ski is dozing.

"Comrades." Val shakes Norba's hand. Ski slowly opens his eyes. "I must tell you what is going on, and you must make a decision."

Norba sits on Ski's bed and Val pulls up a chair. He explains the situation with the *Moskva* squadron, and what is about to happen out on the Gulf.

"I will go, sir." Norba gets his stuff off a chair. "Will the Americans fuel up my plane?"

"Yes, Captain Nelson had them fuel up the fighters, and they repaired the superficial damage to the other plane. Norba, I will wait in the hall so you can say goodbye to Ski." Val walks out and joins the doctor and Captain Nelson. "They will both be out in just a minute."

"Goddammit, Val." The doctor puts his hands on his hips and shakes his head. "You can do this only in a war time situation. Your young pilot could bust his stitches and bleed to death in the cockpit."

"I know, Comrade Doctor, but the lives of a great many men hang in the balance. Those two fighters out there represent the only air cover for our ships. They will fly against superior odds and may die doing it. But for every enemy aircraft that they can get, it gives the ships a chance. We in Russia hold our youth in our hearts, as you do. But they have been trained for this day, and they both understand the risks."

"Shit, I understand, Commander."

The two pilots emerge from the room. Norba is supporting Ski. "We are ready, Comrade."

Captain Rollens walks up to them. "Ski, in normal times I would have you grounded, and I can do the same now. You must understand, there are no guarantees. You could bust your stitches and bleed to death in your plane. Is this your decision? I can stop it, if you wish."

"Captain, sir, you have been very kind and professional with me. And I thank you for your concern. But this is a situation that I must attempt. Norba and I, we can help and maybe spare some of our comrades."

"Just a minute, then. Wait here." Rollens goes down to the dispensary and returns with some syringes. "Step into the room here for a second." Norba helps Ski into the room.

"Ski, pull the back of your pants down." Rollens gives him a shot. "That should kill the pain. Here are three more. This is powerful stuff. Use these only if the pain becomes unbearable. Too much of it will kill you."

"I understand, Comrade Doctor."

Ski can feel the pain leaving his body, and though he walks with a limp, he walks on his own.

"Gentlemen, we must go."

"Excuse me, Commander. But the next time you bring me a patient, is there a chance that I can practice my art? Without jeopardizing their lives, or doping them up for missions?"

Val calls back over his shoulder, "I promise, Comrade Doctor."

Once in the vehicle they head for the field.

"They will be here in just a few minutes, Commander," the driver calls from the Hummer.

"We can go ahead and get on the helicopter, Doctors."

Marino grabs his bag, and the two doctors follow him to the waiting helicopter.

The captain's vehicle stops in front of the Mig; the doors to the hangar are open. Men are climbing up the side of the Mig doing last minute repairs.

Ski and Norba get out of the Hummer as Captain Nelson gets out of the front. "Gentlemen, I wish you the best of luck."

They both salute. "Thank you, Comrade Captain."

They look back into the back of the vehicle. "We will make our comrades at Volstad proud."

"I know you will. I hope everything goes well."

"Goodbye, Comrade."

They pull away and head for the waiting chopper. As they pull up, Val jumps out and runs for the helicopter.

"Good luck, Val."

He waves his hand back to Nelson. Val jumps into his seat and puts on a helmet. "I'm sorry, but I had to talk to our pilots." The crew chief checks to see he is belted in, and he signals the pilot. The Seahawk begins moving forward and turns out onto the taxi lanes. The engines rev up and they begin to move forward.

As they rise into the air, a Cobra gunship joins them. The helicopters, now clear of the field, begin a slow turn to the southwest. Marino leans over.

"We'll be on site in just a little bit' the crash site is about fifty miles south of here."

"Thank you, Commander." Susie goes back to talking with Emanuel about the triggering mechanism. The helicopter with its escort moves over the roads leading into the city. They can see men in uniform directing traffic all along the roads from the south.

"The evacuation seems to be going along pretty well."

Val can see the line of cars heading north. "You're right, Commander. We heard that it is proceeding quite well."

Soon the houses are getting farther apart as the two helicopters begin crossing over bayous and saw grass. Raindrops begin to splatter on the front windows as they head into a small squall.

At the base, Norba gets his flight suit on and helps Ski with his. They finish and walk out into the hangar.

"Sir, we did the best we could in such a short time. But we feel the patches will hold all right." Ski climbs up the ladder and runs his hand over the patches. They seem to be well made. "Thank you, Comrade Chief. It looks good; it will hold."

He climbs down from the ladder and looks at the patches on the engine. All seem to be well made, and they should hold. Although he feels little pain, he walks with a noticeable limp. He walks around the aircraft and sees Norba finishing his walk. He walks up and grabs the ladder to the cockpit.

"Sir, are you sure this is the right thing to do?"

Ski looks into the face of the crew chief. He thinks about how much he reminds him of his own chief at Volstad.

"Yes, it will be OK. Chief, do you have something I could wrap my leg with? It will have to be tight."

"Yes, sir. But it will probably hurt."

"Whatever, chief."

The chief yells to a crewman near a tool cart. "Bring me a roll of speed tape, on the double."

"Sir, this stuff has fixed more problems than a computer."

The chief takes the tape. "Are you ready, sir?"

"Yes, Chief." The chief wraps the tape tightly around Ski's thigh; the compression causes him to flinch. He looks down at the finished product, the wraps of gray tape squeeze his thigh numb.

"Thanks again, Chief."

"Yes, sir."

Ski climbs up to the cockpit and gets in. They have removed the sharp rips in the metal and replaced some cabling. A sailor helps him into his harness and adjusts the straps. Ski puts on his helmet and plugs into the radio. He feels a pat on his shoulder. "Sir, everything seems OK. We'll be moving you out of the hangar."

Ski signals thumbs up, and the ladder is removed. A jolt is felt as the aircraft is backed out and slowly turned to face the runway. The two Migs sit next to each other as the fuel truck loads their tanks.

"How do you feel, Comrade?"

He looks over at Norba. "It's OK. I just might have a hard time doing G-turns to the right."

"Good, Comrade."

The man in front of the plane signals that the fueling is complete. The starting generator is moved in and hooked up. The man looks around both aircraft and signals for them to start their engines. Both jets roar to life as the pilots check their gages. They begin doing their pre-flight. Both planes seem to be up and operating as they should.

"Tower, this is Wolf 1 and 2. Over."

"Roger, Wolf flight. Your escorts are waiting at the end of the runway. You're cleared to taxi to runway seven. Over."

"Roger. Runway seven. We are leaving now."

The man in front of the planes orders the chocks pulled and signals them to another man out towards the field. Norba pulls out and follows the yellow line towards the other man.

As Ski checks left and then right, he sees the crew chief and his men at attention. When they check his eye, they all salute. Ski returns their salute and signals a thumbs up out the open canopy.

They move up behind two F-14 fighters, then all four move out onto the runway. Cleared for takeoff, they accelerate down the runway and into the air. Everyone on the base watches as the four move away from the base towards the southwest.

As they accelerate, their wings begin to move back to a delta configuration. Once they had been the ultimate foes, each created to defeat the other. They now fly as companions from the same pack, the cutting edge of technological death.

MOSKVA BRIDGE
THE GULF

"Sir, this was just received from Moscow." The admiral takes the message and reads it to himself. He looks around and finds the captain and the air officer at the front windows of the bridge. He walks over to join them and watches as the bow of the ship dips into a roller, then emerges, throwing spray.

"It seem to be getting worse, Captain."

"Sir." He turns towards the admiral. "My thoughts are that we have not seen the worst yet."

"I would agree with you. I just received this from Shagan. It concerns both of you." They each read the message.

"This is not good, Admiral. We have deployed the ships and are prepared to fire at your command. But this represents a very potent threat to the force, which we are unable to counter."

"Thank you, Captain. And flight Captain, your view?"

"Well, sir. The Mig-23 is a capable fighter. But we can deal with its threat; it's purely a dog fighter. But the Mig-27, this is another animal. I have flown both.

"The Mig-27 in full attack mode is a formidable foe. When we designed it into its role as attack fighter and bomber, we outdid ourselves. It is a hunter, designed to attack at low levels, with a big punch. And if the information is correct, in conjunction with the Tupolev ECM, we have an aerial problem. The best that we can put into the air is one Yak-38. Against the Mig-27, it has a problem, but against the 23, it doesn't have a chance. And the weather will work to their advantage. We will make contact..." he looks at his watch, "...it's almost 11:30, so within an hour."

"Pass an order out to our escorts that we are at full alert. And in case of a loss of communications, they are free to fire at will."

"Aye, aye, sir."

ON THE ROAD TO CARDENAS, CUBA

The cab strains under Miguel foot as he pushes it as fast as the old engine will go. Trucks are passing by and other vehicles are on the road with him. Passing through some small outlying towns, the traffic increases. His eyes continue to search the road for police or military checkpoints. He knows he will soon be in the city and lost among the crowd. As he looks forward, a dark object in the sky moves along the road heading towards him. He bunches in among some other cars and a truck as the helicopter flies over.

Quintano watches out the window, seeing more and more traffic on the road. "Hell, this is no good. Even if we saw the cab, we couldn't tell it from any of the others out here on the road."

A sense of cold passes through him as he looks down on a group of cars with two cabs in it. He signals the pilot to go around and fly by the group again. They swing back and pass one more time by the group. Again the odd feeling. Quintano writes down the number forty-four off the top of one of the cabs.

"All right, let's head up route five, and hope that they are stuck in the hills somewhere."

Slowly the traffic thins, and cane fields begin passing under them. As they move up the road, a lone figure is walking along the road, his hands in his jacket pockets.

"He sure doesn't look like a farmer. But he is too old for our man."

"Yeah," Brock calls up. "But he was no farmer."

"We'll keep this man in mind. Let's find the checkpoint and come back for a talk with that fellow."

CRASH SITE
LOUISIANA

"We're just coming into the crash site, you'll be able to see it out the right side." Susie and Emanuel look over the crash site with the deep scar on the beach from the fuselage, and the broken front near the surf line. The helicopter circles the area and lands beside the Stallion. The door slides open and the rush of wet air fills the cabin. Marino jumps down first. "We'll meet with the others over in the Stallion."

The doctors climb out and move away from the helicopter. As soon as they're clear, it lifts up and moves down the beach next to the others waiting.

As Marino and the two doctors begin to move up the beach, two armed marines join them. They escort them to the rear of the Stallion. Marino stops and looks up the beach at a group of sailors.

"I'll join you in just a minute. I need to talk to the chief near the cockpit. The others are inside, waiting for you."

Marino goes down the beach, as the two doctors with their escort go up the ramp. Inside a table is set up and the men around it are talking in hushed voices. Colonel Knight looks up and sees the two doctors. He waves them over.

"Ah, Doctors. We need your input on a couple of matters."

They walk up to the table, and a space is made for them. The table holds maps of the area and the aerial photos they had seen earlier.

"Well, Doctors, we believe we have two sites nailed down. Captain Johnson sent two of his men to each site to verify. They have called back in; they're near the bombs now. They will lay smoke when your team goes out to the site.

"Excuse me, Doctors. I'm sorry, let me introduce you to Captain Johnson, and Lieutenant Neal."

"Doctors." They both nod. "And our other DEA agent, Mr. Owens."

"Doctors." He shakes hands with them.

"Well, let's get to it. Mr. Johnson has split his platoon into three groups. One will accompany Dr. Davies, and the other will escort Dr. Reddeer. They will secure the sites before you go in. The third group will maintain the security here at the site." Marino joins them at the table.

"As was discussed, I will be here with the third group at the crash site, along with Commander Marino. The Lanstat set will be on the TAC frequency."

The two marine officers excuse themselves to go get their squads ready.

"I'd like you doctors to take a minute and give me a want list. List any special equipment you might need in the field. Mr. Marino has a list of the technical equipment for you to add to or delete. So let's take a few minutes. Besides, I need to get a cup of coffee. And you two can go up and look the wreck over."

"Thanks, Colonel. We would like to stretch our legs." They walk outside, each to their own purpose. Susie and Emanuel go up to the main part of the bomber.

"Damn, Susie, this is pretty good size."

"Yes." Her eyes follow the edge of the slope and stop at two men talking to Lieutenant Neal. They salute him, then begin walking down the slope to where they are. One is a big man, she guesses six feet, five inches, and about 230 pounds. He carries himself well, and looks in good shape. The other is about six feet, three inches, with just a hint of a belly. Both look definitely like marines in the movies. She and Emanuel continue to look over the bomber, and they climb up to look into the bomb bay. As they climb down, the two sergeants wait nearby.

"I might make a suggestion, Doctors." They both look at the tall sergeants. "The forward cabin is pretty messy, and is beginning to smell a bit."

"Well, thank you," she looks at his collar, "Sergeant."

"Ma'am, you're Dr. Davies, I presume?"

"And you are Sergeant Stanley, I presume?"

"No, ma'am. Gunnery Sergeant Marshall and this is Staff Sergeant Cabolero; we have been assigned to remain with each of you during this mission." Cabolero steps forward.

"Dr. Reddeer." They shake hands. "I'll be with you."

"Great, Sergeant. Can we look at the cabin down there?"

"Yes, sir."

"By the way, what's your first name, Sergeant?"

"Gilbert, sir."

"Do you want to come along, Susie?"

"No, thanks, Emanuel. I'm going to get some juice."

"OK, we'll meet you back at the helicopter." The two men trudge down the beach towards the cabin.

"Well, let me guess, Gunnery Sergeant Marshall. You're with me?" She looks up into the face above her, as the red mustache above his lips widens into a good Irish grin.

"Yes, ma'am. And please call me Gunny."

"Well, Gunny, do you drink coffee?"

"Yes, ma'am."

"I see the tent. Let's go for it." As they're walking to the tent, a sound like thunder rolls over them. Four delta winged jets streak across the sky over the crash and head out to sea. "Damn." The gunny kneels down in the sand. Susie has her hands over her ears. She watches as the gunny stands back up.

"It's a carry over from 'Nam and the Persian Gulf."

"Well, I think next time I'm going to do it, too. By the way, weren't two of those jets Russian?"

"Yes, ma'am. They had the red star on them for sure. I wonder where they are going."

They go up to the tent and join others who are also getting something to drink. Colonel Knight and Captain Johnson talk as Susie gets her juice.

"Well, Doctor, I see you have met Gunny Marshall."

"Yes, Colonel. Apparently he will be my escort."

"Yes, while you're in the field with the squad. Both you and Dr. Reddeer are with two of our most experienced men. They will ensure your safety out there. After talking with Mr. Sandovol, we don't want to take any chances."

Captain Johnson steps forward. "Myself and Lieutenant Neal will be in constant contact with the colonel here on the beach, with the Lanstat, and with the situation room in Washington. Once we have secured the area, you and Dr. Reddeer will dictate the procedures we will follow to extract the bombs."

Reddeer and Cabolero come up the beach and join them in the tent.

"Wow, you were right, Gunny. The cabin is a mess. It's hard to believe that someone lived through it." They get themselves some coffee.

Val is drinking some coffee at the edge of the tent.

"Commander Val, weren't those the jets that flew over the ones at the base?"

"Yes, Colonel, they are going out to join the *Moskva* squadron."

"I heard the latest reports. They're going to have their hands full."

"Yes, Colonel. As we do."

Knight looks at his watch. "It's 11:45 A.M., folks. We need to get going, so as soon as you're finished, we'll meet back at the Stallion."

As Susie finishes her juice, she looks around for the gunny. He had walked down the beach, and now was talking with Mr. Marino and his chief. She and Reddeer leave the tent and begin walking back to the Stallion. A flight of six Blackhawk helicopters flies over and begins landing along the beach. Navy men are on the ground, directing them in with hand held lights. As they touch down, he signals the marines behind him. They move forward and begin climbing into the helicopters. Susie and Emanuel walk up the ramp into the Stallion.

"Dr. Reddeer, we're about to leave."

"Right, Captain. I'll get my jacket."

He turns to Susie. "It was a pleasure to meet you, Dr. Davies."

"Why thank you, Captain."

"My understanding is that you will make the first attempt to disarm. I wish you luck. I just wish they would get the Russian weapons people in soon."

"I agree, we can use all the help we can get."

"I'm ready, Captain. Mr. Marino had my stuff loaded on the helicopter already."

"Ma'am." Johnson gives her a quick salute and walks to the base of the ramp. "Mr. Reddeer."

He turns to Susie. She looks him in the eye and gives him a quick hug. "Be careful, Emanuel. I'll be in contact with you, if I decide to go on my bomb. I think I will be leaving soon also. So I'll call as soon as I get a good look at the thing."

"Right." Emanuel walks down the beach with the captain. As they get near the helicopter, he turns and waves to Susie at the ramp. She returns the wave and watches as three of the helicopters lift off and head inland.

"We're off next, ma'am." Lieutenant Neal walks down the ramp. "If you're ready, we'll get going."

"Very good. Everything is loaded, so I guess I'm ready, also."

As they walk to the helicopter, marines again are loading. As they walk by Marino, he calls after her. "Good luck, Susie." She turns, smiles, and waves back to him as she slides in next to Owens. The gunny gets in across from her.

"Dr. Davies, I got this for you from supplies." He hands her a poncho. "This rain is going to be falling all day. Your jacket may not be enough."

"Thank you, Gunny. I was a little concerned about my jacket."

"You're welcome. I also had Sergeant Cabolero take one for Dr. Reddeer."

The door closes and the engines rev up; they begin to lift. The three helicopters rise up and begin heading northeast. The Cobra gunship pulls up next to them, and she can see the two crewmen. It tilts forward and races ahead of the others.

MOSKVA BRIDGE
THE GULF

"Admiral." The admiral looks at the captain. "Sir, we will not be able to launch the helicopters in this squall. We'll have to wait until it settles down."

"I was afraid of that." He looks out the front of the bridge; water is streaming down the windows.

BACKFIRE

"Also, sir, one of the subs has already turned towards the Cuban ships. He is about twenty miles off the port side; the other one is about fifteen miles abeam of us. They're reporting heavy rollers; it will be tricky getting the techs off."

"All right, Captain, as soon as there is a break in the weather, we'll launch."

"Aye, aye, sir."

QUINTANO'S HELICOPTER
CUBA

The crew chief leans over and taps Quintano on the shoulder. He looks over at him; he is pointing down the road ahead of them.

"I think we have found our lost checkpoint, sir."

As they fly over the police car, a man in a truck is waving his hands. There are three people in the ditch next to the car.

"Lieutenant, bring us around and land in the middle of the road."

"Right." The helicopter banks and lands facing the car and the truck.

"Come on, Brock. I think we have a problem." They get out and walk up to the man in the street.

"Señores, we found the two officers. They are dead in the ditch. Who could have done such a thing?"

Brock nudges Quintano. "Look at the hood, I'd say someone got it there."

"Lieutenant." Quintano holds the radio near his mouth.

Brock goes down the side of the ditch, next to the other man from the truck.

"Sir."

"Call police Captain Bodus. Tell him his two officers are dead and to send out an ambulance. Tell him we believe our man came this way."

"Roger, sir."

Brock climbs back up the bank. "He got one at close range, and the other one was hit twice in the chest. My guess is that one walked up to the car, and the other one was leaning on the fender."

"That sounds right." Quintano eyes are drawn to a glint in the middle of the street. They walk over, and kneel down. "I'd say 9 mm auto, with the cab sitting about here."

"Yes."

They both stand and walk back behind the police car. One of the crewmen from the helicopter has the truck driver off to the side and is getting a statement from him.

"That man on the road."

"Yeah, the non-farmer. If he has been walking along the road, he may have seen our man."

"Lieutenant, remember the man walking down the road?"

"Yes, sir."

"Go back down and pick him up. We would like to question him about all of this."

"Roger, sir." The engines wind up, and he lifts off and flies down the road.

"Sir, I have statements from the men in the truck. They just happened on to the scene, just like it is now. The driver said that they have not seen anyone since they got here."

"All right, let them leave. If we need anything more, we'll get hold of them."

"Yes, sir."

Quintano looks at his watch; it's almost noon. "That means that he has about a thirty minute head start from here. That would most likely put him into the city."

Brock looks around the hills. "Yeah, but he is definitely trying to get to some point along the coast." His eyes follow the road up into the mountains. Three large radio antenna stick up into the air. Quintano follows his line of site. "When we have questioned this man, we will make a side trip to the top of the mountain."

"Thanks, General."

CHAPTER 9

Susie watches out the windows as wetlands pass under the helicopter. Areas of open water and grassland slip away to thick woods and swamp. She looks at her watch; it's noon. She feels a sudden affection for Gary Cooper, as if she too were stepping out onto some dusty street to face off with the evil bad guy. But this time, the bad guy is a million times more deadly and requires more cunning to kill. She looks around the cabin at the others who will be joining her at the site. In her mind, questions rise. Did they really know how deadly this thing in the woods is? What would make them volunteer to put themselves at the gates of hell? Well, for all of that, what the hell was she doing out here? It seemed to be a combination of professional ability and a flair for a dangerous situation.

Rain drizzles off the windows at the front of the helicopter. She thinks of her ranch back in New Mexico. Back home, there is dry hot weather, stark beauty, and her husband. She thinks about how much she would rather be watching tonight's sunset with him. A smile crosses her face. What a team they made. Him, the good-looking hulk rancher, and her, the brainy scientist. Her work at Los Alamos was intent and far-reaching. Her time with him was joy and laughter. Even after twenty years of marriage, the fun was far from gone in their relationship. And even from this distance, she could feel his love with her all the time.

"We will be on site in just a minute."

The pilot's voice over the intercom jolts her back to the here and now. "They are having us land about forty yards away from the bomb. They're afraid we may cause vibrations that would set it off. Do you agree, Dr. Davies?"

"I'd say we should be very prudent around these things. I agree that we need to take every precaution around them." The helicopter begins a slow left turn. A marine on the ground throws out a red smoke grenade and the helicopter lines up on it. The man on the ground begins signaling the pilot. He hovers over the ground and slowly move up to the man. He crosses his chest and they touch down softly on the wet grass. The engine is cut as soon as they're down. The other two helicopters land farther out, and the marines deploy from them and head in their direction.

The door is slid open, and Lt. Neal steps out first. As his foot reaches the ground, it sinks about two inches into the moist surface. "Everyone watch your step coming out; it's real soggy here." The marines move from the front of the helicopter to the lieutenant. "Sir, the bomb is over here." He points to a second marine near some thick grass. They move out into the field and await the arrival of the marines from the other two helicopters.

The gunny jumps down with a loud plopping sound. "It's pretty soft out here, so watch your step." He holds Susie's hand as she climbs down into the mud.

"Soft?" Her shoes sink into the mud. Owens climbs down behind her. They walk through the grass towards the distant marine.

"Mr. Owens, what exactly do we need to be aware of out here?"

"Well, to begin with, snakes, then gators, and last, there are dangerous people. This area is pocketed with drug runners and illegal whiskey stills. Either way, they do not like people coming around their operations. This field we're on was used by one group to drop bundles of pot. The bust cost us two agents."

"Now I feel a lot better. Let's see, we can be blown up, bitten, eaten, or shot. I just knew the odds were in our favor."

As they draw near the bomb, white tape is strung around the area about twelve feet out. The retard fins have pushed the grass down around the end of the bomb. Susie crosses over the tape and approaches the bomb. The fins protrude about two feet out from the back. She kneels down to get a better look.

While she is looking at the bomb, the others have come up around her. One group sets up the Lanstat set, and a radioman joins Neal off to one side. Susie walks back outside the tape. "Gunny, I need to talk to Mr. Marino at the crash site."

"Yes, ma'am." He walks over to Lieutenant Neal.

"Sir, Dr. Davies needs to talk with Commander Marino at the crash site."

"All right, Gunny. Get the rest of the men set out, and I'll contact the beach."

"Aye, aye, sir." The gunny gets the men set out thirty yards from the bomb. He positions the machine-gun on a knoll about forty feet away. They're all wearing helmet mikes, and the gunny positions his to send.

"Everyone, listen up. No one, but no one, gets near the bomb site. You'll challenge. If they continue, you're cleared to fire. Lock and load, and wait for further orders from the lieutenant." In groups of two, the men fan out and form a perimeter around the bomb.

"Bulldog, this is Bulldog 3. Over."

"Roger, Bulldog 3. This is Bulldog. Over."

"Sir, we're at the site. Dr. Davies would like to talk with Commander Marino."

"Roger, hold one."

"Dr. Davies, they're getting Marino now. Please, this is an insecure net. So be careful of what questions you ask." He hands her the mike.

"Lieutenant, how soon will we be up on the Lanstat?"

"They're running tests on it now; it should be lined up in just a few minutes."

"Doctor, this is Marino. What can I do for you?"

"After looking at the situation, I believe we could use about thirty filled sandbags, some rope, and some kind of tarp."

"Roger, Doctor. I'll get it loaded and sent it out to you in just a few minutes."

"Thank you. Have you heard from Emanuel yet?"

"Yes, but they are having to move through a really swampy area. They believe they will be on site in about fifteen minutes. Over."

"Dr. Davies, this is Bulldog 1. We'll be on site soon. The lead team has already begun to set up the other equipment. We'll contact you on this net first and then transfer to the other system. Bulldog 1 out."

"Here." She hands the handset back. He talks for a short time and then clears the net.

"Doctor, the colonel will be sending out a couple of men to help. They're loading the bags now, and we'll load some for the other group also. Gunny, I'm going to check the men and their positions."

"Yes, sir."

As the lieutenant moves out to check the perimeter, one of the helicopters starts its engine and lifts off. It heads back in the direction of the beach.

"The helicopter bringing your supplies will replace that one. They'll shuttle that one out to the other site."

"Right, Gunny. Would you mind getting that case over there? It has some equipment I need to take some readings."

TELEVISION STATION
NEW ORLEANS

"This is KNLT noon day news. We have some fast-breaking stories: the massive evacuation of the southern peninsula and the crash of the Russia bomber, as well as the apparent use of missiles by Cuban forces in the Gulf.

"We'll go live with Darin Bodine in Magnolia." His picture comes up on the monitor behind him. "Darin, can you hear us?"

"Yeah, Greg. We're out here on the 23 near Magnolia. The traffic has been moving north all morning. We talked to some of the state guards and the police, and everything seems to be going as planned. We are told that the towns from Pilottown to Triumph are now considered clear. There have been units from the army alert force out of Alabama arriving at the naval base, and they're relieving the police and guard units. They are being ferried out to their location, and are taking up positions at intersections.

"They are continuing to search for any stragglers. Word has been passed that they will shoot any looters caught in the areas. They are also asking us to move north. So we'll be heading back up to the naval base as soon as we leave here."

"Also, Darin, is there anything new on the crash of the Russian bomber?"

"As of about ten A.M., no one other than the military is allowed on the base. We are getting handouts from the base news office, but it is pretty generic. The place is sealed shut, with armed guards, and a lot of plane activity. We have a film we shot just before we left. We'll roll it for you."

The film comes on as Darin is describing the activity they can see, when he is told to look over at the airfield. "Holy cow, look at this, folks." The camera pans to the four fighters taxing along the runway. The large red star stands out on the two trailing fighters. "Those are the two Mig-29s that landed this morning. They are apparently going to fly out to somewhere in the Gulf."

The four fighters go to full throttle and move down the runway. The camera begins to shake as the noise level rises. They lift off the end of the runway and pass over the camera crews outside the fence. The boom as they go over drowns out all other sounds. "Did you see that? Those things are loaded for bear." The film stops and Darin is back at his location.

"Besides the jets, there are armed Cobras running all over the place. A large group of helicopters loaded with marines left the base also. We presume they are going out to the crash site."

"We're going to move from here, so this is Darin Bodine for KNLT news."

"Thank you, Darin. We now have a live report from Marcey Lane over at the mid-town Radisson. "Marcey, are you there?"

Her picture comes up on the screen. "I'm here, Greg. We just had to move some cables."

"Apparently, there have been some strange goings-on over there?"

"You're right, Greg. About two hours ago, two top nuclear scientists were picked up here at the hotel and flown over to the naval base. The manger said that the military was very polite but also very determined. They sought out the two scientists and had their bags packed and taken to the airport. The scientists were Dr. Susie Davies and Dr. Emanuel Reddeer. Dr. Reddeer's wife was driven to the airport and put on a plane for Los Alamos, where both the scientists work. A little background on them. Dr. Davies is the best known; she has been on many top-level government committees dealing with nuclear waste and tactical weapons. She was sent to Chernobyl and some of the other problem areas of the world where disasters have occurred. Both she and Dr. Reddeer were part of the inspection teams that were sent to Iraq. Their

265

specialty is tactical nuclear weapons and safeguarding procedures for plutonium storage. Dr. Davies is considered to be at the top of her field, and is characterized as being very up front.

"This, as some may remember, caused some red faces for some high level committees in Washington, including one on which Secretary Brant sat. If I remember right, her famous statement to some of the members was, "Gentlemen, try getting some balls." At this point, we have not been able to get any more information on the two scientists."

"Thank you, Marcey. We'll be going to our Washington bureau for some updates on the Cuban situation in the Gulf, after this message."

ULTIMA
WASHINGTON, D.C.

"Mr. Brant, have we got people at the bombs, yet?"

Brant finishes his drink and turns towards the president. "Yes, sir. They should be up in just a few minutes. They will come up on the satellite link, so will have a secure network."

"Excuse me, Mr. Brant."

"Yes, Admiral."

"Sir, I talked with Commander Marino at the site. They're sending Dr. Davies sandbags and rope. She is running tests at the site now."

"Mr. Secretary."

"Yes, General Becker."

"Sir, the evacuation is going along great. The first group from the alert force is on the ground and has already begun moving out into the cities. They are continuing searches for anyone left behind."

"Outstanding, General." The president pushes his lunch plate out of his way. He stands up and walks around the desk. He looks up at the screen showing Evita swirling in the Gulf.

The others at the table finish up their lunches, and have the plates removed. On one of the screens, the area south of New Orleans is projected with a white box showing the two confirmed bomb locations. Three red boxes are also on the map, showing possible locations.

"Have we any news of the weapons people off the two subs?"

Captain Van Nar walks up next to him. "No, sir, not since our last message that an attempt would be made at 11:45. But that was called off because of the rain squalls passing through the area. Also, Mr. President, the speed of the *Moskva* group has been reduced from twenty-five knots to twenty knots. They're in a running sea, and the situation is getting worse. Winds are now gusting up to fifty miles per hour; they may have to recall their helicopters, and additional launches may be canceled. The Cuban forces have closed to within thirty miles and are still moving at twenty-five knots. They will soon be reducing speed, also, because of the sea conditions."

"Thank you, Captain."

"Admiral, will they be able to get their weapons people off the subs?"

"Well, sir, as Captain Van Nar said, the sea conditions are getting worse. In a normal situation, we would not try and remove the people. It is just too dangerous. But because of the situation, an attempt will be made. Besides the obvious danger of the extraction, the Cubans will have the subs spotted cold. As long as they are on the surface, they are in grave danger. Also, if they do get the people off the subs, their helicopters are sitting ducks for the Cuban fighters."

"Well, then, is it worth trying to get these people off?"

"It's hard to say, Mr. President."

"Well, then, Admiral, would you order these people off knowing the dangers?"

"Under these circumstances, yes. No one would attempt this under these conditions normally. But these are not normal conditions; three deadly events are going on at the same time. At this point, we need any edge we can get."

"Thank you, Admiral."

The president walks along the table until he is abreast of Brant.

"Mr. Secretary, I believe that, along with Dr. Davies' assessment of the bombs, the question is whether she believes that she can disarm them herself."

"I agree, Mr. President, that we should pursue a strategy to remove the bombs ourselves. Using the information provided by Marshal Shagan's staff," he looks at the clock, "in fifty minutes, some of our questions will be answered. We'll consider 1:00 P.M. a go if all else fails."

"That sounds good, Mr. Secretary. I'll be talking to Secretary Sholenska so that everyone is on-line."

"Yes, sir." Brant goes back to some paperwork as the president goes back to his desk.

A hissing noise comes into the room from speakers under the screens. The noise snaps and crackles. "This is Bulldog. Over."

"Roger, Bulldog. This is bulldog 2. Over."

"This is Bulldog 1. Over."

"The net is up, gentlemen. We now have to confirm contact with Ultima."

Commandant Swane picks up a handset near him. "Bulldog, this is Ultima. Over."

"Roger, Ultima. Receiving you 5/5. Over."

"Roger, Bulldog. Receiving you 5/5. Over."

"Roger, Ultima. All stations are now on-line. Each position will have someone on-line at all times. Because of the net security, call signs will only be used on the TAC net. Over."

"Roger, Colonel Knight. This is General Swane. Over."

"Sir, it's good to speak to you again. My guess is that we are on the loud speakers in the war room. Over."

"Roger that."

In the background, voices come in faintly. "Sir, sir, we have movement to our front, towards the hedge row."

"This is Lieutenant Neal. I'm handing the headset over to Gunny Marshall. We have some kind of activity near our front." The sound of the mike being handed off comes over the speakers.

"Gunny?"

"Yes, sir, this is Gunny Marshall."

"This is Commandant Swane, Gunny."

"Sir, it's nice to work with you again."

"What's the situation there?"

"Well, I'd say it's not a trophy, but it would be worth a shot. It's a deer scared out of the swamp, sir."

"Well, I'm glad to hear it, Gunny. You're with Dr. Davies, right?"

"Yes, sir. She is measuring radiation levels and looking for a black line painted down the side of the bomb. She has an entrenching tool and has removed some of the mud. As soon as she is done, I'll have her get on the net. Over."

The gunny goes on monitor. "Doctor, they would like to talk to you as soon as you're done."

"Fine, Gunny, it will just be a few more minutes. I haven't got quite enough mud on me. Also, you could help if you wanted."

BRIDGE OF THE *MOSKVA*
THE GULF

"Sir, it is becoming impossible to launch." The rain slams into the forward ports on the bridge. They walk to the back of the bridge to look out over the flight deck. Wind-blown rain whips across the deck. The elevators have brought the two stripped-down helicopters up. Men with lines tied to them move around the two stationary helicopters. "Admiral we have had to reduce speed to keep the squadron together. We are now at twenty knots; the wind across the deck is blowing gust up to fifty-five knots."

The admiral feels the ship dip its nose into the next roller; the spray flies into the air. They walk over to the port side and he watches one of the *Sovremennyy* destroyers bury its bow. The spray flies back along the deck to the front of the bridge.

"Sir, I respectfully submit a protest. We should not expose the submarines to possible attack, and it is suicide to launch these helicopters in this weather. We have pulled in the other helicopters; all ships are operating at full range on sonar and radar. Sir, we have tried. They must understand. We made the good effort, but were not able to comply."

"Yeoman." The admiral walks over to a seaman on duty under arms.

"Sir."

"Yeoman, enter the captain's protest into the ships log." The admiral repeats what the captain told him. "And have the captain sign it."

"Yes, sir." He writes down the message, and hands the captain his pen to sign. He signs his name under the protest, and it is duly noted in the log.

"Have communications get me in touch with Air Marshal Shagan."

The captain moves over, and removes a handset from its cradle, and talks to the comm center. In a few seconds, he talks to someone and then removes the handset from his ear. "Sir, they are getting Marshal Shagan." He hands the phone over to the admiral.

"Sir, this is Admiral Kirsanov. I have logged a protest by Captain Sokolov. I wish you to know that my personal opinion is in full agreement with his assessment. But because we are in grave danger from different scenarios, I will order the subs to the surface and attempt to get the weapons people to the American coast. The weather has turned foul, and we can only guess at the reactions of the Cubans. I wish to add my fullest belief in Captain Sokolov's ability to command and execute the orders that he will receive."

"We are in full agreement with you, Admiral, and we share your confidence in Captain Sokolov. All attempts must be made to defuse the situation in Louisiana. Best of luck, Admiral."

He hangs the phone up and walks up to the front of the bridge, then turns and goes back down the ladder to the combat center. "Lieutenant Pstygo, give the helicopters the coordinates for their intercept with the subs. And Weather, do we have a window?"

"Yes, sir. We believe at 12:30 local time, we will be between squalls. But there will be no more than thirty minutes before we're back in the next front."

"Excuse me, sir."

The radar officer comes up to the admiral. "Sir, we have acquired a track on eight jets on long range. If they continue on their present course, they will be over the squadron in forty-five minutes."

Pstygo leans over the plotting table and draws in some lines. "Admiral, we have now moved within thirty miles of the Cuban force; they continue to move in an intercept course. The submarines are now here; they are twelve and fifteen miles out. We are experiencing a decline in visibility. It will be down to five miles or less within the hour."

"Thank you, gentlemen." The admiral goes back up the ladder to the bridge.

"Captain, we will launch the helicopters at 12:30 local time. Contact the subs ten minutes before launch. They might want to bring the helicopters in with lights, instead of using their radios."

"Yes, sir. The *Otlichnyy* has had to recall its helicopter. The weather will probably cause a recall of the other one also."

"May I suggest that we use the Yak as our spotter. It would be a lot more survivable."

"I agree, Captain. It will relieve the helicopter when it needs to come in."

"Admiral, I have spoken with Pstygo and the others. This could prove to be a very interesting next few hours."

The admiral smiles and looks into the face of the captain. "Sir, you are a credit to the Soviet navy. Not only do you do your job as captain well, you can also put a very hostile situation into some well-chosen words."

CUBA, ON THE MOUNTAIN ROAD

"The helicopter is coming in, Quintano." Brock points down the road.

"Right." Walking back up the side of the ditch, he steps to the side to avoid the blood in the grass. He joins Brock at the police car, and they watch the helicopter settle onto the middle of the road. The side door opens, and Captain Bodus jumps down and walks up to the car.

"Sir." He salutes Quintano and looks at the blood stain on the hood. They take him to the side of the road, and he goes down into the ditch to examine the bodies.

When he reaches the bottom of the ditch, he turns one of the bodies over. His hand makes the sign of the cross, and he lowers his head.

"This bastard will pay; he has killed my brother."

The cab driver joins them at the side of the road. He looks down at the two bodies. The captain looks up and their eyes meet. A cold chill runs through him; he sees rage and hate in the dark eyes.

"Please, señores, I had nothing to do with this. By the Holy Mother, I swear. The man has gone mad. He will kill anyone who tries to stop him."

"What man?" Quintano takes out the pictures of Luís and Miguel. "Was it one of these men?"

He looks at the picture and sees Miguel. "This one, señor."

He hands the picture back to Quintano. The captain comes up from the ditch and grabs him. "And why did he let you live?" The grip around his neck chokes off his air.

"Captain, captain, we need more answers."

He pushes the driver back. "The whole truth, or you will join them in the ditch."

Trying to recover his breath, the driver describes how he picked up the man, and explains the events that lead up to the shootings. He mentions that the man kept saying, "I've done this for you and Cuba."

"Please, that is all I know. Señores, I begged for my life when he did this. I don't know why he let me live. But I thank our Holy Father."

"He has your cab now, right?"

"Yes, señor. It is number forty-four."

"Shit." Quintano reaches into his pocket and pulls out a note pad. He shows it to Brock. "When we were on the road, I had this odd feeling when we flew over this one cab. So I wrote down its number off the top." The note reads, "Cab number forty-four. Check this one."

Captain Bodus gets on the radio, and calls to his dispatcher. "Cab number forty-four—it is to be stopped and the man inside arrested. He has killed two officers, and is to be considered armed and dangerous. Try and take him alive. I want this man for myself."

Quintano takes Brock off to the side. "I have told the lieutenant to run you up to the transmitters. You will have only a short time. I will wait here with the captain and see if I can get some more information."

"Thanks, Quintano." He runs to the chopper, and it lifts off, heading to the top of the mountain where the tall radio masts stick up like thorns. Quintano watches the helicopter as it gets smaller and smaller, working its way to the top.

The sound of sirens brings his attention back to the road. In the distance, a line of cars and an ambulance, their lights flashing, moves towards them.

"All right, I want to know anything else you remember, anything that Miguel might have said that gave you a hint of where he was going."

"Sí, señor."

CAB, OUTSKIRTS OF MALANGAS

As he is driving into town, Miguel sees an open parking place, and he pulls up to the curb. Four young men sitting on a low wall watch the man in the cab. They drink their beers as he gets out and grabs a duffel bag from the back. He sees them and walks over.

"Is there a bus stop nearby?"

They all look at each other. "Yeah, down on the next corner. But why do you need a bus when you have a car?"

"I'm sick of it. I want no more of it" He tosses the keys to one of the men. "Here, you do with it as you wish. It is yours now." And he runs down the street to catch a bus across town.

"The man is loco. He gives us a cab." They look up and down the street to see if someone is chasing the man. The one with the keys walks over to the cab, and looks in the front and back. He walks around the cab, and opens the trunk. "It has a good spare; we can sell that. And it is in pretty good shape." He closes the trunk and tries the key in the door. He opens it up and gets inside. Putting the key in the ignition, he turns it on. It roars to life. He checks the glove box. The others climb in with him. "This is weird; there is over half a tank of gas."

"Let's go for a ride, and then sell the piece of shit to Ernesto."

"Right. Who am I to turn down a gift?" He puts it into first gear, and they drive off into the city.

100-MILE DEMARK
OVER THE GULF

"You're on your own from here out to the squadron. Good luck."

"Thank you, Comrades. It was good to fly with you. Over."

The two Migs continue on as the two F-14 fighters make a banking turn to the right and move away rapidly.

"Ski, are you all right?"

"Yes. My right leg feels like it is asleep. But I'm ready as I can be. Over."

"Good. All weapons are armed. We have two bogies about ten miles to the right at 20,000 feet. I'm guessing two Cuban fighters. Over."

"Yeah, I have them to. We can go to the deck and see if we can loose them. They don't have look-down shoot-down radar. So they may think we're just American jets at the demark. Over."

"Sounds good to me. Here we go."

The two jets drop down below the clouds. They move at moderate speeds to conserve fuel. They level out and skim along at 100 feet above the water. It has a dull gray look, and the rollers moving towards the shore create deep troughs. They see rain on the horizon as they move south.

"Norba, do you see that water?"

"Now I remember why I choose to become a pilot."

"Yeah, it does look ugly. It's worse ahead; the ships are probably taking a pounding."

"I'm picking up four bogies to the east. We'll stay on passive until we know they have identified us."

"Roger. There is a lot of radar operating out here. I'll hold off calling the *Moskva* to the very last moment. They should pick up our IFF signature soon. Over."

"Yeah, and so will the Cubans. If that Tu-16 is in the area, he'll spot us quickly. Over."

"Ski, if we get jumped by the Cubans. I'll go with the fighters. You try for the Tupolev; they said there are two of them out here. With the equipment they have, they could blind the squadron. Over."

"Roger. Only if you promise to leave some of the fighters for me. Over."

"You got it. I'll save as many of them as I can. Over."

The two jets make a slight course correction and continue flying south. Their instruments continue to pick up scans of search radar all around them.

RADIO SITE ON THE MOUNTAINS
CUBA

"Base, this is Brock. Over." He repeats the message on the radio. "Damn." He retunes the radio to the TAC frequency for the Russian fighters. Before he can speak, a voice comes out of the speaker.

"Anyone. This is Lieutenant Beregovoy at Matanzas. Over."

"Beregovoy, this is Commander Brock. What is your situation?"

"Sir, we have not been able to contact anyone for hours. We're being held under guard in one of the hangars. I'm talking from one of the jets we are working on. Our normal radios have been shut down, and there is a lot of activity going on out on the field. They launched eight fighter-bombers a while back, and are getting ready to send eight more out. They're loaded with bombs. What's going on?"

"There going after the *Moskva* squadron. General Morales has gone mad. Is there anything you can do to stop them? Over."

"We have some pistols, but not much more. I'll pass the information on to the others. The guards are getting suspicious. I will have to go."

"Do what you can, Beregovoy. I, too, must go. Good luck."

Unable to do anything else, he turns the set off and goes back out to the helicopter. He swings the chain link gate closed as he walks by. The broken lock falls to the ground as the gate clangs shut.

"Let's go. I'm done here." They rise into the air and begin the flight back down the mountain.

Quintano steps aside as the second body is carried to the ambulance. "Captain Bodus, you can ride with us, if you want. We'll be leaving in just a few minutes." His eyes look up the mountain, and he can see the dark shape of the helicopter coming down.

"Thank you, sir. I need to get into town to lead the search for the man who did this. He will pay dearly for his actions."

Bodus walks over to a sergeant and orders him to drive the cabby back to headquarters. He also orders one of the other officers to drive the car back. He says that he will be flying back to town. The ambulance turns around and begins the trek down from the hills; a police car runs in front of it and turns on its lights and siren. Quintano and Bodus watch the cars disappear down the road. They turn back to the sound of the approaching helicopter as it shifts position and begins coming down near them.

BOMB SITE
SOUTHERN LOUSIANA

"Dr. Davies, your gear is coming in." She looks up from her instruments as a Cobra gunship flies over head. The other helicopter moves off from the site and lowers a pallet down and then moves over and lands. Navy men climb out of the helicopter and begin unloading additional equiptment.

"We need a couple more men to get those sand bags over here." Two men follow the gunny's direction and move over to the pallet. They start to bring the bags up to the tape. Susie has dug around the bomb, and exposed a two-inch black line down one of the fins. "We need some bags along the front here, Gunny. It's seeping all around here. We'll start building up a support around the back side of the bomb."

She pulls more mud from the black line. "Start putting the bags around the back, at least two bags thick. We'll need some shovels to dig a trench. The men from the helicopter bring four shovels up to the site, as well as some rope. She has exposed about six inches all the way around the bomb. She continues to dig down the black line.

"Should we really be doing that, ma'am?" She looks up at Neal with mud splatters on her face. "Trust me on this, OK." A smile crosses her face. "Gunny, get me Mr. Val on the radio."

"Yes, ma'am."

Val is nearby and gets on the Lanstat net; all locations on the net listen intently to the conversation.

"This is Val, Gunny."

"Dr. Davies would like to know how close the black stripe is to the access plate? Over."

"It is three feet down from the beginning of the black stripe."

The gunny passes the message on and waits for a reply.

Susie ties a rope around the end of the extended fins and passes it to a man behind her. "Keep tension on this while they dig out the mud. They dig down two feet, and then back three feet." The bags of sand are handed in and placed up against the side of the bomb. Bags are placed from the bottom of the hole to the base of the fins, halfway around the bomb. A nylon pull strap is put around the top of the bomb and pulled tight around a sandbag.

"That should hold it. We need to remove the mud on this side. Down about four feet, and out about four feet. This thing is in pretty solid."

They begin to dig the mud out and build a short wall of bags out from the bomb. As they dig, water begins to fill the hole. Susie watches as the men dig.

"I think we're going to need some kind of pump to keep the water out."

One of the navy men from the beach walks over to Susie.

"Ma'am, Mr. Marino thought that you might need one. So he had us load a water hog and a portable generator. If I can get some help, we'll have it set up in just a minute."

"That's great. Let's get it set up."

Two men go with him back to the helicopter and carry the equipment back to the site. They set up the generator and the pump, and then hook up the hoses.

"We're ready to put the hog in the hole."

"Let's go with it. Gunny, see if we can get some shoring material out here. I don't think that the sides of this hole will hold. It's too wet."

"Here, ma'am. Mr. Marino is on the handset."

"Mr. Marino, thank you for the pump."

"I thought you might need it."

"We'll need some shoring material to brace the hole."

"Right, I requested it from the ship, they have a shop on board. They are cutting three-quarters plywood into four foot sheets, with two-by-four supports that can be driven two feet into the ground. They are also getting you some two-by-fours for cross-bracing. The necessary tools and nails will be sent out to you as soon as they're ready."

"My compliments, Mr. Marino. You make a good beach master. You seem to have an insight into what we need as we get there."

"Well, that's good. By the way, they're sending in some extra utility shirts and trousers. I'm guessing everyone is getting covered with mud, and is soaked to the bone."

"Well, I'll be. You sure you're not out here watching us?"

"No, but I have to confess, I've done operations in the swamps, and I ran into the same problems that you and Dr. Reddeer are running into. But from now on you'll make the calls. We'll react to your demands."

"Just a second, Doctor." Marino talks with the chief. "All right. I'll pass it on."

"The ship has just called; they have four bracing units ready. We'll have the others soon. There is a mike boat bringing them in. We'll get them in the air as soon as they arrive."

"That's great. Mr. Neal has requested some rations for us be thrown on also."

"They're on their way. The first load for Dr. Reddeer is leaving now. I need to check the load. Over"

"Right. Emanuel, are you on the net?"

"This is Corporal Kent, ma'am. He is looking the bomb over. They see my signal, just a minute."

"Susie, this is Emanuel. Are you there?"

"Yes, how does it look?"

"Well, our bomb landed on a brush-covered sand bar in the swamp. There are bugs everywhere, and the marines have killed three large cottonmouth snakes. The brush has been cut back, and I located the black strip. We're going to hold at that until the supplies get here."

"We're pumping out the seepage, and the hole is falling in as they have been digging. The sandbags seem to secure the bomb well. My test show no leaks or dangers in handling the casing."

"Yeah, Captain Johnson is finishing up with the Geiger counter now. We're finding the same thing. We're just getting some rain. I need to get my poncho. The rain will be on you in just a few minutes."

Susie hands the phone to the gunny. "We'll be getting some rain in just a few minutes."

She gets her poncho and slips it over her head. The men in the hole climb out and lean on their shovels. The hole around the bomb is about three and a half feet deep. They left a six inch collar of mud around the casing. The pump drones on, pulling the seeping water out. The rain begins to fall slowly at first, and then the tempo picks up. The water quickly fills the hole and drives everyone under a nearby tree. As they watch, the mud collar around the casing loosens and slides into the hole. The water washes the mud from the surface of the bomb. The black stripe now stands out against the white body, as do three numbers painted in red about a foot down beside the stripe.

"Gunny, look at the bomb." Susie grabs his arm; she jumps into the hole and pushes water aside. The gunny grabs the phone off the storage boxes.

"Bulldog, this is Bulldog 2. Over."

"Gunny, this is Bulldog. What do you need?"

"Sir, Dr. Davies has found the numbers on our bomb."

Susie calls the numbers out, and feels down below the water. Her fingers run across a hair line cut in the casing. "I think I've got the top of the access panel." She is kneeling in the water, and is submerged up to her elbows.

"The number is 757, sir."

"Hold on, Gunny. Val, they have the number off the first bomb. It's 757."

ULTIMA
WASHINGTON, D.C.

Brant and the others stop what they're doing and listen to the voices on the net.

"It's 757."

Val puts on a headset and joins the net. "This is Val; is Moscow on the net?"

"This is General Kuznetsov. I have the envelope."

Val and the general talk in Russian for a few minutes. A translator has been brought in and sits next to Brant. He listens and passes the information on to those in the room.

"Mr. Brant, are you monitoring?"

"Yes, Commander. I have a translator with us to help with any language problems."

"Good, General Kuznetsov can speak some English, but will probably talk in Russian most of the time. He is standing by with the code cards for the bombs. I would like to explain the 757 number that Dr. Davies called in. The seven is the year it was made; the five is the nuclear armory it was produced at; and the seven is its number in the eight-bomb load. And as soon as Mr. Reddeer can get his bomb uncovered, we will be able to plot the drop course better. The general also said that the *Moskva* squadron is in bad weather, and they are trying to get the weapons people off."

"Yes, we heard that. We'll still hold with the one o'clock period. We're hoping the weapons people can get into the crash site."

"Val this is Reddeer. I have the numbers off our bomb. They're 758. Our bomb is sort of laying on its side."

"I have that, Doctor." He passes the numbers on to Kuznetsov.

"That should help us get some better plots on places for the others, Mr. Brant."

"I agree, Val." He looks up at the screen. The red triangles at their locations on the map go to yellow.

"This is Knight, Mr. Brant. We have moved the two man recon people to check out two more locations. We are pretty sure that at this time we have bomb number six located. We'll know soon; both teams are on the ground."

"Thank you, Colonel. So far so good."

In the background, the sound of men yelling orders comes faintly over the net. They hear directions for bag placement from Reddeer, and the sound of helicopters drifts from the speakers on the open net.

"Val, this is Reddeer. We just received the sand bags. Is Mr. Marino sending out the shoring material?"

"Just a minute." Val talks with Marino for a second. "Doctor, they sent out the first shipment to Dr. Davies. Yours is being loaded on the helicopter now. You should get it soon."

"Thanks, Val—" The words are cut short.

"What the shit? Look out! Shit!" *Bang!* The sound of the gunshot draws everyone's attention.

"What's going on?"

"What was that shot?

"Corpsman, take Dr. Reddeer over there and calm him down."

"This is Brant. What happened?"

"Sir, this is Captain Johnson. It seemed that while Dr. Reddeer was down looking at the numbers, we had a snake get in the pit with him. He is all right; I have one of the corpsmen over with him now. He got a little shook up. It's dead, but it must be about three feet long. The shot was mine killing the snake. We have killed five big ones so far."

"Well, we're glad he's all right. We couldn't figure out what had happened. Thank you, Captain."

The net again settles down. Reddeer and the corpsman walk to the edge of the sand and look out over the swamp. "Are you all right now, sir?"

"Yeah. God, that thing was looking me directly in the eyes."

As they talk, Johnson walks up carrying the snake. "He was a big one." The limp body hangs from his hand. The 9 mm round had hit it just behind the head, and torn it half off. He swings his hand back and lofts the reptile into the air out over the water. It hits with a dull splash. "Well, let's hope that there aren't any more around."

"Sir, we have another Mr. No-Shoulders trying to get by our lines."

Reddeer looks up at the corporal. "Sergeant Cabolero killed it with an entrenching tool. He said that he thinks they all want to go swimming in the bomb hole."

"What? What does he mean? They're all trying to get in the bomb hole?"

"Thank you, Corporal. We'll stow the bullshit."

"Yes, sir." The others around the hole smile at each other.

"Sir, this is Corporal Kent. I believe we have a log with eye balls that just came up to your right."

They look to their right as the alligator lifts its head out of the water. It has the shot snake in its mouth. It tosses its head and the snake disappears down its throat. It watches them for a moment and then submerges.

"Sergeant Cabolero, remind everyone to be alert for gators also."

"Yes, sir. I was just talking to Mr. Sandovol. He thinks there is a nest of snakes to our left front. He hasn't seen this many together in quite a while."

"All right, then, have them clear out a few more feet of brush so we can have a broader clear zone."

"Roger, Skipper."

Men cut the brush back about ten feet using machetes and their entrenching tools.

"That looks good." Cabolero looks over their work. "Anyone else see anything?"

"Yeah, Sarge. I just saw Troy with a Georgia black snake in his hand over by a tree."

"Cut the shit." Johnson's voice comes over the headset.

"Yes, sir."

Reddeer looks at Johnson. "A black snake? You mean there is another kind of snake out here? Is it dangerous?"

"No, Doctor. Not unless Troy has some kind of gender problem."

"Sir, Troy said he has no gender problem. But Corporal Kent has been looking awful sweet lately."

The men on the line laugh together. "All right, gentlemen, let's shape up. I can hear the helicopter coming in. We'll dispense some more rations in a little bit."

"Great, Sarge, let Hitman and Troy have the beans and motherfuckers this time."

"All right, the skipper wants the bullshit off the net. Corporal Kent will give out the rations."

Kent looks over at them. "And Hitman and Troy, you're fucked."

The helicopter flies over them and then comes around. A pallet hanging from it sways back and forth. It slides in to the edge of the sandbar, and the marines pull it in to the shore.

"Keep an eye out for that gator."

Two men kneel on each side of the men working on the pallet, their rifles at the ready in case the gator appears. The ropes to the pallet are unhooked, and the helicopter rises and flies off. The wood bracing is moved up to the hole, and the captain calls for a fifteen-minute break. The men get their rations and eat at their posts. Sergeant Cabolero sits down with Reddeer and the captain near a tree. They open their rations and begin to eat. "What are these meaty things in with the beans?"

Johnson and Cabolero look at each other and laugh.

BOMB SITE, NUMBER SEVEN
LOUISIANA

The men have driven the bracing panels down into the side of the hole and put a row of sandbags along the top. Once the two sides are in, they cross brace them with two by fours wedged into place. The back piece is driven in and nailed and braced with the others. Susie wrestles a couple of sandbags at the bottom of the hole near the bomb casing. Other bags are put on the bottom.

"Here's a rag to wipe the bomb off with." He hands it down to Susie.

"That should do it for now." The cloth cleans the mud smears from the access plate. "We'll wait till one o'clock and see where we can go from there."

The gunny grabs Susie's hand and helps her out of the hole. He notices some black globs on her forearm.

"Corpsmen, over here." A lady corpsmen comes over and he leans over and talks into her ear. Susie watches, wondering what is going on.

"Mr. Brant, this is Susie. We have completed the excavation around the bomb. The pumps are going and we should be ready for the decision at one o'clock."

"Thank you, Susie. We'll talk with President Wayne at that time."

The gunny takes the handset from her and the corpsmen moves up. "Dr. Davies, I'm pharmacist mate Jane Moody."

"What's the matter?"

She takes Susie's two hands, and lifts them up. Then unbuttons her cuffs, and rolls the sleeves backwards. Susie looks down at three two-inch slugs on her right forearm, and two on her left forearm.

"They're leeches."

"Get them off me. Get them off me." Her voice rises as she stares at the pulsating black globs. The corpsman moves her over to some supply boxes and has her sit down.

"Gunny, help me."

Those on the net hear her in the background. "Gunny, get them off me."

"Susie, just sit down. The corpsmen know what to do."

"Gunny, this is Secretary Brant. Is there a problem?"

"Just a moment, sir. Susie sit back down, so she can get them off. Mr. Brant, we have a small situation here. While Dr. Davies was down in the water in the hole, some leeches got on her. We have a corpsman working on her now. I would best describe her as not real happy with the situation."

"My God, leeches?"

"Yes, sir. And they're pretty big."

"Gunny, are you laughing at me?" She holds her arms steady as Jane removes another one.

"No, ma'am, I've been through this myself. It's no laughing matter." He bites his lip.

She sees him bite his lip, and he looks away. "Oh boy, yeah, oh boy. You are going to pay for this." The last leech is taken off.

"Doctor, I had nothing to do with this."

"Drop the doctor shit, Gunny. You call me Susie, and I saw you bite your lip. Look at you now, you're about ready to laugh. And if you do, I'm going to kill you."

"When was your last tetanus shot?"

"I don't remember, Jane." Her eyes focus on the gunny's face.

Jane prepares the needle and gives her a shot in the arm. She goes back to cleaning the bites and putting bandages on them.

"Look at these." She nods her head at her forearms. "I have five ringworm-looking things on my arm, and when I got the shot, you almost broke out laughing then."

"I swear, Susie, I would not laugh at a situation like this."

Jane stands her up. "We'll need to go over to the helicopter and check if there are any more. And you can change your shirt." They walk to the helicopter; she looks back at different times to check Gunny. When she gets to the helicopter, they get in.

Gunny and Neal look at each other and burst out laughing. They put their hands over their mouths to muffle the noise. But in their headsets, a voice from hell comes on.

"Now both of you will pay."

COMMAND CENTER
CUBA

"General, the second flight out of Matanzas is about ready to leave. The first group will be over the target in about ten minutes. They will refuel and then go to their assigned areas."

Morales looks up from his desk and pushes some papers off to the side. "Very good, Captain. Tell Admiral Rivera that I would like to see his entire plan. And Captain, I mean now!"

An army lieutenant knocks and sticks his head in the door. "Sir, we have made contact with General Quintano's pilot."

"Well, what is going on?"

"Sir, one of the suspects apparently killed two police officers outside of Cardenas. Quintano is with the police chief and they are flying into town to try and catch him."

"Very well. Pass on to them that I want to be informed immediately if they make an arrest."

"Sí, Señor General." As he leaves, the admiral and his aides go into the office. They move over to a side table and set out some maps. A soldier from Morales's special forces moves over beside them.

"General Morales, we are prepared to cover our plan to intercept if we must."

"Very good, Admiral." Morales gets up and joins them at the table. "I look forward to this, Admiral."

"General, our forces have been alerted to stand by. We sent out the primary orders, and they are awaiting only the order to execute the attack. As I showed you earlier, we have made some small add-ons to the plan and moved the ships closer, because of the weather. The area is experiencing heavy seas, and visibility is falling. We have a definite advantage in air power, although we are still unable to locate the two submarines." He points to a position between the two forces.

"We believe they are somewhere out in this area." His finger rests about twelve miles to the northeast of the *Moskva* group.

"Our aces in the hole are here. They will intercept at this point. They're laying on the bottom." His finger moves to a map position in front of the Russians. "It will prevent them from being detected by the two *Victors*."

"Very good, Admiral. When will everything be in place?"

He looks at his watch. "It's a little after 12:30. Our best interception time would be around 1:30. This would give the additional fighters from Matanzas time to get on station."

"Very good." Morales moves back to his desk and sits down.

"Give the order, Admiral. We will attack at 1:30."

"Yes, sir."

CITY STREETS
MALANGAS, CUBA

"Hey, that's a pretty new tire."

"Well, you can take it or leave it. You came to me, remember."

"Yeah, I forgot what an asshole you were. We'll take it."

"I figured you would." He hands the money over and rolls the tire into his shop.

"Well, how did we do?" The guys in the cab watch the driver as he gets in. "All right, we have enough for some food and cerveza."

"Hell, that's good enough. Let's get going."

"Yeah!" They all yell out the windows as they pull away from the curb. He turns onto the main street and heads for the center of town. They stop and get some beer and buy some tortes to take with them. Moving through the city, they drive to a park.

They get out and eat their tortes and drink some of the beer. The music from the cab radio fills the air around them. They had not noticed the plain blue sedan that had followed them from the store. It was now parked across the street, watching them.

QUINTANO'S HELICOPTER

"Sir." The helicopter pilot taps Quintano on the arm and points to his headset. "We're getting a call from the police for Captain Bodus."

"Sí." He turns around and signals for Perez to turn on his headset.

"This is Bodus."

"Sir, we have an undercover vehicle that has been trailing the cab you're after. It's parked at Del Sol Park where four guys are drinking beer. You asked to be there when we move in."

"Right, we are coming in now. We'll arrive there in about fifteen minutes. Have a car waiting for me at the parking lot on Blanco Boulevard. We'll move from there and keep the car under constant surveillance."

Quintano hands him a map, and he points out the location of the parking lot. He shows the pilot. They begin to see the buildings of town in front of them.

DECK OF THE *MOSKVA*
THE GULF

The crews on the deck have to hold on to the side of the helicopter to keep their balance. The wind whips across the deck, pelting them with stinging rain. The pilots climb up inside and begin to start up the engines. The full crew is aboard as the engine's wind up to full power. The wash from the blades adds to the fury on the deck.

Admiral Kirsanov and Captain Sokolov watch the two helicopters come to life. The captain looks at the clock. "Sir, we're running a little behind time. We need to turn the ship into the wind to cut the side shear across the deck."

"Very good, Captain." The orders are given and the ship slowly turns into the wind.

The helicopters go to full power as they fight to rise off the deck. The main structure of the ship block the wind. They move to the side as they rise. As they clear the side of the ship, the wind catches then and pushes them up suddenly.

"Sir." The communications officer runs up to the captain. "We need you in the combat center."

"Very well. Bring the ship back to the original course."

He goes down the ladder to the combat center and joins his air captain at one of the radarscopes. "What's going on?"

"Sir, we have just picked up two inbound fighters. Their IFF is correct for the two fighters that were escorting the bomber. We are going to try and contact them." The radioman calls out to the two approaching planes. They listen as the call goes out.

"They're running low over the water. The Mig-23 fighters don't have look-down radar. So far, they are probably undetected. But if we are picking them up, so are the Cuban ships and that Tupolev 16. We'll have to see what their next move is."

"Alert the other ships? They have probably picked them up also. Until we know for sure, they will be considered hostile. This could be some kind of trick."

"Redflare, this is Wolf 1 and 2. Over."

"Roger, Wolf leader. We have you inbound at fifty miles."

"Roger, Redflare. Commander Val thought you might need some assistance. We will be at your position at 1300 hours."

"Wolf leader, we agree with Commander Val. Your presence will be appreciated. Roger, you're at 1300 arrival time. This is Redflare. Out."

The captain rejoins the admiral at the back of the bridge, just as the Yak is lifting off the deck. It raises up. As it clears the ship, the wind catches it from behind and pushes it forward. Retracting its wheels, it turns to the northeast and flies to cover the helicopters.

"Sir, I bring some good news."

The admiral turns to look at him. "We could certainly use some, Captain."

"We have just made contact with the two Migs that were escorting the bomber. They will be on station at 1300 hours."

"Excellent, Captain."

"It seems that Commander Val persuaded them to fly out and join us."

"Very good. Remind me to buy Commander Val a drink when this is over."

RUSSIAN SUBMARINE
THE GULF

"Once again, when we surface, the chief will gaff the harnesses in. Do not attempt to grab them. The static charge will knock you off your feet. It has to touch the hull, before anyone physically touches it. Also, I want the two men with Grails at their stations immediately. You're cleared to fire on any aircraft which appears to be a threat."

"Lieutenant, are your weapons people ready?"

"Yes, sir. We're ready when you are."

"Good, blow the main tanks. Radar on passive. Let's surface."

The commands echo in the control room as each command is passed to the appropriate crewman. The sub rises slowly. The captain leans on the handles of the periscope. He looks around and sees nothing in the area. "Down scope."

"Gentlemen, make sure your safety straps are on. We will be in rollers when we get up."

As the sub breaks the surface, the top hatch is opened and a blast of wind fills the conning tower. Two men climb by the windscreen on top. They fasten safety lines around the periscope and the radio mast. A chief hands them each a Grail missile; they scan both sides of the submarine. The chief climbs up and attaches his safety line to the periscope tube. He is handed a six-foot gaff; they all steady themselves against the pitch of the sub.

The oncoming waves move silently over the deck of the ship from bow to stern. As they hit the conning tower, a blast of spray covers the men. A ship's lieutenant climbs out and moves to the side as the captain joins him in the cramped quarters around the hatch. They both duck behind the wind screen as another wave hits the conning tower.

"Sir, the helicopter is about 500 yards off the port bow. Radar says were being scanned from positions all around us."

"Very well. Contact the helicopter to get in fast. We're not going to be able to stay on the surface long."

"Aye, aye, sir."

He talks to the radio room and has the operator transfer the helicopter up to the conning tower. The helicopter moves in off the port bow. The captain listens as he talks to the pilot.

"Sir, there is a Yak fighter in escort with him. It will come out of the ceiling soon. He asks us not to shoot it down."

"Chief, there is a fighter from the *Moskva*. It's acting as escort for the helicopters. Let the others know."

The chief passes the message on. The helicopter continues to move in. It moves directly over the hatch area and begins to let the cable down. The chief catches it on the first try and brings it against the periscope tube. He then pulls it in and grabs the nylon harness. He passes it over to the captain.

"First man up." The captain pulls more slack, and helps the weapons man into the harness. He grabs on to the cable and signals that he is ready. The captain looks up at the helicopter and gives them a thumbs up. As the winch begins to pull him up, the wind blows them away from the tower. The man dangles forty feet above the angry sea. The wind continues to swing him back and forth. Finally, he is pulled in, and the helicopter prepares to move in to pick up the second man.

CUBAN SHIPS
THE GULF

"Sir, we have picked up three aircraft. And a submarine has surfaced. They seem to be trying to pick up something from it. The other helicopter has moved about four miles to starboard and is waiting."

"They have brought their subs to the surface?" The Cuban captain has a puzzled look on his face.

"Also, we have picked up two inbound fighters. They are coming in from the north. Sir, this could be an excellent opportunity. We could eliminate their two most formidable weapons."

"Correct, lieutenant. Send fighters to intercept the two coming in from the north. Alert the Ilyusin, and have the Tupolev stand by. We may not have a better chance to get the submarines.

And to have them handed to us! This is a mystery, but one we will not ponder for long."

"Have the *OSAs* finished refueling?"

"Yes, sir."

"We'll follow Admiral Rivera's plan. Order them to their jump off point. If there is a response from the Russians, we will not wait for 1:30."

"Contact the ASW aircraft. They're to attack at once. We should not deny ourselves these gifts, so obligingly given us by the Russians."

RUSSIAN SUBMARINE

The down wash from the helicopter blows the harness out of the reach of the gaff. The pilot fights to hover above the moving sub. As the chief attempts to snag the harness, the sub rolls violently to one side. His foot slips on the wet deck and he falls. The safety line pulls around his stomach like a vice. The captain leans out to help pull him back to his feet.

"Careful, chief. We don't want to lose you."

"Yes, sir. I almost had the bastard."

"Sir, radar has four aircraft ten miles directly off the port side."

The captain cups his mouth to yell at the missile men. "We have aircraft off the port side. Be ready if they decide to come our way."

The two men wave acknowledgment and position themselves in that direction. The captain calls for two more missile tubes to be handed up. As the chief tries to get the harness, the others scan the sky.

"Sir, we have five miles, at most, visibility. We'll be cutting it pretty close."

"I know." He tries to hold on to the chief's foot to steady him.

"Sir." The lieutenant cups the receiver handle. "Radar has just been jammed. It's pretty heavy; they're trying to burn through it now. They're saying we are blind, sir."

"Shit." The chief's gaff catches a piece of the harness, and he begins to pull it down. The down wash from the twin rotors causes the men to cover their faces for a second. The hurling water hits them like gravel stones.

As they protect themselves, they fail to pick up the two black jets that have just emerged from the mist. At 400-plus miles per hour, they race towards the men struggling on the sub.

"Inbound, fighter off the port side." The missile men arm their weapons and raise them to their shoulders. The weapons man is hurriedly snapped into the harness, and the signal to lift is given.

At 1,000 yards, the gun pods on the bellies of the fighters come to life. The men on the bridge of the sub see flickers of fire from the guns as the first rounds hit the conning tower.

The captain looks up at the helicopter as metal shards are torn from its side. The chief and the others on top are torn to shreds by the cannon fire. As they fall, both Grails are fired. One streaks off to the south, the other is shot directly into the sea. The helicopter lifts, and rolls to its left. It drops from the sky. The captain's last vision is the helicopter impaling itself on the periscope. The fuel tanks rupture as the fighters flash overhead. A dragon's breath of fire is blown into the open hatch of the conning tower. As fire blossoms from the top of the sub, a second aircraft lines itself up with the sub.

The pilot of the Ilyushin 38 aligns his sight on the target. At 500 yards, he launches an acoustical torpedo and does a banking turn to his left. The torpedo hits the water, and searches the area. It locks onto the floundering sub. The motors drive the weapon forward. It crashes through the outer hull and explodes.

The blast rips the sub in half. It rolls and sinks beneath the waves. In less than a minute, the sea is clear. Whiffs of smoke dissipate in the air, and the surface is seamless once more.

ABOARD THE *MOSKVA*

"Admiral, the *Otlichnyy* has launched two missiles at the aircraft that was diving on the sub. They have gone to full speed to get to the last known area of the sub. We are still being jammed, but have been able to burn through on some frequencies."

"Very good. Is there any word about the sub?"

"Not yet, sir. But the *Otlichnyy* saw an explosion on the horizon."

"Form the other three around us. Tell the *Otlichnyy* to remain outboard of us. Prepare the squadron to launch an attack. We'll go with the best data we have."

As the *Otlichnyy* moves away to the northeast, the other ships position themselves. The group now forms a diamond shape.

SKY OVER DOWNED SUBMARINE

As the two Cuban fighters pull away from their strafing run, their missile alarms go off. They go to afterburners, and dispense chaff and flares behind them. The missiles chase after their prey, but they are at almost their total range. They explode into the chaff as the fighters move away.

SECOND RUSSIAN SUBMARINE

At the other sub, the captain sweeps the sky with his binoculars. He looks at the helicopter off the bow about 300 yards. He picks up the receiver and ducks behind the windscreen as the sea crashes against the conning tower. "Get the chief up here."

As he emerges from the hatch, the wind wipes spray into the small space. "Damn, this is not good, sir."

"I agree, Chief. Do you think we can snag the harness from up here?" They look at the sea and the helicopter.

"To be honest, sir. I don't know."

One of the weapons men comes up into the hatchway. "Sir, I've talked with the others. We request that we be allowed to jump over board, and have the helicopter pick us up in the water."

The captain looks at the man, and thoughts race through his head. Their last contact and the sonar noise from the other sub makes them believe that it is gone. Again he looks at the chief.

"Sir, were sitting ducks up here. It may sound crazy, but I have to agree with him."

"All right, tell the helicopter what were going to do. We'll send you down on the starboard side. That way the swells will take you away from the boat."

"Aye, aye, sir." He yells back down the hatch and climbs out as the other man emerges from below. They climb up and hold on to the periscope housing. A wave hits the conning towers and rolls by. They climb down the side of the tower and await the next swell. The nose of the sub pushes into the next wave, as a wall of water six-foot tall races at the two men. As the water hits them, they release their grip and are swept away from the sub. The captain waves back to them as they float over the crest of a roller.

"Prepare to dive." The chief and the captain climb down the ladder into the conning tower and secure the hatch. The sound of dive alarms fills their ears.

As the sub begins to submerge, two fighters break from the veil of clouds and begin a strafing run at the disappearing sub.

From the opposite direction, a lone fighter also begins a run at the sub. The men in the water watch as the planes race at each other. One fighter turns towards the helicopter, and the other runs for the disappearing conning tower.

The Yak pilot pushes the pickle on his stick, and an Aphid missile slides from its rail. It speeds towards the fighter attacking the helicopter. Picking up the missile, he pulls back on his stick and goes straight up. Chaff and flares pop from the rear of the plane. The Yak now aligns head on with the other fighter. Their guns blaze at each other on a head-on course. But the Mig flinches first; he pulls up and to the right. The Yak's bullets tear into his right engine. Black smoke begins to billow out the back. The pilot dives near the water and heads away to the east.

The Yak pilot pulls his stick and goes after the other Mig. As he turns, a large four-engine plane comes out of the haze. His attention is back to the fighter, and he pursues him into the overcast.

The Ilyushin makes a left turn and begins flying in the same direction as the sub. As it passes near to the men in the water, they see the co-pilot looking at them and the helicopter. A torpedo drops from the bomb bay and splashes into the water near them.

It's acoustical scanner picks up the subs disappearing tail and begins the chase. "Sir, we have a torpedo in the water. Dead astern."

"All right. Release the decoys and prepare to dive to 600 feet."

"Aye, aye, sir."

Two decoys are released and activated, as the sub begins to enter the black lower waters.

"Sir, we have it at 600 yards." He listens to his earphones.

"We have it at 500 yards, and closing. We have three seconds to decoys." The men silently wait as the seconds tick off. "We should have detonation at the decoys." In the following seconds, a loud boom echos in the bowels of the sub.

"Sir, we have a line of sonaboys in the water 1,000 yards to our bow. They have just gone active." The pinging of the buoys echoes on the speakers of the ship.

The men in the water hold onto a nylon strap, tying them together. One of them pulls the pin on a smoke grenade and holds it up into the wind. The helicopter, seeing the smoke, moves in for the pick up. As they hover overhead, they pull the two men on board. As soon as both are secured, the engines go to maximum and their journey north begins.

The Cuban pilot fights the plane to stay on course. The damage to his engine billows black smokes out behind the jet. He looks around and sees no one around him. The Yak must have gone after the other plane. As he looks over his instruments to assess the full damage to his plane. His missile alert alarm goes off. He turns his head to look behind the fighter, and sees no one. His radar is clear ahead.

As he searches the sky, his eyes are pulled down to the surface of the water. He can see the missile launcher on the Russian ship turn towards him. A bright yellow-orange blast appears under one of the missiles as it leaves the launcher. His eyes are fixed on the rising missile. His hand instinctively rolls the stick over, but there is no instant response. He shrugs his shoulders, and the missile rips into the belly of the fighter.

"Tell the admiral that the sub at this location is presumed gone with all hands. But add also that we eliminated one of their fighters."

"Sir, we have a contact at fifteen miles, from the same direction as the jet. We have confirmed a kill by our side by the Yak from the *Moskva*. He was able to get the other fighter, and is now going to escort the helicopter to the American lines. Also, he saw a Ilyushin 38 over the sub."

"That must be what we have on radar. Launch a missile. We may catch him inside the range."

The ship turns to face the Cuban ships and fires a missile at the bogie beyond their sight. As the IL-38 recrosses the path of the sub, two depth charges drop from the weapons bay and splash into the water. They sink into the rolling mass and dive for the depths.

"Sir, we have a missile lock on us. It's fifteen miles behind us."

"Roger." He pushes the throttle forward, and the four big props bite into the air. They begin to race west, out of harm's way.

"Sir, we have a launch. We are the target." They watch the radar scope as the missile races to close the distance between them. The big plane seems to strain forward as the gap between them continues to grow smaller. Chaff is fired out the rear as they make a course change.

"Sir, we are still the target. We are now seven miles ahead of the missile, and it's closing. The big plane is flat out." To try and gain space, it drops flares.

"Sir, we are just coming to sixteen miles. It is now three miles behind us, and still on course."

As they begin a banking turn, the missile also turns. As it hits the sixteen-mile range, it suddenly explodes with a bright flash.

"Thank God." The pilot pulls the throttles back and brings the plane in to a normal cruising speed. The men in the back cheer over the intercom.

RUSSIAN SUBMARINE

"Sir, we have ash cans in the water."

"Very good. Continue the dive. They're shooting blind on this. Let's hope they're wrong."

The men on the sub brace themselves and wait for the coming event. The two depth charges continue to sink deeper into the sea. Soon they leave the light behind and cut through the liquid darkness. At 400 feet, one ceases to sound and a huge explosion rocks the depths. The vibration and pressure slam into the top of the sub. The men are shaken about, but all remain intact. The second one continues on to its selected depth, as it passes 500 feet.

"Sir, 600 feet in five seconds." The words get lost in the concussion of the second depth charge at 550 feet. The explosion bends the periscope mast, and wipes away the others. The sub is rocked and pushed all at the same time. As quickly as it occurred, the sea around the sub grows silent. The groans and creaks of the hull are the only sound. The sub levels at 600 feet and sets a course for the Cuban ships.

ULTIMA
WASHINGTON, D.C.

The president and Secretary Brant are standing in front of the desk, their eyes glued to the screen. The satellite's imaging camera has just played them the opening skirmish between the two forces.

"I can't believe that this is happening. That submarine just blew up, with all those men on board. Morales is going to fucking start a major conflict, for no reason."

"Yes, Mr. President. It is a terrifying turn of events."

The screen expands, and a small white helicopter shape moves away from the area. A jet joins it.

"Sir, I will contact Dr. Davies. Our thought is that the chances are slim for the weapons people getting through." He looks at his watch. "It's five minutes to one."

"We'll give the go ahead to Susie, if you agree, Mr. President."

"Yes, Mr. Secretary. Of course."

He walks back to his chair and sits; he puts his head in his hands. Then he looks back at the others. "By the time this day is through, we'll all have ulcers and gray hair."

"I would agree with you, Mr. President." Brant's hand picks up the receiver. "Get me Dr. Davies at the bomb site."

CHAPTER 10

ULTIMA
WASHINGTON, D.C., 1:00 P.M.

"This is Secretary Brant. I would like to speak to Dr. Davies.".

"Just a minute, sir. Gunny, it's for Dr. Davies, from Secretary Brant."

The gunny walks over to the helicopter where Susie and her corpsmen have been having lunch and staying out of the rain.

"There is a call for you, from Secretary Brant."

She looks at her watch and hops down. She catches up with the gunny walking back to the site. "This could be it, Gunny. We go for the big one. You're hoping I have forgotten all about the leeches, and yours and Neal's thinking it was humorous." He looks over at her with a sheepish grin. "Don't you, Gunny. Mr. Brant, this is Dr. Davies."

"Susie, the situation in the Gulf has now escalated to a full blown attack by the Cubans on the *Moskva* squadron. We are at full alert in the Gulf. One of the weapons teams was killed when the Russian submarine was attacked and sunk."

"My God." She tries to envision the situation out at sea. "What about the other one?"

"They were also attacked. The weapons people were picked up. They're being escorted in by the Yak fighter. They have not had any contact with the sub; we don't know its fate at this time. The chances of the weapons people reaching the main land is considered slim."

"Then we will proceed on our own to disarm the weapons?"

"Yes, you have the full green light from the president and the Joint Chiefs. We can only wish you the best of luck."

"Thank you, Mr. Brant. We're set up to go. I will disarm the first one, and Emanuel will follow my procedures. We'll begin in just a few minutes."

"Very good, Susie. President Wayne would like to say a few words."

"Susie, this is President Wayne. I am at a loss for words to describe the indebtedness of the people of both our countries. It seems in all great emergencies, we have people like yourself and Dr. Reddeer, who come forward to right a terrible wrong. And in this case, you face the wrath of both nature and a man-made cataclysm. My prayers and the prayers of all parties involved go with you. Good luck."

"Thank you, Mr. President. We will certainly do our best."

She hands the mike back to the gunny. "We'll begin disarming the bomb as soon as we get everything together here. By the way, aren't there other channels on the Lanstat?"

"Yes, ma'am. We'll clear a channel out for you." He walks over to the radioman, and explains what they want. He begins to throw some switches, and plugs in a second handset in one of the open ports. "It's ready when you are, ma'am."

She takes the handset and turns it over. It has a touch tone button pad on its back side. Her fingers punch in the area code for Los Alamos and the ranch. The ringing at the other end seems so distant. It rings about four times and is picked up.

"Hello." The voice on the other end sends a scalding chill through her mind and body.

"Hey, cowboy. What are you up to?"

"I knew you'd call. The navy called to say you were on some special assignment. I heard about the Russian bomber. I put two and two together, and figured you'd be in the middle of it.

"I'm just doing some check work and will be flying out tomorrow."

"OK. I picked up Mary and the kids. She told me what had happened. If you see Emanuel, tell him they're fine. Her mother is over with her now."

"Good, I'll tell him. I just wanted to call and say I love you."

"I love you. I know now that whatever it is you are doing is out of the ordinary. You're too ballsy for your own good, Davies."

"Yeah, but that's the way you like your women."

"Yeah, I have to agree. You're everything I could ever want in a woman, and more."

"I'm glad you feel that way. I'm all the woman you'll ever need."

"You're right. I have a couple of steaks marinating with a couple of cold beers. Even a horse blanket for a ride out to bun buster point. All I need is you."

"It sounds great. I will be looking forward to the whole enchilada. I need to get going. I love you."

"I love you. Really more than that, the word doesn't cover it. It's now and forever. I'll always be there for you."

"I know. Goodbye, my cowboy."

He hangs up the phone, and walks out of the barn to the house. Halfway he stops, and his gloved hands remove his Stetson. They curl the brim as he lifts his face up into the clear blue sky. "Please, God, bring her home to me. Amen."

She hands the phone to the operator. The rain hitting her face camouflages the tears in her eyes. "Gunny, we're ready to go. Have Emanuel on the headset in case anything goes wrong."

"Yes, ma'am."

ULTIMA
WASHINGTON, D.C.

Captain Van Nar walks up to the podium. The center screen looks down onto the Russian destroyer *Otlichnyy*. "Sir, the Russian commander Admiral Kirsanov has issued the order to engage the Cuban forces." As they watch, two missiles are fired from the *Otlichnyy*. The two Siren missiles streak from the quad launchers at the side of the ship. The screen showing the radar image of the area is suddenly splattered with false targets. "As you can see, the Cubans have activated their ECM aircraft, as well as the ECM units aboard their ships."

The rear launcher fires two Grail missiles at targets to the east of the destroyer. The four Cuban Mig-27 fighters east of the destroyer lock their missiles on different radar frequencies. Each picks off one of their AS-11 anti-radar missiles. As they disappear, they roll out of range of the two inbound missiles. Again, two missiles leave the forward launchers; these Sirens are aimed at the second Cuban ship. The ship begins to maneuver and fires two missiles to the southeast. The two aircraft from the southeast lock on radar frequencies and rush forward at the ship. As the radar screen cleans its patterns up, two small blips appear. They are coming from the southeast and move directly at the destroyer.

Van Nar looks up to check the screen. "As you can see, we now have two Cuban missiles inbound. They are heading for the destroyer. We have four *OSA* boats approaching from the southeast and three from the northeast. We also have two more missiles launched. The target is the *Moskva*."

The others in the room sit silently as the missiles race for the targets. The imaging camera moves back as more missiles are launched from the other Russians ships at the fighters.

"Holy shit, what a show." Admiral Hillings walks up with Van Nar and looks at the screen. "Mr. President and Mr. Brant, no one has ever seen such a showing. I find it hard to believe myself. This could be the greatest sea battle ever recorded. Everyone has always wondered how all these weapons systems would work. The missile people, the decoy people, the radar folks, and the tactics people. This is the whole spectrum of modern sea warfare, not just a computer model. This event will change the tactics and applied weapons development for years to come."

As the president watches, his lips mumble, "God help us all."

MOSKVA BRIDGE
THE GULF

"Admiral, we have two missiles inbound, off the starboard bow. We believe they are from one of the *OSA* boats. We had a track on three moving northwest; we are having problems locking on the Cubans with our missiles, due to their ECM interference and our inability to launch a helicopter for target guidance."

The ship dips into the next roller, and wind hurls the spray in all directions. The after deck is swept with the wind and rain.

"What is our visibility at?"

"Sir, we are less than five miles. The other Tupolev west of us is now jamming us." The two men look out the front of the bridge as a wail comes over the speakers. One of the front SAM launchers turns in the direction of the inbound missiles and fires two Goblet missiles. They streak from the ship and quickly disappear into the downpour. A sudden boom from the starboard side sends a decoy cloud of chaff 1,000 yards out. The second SAM launcher on the front of the ship turns to starboard. It fires at full depression to the side of the ship. A flash and the following concussion signal that one of the missiles has been hit. The point defense, a 57 mm cannon on the starboard side, comes to life, firing into the downpour. The admiral and the captain run to the starboard side to see the action. Just as they reach the window, a huge orange fireball appears. The concussion from the 800-pound warhead slams into the side of the *Moskva*. Both men hang onto the edge of the port.

"Damn, that was close." The admiral and the captain exchange looks. The forward launchers again swivel and two more missiles roar into the sky. A second missile is launched, almost vertically.

"The damn fighters are trying to draw out our missiles. They're near the max range, and they dart in and out of our targeting radar."

"The hell with the fighters; they can't hurt us any way. We need to concentrate on the inbound missiles and that flight of planes now coming up behind us."

On the *Otlichnyy*, its forward launcher fires two SAM missiles into the path of the incoming Cuban missiles. The point defense weapons come to life, and chaff is fired into the storm. As the *Otlichnyy* maneuvers, its 130 mm dual-purpose guns swing to the northeast and begin firing. A huge explosion in the mist to starboard signals the end of one of the missiles. The 30 mm Gatling gun comes to life and fires point blank into the mist. At one hundred yards, the second missile is hit. It dives and cartwheels towards the ship and explodes. The blast knocks men off their feet, and the ship is rolled to the left.

Shrapnel from the casing and a huge tongue of flame careen into the side of the ship. It tears the captain's jig to pieces, and one of the missile control radars is blown away. The small boat begins to burn as tons of water thrown up by the explosion rain down on the ship. Damage control parties move towards the area.

The Cuban ships maneuver and fire chaff; the missiles divert away from the two and crash and explode in the sea behind them. The heavy ECM coverage of the Cubans has turned the missiles; the sky grows quiet once more.

BOMB SITE, NUMBER SEVEN
LOUISIANA

Susie looks over the tools and walks to the edge of the pit. The gunny's hand grabs hers to help her into the pit. The mud hog is slurping out the water in the bottom of the pit; she hesitantly kneels down beside the bomb. He hands her a headset and kneels at the edge of the pit. She put the headset on and looks at the access plate, then back up at the gunny.

"Well, I think we're about as ready as we'll ever be."

"Yeah." He looks deep into her eyes and pats her on the shoulder. "Susie, you're the best. You remind me of my wife. She had the hardest job in the world, and she enjoyed the challenge every day. She was killed in an auto accident when I was on an operation."

Susie looks at him quiescently. "What was her job, Gunny?"

"Being married to me. Like her, you're both great ladies. Now let's kick this thing's ass."

"I got you, Gunny. Let's rock and roll."

"Emanuel, are you here? Yes, we're just finishing the last of the sand bagging. Good luck, we'll go as soon as you're done. Very good. By the way, I talked to Dave. He picked up Mary at the airport; her mom is at the house staying with her."

"That sounds great. I have to admit, for a guy as big as Dave, he has a heart of gold."

"Thanks, I think he's great also. And in his jeans, he makes those models look lame. He is every cowgirl's dream: tight buns with a brain."

"Ha, ha! You kill me Susie. He is probably the only guy that could keep up with your no-holds-barred, up-front humor."

"That could be. Well, its show time." She puts a grounding strap around her wrist, and the gunny hands her the ratchet with the star-shaped drive.

The others on the net listen in, their thoughts hanging on every word. Like some old radio program, they anxiously wait the next event in the drama.

"Mr. Val, are you here?"

"Yes, Doctor. A reminder—the screws are numbered from the upper left corner. It is number one, and the screw to its right is number two, and so on."

"Right." She takes a grease pencil and puts a number just outside of the cover by each screw. She hands it back to the gunny and looks around the pit. It seems that everyone is frozen; their eyes have a cold stare. She hears the mumbling of a short prayer from behind her.

"Are you ready, Gunny?"

He adjusts his headset. "Yes, ma'am."

"We're ready for the number sequence, Val."

"Very good. Hold one. General Kuznetsov, we are ready for the first series of numbers. It is bomb number 757."

The general lays the envelopes out on the table and picks up 757. He breaks the wax seal on the back and pulls the card out of the envelope; the numbers are printed in bold red at the bottom of the card. In his thick Russian accent, he reads the numbers to Val as Shagan listens while looking at the screen. The numbers are written down in Washington and at the crash site. Val repeats the numbers and thanks him.

"Dr. Davies, the numbers are six, three, five, seven, one, four, two, and eight. I will repeat them again." He goes over the numbers again. "Also, the screws must be removed totally from the casing."

She looks up at the gunny; he gives her a thumbs up.

"Thank you, Val. We have the numbers."

As she raises the ratchet, her right hand moves inside the top of her blouse and she clutches her medicine bag. A gift from the medicine man of Emanuel's tribe, the Lakota Sioux. Her interest in Native American studies had bonded her and Emanuel from the start of their working together. Under her breath she whispers to her self.

"All right." Gunny calls out the first number. "We start with number six." She inserts the head of the ratchet into the screw marked number six. It holds and then slowly gives under the presure of her push. She retracts the screw and hands it to the gunny. He puts it into a plastic bag and calls out the next number. All is quiet on the net as they listen to the numbers being called out and the deep breathing of Susie as she unscrews them from the casing.

"This is the last number; it is number eight." Susie looks at the last screw, and then at the gunny. "Gee, I would have never guessed that." She inserts the ratchet and removes the last screw. "That's it."

She hands the ratchet back to the gunny and slowly lifts the panel from the side of the bomb. Taking out a flashlight, she scans the interior of the weapon. Reaching in, she pulls the connector to the plate cover and hands it up. He takes the panel with its trailing wires and puts it into a bag.

She looks into the interior of the bomb; three flashing squares inside hold her attention. She pushes the last of the red squares, as the button pops forward the light goes out. Moving to the next one, she pushes it and its light goes out also. Then she unscrews a connector attached to a leveler.

"I have disabled the anti-tampering and the tilt devices, and will now pull the cork on the arming switch." She pushes the button; the light fades as she disconnects the cord attached to the detonator. Its spiral stainless steel body gleams back at her from the light of her flashlight. Her hand moves over to the other side of the cavity and pushes a button on the timer. Its illuminated numbers stop on 13:20. The gunny hands her a spanning wrench; she takes it and inserts it into the bomb. It fits onto a locking ring; she turns it to loosen. Pulling out the wrench, she unscrews the ring by hand and brings it out. She hands it to the gunny and reaches back into the cavity. Her hand rests on metal tabs; she pushes clockwise, and the cylinder moves a quarter turn. Slowly, she lifts the cylinder out; it rises six inches and is free of the detonating charge. Backing out of the opening, its shiny exterior looks out of place in the muddy hand. The timer detonator is handed up, and placed in a special box lined with foam.

She looks up at the gunny, and gives a sigh of relief and then a thumbs up. She leans back on the sandbags behind her as a loud cheer goes up from the others. The others on the net hear the yelling in the background.

"Mr. President, bomb 757 is now disarmed."

At the sound of her voice, a cheer goes up from all the locations on the net. The president pats Brant on the back.

"Congratulations, Dr. Davies, from us all."

"Thank you, Mr. Brant. But we still have a lot of work to do."

"Emanuel, the kill switches are to the right as you lift the panel off. The timer is to your left. It is pretty straightforward. Just take your time. The timer detonator is exactly as Val described it. And by the way, who ever estimated the start time on the bombs was right on. This one stopped at 13:20 remaining. We'll have to keep up a good pace to clear them all."

"OK, Susie. I'm going into the pit now. I'll keep in touch."

"Emanuel, Bijjh dinéé bitsli, Ádaa ahólyá." She speaks in his native language. A smile comes over his face as he slips into the pit. He looks around as Sergeant Cabalero sits on a sandbag at the edge.

"We're ready for the numbers for bomb 758, Mr. Val."

The process is again started as General Kuznetsov opens the second envelope. Once the numbers are verified, Emanuel places the ratchet into screw number five and begins to turn it.

The gunny reaches down and grabs Susie's hand to pull her out of the hole. He pats her on the back, "You're good."

"Thanks, everyone. The recovery team can now start getting this thing out of here."

A young marine nearby, shakes his head. "Man, you are one fucking ballsy lady, ma'am."

"Lance Corporal, those are not the words to use with this lady." Lieutenant Neal steps forward.

"Please, Mr. Neal. I take it as a compliment. We have just all come through a pretty shaky time. I was not offended by the remark."

"Very well, ma'am. But we do need to watch what we say."

Susie walks over to the radio, and sits on a case. She listens to Emanuel at the other bomb site. The gunny hands her a fresh towel to wipe the mud off with. "This is great, Gunny."

"You are something else, Doctor."

"I think I need some paper to wipe with."

"Yeah, I'll bet." She pops him with the end of the towel.

Lt. Neal signals to the chopper, and it starts its engines. The two navy men from the beach jump into the pit and fasten a nylon harness on the bomb. They wiggle it back and forth in the mud. After talking with two of the marines at the bomb, they run across the field and get onto the waiting helicopter. It lifts slowly into the air and makes a circle of the site. The marines on the ground signal it in over the top of the bomb. The other marine takes the cable from the helicopter and attaches it to the harness. The helicopter slowly begins to rise. The bomb quivers and then begins to slide out of the grasping mud. They raise it up with the cable and then turn to head for the beach. Two Cobra gunships join it, and they move to the southwest.

"Bulldog, this is Bulldog 2. Over."

"This is Bulldog, go ahead."

"Sir, our first bad guy is on his way to you. Over."

"Roger, as soon as we have word from site two, your squad will be moved to the next site."

"Roger, Bulldog. We're loading extra gear now. Bulldog 2 out."

RUSSIAN FIGHTERS
THE GULF

The two Migs continue over the tops of the waves. Like two trapped animals, their senses seem to heighten. They know they have been seen, but they wait for the hunters' next move.

"Ski, we have two bandits coming in behind us. Over."

"Roger. I've been watching them. I think I have an idea of where the Tupolev is. And then it's anything that pops up."

"Roger. I'll take the two behind us. When I say break, you go up and left. They should stick with me."

"Roger, Norba. I hope we can have dinner tonight together, and tell good stories about this battle."

"I hope so, too. Good luck, my friend."

The two Cuban fighters fall in behind. Their radars scan the two fighters. The missile locks on the Migs go off. The whine fills the two cockpits as they watch their radars.

"Now!" Norba yells into the mic, and Ski goes to afterburners and rolls to the left. Norba pulls the nose of his plane up and heads for the stars through the overcast. The Cubans fire just as the two planes begin to maneuver. Norba dispenses flares and chaff out the back of the plane as he climbs. The missiles rip into the flares and explode harmlessly. They both pull up to follow

Norba into the overcast. They inform the ships that one of the fighters is on its way towards them. They acknowledge and send two fighters from their air cap to intercept.

As Norba breaks through the overcast at 15,000 feet, the glare from the sun momentarily blinds him. His wings tucked against the side of the fuselage, he rolls over and dives at the two fighters. He locks onto the lead aircraft and waits for his tone. The circles and squares on his HUD quiver and move, then the firing circle closes down on the target. He hears the tone, and his hand pickles the first missile off its pylon. Turning the plane to the other fighter, he goes to guns as the two adversaries streak towards each other. The lead plane goes into a barrel roll; he dispenses flares and chaff. But the missile catches him at the apex of his roll; it hits at the middle of his fuselage. The plane explodes and tumbles toward the sea. The second fighter goes to guns. The sky is full of streaming tracers as the two close. The Cuban tries to dive to go under him, but Norba dips his nose and tattoos the fighter from cockpit to the tail. It spins over into a corkscrew dive, smoke and fire belching from the back. Norba regains his original course and calls forward to the *Moskva*. They vector him over the fleet and to the south to intercept the on-coming fighter-bombers.

As Norba brakes from the overcast, he over flies the squadron doing a tight barrel roll. He disappears over the stern of the ships, a sonic boom trailing him.

COMMAND CENTER
CUBA

"General, we have another report."

"Well!"

"Sir, we have received word that the two fighters escorting the bomber have joined the Russian squadron. We have lost two of our fighters."

"Damn!" The general's fist slams into his desk. "I want them down, now! We are just about to launch the main attack. The second wave of attack bombers should be leaving about now."

"General." The admiral looks up from the map. "We have already dealt them a crippling blow with the loss of their submarines."

"I might remind you, Admiral, that only one has been verified."

"Yes, but we are into the final attack positions. The Russian squadron is about to be subjected to the greatest mass attack by missiles in history. Our fighters will get the two lone Migs, and history will record the success of our attack."

Morales looks at his watch; the hands stand at 1:30 P.M. "In fifteen minutes, we will turn the Gulf into the greatest naval defeat the Russians have ever known. These Bolshevik bastards, have had their knee in Cuba's back for decades. We're about to rip their legs off and wave the bloody stubs at the world. We are about to become the sole Western Hemisphere country to stand the Americans back on their heels."

Those in the control room cheer the generals words. They are now caught up in the momentum of the event. The clash of forces at sea has generated an adrenaline rush. The men and women listen as voices from the battle erupt out of speakers. There is a pride—not of the event, but of the resolve of the Cuban spirit.

TOWN PARK
CARDENAS, CUBA

"Give me another beer." His friend hands it to him, but his eyes do not leave the light blue sedan parked across the street.

"Don't look all at once, but I think that we have been followed. That *cabrón* over there keeps looking at us." The others sneak a glance at the car, which is pulled up in the alley.

"Let's go by the apartment and get our stuff."

The others nod their heads and pile into the cab. They pull out of the park and head up the street.

The helicopter circles the parking lot and then descends. They climb out to waiting police vehicles. The captain moves to the lead car. "I want this man taken down to the station and a statement taken. I'll be in the field; we are going to get these guys for the murder of our brother officers."

"Yes, sir." The sergeant directs some others to take the man to the station. He walks to the back of the car and opens the trunk. "Sir." The captain looks in and takes out a submachine gun. "We have just received word the cab has pulled out of the park; our undercover man is still trailing them."

"Good." He turns to Quintano and Brock. "Gentlemen, would you like to get a weapon?" They look into the trunk. Three submachine guns and four shot guns are neatly racked with ammo in boxes beside them. Brock picks up a shotgun and a box of ammo.

"This could come in handy."

Quintano smiles and shakes his head, "Not for me, Captain. I'll stick close to you guys."

The captain gets into the front car, and Quintano and Brock climb into the next one. The cars move out of the parking lot, and head in the direction of the moving cab.

The cab moves through traffic. They keep an eye on the car following. "He is still there. He is definitely following."

"Do you think it's cops or those *cabrónes* from Dehare street?"

"I can't tell. The car looks like shit. Could be either one."

The driver finishes another beer and throws the can out the window. "Fuck him, whoever he is." He pulls down an alley to the next street. They watch out the back as the sedan turns with them. They race up the street; they're on home ground, and they know the area. The sedan speeds up to try and keep them in view. They weave through traffic and take a sharp turn up an alley. They pull in next to a garage, jump out, and run up a flight of stairs to an apartment. One of them goes to the window and watches for the car. The others open a closet and get out automatic weapons.

"There he is." They watch as the car slowly moves up the alley, below the windows. "It's time to teach this *pendejo* whose streets these are." A rifle is thrown to the man at the window. They each grab loaded clips and stuff them in their coat pockets. "Get some more beer out of the refrigerator so we can drink to our coming success." The others hold their rifles up in the air, and yell, "Let's do it!"

"Where is he now?"

"He is parked down the alley, facing away from us."

"All right, let's go." They open the door and run down the stairs to the cab. They back out and accelerate up the alley towards the sedan.

"Captain, I think they have made me. I need to get out of here; they're coming by me now." He drops the mike and turns the key. He shifts into gear. The cab has pulled up next to him. He sees the driver in his side window smiling at him. As the cab moves forward, he sees the man in the back seat. His rifle is aimed directly at him. For an instant he sees the flash of the first shot, and the shattering of the window.

"Yeah, yeah!" the gunner cries out as he half-empties a clip into the sedan. The bullets rip the metal of the door just before they hit the driver.

"All right, all right, I think you got him."

The sedan rolls across an empty lot and crashes into the side of a building. The cab is backed up and brought alongside it. The man in the back gets out and checks the driver.

"This fucking *cabrón* is gone, man."

The radio blares. "Are you there? This is Captain Bodus. Are you there?"

The gunman reaches in and picks up the mike. "Yeah, we're here. What do you want, *cabrón*?"

"Who is this? What are you doing on this channel?"

"I'm the guy who just blew your fucking man away."

"We will get you, asshole."

"Fuck you, Captain Dickhead." He throws the mike back into the car and jumps back in the cab. "Let's haul ass, man."

The cab races away from the car. The wail of sirens can be heard. They work their way to a main street and head for a hideout near the river.

Bodus's car pulls into the alley. There are two cars at the apartment already.

Farther down the alley, the two cars are pulled in behind the sedan. They move past the apartment. The captain gets out and walks up to the passenger side window. Quintano and Brock follow.

"Son of a bitch." The captain slaps the side of his machine gun. "Get me the men in the apartment." He walks back to his car. Brock and Quintano look the car over. Brock puts his finger in one of the holes in the door.

"I'd say AK-47 from the size of the holes. It looks like our saboteur really doesn't want to be caught." Quintano runs his hand over the door. "I guess so."

"Sir." A call comes over the radio. "We have searched the apartment, but we didn't find a lot. Some 7.62 ammo and miscellaneous radios and stereos. Also some marijuana and a small amount of crack. I'd guess these guys to be thieves, with some drug dealing. No political literature or banners."

"Very well. Leave a car here in case they come back."

Another call comes in. "Sir, we have the cab. We're in pursuit. They're heading for the river. They're on Del Sol Boulevard."

"Roger. We're on our way." He throws the mike into the car, and calls for Brock and Quintano to get in. "They're headed for the river. We'll get them there."

MIG-29
THE GULF

As Ski pushes deeper into the squalls, his radar picks up two fighters. They are tracked and designated. At twenty-two miles, two medium range Apex missiles fire forward into the void. He watches their track and then sees the two returning blips. His missile alert signals a lock on him, coming from the on-coming Cuban fighters. Chaff is dispensed, and Ski rolls the Mig over and dives for the deck. The track of the incoming missiles follows his movement; the changing blips mesmerize him on his radar. He waits and then pulls a hard right turn. The plane is brought to almost vertical, and he applies his afterburners. Chaff and flares are flung from the tail of the jet as it rockets skyward. The missiles try and bend their flight path, but they are to close to the surface of the water.

The two slam into the water at the speed of sound and explode. His movements to elude the missiles have brought him over the Cuban fleet. His missile alarm goes off again as two missiles race skyward from the ships. His radar picks up the Tupolev ECM aircraft. It's almost dead ahead. As the distance closes to four miles, an Aphid close range missile leaves the Mig. His eyes watch the closing missiles on his tail.

The captain of the Tu-16 watches out his front window as two Kelt anti-ship missiles leave the wings and fly into the storm. His tail gun begins firing as he dispenses chaff and flares in a hard left dive.

Ski dives with him. The tracers from the twin rear machine guns fly by him. He goes to guns and fires back at the huge shape in front of him. The missile catches it at the right wing engine root; the explosion tears the wing off. He passes over the Tupolev and dives behind it. The two ship missiles lose him and find the huge plummeting bomber. They finish the work; one hits the fuselage at the front of the plane, and the other slams into the tail section. The blast tears the bomber apart, and in flames it crashes into the sea.

His radar picks up three blips to his right at 25,000 feet. Rolling back to ninety degrees, he hits his afterburners and heads for the planes. He becomes aware of another jet coming in from his left. His missile alert goes off. The Cuban fighter closes the distance between them. As he breaks through the clouds into the sunlight, he catches site of the huge Ilyushin 76 tanker, with two Cuban fighters being fueled from it. At his rate of closure, he fires his Aphid missile at the big tanker and goes to guns. The missile hits the tanker in the rear and explodes. The fireball engulfs the two fighters as they fly into the wreckage. They add to the fireball, and the three falls from the sky. He throws the Mig into a right diving turn and chaff and flares fill the sky. But they don't deter the Cuban fighter's missile. It hits the right rear of the Mig. The right engine is shut down, and he tries to regain control. The plane is like driving a truck, and pain races up his leg. Once the Mig is in a slow forward dive, he reaches into his pocket and withdraws another hypodermic. He shoots it into his leg.

"*Moskva*, this is Raven 2. Over."

"Roger, Raven 2. This is *Moskva*."

"I've been hit and will not last long. I shot down the Ilyushin and two fighters fueling. I must have gotten one of the other Cuban fighters, but the other one is coming in behind me.

"Roger Raven, this is Captain Sokolov. You are an air ace in the true sense of Russian heroes. We are proud of your accomplishments; we can now engage the Cuban ships. We salute you, Comrade."

"Thank you, sir. Raven 2 out."

The Cuban fighter behind him has little difficulty following the dark smoke billowing out of the Russian plane. He lines up his next shot.

"Raven 2, this is Norba. Over."

"Roger, my friend."

"Ski, try and get back to the Americans. If you have to ditch, they have ships and planes standing by. Over."

"I'm going down. I can see the Cuban ships. I will attack them with what I have left. Over."

"Good luck, my brave comrade. I will tell your parents of your brave deeds this day."

"Roger, Raven 1. It's been good flying with you. Out."

Arming his last missiles, he fires them at the closest ship. His alarm screams in his ears. The ship is firing up at him as he comes in from behind. The missile hits him in the left engine and the Mig explodes. The debris scatters across the surface of the water.

The Cuban fighter flies over the burning spot on the surface of the water and wags his wings. He looks over at the ships; one of the missiles has hit the trailing ship near the aft gun turret. Crewmen are already getting hoses out to douse the fire. He pulls the nose up and goes back to his patrol station.

BOMB SITE, NUMBER EIGHT
LOUISIANA

"The last one is number six, Doctor."

Emanuel puts the ratchet into the screw head and begins to unscrew it. The men around the pit stand silently as they watch. The only sound is the calling of some birds in the swamp. He removes the screw and hands it and the ratchet to Sergeant Cabalero.

He slowly lifts the cover plate. Using his flashlight, he presses in the first button. He then removes the connector cord and hands it to the sergeant. On his knee in the pit, he rocks back to take a couple of long breaths. The others on the net listen to his inhales and exhales. Nothing is said; they don't want to throw off his concentration.

Using the flashlight, he looks around the cavity. It is as Susie said: simple and to the point. Reaching in, he pushes the button for the movement sensor, and pulls the cord on the leveling device. He pushes the last button, and the arming switch light goes out. He detaches the cord to the top of the detonator and hands it up to Cabolero. He pans the light to the left in the cavity and sees the last glowing light. Pushing it in, the numbers stop at 13:28. Cabalero hands him the spanning wrench, and he removes the locking ring. Reaching in, he turns the cylinder a quarter turn and it lifts out of its chamber. Slowly he removes it from the bomb and hands it up to Johnson. He puts it in the foam case and closes the lid.

Emanuel rocks back on his knees and puts both hands up into the air. "Number 758 is dead." A cheer goes up from the men around him, and the others on the net yell their approval.

"OK, Emanuel, we're on our way to our next site."

"Roger, Susie. We'll clean up here and head out in just a few minutes. Good luck."

"There's no luck to this. We're just good."

"Yeah, you got that right."

"Excellent job, Dr. Reddeer and Dr. Davies. The president sends along his congratulations."

BOMB SITE, NUMBER SEVEN
LOUISIANA

"Thank you, Mr. Brant." Susie hands the headset and mike back to the radio operator and joins Neal and Marshall, who are walking back to the helicopter.

As soon as the Lanstat is packed, it is picked up by two marines and is moved back to the helicopter. Waiting until everyone is clear, another marine places a charge in the pit. He checks the area around him and pulls a fuse lighter. He runs to catch up with the others and yells, "Fire in the hole."

As the helicopters warm up their engines, Susie looks back at the site. The charge explodes and a fountain of mud and water covers the site.

ULTIMA
WASHINGTON, D.C.

"Gentleman." Captain Van Nar steps up to the podium. "We have the launch of two Kelt anti-ship missiles by the Badger ECM aircraft, just before it was shot down. These are two of the largest Soviet anti-ship missiles. Our data is that they weight in at around 10,500 pounds. Our best estimate is one is targeted for the *Moskva* and the other for the *Vladivostok* cruiser. On the radar screen, all inbound missiles from the Cubans are in red circles. The Russian missiles are in yellow circles. As you can see, we are now picking up defensive missiles from the ships."

As they watch, the red circles race at the ships. Yellow circles head towards them. The *Sovremennyy* fires two more at the missiles. They watch as two of the yellow circles collide with the red, and explode. "We have one missile down. The other is still headed for the *Vladivostok*."

ABOARD THE *VLADIVOSTOK*
THE GULF

The long-range point defense canon on the rear of the ship comes to life. Its elevation continues to drop as the missile lowers itself to just above the surface and aligns with the ship. The men on the bridge look out the back port, their binoculars trained into the mist. At three miles, the red painted missile springs into view just above the water. They watch in horror as the huge missile bears down on them. The cannon bursts are plainly visible, exploding around it. The missile size makes it look like an airplane diving into the ship. The captain yells into the ships radio system, "Prepare for impact in the stern." As he watches the missile cross the one-mile mark, two white flashes streak from the sky and hit the missile. The resulting explosion blows water and debris over the stern of the ship. The concussion wave rocks the bridge. The captain looks around the bridge at the others; they all seem to be frozen.

"Very well. We're still afloat, and we have a job to do."

"Get a message off to the Sovremenvyy — good shooting."

ULTIMA
WASHINGTON, D.C.

For a few moments, the scene is quiet. The Joint Chiefs stretch their necks; the president slowly shakes his head. He gets up and walks over to the table next to Brant. "Gentlemen, when will this stop?" Admiral Hillings looks at the board and then at the president.

"Sir, we do not believe that the main action has yet started. These are just the opening rounds. With the fighter-bombers coming in and the *OSA* boats in position, we believe all hell is about to erupt."

"Admiral, what type of insanity would cause this?"

Brant looks up at the president. "Sir, if I could try and explain. This is all the doing of General Morales. We have known for sometime that he gets involved in rather unstable dealings. We know that Fidel is not involved; this is turning into a type of military coup by him in Fidel's absence. At this time we're not sure where General Quintano is. But if he is not dead, he will move on Morales to stop him. We have dealt with Quintano in secret as a go-between for Fidel and us. The Russians have talked with Fidel; he has condemned Morales's actions and is leaving Bogota, Bolivia, to fly to Havana."

"Mr. President, we hope to have our people on their next site by," he looks at his watch, "2:00 P.M."

PALACE OF JUSTICE
CUBA

A phone rings at the governmental palace. On its fifth ring, it is picked up. "This is Judge Palentino."

"Juan, this is Fidel."

"Fidel, you are lucky that I answered the phone. Everyone has gone into hiding. Morales is running wild."

"I know, I talked with the Russians. They told me about Gutaras. My heart is sad, but we must do something."

"Sí, I agree, amigo. But what can be done? He has his black guard everywhere."

"Juan, get in touch with Quintano. Do not go through the command center. Call his base and have him call you there. I'm at the airport in Bogota, use this number." He gives the number to Palentino. "I will wait here until I hear from you. Good luck my friend."

"Sí, Fidel. I will get hold of him."

The judge dials the number to Quintano's base. The phone rings several times. "This is Sergeant Munous. Can I help you?"

"Sergeant, this is Judge Palentino. I need to speak with General Quintano."

"Sir, he is off the base. But Captain Ruiz is here, sir."

"Good, let me talk to him, please."

"This is Captain Ruiz."

"Captain, this is Judge Palentino. I must get in touch with General Quintano."

"He is in the field. It may take a while."

"It is of the utmost importance. I do not want to speak to anyone except him. Do you understand, Captain?"

"Yes, sir. We have been held on base awaiting his orders."

"Excellent, Captain. Please hurry. Have him call me at this number."

The line goes dead as Ruiz finishes writing down the number. He turns to the radio operator and has him call the helicopter on their secret frequency.

"Sir, I have the helicopter. The general is away from the ship."

"Let me talk to him." He picks up the mike. "This is Captain Ruiz. I have a message for the general only. Have him call this number from a ground station." He gives the number, and listens for the affirmation.

"Roger, Captain. We'll get the message to him. Out."

The lieutenant reaches over and changes the frequency on his radio. "General, this is the helicopter. Over."

The walkie on Quintano's hip comes to life. He looks at Brock. "This is Quintano. Go ahead."

"Sir, I just received a call from Captain Ruiz. I have a message. It's for your eyes only."

"Roger, I'll head back to the ship. I'm beginning to think we're chasing the wrong guys anyway. I'll be there in a few minutes." He looks at Brock. "I wonder what this is about."

"I'd guess that it has something to do with Morales."

"You're probably right." He leans forward. "Sergeant, I need to return to the helicopter. Could you inform Captain Botus?"

The vehicles pull over to the side of the road. Botus gets out and walks back to their car. "Sir, I'll send this car back with you. If Señor Brock wants to continue, he can join me."

"Thank you, Captain. I'll rejoin you as soon as possible." Brock gets out and goes with the captain as Quintano's car turns around and heads back for the helicopter.

As Brock and Botus get back in the car, the driver turns around. "Sir, the patrol car in pursuit of the cab is now exchanging shots with them. They apparently knocked out the back window and opened fire on them."

"Well, let's get going. I want these men badly."

The car pulls from the curb and with sirens wailing, races down the street.

COMMAND CENTER
CUBA

"General." Admiral Rivera looks back at the desk.

"Yes, Admiral. Good news, I hope."

"Yes, we have shot down one of the Russian Migs. And they are in pursuit of the other one."

"Excellent, and what did they do to us?"

"We lost one of the ECM aircraft, one of the tankers and three fighters."

Morales stands up and yells. "So when we loss five to one, Admiral. We're doing excellent."

"Well, we eliminated the threat, General."

"How much will the second fighter cost us, then? Maybe four aircraft, so we can declare a major victory." He walks up to the admiral and his aides. "We need to do a lot better. I would hate to think of the consequences if we fail."

"Sir." A sergeant comes into the office. "You have a call on line two. It is President Fidel."

"Very good. Gentlemen, if you wouldn't mind." He ushers them out the door. Picking up the phone, he clears his throat. "This is General Morales."

"General, this is Fidel. I do not understand what you are doing, and I order you to recall all of our forces from the Gulf. You are to put yourself under house arrest. I will be leaving Bogota in just a few minutes. When I arrive in Havana, you will meet me at the palace. Do you understand?"

"Sí, Fidel, I understand."

"I want General Quintano to assume command of the forces. And I want to talk to the next senior officer, now."

"Sí, Fidel, I understand. What I understand is that your time has passed. A new age is about to dawn for Cuba, and its leader will be me. You are a stone around the neck of every Cuban. In your dealings with the Russians, they walked all over you. Well, now is their time to pay. I would suggest that you ask Bolivia for political asylum. If you come back to Cuba, I will shoot you myself."

"Have you gone mad? You're about to throw the lives of Cuban fighters away for nothing."

"Throw them away? Like you did in Africa, and other places in the world? If anyone should wear a bloody shroud, it is you. Now that your amigos the Russians have broken into parts, you yap at the world like a small dog. Well, I'm putting the wolf back inside the hound. Like them, you kiss the Americans' asses. I will deal with them from a position of strength."

"Morales, stop this thing. You will destroy Cuba in your madness."

"Goodbye, old man. Again, do not come back." He hangs up the phone.

He stretches and straightens his uniform, and then opens the door to the outer office. "Everyone, I have just spoken to Fidel." All heads in the control center turn towards him in silence. "He wishes us the greatest success in the coming battle. He only wishes he were here."

A cheer goes up from the men and women in the command center. The news teams gather around him to ask more questions. Then rush to get the news out to the people.

"Admiral." He waves his hand towards the door. "We have a battle to win."

"Have the other bombers taken off yet?"

"General, there has been some difficulty getting them loaded. They're going out with a mixed load of ordnance."

"I don't give a shit—get them going. If they're not in the air in five minutes. I'll give an order to have the loading officer shot. Do we understand each other, Admiral?"

The admiral picks up a phone. "Yes, General."

RUSSIAN WEAPONS PERSONNEL IN HELOCOPTER
THE GULF

"Can that thing go any faster?" The Yak pilot looks over at the little Kamov copter. It is bent forwards, both rotors wiping the misty air.

"We're at max now. This thing is shuddering like hell."

"Roger. We're about 140 miles from the demark line. After that the Americans can help you out."

"Yeah, if we don't shake to pieces first. Our two passengers are a bit nervous."

The Yak pulls in front of the helicopter in a wide circle and flies down his other side, his radar searching for any sign of other planes.

High above them, two radars go active, and the jets roll over into a shallow dive. As soon as they have a lock, their missiles race for the two targets. The missile alarm in both the Yak and the helicopter goes off at the same time. The Yak pulls ahead of the helicopter, turns and races directly over him.

"When I yell break left, do it fast."

"Roger."

The Yak passes over him, and pulls his nose up towards the two attackers. As he rises, chaff and flares are fired out the back. "Break now."

The helicopter slams to the left, as two missiles slam into the sea. The explosion buffets them as they level off. The Yak gets a lock and fires straight up; the two jets go into evasive action and split. They pass each other at high speed; the Yak then goes into a steep diving left turn. As the Mig pulls up, the Yak falls in behind. He gets a lock and fires. As the missile leaves his plane, the alarm in his plane goes off. Both he and the Mig roll over to dive and throw chaff into the sky. His missile catches the Mig just behind the cockpit. Its explosion comes just before his own. Both fighters plummet from the sky and crash into the sea.

The second Mig looks over the crashes, and resumes the hunt for the helicopter. He quickly spots it and flies to intercept. He extends his wings and flies down next to the chopper. For a minute, they both look at each other. He pushes his throttle forward and moves away. He gains speed and does a slow turn to come in from the side. The helicopter pilot begins some evasive maneuvers, even though he knows it will only prolong the inevitable.

As the Mig moves in, he goes to his guns and fires at the elusive little chopper. The machine gun rounds tear up the water as the walk across the surface. The captain pulls the helicopter straight up, but the sound of a few rounds hitting the ship rattles through the compartment. The Mig dives under him, and goes into a slow climb on the other side. He takes a slow left turn to bring the nose around to begin his second attack. The co-pilot looks back into the cabin. Two rounds came through the door, and exited out the other side. "The two submariners—now I know why they choose subs, Captain."

"I wish I had two right now."

"He is coming in from your side. Tell me where he is."

Ninety miles in front of him, a Phoenix long range missile drops from the belly of an F-14 and disappears into the mist.

The Mig slowly lines up his plane for an attack. The co-pilot stares at the jet. He sees flashes from its under belly. "Sir, we have—" The first rounds hit in mid sentence. The exploding glass from the right causes the pilot to veer left. Rounds move back into the cabin, hitting one of the crewmen and one of the weapons people. An alarm in the Mig causes the pilot to pull his nose up. As he does, a round catches the right engine. Smoke comes out of the engine as the Mig flies over them. The captain doesn't understand why he has stopped firing. They are sitting ducks. He watches the Mig fire chaff and flares, and then begin a steep climb. Just as the entire plane is going vertical, a missile slams into its side. The plane disintegrates and falls into the sea.

"Helicopter, this is Sky 1. Over."

The captain struggles to pull it back on the original heading. He is surprised to hear a Russian speaking over his headset. "Helicopter, this is Sky 1, what is your condition?"

He compensates the loss of the right engine, and keys his mike. "Sky 1, who are you?"

"This is American tactical control; we have you inbound. We are sending escort. Over."

"We are in bad shape. We have three dead and the loss of one engine. We have also sustained structural damage to the right side. Over."

"Roger. You should see your escort soon. We have also dispatched Coast Guard helicopters. A Coast Guard cutter is also moving down your line of flight with escorts. Over."

"Roger, Sky 1. We thank you for the help."

"Roger. Remain on this frequency. We will bring you in. Sky 1 out."

The Russian captain looks over the damage to his ship. The 23 mm canon rounds did their job well. The window and part of the door on the co-pilot's side are gone. A fierce wind blows into and around the cabin. The body of his co-pilot shakes with the movement of the ship. Holes are torn in the right side; the crewman and the weapons man are slumped to that side. The other crewman is trying to calm down the other weapons man who is now hysteric. Blood covers the walls and floor of the craft.

The radar intercept officer on the lead F-14 alerts his pilot.

"Sir, we have two bogies due south. Signature would suggest additional Cuban fighters inbound at fifty-five miles. That would put them approximately thirty miles behind helicopter."

"Roger. Give me the frequency of the two fighters."

"Roger. Hailing frequency adjustment. You're clear."

"Roger."

"To approaching Cuban fighters, this is the United States Navy, alert flight. We are responding to a distress call. We thank you for your assistance. But we request you turn back now."

"Sir, their high lark radar will have picked us up by now. If they use their medium range missiles, the helicopter is still in danger."

"Roger. To alert aircraft, take your positions."

The F-14 Tomcats flying in tandem move to each side. They now form one line.

The two Cuban fighters see the blips on their radar go from two to four. Both run a lock on the helicopter.

"American fighters, you have moved beyond the 100-mile demark. We see this as a act of aggression and will take appropriate action."

"Cuban fighters, this is Captain Randall, United States Navy. I have four F-14 Tomcats. If you continue or if any act of aggression is seen, we will assume you have chosen to die for your country. We will facilitate your choice and ensure that outcome. Over."

"Sir, the Cubans are turning back."

"Roger. Three and four, you're air cap. We'll go down to check the helicopter."

Two of the Tomcats climb to 15,000 feet. The captain and his wingman begin a slow spiral dive to do a visual on the helicopter. As they flatten out 300 feet above the surface, their radar locates the Russian helicopter. At 300 feet above the water, the Russian captain fights to control his ship. Black whiffs of smoke trail from the dead right engine.

"Sir, you should have visual three miles off the nose."

"Roger. Have him. We'll pass on each side."

With their wings fully out, the two huge fighters pull alongside the damaged craft. They wag their wings and pull forward. The captain watches the two fighters pass and move forward. They are soon lost in the mist.

"Sky 1, this is the alert flight. Over."

"Roger, Alert. We have you inbound with helicopter. Over."

"Roger, Sky 1. I'd say he will be lucky to reach demark. Over."

"Roger. Alert 1, hold."

"Alert 1, be advised that we show Cuban fighters in a tight banking turn. You have a threat possibility. Out."

The two fighters do a tight roll and pull up at 4,000 feet, facing the Cubans. "Alert 1, this is Alert 3. The bogies have turned and are back on their original course. Sir, we have a launch."

"Roger. You're cleared to fire."

"Sir, we now have two missiles going towards our air cap. And two missiles inbound, towards the helicopter and us."

"Roger." The two fighters do an inverted roll. "I'm going down to pull the missiles off the chopper. You're the shooter."

"Roger." The wingman pulls a tight right turn and speeds away.

The captain pulls an inward loop and dives for the water. As he levels off at 300 feet, the swing-wings pull back against the body. As he passes over the helicopter, he pulls the nose almost vertical and goes to afterburners. Chaff and flares are shot out. The huge signature of the bottom of the F-14 pulls the missiles to him.

"Sir, we have succeed in pulling the missiles off the helicopter."

"Roger, Decon." They climb at a forty-five-degree angle to the missiles.

"Rattler, I think it's time to use all that expensive training you have."

"Roger, Deacon. Call the angles for me."

As they climb, the wingman fires two Sidewinder missiles at the inbound missiles from a forty-five-degree angle to the right.

"Sir, Alert 2 has fired on inbounds."

The two Sidewinders slam into the missiles. The explosions take one with them. The last missile continues to press for the kill.

"Rattler, we are at full ECM. On my command break right and dive. One, two, three, *now!*" As the fighter dives, more chaff and flares are fired. The missile passes over their heads and explodes behind them.

"Holy shit, that was close."

The air cap fighters have also evaded their two missiles and come back on course facing the Cuban fighters. They each target one of the fighters, and at the tone, pickle the missiles away. Two Phoenix missiles fall from the Tomcats and race forward.

The Cubans fired and did a split "S" maneuver, diving on the deck and push forward at full speed. They want to put as much distance as they can between themselves and the American fighters. The risky shots have been their doom. Their alarms activate. They pull up and fire decoys. They begin maneuvering right and left. The onboard radar of the missile locks on its prey. One last turn and the missiles slam into the planes. Chunks of aircraft settle to the surface of the water.

"Alert 3 and 4, we show two bogyes down at fifty-five miles. Over."

"Roger, Sky 1, confirmed."

"Good shooting, gentlemen, and stay alert."

"Roger, Rattler. It's like I always say, 'It's not just a job....'"

The others all chime in, "It's an adventure."

As Rattler's wingman rejoins him, they fly to get back to the helicopter.

"Alert 2, good shooting." He wags his wings.

"You know, Deacon, I love this place."

HELICOPTER
ON BEACH NEAR BOMBER

"Bulldog, this is touchdown. Over."

"Roger. This is Bulldog."

"Colonel, this is Captain Nelson. I have an urgent matter for you."

"Yes, sir."

"Our weather people here at the base have confirmed that the thunderstorms which have been passing over are now being pulled back towards the hurricane. Our out boundaries markers are showing winds that are between fifty-five and sixty knots; they will hit your area in about ten to fifteen minuets. We advise you to ground all helicopters in operation. Duration they believe will be about an hour. It is expected to drop intense rain and lightning."

"Roger, Captain. We'll bring aircraft down. We now have one bad boy in camp. The other should be here soon. Over."

"Excellent. Touchdown out."

The colonel grabs the Tac radio. "All units prepare for high winds fifty-five to sixty knots. All aircraft are to remain at their landing sites; duration should be less than one hour. Over."

The pilot looks back into the cabin, "Lieutenant, we have been ordered to remain at our landing site and sit tight for an hour. There are strong winds and rain coming in."

The three helicopters shut down their engines. Another helicopter with a pallet of sandbags lands in the woodlands near them. A crewman opens the side door and two of them jump out. They pull out a large canister and run with it up to the lead helicopter. The gunny slides the side door open and gets out. He looks around. The sky is overcast, and the wind is moderate.

"Why are we waiting here, Gunny?" Susie jumps down beside him.

"Apparently there is some really bad weather coming in from the north."

They walk in front of the helicopter and look in that direction. The clouds coming at them are coal black, with streaks of lightning leading the way. "I think I would agree with your weather people."

"Yes, ma'am." He walks over to the canister and opens it up. "Well, this is good."

The lieutenant and the aircrew join them at the canister. "It looks like a good supply of sandwiches and coffee. There are some sodas in here also."

"You first, Susie." The lieutenant waves his hand at the canister.

"Gee, I think I'll try the turkey. Do you think it's real?"

Gunny and the lieutenant look at it. "It looks kind of like turkey." A marine from one of the other helicopters walks up to them. "Ma'am, this was in one of the other canisters." He hands her a bag with a note on it.

She sets it down and reads the note.

"Dr. Davies, you didn't look like the coffee type, or a big soda drinker. So I sent along some apple and orange juice. If you need more, please call your friendly Beach Master, Commander Marino."

"Well, that was nice of the commander. I do prefer the juices."

The gunship crews come over and get sandwiches and drinks also. As they finish up, the aircrews are checking their equipment and the choppers. Susie puts her extra drinks into the cabin and slips on her poncho as the first big drops begin to fall. Her hand rests on the side of the helicopter. She can feel the push from the wind as the first gust hits them. They all scramble inside as the first bolts of lightning flash over their heads. Susie looks at her watch; the hands stand at 2:50 P.M.

"I feel sorry for anyone out in this."

The wind slams into the side of the helicopter and pushes it slightly on the wet grass. The rain hits the side of the helicopter like hammer strokes. They all get as comfortable as they can and settle in for the duration.

BOMB SITE, NUMBER EIGHT
LOUISIANA

Captain Johnson gets off the radio and walks over to the others.

"Sergeant, let's get everyone moving. The Colonel wants all helicopters down. There is more bad weather coming this way."

"Aye, aye, sir."

"Doctor, are you ready to go?"

Emanuel watches as they finally get the bomb free, and it rises up into the air. "Yes, I'm ready."

"Good, we have to get out of here, and get to the helicopters. We are going to stand down for a while, maybe up to an hour. We don't want to be caught out here in the swamp."

"I'll take the rear, sergeant."

"Right, sir. Move them out point."

The file of men begins working their way through the mud. Johnson watches as a charge is set in the pit, and he and the demolition man move after the others.

The captain puts his hands up to his mouth and yells, "Fire in the hole." They run forward to join them on the trail. When they're about 100 yards out, the charge detonates in a fountain of mud. Their pace picks up under the darkening sky.

CHAPTER 11

MIG-29
THE GULF

As Norba moves southeast of the squadron, the weather continues to deteriorate. He is flying deeper into the storm track of Evita. His passive radar sweeps ahead; it remains clear. He pulls the nose of the Mig up to gain height. At the higher levels, it gives him the advantages over the Cuban fighters. At 25,000 feet he breaks into the clear blue sky. The bright sun bathes the fighter. At fifty miles, blips begin appearing on his scope. First four and then eight, finally twelve. Three groups of four planes each move towards the ships. As he closes on the group, his equipment alerts him that he is being scanned by strong radar. He turns his head and looks over his right shoulder in the direction of the Ilyushin refueling aircraft.

As he gains more altitude, four of the blips continue on course towards him, and the other two groups break towards the northwest. The four unknowns gain altitude, and spread out in formation. Their speed increases and the distance between the two adversaries closes quickly. The four sleek Mig-21 fighters break through the cloud canopy together. Two level off at 25,000, and the other two climb higher into the sky. From 38,000 feet, Norba watches the planes' progress. He tracks the two lower fighters and gets a radar lock and tone. He fires his last two Atoll missiles. His look-down radar tracks the missiles towards their targets. He throws the nose down, and dives to meet the other two in his realm.

The Cubans also have their mid-range missiles and go into the attack as Norba fires. The two below pull their noses up and lock and fire. The other two roll over and fire from 32,000 feet. The four missiles have him in a box. Pulling his stick back, he dispenses chaff and flares. He goes to afterburners. He rockets towards the heavens jinking and twisting. The lower jets go into evasive action to elude the two missiles. One flies by and disappears into the clouds below them. But the other finds it mark and catches the second Mig in the tail section. The pilot ejects as the fighter begins a flat spin into the clouds. As his parachute fills, he looks up at his comrade and watches him disappear in a steep climb. He looks past his feet; the dark clouds seem to be reaching up for him. His thoughts go to procedures that may save his life in the coming trial. As he slips into the clouds, lightning strikes beneath him illuminate his path. He may be facing a harder enemy now than in his plane.

As Norba twists his plane one more time, the last of the missiles fly past him, leaving white trails in the clear sky. At 45,000 feet he pulls over. With the sun directly over his shoulders, he noses the big jet over and dives at the two fighters.

As the range closes, he is able to make out the shape and type of aircraft he will soon destroy. He had enjoyed flying the Mig-21, even after so many years. It still remained a formidable threat in the air. He visualizes the pilots turning their heads, trying to locate him.

At less than a mile, he fires. An Aphid missile zooms ahead of him, catching the first jet. The second rolls and dives, with him right behind. He goes to cannon and pursues the Cuban fighter. As he lines up the shot, time seems to stand still. The other jet seems to just hang in the air in front of him. The first of the 30 mm cannon rounds fly by its right side; the tracers disappear below. As he adjusts his fire, pieces of the fighter seem to rip off and fly in every direction. Smoke boils from his engine.

From the back, he watches as the pilot ejects. As he rolls over and nears the clouds, his missile alert sounds. He looks back over his shoulder and sees the deadly front view of the Mig-21. Norba feels the hit of the missile, but it does not explode. It has impacted at the base of his left tail fin and has torn a gapping hole through it. As he fights the controls, tracers fly by his canopy. He pulls up and applies power, but he can't escape the machine gun rounds. They tear into the left engine, and an alarm goes off in his cockpit. Rolling over, he dives into the storm below, and shuts down the engine. Black smoke trails away. The Cuban fighter breaks off and turns to rejoin the bombers. Norba's radar picks up groups of aircraft at different distances as he finishes a tight turn and heads back towards the squadron.

BRIDGE OF THE *MOSKVA*

"Sir, we just received a call from Raven 2."

"Very good, and the Cuban bombers?"

"They split behind us and have moved towards the Cuban ships."

"This weather should keep them off us for a while, maybe."

"Maybe." The captain and the admiral look at him.

"Sir, the Mig-27 is a real bulldog. We built it well. Even in this weather, it could make a run at us." The ship lurches and rolls violently. "Well, Captain, that's nice to know. We're having trouble steering, the squadron is fighting for its life, and you bring us encouraging news. A deadly little fighter-bomber that we sold the Cubans is about to attack us. It's a pity we didn't use our missiles and defensive armament against each other. We seemed to have wasted our time worrying about the NATO forces, when in fact, we will probably sustain grievous damages, from our own arsenal."

"Admiral we just received a call from the Raven 1. He has shot down three Cuban fighters. But he sustained damage and is operating on one engine. He is trying to get back over the fleet for added protection." The admiral grabs hard onto the rail as the ship dips and rolls in the storm. "We may not be able to assist him much in this type of weather, Captain."

"Yes, sir. He can still be effective against the bombers using his missiles. And if he has to crash, we have a chance of picking him up." They both grab on as the ship rolls once more. They look out the front windows. The admiral looks at him. "I know, sir, it would be a slim hope of picking him up. But that's the best he has."

"Sir." The air captain joins them. "We have a track on Raven 1. He is losing some fuel; we have him south of us. He is being vectored towards the Ilyushin tanker." The plotting officer Pstygo comes up from below and joins them at the windows. "Admiral, I have some good news."

He looks at the young officer. "Is it that Russian ships are not resupplying the Cubans?"

He looks at him quizzically. "No, sir. We have made contact with the submarine."

"Excellent. We were beginning to give up hope."

"They said that they had sustained some damage but are prepared to fire their torpedoes. They want to know if you want them to fire in tandem with the squadron or to fire as they see fit."

"Pstygo, where are they?"

"Captain, they are twenty miles just off the bow on the port side."

"Well, Captain, how should we advise them?"

"I would advise them to fire on their own, Admiral."

"Very good. Have that sent to them, Pstygo."

"Captain." The admiral looks at the other man. "We seem to be thinking along the same lines as each new situation arrives."

"Thank you, Admiral. From you sir, that is a definite compliment."

WAREHOUSE ON THE DOCK
CUBA

As the police car pulls in, Brock can hear the staccato of automatic gunfire. They pull in behind two police cars parked by the side of a building. As Captain Bodus climbs out, he gives orders for some of the men to join the officers behind the cars in the street. As they move to the position, bullets hit the cars and ricochet down the street. Brock joins him and they look around the corner of the building. The scene on the street looks like a small war in progress. Two police cars are on fire about half way down the block. The cab had run through a gate leading to a two-story warehouse. They had tried to follow but were caught at the gate. Two bodies lie behind one of the cars, and a third is across the street on the sidewalk. Police cars block the other end of the street and are firing into the warehouse. They duck back as rounds from the warehouse hit the wall and spray the cars. Brock and the captain talk over the noise of the gunfire. "Señor Brock, any suggestions?" Brock pulls in a large breath and slowly blows it out. "Well, they certainly have not made it easy."

"Sí." Bodus gets on the radio. "Lieutenant, send a group down the front side of the buildings from your end and try to occupy the building next to them. I'll send a group down from this end to do the same."

"Sí, Captain."

"We have made contact with the local army group that was helping with the storm damage. They are sending over some men and two armored vehicles. They're on their way and will contact you soon."

"Very good. I'll get back to you in a minute."

He tells the sergeant to get men together and move down the street. They check their armored vests and helmets. Brock looks at the men, and then back at the captain.

"Do you have an extra helmet?"

The captain smiles, and gives him his. Brock puts it on and checks his radio. One of the policeman walks up to them and hands Brock a bandoleer of shot gun shells.

"Thanks, that should do it."

Bodus grabs his hand, "Good luck, Comrade."

He goes back to the radio as Brock joins the men on the other side of the street. As soon as he is with them, they start down the face of the buildings. He can see the other group moving also; they cut through a fence and run to the front of the warehouse. The buildings are about 100 feet apart and set back from the road. Their angle along the front of the other warehouses keeps them out of the line of fire. Two men go to the corner of the building and look around. They are immediately fired on; the bullets hit the wall and cement around them.

Brock moves up with the sergeant as others try and open the doors to the building.

"Sergeant, everything is locked. We'll have to shoot it open."

"Sí, we'll shoot it open." Brock walks over and cocks his shotgun. Just as he is about to blow the door open, a cry comes from inside. "Señor, stop, please."

The policeman talks to the men inside as Brock lowers his gun.

"They are the workmen in this building. When the gunfire started, they locked everything up and hid inside."

"All right, let's get them out."

The door is opened and they go inside. About twenty men stand looking as the policemen move in. The sergeant calls the captain, and they take the men to the side of the buildings and send them back to the police cars down the block. Brock goes with the policemen down the center of the building, and they move to a large side door facing the other building. One of the men unlocks it, and begins to slide it open. As he pushes the door, a volley of gunfire slams into the door around him. It catches him and another policeman, and they fall in the opening. The bullets run down the side of the corrugated steel building, tearing holes in the walls. Everyone hits the floor. They get behind boxes and anything else for cover. When the firing stops, they look at each other. Brock looks over the top of the box he is behind. Light beams shine in from the holes in the wall and door. The two men lie still in the opening.

The sergeant sends one of the men on the other side of the opening to push the door closed. He works his way around boxes, and pushes the big door closed. As he does more fire tears into the door, and moves back towards him. He ducks behind some boxes. The rounds rip the metal side of the building. As soon as the gunfire stops, Brock and an officer crawl over the top of some boxes, and reach the side of the door. He reaches out and grabs one of the men on the floor and pulls him back. He takes a breath; the other man is about three feet out. He sets the shotgun down and lies flat on the ground and grabs the man by his arm. As he pulls, a volley of fire hits the door. It takes a random line across the section near him and stops. Brock pulls the man behind the boxes, and they drag him to the center of the warehouse. The sergeant checks both men and gets on his radio.

"Yes, sir. One dead, the other hurt badly. We need some medical help, now."

The echo of gunfire runs between the buildings, then there is an explosion. "Sergeant, you have medical people on their way. That explosion you just heard came from them. They have grenades. You're lucky, Sergeant, that the other group did not run into any resistance. They sent a team of four to assault the warehouse. About halfway across, they were cut down by gunfire. We're waiting for the army to show up with some armored cars."

"Sí, Captain. We will set our position here. Out." Brock and the sergeant look around the warehouse. "This place is full of farm and construction parts." Brock points to a long crate about three feet high. "That looks like a dozer blade. Have you got someone who can drive a forklift?"

"Yeah, me."

The sergeant moves to the back of the warehouse and jumps on the lift. He picks up the crate and drops it ten feet from the door. He parks the lift to the side, and he and three other policemen get behind the dozer blade. They position their weapons to fire at the door across the alley.

A rope is tied to the door. "Pull the door now!" The big door slides sideways and immediately comes under fire. As the door moves out of the line of fire, they open up on the gunman. He is forced to duck behind some boxes as the concentrated fire follows him. As they watch for movement from the other door, a small, dark, round object flies out of the dark void. "Grenade, grenade, everyone down!"

It hits the front of the dozer blade crate; the men duck down behind their cover. The explosion sends shards of hot metal in all directions. The concussion is deafening, and pieces of the crate are thrown into the air. Brock rolls back over and fires across into the door. Another grenade hits the side of the building and explodes. A gaping hole is ripped in the wall above Brock. The men open fire again, driving the man down. The sergeant pulls the pin on a grenade of his own, stands, and tosses it at the other door. As it is flying, he pulls a second grenade and tosses it also.

"Everyone down!" They all duck behind their cover. The first grenade hits and slides into the partially open door. The explosion blows it back and off its runners. It crashes to the floor inside the warehouse. The second one follows the door inside and explodes. Some crates and boxes near the door begin to burn. They fire into the door, and then wait to see what the gunman will do.

"Sergeant, this is Captain Bodus."

He pulls the radio up and talks for a minute, then puts it down. "That was the captain. We are to hold our position until the armored cars get here. So get comfortable."

Brock looks through the hole in the wall. The fire is burning more of the boxes. Black smoke is beginning to pour out of the opening.

MATANZAS AIR BASE
CUBA

The Russian crew chief watches as four Mig-21 fighters taxi into position to takeoff. He moves away from the window and walks over to the lieutenant.

"Sir, the fighters are about to leave, and there are four attack bombers moving up behind them." He looks around the hangar at the guards. "It is now or never, sir."

"Get the men in position, Chief. We'll move when the fighters take off."

"Right." He walks over to some men working on a Mig-23. He explains what will be going on and then moves to another group having coffee in the back. The men break up, and two walk into the hallway past one of the guards. "Got to use the head, all right?" He nods his head, then goes back to watching the men around the coffeepot. Other men work their way up to the front, near the two guards by the hangar doors. As the fighters begin to take off, the lieutenant yells, "Now, Comrades, now!"

The men fall upon the guards and wrestle them to the ground. They disarm them and look back at the guard near the back door. As he starts to move forward, two men jump on him from behind. He is knocked unconscious with a wrench. The men are disarmed, tied up, and put in a cleaning closet "Sir, we have three machine guns and three pistols." He climbs up to the cockpit of the fighter and hands down another pistol and a flare gun. He looks the jet over.

"Chief, are there rocket pods for this thing?"

The chief looks up at him, and then around the hangar."Yes, sir, we pulled them off and put them in the back." They look around and spot the pods on a loading dolly. "How fast can we get them back on the plane?"

"Sir, there is no engine in this thing."

"I know, Chief, but if we can get those pods mounted, we can use a tow vehicle up front and one of the quick start vehicles for power. It would give us a pretty good punch."

"But sir, how would you aim this thing?"

"The front tow would line me up on the planes, and by moving around, we could disperse the shots." The chief shakes his head and yells for the pods to be mounted. "Get the tow hooked up and run the other vehicle under the right wing." He explains what they are going to try to do. The men quickly lay out sixty feet of power cord from the vehicle. The driver of the tow puts on a headset as the lieutenant climbs into the cockpit. He puts his helmet on and talks to the tow driver. He gives the chief a thumbs up. One of the men runs to the controls to open the hangar doors and waits. "Chief, there are two guards on foot in front of the doors. And there are two BTR recon vehicle about thirty feet out." The quick start vehicle starts its engine and the instrument panel on the jet comes to life. The lieutenant throws switches to arm the pods and gives the chief a thumbs up. The three men with machine guns go to the center of the doors, and the chief joins them. He looks around the hangar; the other men have taken cover. "Now, the doors."

As the huge doors begin to open, the guards in front are caught off guard and stare at the huge sliding doors. The chief and the others rush out and open fire on them. The two in front are cut down first. They run at the recon vehicles firing. Men inside move forward and pick up the weapons from the dead guards and join the others at the vehicles. The sound of the four jets taxiing into position has covered their initial move. They overwhelm the men at the vehicles and pass out weapons to men coming up behind them. Men get in to drive the vehicles and man the machine guns on top. The chief gets behind one of the machine guns and signals the other to pull out of the way of the jet that is just coming out of the hangar. The lieutenant yells in the mike, and the tow driver starts forward. The guards on each side of them begin to fire at them, and they return fire. The tow vehicle pulls the jet out and turns it to face the end of the runway. The Cuban bombers are about 500 feet away. The recon vehicles move to each side of the doors and open fire on the guards on each side. Other vehicles begin to move towards them from the front of other hangars. Guards from across the runway begin firing on them; they fire back from behind the tow and from the side of the vehicles. The bombers, seeing the situation, begin to taxi onto the main runway, trying to take off.

"Get down, now!"

The other men firing from behind it lay flat on the ground. As the first two planes turn onto the runway, four rockets are fired from each pod. The noise and smoke engulf the men in front of the plane. The others watch as the 57 mm rockets fly into the two lead jets. In turn, he catches the back of the lead jet and the front of the other. The planes explode from the impact, and then the ordnance on them causes a second huge explosion. Everyone around the area is hammered by the concussion of the bombs and gas going up. The explosion consumes the two trailing jets, and they explode in unison.

Farther down the taxiway, the other four jets are trying to turn around. They turn on a side road and move back in front of the hangars. "Pull me to the right, so I can get a shot at the others." As the tow pulls the jet around, a bullet hits the driver; he slumps over the wheel. One of the men on the ground jumps up, pulls him off, and gets in the seat. Gunfire from a machine gun rakes across the fighter. As the plane slowly turns, the rounds tear holes in the wings and tail. An RPG is fired from a guard near the runway and hits by the tow vehicle. The driver and a man near him are killed. The last bomber moves by the front of the plane when the lieutenant gets ready to fire. "Shit." Looking down, he sees the tow vehicle and the dead men on the ground. He watches the other four bombers move down the hangars to get out of the way. But in front of him are two tanker planes. He smiles to himself and fires a burst of rockets into them. Eight rockets fly across the runway and slam into the two Antonov tankers. The fuel in the planes adds to the explosion. He watches from the cockpit as men begin moving across the runway under the smoke. They are firing RPG at the vehicles, and the hangar is hit by withering machine gun fire. As men are hit, others grab up their weapons and continue the fight. The chief runs out of machine gun ammo and abandons the armored car. He sees the lieutenant and works his way across the hangar. He runs up to the airplane and signals the lieutenant. He points across the field to the control tower. The lieutenant nods his head as he feels the plane move. Cuban troops appear at the burning armored car across the hangar. One goes to his knees and fires an RPG; it hits the plane just behind the wings.

The explosion blows the tail of the fighter off. The chief lines the plane up with the control tower. He ducks rifle fire. Rounds hit the canopy as the lieutenant fires the last of the rockets in two bursts of eight. They leave white trails as they cross the field and explode at the base of the tower. The tower shudders under the first barrage, and is given its death knell by the second volley. An explosion at the armored car near them kills the last of the valiant Russian fighters. The chief puts the tow in gear and drives out of the hangar, with the half fighter behind. As the tower crumbles into the smoke at its base, the chief raises his hand and yells. Machine gun fire from the front hits him, and he slumps forward. The Cubans run up to the plane and fire at the cockpit. The canopy blows and the lieutenant ejects from the plane. The seat kicks off, and the chute deploys.

The Cubans fire up at him. As he descends, he tosses two grenades down. He slumps in his harness as the machine gun rounds find their target. The grenades hit near the gunman and explode. The Cubans search the hangar for any survivors and release the three men in the cleaning room. They mill around the front of the hangar and watch the fires burning across the field and on the runway. Fire trucks try to knock down the flames at the transports and the fighters. Black smoke and the smell of cordite fill the air. It blows across the field and wisps over the thirty-five dead Russians. The four attack bombers again get on the runway; they race down it and lift into the sky. They join the four Mig-21 fighters, leave the burning airfield, and fly north.

CUBAN COMMAND CENTER, 2:00 P.M.

A lieutenant runs into Morales's office. The general is on the phone and looks up. "Sir, the Russians at Matanzas. They attacked the bombers and destroyed half the flight."

"What? What are you saying?" Morales slams the phone down.

The others in the room go silent. The young lieutenant seems dumb struck. Morales gets up, walks up to him, and takes a message out of his hand. He reads the message and crumples it in his hand.

"Get me the guard commander at Matanzas."

He throws the note to Admiral Rivera and storms into the outer office. Rivera reads the note and passes it on to his aids. They can hear Morales yelling at the personnel in the other room. He storms back into the office; his phone begins to ring.

"This is General Morales. What the hell is going on?"

The captain on the other end explains the situation and the effects of the attack. Morales is livid and demands to speak to the commander of his private guard.

"Captain, I want you to take command of the base, now! Are there any more Russians on the base?" He listens and looks around the room. "So all thirty-five Russians were killed?" He nods his head as he listens. "When we hang up, I want you to take the base security officer out and shoot him. That is a direct order from me. Do you understand? Good." He hangs up the phone.

"Well, Admiral? What effect will this have on the plan?"

"Well, General. We will send a quarter less firepower against the Russians. The additional fighters are each loaded with two Aphid close range missiles and two general-purpose bombs. The actual type of bombs is not clearly known. So it is a mixed combination of ordnance. The weapons storage at the base was pretty well used up."

"Damn!" He slams his fist into the desk. "And what about that Russian fighter?"

"We have a confirmed hit from one of the fighters; rocket and machine gun fire hit him. He was last seen falling into the clouds on fire."

"Well, you mean we had some success?"

"Somewhat. We lost three fighters."

"What else is going on?"

The admiral looks at the men around the table. "We have a report from the Ilyushin. They picked up a radio message from a high frequency transmitter."

"So what the hell does that mean?"

"We're not sure. But it is the type of message sent by a submarine trailing an antenna. They tried to get a fix, but it was too late."

"What the fuck? Did you not tell me that we sank the second sub, Admiral?"

"Yes, sir. From the report we assumed it was sunk."

"It is getting real detrimental, Admiral, to assume anything. Do you understand?" The phone rings and diverts Morales's attention. He picks up the phone and talks to one of his guard captains. "Where are you? Forget the ministry and get to the radio station and shut it down. And when you're through there," he turns his back on the admiral and lowers his voice, "send troops over to Bacio Del Sol. I'm sure some of the dogs are hiding at that location." He listens and turns back to face the admiral. "Yes, use whatever force is necessary. Now get to the station and kill that broadcast." He hangs up the phone and walks over to a radio and turns it on. The others in the room listen as the voice of Fidel blares from the speaker.

"I repeat, General Quintano is now in charge of all military forces in Cuba. And General Morales is to be put under house arrest. I will join you soon and put an end to this madness." The message is repeated.

Morales turns the radio off and walks into the next room. The people sit silent. He walks over to a radio and turns it off. "This is an American ploy to distract us from our mission. They have done a good job of faking Fidel's voice. But as I have said, he is behind us one hundred percent. Now we all need to get back to the job at hand." He walks back into his office and closes the door. Walking over to his chair, he sits behind the desk.

"The attack, Admiral."

"Sir, the weather is quite severe. Both our ships and the Russians are fighting fifty to sixty mile an hour winds and intense rain. We suggest the attack be held off until the conditions clear."

Morales just looks at the admiral and picks up the phone.

"Have two gunships sent to the command center, and stand by. Also, have two gunships sent east to find General Quintano. He is now considered an agent of the Russians and is to be shot on sight. Do you understand? Good." He hangs up the phone; his eyes never leave the Admiral's. He looks at his watch; it is 1:20.

"Admiral, the attack will begin in ten minutes. If for any reason it does not, you and your entire staff will be executed. I hope there is no misunderstanding."

"No, sir, General."

WITH THE POLICE IN THE PARKING LOT
CUBA

"General!" The pilot signals Quintano over to the side of the helicopter. "We are getting a radio transmission on the civilian frequency. I think you may be interested." He listens as the voice of Fidel comes out of the speaker. The message is repeated twice and suddenly goes quiet. "What happened?" Quintano looks at the officer. "I don't know, General." He turns the knobs. "But they are totally off the air."

"I think I know. They were helped by General Morales's men."

"Sir." The pilot hands Quintano a handset and plugs in the cord. "General Quintano, this is Colonel Ruiz."

"Ruben, did you hear the broadcast?"

"Yes, sir."

"We will need to move quickly to contain Morales."

"Sí, I have contacted Colonel Guterus at Holguin. He is loyal to you and will back his troops away from Guantánamo at your orders."

"Good, and Colonel Arcenaga at Santa Clara?"

"He was in the field and will get back to me. But I would say you have control of the island from Colon east."

"Very good, we will need to isolate Morales in Havana first, and then into the command center."

"General, we have a report from Matanzas. The Russians at the base attacked the bombers there and apparently blew some of them up. They were all killed in the assault by the base troops."

"I'm in Cardenas. We're still tracking one of the saboteurs. Where are you now?"

"I'm at the base. We were helping the people in San José. I have recalled all our troops and will await your orders. Also, I have placed special guards around your residence, so you need not worry."

"You are a good friend and officer, Ruben. I also fear for my father's well being, with Morales's men on the loose."

"I will dispatch forces to Del Sol immediately. Hold one, General." Someone else talks to Ruiz. Quintano looks around the parking lot and at the town. It doesn't seem to be aware of the forces moving about in Cuba and out over the Gulf. "General, you are in grave danger."

"What has happened?"

"Sir, Morales has issued an order for you to be shot on sight. He said that the message from Fidel was a hoax, and they have shut down the radio station. We also have news that Morales has ordered two gunships to the command post and two others to proceed east to find you. They are leaving from Artimisa."

"It didn't take him long. Ruiz, I will be leaving here soon. Send some gunships to me. Get your group together and meet me on the main highway to Matanzas, about ten miles out. I'll wait for you there."

"Sí, General. We will be there."

Quintano calls the other colonels and asks for their support to regain command of the island. They both agree to follow him. His orders are to back the troops off of Guantánamo and secure all military bases in their areas. If they join them, that is fine. If they refuse, they are to be taken by force. Troops are to move from Santa Claria up the main highway, to join him at Matanzas. They agree and then begin to move on the task before them. Quintano hands his handset back to the pilot and lets him know they will be leaving in a few minutes.

"Any word from the police?"

"No, sir." The ground crew begins checking the helicopter so that it will be ready to go at Quintano's orders. The pilot walks over to the police car and listens to the radio traffic coming from the docks.

BARATARIA BAY CRASH SITE
LOUISIANA

Rain whips the bomb hanging from the helicopter; it swings in a slow arch. Marino and his men wait for it to touch the sand and grab it to ease it down. They quickly undo the harness, and the helicopter moves down the beach. It lands next to the others parked there. The tide has moved out, and the broken cabin sits stranded on the sand. A mike boat from the ship lands near it and drops the front ramp. Men scramble out carrying two wooden crates. A forklift gently picks the bomb up, moves it to the back of a Super Stallion, and places it on the back ramp. The rain continues to beat down on Commander Marino and his men. They get slings around the bomb and run straps over the forks of the lift. It raises the bombs into the air. One of the men puts a plastic cover over the access hole. It is lowered into the crate, and the straps are removed. A solid piece of plywood is nailed on the top of the frame and is winched into the back of the helicopter. Marino and his men get inside out of the storm. They watch as the tops on the bomb boxes are stenciled with their numbers. The other parts are packed in around the casing. Marino picks up the detonator and runs across the sand to the command helicopter. When he reaches the back of the other Super Stallion, Colonel Knight and Val take the detonator case and help him in. They stack it at the front of the helicopter bay and walk back to Marino. He shakes the water off his rain suit and pushes back the hood.

"Well done, Commander. We were watching you and your team. Excellent work."

"Thank you, Colonel. In that this is our first time at this, we have been blessed with some good luck so far. Having that supply ship diverted here is a lifesaver." Val brings him a cup of coffee; it throws steam into the cold air of the helicopter. He takes a deep drink. Marino looks at the other two. "This weather really sucks."

"You got that right. We're breaking the security in half and getting some of the marines into the helicopters for food and to get dried off." As they talk, six marines move up the ramp. They go to the front of the helicopter and get coffee and rations. The smell of wet clothes and ponchos fills the air. A lightning flash sends a silver-blue light into the helicopter. Val walks to the edge of the opening. "We really didn't need this rain."

"I talked with Commandant Swane. He told me about what's happening out in the Gulf. There are some real problems facing the ships out there. He also said that American fighters have shot down some Cuban fighters. They're escorting the weapons people in from one of the subs. The news out there is bad." As they all look out the back, another bolt of lightning illuminates the water lapping at the sand.

BOMB SITE, NUMBER SEVEN
LOUISIANA

The Tac radio suddenly comes to life across the net.

"Bulldog 1, this is Pathfinder 2. Over."

Susie moves her head, but does not open her eyes at the sudden noise from the radio. The smell of wet cloth and mud fills her nose, but the left side of her head is warm and comfortable.

"Bulldog 1, this is Pathfinder 2. Over."

She slowly opens her eyes. She blinks and opens them wide a couple of times. Others in the cabin are also waking and stretching. She lifts her head off of Marshall's shoulder, and looks around.

"I'm sorry, Gunny. I must have fallen asleep." She rubs his shoulder, and stretches in the tight confines.

"No problem, ma'am. I think we all got a little shut eye."

The pilot looks around and turns back into the cabin. "We'll be airborne in a few minutes. The wind is falling pretty quickly now. The path finders have located another bomb. They're calling in to the other team."

"Pathfinder 2, this is Bulldog 1. Over."

"Sir, we may have a problem at our site."

"Roger. What's the problem?"

"Sir, just before the rain hit us, Benson saw a mother pig, with some babies across the stream behind us. And now we keep hearing a bunch of grunting in the brush ahead of us. We think we may have a boar out here. And we're between him and his women."

"What is your situation now?"

"We're in a pit across from the bomb. We cut back about ten feet of thick brush. It's pretty dark in here with all the trees around us. On the map there is a landing site about 100 yards southwest of us."

Johnson looks at his map. "Roger. I have you near a creek."

"One of us will meet you at the site and lead you in."

"Roger. We should be airborne in just a few minutes."

"Roger, Bulldog 1. We'll—" A flash of lightning flares above the two marines' heads. As they look to the front, a large black boar breaks into the clearing. Its tusks, nose, and eyes flare. Benson fires four fast rounds into the air. It starts to move forward. It bellows a grunt at them and disappears back into the brush.

"Holy shit."

"Pathfinder, this is Bulldog 1. What were those shots?"

"Fuck, Captain. The biggest goddamn pig I've ever seen just came out of the bush. Benson fired a couple of rounds to scare it off."

Sandovol grabs Johnson hand. "Ask him if he wounded it."

"Pathfinder, did you hit this thing?"

"No, sir. It just ran off."

"That's good, Captain. If they think that boar is mean now, they should know that if injured he would be about as bad an animal as you would ever want to be around."

"Pathfinder, hold your position. We'll come in to you. Is there a path leading towards the clearing?"

"Yes, sir. We can see about a 100 feet down it, then it turns."

"Roger. We'll pop smoke when we get near you. Shoot only if attacked. We don't want to be hit coming in, all right."

"Roger, sir."

The engines on the helicopter begin to wind up as Johnson hands the mike back to his radio operator. "That's all we need—a fucking pig."

He looks at Sergeant Cabalero. "Well sir." He has a smile on his face. "We may be having a great dinner tonight." A shudder in the helicopter as it leaves the ground forces both men to grab hold.

Listening to the radio, Susie turns to Gunny Marshall. "A pig? Are they talking about a pig? Or maybe a javalina? We have those in New Mexico."

"No, ma'am." The gunny looks over at her. "We're talking about something twice their size and with a whole lot of anxiety."

Susie looks out the window. "Well, let's hope we don't run into any critters at our next site."

ULTIMA
WASHINGTON, D.C.

The marine guard opens the door, and the president's press secretary comes in. He waits while the president finishes a phone call. Wayne sees him and motions for him to come over. He hangs up the phone.

"Sir, with the release of Castro's radio broadcast, the news corps is crying for information. They have that and other reports of major activity over the Gulf. We believe it is imperative you make some kind of statement."

"I know." He gets up and continues to watch the screens. "It's just that right now I have calls coming in from heads of states. They want to know what is going on also."

"Sir, if I could suggest something? A quick press conference with Secretary Brant would certainly calm things down."

"I think you may be right." Brant gets up. "Sir, I will take General Becker with me. He can give them some insight on the evacuation."

"Very good." The president runs his hand through his hair. He sits down on the edge of his desk as Brant gets some paperwork together. Captain Van Nar walks up to the podium.

"Gentlemen, we have additional reports from Cuba. It is now confirmed that Russian personnel at Matanzas attacked and destroyed six aircraft on the ground, as well as associated buildings. Four bombers and four fighters did get off the field; they are en route to the squadron. The visual is on screen two.

"The track of the storm continues and has now pulled the line of severe thunderstorms out of the western Gulf. Both our bomb parties are now back on schedule and will arrive at their next locations in a matter of minutes." The storm whirls on screen three; the ships are interposed as white squares. On screen four, the track of the bombs over Louisiana are under a red line. White circles follow the movement of the helicopter groups. "It is believed now that the Russian submarine we picked up has taken a position somewhere just east of the Cuban ships. It was given the go-ahead to fire at will. It is to be assumed that it is in an attack posture. Our escorts are now on station, waiting for the arrival of President Castro's flight into the Gulf. And a Coast

Guard rescue helicopter has just joined the American escort for the damaged Russian helicopter. He is still fifty miles from the cutter. Sky 1 confirms that it is doubtful they will make the cutter. Thank you, gentlemen."

The president's hand goes to his forehead. He slowly shakes his head. "My God, will this thing not end." He walks back to his seat and slumps into the chair. "I have had to order men killed, and we stand at the brink of a horrendous loss of life." His physician joins him and has him take a couple of pills to help calm him.

"Sir, just take this. It is just a light relaxant." The president takes the pills and drinks a glass of water down with them. The phone on his desk rings, and he picks it up. "Yes, put him through. Yes, Mr. President, and how is the weather in Germany?" Brant and General Becker get their stuff to together and leave with the press secretary. They walk to the main conference room; the noise level is loud as they near the door. "Mr. Brant, I'll go in first and then bring the both of you up to the rostrum."

"That sounds good. We'll wait for you to calm them down."

They wait until the press secretary has the group settled down. The door beside them is opened, and they go in to the rostrum. Brant goes to the podium. The reporters yell questions at him from all directions.

"Ladies and gentlemen, I will only be here for a short update on events. So please, no questions at this time."

Brant describes the situation in the Gulf and the seizing of power by General Morales. He details the events which have transpired and comfirms that American lives are safe. "We had again moved in to rescue a Russian helicopter, which was carrying wounded." He does not mention the firing of missiles by the rescuers. He then has General Becker give an update on the progress of the evacuation and the status of the hurricane. As he talks, a marine orderly comes in and takes a message up to Brant. He quickly reads it and waits for Becker to finish. He thanks Becker and returns to the podium. Again they throw questions at him, and he raises his hand. "Ladies and gentlemen, please. I have just received a message from President Wayne, and I will share it with you.

"A short time ago, General Quintano began to move against General Morales. The commanders in the two districts east of

Matanzas have begun to withdraw troops from around Guantánamo Bay and recall any surface craft or aircraft operating in the eastern section of the Gulf. All offensive activity is now concentrated in the western section of the Gulf." The group cheers and claps.

"Also, President Wayne has dispatched two American fighters to escort President Castro safely into Guantánamo Bay. It was originally planned to have him land in Jamaica, but with the new situation, that plan was dropped. I would like to add that President Wayne is in constant contact with Secretary Sholenska, and he has had conversation for informational purposes with the heads of states in our hemisphere and with our NATO allies. The press secretary has been briefed and will answer questions. But General Becker and I must rejoin the president in the situation room. Thank you."

They all applaud as the men leave, and immediately begin firing questions at the press secretary.

As Brant and Becker get back in the room, Admiral Hillings is at the podium with Captain Van Nar. "Sir." He turns towards the president. "We believe that the Cuban forces are now staging for their attack. The bomber splits are now getting into position, and the two frigates are turning almost due south to cross the front of the Russian squadron." As they watch the board, the arrowhead images of planes around the Cubans move into pockets of four. Hollings looks at his watch; the hands stand at 2:33. "Sir, the attack is imminent."

CUBAN COMMAND VESSAL
THE GULF

"Sir, we have received another message from command." The Cuban captain looks at his executive officer and takes the message. He reads it over and grabs the edge of the front window as the ship rolls. "They now believe that the sinking of the second submarine was misreported. So in all probability we're being tracked by a hunter and killer, which is very good at what it does."

"Sí, Captain. The Ilyushin is moving in between us and the site of the transmission. They have begun to work the area."

"Good. Have the *OSA* boats been told to fire and head due south?"

"Yes, sir. They will fire and meet us at the rendezvous site."

"Good, we'll plot a course back to port from there. I wonder if they're aware of the conditions out here. This order to attack is from General Morales, a land commander. I know Admiral Rivera. He would have waited for this front to pass." He looks at his watch. "Commander, order the bombers to attack. We'll wait ten minutes and commence our attack."

"Aye, aye, sir."

WAREHOUSE
CUBA

Brock and the sergeant lay by the door and look into the other warehouse. The fire continues to spread. Most of the center section is in flames. Thick black smoke billows from the door and seems to fill the interior. They hear gunfire from the front and a single weapon firing from the back. There is a staccato of machine gun fire from the front of the building. "I think the armored cars have arrived."

Brock gets to his knees behind the boxes. "I think you're right." The sergeant yells to the men to prepare to assault the other warehouse. There is a lot of firing, and the sound of an explosion. On the radio, men are ordered to move in behind the BTRs. "Sergeant, this is Botus. Over."

"Yes, sir."

"We're sending an armored car down to your position to enter the building from your side. You can follow it in. We believe there are three gunmen in the front, and the last one is in the back. The fire has cut him off from the others. Good luck."

They all get ready to move. The armored car comes down between the buildings and crashes into the barrier inside the door. It disappears inside the opening, its guns blazing. "Let's move." The men join on the sergeant and Brock, and they run across the area between the buildings. They move to each side of the door, and the sergeant talks to the armored car. He then waves his hand, and they move inside. Boxes are burning across the warehouse and cutting the front off. The car is parked in the middle and has its guns aimed towards the back. They move in beside the boxes and stop at the wide open center area. They can see other officers coming in from the other side. The armored car sits alone in the center of the building, moving its gun back and forth towards the back. Automatic rifle fire ricochets off the side of the armored car. The gunner turns the turret and begins firing. It begins moving towards the back of the warehouse. Brock and the sergeant move along the face of the boxes on their side. The men on the other side fire down the center.

"Grenade!" They all hit the floor. The grenade bounces by the armored car and slides into the burning boxes. The explosion throws burning wood and packaging material in all directions. The boxes behind Brock begin to burn as he gets up and moves deeper into the warehouse. The man in the armored car calls, "Sergeant."

His radio clicks on. "Yes, I'm here."

"We have him in the back corner on your side. There is an office back there. We have pretty well shot it up. But we can't get any closer." There is a lot of firing from behind them and an explosion. Then it all gets quiet, and police officers begin appearing on the second floor walkway. Firemen begin coming into the building from the front and the other side. As they spray the fire, the hissing of steam and their yells can be heard. Brock taps the sergeant. "I'll go down the back side with these two guys." He nods his head as they cut down a side aisle and begin moving down the wall. He moves his group forward and looks around some boxes. The fire from the armored car has knocked down part of the wall of the office.

"Give yourself up, now!" He listens. "This is the police. The others are dead. Put down your weapon, and walk out with your hands up."

Rounds bounce off the armored car and hit the boxes around the sergeant. The machine gun on the armored car fires directly into the back corner. As the gunner stops, the sergeant looks around the corner again. The walls at the corner of the office are shredded by the machine guns. Light shafts poke into the dusty interior. Brock can see the corner of the building, and a foot sticking out. They signal the sergeant that they are going in. Brock raises up from behind a box, with his shot gun aimed at the bleeding figure. "Don't move." The man stares at the muzzle of the shot gun. "Where is Miguel?"

The man has a quizzical look on his face.

"Are you with Libertal?" Police have come up from the other side; their weapons are aimed at the man on the floor. He has been hit twice, once in the leg and side. A bloodstain continues to get bigger, and it drips to the floor. "Push the weapon off your lap, now!" He moves his legs, and the weapon slides off onto the floor. He brings his hands out from behind his back, in each is a grenade with the pins pulled. Looking into Brock's shotgun, he smiles. "This guy Miguel."

"Yeah?" Brock holds the shotgun steady.

"Fuck him, and fuck you." He opens his hands, as Brock and the sergeant fire.

They roll to each side, and the men around him dive for cover. Brock and the men with him dive back along the wall. The explosion tears the wall out behind them and blows the office up. Pieces of boxes rain down on them, and a fire starts in the crates. Brock pushes pieces of crates off himself and one of the others. "Are you all right?"

The sergeant comes over to them. "Shit, that was close. But I don't think these were the men you were after, Señor Brock." Brock brushes himself off and lays the shotgun on a crate. "You're right, sergeant. I don't believe he was politically motivated."

"Sergeant." Captain Botus comes over the radio. "Get Señor Brock out the back of the building. The helicopter is coming in to pick him up."

"Roger. We're leaving now." Firemen move in as they walk out the back door. They walk over to the edge of the dock and sit down on some rope coiled there. They can see the helicopter out over the water, moving in towards them. Brock stands up as the helicopter moves into land. Turning to the sergeant, he shakes his hand. "It was nice working with you, Sergeant. You and your men did a good job." The helicopter lands in the open area and the side door slides open. Quintano waves to him to get on board.

As he climbs in, Captain Botus pulls in next to them. He gets out and runs up to Quintano's window. "General, we have received word from a road block about twenty miles up the coast.

Your man Miguel got out at a fishing village. The police there have followed him to a blue colored house on the shore. They will assist you when you arrive."

"Thank you, Captain." As soon as he is away from the helicopter, it begins to rise and fly out over the water. They turn in the direction Botus gave and fly along the coast.

"I guess we were chasing the wrong men?"

Quintano looks back in the cabin, and smiles. "Yeah, you were right. Well, at least, I got a free shotgun for the effort."

"Well, things have changed since we parted. I'll cover you on what is going on, while we fly."

"Sounds good, General." Brock smiles.

CUBAN ATTACK PLANES
THE GULF

The radio in the Mig-27 comes alive. "Gavilon leader."

"Roger, Luna. This is Gavilon leader."

"Gavilon, this is Luna. The word is go, go, go."

"Roger, Luna. Go, go, go."

The flight leader calls the others and gives the order to attack. Two groups of three drop to the surface of the water and head in towards the Russians. One group from the right front, and the other from the right rear, fly through the storm twenty to thirty feet off the water. Each group forms a "V" shape. They display no forward radars and fly vectors from the Ilyushin ECM tanker south of them. Two bombers cross over the Russian fleet at 40,000 feet. Fighters dash in and out at different altitudes to draw missile fire from the ships.

The *Otlichnyy* has moved in front of the *Moskva*. ECM transmissions from the plane south of them dot the screens of the squadron. The ships bury their bows into the oncoming swells and rise high above them at the crest. At ten miles, the three bombers from the front rise up and lock on radars from the ships. They fire anti-radiation missiles and split to attack the three ships in front of them. One turns to the lead ship, one turns to the cruiser, and the middle one turns directly at the *Moskva*. As they race in, their radars lock on their targets, and they're laser range finders set the distance. They fire anti-ship missiles and set for bomb runs. The *Otlichnyy* at the lead turns towards the attackers and is caught in the trough of the oncoming swell. It hits the side of the destroyer and rolls it ten degrees. As they bring the ship back on course, the first anti-radiation missile slams into their Top Steer antenna and explodes. It tears half of it off the mount and it falls on the navigation radar just below it. The forward missile launcher fires as the bow dives. The missile hits the top of the wave and disappears. The point defense cannons in the rear turn and begin firing into the rain. The port side Gatling gun begins firing. A second missile hits the Big Net radar on the *Vladivostok* as the forward missile launcher swings forward and fires two missiles. The point defense cannons on the front port side fire into the rain. A side Gatling gun turns and fires as chaff is automatically fired in two directions. The first anti-ship missile hits the *Vladivostok* at the base of the central tower. A gaping hole is blown into the side. Backup units come on as half the radars on the tower are knocked out. As the third anti-radiation missile hits the surveillance radar on the *Moskva*, its anti-aircraft cannons on the port side begin firing. The topsail radar stands shattered on the masthead. The two Goblet launchers at the front fire as chaff is fired.

Two missiles are fired at the plane attacking the *Otlichnyy*. The second anti-ship missile hits the *Moskva* just behind the cannons on the port side. It blows a huge hole in the deck and knocks the cannon out.

BRIDGE OF THE *MOSKVA*

Admiral Kirsanov moves across the pitching bridge to assess the damage to the port side. He grabs hold as the ship drops into a trough, and he looks out the front windows. As the ship tears its bow out of the water and raises on the crest, a black shape appears directly ahead. The cannon fire from the bomber rips into the face of the bridge. It catches the admiral and the helmsman as rounds explode against the back wall. The ship falls off to the left. The blood-smeared wheel spins at the helm. Captain Sokolov climbs up the pitching ladder as the ship wallows violently. He reaches the bridge, and the ship pitches over to starboard. The rain and wind rush in through the shattered front windows. He grabs a phone near him and yells to the combat center. "Move the helm to mid-ship. Bring it back to the original course." He lets the handle drop from his hand and strains to reach the front of the bridge. The ship takes another violent roll to starboard. He grabs the chair near him and tries to get to the admiral. Medical and damage control teams are coming onto the bridge. He looks down at the admiral. The 23 mm rounds have almost torn him in half. He grips hard on the rail and can feel in his hands and feet the ship trying to come back around. As the men try and block the shattered windows, both forward launchers fire into the sky. Tracer rounds fly from the Russian ships in all directions. The medical people treat the others on the bridge who were hurt during the attack. They put the admiral and the helmsman in body bags and move them down the ladder. The captain only has a few seconds to think of his fallen comrade. The admiral was not just his senior officer, but also a close friend. He had learned many things, which were not written in books, from Kirsanov. He opens the side door to the bridge and steps out into the howling weather. The stinging spray hits him in the face and revives his thoughts. As he looks around, the noise of explosions override the wind. Rocket flashes and tracers seem to be flying in all directions. He gets back into the bridge and closes the door. "I want a full run down on the damage to the ship and to the others in the squadron."

The missile from the *Moskva* catches the bomber that attacked the *Otlichnyy* at the front of the group. It explodes and falls into the sea. The bomber attacking the *Moskva* has turned south and lines up with the destroyer. It closes the distance quickly, just above the water. The main guns on the *Osmotritelnyy* turn towards it. The twin mounted 130 mm rapid-fire cannons spew shells into its path. The plane's cannon fire rakes the side of the ship. It pulls towards the front and releases its two 1,000-pound bombs. When it banks to run out from the ship, the ship's forward cannon hits it with two shells. It explodes in a huge fireball. The two bombs sail forward towards the ship. It lowers its bow into the next trough as they seek their target. The first one flies over the forward deck at ten feet, hits, and explodes in the sea. The second bomb catches the gun turret at a low angle. The explosion tears the turret out of the deck and rips a hole towards the starboard side. Ammunition explodes in the feed mechanism from below decks.

Two missiles on the launcher above and behind it are blown away. Shrapnel from the explosion hits the front of the bridge and the radars above it. The last bomber sets his attack angle; he is coming at the trailing destroyer head on. He can see the flash from the forward cannons and a missile firing. As the captain on the *Sovremenyy* watches the missile firing forward at the oncoming jet, he is told that two inbound missiles have been fired by bombers from the port side stern. Three inbound fighters have been picked up. The three bombers from the southeast split, and each heads for their assigned ship. One at the trailing destroyer *Sovremenyy*. One at the cruiser *Vladivostok* to the right, and the last head-on at the *Moskva*.

The head-on fighter evades the oncoming missile and goes to cannons, raking the front of the ship. He releases his bombs, and slides by the starboard side of the ship. The rear missile launchers and the cannon turn to the closer threat and fire at the departing bomber. The anti-radiation missile hits the topsail radar and destroys it. The incoming missile hits the helicopter storage hangar; it destroys the hangar and helicopter and knocks out the port side rear missile control radar, as well as the spaces below it. Fire rages from the burning helicopter and fuel. Fire control teams begin hosing the fire, trying to reach injured and trapped men in the rear spaces. The bomber attacking from the rear is forced to veer away from the ship because of the shells from the rear gun mount. As it turns behind the stern of the ship, the shells find their target. The 130 mm shells tear the bomber to pieces. Its other weapons explode as it cartwheels into the sea. On board the *Moskva*, Captain Sokolov orders the ships to close up. Point defense on the port side, fire to the east of them. It takes the anti-radiation missile first and kills it in flight. The 57 mm mount shifts to its next target and begins firing. The forward mounts on the trailing *Sovremennyy* fire into the paths of the other two bombers. The rear launchers and guns of the *Vladivostok* join in. An incoming missile explodes to the rear of the *Moskva*. The pilot goes to his cannons and rakes the ship. His two 1,000-pound bombs sail towards the ship. He turns and flies between the *Moskva* and the cruiser *Vladivostok*; their combined gunfire shoots it down. The two bombs hit fifty yards off the port side. The ship shudders from the concussion. The anti-radiation missile from the bomber heading for the *Vladivostok* hits it in its rear facing bass tilt, and and it explodes. A missile launched from the rear of the cruiser takes out an inbound missile. The bomber attacks directly from the stern. The rear launcher sits idle, its guidance radar shattered. The bomber dodges the ships cannon fire and releases its weapons load. His cannons walk the length of the ship, and he turns east, firing flares and chaff. The forward guns fire in his path, and two missiles chase him into the storm. They find their mark two miles from the ship. The two pods dropped by the bomber straddle the rear missile launcher, and napalm explodes up each side of the ship. "Captain, the *Vladivostok* has been hit with napalm, sir."

"Napalm!" He runs to the port side. The burning cruiser has tightened up to 300 yards. From its stacks to its stern, it burns furiously. As he watches, his eyes are pulled up to a black object in a vertical dive above the cruiser. Two dark things detach, and the bomber veers away from the ship. He watches as missiles try and catch the fleeing bomber. Like in slow motion, the falling bombs drop on the cruiser.

One hits in the water right next to the ship, but the other one finds its mark. It hits the cruiser on the rear launcher; the blast is huge, orange and red. The launcher and the helicopter storage hangar disappear, and a huge gaping hole spewing fire remains. "Shit!" Captain Sokolov turns and calls out as the first bomb hits the flight deck, just behind the super structure of the *Moskva*. The second hits in the middle of the flight deck and punches through to the hangar deck. As it enters the hangar deck, the 1,000-pound bomb detonates. Everyone on the ship is thrown to the deck; anything loose flies through the air. At the back of the super structure, a forty-foot gaping hole is blown in the deck. The hangar doors at the rear of the super structure are blown in, and fire and smoke swirl out. The second bomb tears through the forward elevator and rips a fifty-foot hole in the deck. The helicopters stored below are crushed against the sides of the ship. They burn and explode in the fire raging on the hangar deck. The captain and the other men on the bridge slowly pick themselves up. Calls for help blare out of the speakers, and fire alarms clang throughout the ship. The captain picks up a phone, and looks out the back ports of the bridge. Smoke covers the rear of the ship.

"Damage control, what's our situation?"

"Sir, we have a serious fire on the hangar deck. Half of the sprinkler system was blown away. But the other half is on now. We are just getting hoses back into the area, and we will probably have to seal the starboard side. We're taking water in from ruptured hull plates."

"What about the people down there?"

"Sir, were looking at a possible ninety to 100 dead. And some we will not be able to get to."

"Keep me informed. Do your best, Comrade."

"Thank you, sir. We will do all that is possible."

MIG-29
SKY OVER GULF

Norba watches his radar; the tanker is almost directly above him. One jet eagerly takes on fuel as another slowly backs off the drogue. Five others hang to the side, waiting their turn. The tanker updates the ships on the movement of the Russians and gives them their coordinates. Norba pulls the nose up, gets a lock on the huge blip, and fires. "This is for Ski." His last missile races up and out of the clouds. It locks on to the belly of the tanker. Alarms go off on all the fighters and on the tanker. It disengages the fighter and banks to the left. But it hardly gets into the turn when the missile hits. It tears into a fuel cell and explodes. Pieces of the tanker fall into the clouds. The five waiting fighters circle the now empty space. They are ordered southwest to rendezvous with a new tanker and the ships. If they have to ditch, the boats can pick them up. Norba applies power to his sole remaining engine and accelerates away. He sets his course for the north to try and reach the Americans.

CUBAN ATTACK BOATS

"Sir, we have lost contact with the tanker." The *OSA* captain looks over the windscreen of the boat. "Keep trying. We're about to fire."

"Captain, we have contact with a fighter. The tanker has been shot down. We are ordered to fire what we have and head for the rendezvous area."

"I second that. We're showing less than half a tank of gas."

"Signal the others to fire on my command. And tell them to add some deflection and hope the infra-red homing will correct it in final flight."

"Stand by to launch."

The four boats pull up in line and await the command to fire. The commander does a final check on his charts to ensure that they are within the forty-mile range of the Styx 2B missiles.

"We'll fire our last two and get the hell out of this weather." He does a final check. "Fire one." The first missile leaves it launch tube. "Fire two." The second missile launches and flies into the overcast. The other three boats fire their missiles and turn to close up with the commanders boat. The four turn southwest in a diamond formation, and head for the rendezvous area. Twelve missiles fly for the Russian squadron from the west. Nine more are fired from the *OSA* patrol boats from the southeast. They turn and head for the rendezvous area.

ABOARD THE *MOSKVA*

"Sir, the *Otlichnyy* is reporting twelve missiles inbound from the west. And the *Sovremennyy* is reporting nine from the southeast. It is believed that they're coming from the *OSA* boats."

"My God, that's all we need. Order decoys fired from all ships and come to due north. Engage them as soon as possible."

"Aye, aye, sir."

"Captain, its damage control."

He takes the handset, "This is Sokolov."

"Sir, we are making headway with the fires on the hangar deck. We had to seal off the starboard fuel bunkers under the hangar deck in the stern, and we'll have to flood the port bunkers to bring the ship back on an even keel. Also, the blast caught most of the aircrews in their ready room just off the hangar."

"Very good. Keep me informed." The destroyers fire decoys of chaff and infrared flares out into the paths of the incoming missiles. Replica decoys are fired out from the destroyers, and they deploy. The floating reflectors take on the signature of the ships. The destroyers have formed on the *Moskva*: one on its stern, the next just to starboard, and the third just off the starboard bow. The *Vladivostok*, still fighting fires and down to three-quarter speed, moves to a point off the port bow. All operating launchers turn towards the threat. Rapid bloom chaff forms around the ships, and any working ECM are actively operating. Missiles begin to launch from the different ships and race to their counterpart. Both of the forward launchers on the *Moskva* fire a second salvo. "Sir, they're turning towards the decoys. We think they were fired with old coordinates."

"Excellent." The captain raises his binoculars and looks to the west. A new line of flares drops in the mist; it causes a weird red glow out from the ships. As he watches, missiles find missiles, and a chain of explosions lights the western sky. He turns his glasses to the south, and more explosions light the dark storm clouds.

"Sir, we still have five inbound from the west and four from the southeast. They are showing a deflection to the decoys." He looks out the port side as another salvo of missiles rocket from the squadron.

Again, explosions flare in the mist around the ships. Three of the missiles from the west find the decoys and explode to the rear of the squadron. Two from the southeast explode in the chaff and flares. A gentle rain begins to fall on the ships, and the only sound is the wind. The men on the bridges of the ships look at each other and wonder what is next. Men below rescue shipmates and fight fires. They throw twisted chunks of steel over the sides and carry the dead to the medical ward in the center of the ship.

"Captain, the *Vladivostok* is settling in the stern. They have lost the main shaft on the starboard side. They will have to reduce speed to ten knots."

"Reduce our speed to match theirs and signal the others to follow suit. Inform the cruiser that we have fought together, and we'll remain together to the end." The captain joins the damage control officer, and they go through the combat control center and out a side hatchway. They walk down the starboard side on the deck overlooking the flight deck. Twisted metal blocks part of the walkway. They maneuver through it and look over the railing at the damage. Smoke from the fires still billows from the holes in the flight deck. Crews have contained the fires just behind the super structure; he looks down and sees men carrying stretchers on the deck below. It looks like a giant bullet hole. Below the flight deck, steel frames are smashed flat. The second hole is ringed with steel plates peeled up three feet above the deck, and an angry red glow fills the void. He shakes his head; the damage is almost unbelievable.

"Captain." The damage maintenance officer—DMO— points to the starboard side. He follows his finger; the side of the ship has been pushed out. It looks like a huge hammer had slammed into the side. "Sir, the bomb has ruptured the hull in that area."

"I see." He looks out at the destroyers to the side. They have crews putting temporary covers on holes in the decks and superstructure. The front of the *Osmotritelnyy* is nothing but smashed and twisted metal. He turns to the officers around him. "By someone's grace, gentlemen, we are still afloat. Let's hope our luck holds." They walk back to the combat center, and check on the position of the Cuban ships and planes.

RUSSIAN SUBMARINE

"Sir, we have sonobuoys in the water. They are approximately at our transmission site, in a line moving towards us. Also, the *OSA* boats southeast of us have turned southwest and are leaving the area. The explosions earlier we believe were their missiles attacking the squadron."

"All right, get me a preliminary firing solution on the ships."

"Have the aft torpedo room load a decoy torpedo and stand by." The men slide the type-65 torpedo into the rear tube. Its thirty-mile radius and forty knot speed will serve it well against the circling ASW aircraft. They load and stand by for firing. "Sir, sonar has us at 9,000 yards and parallel with the stern of the lead ship. With their course change, we believe they are also withdrawing from the engagement."

"Not for long. I want a four shot spread at five miles. Confirm that the forward torpedoes are the type-65s."

The executive officer calls forward and confirms the weapons. "Sir, they are confirmed and are now coming up ready to fire." Lights on the weapons panel come to life, showing the four forward tubes ready and the aft tube ready. The fire control officer stands ready.

"Set the decoy to go active at 1,000 yards. The forward torpedoes should go active at 3,000 yards." All parameters are keyed into the torpedoes. "Bring us up to 200 feet." The submarine turns to the west as it rises.

"Sir, 200 feet, opening outer doors. We are free to fire, sir."

"Fire one, fire two." The torpedoes are blown from the tubes and race for their targets. "Fire the aft torpedo and take us down to 400 feet and full speed. I want to get ahead of them." The submarine dives at thirty degrees and levels off at 400 feet as it pushes forward in the dark depths.

CUBAN COMMAND SHIP

"Captain, we have torpedoes in the water at 8,000 yards." The Cuban captain and other officers move to the starboard side and walk out on the flying bridge. They look through their binoculars in the direction of the torpedoes.

"Arm the RBU and stand by to fire." The RBU-6000 ASW rocket launcher is activated and swings in the direction of the oncoming threat. Two of the rockets fire and are closely followed by two more. They fly out and splash into the water. A huge explosion and a geyser of water shoots into the air. "Give me ninety degrees to their course at flank speed." The ships begin their turn as the launchers continue to fire.

"Sir, they have gone active. There are still three in the water." Both ships continue to fire rockets. The three-inch guns begin to fire at the torpedoes. Explosions are dotting the water. The ships continue to turn as two more explosions signal the end of more torpedoes. "Sir, the last torpedo is trying to match our turn."

"Very good." The launchers fire another salvo. Their aim is true and the torpedo explodes. "Bring us back to our original course and back to three-quarter speed. Prepare to launch our last missiles."

"Sir, the Ilyushin aircraft has located the submarine. It is moving at flank speed due east of our position."

"Very good." The captain looks around at the other officers. "Apparently our attacker is a shoot and run type of officer."

The others laugh and congratulate the captain on his success. "Sir, the Ilyushin has provided us with the firing coordinates of the squadron. They have slowed to twelve knots. The reports from the bombers say they have sustained many hits. We are ready to fire on your command."

"Well then, gentlemen. It looks like we will deliver the coup de grace to the squadron. Order the missiles to be fired." As the ships continues to turn, the missiles fire from their decks, two from each. They disappear into the clouds heading east.

RUSSIAN SUBMARINE

"Captain, all tubes have been reloaded and set to go active at 1,000 yards."

"Very good. Stand by."

"They will turn at ninety degrees." The captain smiles. "Sir, they are continuing their turn. They will cross the bow at 3,000 yards in one minute."

"Stand by to fire." They had run ahead of the ships, and during the confusion, they had turned. They now wait at 200 feet. The captain guessed their maneuver correctly, and the prey is coming to the killer. It hangs in the black water as the Cuban ships turn their bellies to it, getting back on course. "Sir, five seconds. One, two, three, four, five."

"Fire all tubes." The weapons officer pushes the button and the sub shakes from the launching. Four homing torpedoes race for the kill.

CUBAN COMMAND SHIP

"Captain, we have torpedoes in the water on the starboard side at 2,500 yards."

"What?" He again moves to the outside bridge. He orders the ship to come about, hard to port at flank speed. It wallows in the water, trying to comply with his commands. They're almost thrown off their feet as the ship lumbers to turn.

"Sir, they have now gone active, and we show them at 1,000 yards." The second ship is turning inside the lead ship and cannot fire his weapons at the torpedoes. The captain orders the RBU rockets fired as the ship leans into the port side. The sonar homing on the torpedo's locks onto the huge side of the lead ship as the second ship passes behind it. They lock and race for the kill. They hit the frigate first in the stern, then spaced from there to the bow of the ship. The explosions rip huge holes in the sides. The aft fifty feet of the ship rips away in the blast. The driving turn continues to push it into the sea. From the other ship, it seems to be diving. As the water reaches the bridge, a message comes over the speakers. "This is ASW-1. We have sunk the submarine due east of your position. Have a safe trip."

The Russian submarine hangs at 400 feet. The noise of the kill and the sounds of the sinking ship echo in the hull. The screams of crushing steel bulk heads echo in all directions.

RUSSIAN SUBMARINE

"Captain, the second ship is now at 8,000 yards and moving due west. She was probably behind the lead ship. Also, that explosion we heard due east of us was probably the Ilyushin destroying the decoy." The captain looks around the control room. "Take us down to 500 feet and plot a course after the other ship." The submarine dives down and turns to pursue the other ship.

"Sir, we have sonabouys in the water at 5,000 yards in front of the bow. They are between us and the ship, and they have just gone active." The pinging echoes in the water around the sub as the airplane flies in ever-wider circles. "Break off and plot a course back to the squadron. We'll slip out of the area." The sub turns towards the ships and moves away in the blackness. As they move in, the depth's water passing over the sail of the sub is disturbed by the half-open hatch over the periscope. The earlier explosion had jammed the door partially open, and it now accentuates the hull noise. In the darkness the men relax, the thick dark coat of water around them. As they congratulate each other on the sinking, six sonobuoys drop into the water over their heads. "Sir, we have sonobuoys in a parallel line with the ship."

"Shit, give me ten degrees to port and full speed."

The men in the control room silently move back to their stations as the buoy pattern is displayed on the board. "It may have been a fluke, him dropping so near." The plane flies over and rechecks his readings, then lays a second line of buoys. "Sir, he has just laid a second line of buoys. They are parallel with the port side of the ship. We are now in the middle of a lane."

"Damn, he knows we're here, and now has us cold. Prepare to launch decoys, and dive." The Ilyushin takes a wide turn and pulls around into the lane to attack. As his bomb bay doors slowly open, he adjusts his course. The big plane drops down to 100 feet above the water. At 500 yards from the drop, a Mig-29 drops in behind him. The first burst of canon fire catches them off guard, and the pilot tries to turn to the left. Norba adjusts his shots and rakes the starboard engine and the fuselage. The big plane bursts into flames and slams into the water. Norba looks around and, not seeing anyone, he continues his flight north. He thinks to himself how lucky he was to happen onto the Ilyushin. The men in the sub wait for the splash of the depth charge or a torpedo. What they get is the explosion of the plane hitting the water.

"This is weird, sir. But I think the aircraft has just crashed into the sea."

"What? Crashed?" He moves over to the sonar operator.

"Yes, sir. There are pieces of something sinking to the bottom." They continue on and leave the trap of the buoys, not understanding what had happened. But they are glad it did.

RUSSIAN FIGHTER

As Norba passes west of the squadron heading north, his radarscope tells him they are again firing at a missile attack. He checks to the front, and all is clear. He eases back on the throttle to conserve fuel. The dark clouds to the east flash at times with lightning. He puts the low hanging cloud 500 feet above him and the sea 500 feet below. He checks his fuel and tries to figure his chances of getting back to the American base or at least ditching near a naval ship. His eyes do not pick up the sleek dark shape coming in behind him. It maneuvers directly behind the crippled jet. With its radar on passive, no alarm screams in the cockpit. Norba checks his scope again and looks to both sides. Everything is still clear; he looks up to the mirror to look behind him. The conical intake of the Mig-21 stares back at him. Before he can move, the cannon rounds walk up the center of the jet and blow the canopy away. Smoke streams from the right engine, and chilled wind blows across Norba's body. His eyes open wide as his fighter collides with the water. The Cuban pilot circles over the site and wags his wings. He then flies south to join the others at the rendezvous site. He thinks to himself how fortunate he was to find the Russian Mig in all this confusion.

BRIDGE OF THE *MOSKVA*

"Captain, we show the area clear."

Sokolov nods to him and looks out at the other ship. He think to himself, "How fortunate to have escaped this last wave of missiles."

"I want a status of the ships, and get me through to Marshall Shagan." As the reports come in, they are processed and sent on to the captain. He and his executive officer pore over the reports and make suggestions for their next move. "Sir, your call to Marshal Shagan."

"Sir, this is Captain Sokolov."

"Captain, it is good to hear your voice. I know that things do not go well with the squadron."

"Yes, sir. Admiral Kirsanov is dead; he was killed in the air attack. He died with great honor, sir."

"We are saddened by his death. And extend to you and all your men, our thoughts in this brave hour. The Americans have updated us on your situation, and they are standing by to assist in any way they can."

"Thank you, sir. I have been reviewing the damage to the ships and the death toll. We stand at 390 dead and another 500 wounded. The destroyers and the *Moskva* are maintaining themselves, but the *Vladivostok* is in critical condition. Unless things change drastically, she will be lost. The captain has contacted me, requesting his wounded be moved to the other ships, and that his complement be reduced to a skeleton crew."

"You have hard decisions to make, Captain Sokolov, and a large set of shoes to fill. But like Admiral Kirsanov, we have the utmost confidence in your decisions. We have decided to advance your promotion to admiral as of now, instead of waiting until you return home."

"I thank the supreme command for their confidence, and I will bring honor to my mentor."

"Very well put, Admiral. Is there anything that we can provide to you?"

"At this point we are unable to target the Cuban ships; they knocked out our surveillance. And we cannot launch a helicopter to spot for us. The risk to the crew from fighters is too high. If there was some way to get those coordinates, we could turn the tables on them."

"Very well, we will seek a solution to your dilemma. I will contact you again with the answer to your request. Good luck, Comrade Admiral."

Sokolov hangs up, and calls the cruiser. After a short discussion, plans are made to lift off the wounded and disperse them to the other ships. The destroyer *Otlichnyy* is able to launch its helicopter. They begin to lift wounded off the cruiser. Sokolov's officers gather around him. "After the wounded are removed, we will begin moving the able-bodied seamen. Check with each ship and the *Vladivostok* to match positions that have been voided by the attacks. Send electricians, radar operator, or techs, to the ships that have lost these men."

The officers leave and begin to match jobs with requirements on the ships. The weapons officer comes up from the control center, and joins Sokolov. "Sir, we are reloading the side guns. One was down to ten rounds left. We are at sixteen remaining missiles for both front launchers." Sokolov tries to calculate a number. "Sir, I'll save you the time. We have fired thirty-two missiles so far. Under another aerial attack, we will run out. I have checked with the other ships; they also are running short on missiles. And some of the cannons are down to less than 100 rounds. We still have a very impressive stock of anti-ship missiles."

"Very good, keep me updated on our munitions stock."

He watches as the helicopter moves between the ships, and he wonders what will they throw at them next.

CHAPTER 12

RUSSIAN HELICOPTER
THE GULF

"Cutter, this is air rescue. The Russian helicopter is going in. Over."

"Roger, Rescue. We have you thirty-five miles south of our position."

"Roger, Cutter. We have light rain. We'll snatch three and fly to you. Over."

"Roger, Rescue. We'll continue on course to you. We have moderate showers at our location. Deck crew will be standing by. Over."

The Russian pilot fights the stick and brings the helicopter to a shaky hover. Lights blink on his instrument panel: low fuel and hydraulic pressure. He alerts his crewmen to be ready to ditch. As he hovers, the Coast Guard helicopter comes to a hover just to the right side of him.

The sea below is rolling swells as he descends. The waves reach up and skim the bottom, then fall away. The inflatable pontoons on the wheels settle into the water. The captain kills the engines and starts to unbuckle his harness. The helicopter noses into a trough and buries itself into the oncoming swell. The spinning rotors flay to a stop in the sea. The helicopter rolls on its left side.

The Coast Guard helicopter moves over immediately, and a diver sits ready to jump. The bodies in the cabin fall across the men, they hang from their harnesses. The pilot is caught under the hanging body of his co-pilot. The water begins pouring in through the holes on the right side. The crewman pushes the weapons man up through the open side hatch. Water slopes over the edge and falls on him as he tries to reach the pilot. As the weapons man climbs on to the side of the sinking helicopter, he looks back into the cabin. Then he looks up at the helicopter over head.

The pilot sees him and the fear on his face. He keys his outside speaker. "Remain on the helicopter. Do not move. We will get you off." He looks up at the source of the sound and screams.

"We're in, sir." The two jumpers in the back leap into the water.

"Damn, we're going to loose this guy if they don't get to him fast." The divers fight to reach the helicopter; they are swept towards it and then away. Water swirls around the body of the helicopter, and it wallows in the water.

"Do not move. We have people in the water to help. We will get you. Shit." The weapons man dives in over the back of the helicopter, and is swept away. "Son of a bitch, did he have a life belt on?"

The co-pilot keeps looking at the two men in the water. "I don't know, Captain."

"Sir, one of the divers is on the side of the helicopter."

The diver has the cable attached and climbs down into the cabin. The other diver is on the front of the helicopter at the co-pilot's door. The captain is pinned on his left side; his crewman has the buckles undone. The diver grabs the crewman and points him to get out. The other diver puts his hand through the holes in the door, and releases the co-pilot's body. The limp form lands on the pilot's chair, then slips to the floor of the back cabin with the other bodies.

The diver with the cable signals the other diver to save the other crewman. When he gets onto the side of the helicopter, he takes the cable. Attaching it to his harness, he puts a sling around the Russian. They are immediately lifted off the wreck and up into the hovering helicopter. As soon as they are on board, the cable is sent back down.

The diver helps the pilot pull himself up out of the seat. The bodies in the cabin now float in the rising water. As the pilot and the diver begin to climb up out of the cabin, the helicopter shudders, and a flood of water throws them back.

"Captain, the helicopter sank. I could see them in the cabin."

The water is dark and cold as the diver searches for the pilot. Bodies seem to fill the cabin; he grabs the pilot by his collar and kicks for the opening above him. As he pulls the pilot out, one of the bodies is pulled out with him. He looks up and kicks for the surface.

"Any sign?" The pilot holds the helicopter in its position.

"No, sir. It took them both down. It's got Chief Peck."

As the chief kicks for the surface, he locks his legs around the pilot. He tightens his grip on his collar and pulls a lanyard. His life vest inflates, and the two race towards the surface. As they rise, the chief looks directly above. As they near the surface, he sees the shape of the helicopter through the water. They break the surface as a dye marker in the vest sends out its green-yellow color.

"They're up, sir." He signals the cable to be lowered. The chief holds on to the pilot as they lift to safety. They get them on board. The pilot is given oxygen and checked out. The chief leans back against the front wall of the cabin and puts a headset on.

"Chief, are you all right?"

"Yes, sir. Just a little winded."

"That was a hell of a rescue."

"Thank you, Captain."

"I just have one request, Chief."

"Sir."

"Next time, not so dramatic. You scared the shit out of us."

"Aye, aye, sir."

They fly out in the direction of the weapons man. Two fighters fly off to their sides, searching the water for any sign of him.

"Rescue, this is Escort 2. I think I have your man, about 200 yards off your port side. It doesn't look good. Over."

"Roger, Tomcat." The helicopter leans over and in seconds they hover above the man floating face down in the sea.

"Cutter, this is Rescue. We are retrieving the body of the last crewman, and will ETA you about fifteen minutes."

"Roger, Rescue. Cutter out."

ULTIMA
WASHINGTON, D.C.

The president and the others sit silent and stare at the screen. The imaging camera moves over the squadron. They watch the helicopter move between ships.

Admiral Hillings gets up and walks to the podium. Captain Van Nar stands staring at the screen. "Mr. President, we have just witnessed the greatest modern sea battle since World War II." The camera scans across the *Moskva*. A glow still shines from the bomb crater in the flight deck.

"We can assume that the cruiser is lost." The camera sweeps across the stern, and then on to one of the destroyers. "Here is what saved the day." The camera looks at another destroyer.

"The *Sovremennyy* destroyer has shown itself to be really tough. We were aware of the shortcomings of the *Moskva* and the *Vladivostok*. They're both under-armed. But the destroyers have proven themselves gallantly."

"My God, Admiral." The president looks at his watch. "In less than thirty minutes, hundreds of lives have been lost. Ships and aircraft are lost, and for no reason."

"Yes, sir." The admiral walks back to his chair. "Mr. President." The admiral grabs the back of his chair, and looks at Wayne. "Sir, both the Russians and us have been working on these weapons in the name of mutual destruction. We have run computer models, test fired them, and let others fire them in battles. We have brought the art of electronic warfare to an all-time high. We are in an age of technological wizardry, where smaller means more destructive. And you must remember, sir, if either side had used nukes, this entire scenario would have lasted less than one minute."

"I understand, Admiral. But are there lessons to be learned from this. What can we say when a madman casts this kind of destruction on the world?"

"Sir." The admiral sits down. "That is the job of the peacemakers. That is the focus of what you and your administration does. Those of us around this table are here to protect and defend. We don't make policy; we enforce it. When a military commander tries to combine both entities under one set of rules, the outcome is, historically, dictatorship and conflict."

Secretary Brant's phone rings. He talks to the other person and then puts him on hold. "Mr. President, this is Marshal Shagan on the phone. He has a request to make of you."

"Marshal Shagan, what can we do for you?"

He listens and then talks with Secretary Sholenska, looking at the screens and then back to the men at the table. He nods his head, and hangs up.

"Gentlemen, Secretary Brant will brief you on the request made to us by Secretary Sholenska and Marshall Shagan."

Brant stands up and steps to the back of his chair. "After talking with Admiral Sokolov, we have learned that Admiral Kirsanov was killed in the air attack. The Russian squadron's ability to see beyond thirty miles has been knocked out. They are using base line radar for point defense purposes. They are unable to repair the damage done by the anti-radiation missiles to their long-range surveillance radars. They have made a request of the president to see if we can provide them with the targeting of the Cuban ships and the location of the fighters coming from the south."

"Mr. Secretary." General Lane leans forward on the table. "We can have Sky 1 contact him on the fighter-bombers coming in from the south. They have a Russian speaking operator on board. As for the targeting of the Cuban forces, we can provide them with a downlink off the satellite. They can even transmit corrections in flight."

"Very good, General. Can you make that happen?"

"Yes, sir. We're on it now. I'll let you know when we are ready."

The president suddenly stands up. "Hell! I forgot about the bombs, with all the excitement out in the Gulf."

Captain Van Nar steps up to the podium. She uses an electric pointer and highlights the screen showing the bombs. "Sir, the helicopters will be landing about now. As you can see, they are almost on top of the bomb site. They should be back up on the Lanstat net very soon." She moves her pointer to the radar screen. "The Russian helicopter was forced to ditch at sea. The

Coast Guard rescue helicopter has picked up two survivors and one dead. They are en route to the cutter under escort.

"We have tracked the new group of attack aircraft that left Matanzas. They were forced to fly around some weather and are now nearly directly south of the squadron. We estimate they will be over them in approximately one hour. We also have a bunching of fighters over the *OSA* boats heading southwest. The frigate is also moving in that direction. I would like to point out also that half of Captain Emmett's Sambora effect is now in place. And the jet stream is falling to the south, drastically. Also, there is a full moon tonight."

The president looks at Brant. "That's must be why all this weirdness is happening."

Brant nods, "You may be right, sir. We are certainly having something beyond a bad hair day."

BOMB SITE, NUMBER SIX
LOUISIANA

"Captain Johnson, there's our landing site."

"Roger." He turns to Cabalero. "As soon as we get down, take a couple of men with you. Clear the trail into the bomb site. I'll call Corporal Milton and tell him to look for red smoke."

"Aye, aye, sir."

As they settle to the ground, Cabalero slides the door open and jumps down. He signals two men forward from the other helicopter. After explaining what they're going to do, they check their weapons and head towards the bomb site.

Johnson gets the others around him and explains the situation around the bomb; he checks his map. "We're backed up on a creek. We'll need some chain saws and some axes. Then we'll call in the lift helicopter." Four marines run over to the lift helicopter, and the chief gives them the equipment. They rejoin the others as they begin to move towards the site. The radioman walks with the captain as he calls into the site. "Pathfinder 2, this is Bulldog 1. Over." He tells them to look for red smoke from the forward element.

Cabolero and the other two near a split in the path; one goes along the creek. As one of the marines steps forward, his foot slips into a hole in the wet grass. He falls into the brush on the side of the trail; the noise reaches the bomb site.

"Come on, come on in, you fucking pig."

Cabolero signals everyone down, and gets the smoke grenade out. He pulls the pin, and rolls it down the path. The pop of the grenade draws their attention. As the thick red smoke fans out across the trail, Cabolero calls to them.

"This is Mr. Pig. We're moving in now."

"You're the other Mr. Pig. Come on in."

Out of the red smoke, the three marines move up to the site. As they near the site, Cabolero calls out, "You here! You two move out to the slicks. They will take you back to the beach. Get some food, and coffee. They will then lift you to the next site, or if you want, see the lieutenant and they will send out two replacements."

Two marines step down the trail as they talk. They see the captain setting up the perimeter.

"We are the fuck out of here." They get their stuff and get ready to leave. "Sarge." Milton turns back to Cabolero. "Watch yourself—that fucker is big." They move down the trail and pass the others who throw pig jokes to them. As they pass, the captain walks over.

"Corporal, you guys have done a great job finding these things. Get some food and dry out a little. Maybe we'll see you at the next site."

"Aye, aye, Skipper. And watch out for that pig, sir."

Johnson, Sandal, and Reddeer join the others at the pit. Cabolero has men going up the trees behind the site to cut branches down. Emanuel climbs into the pit with the bomb.

He looks at the bomb stuck in the grass and vines at the edge of the pit, and then looks up. It tore a hole in the canopy of tree branches above them. He looks around at the pit, which is really a round area worn out by animals going down to cross the creek running about twenty-five feet away. The water moves quickly, carrying branches and other debris with it. The men in the trees begin cutting away the overhanging limbs and branches. They fall onto the short sandy edge along the creek and into the water. A navy chief points to other branches that need to be cut. Then he goes back to his radio to call the helicopter in.

Johnson and Cabolero stand off to the side with Sandovol. "I've got the perimeter set up along the trail about 100 feet out." Johnson's finger runs along a line on the map. "I'll walk the perimeter and see how everyone is doing, Skipper." He slings his rifle. "They will have the Lanstat up in a few minutes. I just want to make sure this pig thing doesn't get out of hand."

"Captain, would you mind if I went with Gilbert?"

"All right, Mr. Sandovol." Johnson folds the map and puts it away. He calls after Cabolero, "Watch yourself out there, Sergeant."

Johnson watches as Emanuel digs around the bomb to find the black strip. Two marines with shovels stand by to begin digging out around the casing. The sawing has stopped, and the last of the large branches is tossed to the side. The chief talks on the radio, and the sound of the incoming helicopter fills the air. Johnson looks up as the body of the helicopter slides over the opening; it winches the pallet down onto the sand by the creek. As soon as it is released, the men start moving sandbags up to the pit.

Cabolero and Sandovol walk along the path, heading towards the middle positions. They have talked with the marines at two points along the trail. The perimeter formed a curve from the creek on the left, back to the spot where the two trails crossed. The storm clouds overhead cast a dark gray light on everything around them. They move up to the two marines in the center.

"Yo, any Pig sign?"

They both have their rifles aimed forward from the hip. "We haven't seen him, but something is moving between us and the next post down the trail." They point to their right as a cracking sound comes out of the dense brush to their front. They all stand silent as it stops. Cabolero unslings his rifle and looks into the deep dark green growth. After a couple of minutes, he relaxes his hands on his rifle and lowers it.

"Well, whatever it was, it—" The words stick in the air as a loud grunting scream comes out of the brush to their front. It seems so close that Sandovol draws his pistol, and the two marines and Cabolero fire into the thicket. Each fires a couple of rounds, and then listens. The sound of something moving to their right deep in the brush fades away.

"Holy shit." Smoke drifts from the muzzle of Cabolero's rifle.

"Corporal Milton was right. There is some kind of demon fucking pig out here." Sandovol looks at the Sergeant, his 357 pistol still in his hand. "OK, let's shut down. We need to keep our heads with this fucker."

His radio comes on. "Cabolero, this is Johnson. What were those shots?" He looks at the others as he keys the radio.

"Sir, we had a visit from Corporal Milton's pig."

"Did you get him?"

"No, sir. He keeps moving across the front here between us and the fork in the trail. And I might add, from his sounds, I think he is really pissed off. Sandovol and I are moving on to the next post. We'll be back in a few minutes."

"OK, Sergeant. They have the bags going up around the casing. We'll be able to get started in about fifteen minutes."

Cabolero calls each of the posts and has them move so they can see each other. He looks both ways. The adjacent posts wave back to him.

"Sarge, I think we should grenade the fucker." The words come across Cabolero's headset. "This is post four. We're locking in. Fuck Milton's pig." The two marines load their 40 mm grenade launchers and lock them in.

"This is Cabolero. Don't go firing fucking grenades inside the perimeter. We have marines all around. Make sure of your direction of fire. Has everyone got that?" They all answer up and acknowledge.

As Cabolero and Sandovol move up the trail towards the next post, the sound of a rifle grenade being chambered come from behind them. With his rifle at the ready and Sandovol's pistol out, they move up the dark path toward the next two marines.

"This is post five. We have Mrs. Milton moving to our left. She sounds real fucking pissed."

"Good, move the bitch towards us." The guys at post four stare down the trail towards post five and wait. The sergeant and Sandovol reach them just as a huge grunting and screaming pig appears on the trail fifty feet in front of them.

"Holy shit, it's Milton's mom." The huge boar moves towards them, its tusk bared. Then it leaps back into the brush and disappears. The rounds from the two marines walk up the

379

trail and into the brush where it disappeared. Another line of fire comes from the other post and walks up the trail. Then there is the thud of a rifle grenade going off. It crashes into the brush, out from the perimeter. The guys at post four join in with two grenades of their own. Explosions rip into the swampy woods, out from the perimeter. Rifle fire follows the grenades into the brush.

"Cease fire, cease fire, goddammit," Cabolero yells over the radio. "Mrs. Milton is gone."

"Sergeant, what the fuck is going on?" Johnson yells into the mike, as everyone around the pit hits the ground.

"Sir, Mrs. Milton just jumped onto the trail between post four and five."

"Gunny, tell them to knock it off with the fucking grenades."

"Yes, sir. We're at post four now."

"Good. Hold there. I'll meet you there."

Johnson grabs his rifle, and he and the radioman move down the trail to post five. As he reaches the men, a gunship flies low over the trees. "Bulldog 1, this is Gunslinger. Do you require fire support?"

"Gunslinger, we do not require support at this time."

"Roger. We'll stand by."

"Let's move." They move up the trail to post four and join the gunny.

"Gunny, this shit is getting out of hand. Now we have the fucking gunships going after Milton's pig."

The crushing of underbrush passes by the front of the post. They stand silently, and Johnson watches as the muzzles of everyone's weapons follow the noise. "It's her again, sir."

"Mrs. Milton is moving."

"Gunny, let's move up to post three." They move forward and leave the two marines at their post. As they near post three, more noise from the brush stops them. When they are about forty feet from the two marines at post three, they point and yell, "Behind you, sir. It's Mrs. Milton."

Johnson swings around. Ten feet away, 300-plus pounds of boar stands glaring at him. It grunts and screams and moves towards him. The sound of Sandovol's pistol next to his ear freezes the boar. It lunges forward and runs into the brush. Rifle fire from those around him and from the other post tear up the bushes where it disappeared. The sound moves away from them in the brush. The thud of a rifle grenade comes from behind him. Two more from post four follow it. They explode out in the swamp.

"Cease fire, cease fire." The gunny helps Johnson to his feet.

"Goddamn, Gunny. That was the ugliest and meanest looking thing I've ever seen. It seems Mrs. Milton is real pissed off now."

"Let's move on to post two."

"Yes, sir."

They move down the trail. Everyone, including Johnson, has their rifles ready. The sound in the brush moves around in front of them as they get to post two. Johnson grabs the handset from the radioman.

"Gunslinger, this is Bulldog 1."

"Roger, Bulldog 1."

"Cruise around the front of our perimeter and see if you can see Mrs. Milton. Over."

"Roger, Bulldog 1."

Johnson watches as the gunship begins moving across the front of their position. Just in front of post three, they hover. The grunting and screams of the boar carry on the wind.

"Bulldog 1, is Mrs. Milton a big ugly fucker?"

"Roger, Gunslinger. We hear her singing from here."

"Well, she is standing on a little rise about 200 feet in front of your perimeter. The bitch is jumping up at us and from the look on her face, I'd say major PMS."

The barrels spin as the rounds fly forward. They rip the trees and bushes to pieces on the rise. The boar jumps down and runs into the brush. The firing stops. The helicopter swings around and moves across the front of the perimeter.

"Shit, Bulldog 1. Have each of your positions throw smoke. That fucking Mother Milton is running around all over the place."

Smoke blossoms from the different posts. The helicopter swings around at post one and moves in front of the perimeter, firing both its 20 mm cannon and its gun pods. Everyone hits the ground as rocks, bushes, and ricochets fly in the air. He ceases fire at the front of post five. A section of swamp thirty feet wide and 400 feet long is laid waste by the gunfire. Trunks of downed trees burn, and the ground is all churned up. As they cross back over the front, their rotors blow the smoke away. On a pile of twisted tree trunks, the boar rises up and screams at the gunship.

"Holy shit, Bulldog. The fucking thing is standing on a tree trunk, and it is fucking pissed. It's too close to your lines for us to fire. Mrs. Milton is majorly bent."

"Roger, Gunslinger. Keep an eye on that thing."

Sandovol comes over to Johnson and Cabolero. "Shit, I've never seen anything like this. But I really like going pig hunting with you guys."

"Thanks." Johnson hand the handset back to the radioman.

"Bulldog, this is Gunslinger. Mrs. Milton is on her way into your front."

The grunts and screams of the pig roll down the trail from post three. Shots ring out, followed bye a cry for a corpsmen.

Cabolero leads them back down the trail. One marine is down, and the other has his rifle aimed into the perimeter. A corpsmen works his way up the trail from post five. They move up around the two marines. The one on the ground has a wound in his left thigh. His buddy holds the pressure point and points into the perimeter.

"Shit, Gunny. That fucking Mrs. Milton came out of the brush and took us both out." The corpsmen moves in and begins working on the downed marine. He looks up at the captain. "Sir, we need a dust off. Milton's pig torn the artery in his leg." In minutes a helicopter is readied. They pick up the marine on a poncho, and carry him to the helicopter.

"Sergeant, pull everyone back to the pit." The marines move back to the pit and take up positions on each side, facing into the brush.

Johnson walks up to the pit. The casing has been sandbagged, and the access plate is visible. They finish securing the bomb. Emanuel looks up at Johnson.

"My God, it sounded like a war out there, Captain."

"It is a war. Between us and some fucker from another time."

"Sir, it's Bulldog."

"This is Bulldog 1. Over."

"Captain, what the fuck is going on over there? We heard the explosions and gunfire, then the gunship cut in. Do you need more fire support?"

"No, sir. We can handle this thing now. We have formed around the bomb. Milton's pig has taken out two marines. They're being lifted back to the naval station."

"Hold one, Captain. You're telling me that all of that fire power was for a pig?"

"Yes, sir. But not an ordinary pig. The bastard is possessed."

"Mr. Johnson, I'm on my way to you to see this bastard."

"Aye, aye, sir. I will send some men out to escort you into the site."

"That will be all right. I'll have my radio operator with me. Bulldog out."

Johnson stands up and looks over the men lying prone on each side of the pit. "The colonel will be joining us in a few minutes. He wants to see the pig from hell."

Colonel Knight gets his rifle and calls his radioman over to leave. He notices Milton getting some coffee. "Corporal, apparently a pig named in your behalf has first squad and your company commander pinned down."

"Sir, I can believe it. That bastard is huge and pissed."

"Very good." Knight goes outside and lets Commander Marino know what is happening. He calls over to the marine sergeant on the beach. "I need one of the machine guns and two men." The sergeant pulls one of the guns and sends it and the gunner with the Colonel. "Good hunting, sir." The sergeant salutes as the helicopter begins to lift. "Right sergeant." Knight smiles.

They fly about fifteen miles east of the beach and land near the other helicopters. Two of the pilots have rifles out and are watching the brush and trail that lead to the site. The colonel gets his directions from them and calls forward to Johnson.

They reach the fork in the trail; Knight looks over the devastation from the gunship. "Shit, we'll probably have the fucking park service all over our ass for this." They signal the pit and start down the trail. The marine with the M-60 walks in front, with the others following. The colonel walks at the rear of the column. About fifty feet from the pit, a cry goes up.

383

"Behind you, it's Mrs. Milton."

The colonel looks over his shoulder. The boar is about ten feet behind him, teeth flared and grunting. It moves forward and squeals. The marines around the pit can't fire because the men on the trail are in their way.

"Run, goddammit!" The colonel and his men run for the pit. The boar ducks back into the brush as the colonel dives into the pit over Johnson and Cabolero. The four marines roll in the mud as the others fire up the trail.

"Bulldog, this is Gunslinger. We think Mrs. Milton is about 200 feet to your left front. There is something crashing through the thicket."

"Gunslinger, this is Bulldog 1. Are you sure it's Mother Milton?"

"We can't tell because of all the brush. Pop smoke down the trail, and we'll clean her up."

Johnson looks at Knight. He nods. "Gunslinger, we're throwing smoke now." Cabolero pulls the pin and throws it down the trail.

"Got you, Bulldog. We're in."

They all get down as the gunship circles over the center of the front and begins firing as it moves towards the creek. The noise is tremendous, and wood and dust fly in the air. A new swath of destruction is torn in the swamp. The gunship moves slowly over the area and hovers over the creek.

"Shit, Bulldog."

"Yeah, did you get her?"

"No, but we fucked up Bambi. Also, we scared out a bunch of oversized rats. They're on the trail looking around. And about six alligators are coming your way also. They're in the creek."

"Hold one." The helicopter swings around and moves forward.

"Bulldog, Mother Milton is on a downed tree trunk. Its time she fucking dies. Hit the deck."

Everyone ducks as six rounds fire from the helicopter, then there is only a whirring sound. The sound of the cannon spooks the group of nutria on the path, and they charge the pit. The smoke clears, and the new threat races at them. Sandovol sees them and yells out, "Don't fire. They're just nutria. Lay flat, and they will just run by."

The marines on the left of the pit bury their heads as the nutria run over them and dive into the pit. They run over everyone in the pit and break for the creek. Two alligators had begun to pull themselves out of the creek by the pallet. When the nutria hit the water, others join them in an attempt to catch an easy meal.

"Bulldog, Mrs. Milton stuck her ass up at us and dove back into the brush. We're low on gas and need to reload. The other ship will be back in a short while. It escorted the medivac unit back to the base. We'll be back in a little while. Over."

Knight gets up and looks around. "Mr. Sandovol, is there any other fucking creature of nature out here that will attack this position?"

Sandovol stands up with him. "Well, I would keep an eye out for snakes. With all the shooting, they're probably moving around."

As they look down the trails on each side, they watch them crawl over the path towards the creek. Cabolero checks their positions and keeps a look out for snakes.

"Sir, the Lanstat is up on bomb number six. We're ready to go."

"All right. Doctor, are you ready?"

"Just a minute, Captain. I have never seen anything like this in my life. I just need to relax for a minute, and get over the trampling by those oversized guinea pigs."

A loud grunting comes from the front, accompanied by a high-pitched squeal.

"Bulldog, this is Razor 1. Over."

The colonel picks up the handset. "Roger, Razor. This is Bulldog."

"We will assume your firing missions until Gunslinger gets back. We're on station, coming in over your landing site." The howl of the engines over the trees turns everyone's eyes towards the landing zone as two Harrier jets ease forward. "Razor, this is Bulldog. We will not need additional fire at this time. Over."

"Roger, Bulldog. We'll stand by." The two jets move forward and climb into the sky.

The colonel looks around. "That's all we need, a fucking air strike on a pig."

"We're ready to start, sir." Johnson puts the headset on and calls for the first number.

BOMB SITE, NUMBER FIVE
LOUISIANA

As the helicopter settles to the ground, the gunny slides the door open and jumps out. He signals the men on the other helicopters to form off to the side. The lieutenant and Susie join them as the engines on the helicopters shut down.

One of the men from the bomb site emerges from the trees at the side of the landing zone. He talks to Lieutenant Neal and Gunny. They all walk over to the others.

"All right, listen up." Neal has his map in his hand. "We're about 100 yards from the site. We'll be crossing three creeks; two are knee level. The third one is about six feet deep, but the current is slow. So keep in touch with your buddies. We don't want to lose anyone. All right, Gunny, let's move out."

"Sir." A lance corporal steps forward.

"Yeah, Folly. What is it?"

"Well, there is some pretty weird shit coming in on the TAC net. Is team one being attacked by a pig?" The men all laugh.

"Well, I'll tell you. Gunny and I can't quite figure out what is going on, either. Hold on." He grabs the handset from the radioman. "Bulldog 1, this is Bulldog 2. Over."

"Bulldog 2, this is Cabolero, sir."

"Gilbert, what the hell is going on over there?" They move over to the helicopter so everyone can hear the conversation on the speakers.

"Well, sir. It's hard to explain, but right now, a marine unit is pinned down by a 300-pound pig."

"Damn, it sounds like he's a real swine."

"Yes, sir. We are definitely getting porked."

The men around the helicopter laugh as a new voice comes on the net. "This is Bulldog, Mr. Neal. I would suggest we hold the pig and pork jokes till after the operation. We certainly don't need anymore hams on the net."

"Aye, aye, sir. We'll get the lard. Out."

"Roger. Bulldog out."

He hands the set back to the radio operator. "Let's go, Gunny."

They follow the scout to the edge of the landing zone, and enter the thick vegetation. An animal path winds over a small knoll and down into a creek. The sky above darkens. The shadows of the trees give the place an eerie look. They all cross the creek and move deeper into the swamp. The group bunches up a little as wet foliage around them pulls at their clothes.

A marine in front of the gunny trips on a root and goes down. Gunny falls on top of him, and Susie and Neal pile on. As everyone tries to extract themselves from the mud, they start laughing. "Here." Gunny grabs Susie's hand and helps her up.

"Is this part of the normal procedure on jungle trails?"

Susie laughs as she brushes herself of. "Yes, ma'am. We plan on falling down about three or four times a day." The gunny turns to the others. "We need to spread out a little more."

They soon reach the second creek; it's twenty feet wide and only about five inches deep. They all watch their footing on the loose rocks. It empties into a large pond or lake; they can only see flashes of it as they move up the trail.

"Gunny, were you in Vietnam?"

He keeps moving forward. "Yes, ma'am. Myself, Staff Sergeant Cabolero, and Colonel Knight. We were also together in Kuwait during desert storm."

"Was it like this in Nam?"

"Yes, except someone was out there trying to kill you. We lost some good marines over there. Watch out for the root." She hops over the gnarled root in the path as they come up to the last creek.

"Shit, you weren't kidding about this one." Gunny talks to the scout.

"Yeah, the bottom's pretty firm, and the current is slow. He'll go first."

He eases into the water, and holds his rifle above his head. The water in the middle of the creek comes up to his shoulders. He climbs up on the other side. "All right, who's next?"

Four marines grab the Lanstat case and lift it over their heads and wade into the water. When they reach the other side, they drag the set up the bank. "We're next." Owens and a marine ford the creek together and climb up the other side.

"All right, Susie. I think you had better hold on to Mr. Neal and myself. It's a little over your head."

"That would be nice." She gets between the two and puts a hand on their shoulders. As they get in the water, she pulls herself up. She floats as they move across the bottom. When they reach mid-stream, Owens yells at them, "Stop, stand still."

They stand in the middle of the creek, and Susie dangles between them. They look slowly around and don't see anything. "What's the problem?"

"Stand still and don't make a sound. I think you have a gator in with you, about ten feet from Lieutenant Neal."

Susie looks around Neal's head as a huge dark green head rises out of the muddy water. It has an animal in its mouth, and it looks around.

"No one move." Owens softly speaks to the others. "No quick movements. It has food. So I think it is trying to get back to the main channel in the water. Just stay still."

The alligator snaps its head up and gets a firmer grip on the large rodent in its jaws. It looks around slowly; the large body joins the huge head. It slowly rises to the surface. Susie's grip on the others tightens as the monster moves slowly towards them.

As it nears them, she looses sight of the head. She slowly turns her head to the front as it passes by. The dark bumpy hide almost obscures the cold dead eye as it passes. It looks deep into Susie's eyes and moves on. As the feet go by, they rub across the three. She can feel the others tighten up as it passes. It seemed that it moves in slow motion. The huge, thick tail moves back and forth in the water. It hits them and then moves on.

Susie looks around the gunny's head. It reaches the main channel and disappears.

"All right, move. Get out of the water," Owens calls to them.

The three seem frozen in the middle of the creek. "Come on. Get the fuck out of the water." They look around and quickly move to the bank and up onto firm ground.

"Oh, my God. Holy shit." Susie storms in a circle and begins crying and yelling. The gunny and Neal stand and look at each other and blow out large breaths.

"It's you two." She turns on them both. "You two, you keep getting me caught up in these situations. My God, that thing was huge. It would have killed us. It's you two. Damn it."

She swings both hands and hits them each in the chest, then puts an arm around both and pulls them into a hard hug. She cries softly as they all hug.

Gunny looks at Neal. "Sir, did you feel the water get warm all around us?"

He nods his head. "Yeah, you too, Gunny."

"Yes, sir. I pissed my pants when it passed. And I'm proud of it." They both start laughing. "Me too, Gunny."

Susie pushes away. "See there you two go. Making fun of a horrible situation." She turns away from them and then looks back at them. "I pissed mine, too."

They all laugh as they get their gear. Owens walks over. "You folks did good. That was a big one. I'd guess fourteen feet."

"Everyone is over. Let's move."

A short way up the trail, the end of the bomb protrudes from the ground. An open space near it runs down to the shore of a large pond or lake. The helicopter is over the water, and they are bringing in the pallet. Susie watches the surface of the water as some alligators thrash their tails and disappear under the water.

While they get the pallet unloaded, she digs around the top of the bomb. She locates the black strip and digs down to get the number. The radioman set up the Lanstat and hands a headset to the gunny. "We're up on the net, Doctor."

"Good, Gunny." She gives him the finger.

"I'm sorry, Susie."

"Then tell them that we have bomb number five." She smiles.

Neal sets the perimeter as the gunny calls for the numbers on the access plate.

ULTIMA
WASHINGTON, D.C.

"Mr. President, we now have both teams at their sites."

Captain Van Nar points to the screen of the bomb tracks. "We have confirmed bombs number six and five. They are finishing up the digging and securing around bomb six; number five is beginning the removal of the access plate.

"An unclear situation at bomb site six has prompted the deployment of two F-18 fighters as air cap and two marine Harriers for close air support. Casualties were air evacuated, and a gunship was used to suppress the aggressor. We had an R4 reconnaissance aircraft do an over fly and take some pictures. They are being processed at NAS New Orleans. They will be sent to us as soon as possible."

Brant looks over to Commandant Swane. "That's a lot of firepower over bomb six."

"Yes, sir. We're setting up a second channel to the site. The battalion commander is now at the site. We'll get a firsthand account of what is going on."

General Lane walks up to the podium. "Mr. President, we have discussed the requirements of the ships with Marshal Shagan's staff. Sky 1 should be making contact as we speak. We'll be linked through to Admiral Sokolov."

"Ultima, this is Sky 1. Over."

"Roger, this is Ultima."

"Sir, Admiral Sokolov is on the line."

"Admiral, this is General Lane."

"How do you do, General."

"Admiral, we have the link with Sky 1. They will supply you with the data on the approaching Cuban jets. And Admiral Hillings's group is set to link you with a satellite for your missiles."

"Thank you, General Lane. Your assistance is greatly appreciated. Is Admiral Hillings with you?"

"Yes, hold one." Hillings goes to podium.

"It is nice to hear from you, Admiral Sokolov."

"Admiral Hillings, we meet again. I hope you and your family are well."

"Thank you, yes."

"This is good. We have done the modification on the ship to link with your satellite. A radar scope has been set aside. It is ready to go when you are."

"We are ready. It is time to turn things over to the technicians."

"You are right. I must prepare for our next move."

"You have fought well, Admiral Sokolov. We send our condolences for the loss of Admiral Kirsanov."

"Thank you, Comrade. We will share a drink when this is over."

"Do svidaniya."

Hillings turns to the president. "Sir, with your approval. As they continue north, we will alert them to their next threat."

"What threat, Admiral?"

"Sir, we have located the Cuban submarines. They are directly in their path in an area we call the Petrified Forest."

CONTROL CENTER
CUBA

"General Morales, we must move now to save our fighters out in the Gulf. They will begin to drop into the sea if we do not get a tanker out to them. The frigate has eluded the submarine and can give fuel to the *OSA* boats."

"Admiral Rivera, the Russians at Matanzas, they blew up our last two tankers, and I have a revolt on my hands from officers loyal to General Quintano. I'm afraid your inability to sink the Russians has cost us dearly."

The general walks up to the admiral. "I have a question. Why didn't the Russians fire any missiles at the ships?"

"Because our brave pilots have knocked out their long-range radar. And they can't afford to send a helicopter out beyond the ships. Our fighters would shoot it down."

"So we have a second air strike and the submarines left to stop the Russians?"

"Yes, General. By the time they reach the squadron, they will not be able to return without refueling. We could recall them so that we don't lose more good men, General."

"They have their orders. They will stand, Admiral."

"General, we have ordered them to death."

"Admiral, I would watch my statements at this point. All officers are under suspicion. Do you understand?"

Morales turns his back to walk away. Rivera grabs a letter opener and plunges it into the general's back. He falls forward, and grabs the desk. Blood appears around the wound and spreads across his uniform.

Rivera lifts the knife again. "Long live Cuba."

As he goes to plunge the knife a second time, the guard at the door cuts him down. A second guard fires, and Rivera's three aides join him on the floor.

"Get me a doctor, now." The guard helps Morales out of the office and down the hall to the dispensary. "Have their bodies moved out and thrown on the pile of those other traitors."

"Yes, sir."

The doctor gives him a shot to kill the pain and removes his shirt. The knife had gone into his upper shoulder and cut into the muscles. The doctor cleans the wound. Morales yells for him to hurry up. "General, the wound is about three inches deep. You're lucky. I can stitch it up for now."

"Do what you must, Doctor. But I need to be on my feet and dealing with the traitors around me." The area around the wound is numbed, and the doctor stitches it up and applies a bandage. Morales walks back to his office and gets a clean shirt out of the closet. The guard helps him put it on as the last body is carried out of the room. A guard comes into the office. "General, your gunships are parked at the side entrance."

"Well, somethings still work. And the other two, where are they?"

"They have moved up the coast to Matanzas. They had contact with General Quintano. He is on the beach, and they have a saboteur trapped in a blue house."

"The pilots have their orders, correct?"

"Yes, sir."

MORALES'S GUNSHIPS
EAST OF MATANZAS

Two Hind-D gunships fly out over the water and head east along the coast. "General Quintano, this is Lightning flight. We are to give you close support if needed."

"Roger, Lighting flight. I am on the beach, just off a blue house. We have one of the saboteurs trapped inside. And we're trying to talk him out."

"Roger, General. We're coming in from the water. We see your helicopter on the beach and the house just behind."

The two gunships swing out and then come in towards the beach. Quintano's helicopter is directly ahead.

"General, you're in the helicopter."

"Roger. Land west of me. I have been placed in command of all Cuban forces. General Morales has been relieved of command by Fidel. So I order you to land next to me, now."

The second helicopter swings to the right and heads into land on the beach. The front one hovers 100 feet off the water. "Sir, I have not received those orders. So I will help you in this situation."

From 300 feet away, the gunship launches rockets into Quintano's helicopter. It explodes in a ball of fire. It then turns its attention to the blue house, and a second volley of fire is sent slamming into the structure. The house is leveled in a mighty explosion. "I hope we have been of service, General Quintano?"

"You have." The pilot looks up and down the beach. His forward guns spray the area around the burning helicopter. From dunes behind the beach, two handheld Grail missiles fly at the gunship. They see the white trail as the missiles hit the Hind, and it falls burning into the surf below.

The other helicopter has landed and turned its engines off. Quintano and his group come out of the dunes. He orders the crew out and watches as the men walk to the front of the helicopter. When they are on the beach, they move forward.

"Smart move, Captain."

He salutes as Quintano walks up. "Sir, we of the regular army are not involved in this. Morales's special guard flew the other ship. We heard the radio broadcast. We are ready to join your forces."

"Thank you, Captain. But what I need is your helicopter. We'll take it from here. You and your men will be driven into Cardenas to join the other forces there. You will be welcomed into the group."

The captain again salutes. "Very good General." They get their things out and walk up the beach to a waiting police car.

Brock and Quintano stand in front of the helicopter. They look at the burning house. A policeman runs up to them.

"Sir, we found one body in the rubble. These papers were on him." They look at the charred papers and look at Miguel's ID card from the airbase. "Thank you. We have found our man."

"Officer." Brock walks over to him. "When I was on the other side of the house, I saw a trail that leads up the shore. It may pay to check it. We still have one man running free."

"Sí, señor. We will check."

"Still on the hunt." Brock turns back to Quintano. "Yeah, I think he went up that trail."

"We have bigger fish to fry. We need to meet Vargas and the others on the road to Matanzas. We have to stop this insanity as soon as possible."

Quintano climbs in behind the pilot as Brock jumps in with the two crewmen. The big gunship comes to life and rises into the sky. It heads for the crossroads outside of Matanzas.

BRIDGE OF THE *MOSKVA*
THE GULF

The admiral stands next to the plotting board and watches as Pstygo works with the technicians. They stand around a radar-scope, turn knobs, and throw switches. "I think you have it." Pstygo pats the man on the back.

He turns to Sokolov. "Sir, we have the satellite link in place."

"Very good. Set the coordinates to the Cuban group."

The weapons officer watches the screen as the sweep hand moves across the face.

He looks back at Sokolov; the red and green lights of the radar sets color his face in odd hues.

"Admiral, we have three targets: the frigate and two pods of the *OSA* boats. We can target each group with one of the destroyers and have the *Vladivostok* fire her missiles in tandem."

"Have the cruiser fire on the frigate. How many does she have remaining?"

"Two sir. We'll take command of them as soon as she gets them away. The captain is in the control center and requests to speak to you."

Sokolov picks up a handset and talks to the captain of the cruiser. "Very good, Captain. We wish you the best of luck." He hangs up the phone and rejoins the weapons officer.

"The *Vladivostok* captain has requested that he be allowed to detach from the main group and steam due south. He will be down to twenty-five officers and men. They will do their best to keep the fighters off of us. As soon as you are ready, they will fire their missiles and come about."

"Yes, sir."

The admiral climbs up to the bridge and goes out onto the flying wing on the port side. A speaker blares on the ship. "Stand by on the ship. The *Vladivostok* will be firing missiles in five minutes."

He watches the twin launchers on the starboard side rise up into position. The covers over the front of the missiles move out of the way. Men on the other ships stop what they are doing and watch the cruiser. They cheer as smoke billows from one tube and the missile launches. The second missile quickly follows it. The ships are informed that missiles are on their way to the Cuban frigate. Men around the admiral clap and cheer as the missles disappear into the mist.

The cruiser moves out in front of the other ships and slowly turns. It passes by the squadron on the port side. The captain has ordered flags and pennants raised. Its lights are all turned on. As it passes, the captain calls out over loud speakers, "At your leave, sir," and doffs his hat. The admiral picks up a handset and calls back. "Good hunting, Captain." Sokolov grabs his hat and waves it in the air. The crewmen all wave their hats and yell encouragements to each other. The foghorns aboard the ships blare out over the water. The cruiser moves to the south and heads into the mist.

The admiral goes back inside and crosses to the other side of the ship. He looks over the three destroyers and watches as they prepare to fire their remaining missiles.

The weapons officer joins him on the flying bridge. "Sir, the missiles from the *Vladivostok* will impact the frigate in approximately nine minuets. Their range was just over 100 miles. Flight time is twelve minutes. They should get quite a shock when those SS-N-3 warheads come in. It's over 4,000 pounds of high explosives." Sokolov looks at his watch; it is 3:20.

He watches as the three destroyers pull away from the *Moskva* at a thirty-degree angle. "What is the range of the *OSA* boats?"

"Sir, they are about sixty miles out. We'll cut it close; the SS-N-22s aboard have a tactical range of about seventy nautical miles. The two forward destroyers will fire two each at the main pod; the stern destroyer will fire two at the second pod. That will leave us with two missiles remaining on each ship, sir."

"Very good." The speakers blare across the water and on the ship. "Missiles being fired, three minutes. Clear all deck areas forward." The men on the *Moskva* join the admiral in watching the destroyers set up to fire. The weapons officer looks at his watch. "It should be right about now, sir."

Missiles streak from the forward two destroyers, and another fires from the last one. As soon as they are clear, a second missile launches. The smoke trails disappear into the mist.

As soon as they have fired, the destroyers begin to maneuver into positions around the *Moskva*, one on each side and one astern. Sokolov moves back inside the bridge. "Commander, bring us up to fifteen knots."

"Aye, aye, sir."

ULTIMA
WASHINGTON, D.C.

"Mr. President, the Russians have launched their missiles against the Cuban ships." The president looks up at Van Nar, and then at the screen. Little circles leave the Russian ships on the radar screen. On the imaging screen, rockets fly off the destroyers.

"Sir, the squadron is picking up speed. The cruiser is heading directly into the path of the attacking Cuban aircraft."

Admiral Hillings watches and walks up to the podium. "Sir, the cruiser is in bad shape and is slowing down the others. They have been evacuating their injured and non-essential personal. Our estimate would give the cruiser about four more hours before it sinks. They will attempt to disrupt the aircraft and fight to the end."

"A brave act that will stand out on a heroic day."

"Well said, Mr. Brant."

They listen as numbers are called out at the two sites. Val verifies them with General Kuznetsov, and he passes them on to the two teams. "We are ready for our next number at site six."

The general reads a number, and Val verifies it. "This is site five ready for our next number."

"Your next number is four."

"Roger, site six. Four."

"Roger, site five. Four."

The interpreter next to Brant grabs his arm. "Sir, stop them now." Brant is taken by surprise. "Sir, the number. Stop them."

"This is Brant, Stop, stop. Both sites check in. We will stand by."

"Val, this is Brant. Our interpreter believes there is a mis-call on the last number."

Val checks his card, and checks with the general in Moscow. "Well, I show number four for site six, and number seven for site five."

"Val, we show both sites verifying number four."

"This is site six, we have number four."

"This is site five, we also have number four."

"Site five, you have the wrong number. You should be removing number seven."

Both sites verify their numbers with Val. "All right, I think we have everything straight."

"Val, this is Brant. We're all under a lot of pressure. May I ask that we do one site at a time? It's critical only through the access plate screws."

"I agree, Mr. Brant. We'll conclude site six first. Is that agreed?"

"This is Susie at site five. We'll take a break while Emanuel finishes his access panel."

"Thank you, Doctor."

The president walks over to the interpreter and shakes his hand. "Thank you, Mr. Droski. We could have had a terrible accident here." Droski thanks him and goes back to monitoring the Russian conversation. Brant walks over by the president and gets a glass of tea. "Thank God Droski caught that."

The president nods. "We don't need any more excitement."

BRIDGE OF CUBAN FRIGATE
THE GULF

"Sir, we have an inbound missile at ten miles."

The Cuban captain moves towards the starboard side as the first boom of the decoy system goes off. The twin 30 mm canons towards the inbound missiles begin firing. The captain looks back at the men on the bridge; they stand stunned. He looks back in the direction of the missiles when the first one hits.

The first missile hits forty feet from the stern; its 2,000-pound warhead rips the side of the ship. The second missile hits thirty feet forward of the other. The blast kills everyone on the bridge, and tons of water race into the disembodied ship. It wallows to starboard, and secondary explosions rip deeper into the core. It rolls onto its wounds, and sinks beneath the waves.

A coal black cloud of smoke stands above the spot as a marker, then it is quickly blown away in the wind.

ON CUBAN *OSA* BOATS
THE GULF

The men on the *OSA* boats are watching the lines as the two-lead boats tow the two others. They are beginning to break into calmer water, and they look forward to meeting the frigate for fuel and other supplies. The radars on the two forward boats pick up the missiles at ten miles. Alarms go off as the boats' captains look over their sterns into the mist.

The first missile races in and explodes twenty feet above their heads. The 800 pounds of high explosive flattens the lead boats. In quick succession, the other three explode above the remains of the boats. When the smoke clears, wreckage and bodies dot the surface of the sea.

The second pod of the three *OSA* boats sees the explosions on the horizon dead ahead of them. And in seconds, they too join their comrades in the deep when two missiles pound the small boats into rubble.

Near the spot of the explosion, a Mig-23 crashes into the sea. High above, a lone parachute blooms and its cargo swings towards the dark water. A mile farther south, a second Mig runs out of fuel. Its pilot punches out as the fighter drops its nose down and falls from the sky.

BRIDGE OF THE *MOSKVA*
THE GULF

"Admiral, we have sunk the frigate and destroyed the *OSA* boats. We also were able to observe that two of their fighters apparently ran out of fuel and crashed."

"Excellent shooting, Lieutenant." The weapons officer smiles and requests permission to pass the good news on to the other ships. As the loud speakers on the ships dispense the news, a cheer goes up from the men on the ships. Sokolov looks over the back of the *Moskva* as damage repair crews work to remove and cover holes in the ship. The other ships have crews working also. They head into a gentle shower. Farther ahead, a black wall of clouds rests on the water.

Sokolov walks down to the combat center and calls Air Marshal Shagan. He tells him of their success in sinking all the Cuban surface combatants. He also relates the casualties and damage estimates. Shagan puts his call on the loud speaker so that the others in the room can hear.

"We salute you, Admiral Sokolov. You have won a great victory. But we have not gone unscathed; we have lost many brave comrades this day. There will be many tears shed in our homeland.

"I talked with Admiral Hillings. Your journey continues to put you and your brave comrades in harm's way. They have news for you on the Cuban submarines.

"Admiral, please pass on to your men that we at the war ministry are made proud to be in the Russian military by your deeds."

"Thank you, Air Marshal Shagan." Sokolov hangs up the phone, and looks at his watch. It's 3:30 P.M.

"Get me a line through to Admiral Hillings, please."

"Aye, aye, sir."

ULTIMA
WASHINGTON, D.C.

"Gentlemen." Van Nar stands at the podium. "We have confirmation: all Cuban surface ships were sunk by the Russian missile attack. The squadron is now proceeding north at fifteen knots. We were tracking eight fighters staged near the *OSA* boats. Two have now crashed into the sea. They are running out of fuel."

Van Nar listens over her headset. "Admiral, there is a call coming through from Admiral Sokolov."

Hollings turns in his chair and faces the screens. "Please put it on the loud speaker."

"Admiral Sokolov, are you there?"

"Yes, Admiral Hillings. Marshal Shagan asked me to contact you regarding the Cuban submarines."

"Yes, we have news for you. I would like to add that your destruction of the Cuban ships was very thorough."

"Thank you, Admiral. But it is sad that we were forced to take such extreme measures. Good men on both sides have died in defense of their comrades."

"We have a location on one of the Cuban submarines."

Sokolov moves in next to his plotting officer, Pstygo.

"About an hour ago, one of them surfaced to recharge his batteries. We have tracked them for the last two days. They are hiding in an area we call the Petrified Forest." He reads off the coordinates for the area. Pstygo runs his finger over the map and points it out to Sokolov.

"I see it, Admiral. We call that area the Frozen Forest."

"Good name. We both view the sub-surface formations in the same manner. We believe the second submarine will surface in a while and recharge its batteries also. We are estimating your arrival in the area at around 9:00 P.M. given your present speed."

"I agree. We will meet them in the darkness."

"Yes, we also estimate your *Victor* class submarine will arrive on your base course in about two and a half hours. They will be twenty miles ahead of you."

"Excellent, Admiral. My plotting officer fully agrees with your estimates. We will attempt to make contact with the submarine as soon as possible. They are unaware of the threat before them."

"Very good. You are provided with the satellite link for navigational purposes. And Sky 1 will keep you informed of the airborne threat."

"I again thank you and your Joint Chiefs for their assistance at this time. Sokolov out."

"Admiral." Hillings turns towards the president. "What is this place you call the Petrified Forest?"

"Sir, it is an area where undersea currents have carved out tall spires of rock and canyons. They are from 200 to 1,400 feet deep. It is an excellent place to hide for a submarine. The rock formations and canyons make location difficult, so they can move about almost invisibly."

"I see. Thank you, Admiral." The president's eyes move over to the screen showing the storm. It swirls with a dark black eye in its center. The bomb locations being worked blink on the next screen.

BOMB SITE, NUMBER SIX
LOUISIANA

Emanuel slowly finishes turning the last screw on the access plate and hands it and the screwdriver over to Cabolero.

"That got it." He leans back as a gentle rain falls from the darkening sky. The marines around him lie in the mud, facing the thick brush. As he wipes his face off, gunfire suddenly erupts from the direction of the landing strip. The tracer rounds cross into the tangled mass at the head of the trail.

"LZ, this is Bulldog. What the hell is going on?"

"Bulldog, Mrs. Milton came bolting out of the brush and tried to get one of the choppers. She went back into the trees towards you."

"Roger. Bulldog out."

"Bulldog, this is High Cap. Over."

"Roger, High Cap."

"If Mrs. Milton crosses above 5,000 feet, she's chitlins."

"Roger, High Cap. Bulldog out."

"Holy shit, something tells me were not going to hear the end of this for a while."

A smile crosses Johnson's lips. "I think you're right, Skipper."

Emanuel looks around. The gunfire had driven him into the side of the pit, and he brushes chunks of mud off. "My God, does that thing ever settle down?"

"Sergeant, let Val know we're done with the plate. We are proceeding to complete the disarming. Dr. Davies can start on her bomb now."

"Roger." He passes the word on as a crashing of branches makes them all look across the path into the wall of brush. Knight pulls his pistol and has it at the ready. Johnson is in the kneeling position with his rifle at the ready. Cabolero slowly removes his sheath knife.

"Skipper, it sounds like he is right in front of us."

He points with the knife in his hand. "You're right, sergeant."

"I suggest you finish this thing off, Doctor, so we can get the hell out of here."

"Right." Emanuel kneels in the mud and using his flashlight, reaches in and disarms the timer. His hand moves to the detonator switch and turns it off. With pliers he loosens the locking ring and hands them to Cabolero. His hand turns the detonator, and just as he begins to lift it out, a huge pig crashes out of the brush on the other side of the creek. It snorts and squeals.

The detonator slips from his grip as he, like the others, looks over at the new threat. Lighting flashes as the pig runs back and forth on the shoreline, grunting and squealing.

"Sir, should we take it out?" A marine next to Knight kneels and takes aim. Knight watches the large pig kicking sand and yelling across the creek at him and the others.

"No, not unless it starts crossing the creek."

Emanuel regains his composure and reaches into the void and lifts the detonator up and out into the air. He starts to stand as a bolt of lightning turns the area silver-blue. The crash of the thunder is matched by the crash of the brush behind him.

As he turns to look at the source, a huge black form rushes across the opening at the men in the pit. It's initial cries lost are in the trailing concussion of the thunder.

"God." The word sticks in his throat and hangs in the air as the boar rushes at him.

The sudden apparition facing them stuns everyone. Knight rolls on his back and fires a round into the side of the boar as it lunges into the air.

Cabolero pushes Emanuel and the detonator aside and takes the full brunt of the attack. His knife buries to the hilt in the belly of the beast. Its momentum drives both of them over the edge of the pit and down the slope to the edge of the creek. Cabolero lies on his back, his feet pointing up the slope as the boar rolls over and regains its footing. It looks across the creek at its mate and forces out a long loud squeal. Then it turns towards Cabolero, its tusks bared. It rushes at him as he tries to rise in the mud. Three shots tear into the side of the boar. The impact knocks it into the creek.

Cabolero looks up the slope as Johnson lowers his smoking rifle. A cheer goes up behind him, from the others. Johnson walks down to Cabolero and gives him a hand up. "Thanks, Skipper."

"Simper fi." His eyes are still on the huge body floating in the water. They shake hands.

A corpsman checks Cabolero as the colonel joins them at the creek bank.

"Mrs. Milton was one tough bitch. I'm sorry it had to end this way."

"Yeah." Johnson looks up at the other pig. It grunts and disappears into the brush.

Cabalero walks into the water and pulls his knife out. He grabs its tail and cuts it and one ear off. He walks up to Johnson.

"These are yours, sir."

As the men join them on the bank, others pack up the Lanstat and put the detonator into its case. The bomb pick-up helicopter is warming up as two navy men secure the harness on the bomb casing. They walk up the slope to the trail.

"Bulldog, this is the Grim Reaper. Over."

"Roger, this is Bulldog."

"Sir, we are being told that Mrs. Milton has been capped."

"Roger that. We're pulling out, Reaper. Bulldog out."

Emanuel joins them on the trail. He sees the ear and tail that Johnson is holding. "My people believe that the bravery of a warrior is proportionate to the bravery of his foe."

Johnson holds the tail up, and they all look at it. "Then we were fortunate today. We were tested by an honorable foe."

Emanuel watches as the three marines turn, facing the creek, and render a salute.

They can hear the helicopters warming up at the LZ. "Let's move." Knight takes the lead, and they head back up the trail. As they walk up the trail, the two gunships fly overhead. They hover out of the way as the pick-up ship comes in, and they hook the bomb up. With a tug it is lifted into the air and begins the flight to the beach. The two gunships hover over the floating pig. They both dip their noses then pull up and fly back to the LZ to escort the team to their next site.

Johnson waits until all the others are aboard the helicopters and then jumps up into his seat. "We're out of here." The motor revs up and the helicopter begins to rise up into the air. "Well, Doctor." Knight looks over to Emanuel. "Let's hope the next one is a little less involved."

QUINTANO'S HIND-D
CUBA

Quintano rests his head against the pad behind his seat and closes his eyes for a while. The droning of the engine inside the big Hind-D gunship sent shivers of power through the body. He enjoyed these helicopters; they displayed brute force like nothing else. The three gunships moved quickly across the rolling hills behind the beach leading to the main highway to the west. Brock looks out the side window at the gunship next to them. Its camouflage seemed to highlight its brutal nature. The weapons stores on his side is poised for action, and the nose gun moves back and forth.

Quintano opens his eyes and looks towards Brock. "I sense you like this helicopter better."

Brock smiles. "General, where were heading, this brute will carry the day."

Quintano nods his head. "I agree."

They pass from the foothills and turn west when they hit the road. As they fly west, they pass over lines of trucks and armored vehicles. Every thing is moving towards the junction at Santa Angelo. They pass by troop helicopters moving towards the rendezvous.

The pilot calls back to Quintano. "Sir will be landing in just a few minutes. They are routing all aircraft to a large field just north of the main road."

"Very good." He motions to Brock. "We're down in just a few minutes."

"Right." Brock can feel the change in the seat as the helicopter begins to slow down and do a slight right turn. The three gunships form a line and land next to a line of troop ships already on the ground. As they settle to the ground, a truck carrying Captain Vargas moves in from the side. Brock opens the hinged doors on his side, and he and Quintano step out onto the grass field.

"General." Vargas waves his hand out the window as they pull up. "Sir, we have a command post set up at the edge of the roadway." They get in and head to the intersection. The truck pulls in behind two ACRV-2 command vehicles. Their rear doors open. As Quintano gets out, he can see men leaning over a plotting table in one of the vehicles. Men are moving between the two, and radio operators in the vehicles are directing forces moving on the road. As they walk up the ramp into the vehicle, a stout officer at the table turns and then calls the men to attention.

Quintano salutes. "Gentlemen, continue on, please."

He extends his hand. "Zino, I'm glad you're here."

"Thank you, sir. We have a mixed group of staffs here, but I was able to bring most of my own with me. We are at your service, General."

"Like always, you come well prepared. Let's see where we stand. It is paramount we move quickly." The men pour over the outstretched maps on the plotting table. Zino and Vargas brief Quintano on the location of troops and the steps taken by Morales to counter them. Zino uses a pointer on a wall map as Quintano leans against the plotting table, drinking a cup of coffee.

"I have taken the liberty of dispatching a mechanized company to this point five miles from the naval base. We have recon BRDMs out on all roads leading towards Havana. We have tanks on the road; they will reach us in about an hour at this location. They can be off loaded at the locations you wish."

His pointer moves towards Malangas. "I have dispatched two companies of mechanized infantry to this location, three miles from the main entrance. Our scouts have not reported any movement of Morales's troops as they edge their way towards Havana."

Quintano takes a last drink and nods his head. "Excellent as always, Zino. I agree with you on the deployment. It will save us some time. I will take the attack to Malangas with two of the gunships. Zino, I would consider it a favor if you would assume the command of the troops at the naval base."

"Yes, sir."

"Very, good. I would like you to take the last gunship and an air unit. We must move quickly. Morales can still do a lot of harm." Quintano looks at his watch; it is 3:45. "In forty-five minutes, we will jointly attack both the air base and the naval station."

Zino checks his watch. "Sir, I will retire and join the force outside the naval station. The scout informed me that there were some tanks at the location." He motions one of his staff over, and they both go to the front and get their gear.

Quintano walks up by them. "It does not seem right to ask you to take this mission without some incentive. Good luck, Colonel Zino." They shake hands.

"Thank you, sir. We will launch our attack at 4:30." He and his aide move out and are driven to the last gunship. It brings its engines up and is soon on its way. A line of air assault helicopters rises up and begins to follow the gunship.

"Well, Captain Vargas. It seems that you will be moving up the main road towards Havana."

"Yes, sir."

"The road is clear to Colon. Send a force from there to Guines. As you continue towards Havana, we should meet again outside of Matanzas."

"Yes, sir." Vargas turns to the staff. "Prepare to move out as soon as the general is airborne."

Brock and Quintano pick up some extra ammo and walk out to the waiting truck. Quintano turns at the bottom of the ramp and walks back up to the top.

"Captain Vargas."

"Yes, sir."

"You have done a fine job."

"Thank you, General. We will continue to do a fine job."

"Very good, Major. Carry on." Quintano smiles as Vargas salutes.

Quintano and Brock are driven out to the gunship, and he talks to the commander of the airmobile group that will be flying with him. They climb in, and the ship pulls up into the air. Another line of assault helicopters rises in their wake and follows them out.

Vargas continues to direct the preparations for moving on when he suddenly stops. "Did Quintano say 'major' when he left?" His staff gathers around him, laughing. "You are so busy we thought that you missed it. Congratulations, Major Vargas, from us all."

"Thank you, gentlemen. Now let's move."

COMMAND CENTER
CUBA

"Excuse me, General."

Morales looks up from his chair. "Wait." He puts his hand out. "Doctor, I need another shot. The pain is getting worse." The doctor gives his shot as the lieutenant briefs him on the latest developments.

"Sir, our scouts have contacted forces outside of the air base at Malangas and the naval base. We believe that an attack is imminent on both locations."

"Do we have forces moving towards them? And do we have any additional news on the two gunships that were sent to remove General Quintano?"

"We have troops moving up from Pinar Del Rio to positions around Havana. There is a central force moving from Santa Clara up the main highway. We cannot confirm the loss of General Quintano. Two helicopters were destroyed at the contact site. And we have not heard his voice on the TAC nets. But three gunships did land at some command trailers, and then left in different directions. The center force is now on the move, and tanks are being shipped by truck towards the front of the column."

"Shit." He bangs the desk with his left hand.

"How soon will we have the forces from Pinar Del Rio?"

The lieutenant looks at his watch. "Sir, in about an hour the lead elements should be arriving in the capital."

Morales looks at his watch. "You're saying 5:45? That is the soonest that they can get here?"

"Yes, sir. We have three companies of air assault troops available from Bauta air base and eight gunships."

"Then send one company to Malangas with two gunships. And sent another company to Malazus with two gunships. Have the other four start to move down the road towards Colon. They should be looking for any scout vehicles they may have sent out. If they contact the main force, have them attack, then withdraw back to Malazas."

"Yes, sir. We have six fighter-bombers at Bauta. They are being held in reserve."

"Is there any word from the fighters that went south on a special mission?"

"Yes, sir. They landed at the airfield outside of Maracaibo to refuel."

"Very good, very good. Finally some good news. They're right where they should be. I want to be contacted immediately if they call."

"Yes, sir." He leaves the room and shuts the door.

A captain of Morales's special guard pours him dark rum and hands it to him. "Sir, we can deal with Quintano and the others. Especially if the plane with Fidel on it crashes at sea. Quintano's only thread of authority is a short radio message." The general drinks down the dark fiery liquid, and slides the glass onto the top of the desk.

"We'll wait until we get the troops from Del Rio. Then we will move against Quintano and the others. I'm going to lay down for a while. Wake me if there is any news."

He walks into a side room and lies down on a cot. He rests his head on the pillow and closes his eyes. The pain in his shoulder stabs and then melts away.

ULTIMA
WASHINGTON, D.C.

Captain Van Nar walks up to the podium. "Gentlemen." Those in the room look up at her and the screens. "We now have bomb number six at the beach location. The nemesis of team one was killed at the location. The team is now airborne and en route to its next location."

She pushes a button and one of the screens displays a map of Cuba. Lines appear in different colors. She uses her pointer to emphasize certain locations. "We are showing General Quintano's forces at these locations and positions. We believe that an attack at these locations will occur in the next hour."

The screen on the Russian fleet pulls back and shows the locations of all the ships. "The first wave of Cuban fighter-bombers will be within range of the *Vladivostok* in fifteen minutes. They are in contact with Sky 1. We believe that the sea action will commence at 4:00 P.M."

She points to the bomb track screen. "Dr. Davies is now removing the last of the screws on the access plate of bomb five. They will probably be airborne shortly after 4:00 P.M." She points to the screen showing Evita spinning with its dark eye staring back. "We have a hurricane flight coming out of Florida. It will enter the storm at approximately 4:10. We have escorts up to the point of entry. All Cuban airspace behind the storm is clear. All picket ships have been moved east and west of the storm track. Thank you, gentlemen."

The president watches as the number six bomb location on the screen goes yellow. But the other five circles remain red. His eyes are drawn to the swirling mass of the storm. The dark eye seems to look back from the screen in defiance.

Brant walks over to him. "Sir, we'll have the reports on the storm and how the evacuation is going. They will be here at 4:00."

"Thank you, Brant. I hope that we will be receiving some encouraging news."

"Yes, sir. We are doing pretty well so far. I only hope our luck continues."

BOMB SITE, NUMBER FIVE
LOUISIANA

Susie hands the screw and the screwdriver to the gunny. "Let the beach know that the plate is off and the sensor is disarmed."

She leans back and rocks on her knees in the mud, and she pulls out her small flashlight. The sky continues to darken. She looks beyond the pit at the open water of the lake. In the shadows of the pallet on the beach, two large shapes move low up the beach. The others are facing the pit or outwards into the brush.

"Ah, Gunny. You might want to have someone check the pallet on the beach. I think a couple of your swimming buddies are trying to join us." Neal and Marshall look back over their shoulders at the edge of the lake. Owens stands up.

"Shit, what the hell are they doing?" Neal rises next to Owens.

"Let me have a couple of your marines, and I'll get rid of them."

"Right." Neal motions a couple of the men over to join Owens.

"We'll work our way down to the edge of the water and just drive them back."

They shine their flashlights on the two intruders. Their incandescent yellow eyes shine in the light. One of them gives out a long hissing sound as the men move towards them. Neal kneels at the edge of the pit, his rifle at the ready. Owens and the others yell and slap the stocks of their rifles to scare them back into the water. One turns and hisses, then drags itself quickly into the darkening water. The other rises up on its short legs and suddenly moves at the men.

"Shit!" The three men turn and run back up with the others.

"That was pretty good, Mr. Owen." Susie watches as the dark green form lowers itself down and opens its mouth. The pink and white of its teeth and gums stand out in sharp contrast to the dark colors around it.

Hiss. The jaws snap shut.

"Fuck this." Neal stands up and fires off four quick rounds into the air. The alligator looks and then turns and slides back into the water.

"Well, that should do it." Neal lowers his weapon.

"Very good, Mr. Neal. The direct total fright package. Man's ultimate tool for getting the respect of lesser creatures."

Susie goes back to the bomb; the light in her hand plays off the switch for the detonator. She throws the switch and removes the connector. Next she pushes the switch on the timer. The gunny hands her the pliers, and she disengages the locking collar on the detonator.

"Here." She hands him the pliers. She reaches in and turns the detonator. She slowly lifts it out.

"Clear." She hands it to Neal. "We're out of here."

Neal puts the detonator in its case and hands it to one of the navy men as the others slip the harness over the casing.

"Ultima, this is team two. We are securing this site."

"The package is being wrapped now. Over."

The gunny hands the radio gear back to the marine now packing up the Lanstat. He walks over to Susie as she walks out of the pit with Owens and Neal. The sound of the incoming helicopter echoes over the water to their front. Its running lights shine out across the surface. Dozens of yellow eyes stare from short stocks above the water.

"Let's get out of here. Gunny, saddle them up."

As they near the edge of the first creek, Susie looks back and watches the men hook up the harness and pull the casing out of the hole. The helicopter picks up the other naval men and leaves heading south.

"We need to wait here for a minute." Neal moves by them and signals two marines standing on the top of the slope.

"We're all set. Everyone down." They all kneel down along the trail.

"Fire in the hole!" The marines at the top of the slope pull the pins on grenades and throw them into the creek. Susie hears them hit the water and then the blast as they both explode. Mud and water fall on everyone along the trail.

"Christ, this had to be one of your ideas, Mr. Neal."

"Yes, ma'am. It's new, it's innovative, and it works." The lead marines throw illumination grenades along the shoreline. They pop and hiss in the mud. They begin moving across, with two men on the shore providing cover. Susie and the others float across the creek.

"I doubt that you will be receiving any wild life awards this year, Mr. Neal."

"That may be true, but the team loves me."

The men around them all sing out, "Aye, aye, sir."

They cross the second creek and move towards the last one. The sound of the helicopters warming up comes from up ahead of them. They reach the edge of the last creek and wait for everyone to join up. As the lead men shine their flashlights across the creek, two triangular heads rise out of the water.

"Excuse me, but are the rocks growing heads?" Susie looks at Neal and Gunny.

They both shrug their shoulders. "They're snapping turtles." Neal pushes by. "Get me a couple of branches." They hand them to him and he wades out into the creek. He waves the branch in front of the first turtle, and the snap of its jaws echoes in the air. He lifts the turtle up and tosses him into the deeper water. He does the second turtle and waves the others forward. "It's clear." They all move across the creek and load the helicopters. As they lift into the air, the co-pilot leans back to talk to Neal.

"We have been ordered back to the beach. The first team will also be there."

He leans forward towards Susie. "They want us back at the beach. We should be there in just a few minutes."

She smiles knowingly and pulls her field jacket tighter around her neck. She glances quickly at her watch. It's 3:58. She thinks to herself that they have done well to have disarmed the fifth bomb by now. She leans back and closes her eyes to catch a few quick moments of rest.

CHAPTER 13

ULTIMA
WASHINGTON, D.C.

Captain Van Nar walks over to Admiral Hillings and then moves on to Secretary Brant. They talk in low tones, and he nods and reads over a message that she handed him. Others in the room are on phones and talking to one another. She leaves Brant and walks up to the podium.

"Gentlemen, we will have a couple of reports on the storm and also on the state of the evacuation in southern Louisiana. Also, a request has come in from the Russian fleet commander. Admiral Hillings will discuss this matter."

"Perhaps we should consider the request from Admiral Sokolov first." The president looks over at Brant and back at Hollings.

"Yes, sir. We will consider this issue first." Brant looks over at Hillings. "If you would, Admiral." As Hollings reaches the podium, he puts his notes down. "Mr. President, the request from Admiral Sokolov is for a tactical channel from the satellite. It's to control their SS-N-14 missiles. We are not recognizing the need for the channel, but would have no problem complying with your directive, Mr. President."

"I wonder what it would be used for."

"We would guess mid-course corrections on the missiles. But with no surface units of the Cubans in the area, the missiles are useless. And the *Moskva* has all the anti-submarine missiles it needs."

"Well, we can only go with Admiral Sokolov. I would tend to think he has a plan of some sort." Brant looks back at the president.

"I agree Mr. Brant. Admiral, please provide Sokolov with the channel he has requested."

"Yes, sir. We are in contact with them and can down link to them in a few minutes." The admiral walks over and gets on the phone to the comm center. He then gets on the phone to Sokolov as Captain Emmett walks up to the podium. He checks his mike and has the screen with the storm on it focus down, so that the eye fills the screen.

"Mr. President, you are now looking at one of the most dangerous natural events ever seen by man. The eye has now compressed down to thirdy miles across; the Sanboro effect is at full strength. Estimates on wind velocity are entering ranges never before recorded. We have estimated gusts of up to 300 miles per hour. At the edge of the eye, we have what appear to be vortexes which are forming on the trailing face of the eye. We believe that there are waterspouts forming near the trailing edge. And from the looks of the water inside the eye, some type of anomaly is occurring."

He pushes a button, and the screen moves back. "The storm is now 110 miles across, and is on a direct line to New Orleans. When we can get the storm chaser inside, we'll get the definite answers on Evita. From what we're seeing at this time, this could be the worst hurricane ever recorded. It has moved beyond our normal method of categories. We should be getting live updates from the C-130, after it gets inside.

"We have the storm moving at twenty miles per hour; the leading edge of the eye will make land fall at approximately 4:00 A.M. tomorrow. We have seen killer storms in the past, and endured them against our coast. What we have here is pure death. Nothing will withstand the impact of this storm. Are there any questions, gentlemen?"

"How soon will the C-130 be in the storm?"

Emmett looks at his watch. "They will enter the outer canopy at 1610 our time. They will be coming in from the northeast." He points to the top of the storm and has a computer track drawn over the storm. The green dotted line enters the storm and flies completely around the eye, and then turns into the eye on the southwest quadrant. It flies around in the eye and leaves the eye out along its original in flight track. Emmett picks up his papers and steps away from the podium.

"Mr. Emmett, please remain in close contact with us on this storm. I would like an update as soon as the storm chaser is inside the eye, or when there are any new developments."

"Yes, sir, Mr. President."

General Becker walks up to the podium. There is a screen showing southern Louisiana. He picks up the pointer and aims the laser onto the screen. "Mr. President, the evacuation of the bomb area is progressing at a quick pace. We have twelve hours until the full impact of the storm hits the coast. We now have elements of the alert force on patrol in all areas now shaded in yellow." Over half the area is shaded over and the location of the forces are shown as black triangles on the map. The main roads are highlighted in blue.

"We have helicopters from all services crisscrossing the areas looking for anyone not picked up yet. We have received word of people out in fishing boats and camping, who are being air lifted to evacuation points. We have pictures from the news helicopter at KNLT. They're pre-empting all of their normal programming and going with a live report on the evacuation and the storm itself. We'll put the latest report up on screen one."

The screen comes alive with Marcy Lane, standing next to the main highway from the south. Cars are passing behind her in an orderly manner. A drizzling rain sweeps the scene. "The evacuation continues to move north in an orderly manner, and we have talked with the military officers. We are not allowed any farther south of here, but they are guarding the now-deserted towns and hamlets."

The screen goes quiet, but the pictures remain. There are scenes of the traffic going north, and the police and national guard troops directing traffic. The lot around the superdome continues to fill. "We have two of the local officers with each group of soldiers. They will remain with them until 0200, and then they will be air lifted to the dome. The military personnel will be lifted out at 0300 to the naval station."

"Very good, General Becker. Things seem to be going quite well."

"Yes, Mr. President. We are now at about sixty percent completion."

"General, have all precautions have been taken to ensure that everyone is out of the area on time?"

"Yes, Mr. Secretary. We have helicopters standing by at all locations. We will have secondary ships on standby, in case of a failure. They will be dispatched to the area and the downed helicopter abandoned. We will get everyone out."

"Every thing seems to be in full gear, and in full control."

"Thank you, General."

CRASH SITE
BARATARIA BAY

Susie is jolted as the helicopter swings around to land on the beach. They settle in next to the one from team one. They climb out and walk over to the main command helicopter and are welcomed by Commander Marino and Val. Knight and Emanuel are at the front getting some coffee as they walk in.

The marines move to the other Sea Stallion. A tent has been put up near the rear door. They get hot food and replacement gear. As team two walks in, they all grunt like pigs. Marshall leads the team in as Sergeant Cabolero walks up to him. "Shit, Gilbert. We were told that you threw tonight's dinner into the fucking creek." They shake hands.

"Yeah, were talking cong pig here." The gunny drops his gear and walks with Cabolero over to get some hot coffee. Cabolero tells him the story of the attack of Miss Milton. Some of the aerial photos are laid out on a table. The gunny looks them over with others in the platoon. "Holy shit, Gilbert. You and those crazy gunship jocks tore the shit out of the place."

"Yeah." Gilbert smiles. "We heard you and L.T. took a swim with one of the local bad boys."

"You heard right. Apparently he didn't like the smell of shit in the water."

Gunny looks around. "Both teams, make sure you change your socks and draw any other gear you need. The ship has sent in everything from field jackets to underwear. Make use of the stuff to get dry."

He and Cabolero walk up into the Sea Stallion. They join Captain Johnson and Neal near the stored bombs. "They look pretty docile, Skipper."

"You're right, Gunny. Let's just hope we get the other four in here without any problems." They move off to one side. The four drink their coffee and discuss the operation so far.

Knight gets on the radio to Ultima and talks with Commandant Swane. Susie and Emanuel hug, and he gets her some hot cider. They both sit down on some wood crates and discuss the events of the day. The hot liquid feels good as Susie listens to Emanuel's story of the pig attack. She punctuates her listening with a smile at the events. She enlightens him on her adventures with the alligator in the creek. They soon turn to discussions about the bombs and what each has done that may expedite the disarmament.

The radio on the Tac net switches from normal conversation to one of urgency.

"Bulldog, we have a bogie coming in at your location from the north. Two gunships are in pursuit. Over." Knight looks back towards the radio and puts his hand over the handset. "Get Captain Johnson on this."

Johnson's radio man runs over to the back of the helicopter, and calls in to him. "Sir, they want you at the other chopper. We have some kind of inbound hostile."

Johnson and Neal sprint across the sand towards the other ship as two Harrier fighters fly low overhead. The noise is deafening as they cross over the hill behind the beach.

Knight calls to them as they reach the top of the ramp. "Captain, you have an inbound. Deal with it."

"This is Bulldog 1. Give me a status on the bogie."

"Roger, Bulldog. We are coming up on it now; it looks like a Bell Ranger. Our guess is a news helicopter. He is flying on the surface of the water below the tree line. We're coming up on each side of him now. We're about five clicks northeast of your position."

"Escort him out of the area. Over."

"Roger, we have a positive on him. It's a news team from KNLT. We're hailing now."

The camera pans around and focuses on Darin, with the gunship directly over his shoulder. The soundman in the front seat waves back to him.

"They're ordering us out of the area. If we continue on our present course, they will be forced to open fire on us."

"All right, let's roll 'em. This is Darin Bodine, from KNLT news. We are about four miles from the crash site of the Russian bomber. We have, as you can see, an escort of marine gunships. They have ordered us out of the area. Our question is, What is so sensitive out here?"

The pilot calls back. "They're ordering us out now. What are we going to do?"

"Again we have been told to change course, or they will open fire on us. Our pilot has asked why we can't film the crash site, if it was all right this morning. Hold on, one of the ships is pulling in closer. I can see the gun on the front of the gunship turning towards us." The camera pans out to the closing Cobra. The 20 mm multi-barreled cannon swings towards the front of the news helicopter. The camera captures the burst of flames as the gunships fires a line of tracers in front of them.

"Holy shit!" The noise of the gunfire staccatos across the air waves. Darin's face appears on the screen, with the gunship behind him. "They have fired at our news team. We will have to break off contact and move from this area." Before he can finish, a second blast of cannon fire roars into the path of their helicopter. The pilot calls back, "We're out of here."

He slams the Ranger into a hard diving turn and races up a side creek. The blades of the rotor hit the overhanging foliage along the bank as they race ahead. The move caught the two gunships by surprise. They turn to try and catch up with the news helicopter. The camera swings around and looks directly out the front window as they race up the narrow creek.

"Holy shit, Bob. We're going to die."

"Hold on, we're going to jump this hedge row ahead and get the hell out of here." Darin slides in front of the camera as the helicopter swings from side to side. "We're leaving this area as quickly as possible."

His hand grabs a strap on the side of the cabin to help steady him as he narrates their roller coaster ride. The pilot pulls the helicopter up at the last moment to skim over the top of the hedgerow.

"What the fuck?" As they clear the trees, two dark forms hang in the air in front of them. The two Harriers have their lights flashing as the distance between them closes. The camera is riveted on the two, when the burst of machine gun fire from them streams out into the darkening air.

"Shit." The pilot throws the helicopter into a right banking dive. The 25 mm cannon rounds strike the helicopter in the engine and tail area. Smoke billows out as they go into a noseward plunge in a wide field heading to the beach. The pilot pulls the nose up and the helicopter slides across tall wet grass, the rotor blades whips grass and mud into the air. They come to rest at the side of a swampy bog.

"Shit." The pilot looks around. "Everyone out, now." The men scramble out the doors and help get Darin out. He'd hit his head on the back of the pilot's seat when they hit. The two techs rush back and get their equipment out as the smoke from the engines turns coal black and flames begin to appear near the main rotor shaft.

"Let's move a little farther out. There could be an explosion." The two Harriers fill the air with the noise of their engines as a squad of marines from the beach works their way out to the downed helicopter. Johnson and Neal stand on the mound behind the beach, watch the events, and talk to the squad in the swamp. The others have come up the mound to see the action. Susie lowers the binocular she borrowed from Lieutenant Neal. "I'm not certain, but I would say we have just shot down a news team."

"Yes, ma'am. The assholes are lucky to be alive, pulling a stunt like this." Johnson listens on the radio as the team from the beach reaches them. "Roger. Bring them back to the command center. Out." A corpsmen looks at Darin's head as the others are held off to one side. "Keep your hands on your heads, assholes."

"He'll be all right. More blood than wound." The corpsman puts a bandage over the cut on Darin's head.

"Good, now single file up the path, fuck-sticks." Under guard, the line winds its way back to the beach.

"Hold them over near the front of the command ship, Neal. I'll go get the colonel."

"Right." Neal watches Johnson walk back to the helicopter, and he and Knight talk near the back ramp.

As the line arrives at the marines in the perimeter, a loud explosion behind them draws everyone's attention. The burning helicopter explodes in a loud boom. The four men are brought over the mound and held at the front of the big Sea Stallion.

"This is bullshit! We're KNLT news. And I want to talk to whomever is in charge here. And you don't need to keep pointing those rifles at us."

"I'm in charge." Darin swings around and looks up at Knight. "And I wouldn't be too bent out of shape. You are in a secured area and facing a pretty long list of charges. Bottom line is, you're lucky to be alive, and your asses are in a big sling."

KNLT STUDIOS
NEW ORLEANS

The news director at KNLT stares at the screen. "Jesus, I don't believe what I just saw. Do we have any word from the helicopter? Were those jets sitting in the air on that last set of shots?"

"Stan, Marcey just got back from the checkpoint. And yes, those are those jets that can hover. We're trying to contact the government on word about the team. We're pretty sure that the helicopter is down, that was the last thing that the pilot said."

"Get me Marcey. I want this on the air as soon as possible." Marcey walks out on the news set and puts her bag down near a desk behind the cameras. Stan comes up on the loud speaker. "Marcey, don't sit down. We have a killer tape from the team with Darin. We think they have been shot down by the marines out near the crash site."

"Shot down! Good God, are they all right?"

"We don't have confirmation. Get up here so you can review the tape."

"You do know I have been working out there all day, and I'm bone cold and tired."

"The hell with that shit. You're going on in about five minutes."

"I need to change and do my hair."

"This will put you up on the national net, guaranteed."

Marcey takes a deep breath and stretches. She then heads up to the control center to view the tape. "Stan, have you heard anything about Darin's team?"

"Not yet. Just sit down and look at this tape. Jake, run the tape for Marcey. We have the script people working up a dialogue run for you now. We contacted CNN. They will run you live from here. So as soon as you're ready, we have a go."

"Stan, there's a call coming in on line three. It sounds like a government type, and they have Charles on the line with you."

"Shit, that's all we need now — the station owner and the government at the same time." He picks up the phone and pushes the button.

"Stan, this is Charles. I have Captain Nelson on with us. He is the base commander at NAS."

Marcey finishes watching the tape. "My God, this tape is dynamite. But have they heard anything about the boys?"

"Yeah, that was Charles and the base commander. The boys are under arrest at the site and will be transported back to the base. We'll have legal head over to try and get them released. Now, let's get the reel on the air."

"Right, I'm heading for wardrobe and to get my hair fixed." She runs to the door and disappears down the stairs.

BRIDGE OF THE *VLADIVOSTOK* CRUISER
THE GULF

"Sir, the forward battery is prepared to fire. All operating systems are up. We will have twelve missiles to launch. After that, we will be dependent on point defense and eight Grail missiles. After that, we throw tools."

"Very good. Have the emergency rafts ready on the port side. Have only essential personal at their stations. The rest will stand by amid-ship."

"Very good, sir."

"Have the missiles fire as soon as they acquire a target. You may fire at will."

"Aye, aye, sir. Forward battery commence firing." The forward facing fire control radar locks on a target and fires. The Goblet missile quickly disappears into the heavy mist. A second is fired right behind it. Two of the Mig 27s break off from the others and press the attack at the crippled cruiser. They each launch an anti-radiation missile at the ship. They go into evasive action to elude the outbound missiles from the ship. The four remaining Mig 27s shift position to fly farther west of the ship. They continue on to the main squadron.

The point defense system comes on and fires into the falling rain. It catches one of the missiles as it skims in over the water. The second missile slams into the radar and rips it from its perch. The captain looks around the bridge as two more missiles launch from the forward mount. He keys the intercom. "Abandon ship, all hands. Abandon ship."

The cruiser wallows in the waves as the forward launcher reloads. It stands frozen, as the directions from its fire control radar go dead. The two fighters move to the west of the ship and turn to make a run in on the dying sea beast. The two safety rafts are secured together as the captain hands the ship's log to his lieutenant. The captain looks around; the sea is slowly working its way up the deck from the stern. "Sir, everyone is on board. We are ready to leave, sir." The captain steps into the raft, and the lines holding them to the ship are released. The two red circular rafts begin to drift to the east. They move as if pulled by some unseen force towards the center of the storm.

The two Cuban fighters come in low over the waves. As they near the cruiser, the last rounds in the point defense system expend themselves. The guns go silent, as the jets do their last adjustments. The two Migs race in at the silent giant. They fire rockets, and each releases a 1,000-pound bomb. As they streak over the ship, the first bomb hits amid ship. The second hits at the base of the bridge. The explosions rock the men in the rafts. They watch as the ship tries to bring itself back to a perfect trim. But it continues to roll to the starboard side. It pushes its bow down into the sea. It slides burning into the Gulf and disappears beneath the waves.

The two fighters fly over the rafts and then head into the mist, flying north. The men on the rafts secure the hatch opening and then lay back against the sides. The captain stores the logbook in a waterproof bag. "I want a seamen on the lines between the rafts at all times." He takes a radio out and talks to the officer on the other raft. "Gentlemen, a salute to a grand and heroic ship: the *Vladivostok*. Hooray, hooray." A faint cheer is heard from the other raft. They all lean back as the raft lurches and slowly rotates. They can feel the strength of the sea under them as they drift deeper into the storm.

ULTIMA
WASHINGTON, D.C.

The imaging camera draws back. "Gentlemen, the *Vladivostok* has been sunk."

The president slowly shakes his head and looks over at Brant. "Mr. Brant, when will this end?"

"I don't know, Mr. President. We would hope that this could have been averted."

"Admiral, what are the chances for the men in the life rafts?"

"Sir, the men are in the Russian copy of our cold weather survival raft. It is designed for the North Sea area and is very efficient. The problem that they face is that they are being pulled into the storm at close to eighteen knots. The figures we have are not good for them. They will be pulled into the eye. There are no surface units that have a chance of a rescue."

"And if they are pulled into the eye, Admiral?"

"Sir, they will be killed."

"Admiral, is there nothing we can do?"

"Mr. President, we may have one chance. We have the *Atlanta*, the attack submarine we pulled off the squadron. It is just north of the demark zone. It may have a chance. I'll make the calls, sir."

"The down link with the satellite has been given to Admiral Sokolov."

"Sir." Van Nar points to the screen. "The *Sovremennyy* destroyers are turning out board from the *Moskva*. We believe they are preparing to fire their missiles."

THE BRIDGE OF THE *MOSKVA*
THE GULF

"Sir, the destroyers are getting into position now."

"Very good." He uses his binoculars, and watches the ships turn five degrees off the base course. The sky and the sea around them have turned black. The storm has smothered out the last of the light.

"Admiral, we have the satellite link. We will have a good track on the planes in just a few minutes."

"Thank you, Mr. Pstygo. Have we made contact with the submarine?"

"No, sir. The American Sky 1 has confirmed the sinking of the *Vladivostok*. They are tracking survivors. They will try and mount a rescue."

"Good, they are a brave crew. And it was a brave ship."

"Yes, sir. They are transferring the data to the ships to program their missiles. We will be ready to fire on your command."

"Give me the running status on the fighters, Mr. Pstygo."

"Sir, we have them at forty miles southeast. There are two groups. One flight of six and a second flight of two farther east."

"Concentrate on the largest group."

"Sir, they are at thirty miles and closing."

"Stand by to fire." He looks through his binoculars at the ship to the direct port side.

"Sir, they have just passed the twenty-five mile range."

"Commence firing, Mr. Pstygo."

"Aye, aye, sir." The first volley of three missiles fires from the destroyers; they arc up and away from the ships and turn to the southeast. The second group of missiles erupts from their tubes and follows the first group. The ships reposition themselves back to the original course.

As the SS-N-22 anti-ship missiles level out, they fly 200 feet apart over the surface of the Gulf. The second wave follows suit and flies thirty seconds behind them. They receive corrections from the satellite and readjust their flight. The weapons officer on the *Moskva* stands poised over the command panel. His finger positioned above a large red button, he looks across the room at

Pstygo. His eyes glued to the radarscope, the red and green lights in the room run patterns across his face.

ULTIMA
WASHINGTON, D.C.

"Admiral, we believe we know what they're going to do with the missiles."

"Go ahead, Captain."

Van Nar points to the screen showing the oncoming fighters. "They have no chance of hitting any of the fighters with these types of missiles, and at twenty-five miles, the fighters will fire missiles to try and knock them down. The staff believes that they are using the missiles in a barrage explosion into the path of the fighters. It should be rather spectacular."

"I don't understand." The president looks at the admiral.

Hillings smiles and shakes his head. "Sir, Admiral Sokolov is about to test a theory held by both us and the Russians: in a last ditch effort, the anti-ship missiles could be used to form a barrage type screen against attacking air groups. We are seeing many speculations pulled from theory and applied. They will explode the missiles into the path of the fighters and hope for a kill."

The missiles on the screen race towards the fighters in two lines of three. "They're using the down link with the satellite for last minute corrections and the detonation commands."

CUBAN FIGHTERS
THE GULF

The darkness has forced everyone to now depend on the machines that see with no eyes. The Cuban fighters pick up the inbound missiles on their scopes. "What the hell." The flight leader checks his screen. "We have what appears as two flights of cruse missiles inbound."

"Roger." His wingman targets and fires a missile at the lead group. Two other missiles are fired; they flash into the darkness and disappear. "Let go up to 2,500 feet and move farther west." The formation adjusts its height and does a slow turn to the west.

The Russian missiles also correct their course. They sense the Cuban missiles and go to evasive action. Flares and chaff are fired into the air. The far right missile in the lead group tries to move but is struck by the missile. It explodes in a huge flash of orange and yellow. Two missiles fly by and explode in the sea. A command is sent to them, and at a critical point, they are pulled up into a forty-five-degree angle. They rise into the sky. "Stand by," Pstygo yells across the room. He watches the scope as more missiles are fired from the Cubans. "Now!" He turns towards the weapons office. His thumb presses the red button.

"Stand by, second group." The button is reset as two bright blips flash on the radar screen. Another of the missiles is hit and explodes prematurely. "Stand by." Pstygo looks at the weapons officer again. "Now!" He sees his thumb depress the red button a second time. Looking back at the screen, two bright blips erupts, and a third blip falls from the group and tumbles into the sea. A cheer goes up in the command center. "We got one, sir."

The flight leader watches his radar as the two lead missiles suddenly rise into their flight path and explode 100 yards in front of them. The flash fills the night before them, and then the concussion wave hits the planes. "Disperse, disperse." The fighters begin to pull away at different angles. The second two missiles explode. The compression wave races up the intake of one of the jets. An alarm goes off in the cockpit as the plane rolls into a dive. "Flame out. I have a flame out. I'm attempting to restart." He keys the restart panel: nothing. He hits it again, and one of the engines fires to life. It comes just in time to accelerate the fighter into the sea. It explodes as the others try and regroup. "Sir, we lost number four. He is down."

"Sir, this is five. I have damage to my hydraulics and electrical. I can continue but will not be effective."

"Roger." The flight leader looks over his instruments. They seem to be functioning. The sudden barrage has shaken up the entire group. "Form on me. They will pay for this."

ULTIMA
WASHINGTON, D.C.

"Sir." Van Nar points to the screen. "They have knocked down one of the fighters, and we believe they disabled another."

"My God." Hillings shakes his head. "This is definitely a day of learning for all parties. We will be looking at these tapes for a long time."

"Mr. President, I have contacted the *Atlanta*. They will attempt to rescue the men from the cruiser."

"Thank you, Admiral. Perhaps we may be able to salvage a thread of hope from today."

"Gentlemen." Van Nar points to the screen showing the squadron. "Admiral Sokolov is using the radar from Sky 1 to target his missile batteries at this time. He is showing the fighters' no-radar emissions."

"That's great." The admiral turns to Brant. "He is not giving them a guide to use their anti-radiation missiles. He is trying to lure them in close before he goes active. His missiles are only good out to twenty miles. If they don't have stand off weapons, they will have to go in after the ships."

Van Nar points to the squadron. "His dispersal of ships has the *Moskva* covering a 180-degree front, while the destroyers will cover the sides and rear of the group. Their major problem now will be the amount of missiles and ammunition left to them."

C-130 STORM CHASER
THE GULF

"Sir, we're showing winds of up to seventy miles per hour and a real good chance of wind shear along our track."

"Roger." The pilot of the C-130 can feel the forces striking the plane as they fly deeper into the storm. The weather equipment on board is working and transmitting its data by satellite. "How far to the eye?" He calls back to navigation. "Sir, we're fifty miles out. We'll adjust as we get closer to go with the spin. Then we'll enter the eye on the southwest side."

"Roger." He looks over at his co-pilot. "This could be a real handful."

"Yeah, Captain. As we adjust west, we're picking up speed." As they go deeper into the storm, lightning flashes tear through the darkness outside. Rain slams into the front of the big plane, and it rocks with the concussion of the thunder around it.

"Sir, we have picked up an additional fifteen knots in wind speed."

"I'm going to bring us in line with the spin. We'll move in as we circle this lady." He brings the plane in line with the swirl of the eye. The plane jolts forward. He checks his air speed. "Shit."

"Sir, we have just gained a fifty mile per hour tail wind. As we get closer, we are continuing to gain. At a very substantial rate, I might add."

"Roger." The plane buffets in the turbulence.

"Sir, radar shows we are about to enter within five miles of the eye. The track just outside of the eye is showing winds in excess of the 110-plus range. We're aimed to enter it slowly to the port side." The captain brings the plane into a gradual left turn to ease into the band of rushing air. As the left wing moves in, it buffets and is pushed forward. As the first engine breaks into the rush, the plane lurches forward. As the fuselage moves deeper into the wind, the big ship is driven forward. The pilot fights the controls as they race around the storm eye. "Sir, our earlier estimate was short. We have picked up a tail wind at over 140 knots. Excuse me, sir, revise that. We are now at 150-plus."

"Christ." The co-pilot is ready to assist if called on. "Sir, we are now at a category five on the scale. Winds are now at 165 knots and rising."

"Roger, we can feel it in the controls."

"Sir, we are starting to overrun the engines."

"Roger, cut back to three-quarters power."

"Sir." The co-pilot points at the air speed. "We have just passed 270 knots." The rain on the skin of the plane sounds like gravel in the loading bay.

"Sir, this is radar. I'm picking up some odd readings at the rear of the eye. There seems to be a vertical wall. My best guess is a vortex of rising air at over 200 miles per hour. I would suggest we steer clear. Also, I'm picking up a large anomaly about 200 yards in front of the wall." The pilot maneuvers the plane to give the rear of the eye a wide birth. As they pass directly behind the vortex wall, hard objects in the storm hit the fuselage. The windshield is hit by small fish that also strikes the engines. "Christ." The co-pilot looks out the front windows. "Shit, we're being hit by fish at 10,000 feet."

The pilot fights the bucking of the plane. The smears on the windshield resemble a car caught in a bug storm. As the co-pilot looks out the side window, a large black object slams into the starboard outboard engine. The cowling explodes as the prop is bent back and stalls. A tongue of flame erupts from a crack in the pod. "Shit, we have a fire in number four." The plane lurches as the pilot fights to stabilize with the loss of the engine. The co-pilot hits the controls for the extinguisher for number four. The fire disappears in a blast of foam; the prop sits tilted at a forty-five-degree angle.

"Sir, we're coming around to our inbound track to the eye." .

"The hell with that. We're going in now." The pilot turns the big plane into a left turn. They rush through the swirling clouds and rain. He puts full power on the remaining engines and forces them through the rim of the eye. They are suddenly bathed in sunshine, and the howl of the wind is gone. They have reached the center of the beast, and all is quiet.

BEACH
BARATARIA BAY

"Sir, we need to take Mr. Bodine over to the med tent. He can use a couple of stitches in his head wound." Knight looks the group over. "Get them over to mess tent, and let them have some coffee." The wind drives a quick squall over the beach. The rain pelts the group as they run for the mess tent. Once inside, they get some coffee and sit down on some benches. Groups of marines are getting food and drinks around them. Bodine walks with the corpsman across the sand and passes behind the Sea Stallion with the bombs. A sudden gust of wind blows the tarp across the opening aside. The navy men from the ship are just loading the number four bomb into its crate. "Holy shit!" Bodine stops and stares at the men working in the lighted interior. The corpsman grabs him by the arm and pulls him forward. "This way. Move."

They run into the med tent, as the rain pelts the canvas of the tent. The corpsman sits him down, and he and the other corpsman work on his wounds. "Were those bombs in the back of that helicopter?"

"Sir, I have a suggestion for you. You saw nothing, and you know nothing. Do you get my drift?"

"Right." They clean the wound. "Shit, that hurts."

"All right." The corpsmen uses butterfly Band-Aids to secure the wound. He puts a compress over it and bandages it into place.

A marine guard shows up and walks up to him as they finish tying off the bandage. "Sir, Colonel Knight would like to talk to you at the command ship."

"That's great. I have some questions for him."

Portable lights are being set up around the perimeter of the two Sea Stallions. A tarp hangs down, covering the back of the helicopter with the bombs. As they reach the back of the command ship, Knight stands at the top of the ramp. Bodine walks up into the helicopter. "Mr. Bodine, some coffee?"

"Yes, Please." His eyes look around the inside of the ship. He sees Susie and Emanuel at the front of the helicopter, and a man speaking with a Russian accent talking to a marine captain. Traffic on the Tac net blares at times, and a navy commander is talking with someone about portable lights. Knight hands him his coffee. He takes a slow drink and looks into Knight's face.

"Well, Mr. Bodine. It seems we have a major problem with you and your film crew."

"Let me say, Colonel, there is something going on out here that has nothing to do with the coming storm. And I think that it deals directly with that bomber out there."

"We're going to fly you and your team back to the base. They will make the decisions on what will be done with you." Knight turns and begins to walk away.

"Colonel, I know you have bombs in the other helicopter." The interior of the helicopter goes silent. The colonel slowly turns and looks at Bodine. "Colonel, the wind blew the tarp aside. And at the rear of this helicopter are two of America's top weapons experts. And the gentleman with the captain is obviously Russian. It doesn't take a genius to put it together."

"I would like you to wait with your crew over in the mess tent. I'll get back to you in a few minutes." The marine guard comes up and escorts him out of the helicopter and over to the mess tent.

Knight moves over to the Lanstat. "Ultima, this is Knight. I just talked with the reporter from KNLT. He has guessed that we are dealing with bombs out here."

"Knight, this is Swane. We have just watched a news flash from their station on CNN. It showed the gunships shooting at them and the final shoot down by the Harriers. They also covered the removal of both the doctors from the hotel. They have almost put the story together on their own."

"Colonel, wait one. The president and Secretary Brant are discussing the situation with their advisers. We should have a decision soon."

"Roger, I'll hold on." The Colonel cups his hand over the mouthpiece. He looks at his watch. "It's 1625, Captain." Johnson leaves the Tac radio and walks up to where Knight is in the front. "How do we stand, Mr. Johnson?"

"We have contact with Pathfinder 2. They have located one of the bombs in a house. From what we're getting, it's not a pretty sight."

"That's Dr. Davies' team, right?"

"Yes sir. Pathfinder 1 is on the ground. They say it's pretty wild. They're moving up to the suspect site. We should hear from them soon."

"Good. Brief Mr. Neal and Dr. Davies on their site. And we'll get both groups in the air by 1700. They're flying in more of the portable lights."

"Aye, aye, Skipper. We'll be ready."

"Thank you, Mr. Johnson. Your platoon is doing an excellent job." Johnson had taken a couple of steps; he turns back towards Knight. "Thank you, sir. Then we must do better."

Knight smiles and shakes his head. Johnson gives him a nod and calls Marshall and Cabolero over. They talk for a while and leave the helicopter. Johnson goes back to the radio and waits to hear from the other team.

"Colonel Knight, the president is being advised to go public with the information. They're trying to decide the best way to present it to the public. As of right now, hold the news team at your location. We'll be getting back to you soon."

"Aye, aye, sir."

OUTSIDE THE NAVAL BASE
CUBA

"Colonel Zino, as you can see, the one tank is positioned near the main entrance, and the other one is behind the command center covering the boats."

"Right." Zino backs down from the knoll. He calls the platoon commanders over to him. "We will have to neutralize the tanks quickly. You have seen the damage they can do on the road in. We'll assign one of the Hinds to each tank to take it out quickly. The troop helicopters will land," he points to a lay out of the base, "here, between the barracks and the command center. This should isolate the naval personnel being held there. We will come in from the front gate and make a run for the command center."

"Sir, has any attempt been make to contact the base and ask them to surrender?"

"Not yet, but I will call Captain Perez at exactly 4:30. At that time, we will have a definitive answer. If they choose to fight, we go immediately."

"They know we're here. One of their scouts picked us up earlier."

"Right." Zino looks at his watch. "It's 1428, gentlemen. I will make the call." He walks down to his command vehicle; they hand him a handset out the back. The radio in the command center receives Zino's call sign. "Sir, we have a call from Colonel Zino. For you." Perez picks up the handset. "Well, Colonel, is it? I see that we can all give ourselves whatever rank we want. That must be the mindset of mutineers."

"Perez, surrender your troops. We are taking over the control of the base."

"How interesting, my orders from General Morales are to repulse any attempts to take the base."

Zino signals the others to begin the attack. "Then you can die for your General, Captain." He drops the handset and gets into his armored carrier. He moves to the front of the column.

Mortars begin to fire off to his left. They concentrate on the main gate, the tanks, and the command center. Two BPM combat vehicles run forward on each side of the column. As they come over the rise leading to the base, they target their Sagger missiles and fire at the tanks and the reinforced guard shack. At the same time, one of the Hind gunships is coming in from the side.

One tank begins to maneuver as the main gun fires at one of the lead vehicles and blows one of its treads off. Its top gun fires at the approaching Hind helicopter. It moves behind a building as the two Sagger missiles hit the guard shack and the building next to it. As it pulls back towards the main buildings, it fires again. The shell passes over the top of the lead elements and hits the knoll next to the column. The forward BMP races for the guard shack and fires its 73 mm cannon point blank into the structure. Its machine gun sprays the area.

An RPG fired by the guards bounces off the top of Zino's vehicle and explodes in the air. The tank fires at the lead vehicle. The round falls short and craters the road. The undernose rotary cannon on the Hind rakes the tank. As two Swatter missiles are fired, tracers from the tank arc up towards the helicopter. The two missiles hit. The tank explodes as the stored ammo aboard explodes. The guards at the gate are taken out as Zino's command vehicle crashes over the rubble of the shack and presses on towards the command center.

The BMP stops at the gate, and its eight troops get out and secure the area. The Hind swings back around and fires a barrage of rockets from its pods, at a machine gun position near some buildings. The assault helicopters land in the road in front of the naval barracks. As the Hind flies over the boat docks, it fires on the command center from behind. Not seeing the tank, he swings back to give support to the assault group.

As the men clear the helicopters, the Mi-8s lift to add their rockets to the fight. A cannon blast from the cement storage building throws a HE round into the third helicopter as it starts to lift. It explodes in a ball of fire. The Hind swings around and fires its cannon into the building.

On one of the *OSA* boats, its two 30 mm guns fire at the helicopters and the gunship. Armored vehicles make their way down the roads of the base to help cover the men assaulting the barracks. The tank fires at one of the lead personnel carriers, and goes long. The shell hits a building next to it and obliterates it.

The cannon on the Hind fires to suppress the guns of the boat. It fires a load of rockets into the building the tank is hiding in. The building explodes in fire and debris. The second Hind fires at the boat as it pulls away from the pier. A Grail missile is fired as the boat pulls away. The helicopter fires flares and chaff as it maneuvers to avoid the missile.

As the smoke and dust settle from the building, the tank emerges from the smoke. It runs towards a group of armored cars, firing as it comes. The first shell rips into a vehicle and blows it off the road. The tank keeps moving forward to close with the others and to avoid the fire of the helicopter.

The weapons squad from the helicopter lines up their AT-4 anti-tank missile and fires it into the side of the tank. It explodes and burns as the ground troops move in from the barracks and the buildings around the command center. The Hind lines up and fires a burst of rockets into the command building.

As the smoke clears, a few shots are heard. Then it goes quiet. The few men remaining in the command building surrender to Zino and his forces. He pulls his command vehicle up on a point overlooking the docks. The escaping *OSA* boat is racing at full speed out to sea.

"Shit, can we get that bastard?"

"Sir, we will need the Hinds with us as we move on. They could go after it, but I think with their guns and firing those Grail missiles.... It's your call, sir."

One of his lieutenants runs up to him. "Sir, the captured guards from the command center say Captain Perez is on that boat." Zino slams his fist into his hand and stomps his foot.

"Sir, if we could be of help?" Zino swings around and looks at a young naval officer. "And what help is that, Lieutenant?"

"Sir, have your helicopter give me some point data on the boat. I'll hit it with one of the missiles off the 221 boat."

"Ha! I love it." He goes to the back of the vehicle and has them contact the helicopter. "They're ready when you are, Lieutenant."

He runs down to the boat with other men on his crew. They fire up the engines and turn on their equipment. He calls the helicopter, and it swings out to sea to fly parallel to the escaping boat. They throw the mooring lines on the dock and pull the boat out into the main channel. Zino listens to the boat and the helicopter exchange data. A call comes over the radio from the boat. "Stand by to fire."

The troops on the shore line the area overlooking the docks as the boat crew pulls the cover off a missile tube. They button up the boat and stand by. "Fire one!" The cry comes over the radio. Zino and the others watch the flash of the rocket and the launch over the bay. The large Styx missile flies in the direction of the running boat. Zino and the others watch through their binoculars as the missile races towards its target.

"Sir, we have a missile inbound." Perez looks through his binoculars to try and see the threat. As he swings his vision back to the base, a huge red winged bomb skims above the water. Before he can order evasive action, the red monster explodes into them. A huge ball of fire erupts into the air, and the boom races back to the men on the docks.

"I believe we have ended Captain Perez's career goals."

"Yes, sir. The naval personnel are taking care of the wounded. And we are reloading the troop helicopters."

"Good, Captain. We'll go as we discussed. You take the main column up the coast road towards Malangas. I'm going with the troop helicopters and the gunships, in support of General Quintano."

"Sir, we have a call from Captain Vargas." Zino goes to the back and talks with Vargas. Then he rejoins his staff at the front. "Good news. Vargas has a group of six tanks coming to you on carriers. And ahead of them are four ZSU-23s, just in case they send jets from the eastern bases. They will join you on the main road. Take care, gentlemen. We'll see you at the air base."

"Yes, sir." They watch Zino board one of the helicopters and lift off towards the west.

"Let's move out." They load up the vehicles and move back towards the main gate.

MALANGAS AIR BASE
CUBA

"Command, this is flight four, from Pinar Del Rio. We are bringing in two gunships and four troop ships to assist you. Over."

"Roger, flight four. You're cleared to land on the eastern side of the field. We are still fighting fires from the earlier fighting. Welcome aboard."

"Captain, we have a flight in from Del Rio to help us."

"What flight?" He looks across the field as the troop ships land in front of the hangars. The fires block his vision. "Get me the command center. I want to check this out."

"I think we made it, sir."

"Right." Quintano and the others scramble out of the helicopters and disperse into the hangars. Brock and Quintano run up to the hangar with the Russian aircrews. A couple of shots are fired, but the security forces lay down their arms as they move through the building.

"My God." Quintano and Brock enter the hangar bay. Burned out vehicles and a blown up jet stand near the main doors. As they walk in, the bodies of the Russians have been pulled in and now lie in rows on the hangar floor. "We will get revenge for this atrocity, my friend." He grabs Brock's arm and pulls him with him. "Let's move. We don't have much time until they find out the truth."

One of the gunships moves to the end of the runway. It lands and its troops jump out and move into the anti-aircraft sites. Once secured, it joins the other one at the end of the field. Darkness covers the movement of Quintano and his troops as they move towards the command center.

"This is Captain Lopez at Malangas. Did you send a flight from Pino Del Rio to help us defend the air base?"

"Wait one, sir." The operator calls over to the officer on duty and asks about the flight into Malangas. He shakes his head and walks over to Morales's door. "Sir, we have a call from Malangas about a flight of gunships and troop ships landing. He had not received word about the flight."

"No shit!" Morales jumps up and runs pass the lieutenant and grabs the radio mike. "This is General Morales. We have not sent any troops in from Del Rio. Stop them before they can land. It's got to be Quintano's forces. Do you understand?"

"Yes, sir." The radio goes dead. "Sound the alert. We have mutineers on the field."

Quintano's forces move across the runways and head for the hangars on the eastern side of the field. Morales's guard unit begins firing at the men on the field. Three armored vehicles move away from the command center as one of the gunships opens fire with its cannon. It follows with a rocket attack. The second ship lines up on a BMP and fires an anti-tank rocket. The blast from the rocket knocks the vehicle on its side in flames. Tracers from machine gun emplacements arc up at the two gunships. One of the BMP vehicles gets to the main runway and begins firing at the men moving in the dark. They fail to pick up the AT-4 crew set up at the side of the runway. They line up the sights and fire almost head on into the vehicle. It explodes in a ball of flame. More gunfire opens up on them from the front and to their side. Quintano's men, working their way up the building to their left, come under heavy fire from the building to their front.

They reach the other side of the runway and move up to the edge of the eastern taxi strip. The gunship fires its cannon into the last hangar on the eastern side to suppress the heavy fire. The other gunship swings around to attack the positions in front of Quintano. It fires its cannon and begins to fire a rocket barrage when two flashes near the command center race through the air and slam into the side of the helicopter. It explodes in a rain of fire over the runway.

"Shit." Quintano rolls over on his back to look at the attack on his left. The other gunship fires a load of missiles at the command center and rolls back over the hangars. His radioman yells over the gunfire, "Sir, we have people in the end hangar. They're moving up to our right." Two flares fired by Morales's men suddenly light the night. The silver-blue light bathes the runway area; he looks at his men lying in the grass. They start receiving RPG fire from the hangars. It explodes along the taxiway and in the grass.

439

Suddenly, two gunships fly low over their heads, firing their cannons and rockets in and around the command center. Another is to their right, firing into the buildings. They turn and fire at any sign of threat, and they move up and down, firing into the buildings. As Quintano watches, four troop ships land on the main runway and discharge troops that run to join his men. A stout figure, silhouetted by the burning gunship, directs the men forward as the helicopters lift off. He moves up to where Quintano and Brock are lying in the grass.

"I hope you don't mind if we join your party, General."

"Colonel Zino, you're always welcome." The Mi-8 troop helicopters add their rockets to that of the gunships as Quintano's men move steadily forward. The fire from Morales's men dwindles to sporadic rounds. "Sir, by your leave, I'll conduct the mopping up of the base."

"It's all yours, Colonel." Zino moves out and joins the lead elements moving against the command center. As Brock and Quintano watch, the medical personnel check the dead and wounded along the grass strip.

STORM CHASER
THE GULF

"Sir, we're launching sonabouys."

"Roger." The pilot adjusts the trim on the plane. He puts the plane in a slow turn to bring them around to face the trailing edge of the eye. "Sir, we're reading twenty knot surface flow, running at the face of the...." The words die slowly. "Shit, sir, look about 400 feet in front of the vortex wall."

The co-pilot leans over to see out the pilot's window. "What the hell is it?"

"Get pictures of this thing."

"Sir, the cameras are running."

The pilot looks over at the co-pilot. "We are the first to ever film a whirlpool at sea. Those damn winds are running this thing in front of the wall." The plane flies as close to the back of the eye as they can, and films the spinning hole. "Sir, laser measurements say it's 230 feet across. It's feeding debris into the vortex." They watch as the trailing wall runs with streaks of yellow and brown.

"Best guess is that it just pulled in a huge load of sea weed. It seems to blow out at 3,000 feet. That's why we got hit by the debris behind it."

"Is the data going out all right?"

"Yes, sir. They may not believe it, but we are sitting in the middle of a force five-plus killer storm. God help the coast this thing hits."

"I'd say right now, God help us. We're out of here. Navigation, give me a heading out of here and home."

"Sir, take a heading on a slant due north. We should be able to fight our way out."

"Roger." He brings the big plane in line with the side of the eye and pulls slowly into the north side. The plane lurches forward, as they work their way back out of the winds. Once they're clear, they set a course back to their base in Florida.

ULTIMA
WASHINGTON, D.C.

Captain Emmett bursts through a side door and moves to Admiral Hillings. He shows him some maps and they both get up and walk to the podium. "Mr. President and Mr. Secretary, Captain Emmett has some startling news of the storm."

"Everyone, the data sent to us by the C-130 aircraft is nothing short of unbelievable. It took readings of winds at close to 250 miles per hour, and at the trailing edge of the storm is a vertical vortex with winds in the 300 miles per hour range. The storm is beyond a force five; this thing is beyond definition. Because of the angle of the satellite, we are unable to look vertically down on the eye.

"Running ahead of the trailing edge is a 200-foot wide whirlpool. They have filmed all of this, and it will be processed in Florida and sent directly to us. The plane suffered the loss of one of its engines during the flight into the eye. They were hit passing by the backside by fish and seaweed. They're en route back to base. We hope to see the pictures by 5:30 or so."

"Captain, what will this thing do when it makes landfall?"

"Mr. President, if I could get an easel. I'll try and draw a picture of the events that will occur." An easel is brought up and placed next to Emmett.

"Sir." He draws a large circle. "The face of the eye will push on to landfall with winds in excess of 200 miles per hour. But before that occurs, the leading edge will push a tidal surge forward as the seabed gets shallower. Our best guess is twenty-five to thirty feet.

"The eye will then ride in on top of the destruction of the surge. The leading wind will tear the path to pieces, the trailing vortex will then destroy anything remaining and throw it up to 3,000 feet into the air.

"Sir, nothing will survive in the path of this thing." He puts his marker down. "Evita may become the worst natural event to hit our shores which has ever been recorded."

"My God." The president looks at the swirling mass of clouds.

"Sir." Brant joins him. "We believe that we should go public with this news of the storm and the bombs."

"I know," the president sighs.

"We believe that we will be able to disarm the bombs before the storm hits. I'm told that Dr. Davies will be leaving soon for the number three bomb, and the search team is working on the number four bomb." He looks at his watch; the hands stand at 4:45 P.M. "We still have enough time to defuse this situation."

The president nods. "I want you with me at the news conference."

"Yes, sir. I'll get the staff going on the release, and then have you check it."

"Thank you. And General Becker, I would like you also to give a talk on the progress of the evacuation."

"Yes, sir."

"Gentlemen, we believe that the Cuban fighters have now acquired the Russian squadron. They are approximately forty-five miles out. The two that attacked the cruiser are now joining up with the main group. Two of the Migs are moving forward." The screen shows two jets pull away from the others.

"We believe that these are carrying the anti-radiation missiles. They will attempt to knock out the remaining radars. But

Admiral Sokolov is using Sky 1 for targeting. They will not light up their radars until they get them inside the twenty mile range." Admiral Hillings rotates his chair towards the president.

"Yes, sir. This should really piss them off. They should have been bathed in radar by now. And I know they will figure that the previous attack knocked them out."

BRIDGE OF THE *MOSKVA*
THE GULF

"Admiral, we have two fighters now thirty miles out."

"Very good. Keep all radars in passive. We're well within range of the AS-9s they're carrying. We will continue to try and bring them in."

The air captain joins him; the ships are running with no lights in the darkness. Their seaman ship is tested by the conditions. All remaining weapons are turned in the direction of the oncoming threat. Sparks from welders can still be seen at times on the destroyers, as repairs to the damaged areas continues.

"Sir, I think that they may be carrying the AS-B missiles. They will have to be in close to get a shot. Because of the mix of stuff dropped on us before, I believe that they may be running with few of the precision munitions."

"Very good. We don't have to worry about any missile bombs. Just the big iron ones, right?"

"Sir, I didn't mean to imply there was no threat."

"Air Captain." He puts his hand on his shoulder. "I was just having some fun." A smile crosses his face. The radars on the lead planes bath the squadron, then go passive. The pilots don't understand why there are no transmissions from the ships. They ease closer to the squadron from their western side. Reporting back to the main group, they continue on as two break off and begin to climb for altitude.

"Admiral, the *Otchyannyy* will allow the fighters in to twelve miles, then light it up and fire. The two are still lingering at around eighteen miles. We seem to have confused them. Two have broken off from the main body and are gaining altitude now."

"We know what they're up to."

"Flight leader, we are still not receiving any emissions from the squadron. It seems that the first attack may have taken out their radars. From the reports, the remaining ships have extensive damage."

"Roger, we'll move in."

"No, wait until we are all in position. We may have a major element of surprise. We will hit them all at once."

"Roger, we'll wait for your arrival."

The Cuban flight leader looks around in the dark and thinks to himself, "They must have had some type of tracking to have fired their anti-ship missiles. And they will pay for that." The jets cut through the dark sky and begin to position themselves for the attack.

Sokolov goes out to the flying bridge on the port side and looks through his binoculars towards the south. A brisk wind blows, and spray from the bow mists by him. The darkness cloaks his ships but also shields the hunters stalking them.

"This is flight leader. Commence attack. I say, commence attack." Two approach from the stern, two from port, and two fly high over the top of the squadron.

"Sir, the attack is commencing." The air captain and one of the ship's radiomen join Sokolov with a headset on. The two attacking off the port side break the twelve mile line first. The Qtlichnyy's fire control comes on first, and it fires it rear launchers. The two Sam missiles flame from the ship. The forward launchers on the *Moskva* pivot and fire almost vertically. They race straight up into the sky. The other ships have gone active and missiles fire in all directions. The two Migs off the port side fire anti-radiation missiles at the destroyer. The point defense system activates and fires. A missile hits the front dome radar at its position near the hangar. The rear guns swing and fire forward along the side of the ship. The forward 30 mm guns catch the second missile, and it explodes off to the side.

The two jets attacking the rear of the ships fire AS-7 anti-ship missiles. Two run at the *Sovremennyy*. Two run in at the *Moskva*. The ECM equipment on the ships blasts into the dark night as chaff and flares are fired. The world around the ships is bathed in the glow of red and white flares. Tracers fly in all directions. The 130 mm guns begin firing at full rate, the shells exploding out in the night. The Migs from the side go to their guns as they near the destroyer. The 23 mm tracers begin running up the side of the destroyer. As a missile from the *Moskva* catches one, it explodes in a ball of flame.

The other Mig releases its 500-pound bombs as it pulls its nose up over the bow of the ship. They crash and explode between the destroyer and the *Moskva*. The admiral is thrown off his feet by the blast. The forward launcher fires point blank and catches the Mig as it pulls away in front of the squadron.

As he gets to his feet, an explosion high in the sky catches his eye. The missiles hit one of the Migs. The forward launchers pivot and fire vertical again. Two more missiles streak straight up. The Migs at the rear go to guns and fire pods of rockets along the side of the destroyer, and a 500-pound bomb is released. It hits the rear mast and crashes into the funnel and the helicopter hangar. A large orange blast smothers the area.

The Migs fire along the destroyed landing deck of the *Moskva*, and a 500-pound bomb hits at the stern and bounces along the deck until it explodes over the hole made by the earlier bomb. A fire is ignited by the blast. Each Mig turns to the side and begins firing on the destroyers. They fire rockets and drop 500-pound bombs as they cross over the ships.

A missile hits one as it fires flares and chaff. The other is raked by the 30 mm guns and crashes into the side of the *Otlichnyy*. It explodes on the starboard side between the smokestack and the forward superstructure. Fire flares from the crash site and spreads forward and aft.

The Mig diving from above drops its bombs and pulls to the east. As it flies over the starboard destroyer, it fires two rocket pods and goes to its guns. It rolls over the ship and goes to afterburners as three missiles are fired from the ships. It evades one of the missiles, but the other two find their mark. It explodes in the night sky.

The two 500-pound bombs fall on the *Moskva*; one hits on the second SAM launcher and explodes. The blast blows the windows out on the bridge. Fire rages across the front of the ship.

Checks are made of the area around the squadron. The sky is clear. They are told by Sky 1 that the entire area is clear. The admiral picks himself up as medical personnel move around the bridge treating the injured. Some of the men are dead, and the fire on the bow flares, throwing odd shadows on the walls. The damage control teams on the ships move into action and begin fighting the fires and stopping any flooding. All four ships continue forward into the night, flames flare on each of them. The admiral goes out on the flying bridge and checks the ships on each side. "We are fortunate to have survived." He orders the ships to slow to ten knots and to assess the damages to the squadron.

BEACH
BARATARIA BAY

Lieutenant Neal and Gunny walk over to Susie and Emanuel. "Dr. Davies, we need to talk to you about our next bomb."

"All right, so what is the mystery of this one?"

"Well, the team was told by the local police that the residents of a certain house have not been accounted for. They made an aerial fly over and didn't see anything. We were searching about a mile north of the position. The team had no luck finding the weapon. It was calculated that at the time of the drop, the bomber was throwing random ECM bursts, and it was obviously damaged. So our computer's best guesses were off. The course was more erratic than was previously thought.

"The team moved south and met the local deputies. They asked them to check the house. Well, they found the bomb."

Susie looks at him. "In the house?"

"Yeah. They also found the two missing people. The gunny and I thought that you may want to pass this one to Dr. Reddeer. From the reports, it's a real mess. The body of the male is pinned in a wall by the retard fins."

"Thank you for your concern, but I did internship in pathology. And I hold a degree in nuclear medicine. I've seen some pretty grisly sights."

Gunny turns to Neal. "Sir." He puts his hand out. They shake hands. They walk over to Johnson and tell him of her decision.

"Very well." Johnson sticks his hand in his pocket and pulls out two five dollar bills. "Here, you were right." They both look back at Susie and have big smiles on their faces.

"So, my two protectors were taking bets on me."

"Doctor." They begin walking away. "It's 1658; we'll be leaving in a few minutes. Your equipment is on the helicopter."

"Very good, gentlemen. And I use that term sparingly with you two." Commander Marino comes up the ramp as Neal and Gunny go out to get the men ready.

"Good, both of you are together." He walks up to Susie and Emanuel. "We are searching everywhere for more generators and self-contained lighting. They will be brought in to your sites. We're losing local power because of the storm. We're also hitting the rental companies in New Orleans. So one way or another, their will be light."

"Thank you, Commander. We both appreciate your taking care of the supply issues. You're doing a great job."

"Why, thanks. Do mention that to Captain Nelson when this is over."

"You've got it, Commander." He moves on to talk to Colonel Knight as Susie gets her things together. She gives Emanuel a hug and moves to the ramp. She looks outside; a slight drizzle has started. She runs down the ramp and across the wet sand to the mess tent to join the others.

Commander Marino goes up to Knight as he is putting down the handset. "You asked to see me, sir."

"Mr. Marino, we have a another problem. That was Captain Nelson on the radio. There is another heavy storm coming in. We may have to ground everything for a couple of hours. So he has suggested we get personnel to their drop points quickly. Dr. Davies' team is leaving for their site. But we still have not heard from Pathfinder 1. We'll need to have the supplies dropped as quickly as possible, then prepare for the shut down. They are predicting winds of fifty to sixty miles per hour across our zone in about thirty minutes."

"Aye, aye, sir. We have Dr. Davies loaded now, and will have on-site lighting and generators at the site. It's the second site. If we don't hear from them soon, we may have to just have them sit it out."

"Right, and the news crew?"

"They're leaving now also. They are going to be flown back to the base and held there."

"Good, we don't need any other problems."

"Colonel, I talked to the captain of the supply ship. He let me know that they are registering an abnormally low tide."

"I noticed that the water around the bomber cabin had gone out."

"Yeah, they're saying that the incoming high tide at 0300 tonight will come in hot and heavy, because of the storm."

"Shit, we'll look for a site further inland."

"Yes, sir. I'll get on the provisions and equipment." "Thank you, Commander. You and your people are doing an outstanding job under adverse conditions."

"Thank you, sir."

As Marino is leaving, he goes to drop a field jacket off for Val. He walks up behind him. "I didn't see you when I came in."

"I was over at the mess tent, getting something to eat and some coffee."

"I think you're going to need this." He hands him the jacket.

"Yeah, it is getting a bit cold. Thanks, Commander."

Marino goes out into the rain and gets his chiefs together. They get on radios and begin to hook up cargo nets to the supply helicopters. The four newsmen are brought out and loaded onto a shuttle helicopter going back to the base. The crewman from the helicopters runs into the mess tent. "Sir, we're up and ready to move when you are."

"Roger, Gunny. Let's get everyone loaded."

"All right, team two. Let's go." The men file out into the rain and run for the helicopters.

"Hang in there, Dick." They shake hands.

"Right, Gilbert. Watch out for pigs." Cries of "Semper Fi" are yelled between the recon marines as team two moves out.

"Doctor." Neal waits for Susie, and they run across the sand to the door of their helicopter. The gunny helps her on and then climbs in and pulls the door shut. The smell of wet clothing and gear fills the cabin as the helicopter lifts from the sand. The spinning blades throw whirls of wet mist; the lights from the ship make rainbows as they lift into the air.

"So what was the bet with Captain Johnson?"

"Doctor, it was done in the most ethical of manners."

"Well, I'm waiting."

"He said that when you heard that a dead guy was with the bomb, you'd let Emanuel take it."

"And." She cocks her head at the two.

"Hell, we told him you had the balls of a Brahma bull and would not pass it off."

"Well, how nicely you put it? And my share?"

"Please, Doctor." Gunny looks at Neal. "We would not allow you to let down the professional and ethical standards of your profession by presents of dirty money."

"You know something, both of you are totally full of shit."

"Yes, ma'am." Big cat grins cross their faces.

ULTIMA
WASHINGTON, D.C.

"Mr. President, Secretary Sholenska is on the phone for you." The president moves back to his desk and picks up the phone.

"Mr. Secretary, I'm glad we will have an opportunity to cover some new events. Yes, we have been following the attack on the *Moskva* group."

"President Wayne, we have talked with Admiral Sokolov. They are in a bad way, and we have regretted the loss of the *Vladivostok*. Admiral Hillings has informed Marshal Shagan of the attempt of the submarine *Atlanta* to rescue the remaining crew. We were a little alarmed by the sudden presence of the news helicopter near the crash site."

"You're right. That is the subject I needed to discuss with you. Some of my staff believes that we should go public with the bombs and the explanation of the accident."

"Oh, Mr. President. We beseech you not to follow that line of thought. If the news of these weapons were to get out, it would cause a great rift in the delicate fabric of our new democracy. Those opponents of the new government and the changes now going on would have a cause to celebrate. It could lead to a revolt. It is imperative that the weapons be secretly returned and destroyed. The others are now disarmed and neutralized. The eight you are dealing with are the last ones. This issue is of the highest security."

"I understand your government's position. We will continue to operate under full security. The news team is being moved back to the naval base for interrogation. I have been told that Dr. Davies is en route to a verified site and that we have teams on the ground near another."

"That is great. Things seem to be developing in our favor. Although our weather people are very excited by the natural ferocity of the inbound hurricane."

"Yes, we are hoping for a conclusion of this situation before it hits land. Admiral Hillings will be discussing the deployment of sea tugs and assistant vessels for the *Moskva* squadron."

"Yes, they have been talking. We still request that your forces remain out of the combat zone so that you will be relieved of any blame in the un-provoked attack by the Cuban forces."

"Very well. Thank you, Mr. Secretary."

As he hangs up the phone, the imaging camera focus on the Russian squadron. Using heat-imaging, fires on each of the ships flare on the screen. "Mr. President, the squadron has again been mauled by the Cuban fighter-bombers." Hillings points to different ships and describes the damage. He pauses on the *Moskva*. The glowing hole at the front of the ship blazes. "They," he points with the laser pen, "have lost their two forward missile launchers. And it appears that the forward anti-submarine launcher has received some damage. With the threat of possibly engaging two Cuban submarines, it is imperative that the forward launcher is operational." On a large map of the area, the admiral covers them on the positions of American vessels ready to go to the squadron's aid. "We hope that they get close enough that we can assist."

BEACH
BARATARIA BAY

"Bulldog, this is Pathfinder 1. Over."

"Roger, this is Bulldog."

"Bulldog, we may have stumbled into a hot LZ. Over."

"Pathfinder, repeat last. Over."

"Bulldog, we have reached the bomb. Preliminary exam shows someone has been walking around the bomb. It appears to be two sets of prints. We keep hearing odd noises from an island out in what appears to be a wide canal."

"Pathfinder, hold one."

Johnson and Knight move over to the radio. "Pathfinder, this is Bulldog 1. I repeat, you are calling in a hot LZ. Remain where you are and secure your position. We will be airborne in a few minutes. We should be at your site in about ten minutes. We'll land at the LZ-14 on the map."

"Roger, Bulldog 1. Pathfinder out."

"Shit, who would be out in this area?" Johnson's finger points at the swamp on the map.

"Gentlemen." Sandovol looks over the map. "You are definitely in Indian country. It could be drugs or alcohol and smuggling. I might add, these are people who do not wish to be found."

"Great." Johnson calls Cabolero and tells him to get the group ready. The sound of the helicopters warming up echoes in the air.

"Bulldog, this is Pathfinder 1. Over."

Knight grabs the handset. "This is Bulldog. Over."

"Bulldog we have found two trip wires near the site. Whoever is out here knows what they're doing. Also, there is the smell of burnt wood in the air. And we can hear people moving things. Over."

"Pathfinder, pull back to the LZ and wait for the rest of the group. We'll go back in with some force."

"Roger, Bulldog. We'll meet the group at the LZ. Out."

Milton grabs the man with him and points towards the trails out. He leans forward and whispers, "We're out of here. Back to the LZ and wait for the others."

As they get ready to go, a branch cracks somewhere in the dark. The marines freeze as the sound of other footsteps in the brush reachs them. Milton hits him on the shoulder and points down another trail. They slowly move forward, their weapons at the ready. The inky darkness covers them and the unknown men in the brush. They move up the trail and reach the edge of the landing zone. They can hear people moving up behind them on the trail.

"Let's move out into the field and take up a position near that fallen tree we passed."

As they move low across the grassy field, lights go on in the brush. They can see men moving in the lights. "I count at least ten men moving around the edge of the field." A light from the edge of the trail plays over the tree trunk. "Bulldog, this is Pathfinder 1."

"Roger, Pathfinder 1."

"We definitely have a problem out here. We're behind a fallen tree out in the LZ. We have bad guys across our front. We can make out about ten armed men."

"Hold where you are. We're inbound."

"Roger. We'll throw smoke when we see you."

As Milton turns towards the trail, about four lights fall on their position. The lights are quickly followed by automatic rifle fire. The tracers fly over their heads and disappear into the swamp behind them. One of the men in the brush lights a bundle of four sticks of dynamite and throws it at the front of the tree. The men duck down as the sparks from the fuse burns into the blasting cap. The explosion rocks the tree, and water and mud fly in the air. The two marines hug the earth as the air clears. Milton slaps his buddy on the shoulder. They both rise up and fire into the brush at their front. The men in the brush fire back at the sudden shooting.

"Fuck this." Milton locks in a 40 mm grenade and fires at the head of the trail. The explosion catches them off guard. The men are yelling to one another and firing as they move back into the bush. "I think we got their attention. So let's try again." Milton fires a second grenade deeper into the brush. A scream of pain reaches them, and then there is more firing. The shooting falls off, and all is quiet. They check the brush line and wait for the others to arrive.

CHAPTER 14

BRIDGE OF THE *MOSKVA*
THE GULF

Sokolov looks out the front of the bridge. The flames from the fire flare up. Emergency lighting fills the bridge with red light. Men are carrying the wounded to the dispensary. The damage control teams are working to repair the broken windows, and others fight the fires from the bomb damage at the front of the ship. As Sokolov looks ship to ship, fires rage on each.

"Admiral, the *Osmotritelnyy* is in real trouble. The fighter hit the main stack. They will have to cut a lot of it away." He raises his binoculars and can see figures moving in the light of the fire. "They seem to be getting the fire under control." The men on the destroyer use axes to chop parts of the fighter off and throw them over the side. The fire hoses spray the mass of twisted metal to cool it down.

A quick moving squall helps fight the fires. Broken and destroyed equipment is pushed and dragged to the sides of the ships and is dumped into the sea. The fire fighters push forward in the twisted passageways at the front of the *Moskva*. Torches are brought forward to cut through smashed beams and twisted plates of steel. They cut through to the feed magazine for the top SAM launcher. Men on the main deck shoot water and foam down into the gaping hole, and throw chunks of twisted metal over the side. The launcher is gone, and the feed mechanism has been smashed downward. It is bent and crumpled through the lower decks.

As soon as they cut a passage by the feed mechanism, the damage control officer works his way by and opens the hatch to the next compartment. The second SAM launcher is bent and twisted on the main deck. The fire had been contained in the aft

453

compartment. Pieces of the upper deck hang down in the room with a large cylinder in its middle.

"Shit. Chief, look."

He works his way up to the officer and looks up at the damage. "We have a big problem, sir. You need to contact the bridge and keep everyone out of the area."

"Yes, sir." The officer works his way back through the compartments, and grabs a phone in the main passageway. "Sir, you have a call from the damage control officer."

Sokolov grabs the phone and listens as the damage control officer describes the damage. He shakes his head while he listens. "I agree. Get started as soon as you can."

He goes by the men working on the bridge and down the stairwell to the combat control room. Pstygo and the air captain are looking over some scopes at the side. "Gentlemen." They join the admiral at the main plotting table. "We have a bad situation up front. It seems that the dive bomber dropped two bombs. One exploded. The other one is wedged between the second and third decks. We don't know if it is a dud or what. They're trying to clear the material around it away."

"Sir." Pstygo looks across the table into the admiral's face. "We have lost the forward sonar and control of the ASW launcher. My guess is that the bomb has cut the cables." The weapons officer joins them.

"Sir, I'll be going in with the damage team. We'll need to remove the other ordnance from the two destroyed launchers."

"Admiral, with your permission, I would like to join Mr. Beregovoy. While with the air service, I went through a course to disarm and neutralize aircraft ordnance."

"Very well, Kruglov. I want to know what is going on down there at all times. Lieutenant Major Yefimov will be on the bridge with me to direct the ship if need be."

"Aye, aye, sir." They move down a ladder into the bowels of the ship. As they move forward, the smell of burnt paint and cordite fill the air. Men are venting the smoke as others pass pieces of debris up the ladders. They meet the damage officer and move forward to look at the bomb.

"How is our course, Pstygo?"

"Well, sir. If things get any worse, we'll be operating on dead reckoning. We're about as blind as a major ship can get. If not for the down link, we would be on the decks shooting flares in front of us."

The admiral pats him on the back. "You mean we have become seamen again, and not just operators of technical wizardry."

RECON 1
SWAMP

The swamp has become quiet. Milton checks the area in front of the fallen tree. The lights have disappeared up the trails, and the blowing wind races over his face. Behind them, the open grassy area sways back and forth, and in the distance the flashing strobes of the oncoming helicopters blink in the blackness. The two gunships come from the sides and streak across the field. "Pathfinder, this is Night Moves. Over."

"Roger, you just passed over us. I'm going to throw a flare out from our position for the slicks."

"Roger, Pathfinder. We're going to IR out in front of you. Night Moves out."

"Cover me. I'm going to pop a flare out in the field." As Milton works his way out in the tall grass, the other marine rests his rifle on a twisted root at the end of the trunk. He watches Milton disappear into the darkness of the field. His eyes search the brush line for any movement or light. The sounds of the helicopters fill the air. Milton stops at a point about 100 feet from the fallen tree. His eyes search the area. Everything seems to be quiet. He takes out the flare grenade and pulls the pin. He takes one more quick look around the area.

He waits until the helicopters are about 300 yards out and pops the spoon on the grenade. It flares to life, and he tosses it out away from him. From his kneeling position, he sees the helicopters line up on the flare. The sudden burst of gunfire catches him off guard. A flare flies into the sky from the trees as two rounds slam into his back. He falls forward into the wet grass.

The marine at the tree is suddenly caught in the silver-blue light as gunfire rakes the tree. He rolls back and grabs the radio.

"Bulldog, abort the landing. Abort. We're under fire, and Milton is down." The incoming helicopters veer away from the site and circle back away from the field. The gunships roar back over the tree line. As two more flares are fired at them, their IR equipment goes pure white from the bright light. "Pathfinder, this is Night Moves. We see you at the log. Our target area is at your direct front. Over."

"Roger. The bomb is on your right quadrant. It is about 300 feet up the path and over fifty."

"Roger. We're strapped. We're going to teach these guys the cracker half-step."

"Night Moves, this is Bulldog 1. Over."

"Roger, Bulldog."

"Make damn sure you put your ordnance away from the bomb site, or we all go up in one big light."

"Roger. I'm packing two gun pods and two missile pods."

"Roger. We're on our way in; we're down about 400 yards from Pathfinder. We're on our way in. Hold your fire to only forward of the fallen tree, and no rockets. Over."

"Roger." As the two gunships maneuver into position, two more flares are fired into the sky above them. As they pop and begin to descend from their parachutes, tracer rounds begin to fly up towards them. "Shit, we're taking fire from three different locations." As the two gunships line up on the tree line, bullets hit along their sides. "Son of a bitch. We're hot."

The forward 20 mm cannons come to life and rip into the trees. The helicopters slip sideways and hover over the fallen tree, their nose guns moving back and forth across the front. Gunfire from the far left corner of the field flies at them. The nose guns rotate in that direction and fire. The tracers from the cannons explode into the brush and trees, cutting everything to ground level. One gunship stays over the fallen tree as the other one moves off to his left, to the edge of the field. The front is now in crossfire between the two.

"Pathfinder, this is Bulldog 1. Over."

"Roger, Bulldog."

"We're coming in directly behind you. We're in the field. We'll work our way up to your location."

"Roger, Milton is down about 200 feet to my left." He raises and looks around the end of the log at the trail. A spark of light near the mouth of the trail catches his eye. Then two sparkling bundles are flying in the air at the log. "Shit." He rolls back as they hit on the other side of the tree.

"Bulldog, watch for—" The blast of the dynamite slams the tree into his back. Mud and water are thrown into the air. The gunship is caught in a shower of debris. "Shit." The helicopter is pushed up from the blast, and mud and grass cover the front of the canopies. It swings to the right and fires along the left edge of the trail.

"This is Bulldog 1. Over." Only static comes back to Johnson as he and the others kneel in the grass. He looks over the field in front of them; his night vision gear sweeps the field. He can see part of the tree, but no one behind it.

"Mianno, can you get to the radio? Over."

As he lies at the base of the tree, his hand finds the receiver. "Roger, Bulldog. I'm down. Over."

"Hang in there. We're about 200 feet behind you. We're coming in. Over."

"Roger."

"Cabolero, take a fire team over to where Milton is."

"Right, Skipper."

Johnson and the others move up to the fallen tree. The machine gun is set up facing up the main trail. A corpsman moves up to where Mianno is lying. "We have you now. You'll be all right." Johnson moves over to the end of the tree and watches the men moving towards Milton.

He watches two unknown figures rise up in the grass. "Check him. Make sure he's dead." The other man turns towards the tree. "We'll get these bastards now."

The man kneels and prods Milton with the barrel of his shotgun. Milton's hand grabs the barrel and pushes it to the side. It fires and tears into the left side of his flack vest. His knife plunges into the figure's stomach, and he falls backwards with a scream of pain.

The other man turns from the tree and brings his rifle up. "Your dead now, you fucking fed."

"I don't think so." The man looks up in time to see the flash from five M-16 rifles. He is thrown back by the rounds and sprawls in the mud. Cabolero moves up next to Milton. "We got you now."

"Shit, I was sure I was toast. I was glad to hear your voice, Sarge. I'm a little fucked up."

"So what's new, Corporal?"

"Bulldog, we have Milton."

"Roger. I saw the two assholes raise up. You got them before we could get any shots off."

"Roger. The corpsman is going over him now. We're going to have to dust this guy out of here."

"Right. We have to get Mianno out too. Can you get him back to the LZ?"

"Roger. Three of us will be coming in to your position."

"Right. We're also sending Mianno back now. Out." As Johnson hands the receiver back to his radioman, a gust of wind and rain hits their position. Lightning flashes over their heads and a real downpour begins.

As Cabolero moves through the grass towards Johnson, the wind and rain beat down on him. As he goes by a clump of weeds, the lightning flashes. A form rises up and a knife glistens in the light. He grabs the arm and they both fall into the mud. He drives his fist into the chest of his attacker and forearms him across the face. His hand goes to his belt and his own knife is drawn and plunged into the man. He goes limp in Cabolero's hands.

"Shit, they're in the field." He yells it out over the rain to the men behind the tree. Bursts of gunfire rake the ground around him and around the men at the tree. One of the marines with him is hit in the arm and goes down. Johnson and the others fire into the field. Tracers fly back and forth. Cabolero drags the wounded marine in behind the tree with the others.

"Shit! What the fuck is with these guys?" Sandovol moves over next to them.

"We must have stumbled onto a big smuggling group, or dope."

"Night Moves, this is Bulldog. It's a free fire zone from the tree to the brush in the field. There are some of them out in the field with us."

"Roger. We'll make one pass from the trail to the other side of the field. But we're going to have to set down in the LZ. The wind and rain are getting worse."

"Roger. We're heads down."

Gunfire hits the tree as the firefight from the field explodes in intensity. Tracers arc up at the helicopters as they line up on the field. Both gunships open up with their two gun pods and move across the front of the tree. One locks on the left side of the field and the other takes the trees to the front. The rocket pods on the helicopters flame to life as they unleash all seventy-six missiles onto the target zone. The exploding missiles light up the field and shred the trees. They move back towards the LZ and land next to the others. The wind screams in the air as it drives the rain before it.

Cabolero moves over next to Johnson. "We're talking a monsoon here, Skipper."

"You got that, Gilbert. Nice moves out in the grass."

"Thanks. What the hell is with these guys?"

"We're near something big." Sandovol pulls his collar up. "I think probably moonshine and shit like that. These guys get a bunch of local assholes, and then bring in mercs for protection."

"I'm going to call the colonel. We need to secure the bomb site. Get a team together and try and secure the trail. This shit is affecting them the same as us."

"I would like to go in with Cabolero. I might be able to help them spot the main base."

"All right, Sandovol, but go in at the rear of the group."

"Bulldog, this is Bulldog 1. Over."

"This is Bulldog. Captain, the sky looks like Nam over there."

"Roger. We have three down. They're being taken back to the LZ. We have lost our air cover. We count nine bad guys down so far. Sandovol thinks they're mercenaries."

"Shit, I'm coming in with two more squads. We'll use the Jolly Green. It should be able to get through to you." Val is moved over to the other helicopter, and marines fill the interior of the big helicopter. Knight runs over to talk to Marino and Val. "We'll leave two fire teams for security. I'll call you from the site."

"Good luck, Colonel."

Knight runs up the ramp, and the big helicopter begins lifting into the sky. The helicopter fights its way to the site. Knight gets on a radio and calls Nelson at the base. They discuss the situation and that wounded will be flown in as soon as they can get airborne.

"That sounds good, Colonel. Captain Rollens has a trauma unit set up. He is in contact with the corpsman at the scene. The storm has them on the ground. They will have to sit it out until they can get a window."

"You have bad weather to 5,000 feet. You have two AVC's over you. If you require more support, call them down."

"Roger. Bulldog out."

The wind shakes the big Sea Stallion as it closes on the landing site. The pilot is in contact with the helicopters on the ground. As they get near, flares are thrown out by the men on the ground. The pilot and the co-pilot strain to see in the blackness. Their radarscope picks up the landing site, and the flares glow through the wipes of the blades on the window. "Bulldog, we have the LZ. We'll pass over the field and come in from the west."

"Roger." Knight turns to the men. "We'll be down in just a minute. Get everyone checked, Sergeant."

The men check their ammo and other equipment. As the helicopter flies over Johnson's head and begins the turn, tracer rounds arc up from the island in the canal. They swing the big helicopter to avoid the incoming fire. But rounds hit along the right side of it, and tear holes in the metal skin.

"Holy shit." Knight steadies himself. As the helicopter maneuvers in the darkness, they swing around and drop down next to the two gunships. As they settle down, the rear ramp is lowered, and the marines pile out the back.

"Set your perimeter." Knight points towards the next field. He runs up to the Seahawks and checks with the corpsman working on the injured.

"We have three down, two gunshot wounds, and some broken ribs and a broken hip."

Knight looks at the sky, and around the area. "Can you move them onto the Jolly Green?"

"Yes, sir. They're stable, but two are in mild shock now. They're set up at the base to deal with them as soon as we can get them out." Crewmen from the helicopters help carry the wounded men to the Sea Stallion. They take them up to the front of the bay area and run back through the rain and wind to their own ships.

Two of the corpsmen work on the wounded as the third talks to Rollens back at the base. They get them stabilized and get their equipment ready to rejoin the marines in the rain.

"Sir, I'll stay with the wounded. They will be going back in with you."

"Thank you, Chief. We'll be moving out now." The crewmen from the helicopters stand out in the rain in ponchos, their M-16s ready to defend the helicopters. They watch as Knight and the two corpsman disappear into the darkness.

"Bulldog 1, this is Bulldog."

"Roger, Bulldog."

"We're just coming into the field behind you. This rain and wind are playing hell with this night vision shit."

"Roger, we're about 100 yards to your front right. I have a squad going up the trail to try and secure the site. That gunfire you got is from a spit of land running out from the bank about 300 feet. It forms a little island in the canal."

"We're in the field and are coming in abreast, in case there are any more bad guys out here."

"Roger, hold one. Bulldog, we have your point man. He just made contact with our perimeter." The marines move across the field, their weapons ready. With their night vision equipment on, they scan the field for any movement. "Bulldog, I have two bad guys in the grass. The gunships got them. These guys are all in camouflage gear with AK-47s and a H&K."

"Roger. We're at the tree perimeter. Move your people up even with us." The men furthermost out signal with their flashlights. They now form a line across the field, with the men at the tree forming the base. The colonel joins Johnson behind the tree. "I have Cabolero with a squad on the main trail." He points with his flashlight on the map. "It looks like the bomb is right here."

"Good, I'll work the field while your team goes in support of Gilbert's group. This fucking rain is unbelievable." The wind lashes at the wet utilities of the marines lying along the trail. Cabolero moves forward. A second trail breaks off to their right. Sandovol moves up next to him as the point man moves forward.

Cabolero brings two men up with him and signals them up the side trail. Sandovol moves out with them. The point man crawls over a slight rise and searches the area. In his goggles, the sudden flashes of lightning flare and dissipate in the green light. Something moves to his front from the right to the left. He can just see the top of the man's back and head. He seems to be moving down a side trail next to the water. Cabolero crawls up next to him on the side of the trail. Water runs off the trees and plants, and rivulets flow down the path. He signals the marine to take a position at the junction of the two trails. He and the other marines move to the left side of the trail and move along the canal towards the site. As they start up the trail leading to the bomb, Johnson contacts Cabolero and lets him knows that they are coming in behind them. He clicks the mike button in response.

As they round a curve in the trail, he can see two men kneeling in the mud. They seem to be burying something. A crash of lightning makes both men look around. They have night vision equipment on, also. He lies still as the two look up the trail; one raises up on one knee. He seems to stare up the trail at Cabolero. He reaches over, hits the other man on the shoulder, and starts to move away towards the path along the canal.

An explosion from another trail rocks the ground under him as Cabolero pulls his rifle up to fire. The two men turn and fire in the direction of the blast. Cabolero and the other marine open fire on them. The two men fall back into the water. He gets up and runs to the spot where they were kneeling. The retard fins of the bomb are dug out. A piece of the white body is showing.

Johnson and the other men get to the split in the path just as the marines open up on a sandbar running over to the island. The mercs kneel in the shallow water and fire at Cabolero and the other marine. The rounds tear into the trees and brush. A machine gun opens up from the island at their position. An M-60 machine gun drops next to the marine at the fork, and they open fire on the sand bar. A second gun is positioned on the trail towards the bomb, and it opens fire on the men firing from the island.

Knight and a fire team split off the trail and go up the path that Sandovol and the other marines took. Johnson and two fire teams position themselves along the path up to the bomb. Johnson dives into the mud as rounds hit the trees and mud around him. The rain and lightning are intense as Johnson empties a clip at the flashes of rifle fire from the island. "What the fuck is going on?"

"Put some grenades along the brush line of the island."

The plunk of the grenade launchers adds to the noise of battle. The explosions rip into the heavy brush and blow mud and debris in the air. A grenade lands on the sandbar and blows the two men into the air. A flare is fired directly into the brush behind Johnson and Cabolero. Its silver light silhouettes the men on the ground. A machine gun rakes their position. Johnson kicks the flare into a hole with his foot and pushes mud on it. "Shit, put a couple of rockets into that shit."

Two marines pop Laws canisters and aim behind the brush. They fire deeper into the island. The missile hits and explodes, and a secondary explosion throws a huge fireball up and out of the trees. "Shit, what the hell did we hit?"

"Probably grain alcohol." Knight moves up next to the others. "We have people down. That explosion we heard coming in was Sandovol and the two marines. They hit a trip wire fused to dynamite. Sandovol and one of the marines are dead. The other is in bad condition. They're moving him back to the chopper."

"Shit." Cabolero crawls up next to the bomb and begins digging in the mud. Johnson watches him as he digs with his hand. "What the hell are you doing?"

"The two we shot near here were burying something next to the bomb. It might have been more fucking dynamite."

"Shit." Johnson crawls up on the other side of the bomb, and begins to dig in the soft mud.

A burst of gunfire from the island catches both men in the open; it hits near them and then walks over the top of them. The men along the bank fire back and fire more grenades across the water into the trees. One of the M-60s sets up near them, as the two men with the gunner set in.

Two navy men join them, carrying sandbags, and they start to dig up wet sand and fill them. As they get them filled, they stack them at the front of the bomb. As one is placed, a volley of shots rings out. One of the navy men is hit in the side. He rolls back into Knight. Another round catches the top of Johnson's leg.

"Fuck, I'm hit." He can feel the stinging burning across the back of his leg. His hands grab the mud and squeeze. It runs out between his fingers as they compress. Knight pulls him back in the depression; the corpsman is working on the navy crewman. He opens his shirt and puts a field dressing on. The moaning of the man can be heard above the wind and rain. More shots ring out and are answered by the machine gun. The man is give a shot of morphine and is pulled behind some trees. A cry of agony echos across the water as the machine gun finds its target.

"Sir, where are you hit?" The corpsman crawls up next to Johnson.

"Across the back of my leg. It burns like shit."

"Hold on, sir." He cuts his trousers away from the wound. The flashlight on his web gear shines on the exposed area. A wound five inches long and a quarter inch deep scars the back of Johnson's leg. The rain and blood mix and run down into a pool. "No major arteries, but you need to get this checked out by the doctor back at the base." He puts a field dressing on it and pulls it tightly around the leg. Johnson grimaces as the pressure is applied to the wound. "Shit, Doc."

"I know, sir. I'll give you a shot. We should get you back to the helicopter with the others."

As the needle is pulled out, the pain seems to dissipate. "I'll be all right. It is just a little sore." Knight gets on the radio with the helicopter. Water is running down the depression they're in, and it is falling in a small waterfall into the bayou.

"Johnson, they're requesting to lift off with the wounded. If you want to go back, we need to get you back there now."

"No, I'll be all right. I'm going to finish this thing."

Knights back on the radio. "Can you get out all right?"

"It may be close, but the doc is saying if we don't get them out, we'll have more dead marines on our hands."

"Roger. Good luck. Bulldog out."

ULTIMA
WASHINGTON, D.C.

"Shit." The commandant puts the phone down. The others in the room look in his direction. He gets up and goes up to the podium. "Mr. President, I just got off the phone with the team down at site five. They have inadvertently stumbled onto some kind of smuggling site, probably drugs and alcohol. It has turned into a real firefight. We have two dead and five wounded." The president puts his phone down. "My God."

"Yes, sir. They have also accounted for nine dead bad guys and the number is climbing. They're flying out the wounded now. It's pretty grim out there. Also, we need to pass on to the DEA that one of the dead is their man Sandovol.

"The marines at the site are now cut off from air support by the gunships. The storm is hitting them with fifty to sixty-five mile per hour winds and a torrent of rain."

"Sir." Brant gets up and walks over to the president's desk. "We need to get the news conference going. The films from the KNLT helicopter have generated more demands for questions. We can connect the action going on out there to these moonshiners, to account for all the firing and explosions they see from the tops of the buildings in New Orleans."

"Right. Get on that, would you, Mr. Brant?"

"Sir, the bomb site is in our hands. They're attempting to secure the area around it. Dr. Reddeer has been moved up to the area, and the Lanstat is being set up now."

"Thank you, Commandant Swane. Your marines are earning their pay on this one."

Captain Van Nar gets up to the podium. "Sir, we have radio contact with team two. They have arrived at the bomb number three site. We are advised that the power in the area is knocked out, so they are setting up portable generators. They should be up on the Lanstat in a short while."

"Well, let's get ready for the news conference. We will need weather, evacuation, and status on the operation in the swamps."

"Right, Mr. President." Brant and the others work to get everything together for the news conference.

BOMB SITE, NUMBER THREE
LOUISIANA

A Louisiana state trooper directs the helicopters down onto the road running in front of a two-story house. As they touch down, a crewman from the lead ship gets out and takes over direction of the others' landing. A bright light shines out of the darkness and pans over the landing helicopters. "Thanks for the help. And can you kill that light?" The trooper waves his hand and heads back up to the line of parked cars and the light. It blinks out as the last of the helicopters settles down. Police cars are parked, blocking the street. Their lights shine off the wet skins of the helicopters.

When all the helicopters are down, they cut their engines. The three troop ships sit in the middle with a gunship at the front and rear. "Well, Doctor?" The gunny grabs the handle of the door. "Let's go." Susie pulls the collar of the field jacket up around her neck as the door slides open. The wind gusts in with a freezing breath and a chilling rain. They jump down and follow some of the other marines up to the garage of the house. Their flashlights play over the wet driveway and the plants along its edge.

They join six troopers in the garage who are keeping dry from the rain. Some navy men are working on a generator. Their flashlights shine off the red frame and give their faces a ghoulish glow. "We almost have it. We'll be on-line in just a few minutes." The two pathfinders come into the garage from a side door into the house. They walk up to Neal and Gunny.

"Sir, we have held the house off limits from the police. It's a real shit situation inside. The troopers have been great; they turned back a news team that heard something on their radio. They're parked down the road behind the troopers' cars."

"Yeah, when we came in, they shot us with their strobe light."

"Gunny, stay with the doctor. I'm going in to look at what we have."

"Right, sir."

Susie talks with the troopers as they have some coffee to help cut the cold. The men at the generator pull the cord and it springs

BACKFIRE

to life. They hook up some cords and the garage is suddenly lit. The light shines out into the dark rain and wind. Susie walks to the edge of the light and looks up and down the street. Except for the police cars' flashing lights, all is pitch black.

The door from the house opens, and Lieutenant Neal walks down the steps into the light.

He is white as snow and visible shaken. "Sir, are you all right?" A corpsmen moves over to him.

"Yeah, I just need a minute." He walks out of the garage and looks up into the angry sky as the rain washes over him in sheets.

The navy men run lines from the generator up into the house. Neal steps back into the garage as a lightning stroke flashes behind him. "Sir, are you all right?" The gunny puts his hand on his shoulder.

"Yeah, what a fucking mess in there. We have two people down, and one is with the bomb. Set your men up around the ground floor of the house and see if Susie is ready to have a look."

"Right." Gunny gets the men and sends them into the house to different rooms.

Susie walks over to Gunny and Neal. "Are you OK, Mr. Neal?" He looks into her eyes; Susie can feel the coldness.

"Yeah, but we need to talk before we go inside." The gunny joins them, and Neal talks to them in whispered tones. "The bomb came in through the window facing east. The man and woman living here must have been having breakfast. It killed them both. The shit part is that it caught the man and pulled him with it. It went through the opposite wall; the retard fins pulled him through with it. It's a mess, so if you're ready, we'll go back in and get this thing taken care of."

They walk up the stairs and go into a side hall; one way is to the kitchen, while the other leads to a family room. One of the navy men comes down the hall and goes into a bathroom. The sound of him throwing up comes through the door.

"This way, through the kitchen." Neal leads the way. The light from a flood light shines on the huge hole torn in the side of the wall. Susie looks around the room, the body of a woman lies off to her right. Someone has covered her up; her legs protrude from the blanket. It is soaked with blood; its smell fills the room.

The wind and the rain blow in through the hole. "Damn, it's cold in here." Susie rubs her hands together. They move deeper into the house. Her eyes follow the track of the bomb and stop at the opposite wall. The body of a man is protruding from it, from the hips down. Blood is spattered everywhere. The retard fin of the bomb has him impaled. "Jesus." Gunny walks up behind the body. The floor is sticky from the blood from the two victims.

"This way, Doctor." Neal leads them to a doorway that leads into the dining room. The others follow as they come around the corner. Susie catches sight of the bomb protruding through the wall. The outer white body is covered in red rivulets; they look like they were painted on it. She catches sight of the upper torso of the man. He seems to be lying on the top of the bomb, his mangled arm hangs down beside it. The wind causes the arm to swing. Blood is everywhere on the walls and floor.

Susie moves in close to the casing to check the number. As she bends over to check it, the lights go out, and the smell of the drying blood fills her nostrils. "What the fuck? Get those lights back on." Flashlights cut through the dark.

"Doctor, are you all right?" Gunny moves up beside her.

"Yeah, I'm fine. I need some light on the casing."

He hands her his flashlight, and she squats next to the access plate. The light shines through the transparent coating of blood on the bomb. "We have number three. Let me know when we're on-line, and I will need some rags to wipe the casing off." The lights blink on and again flood the room. Laura brings some dishtowels and a bowl of water. She wets the rags and they both begin to wipe the casing off.

"Susie, I'll get something to cover up the man's face."

"Thanks, it would make things easier." As she wipes the bomb, the lights again go out. She can hear men cursing out in the other room. She feels a hand grab her around the wrist and squeeze. "All right. Who's the clown?" Flashlights go on and fall on the casing. As the light moves up to the top of the casing, it illuminates the hand on her wrist. She looks at the hand and then up at the mangled face. A bloody froth drips from the flesh, and a mournful sound fills her ears.

"Mmmm helpmmmmm."

"Oh, my God. He is alive. This man is alive." She pulls her arm back, and the bloody hand drops and swings. The moaning is heard again.

"Oh, God. Didn't anyone check him for vital signs?" The corpsmen move in and check. They shake their heads. One gives the man a shot of morphine. They continue to check.

"We don't know how he is surviving. His pulse is so low you can hardly feel it. And his blood loss...half the wounds are in the wall."

Gunny and Neal move up with Susie. She cups her face in her hands. "You all right, Susie?"

"God, Gunny. He has been alive for hours, probably hoping someone would come to help him."

"Susie." Gunny puts his arm around her shoulders. "They're trying to help him, but it is a lost cause. He is so torn up, he won't make it."

The lights continue to blink on and off. Neal yells out at the men in the garage. "Get these fucking lights fixed!"

One of the navy men sticks his head in the door. "Bulldog you have a call coming in."

"Susie, let's step out into the garage and let them work on this man."

As they walk out the door into the garage, one of the navy men working on the generator steps up to them. "Sir, we have a towed generator coming to us. This rental thing is a total piece of shit."

"All right, Chief. Do the best you can."

"Yes, sir." The radiomen have set up the Lanstat set off to the side of the garage. "We're up, sir."

Neal picks up the handset. "This is Bulldog 2. Over."

"Neal, this is Bulldog. We have a Stallion en route with wounded. They are going to land at your location, and then transfer them to ground transportation."

"Roger, Bulldog."

"Neal, we're hot, and I need some of your people. When they get the wounded off, load as many as you can spare. This thing has turned into a real shit storm. Over."

"Roger, we'll get prepared to load as soon as it gets here, over."

"Neal, your people are coming in hot. Bulldog out."

"Shit." Neal puts the handset down and looks around the garage as the generator craps out again.

"This thing is a piece of shit. Grab the other side of this thing." Two of the navy men grab the generator and carry it out into the rain and heave it out onto the front lawn. One of the troopers runs up to them. "We have a call. They're escorting in a towed generator and a couple more ambulances. They're about five miles back." The trooper holds his hat down as the rain slashes them.

"That's great news. Thanks, Officer."

Neal runs over to the door to the house and calls for the gunny. He makes his way to the garage, and they walk to the front of the garage as Neal unfolds a map. "Gunny, Bulldog is in a hot LZ. They're requesting as many men as we can spare. They're going to land a Stallion here and transfer the wounded to ambulances. They think it is safer than flying in to the base."

"Shit, I can hardly believe that anything is in the air." He looks out the front of the garage. The wind whips the rain, and it swirls in the beam of the flashlight. One of the navy men runs out in the rain, down the driveway, and into the middle of the street. He calls a couple of the troopers over and explains what they need. The men run back to the others, and they begin backing up the police cars and keeping everyone back. The sparking flares throw a red hue on the wet asphalt as the troopers throw others out. The flares form a box for the incoming Stallion.

"Gunny, I see two fire teams going with me, leaving one with you and Dr. Davies."

"Aye, aye, sir. I'll get the men ready." He goes back into the house and brings out the men. They get together at the side of the garage. Susie walks over to Neal and watches the men in the street. Neal explains the situation to her.

"Check your equipment. There is ammo and other gear on the Stallion. The lieutenant was informed it is a hot LZ. Get mentally ready." The men check their equipment. Susie's eyes are drawn to the sudden flashing of lights from the east. The convoy of emergency vehicles, led by troopers, works its way up the road. Their lights twinkle and sparkle in the falling rain. The howl of the wind drowns out the sound of their sirens. They wind like a snake around fallen trees and branches, and splash through streams of water running across the road.

The navy man in the street begins to signal towards the west with two flares as the landing lights on the Stallion try to cut through the blowing rain. The big helicopter is buffeted by the crosswinds, and it fights its way towards the glowing box of flares. It flies over the house and swings around to land from the east. As soon as it touches down, the back begins to lower. As soon as the ramp touches the ground, a trooper signals one of the ambulances in. It drives in behind it and swings the rear of the vehicle facing the back of the Stallion. The EMS personnel run up the ramp and begin carrying out the wounded. As soon as they are loaded, they pull out of the way and another pulls in to load. The marines in the garage watch silently as the wounded are unloaded and the body bags are carried out. A figure in a flight suit and helmet walks halfway down the ramp. A long cord attached to the interior of the helicopter trails out behind him. He looks around as the last of the ambulances is loaded. He looks up towards the house and his hand circles in the air above his head.

"Let's move." Neal leads the men down the driveway and up into the rear of the helicopter. As soon as they are loaded, the ramp begins to close. The Stallion slides forward as the huge blades whip the rain and wind into spinning vortices. It slowly lifts into the air and begins moving off towards the west.

"Gunny." The corpsman takes him off to the side. They speak in whispered tones. "Gunny, the man inside cannot be saved. What Dr. Davies heard was not 'Help me.' The man is begging to die. We don't know what to do." Marshall goes inside with the corpsman and kneels down next to the man. He tilts his head to hear the muffled voice. A small bubble of blood and saliva forms and pops as the torn mouth slowly speaks. "Kill meee, killll meee." The dangling hand swings up and grabs Marshall on his forearm. "Semper Fi, Gunny." The hand slips off and swings in the cold air. Marshall stands up and walks back to the corpsman. His flashlight passes over the red hand print on his sleeve. "Shit." Marshall looks around in the dark as one of the marines left with him walks up in the darkness. He holds up a picture and pans his flashlight on the photo. It shows a group of marines somewhere in Vietnam.

"This guy was a E-5 in Nam, with the Third Division. He won a Bronze Star." Marshall's eyes run over the photo. It reminded him of the one with him and Cabolero. The other marine disappears back into the darkness. He turns back to the corpsman; their flashlights hang from their web gear. Their faces are lost in the darkness. Marshall looks back at the figure by the bomb. "Suggestions, Doc?"

The corpsman holds up syringes filled with a yellowish fluid. "There is enough pain killer in this to put him to sleep forever. We'll kill him trying to get him out of that fucking wall. There is no hope."

"I feel kind of shitty about this, Gunny. We're here to save lives, but this is something else."

"Give me the syringe." He hands it to Marshall.

"Thanks, Gunny. I owe you one."

The gunny walks over and kneels down next to the bomb. In the dark, the others could not make out what was being said. In the glow of his flashlight, the torn hand again rises and grabs Marshall's forearm. The room is quiet except for the howl of the wind in the kitchen. Susie walks into the room and stands quietly in the dark. A corpsman holds a flashlight on the man in the wall; she sees a syringe pass through the light and stop near the man's head. A deep voice comes out of the darkness. "Marines, a warrior goes on to Valhalla this night. He will save a cup of mead for us."

The needle is pushed into the man's neck, and the plunger sent home. He retracts the syringe and hands it to the corpsman. He moves to get out of their way as they check the man. They work with flashlights and huddle over the man in the wall. After a few minutes, they step back. The corpsman turns towards the gunny standing in the dark. "Gunny, this marine is now with his wife."

Susie moves over next to Gunny and grabs his hand in the dark. "You're a good man, Gunny Marshall."

He gives her hand a squeeze. "We need to expedite this bomb. Good people are dying for these pieces of techno shit. We should be ready to go as soon as they get the body extracted from the wall." One of the navy men comes in from the garage with a chain saw. "They're going to have the generator hooked up in a little bit. It's backing up the driveway now. I'll trim the wall back around the body so the corpsman can get him out."

"Right." The gunny and Susie walk out into the garage as the five-ton truck backs up to the open door and stops. The navy men begin to pull cables off the truck and run them in to the panel for the floodlights. They lay the cables out, and the truck pulls down the driveway. They watch as the big generator on the back of the truck is started. It kicks over and stalls, then kicks over and bursts to life. The drone of the generator is added to the howl of the wind.

They both get something to drink as the sound of the chainsaw drifts to them from inside the house. Tarps from the truck are carried in and moved into the house. A corpsman goes out to one of the emergency vehicles and comes back with two body bags. "We'll be done in just a few minutes."

"Thanks, Chief."

ULTIMA
WASHINGTON, D.C.

The press secretary stands next to the door as the president and Admiral Hillings come down the hall. "Sir, we're ready as soon as you want to begin."

"Thank you. We aren't going to have much time. So no questions until the end."

The press secretary goes in and walks up to the podium. The president waits as he calms the reporters down and sets the parameters of the briefing.

"Ladies and gentlemen, the president."

Wayne walks out to the podium and looks the assembled group over. He takes a drink of water and arranges his notes. "Ladies and gentlemen of the press, Admiral Hillings and I will try and bring you up to speed on the events in the Gulf. First off, I have been in contact with Secretary Sholenka concerning the crash of the Russian bomber. I am also in contact with Fidel, concerning the engagement of Russian and Cuban forces in the Gulf. We believe that my discussion with Fidel will grow to include mutual agreements on issues between our two countries. At this time, the forces of General Morales are being driven back by General Quintano. We have maintained a full alert in the Gulf to ensure that the situation does not reach American soil. I'll have Admiral Hillings brief you on the military actions and on the evacuation now in progress in southern Louisiana."

The admiral briefs them on the ongoing situation and covers the evacuation progress. He explains the scope of the alert and the positioning of the American ships. He looks at his watch. "We can take a couple of quick questions, then we must get back."

"Sir, sir." The reporters jockey for recognition. The admiral points to one of the men up front. "Sir, we're all getting reports of explosions and gun battles in the swamp, and of possible bombs from the Russians. Is there any truth to what we're hearing?"

Hillings looks back at the president, and he nods his head. "There are two teams of marines operating in the swamps of southern Louisiana. When the Russian bomber flew over the state, it was carrying some new top secret anti-submarine weapons. They were not to be used in the western area, but in the choke points in the North Sea. These weapons each have a 2,000-pound warhead. The ground units are recovering them as we speak." The president walks up to the podium.

"Excuse me, Admiral. The marines have stumbled onto what appears to be drug and smuggling operations in the area. They have come under fire and were forced to defend themselves. With the storm coming in, it was deemed best to put the area under military control."

"Sir, we have heard that Drs. Davies and Reddeer are operating with the marines. Their specialty is nuclear weapons, correct?"

"That is true, but they are also highly trained in the disarming of heavy munitions. These particular weapons have anti-tampering devices and timers on them. We were fortunate to have them in the area. They are working with the naval ordnance disposal unit from the base in New Orleans." The door at the side of the stage opens, and Captain Emmett joins the group. The president looks back and seeing Emmett, turns back to the news people.

"Good, we have Captain Emmett with us to tell you about the storm. It seems that Evita has turned into a rather formidable she-beast. Ladies and gentlemen you must excuse Admiral Hillings and myself. It is imperative that we get back to the situation room." They stand as the president leaves.

The press secretary comes back to the podium. "We'll have Captain Emmett show you the latest on the hurricane, as well as some pictures just received from the C-130, which was damaged when it entered the eye of the storm." Emmett gets to the podium and begins his talk about the storm. He gets set to show films from the storm chaser.

As Wayne enters the situation room, Brant is standing, looking up at one of the screens. Wayne looks at the screen. A huge black hole is spinning in the sea. It looks like some huge lamprey's mouth, sucking in the atmosphere above it. "My God. What is that?"

"It's part of the film sent in by the C-130. That's the whirlpool at the front of the rear wall in the eye." As he watches the screen, he can hear numbers being transmitted over the Lanstat system. The yellow box on the bomb site at number three blinks on and off. "We're transmitting the numbers to Dr. Davies at site three. She is removing the access cover now."

BRIDGE OF THE *MOSKVA*
THE GULF

"Admiral, the *Otlichnyy* is now down to ten knots."

"Very good, Mr. Yefimov." Sokolov walks over to the starboard side and looks at the ship with his binoculars. Fire is still burning on the port side, and lights play off twisted steel. Gaping holes are torn into the ship. Once-polished launchers and radar equipment hang at odd angles.

"Sir." Pstygo joins the admiral. "We have just received a transmission from the Americans. Both Cuban subs have surfaced and recharged their batteries. But they are detecting only one still in the Frozen Forest. The other has moved into the Gulf on a course aimed directly at us."

"Very good. Let's hope they can clear the bomb so we can activate the forward launcher."

The admiral is called to the phone. He listens as Kruglov describes the situation near the bomb and what they think can be done. "They're still knocking down some fire forward and on the first deck. We have extra lighting coming in from amid ship." He squeezes up against the bulkhead as men carry cables forward. Men are down to tee-shirts or no shirts. The heat is over 100 degrees in the compartments. Sweat runs off the men as they remove twisted steel from around the bomb and haul it up the ladders to be thrown over the side. Hoses for the men fighting the fires forward trail through the compartment and disappear down into the bowels of the ship. The lights blink off and on as an angry glow comes from the forward compartments.

Beregovoy joins him at the phone, his shirt drenched in sweat. Kruglov finishes his call and hangs up the phone. They both lean back on the bulkhead as men struggle to carry a large piece of metal out and up the ladders.

"I think it is a complete dud." His hand wipes his brow.

Kruglov looks at him. "That's great, in that we have a fifty-fifty chance of being right."

One of the sailors works his way through the door. "Sir, we have all the metal cleared from the bomb that we can. The chief wanted you to know."

"Right, Comrade. We'll be right there." The smell of burnt paint, acetylene, sea water, and sweat fill the room as the two lieutenants climb ladders on each side of the bomb. They stare at each other over the crushed tail of the bomb. The room gets quiet as they are left alone with their charge. The heat in the lower decks seems to be using the bomb hole in the upper decks as a chimney. The heat near the ceiling is intense. "Shit, it's hotter than hell up here. See, I told you the stabilizing fins are smashed down over the back, and the fuse is totally fucked up."

"You're right." Kruglov looks up through the hole and can see the smoke curl into the blackness. The hole is huge where the bomb hit near the launcher. He climbs up higher and sticks his head through the floor of the first deck. Oily, sooty water drips down on his shoulders and arms. Its coolness soaks through his shirt. "You know, we might be able to pull this bastard up through the hole and throw it over the side."

Beregovoy has slid forward and looks over the side of the bomb along the bulkhead. Two terminals on the wall are torn to pieces. Cables running from them hang limp, draped over the steel plate.

"Shit, the feed terminals for the forward launcher is gone. And it took out one of the power terminals. Unless we can get this thing out of the way, we're screwed."

"It sounds like an honest appraisal of the situation." The sound of the admiral's voice brings both young lieutenants down from their ladders. He catches the eye of the chief running the damage control teams and waves him over. "Comrade Chief, what is our situation forward?"

"Not good, Comrade Admiral. When the other bomb exploded on the number two launcher, it buckled the bulkheads all along this passage. We have the fires pretty well knocked down, but there is a lot of damage." Some men walk by carrying pieces of cables and steel twisted into weird shapes. Other men carry a man between them and work their way back to the dispensary.

"That's the other thing, Comrade Admiral. The heat in the forward compartments is intense. We have lost about six men so far just from that. If we vent up through the hatches, we get this damn storm right down the hole."

"Very good, Chief. I know that you and your men are doing all that can be asked of you. Please pass on my personal commendation of a job well done."

"Thank you, sir. We'll get our ship through."

"I have the utmost confidence that you will accomplish just that."

"Well, gentlemen. What is our next move?"

"Comrade Admiral." Kruglov points to the hole above their head. "I think we can pull it back up and dump it over the side. We have some chain falls that can handle this."

Beregovoy looks at his friend. "Sir, we both think this is a dud. So that could be our best chance of getting rid of this thing."

"Very well. Get with the chief. He'll get the men and equipment you need. It is imperative that we regain control of the forward launcher, or that submarine will have us cold."

"We'll get going on it, Comrade Admiral. We suggest that you may want to move to another area, just in case were wrong, sir."

"Very good, gentlemen. I wish you good luck, for all our sakes."

As the admiral moves back down the core of the ship, fire damage and water seem to be everywhere. As he works his way back to the lower hangar deck, the damage seems to be get worse. When he walks out on the platform that looks over the bay area, it takes his breath away.

"Good God." His eyes jump from one burnt and mangled helicopter to another. The length of the bay is burnt black from the fires. Two huge holes above his head look out into the storm. Rain falls on the lower deck and runs in rivulets towards the sump pumps groaning away.

The destruction in the hangar bay is almost complete. The ship lists to the port side. Men move about, their skin stained black by the soot and oil. The admiral's mind is consumed by the loss of life and the damage to the ships in his command. The magnitude of his losses and the questioning of his commands would fold a weaker spirit. "Sir." The damage control officer joins him on the platform.

"Yes, how are we doing?"

"Sir, we should send a letter to the builders in the Nosenko Yard in Nikolayev. We have been hit by everything and we're still afloat."

"It does seem to be a miracle. But we still have the storm and the Cuban subs in front of us."

"Yes, sir. If you'll excuse me, we're trying to set up the hoist to pull that bomb up."

"Yes, I need to get back to the bridge."

Even with the many men working about him, the admiral feels alone. As he gets back to the bridge, he goes out on the flying bridge and looks at the heavily damaged escorts. The flashes of cutting torches and welders flare like sparklers on the ships. He walks over and looks down on the men on the starboard deck. They are putting together a make shift A-frame. They all have safety lines on and are battered by the wind and the rolling of the ship. The welders work their art on twisted pieces of metal and pipes. The large chain fall lies on the deck, waiting for its time.

QUINTANO'S HELICOPTER
CUBA

The co-pilot leans back and signals to Quintano. He points to his headset. "This is Quintano. Over."

"General, this is Vargas. We have reached Guines. Morales's people have pulled out. We are moving towards San José de las Lajas. Our scouts have seen tanks in the area."

"Very good. Keep pressing the attack forward. Zino has people moving down the coastal road towards Havana, and a battalion is coming towards you on the main road."

"Roger, we are unloading tanks now. We have two Shilka tracks up there. They're picking up some gunships coming down from Havana."

"We'll be there in a few minutes. Hold at the intersection just outside of town."

"Roger. Vargas out."

The helicopter shifts back towards the east and joins the line of lights on the road below. A series of rolling hills separates them from the forward elements of the group. The helicopter is talked down near a group of parked BTR-60 armored personnel carriers. Quintano and Brock walk over to where Vargas is standing. He is talking to some of the staff. As he walks up, Vargas salutes, and they walk into the rear of the command vehicle. A plotting board in the center is marked with symbols showing the position of known forces.

"It is looking good, Vargas." Quintano runs his finger over the map and checks on Zino's position.

"Sir, we have six tanks deployed here along the road into Lajas. They have eight BTR personnel carriers in support. There have been two Hinds crossing here behind their lines. We have remained on passive radar. We doubt they have locked in on our Shilka units. We're moving up the tanks now. These hills have proven to be a blessing."

"Let's run the gunships farther south, then have them get a look at the area around Havana. Also, I would like to go forward and get a look at the ground up to the tanks."

"Yes, sir. We have one of the BTR-40 scouts leaving in just a minute. He'll be able to get you up there."

"Sir, there is a call for the general."

"This is Quintano. Over."

"General, this is Zino. We have run into a tank company with gunship cover. We're moving up our triple A and some of our tanks. We got two of them, but lost three scouts in the process. My guess is that we're due north of your position on the coastal road."

"Roger, Colonel. We will open our attack in about forty-five minutes."

"Sir, that will be fine. We should be in position to move at the same time."

"Good luck, Colonel."

"And to you also, General. Zino out."

"Well, Mr. Brock, do you want to stay here or move up forward?"

"Hell, I came this far, Comrade General. I'll stick with the action." They move out to the waiting scout and drive off into the dark night towards Havana. As they leave, the two gunships lift off and head towards the south. The scout commander calls ahead and gets a position to meet with one of the lead units. Quintano and Brock stand up in the turret and look out over the six Sagger anti-tank missiles mounted on the top. The cool night air blows over them as they move up the dark road.

FIDEL'S FLIGHT
COLUMBIA

"Maracaibo, this is Cuban air flight 111. Over."

"Roger, flight 111. We have you due east our location at 30,000 feet. Over."

"Roger, Maracaibo, we are continuing on to Havana. Over."

"Roger, flight 111. You are cleared. Have a good trip."

The airliner passes out into the Caribbean Sea. Its radar sweeps ahead. All seems clear. The captain informs Fidel's aide that they are now over water and heading towards Jamaica. As the liner settles in on its course towards Kingston, the tower calls down to two Mig-21 fighters.

"We just had a check-in by flight 111 for Cuba. That's the flight that you are to escort, right?"

"Thank you, tower. We need a clearance to leave as soon as possible."

"Roger, we can facilitate you in a few minutes. Use taxi way three, and hold at the line. Over."

The sleek Migs move down the taxiway and wait just off the runway. They get their clearances and pull out. The planes stand still for a minute. Then with fire blowing out the tails, they race done the runway and lift into the sky at a forty-five-degree angle. The boom of the departing planes blasts the quiet of the surrounding area. They level off at 15,000 feet and drop in on the course behind the airliner.

In the darkness east of them, another pair of sleek forms maneuvers over to the track of the liner. They drop to 10,000 feet and come in line with the two Migs. Their radars run on passive. The Hornets run without lights. Northeast of the planes, an A-6 Intruder scans the aircraft and transmits information to the two Hornets. The hunt is on as the fighters move up closer behind the Migs.

ULTIMA
WASHINGTON, D.C.

"Mr. President, President Castro's plane has just gone feet wet. It is being trailed by two Mig-21s with our fighters plugged in behind them."

"Is everything in place? It would not pay to lose Fidel after we promised to escort him into Guantánamo."

"Mr. President." Brant turns back towards him. "According to all reports, everything is in place. It is now up to the two marine fighter pilots. They are well trained and know their mission. The outcome is in their hands."

Captain Van Nar walks up to the podium. "Gentlemen, we have received word from Sky 1. They are receiving radio traffic that suggests a major engagement will soon transpire at the eastern approaches to Havana." The screen above her shows a map of western Cuba.

"The forces of General Quintano are at the locations shown by the blue triangles. The red triangles are the forces of General Morales. The forces of General Quintano now control three-quarters of the island. Also, the Russian squadron has now slowed to eight knots. The damage inflicted by the Cuban fighters is severe. Our estimate is that at least two of the *Sovremennyy* destroyers will not make it to the demark line."

Admiral Hillings walks up to the podium. "Gentlemen, I have just spoken with Admiral Sokolov. He is aware of the submarine threat, but at this time they are almost defenseless. The *Moskva* has a 2,000-pound bomb stuck in the forward part of the ship. They are trying to disarm it as we speak. They will have a short break in the weather. No rain, but still heavy seas."

Over the speakers comes the voice of Val reading the number seven screw to Gunny Marshall. It is cut in by a voice that sounds like it is coming out of a deep hole. "We're receiving fire from three locations. We believe that the bomb is wired with explosives. The weather sucks."

"Who is that?"

"Sir, we believe it is team one trying to set up the Lanstat. They had to move the equipment already because of hostile fire."

"Let's hope their situation gets better soon."

"Yes, Mr. President."

BOMB SITE, NUMBER FOUR
LOUISIANA

The big helicopter fights its way forward as lightning strikes probe the earth for weak points. The rain lashes the length of the ship as the pilot fights it over into a banking turn. "Bulldog, this is Bulldog 2. Over."

"Roger, Bulldog 2."

"We are inbound on the final leg. We will be landing at R5-3 on the map. Over."

"Roger, R5-3. We are receiving fire from near the river. You are coming in hot, I repeat hot."

"Roger, we're in now. Over."

The Stallion lands on some tall grass and sand. It begins to sink into the swamp. The rear door begins to open. "More throttle." The pilot holds the helicopter as steady as he can. He calls back to Neal. "We're landing hot. If we go all the way down, we'll sink in this shit."

"Roger." Neal tells the others and moves to the rear ramp. It lowers till it is straight out from the back of the ship. They move to the sides of the ramp, and drop about three feet into the mud. They exit off to the sides as soon as they are clear. The ramp is lifted, and the Stallion, which is running at full throttle, hovers three feet off the deck. Rounds from the front begin hitting the Stallion as the pilot pulls back on the stick. It arcs upward and is gone. Neal's men move forward in knee-deep water as rounds fly over their heads. They wade up the side of a grassy knoll. They can see muzzle flashes directly to their front. Neal calls the men on the extreme right side of the perimeter. "Bulldog 2, those are the bad guys. We're about ten degrees off their flashes. They're about 100 yards out. Over."

"Roger." Neal hands the handle back to the radioman.

"Lock in some grenades. I want a pattern." He holds his arms out and shows them the area. Six marines take up a position at the base of the knoll and aim their launchers in the air.

"Now!" Neal drops his hand, and all six launchers fire. The men at the top of the knoll fire into the area of the flashes. "We're moving over the top of the knoll. Give us about a twenty count, and then fire a second load of grenades."

As they move over the knoll, the 40 mm grenades begin hitting about 100 yards out. The explosions are muffled in the howl of the wind. Once over the knoll, the ground gets firmer and the men begin advancing abreast. The wet grass is two feet tall, and stubby trees and shrubs cover their movement. The men drop to one knee as the second salvo of grenades flies forward. The men on the knoll fire from the prone position as the grenades explode in the darkness. They begin moving up animal paths in the brush. A loud explosion goes off to their left front. The men all drop to one knee and look around. The radioman runs up next to Neal and hands him the handset.

"Bulldog 2, your suppression fire moved them back. We think they are going to either run or cross over to the island. That explosion was caused by one of them who crawled up along the riverbank and tried to toss some dynamite into our lines. It must have hit a tree branch or something; it fell back towards him. We got the shit scared out of us, and some mud. Over."

Knight moves up behind the men. "Get some flares out over the river. Let's see if we can catch these bastards in the open."

"Bulldog 2, we're going to put some flares out over the water. Move your team up to the bank. Over."

As they continue to move forward, they come upon two bodies in the grass. They check them and then continue forward. High in the sky, two flares burst to life and throw a silver-blue light over the river. Knight and the others search for any sight of men in the water. Neal's group continues moving forward. "Bulldog 2, we have your left flank in sight. Over."

"Roger, Bulldog. We're continuing up to the edge of the river."

"There." Knight points to four heads bobbing in the water. "They're swimming for it."

Gunfire from the island cuts along the top of the riverbank as the flares dive into the river. Two more are fired into the air and closer to the island. An M-60 from Neal's group sets up and opens fire at the island. Others join in and rake the brush and trees. The men around Knight fire at the island as the men in the water climb out onto the shore. They turn and fire from the small beach. The crossfire from the marine positions cut the fight short.

Neal moves up with Knight. "We have two dead in the field and another one down by the edge of the river."

"Good work, Lieutenant. Do you have any casualties?"

"No, sir. We had one of the men hit in his flack jacket, and some cuts and bruises."

"Very good. I want you to take the right side of the line. Your men and two fire teams from Johnson's group should stay at 100 percent. We don't know what else these assholes will pull."

"Aye, aye, sir." Knight works his way back to the bomb. Gunfire still comes off the island to the left. He watches as Cabolero and Johnson continue to dig with their hands around the bomb. "I think I have it." Cabolero hands dig deep into the mud hole he is working on. He lifts a cluster of eight sticks of dynamite out of the hole.

"Shit." He pulls the caps out of two sticks and throws the bundle into the river. He tosses the wire with the caps down the embankment at the water's edge. Both he and Johnson give out a long sigh of relief and roll over onto their backs. The rain pelts their faces.

ON THE ISLAND

Two men huddle behind a log wall. They slowly rise up and look over the top. The shore line looks dark and is quiet after that last big exchange of fire. "Is Shamone ready?" He looks around. A figure crawls up to them. "Just blow the fucks up, so we can get out of here."

"Is anyone still on the other side?" "Listen LaRue, who gives a shit? I think there are some people who were going after the helicopters. But who gives a shit? We either go now or die in this hell hole."

Shamone moves back to the boat. He walks around bodies lying about. This had been a perfect place, for their operations. The access to the river at the back of the island meant they could move their drugs, alcohol, and cigarettes all over the state. Now that they knew where the place was, it was time to move on. He rests his hand on the side of the boat; its clean fiberglass hull is smooth. They had been able to get ten boats off the island, loaded. These were the last ones; the others were working their way up the river, staying in the shadows.

Lenny holds eight pairs of wire in his hand. They have been separated into two tightly twisted bundles. He holds them over a car battery. "Have the guys start shooting, to get their attention." Eight men near them, lean over the top of the log wall and fire at the bank across the river. Their fire is answered immediately. They duck down and move down the path to the boats.

"That should piss them off. Fucking feds." He touches the two bundles to the terminals on the battery. All along the shoreline by the marines, the planted dynamite explodes. As it moves down the bank, it hits the wire for the bomb. The blasting caps pop at the river's edge. He throws down the wires, and they run for the boats. As soon as they're on, they pull into the main channel and head north.

The explosions catch the marines off guard. Anyone standing is blown off his or her feet. Mud and water rain down on the marines along the river. Cabolero and Johnson bury their heads into the mud. As the concussion subsides, they both raise their heads and look around.

Knight was moving back down the trail behind the bomb when the explosions hit. He had just met up with Reddeer; they were both thrown into some broken tree branches: the result of the earlier booby trap that had killed Sandovol.

"Shit." Knight rolls over and pulls a broken branch out of his side. A corpsman moves up to him and checks the wound. His arm and side sting with pain. Reddeer is on some rocks; he holds his side as he crawls back on the trail.

"Sir, you have a nasty cut along your ribs. You're going to need some stitches." He places a field dressing on the wound and checks his arm. "I'm not sure, Colonel, but you may have dislocated your shoulder. I'm going to have to rap it down."

"Shit." Knight looks back at Reddeer. "Doctor, are you all right?"

"I feel like I had my ribs kicked in. Shit." As the corpsman wraps his shoulder, Knight can hear the calls from others for corpsmen. When Knight is finished, the corpsman moves over to work on Reddeer.

"Well, Doctor." The corpsman opens his shirt. "I would say you have some broken ribs and some nasty cuts." He binds around Reddeer and puts bandages on some of the cuts. The falling rain soaks the bandages as soon as they get them on. As they shakily get up, the corpsman moves on to help others. "Let's get up to the bomb." Knight can feel the pain in his side and shoulder as he walks forward. Reddeer gingerly hold his arms against his side and moves forward slowly.

Johnson and Cabolero get up on their knees next to the bomb as Knight walks up. The rain and the explosions have loosened the dirt around the casing of the bomb. The ground suddenly slumps and carries both Cabolero and Johnson over the side of the embankment. They slide to the river's edge in the churning mud. They catch themselves at the water's edge and crawl out on all fours.

As they look back up the bank, a flash of lightning tears across the sky. Their jaws drop when they look back at the bomb. The earth that took them over the bank has been striped from the bomb casing. Its body is almost completely exposed.

Knight drops down behind the bomb and locks his legs around it, and grabs two of the retard fins. The navy man behind him grabs him by his web gear, and in turn he is grabbed by the radioman. Cabolero and Johnson fight and scramble up the muddy slope. Their fingers and toes dig for footing in the wet ooze. "Shit!" They both yell as they reach the bottom of the bomb. They both plant their feet and push their shoulders to secure the bottom.

"My God, get some people over here. We're about to lose this fucker." The web gear pulls against his shoulder and pain wretches his body. "We're in deep shit." Reddeer reaches in and grabs one of the retard fins.

Marines pile over the edge of the embankment and form a human wedge against the lower part of the bomb. Others throw nylon straps around the upper portion and pull them back. They tie off the top of the bomb to the trees behind them. The eight bodies below push to hold the casing steady.

Knight slowly releases his grip and slides of to the side, his body racked with pain. Neal moves his men in to fill gaps in the line and set up covering fire for the men below.

Neal and the radioman pull Knight back and lean him up against a tree. "Sir, we'll take it from here. Corpsman, check the Colonel."

"Sir, we're up on the net."

Neal kneels in the mud. "Ultima, this is Bulldog 2. Over."

"Roger, Bulldog 2. What's your situation?"

"We're in a bad way. Colonel Knight is down, and we have about ten wounded. They set off dynamite planted along the riverbank. It almost blew the bomb into the river. We have Bulldog 1 and about eight other marines using their bodies to hold the casing up. The helicopters are down, and the weather is killing us. We have a large exposure of men on the bank, and we don't have the resources to protect them. Over."

Commandant Swane picks up the handle. "Son, are you in contact with your air support flight?"

"No, sir. We lost the radioman in the explosion."

"Mr. Neal, I'll take care of your air support. How is Colonel Knight?" Swane looks back at his aide and scribbles a quick note. The aide gets on a handset and calls out on the TAC radio.

"Sir, he has some broken bones and some bad wounds. He held the top of the bomb with his legs when the ground gave way. He is going in and out of consciousness."

"Hold on, Mr. Neal." Swane switches over to the TAC net.

"Viper flight, this is Ultima. Over."

"Roger, Ultima. This is Viper leader. Over."

"Viper, we need a run on the island off their position."

"Roger, Ultima. We have two ready to rock. Over."

"Viper, I will patch you in to Bulldog, for best angle." Neal gives them the coordinate with their positions.

"Roger, Bulldog. We have a radar target. We'll make a run from east to west. Keep your heads downs. Over."

"Roger, Viper. Bulldog out."

Neal quickly has the word passed on the impending attack. He yells down to the men pressed against the bomb. They should stand by. They sit and wait as the wind and rain slashes at them.

Suddenly from the east, a noise challenges the wind. The two Harriers drop down above the field to the right of Neal's position. The scream of their engines brings comfort to the men on the ground. They position themselves facing the island, and arm their stores. A second radio is brought up from the helicopters, and Neal gets on the Net.

"Viper, we have you just east of our position. We can see your running lights. Over."

"Roger, Bulldog. We cannot see your position. We're totally on scopes. Can you give us flares along your perimeter? Over."

"Roger, Viper." Flares are thrown out along the riverbank. "We have you. We're on target. Duck your heads." Rocket pods are fired from both the jets; they tear up the length of the island. Secondary explosions throw fireballs high into the sky. The rockets sizzle through the air and pound the island. They cut in their 30 mm canons and move across the river and over the island. Even in the pounding rain, fire rages from exploding alcohol.

"Bulldog, we have targets on radar about a mile north of the island. Shall we pursue? Over."

"Viper, this is Bulldog 2. I don't have the authority to authorize those targets. Over."

Swane's voice cuts into the net. "Viper, this is Ultima. I have the authority. These bastards are going down. Over."

"Roger, Ultima. We're in pursuit. Out." The two Harriers drop on the course of the river and move after the departing boats.

The marines on the shore cheer as the planes move on. Neal has the wounded moved to a clear spot near the fallen tree. Emanuel sits in the mud next to the casing and wipes off the access plate. He calls to Val and gets ready to begin the removal of the screws. As he turns the first screw, pain runs up and down the side of his body. But the groans from the men down below tell him that he is not the only one hurting.

ULTIMA
WASHINGTON, D.C.

Captain Van Nar walks up to the podium. "Gentlemen, we now have Dr. Davies working on the inside of bomb number three. We estimate disarmament in the next fifteen minutes." She slides some papers around, and looks up at the screen. "We now have Dr. Reddeer beginning the removal of the access plate on his bomb. At this time, we do not have any pathfinder marines looking for the last two. The weather in the area is too intense. Captain Emmett will now bring us up to speed on the status of the storms in the area." Emmett collects his papers and heads up to the podium.

"Are we going to get a break in the weather soon?"

"Yes, Mr. Secretary." He speaks to the controls and has the screen showing the storm enlarged. "We're seeing a break in the rain crossing the coast." He points with his light pointer. "It should pass over them in about thirty minutes. This should get the aircraft off the ground and help with the transfer of the wounded back to the base. That will also allow us to drop the marine pathfinders at the last two bomb positions."

"What about the men in the Delta?"

"I have discussed that with General Becker. All forces south of Port Sulfur are to be moved north by midnight. At 0200 we'll move the remaining forces back to the Dome and the outskirts of the city. After 0200, all activity south of New Orleans must be secured. The eye will be fifteen to twenty miles off the coast."

"What about the Russians?"

"They will get some breaks in the weather, but all in all, they're in for continued high seas and bursts of rain."

"What about the submarines coming at them?"

Hillings takes the podium. "Thank you, Mr. Emmett. As Captain Emmett has said, the weather is against us all in this operation. The surface conditions will have no effect on the Cuban submarines. Actually, it will favor their attack."

"What about the Russian submarine, Admiral?"

"Mr. President, they have not been able to contact it as of yet. It will have to deal with either both or at least one of the Cuban boats. If one gets through to the squadron, Morales may have achieved his end game."

"What about our submarine, the one going after the Russian men in the rafts?"

"Yes, sir. The *Atlanta* is running at full speed to attempt to recover them. At the present rate of closure, the rescue will occur in the eye of the storm. This will be no small task. The commander may have to make some very real life-and-death decisions in dealing with the rafts, the men, and the boat under him."

"Thank you, Admiral."

Brant walks over to the president's desk. "Sir, I talked with Admiral Hillings and the others on the disposition of the bomb teams. With your approval, we will return all personnel to the base, sort out the wounded, and get everyone fed and rested. The advanced teams will leave from there to find the last two weapons."

"I agree, Mr. Secretary. These people must be running on empty by now."

"Yes, sir. Also, from the reports we're getting from the area and around the news wires, your explanation of the Russian mines is holding fine."

"Great, that should keep the news people at bay for a while."

"The same information was released to the Russian wire services. We should be getting a call from Secretary Sholenska soon."

"I agree. After that, we'll need to get going."

"Yes, sir."

The president stands up and walks up to the podium. "Everyone, Secretary Brant and Admiral Hillings will be leaving for a working dinner with the leadership of both houses, so that they are on-line with what has been transpiring through out the day. We will return at approximately eight o'clock. I have requested that dinner for everyone be set up in the cafeteria at 6:30. I'm hoping that we can all take a little time to relax. General Becker will be senior in command. If any thing needs to be sent to us, he will be our contact point. Thank you all for your excellent work during these trying hours." The phone at the president's desk begins to ring. He walks over and picks it up.

"Mr. Secretary, yes, I figured you would be calling soon." He listens intently and nods his head. "Very good, we hoped that the cover story would be convincing. Fine, I will contact you in a couple of hours." He hangs up the phone and turns to the group. "Well, it looks like everyone has bought the mine story. He is very pleased that this issue will be terminated without a big internal upheaval in the Kremlin. Gentlemen?" He gathers up some papers, and the three men leave for their meeting.

BOMB SITE, NUMBER THREE
LOUISIANA

Susie pulls the plug on the timer and removes its harness. She hands it back to Gunny. The wet wind blows in from the hole in the wall, and a fine mist settles over her and the others. When they removed the body, the wall above the body was cut away. She rubs her hands together to warm them up. "We just about have it, Gunny." He hands her the wrench. She puts her hands down to change her position. When she brings them back up into the light, both palms are red. "God, I forgot." He hands her a towel to wipe the blood off. She throws it to the side and goes after the locking ring. Soon she removes the detonator and hands it to Gunny. "We're clear. It's dead."

The men in the house all cheer, and Gunny helps Susie to her feet. Her knees are stiff from kneeling in the cold. The navy men move in to extract the bomb through the hole in the wall. They will wait until they can get a helicopter in to pull it out. A corpsman pours sterile water over Susie's hands and has her wash with a disinfectant. She thanks him and towels them off. Gunny goes out to the garage and calls, confirming that their bomb is clear. He comes back inside.

"Well, Susie. I think your going to like this. All units have been ordered back to the base. We're to refit and get something to eat. It looks like the other team took quite a beating out there. I don't know the extent of his injuries, but Dr. Reddeer was hurt in an attack at the site."

"Oh, my God."

"He is working on the other bomb, so it may not be too bad."

"How are we going to get out of here?"

"We should be able to fly out in about fifteen minutes. The storm is breaking up, but there's more on the way."

"We could all use a little rest." She looks at her watch. "It's a quarter past the hour. I know I need to get something to eat and lay down for a while."

"Well, you have done a great job, Doctor." A grunting sound pops from Marshall's mouth as Susie pulls back from the punch in his side. "I mean, Susie."

CHAPTER 15

BOMB THREE
INSIDE THE HOUSE

Susie and Gunny move to the side of the kitchen as the two bodies are moved into the garage. The navy men in the kitchen tie harnesses on the bomb and run a line out the hole in the wall. An ambulance backs up the driveway and loads the bodies, then moves into the night.

The men in the garage pack up the Lanstat and get it ready to move. Gunny walks out into the garage and talks with one of the troopers. "We'll be pulling out as soon as the rain slacks off. We want to thank you and your people for your assistance." They shake hands.

"Anytime, Gunny. We'll move everyone out and head into town."

"Right, thanks again."

The trooper nods and walks down the driveway. The rain is beginning to slacken and the winds have died down. He can see the crewmen on the helicopters checking them and preparing them to leave. The trooper talks with his men, and they begin moving their cars. The TV van is turned around, and it joins the convoy of bright, spinning lights. They head for the city. As they get farther away, it looks like an iridescent worm moving in the dark. "Susie." Gunny leans into the door. "We're about ready to get out of here."

She joins him in the garage as the two gunships start their engines. Their running lights flash in the darkness. They are checked by the navy men on the ground and given the signal of all clear. They both lift quickly into their element and sweep over the house.

The other helicopters begin warming up their engines. One of the Blackhawks lifts off and flies to the back of the house. It lowers its cable and the navy men pull it up to the house. They hook it to the line from the bomb. The two gunships move up along side the hovering Blackhawk. Susie and the others go out the back of the garage to watch the extraction. The Blackhawk, following the directions of the man on the ground, slowly backs away. The cable goes tight, and the bomb is slowly pulled back out the hole. As soon as it is clear of the house, the helicopter moves above it and begins reeling it up into the air. A tarp wrapped around it flutters in the wind as the helicopter turns and begins to fly towards the base. One of the gunships flies as an escort.

"Susie, we're set to go."

"Right, Gunny." They move with the other marines down the driveway and load up. The navy men break down the lights and load the generator. As the helicopters lift off the street, they circle around the house. The lights go out, and it joins the others on the street, veiled in darkness.

"I'm looking forward to this break, Gunny."

"So are we. Everyone could use some food and a little rest."

Susie's nostrils pick up the faint smell of drying blood from her jacket. As the helicopters turn on the final leg to the base, she closes her eyes and leans her head against Gunny's shoulder.

BOMB SITE, NUMBER FOUR
LOUISIANA

"Corporal, stay with Dr. Reddeer. I'm going to check the men at the tree and get the wounded loaded."

Neal moves down the trail with the radioman and two riflemen. They stay out of the way of men carrying the wounded in ponchos to the tree. The corpsman works with the men, moving from one to the other.

"How we doing, Doc?"

"Sir, we need to get going as soon as we can. The colonel is in partial shock, and some of the others are getting near it."

"Right." Neal grabs the radio and calls back to the helicopters.

"Bulldog, this is Night Moves. We're going up first. The Jolly Green will be ready soon."

"Roger, Night Moves. We're going to start moving wounded towards you. Things seem to have settled down."

"Roger, Bulldog."

"Bulldog, this is Viper."

"Roger, Viper."

"We have the two boats. They're in the main channel, and trucking."

The Harriers fall in behind the two boats as they race up the channel. They arm their pods and set the guns. As they move up, the boats go into evasive maneuvers. LaRue stands at the back of the boat and points out the running lights trailing them. "We have company, goddammit."

Shamone looks over his shoulder and begins to throw the boat into hard right and left turns. "When they get closer, shoot the fuckers down." The men along the back of the boats open fire on the two sets of lights. Their tracers arc into the night sky.

"Viper 2, you have the one on the right."

"Roger." He moves more to the right as the two jets drop down to a hundred feet above the river. The sensors on the planes target the boats, and they both open fire. The belly of the Harriers lights up as the 25 mm guns fire into the darkness.

The boats are thrown into hard turns as the rounds hit the water and explode behind them. The men on board are thrown to the deck as the boats careen across the water.

"Shit, Shamone. You about killed us, you asshole."

"Fuck you, and shoot those bastards down. We have about a mile to the Divan Bridges. We may be able to lose them in the pilings." Both boats bristle with flashes from the rifles. The rounds fly by the closing jets, but some hit their mark.

As the two boats take a hard left jag, the number two Harrier fires a burst of rockets at his target. The second boat drives into the cluster of missiles. The boat disintegrates in the fiery blast.

"Shit." LaRue looks over at the explosion as a second burst of gunfire cuts across the back of their boat. One round finds it mark and blows a foot-long hole in the upper transom.

"Shit, fuck this. Get this thing into the beach. We don't have a chance out on the water."

"I agree." Shamone throws the boat into a hard right angle and heads for the opposite bank. "When we round the bend up here, there is a park or something on the headlands."

"You're right." He throws the boat into an other turn as gunfire rips the water ahead of him.

LaRue looks ahead of the boat. "I think it's right through there." He points in the darkness.

"Am I supposed to be able to see where you're pointing, asshole? Take the wheel; it's your show."

LaRue grabs the wheel, throws the boat into a hard turning angle, and heads for the shore. The boat races into a small lagoon and up a boat ramp at full speed. It is launched into the air and lands about fifty feet ahead, on the wet grass. It flings bodies out as it slides on its side and plows into a baseball backstop at speed. A blast of rockets from Viper 1 walks the route from the boat ramp. The boat joins the exploding rockets in a fireball. The Harriers fly over and bank left to get back to the helicopters. The dead and injured from the boat litter the ground from the boat ramp to the baseball diamond.

"Bulldog, this is Viper."

"Roger, Viper."

"We have bounced your two boats. We'll rejoin you at landing field. Over."

"Roger, Bulldog out."

Neal looks over the dark field between them and the helicopters. "Let's move."

Those able to walk are helped by other marines; others strain under the weight of the stretchers. Point men walk ahead of the group in case of attack. Neal watches them disappear into the darkness. "We'll hold the perimeter until they extract the bomb." He and his team head back towards the bomb site.

Reddeer strains to concentrate on the access panel. Pain sweeps across his back and chest. The men in the hole are feeling the strain of the wet and cold. Each stands his ground, pushing on the man ahead. Johnson and Cabolero feel their bodies going numb from the pressure of the others. They console themselves with some well-chosen words about the weather and the cold. The flashlights from the corpsman and the others swing back and forth from their web gear as they walk down the path. The corpsman comforts the colonel as he drifts in and out of consciousness. The only other noise is the sucking sound of their boots pulling out of the mud with each step.

"Sir, we'll have you on the helicopter and headed to the base in just a few minutes." They only have to cross over a dike with trees on it, and they're within sight of the helicopters. The point men cross over the dike and drop into the next field.

As the line of wounded reach the base of the dike, the lead men start up the side.

About fifty feet to their right, two figures rise up out of the grass. They kneel in the darkness and level their weapons.

The corpsman leans over. "Sir, were almost there." His next words are lost in the hail of gunfire; he is hit in the arm and the neck. He falls across the colonel as the stretcher bearers drop it to the ground. Over half the men are hit in the first volley. The men in the dark pop out their spent clips and send another home. One of them pulls the pin on a grenade and lobs it at the men. They drop back into a ditch and run along the dike towards the river. The point men have come back over the dike, and they fire into the swamp. The grenade falls near the center of the men.

"Grenade, grenade!" The men around it try to shield themselves. Their flashlights fall on the smoking orb. A figure comes out of the dark. He throws his body onto the grenade. "Semper Fi!" The explosion is muffled under him in the mud. His body is lifted off the ground and thrown to one side, his utilities smoking.

Neal and his men are at the split trail when the gunfire begins. They run back to the tree and then down the trail. As they run, they begin firing from the hip at the muzzle blasts from the two men firing. They yell as they come up the path. The explosion throws a orange light as they keep firing into the field. When they reach the group, the point men come back down the dike and fire up the edge of the trees. Cries come from the men as they reach them.

"Corpsman, corpsman, I'm hit, I'm hit!" The two point men and three other marines move into the field following the two shooters. Men from the river at the front of the field move back towards the firing. Neal and the radioman help one of the men shot in the leg. The men at the helicopters hear the shooting, and some move towards the firing. Night Moves gets into the Cobra and begins to prep it for flight. His gunner is climbing in as rounds slam into the side of the ship. Four rounds suddenly splatter the glass near Night Moves. They hit the glass and the armored shell around him. The gunner falls into his seat and closes the canopy. "What the fuck?" His fingers flip switches and the engine comes to life. He watches crewmen from the other helicopters firing into the dark to his left. The flashes of rifle fire blink in the dark.

He brings the engines up to speed and signals to the ground crew that he is out of there. Gunfire continues to hit the other helicopters. He lifts about fifty feet into the air and turns towards the attackers. The gunner brings the 20 mm cannons around and fires at the area that the rifle fire is coming from. As the three barrels spin, a tongue of flame lights up the bottom of the Cobra.

"Yes," Night Moves yells over the radio. "Bulldog, we're up and strapped." The other Cobra lifts up next to him, and they move towards the river. Marines from the forward perimeter move in to help with the wounded.

"Shit." Neal looks over the men on the ground. He grabs the handset from the radioman.

"This is Bulldog 2. Get the Jolly Green over here. We must have ten to twelve people down. We're popping flares now."

The Stallion roars to life and warms up as the crewman checks the exterior of the ship. He runs around to the back and up the ramp. The big ship lifts off the ground and moves into the next field. Flares light the landing area. It moves quickly over the ground and lands in the middle of the flares. The ramp is lowered, and men rush to load the dead and wounded.

A corpsman runs up to Neal. "Sir, we need to move. We have one corpsman down and one critical."

"Where is Colonel Knight?"

"Over here, sir." The corpsman leads him over to the still smoldering body.

"Holy shit." The body is unrecognizable.

"He threw himself on the grenade. He saved all the men around him. I have never seen anything like it. He's a hero."

Two men roll out a body bag and lift the body into the bag. Men quickly search the area, looking for any other wounded. "Doc, we have everyone. You're out of here."

The corpsman runs to the helicopter and up the ramp. It lifts into the night and races for the base. Neal and the others on the ground watch the lights recede. Neal orders the other helicopters to move into the next field by the tree. The gunships continue to fire near the river. A burst of rockets showers down on the bank.

"We have two down near the bank, Bulldog."

Neal grabs the handle. "Roger. We're coming in behind you." They hear the thump of rifle grenades as they near the riverbank. The explosions light up to their left front.

"This is Bulldog."

"Straight ahead, Bulldog, about 200 feet. We got one of them. The other ran down the bank along the river.

Neal joins the other marines on the riverbank; he looks down the bank with his night vision equipment. The bank is clear in some places, but twists and turns with brush and trees. "Night Moves, this is Bulldog."

"Roger. I sent the other ship to escort the wounded back to base. Over."

"Right. We're going to throw out flares along our forward perimeter. Anything south of that is a free fire zone."

"Roger. We had two on the thermal. They're moving south along the bank. We rocked the area and have not seen anything moving since. Your bad guy is coming this way. We'll keep a look out for him."

"Roger, Bulldog out."

The Cobra swings back over the area, the vision on the thermal shines out in bright green. The gunner scans the area and finds a sudden hot spot up a branch channel.

"I think we have him, bro. I'd say they had a boat stashed up that channel."

"All right, lock on him. I want this cracker." The gunner looks over his panel. "We're showing no rockets. We're down to the gun."

"Guns are fine with me. Let's take him."

"Woo, I have your other bad guy running along the bank. He's heading for the boat." The man in the screen runs in a green and white world. He can see the lights on the helicopter and hopes they have not picked him up. "Give him a burst."

The gunner follows the orders and the gun swings to track the runner. He lines up the shot, and presses the button. Five shots fly into the trees as the figure darts down an incline to an open area along the river.

"Shit." The gunner comes over the headset. "We're dry, mother."

"You're shitting me." The barrels spin under the nose. The man on the ground picks up the whining of the gun motor. He knows they're out of ammo. Night Moves turns and faces the man on the beach. He runs out into the middle of the open area, and stops. The men in the helicopter see him slowly raise his hand into the air. He gives them the finger.

"Motherfucker!" Night Moves is livid. "He just gave us the finger. I'm going to crash this fucker into him. I don't give a shit. This asshole is going to die."

He holds the helicopter in a hover, and they watch the figure run down the beach and over a knoll. "Night Moves, are you there?"

"Roger, this is Night Moves."

"This is Viper. We're coming in behind you. Do you have a target?"

"We sure do. We think the fuckers have a boat stashed over that knoll. The bastard just gave us the finger."

"We'll assist you in getting your honor back. Over." The two Harriers move up to each side of the Cobra. All three aircraft hang in the air and wait the next move of the men on the ground.

"He's coming out." They all swing out over the river until they are facing up the channel. "We have him. Stand by."

As the boat slips out from under the canopy of trees, a volley of rockets flies from the two Harriers. They take the boat and everything around it down in a mighty blast. The thermal images scan the area. Nothing is left.

"What a show! You guys are good."

"Roger, Night Moves. We were glad to be of service. Semper Fi. We're out of here."

They rise up into the air and begin moving forward. Their lights are soon lost in the clouds.

"Bulldog, you're clear. We're moving back over to the other ships." He does a rolling turn and heads for the field.

Neal sets up a perimeter around the helicopters and goes back to the bomb site. When he gets there, he sees that Reddeer has gotten the access plate off and is getting ready to start on the inside. He pans his light over the men holding the bomb; they form a human mass against the casing. As Reddeer begins to reach into the cavity, he pulls his hand back and falls forward. He slides headfirst over the edge of the bank, landing on the men below. His body is limp as it slides over them and lands in the mud.

"What the fuck?" A cry goes up from the men. Neal keeps his light on the doctor as a corpsman and others jump over the side to retrieve him. "The doctor has fainted. Hang on. They're trying to get him back up now." Others on the top grab his arm and pull him back up the bank as those under him push up on his feet. They drag him up along side the bomb, and they pull the corpsman up to look at him.

"What happened?" Reddeer looks around and shakes his head.

"You fainted, sir. I think you may have more than some broken ribs. I'm going to give you another shot and pass an ammonia inhalant under your nose." He gives him the shot and crushes the glass vial in his fingers. He then passes it under his nose.

"Oh, my God. I'm all right. Shit, that really wakes you up."

"Yes, sir. I'll hold you by your web gear so you won't slip." The corpsman slides in behind Reddeer and holds on to the straps across his back.

Reddeer disables the detonator and removes the harness. He then turns the clock off and hands the wire harness to Neal. He takes the wrench and goes inside to remove the detonator. As he reaches in, the corpsman feels his body go limp.

"Doctor." He pulls back on the straps as Reddeer's head hits the casing. Neal takes one of the inhalers, quickly breaks it, and shoves it under Reddeer's nose. His head jerks up right, and he breaths heavy.

"Hang in there, Doc. You're almost done." Neal pats him on the shoulder.

"I'm sorry, everyone. I know this is difficult for us all." Words of encouragement fill the air from the men down below. He puts the wrench back inside, frees the locking ring, and removes it. He slowly lifts out the detonator and hands it to Neal.

"We're fucking clear." A cheer goes up from the men below as Reddeer slumps to the side of the bomb. They drag him up the trail, put him on a stretcher, and move him back to the helicopters.

Neal and others shine their lights down on the men. "All right, the men farthest back can begin to move off to each side." They begin to unpile and move away until only Johnson and Cabolero are left. They can hardly move from being pressed into the casing and the mud.

"You go first, sir."

"Right." Johnson pulls back from the casing and is helped up the bank.

"I'm going to move. Stand clear." Cabolero pushes himself off to the side and lands in the mud. The casing hangs in place, then kicks out at the bottom. It falls until the straps on top catch it. More mud is sent down the bank. Others help Cabolero to his feet and up the bank. Both he and Johnson can hardly walk, so others help them back to the helicopters.

The navy men hook the straps on the bomb up to the winch line from the helicopter. It hovers above them for a moment and then lifts off into the night. Two other gunships arrive and move in to escort the bomb back to base.

The Stallion is loaded, and Neal checks the others. They do a head count before the Stallion lifts off with one of the Blackhawks. Neal watches as the last of the men are loaded, then he climbs in with Johnson and Cabolero.

"Sir, we're ready to leave. Our head count shows everyone is out of here."

"Thank you, Mr. Neal. You have done a good job. I suggest you have one of the gunships run a quick search over the area, just in case."

The engines warm up as Neal contacts the gunships, and they do a quick search of the area. Their halogen lights are brilliant in the darkness. They criss-cross the fields as the Blackhawks lift off.

"Bulldog, we see no friendly force on the ground. I don't think we have to worry about the bad guys. The local scaly morticians are pulling them into the water."

"Roger. Bulldog out."

The gunships join them, and they head for the base. The fires on the island still burn as they pass over it. In the light, Johnson can see bodies lying around.

"Sir, we have been ordered back to base. All elements are being brought in. We'll get something to eat, and then send out the pathfinders on the last two bombs."

"Good. How is the old man?"

"You didn't know, sir. Colonel Knight was killed at the ambush. From what I could gather, he threw himself on a grenade."

"Shit, what a fucking mess this thing is."

"Sir, you're in command of the unit now."

"Yeah." Johnson looks out the window as they fly back in silence.

ULTIMA
WASHINGTON, D.C.

Captain Van Nar walks up to the podium. "Gentlemen. We have verified that the number four bomb is en route to the base. All units have now cleared the ground and are proceeding to NAS New Orleans." The triangle at the bomb site goes green.

"We are receiving reports on the status of the wounded and dead. We have twelve marines in guarded condition, and we have six dead. We have one corpsman in critical condition and a second is dead. Mr. Sandovol was killed at the site, and Dr. Reddeer is in stable but guarded condition.

"From the report we have received, there are approximately forty-plus KIA from the opposing force. No attempt is being made to recover the dead.

"We have also confirmed that the commanding officer, Colonel Knight, was killed at the scene. Reports from the field state that he died by throwing himself on a grenade to save his fellow marines. A heroic act of courage."

She leaves the podium. "Thank you, Captain." General Becker turns back to the papers in front of him. "Commandant Swane." The general looks up at him. "I know that Colonel Knight was a personal friend. His loss is felt by us all. He has brought honor to your corps."

"Thank you, General. This act of personal heroism mirrors his action in Nam. He was an excellent leader and one hell of a marine." General Becker shakes his head. "I can believe that this has been a costly recovery. We can only hope the last two will come easy."

"Captain Van Nar, as soon as everyone is at the station, we will need a conference call set up when the president returns."

"Yes, sir."

BEACH
BARATARIA BAY

Commander Marino and his beach group search the area. As the Stallion with the bombs lifts off, part of the marines at the site leaves with them. Others board Blackhawks and load the command Stallion. Val stands at the back of the ramp and watches the men loading and securing the area. Marino walks up next to Val as the others get on board.

"I think we have everything." He double-checks the area. He calls on the radio to the supply ship as it loads its last boat. He thanks them for their help and wishes them a good trip to Galveston. They are glad to get out of the storm track. As they secure the landing craft, the ship is beginning to turn away from the coast.

Marino keys the pilot as he and Val walk up the ramp. The Stallion crewman checks around the helicopter as the pilot brings the engines up to speed. He runs to the back and up the ramp. He talks to the pilot as he slowly raises the ramp. The big helicopter lifts up, and turns towards the northeast. They head back to the base.

AIRFIELD
NAS, NEW ORLEANS

As the helicopters from Susie's group land, trucks back up to them and the marines and naval personnel are loaded and taken to a mess hall to be fed. Susie gets out with Gunny and walks around to the front of the helicopter. A couple of hangars down, trucks have been parked in a row extending from each side of the hangar.

"The trucks are there to shield the operations with the bombs."

The helicopter from the last site appears with a gunship. They hover over the area inside the trucks, and lower the bomb to the tarmac. It is unhooked and moved into the hangar; the helicopters turn to the sides and land near Susie and Gunny.

"Susie, we need to get going." Gunny grabs her arm and leads her to the car.

"Gunny, I want to go to the hospital. I'm very concerned about Emanuel." They move up the road towards the base commander's office. "Susie, I need to take care of the men." He calls forward to the command center and explains the situation. They are cleared to the hospital.

"Here you go, Doctor. As soon as you have confirmed Dr. Reddeer's condition, the car will be waiting to take you to the commander's office. The men are in the barracks next door; I'll make sure they're all right. Just call me on the radio, when you're ready to leave." He gives her a radio; she snaps it onto her belt.

They get out, and Gunny heads for the barracks. Susie and Laura walk into the emergency entrance. People seem to be running everywhere; men push a gurney up and down the hall.

"Give me another hemostat." Captain Rollens works on the neck wound of the corpsman that was with Knight. He has stopped the bleeding and continues to close the torn flesh. The lights flicker, and then go out. He holds the suture in the air and waits for them to come back on.

"For God's sake, can we get the back-up generators on-line?" The nurses hold flashlights and shine them on the working area. The lights blink on and then off. He continues to work and finishes the last stitches. Rollens steps back. "Bandage him carefully;

he is one of us." Others move in and begin bandaging the neck wound. The wounds on his legs have been bandaged. As soon as they're done, he is moved to the recovery room. Rollens follows the gurney out the door and into the hall. He watches as other doctors work on men in the hall and prep them for the operating rooms. Men and women in green surgical outfits run up and down the hallways.

Nurses tend to and comfort the young marines in the hall. They begin removing the blood-soaked utilities and helping the doctors give emergency treatments to ease the trauma of shock. Rollens sees Susie and walks down the hall to her. On the way, he grabs the head nurse.

"Mary, we need some more whole blood and some type A. We'll need it stat, and ask the maintenance officer if he is getting a handle on these lights."

She nods. "It's just like Nam, sir." She turns and moves down the hallway.

"No shit, Mary. You hit it on the nose: somehow we have gone in country."

He reaches Susie. "Dr. Davies, are you all right?"

"Yes, Doctor. I'm very concerned about Dr. Reddeer."

"You're covered with blood. What the hell happened?"

"We had two people killed at the scene. It was bad."

"Shit, this whole thing reminds me of Nam. We go out to recover some bombs, and end up in a damn war." He looks over at a young marine. "Get this man into surgery, have him prepped. I'll be right there."

Laura comes back and joins Susie and Rollens. Tracks of tears have washed the dirt and grime on her face in lines.

"Sir, is Chief Turvey going to be all right?"

Susie puts her arm around her and hugs her. Rollens slides his mask back up on his face. He reaches out and puts his hand on her shoulder. "Laura, we have done all that we can. Now the love and good thoughts of people like you will have to pull him through. We're all praying that he will get through the night. I have to go. Dr. Reddeer's helicopter will be coming in soon. Doctor, you can use my office if, you want." He turns and moves up to the swinging doors of the operating room and vanishes.

"Laura, let's go wait in his office." Susie helps her to the door, and they sit, looking out into the hallway. Susie holds Laura as she softly cries. "Chief Turvey is such a good man; he has helped every corpsmen in the group. He would take the extra time and suffer the same problems with you. God, I hope he makes it."

"We all do, Laura." Susie hugs her closer as a tear runs down her cheek. It drops onto Laura's wet hair. They sit quietly in the dark. The light from the hallway spills over their feet.

Marshall had noticed a C-130 in from Lejeune on the pad when they came in. He walks up the path to the barracks and goes in. Along the wall are tables set up with utility jackets and trousers. On another are skivvies and tee-shirts. On another, armorers from Lejeune work on the weapons of the men. He sees Sergeant Chuan directing some men to finish up and be ready to deal with the marines coming back from the mess hall.

"Sergeant Chuan, it's good to see you. When did you get in?"

"Just before you, Top. We brought in some armorers, new ammo, and some new utilities for everyone. We also brought in twenty guys from the Third Platoon."

"That's great. They were hit pretty hard at the other site."

"They should be back from chow in a few minutes. We got a call that the other team is on their way in. It looks like you could use a shower yourself, Top."

"Yeah, I'm going to check the men at the hospital, and then I'll take you up on some new gear."

"Let's have your weapons, Top. We'll get them cleaned and ready for you."

"Thanks, Chuan." He hands over his rifle, pistol, and a bandoleer of ammo. They put a piece of white tape on the stock and write his name on them. "We'll see you back here in a little while, Dick."

"Right." He pats Chuan on the back and heads for the hospital.

As Marshall crosses back to the hospital, the first group of marines from the other bomb site begin arriving in trucks. The base maintenance group is moving towed generators in next to certain buildings. Teams hook up emergency wiring.

"Hey, Gunny," the men in the trucks call out as they pass. Just as he gets to the emergency entrance, a truck pulls up with Neal, Johnson, and Cabolero. They climb out and support Johnson towards the door. Marshall runs over and takes Cabolero's place. "Let me have him, Gilbert. Shit, you can hardly walk yourself."

"Thanks, Dick." He and Neal take Johnson in and hand him over to the orderlies. He lays back on the gurney. "Mr. Neal, make sure the men are being dealt with."

"Yes, sir. Gunny is with me now. Everything will be fine." One of the corpsman from the field helps push him down the hall. As another corpsman holding a bag walks down the hall next to Dr. Reddeer.

Dr. Rollens comes out of the operating room and sees Reddeer in the hall. "Get Dr. Reddeer into OR, stat. I'll be right there. And get Mr. Johnson into Dr. Thomas." He looks down the hall at the corpsmen helping.

"You people from the field, we'll take it from here. Join your units; we'll call you all over for a meeting later. Besides, you're getting mud all over the place."

Susie gets up and goes to the door as Emanuel is pushed by. A nurse holds a bag of solution above him as they push him through the door to the operating room. Captain Rollens stops by her on his way to look after Reddeer.

"Dr. Davies, he has passed out. His vital signs are strong. I think every thing is going to be all right."

"Thanks, Doctor."

"Susie." Marshall walks up. "You need to get something to eat and get a change of clothes. We're in radio contact with the hospital. They will call on Dr. Reddeer." He gets Laura and Susie and walks them down to the waiting car. "Thanks, Gunny. I need to lie down for a while." Susie goes limp in his grasp; he picks her up and puts her in the back seat of the car.

"I'll take it from here, Gunny."

"All right, Laura. Take good care of this marine." The car pulls out and heads for the barracks.

Marshall goes back in and checks on the men. He goes over the list of the dead with the duty doctor. "Thank you, sir. We lost some good men out there."

"I know, Gunny. We lost some of ours also. It's been a hell of a night. And it's not over yet."

He meets with Neal and gives him the list. He covers him on what is being done at the barracks. "Sir, you could use a shower and some chow yourself."

"Right, Gunny. I'll meet you at the barracks in about an hour."

"Aye, aye, sir."

Marshall sees Cabolero off to the side; a nurse finishes up with him. He stands and walks towards him. "Well, Gunny, it has been one hell of a night. Let's get over to the mess hall and get something to eat."

"I hear that." Cabolero puts his hand on his shoulder, and they go out the door.

They walk over to the mess hall. The smell of steaks cooking fills their nostrils. They go inside and join others in line. The navy cooks have steaks cooking on the grills with potatoes and gravy. As they go by, they fill their trays with everything. Sitting down, they dig into the food. They enjoy their meal. A navy chief comes out from the line and talks with some of the marines eating. He works his way over to Marshall and Cabolero.

"Gunny, if there is anything else you or your men need, we'll be on duty all night."

"Hell, Chief, this is the best chow I've had in a while. These steaks are great." Cabolero takes another bite of his steak. "It's great, Chief. Everything is fine. From the sound of them, they are really enjoying the meal."

"Good, you guys needed a good meal." The chief goes back to the line as another group of marines comes in. After their second trip through the line, the two sergeants top off their meal with a last cup of coffee.

"I feel like I'm going to fucking explode." Cabolero puts his cup down.

"I know the feeling. Let's get over, check on everyone, and then get some rest." They both get up and head for the barracks. As they walk down the path, they see a dark figure sitting on a bench near the entrance to the barracks. Cabolero nudges Marshall. "What do you think, Gunny?"

"I don't know, but he is one of ours." They walk over to the young marine on the bench. He hears them coming and looks up. He quickly wipes his eyes, and clears his throat.

"Are you all right, son?" Marshall sits down next to him.

"Yeah, Gunny. I just needed to be alone for a while."

"All right, but get some chow and some new utilities. You need to get some rest." Marshall pats him on the back and gets up to leave. His hand is wet and sticky. He holds it up in the light, and the palm of his hand is red. Cabolero sees it too. "What the hell?"

"Son." The two seasoned sergeants sit down on each side of him. "You're bleeding."

His hands go to his face, and he leans forward. "I was right there. I heard the Colonel and the explosion. It killed my two best friends." His voice is caught up in a choking sob.

Cabolero takes his flashlight and checks his back. Four ragged holes along his side are soaked in blood. "Shit, Gunny. We need to get this boy over to the hospital."

"I don't deserve it. They died, and I didn't."

They each grab an arm and lift him to his feet. "Son, both myself and Sergeant Cabolero know what you're feeling. We lost a lot of friends in Nam, and we all asked the same question: why them and not me?"

"It's just the draw, boy. It's their time and not yours." Cabolero pulls his arm across his shoulder to support him. "It just doesn't seem right." As they walk to the hospital, he staggers between them.

Cabolero looks over at Marshall. "I think I know who this is. The corpsman said that one of the marines on the trail got up and started firing at the ambushers. He was yelling for someone to help his friends. He emptied four magazines before anyone else got to them. They think that it broke the attack."

"I'd say it probably did, Gilbert."

The young marine shakes his head. "I apologize, Sergeant Cabolero and Gunny Marshall. I didn't mean to cry."

"Hang in there, son. We're almost there." They pick up the pace and race for the doors of the hospital. As they burst through the doors, they call out for help. "We need help, we have a wounded marine." They stand silhouetted in the light; their muddy utilities and faces seem out of place. "We need some fucking help."

Mary the head nurse reaches them first. The young marine has gone limp.

"Get a gurney, and we need a doctor in OR three, stat." The young marine turns his head towards Marshall. "I'm sorry, Gunny Marshall."

"Sorry, bullshit. Listen, PFC Coffman, you're one hell of a marine. And understand this, there is no man who hasn't cried for lost friends. Now they're going to take care of you and get you well. I expect to see you in formation soon, Coffman."

"Aye, aye, Gunny."

They lift him on the gurney and race down the hallway. "Make a hole. We have a wounded marine."

Marshall looks at Cabolero and shakes his head. "Were we ever that young?"

"Shit, I don't know, Dick. Who says we're still not that young? We're still here."

Mary takes them both by the arm. "All right, you two. You need to take care of yourselves now. We'll deal with young Mr. Coffman."

"You're right, ma'am." They go out the door, and head for the showers.

Dr. Rollens comes out of OR and makes his way to Mary at her station. "What's the word on the blood, Commander?"

"I tried the local blood bank. They're a little hesitant to let much go because of the storm coming in. They're sending over some now."

Rollens looks at the note pad. "We'll need more."

"Yes, sir. I got on the military channel, and I have a shipment coming in from Fort Benning. It is en route now."

"Great, Mary. They're running x-rays on Reddeer now. I think he has a pretty severe concussion, besides having all the ribs on his right side broken."

"This has been a night to remember. We're also getting the dependents in who were hurt in the last storm front that passed through. I'm not sure that we have seen the worst yet."

"Doctor! Doctor Rollens, we have a flat line on Chief Turvey." They can both hear the alarms from the machine, as they run down the hall towards the recovery room.

Susie finishes her shower and slips into a nightgown. She whispers thanks to Chief Lange for getting her stuff for her. She feels good after the shower and a hot meal. The warmth of the blankets caresses her as the soft fingers of sleep pull her into welcomed slumber.

TWO A-10'S
THE GULF

"Sky 1, this is Warthogs. We're feet wet. Over."

"Roger, Warthog. Your cleared to NAS New Orleans. Over." The two A-10 Thunderbolts turn to the new heading and fly over the water at a thousand feet.

SOUTHERN APPROACH TO HAVANA
CUBAN CENTRAL HIGHLANDS

The men crawl up a trail and move up to the base of some low bushes. They speak in low tones and train their night vision scopes on a valley leading down to the junction of the main roads. "Just to the left of the road, General. We think it is a T-72. There are three more farther up the road."

Quintano moves the scope; the green white images change from bushes and trees to the blunt outline of the right half of the turret. The barrel points forward through the foliage of the bushes. He moves the scope to the middle of the crossroads. A scout BTR-40 lies on its side, smoldering. The bodies of its crew lie strewn around it. When he moves the scope back to the tank, he can see a man lying along the side of the turret. He too is looking through a night scope.

"General, we have a Hind helicopter that has come out and then gone back up the road."

The silence is suddenly broken by the sound of explosions to their north. Lights flash and tracers can be seen in the air. They move back down from their vantage point overlooking the roads. A figure runs up to them. "Sir, the force from Colonel Zino is being attacked by helicopters. They are also engaging an armored battalion. They're about ten miles up the road."

"Sir." Ruiz takes out a small light and shines it on a map. "We're going to run two BTR scouts across the road here. They're armed with ATGW missiles. It should catch them by surprise. We'll run two up to the crest of the hills here and fire straight up the valley. We'll open with a volley of rockets from four BM21s, here, sir."

"How soon will the tanks be here?"

"We should have the first ones here in about twenty minutes. The ZSUs are both set up in case of attack by helicopters. We have two AT-4 crews set up to move forward. They are here and here. They will set up along the road, in case one of the tanks tries to run out." The firing north of them increases. The sounds of war are coming closer.

"It looks good. We need to move now, Major." Ruiz grabs a handset from his radioman and orders the attack to begin. Immediately, the night is filled with the *swish swish* of 122 mm rockets being fired. They roar into the opposite valley. The explosions shake the ground. The two scouts north of the crossroads race down a hill and then start their run to the opposite set of rolling hills.

The tank seen by Quintano crashes through the bushes and climbs up a slight grade to the road. The main gun swings north and fires at the racing scouts. The round explodes at the rear of the trailing scout, throwing huge chunks of asphalt and grass into the air. As it moves forward, a second tank rumbles down the road behind it.

Two of Quintano's armored cars move forward beside the road where it curves around and faces the crossroads. They quickly line up their targets and fire. The lead tank moves north towards the scouts. It fires again at the running scouts. The second tank, seeing the flash of the firing rockets, fires at one of the scouts near the road. The round explodes next to it and knocks it on its side.

The missiles fired hit the first tank. One hits the engine compartment. The other glances off the back of the turret. The engine compartment bursts into flames as the tank fires another round.

The AT-4 team near it has set up. They slam their missile into the side of the tank. The following explosion blows the turret off.

The second Morales tank fires and catches the road in front of the BTR. It races backward at full speed. The AT team on the south side sets up to fire. But a shell from the tank finds them first. The round hits the road near them and blows a huge hole where they were. Machine gun fire from the tops of the hills rains down on the tanks. Soldiers with RPGs fire down on them as the tank machine guns rake the hills. Another tank rumbles out of the ravine and moves north. Its machine guns fire up the side of the road. Its main gun fires at the top of the hills.

Flares fired by Quintano's forces bathe the crossroads in silver-blue light. The tank at the crossroads fires up the valley and lobs shots over the hill. They hit on the road and in the fields behind Quintano and the others. From the north, a Hind gunship attacks the tops of the hills. It fires a burst of rockets along the ridgeline, its machine gun racking the scattering troops. It turns up the ravine into which the two scouts ran. They are setting up to fire at the tank, moving north. The gunship fires a Swatter AT missile into the lead vehicle. It explodes in a fireball. The second scout tries to use his speed to out-maneuver his attackers. It pulls into the open with its machine gun firing. The tank on the north side fires at the running scout. The shell goes long and explodes behind it. The integrated fire control system resets and fires. The Heat round catches the scout in the side, and it disappears in a ball of flames. The tank moves back to the other T-72 at the crossroads, and they both withdraw up the main road to the west, firing as they go.

The Hind gunship passes south on the main road, then turns west and circles back over the retreating tanks. It crosses the intersection, firing up the main road to the east. It moves up the road firing. As it clears the curve in the road, its low light sensors search for vehicles.

The microwave acquisition radar on the ZSU acquires the gunship, and the four 23 mm guns fire bursts of fifty rounds. The 200 rounds catch the gunship almost head on, and they tear it to pieces. Both ZSUs go active and sweep the area. A second volley of rockets scream into the air. They race over the heads of Quintano and his staff. The valley to the west is again racked with explosions. Sudden explosions draw the staff's attention. Incoming rounds begin exploding along the road to the east.

"General, it looks like 122 mm field guns. There must be a battery off to the northwest."

Quintano looks back over the equipment staged in the fields. "We're all bottled up here. We need to continue the attack. As soon as the tanks arrive, we will move. We need to get more scouts out and try to hook up with the troops coming down from Zino's position."

"Sir, we're going to send the gunships after the artillery."

"Good."

As shells continue to fall, men on the road call forward to the command vehicle. Quintano and the others move back down the hill. Some of the shells are beginning to find their marks. A truck explodes in the rear.

"Sir, we have a call from the rear. The tanks are moving up now and should be here in about ten minutes." They move inside the command vehicle and look at the map on the center table.

"We have Zino's group here and a splinter group coming towards us on the main road. We need to send a battalion southwest on the road and send the main force due west."

"Yes, sir." Vargas points to a series of ridges ahead on the western road. "This would be a perfect place to dig in."

Quintano nods. "I agree; the tops of the mesas. We'll turn the southern group here and hope that Zino's group can break out. If things go right, will have this force surrounded."

"Let's get this thing on the road."

As they walk outside, the first of their tanks are passing on the road. They are followed by units in MT-LB tracked vehicles. Captain Vargas signals his scout up. "Sir, I will be joining the southern force for our end run."

Quintano grabs his shoulder. "Vargas, I'll see you in Havana."

"Yes, sir." His vehicle moves in behind a group of ten tanks turning south on the main road. Soon, all units are on the roads. Quintano moves forward up the western road towards the mesa. His forward elements are making contact with Morales's forces. He watches as a group of 122 mm self-propelled Howitzers set up and join in the attack on the mesa. The flashs from their muzzles throw red-orange light on the command vehicle.

ULTIMA
WASHINGTON, D.C.

Van Nar walks up to the podium. "Gentlemen, we are receiving updates on the fighting in Cuba. It is 7:50. President Wayne will be returning in a short time. General Becker has asked that all staff prepare for a briefing to bring him up to date on all issues."

F-18 FIGHTERS
THE GULF

"Vanquish leader, this is Prowler. Over."
"Roger, Prowler."
"Your assassins are beginning to move up on target. You are 1,000 yards behind. We'll make contact with flight 111 at 110 miles. Over."
"Roger, Prowler. We'll stand by. Over."
At 110 miles, the pilot of the Ilyushin airliner has his co-pilot change radio frequencies. He calls out to the Prowler. They are told what to do, the distance that the fighters are behind them, and to have everything secured. The co-pilot explains to Fidel and the others what they will be doing in the next few minutes. He is secured in his seat; the others prepare themselves for the upcoming maneuvers.
"Flight 111, this is Prowler. Over."
"Roger, Prowler."
"Flight 111, in five minutes, at 1955 hours, execute a hard-breaking left turn. Continue turn until contacted to stop. Over."
"Roger, Prowler." They watch the clock and prepare for the turn.
"Vanquish leader, trap is set for 1955 Zulu. Good hunting. Over."
The two Hornets set up at a thirty-degree angle on the Migs and move up for the kill. All weapons are armed and ready. In the black night, the hunters still do not realize that another predator is tracking them. The pilots all watch the time as the minutes and then seconds tick away.

The Ilyushin pilot watches the last seconds vanish. The read out is 1955, dead on. "Here we go." The others all grab on to something as the pilot twists the yoke to the left and the big airliner pivots on it left wing tip. The sudden breaking turn catches the Migs by surprise. They push over into a steep banking turn. Their radars go on and begin seeking the target as they come back around.

As the Migs turn, they present a full silhouette. The radar ranging gun sights on the Hornets automatically set up the correct lead. They come at the Migs straight in.

The alarms in the Migs go active as the Hornets sweep them. They turn their heads and look out the top of the canopy as the first blasts of 20 mm canon rounds tears into their exposed tops. The pilot in the lead Mig is caught and killed in the first blast. His plane slides up into the path of the second fighter. Cannon fire still hits them as they merge into a singular fireball. The Hornets break off to each side of the explosion and move back to pick up the Ilyushin.

"Flight 111, break off turn and resume original course. Threat aircraft are destroyed. Over."

The airliner is brought back on course, and the two Hornets move up on each side. Their running lights flare in the darkness. "Vanquish leader, this is Prowler. Over."

"Roger, Prowler. We have taken up positions on each side of the intended victim. Over."

"Roger. We'll rendezvous in fifteen minutes. Your execution, gentlemen, was perfect. Over."

"Roger, Prowler. I would say that the gun camera shots will be spectacular. We'll rendezvous soon. Let's get the president back to his island. Over." The planes set their courses for a direct flight into Guantánamo.

RUSSIAN SEAMEN IN RAFTS
THE GULF

The men in the raft are thrown violently as a wave and the winds hit them. The ropes that lash the two rafts together strain and pull at the tie down cleats. "Sir, I'm afraid that the strain on the ropes will tear out the side of our raft. It must be doing the same to them." He looks at the ropes as the raft is again sent spinning and slamming down another roller. "Raft 2, this is the captain."

"Roger, sir. This is Raft 2."

"What is your condition? Over."

"We are having a problem with the tether lines. They are tearing the cleat out of the raft. We're being thrown around like a top."

"Right, we're in the same condition. I believe that we may loose both rafts if we remained tethered." Silence fills the air as the men on both rafts listen to the captain. "Sir, we agree."

"Very well, prepare to cut the lines." One of the seamen on each raft crawls over to the ropes and prepares to cut them. "Cut now." The ropes are severed, and the rafts settle into the swells.

"Gentlemen, I wish us all the best of luck. We will keep in contact every half hour."

"Aye, aye, sir." The men lean back against the side of the raft and await the next violent action of the sea and storm.

BRIDGE OF THE *MOSKVA*
THE GULF

The admiral glances from the damage reports to the sparking welders. The men on the deck fight the slashing wind and rain. As the bow dips and cuts the top off the oncoming roller, it fights to be free and throws water up into the wind that rolls over the deck crew. The men are thrown about as their tethers strain to hold them. As men are drained of strength by the elements or are injured, others replace them from below.

On the first deck, men bring mattress and pads in and put them around the room. On the deck below, Kruglov and a chief finish securing a pulling eye on the back of the bomb. Beregovoy directs the placement of pads around the hole above them.

The damage control officer leans down into the hole from the first deck. "They almost have the A-frame ready. The weather on deck is getting worse."

"All right. We're ready to go as soon as they are."

A braided cable is passed down from the main deck and is pulled through to the second deck. Kruglov connects the end to the pulling eye and climbs down. "We're all set. Contact the admiral and clear out all non-essential personnel."

"Aye, aye, sir."

The chief begins moving men out and having forward hatches dogged down. Beregovoy calls up to the bridge and tells them they are ready. The winch is run from inside a room at the base of the bridge. The chief pushes a button and the cable goes tight. Kruglov puts on a headset and directs the pull of the line. As the line pulls up, the bomb casing grinds with the metal of the ship. The bomb seems to adhere to the metal, then begins to slide upward. The metal screams in resistance as the bomb is extracted. It pulls clear of the bulkhead and swings out into the room. Men with timbers and mattresses stabilize it in the center of the room.

The bomb hangs in the room, as the ship seems to move around it. The bow dips and seems to bring the forward bulkhead at the bomb. Men with mattresses push back on the casing to keep it from hitting anything. They all hold their breath as the ship rights itself.

Beregovoy gets the men on the first deck ready to receive the bomb. Kruglov's men begin to maneuver the bomb up through the hole. They wait for the ship to align the hole, and the bomb is raised part way up. As the ship rolls back, it is lifted up into the first deck compartment. The shortening cable swings the bomb suddenly from side to side. Men with pads rush in to try and stabilize the swinging monster. It catches two men and presses them into the aft bulkhead. Others go to their aid as their screams fill the closed compartment. Beregovoy calls for medical assistance to help the men crushed by the bomb as others try and stabilize it.

The heat in the compartment seems to merge with the sweat of fear from the men holding the bomb. Again it hangs straight like a surveyor's plumb as the room gyrates around it. Kruglov works his way up to the men on the main deck. Wind and rain continue to lash at the ship, sweeping the decks clean. He talks with the men below and gets his team of men ready to pull the bomb up into the elements. The admiral orders all available light thrown down on the deck area around the A-frame. The rain dives through the lights like glass shards. The lights seem to give the sea an even more ominous look as it crashes over the bow. The black water moves by the ship like undulating plastic.

"Sir, we have a call from the *Otlichnyy*. The captain says he cannot save the ship. They are requesting assistance." He goes down to the combat center and talks with the captain. As he hangs up the phone, he looks over the radar. The ships are buried in the storm. He picks up the phone and talks to the *Sovremennyy*. The others watch as he speaks in low tones. He hangs up and shakes his head.

"Mr. Pstygo, give full assistance to the *Sovremennyy*. They are going to attempt to remove the men on the *Otlichnyy*. We have lost another vessel." He moves back up the ladder to the bridge, walks to the starboard side, and looks over the *Otlichnyy*; it is listing to starboard. It has all running lights on as wave after wave break over the side into the gaping hole at mid-ship.

"Sir." Pstygo comes up onto the bridge. "We may have a break in the weather. This front is passing by us; it looks like a lull before the next one. At best, we may have about an hour. By the time *Sovremennyy* gets up beside *Otlichnyy*, they may have a chance."

"Good, we need some good luck. I think we have earned a little."

FLIGHT HANGAR
NAS, NEW ORLEANS

As a driving rain passes over the base, the second Harrier is pulled into the hangar. The crew chiefs walk around the two jets and two of the Cobras as the maintenance officer finishes his walk. "Gentlemen, all four of these aircraft are now deadlined." He walks to the left side of Night Moves helicopter. "Hell, this thing has eighteen hits in it. And I know he came in with low hydraulics."

"Sir, he is not going to be happy to find out he is grounded.

"I understand, but this equipment is too valuable to lose, pushing in this type of weather. Are we in agreement, gentlemen?" Both the naval and marine crew chiefs answer in the affirmative.

"Good. We'll have to let them go for now. We need to make sure that the area is secured for the storm. Chief, have the marine crews help."

"Aye, aye, sir."

As the captain walks away, the crew chiefs gather their men and begin working out assignments to prepare for Evita.

ULTIMA
WASHINGTON, D.C.

Secretary Brant comes in to the room with Admiral Hillings following him. He puts some papers down on the table and asks for attention.

"President Wayne will be here in about," he looks at his watch, "thirty minutes. He is still in conference with the senators from the Gulf area. We will have reports updated at that time. He spoke with Secretary Sholenska. Apparently, the squadron is losing another ship." His eyes go to the middle screen; the shape of the ships is changing as one of them begins to pull up alongside one of the others.

Admiral Hillings walks up to the podium. "We want everyone prepared for the 2030 meeting. We'll need an open line to Base Commander Nelson in New Orleans. Thank you."

RUSSIAN RAFTS
THE GULF

"Sir, I can't raise the second raft."

They are all thrown to one side and then the other, as they slide and spin down the face of the roller. He hands the radio over to the captain. "Raft 2, this is Raft 1. Over."

"Roger." Static. "We read...." Static. "Luck...." Static. He holds the radio in his hand, and only the hiss and crackle of static fills the air.

"We all wish them and ourselves well in the coming hours." The men in the raft sit chilled in the light of a flashlight. Then one of the senior chiefs begins to sing an old Russian sea chantey. The others join in.

NAS
NEW ORLEANS

Two Humvies sit in front of the base command center; the rain lashes them in sheets of water. They sit calmly, awaiting the command to move.

"We will have a window in the weather soon, sir." Nelson looks over the maps, then out the window. The rain pelts the panes of the glass like buckshot.

"We'll send two pathfinders on land to try and secure the number two bomb. We'll fly in the support helicopters when the weather breaks."

"Aye, aye, sir."

The pathfinders leave in the two Hummers and head to the location that looks the best from aerial photos. The rain and the wind cross their windshields as they leave the base. They are waved through by the armed personnel on the road. The corporal looks over the map and points to a circle. The driver turns up a side road and races into the night.

ABOARD THE USS *ATLANTA*
THE GULF

At 600 feet under the raging surface, the graceful lines of the *Atlanta* are lost in the inky black water. It pushes southwest at thirty-two knots. Its target: the eye of Evita. The long range BQQ-5 sonar in the nose searches the inky void for any sign of trouble. The men in the hull go about their jobs, as the executive officer and the captain meet with a damage control team.

"Gentlemen, we need everyone's ideas on the best way to deal with the rescue. We will have to move quickly to secure both the rafts and to recover the crew as quickly as possible."

The men discuss different ways of getting the men into the hull, and the weather officer covers them on what conditions to expect on the outside of the hull. They can all feel the boat racing through the water. It registers in a sixth sense to the submariners. As the captain and the others plan their tactics for the rescue, the ship proceeds with the others doing their assigned jobs. The officer on the deck scans the various status boards and checks their position. The big frontal sonar is picking up underwater avalanches and a huge hissing noise to the front. The short range BQS-15 checks for closer targets. The officer on the deck moves back from the periscopes and watches the plot of the boat over charts of the area.

"Sir, we are about to launch a bath thermograph."

"Roger." The COB looks over to the planesman and the helmsman. All seems in order. The sonar watch officer passes on an alert from one of the technicians. "Sir, we have a mike contact at 1,000 yards." The sonar display on the BSY-1 scope changes. The waterfall pattern on the scope goes from regular intervals to extend patterns. The engineering officer calls forward. "Sir, we have a fifteen-degree drop in temperature on the hull."

"Sir, anomaly is 700 yards and closing."

The COB takes a few seconds to analyze the information. He looks around at the men in the compartment, and he reaches up and hits the crash alarm. Klaxon horns begin blaring throughout the boat. Men rise up from bunks and run to their stations. The captain jumps up and goes to the door of the wardroom.

"Give me ten degrees up angle on the planes." The dive officer passes on the command.

"I want full astern." The message is cranked on to the engine order telegraph. "Bring us up to periscope depth." The tilt in the ship is felt as the nose starts to rise. "Sir, anomaly 100 yards."

The captain reaches the control room just as the forward momentum of the boat pushes it through the thermal. A hundred feet of the boat passes into the thin warmer water, and the nose begins to drop. The full bulk of the 320-foot hull throws its 6,900 tons towards the sea bottom. It slides on the thermal at a forty-five-degree angle as the helmsman pull back with all his strength.

"Shit." The diving officer puts his foot on the console and grabs the yoke to assist the helmsman. The falling COB hits him from behind; they tumble to the front of the compartment. Men all over the ship fall forward towards the front of the boat as the ship plunges for the depths.

"Sir, 900 feet." The depth gauge continues to climb. The engines reverse to full astern; the hull shudders in response. Men lay hurt at the front of the control room. The dive officer pulls himself up to a sitting position. Blood runs down his face from a gash in his forehead. He wipes it away and reaches down to help the chief. Another man joins him, and they put his feet against the bulkhead. Because of the angle of the boat, he is almost standing up right. The captain works his way to the plotting table. He quickly gets a visual status of the room.

"Sir, 1,200 feet. Bottom depth is 3,000, sir."

The captain checks the ballast control panel. He sees the COB lying unconscious at the front of the room, with the diving officer next to him.

"Shit." The angle causes each movement to draw all available energy from their bodies. A misplaced hand or foot, and you tumble to the front of the control room. The helmsman and the planesman hang towards their consoles from the seat belts on their chairs.

"Sir, 2,000 feet." Beads of sweat begin falling from the men still at their positions. The COD orders a full emergency blow, but no one is at the control panel.

"Full emergency blow," the captain yells towards the diving officer, who is standing vertical at the front of the room. He begins to work his way up to the ballast control panel. The captain is pinned against the plotting table, and the executive officer is held fast by the number two periscope.

"Sir, 2,400 feet." The diving officer climbs up the panel and works his way to the control station. He stands vertically between the helmsman and the planesman, trying to reach the two mushroom-shaped valves above the ballast control panel. The captain has worked his way over to the aisle and climbs over beside him. He climbs up the panels and gets his hand on the top valve; they both crank the valves wide open. The plummeting monster shudders as the hull fights the forces pushing at its skin. It feels its ballast tanks filling and its nose beginning to rise. The nose skims an undersea knoll, and the hull slides through the soft mud and sand. It throws mud and debris into the wake of the passing giant. It fights to obey the command to surface. "Sir, 2,800 feet, and we're beginning to rise."

A cheer goes up from the men on the ship as their boat fights to regain control. It pulls itself to a level position and then reverses its angle. The nose rises at a fifteen-degree angle and throws men back in the opposite direction. It races for the surface, the depth gauge reeling back to zero.

"Sir, 2,200 feet and rising.

"Sir, 1,800 feet."

Men are picking themselves up and going to the aid of the injured. The captain and the COD work their way to the plotting tables. Strange sounds reverberate through the hull as they continue up. "I want a full damage report."

"Sir, we're 800 feet. Prepare to surface."

"Everyone, hold on."

The huge rounded nose of the submarine breaks through the surface and rises into the air. The sail follows it, and the bulk of the submarine settles back to the surface.

"Give me two-thirds forward power and activate outside radar. I want a full scan."

A call from the forward torpedo room reports ruptured plates. They are taking water.

Tubes one and three are crushed forward. The ship is violently thrown by the waves and wind on the surface. The radar scan shows they are fifty miles into the storm and are facing even worst conditions farther in.

The COB talks to the reactor room. "Sir, we have no problem with the reactor, but they are taking water in from the bilge tank and the condensation bay. The pumps are dealing with it, but we have sustained damage along the length of the hull."

"Very good. Communications get me Sky 1 on the radio." The captain of the *Atlanta* is patched through to Admiral Hillings. They discuss the situation and agree on a course of action. As others in the room watch, the shape of the submarine on the screen reverses course. The captain hangs up the phone. "Set in a course back to base. Take us down to sixty feet. We'll be on full alert until we clear the storm. God help the men on the rafts." The submarine slowly submerges, with only a periscope still rising above the water.

ULTIMA
WASHINGTON, D.C.

Admiral Hillings hangs up the phone and confers with some of his staff. He gets up, walks up to the podium, and confers with Captain Van Nar. "Mr. Secretary, the rescue attempt by the USS *Atlanta* has been aborted. They have sustained some major damage."

"What happened? An attack by those two Cuban subs?" Just as Hillings is about to answer, the president comes back in the room.

He looks up and sees the admiral at the podium. "Excuse me, Admiral. Please go on with the briefing."

"Sir." Brant gets up and walks back to his desk as the president sits down. "We have just received word that the rescue submarine *Atlanta* has been forced to turn around due to damages."

The president looks at the screen. "My God, what happened?"

"Sir, I discussed the situation with the boat captain. They ran into a thermal incline; the storm and other natural elements caused it. I have a general call out on the ELF and VLF systems for any boats in the area, which might have a chance to assist."

"My God, I just got off the phone with Secretary Sholenska and Marshal Shagan. The Russian squadron is about to lose another ship, the *Otlichnyy* that was damaged in the air attack. I pray that there is an end to this loss of life."

Brant slides a paper in front of him. "We will go on with the briefing, Mr. President. But as you will learn, this is becoming a most costly operation. And we still have a way to go."

The president reads over the list of names on the paper. "Commandant Swane, is this the Jim Knight I met last month? The one being considered for promotion?"

"Yes, sir. He was being groomed to take over command of the Second Marine Division at Lejeune."

"My God, and all these others. We all owe these people a great debt. It amazes me. We put these young men and women in a situation never before encountered. And through their attention to duty and combined bravery, they make it seem like something they have trained for months to do. For all the faults in today's society, in these times of trouble, the youth of America step forward and adorn themselves in glory."

The president and others are briefed on the bomb site recoveries and the situation at present. Captain Nelson from the base covers them on the situation at the base and the plans for the next recovery. Each situation is covered: weather, the Russian squadron, the evacuation, and the time table for the arrival of the eye.

Van Nar goes up to the podium. "Our last report is on the continuing battle in Cuba."

"We have President Castro safe and inbound. We have an ETA for him of 2200 hours at the Guantánamo facility." The screen in the center pulls down to the western half of Cuba. The forces of Morales are shown in blue, while those of Quintano are shown in yellow. Van Nar points to the screen.

"As you can see, Colonel Zino continues to consolidate his position here at Guanabacoa. As new forces arrive, they are being sent west. He is slowly encircling the city of Havana. There is a large battle just north of Guines. This is the push from General Quintano's forces. He has also sent forces farther west towards Guira de Melena. We believe this force will split and go north towards Havana, and west towards Artemisia. This will cut General Morales off from the western part of the island and isolate Havana."

"Sir." Admiral Hollings turns his chair towards the president and Mr. Brant. "Commandant Swane has spoken to the marine commander at Guantánamo. They are in contact with the fighter escort and are still looking at an ETA of about 2200 hours. We have asked President Castro to observe a radio silence until he is on the ground, in order to prevent any attempt by General Morales to intercept the group with other fighters."

The president takes a deep breath and stretches his shoulders in his chair. "Well, let's hope that when he does arrive, he can put a stop to the fighting."

"Yes, sir."

CENTRAL PLAINS
CUBA

"General, the forward element." He points to their position on a map on the plotting table. "They are requesting AT teams and some tanks. They're in a fire fight with a mechanized infantry battalion supported by tanks."

"Tell him we'll get them to him as soon as we clear them out of this ridge line."

"Yes, sir."

His attention is drawn out the back of the command vehicle as a brace of missiles lands down the valley. He heads outside to get a better look. He walks about thirty feet to get a better look. Incoming artillery lands near the road. Burning trucks and other equipment lay smoldering in the dark. A battery of 122 mm rockets screams into the dark sky.

On the road, Quintano's tanks race up the road leading to the top of the west mesa. They climb up the winding road to reach the top 400 feet above Quintano's position in the trees.

Boom. The blast catches Quintano and some of his staff like a scythe. They are thrown off their feet and sent sprawling into the mud and grass.

"What the hell?" Quintano looks back at the command track. Fire belches from the opening in the back, and a BTR-40 burns next to it. Automatic weapons fire rakes the area around them, and tracers arc over their heads at the trucks on the road.

"There in the arroyo." A man behind a tracked vehicle fires at someone off to the right. "Over there." Some others join him and open fire.

"General, are you all right?" A sergeant runs over to him and grabs his arm as he rises to his knees. "What the hell is going on?" Quintano, dazed, looks around as others with him begin to rise.

"They must have sent an AT team down the arroyo, over to the right. They're behind that track, over there." As he gets to his feet, two Spigot AT-4 missiles slam into the track. The vehicle explodes, sending everyone to the ground.

Two T-72 tanks pull off the road and begin maneuvering around the command position, firing point blank into the dark gash in the side of the mesa. The concussion of the guns is deafening. A swirling funnel of dirt and mud runs from the muzzle blast to the point of impact. The shells rip into the brush and trees, as an arc of yellow and orange flames light up the night. The machine guns on the tops are fired up the trail leading back up the mesa. The main guns blast the terrain farther up the trail.

Quintano runs over near the burning track and picks up a PKM machine gun and some ammo pouches from a dead solider. He runs up behind the lead tank, opens up the comm box, and takes out the handset.

"This is General Quintano. Did you get them all?"

"Sir, we believe we have cleared out the lower area. But the trail turns about 300 feet up the arroyo."

"All right. Pull out. We'll take it from here."

"Roger, sir."

Quintano puts the handset back, closes the lid, and moves back out of the way of the tanks. They begin to move around the burning track as an RPG bounces off the sloped armor on the side of the turret. It disappears into the dark and explodes on the ground farther out. A second one hits between the two tanks as they pull back to the road.

Quintano hooks a side mount of ammo, feeds the belt into the gun, and chambers a round. He tilts the barrel up to fire about 100 feet up the side of the mesa and fires a burst. The tracers walk along the edge of an outcropping, driving the shooters back. He runs up the trail past some burning trees and charred bodies, firing up the trail as he goes.

One of the captains on the staff sees what Quintano is doing and runs over to a sergeant as two MT-LB tracks pull up. The backs open up, and ten men file out.

"Sergeant, quick. Get some men and go after the general."

"Shit, that's him on the trail."

"Half you men come with me. The other half secure this area." Ten men fan out and begin working their way to the mouth of the trail. The sergeant moves quickly up the slight grade. He can see Quintano firing up the trail, which turns to the left. As they move up, the sergeant sees a dark figure rise up to Quintano's right.

Quintano catches a movement out of the corner of his eye and turns to face his attacker. He holds the machine-gun up to block a downwards swing of the man's AK-47.

The metal of the two weapons clanks together. He stops the full downward force of the blow — but not before the bayonet cuts into his shoulder at the base of his neck and drives him to his knees in the loose gravel on the trail. His assailant lifts the weapon for a final thrust. Quintano looks up at the point of the bayonet as it begins its downward path. The man is thrown back as three bullets rip into his chest. He falls next to Quintano on the path.

"Sir, are you all right?" The sergeant grabs his arm to help him up, and Quintano wrenches in pain. "Shit, get a medic up here and secure the path up ahead."

Men move by them and start the climb up the trail. It turns again about 100 feet ahead. The medic puts a pressure bandage on the wound and gives him a shot of morphine. He helps him up. "Sir, we'll move you back down the hill."

"No, Sergeant. I started up this trail, and I'm going to the top. We need to get some light on the subject. Call in some illumination."

"Yes, sir. And sir, this time we'll all go up together, instead of launching a one-man assault. By the way, sir, it would look real bad on my service record to lose a general."

Quintano reaches down to pick up the weapon, and a sharp pain shoots across his back.

"A suggestion, sir. You stick to a side arm in your left hand."

"I agree, Sergeant. Please contact the command group and tell them I'll meet them at the top of the mesa. After you, Sergeant." They start the climb, their boots slipping in the loose gravel on the up-hill trail.

BRIDGE OF *MOSKVA*
THE GULF

Admiral Sokolov scans the *Sovremennyy* as it slides up next to the *Otlichnyy*. Lines are being fired from the ship to the crippled destroyer; searchlights from the destroyer and from the *Moskva* flood the area. Hawsers are pulled to the stricken *Otlichnyy* and secured. The wenches on the *Sovremennyy* begin to pull the two ships together. As they grow closer, the water between them is squeezed up into twenty-foot waves. They rush along the sides of the ships, scouring any loose material from the decks.

"Give us a few moments of peace." The admiral's voice is low as he utters the words.

Yefimov nearby overhears him. "I agree, sir. We could use a period of calm. The men on the *Otlichnyy* deserve a chance to live. They have fought bravely this day."

Sokolov moves past him. "True, Yefimov. They and all the others have distinguished themselves." He moves to the front of the flying bridge and looks down at the men struggling with the A-frame on the forward deck. The sea continues to roll over the side of the ship and pull at the men on the deck. Their safety lines are strained to retain them.

"Sir, Lieutenant Beregovoy says they are ready to make the last pull to get the bomb on the main deck."

"Thank you, Yefimov. Let us hope they are successful." The men below decks stream sweat as they use mattresses to try and control the swing of the bomb. Beregovoy talks to Kruglov in the ready room off the main deck as he gets into his foul weather suit. Six other men stand ready to go out on the main deck with him. The chief near the door watches the waves crash over the bow and sweep around the A-frame. "Sir, it's bad out there. The water on the deck is running about three feet deep."

"All right, Chief. Time us as the bow starts coming up. Beregovoy, we're ready to go onto the deck. The chief will call the time."

"Roger, Kruglov. Be careful." He lays the headset down, goes to the front of the line, and hooks his safety lines to the steel cable.

The chief watches the bow fall, just as it scoops up the top of the roller. He yells to the men at the door. They break out onto the deck. Water to their knees rushes around them. They take up their positions as the bow raises into the air. "Pull." Kruglov's voice is lost in the howl of the wind.

"Now." The chief signals the winch to start. He lets Beregovoy know they are lifting. As the winch tightens, the base of the bomb pulls into the hole. But the ship takes a hard right roll, and it catches in the shredded deck plates.

"Shit." Beregovoy's men try to hold the bomb steady as the ship comes back to the left. The winch pulls as it aligns with the hole, and the beast is pulled clear. As the bomb disappears up the hole, the men in the compartment move quickly out the aft passageway and clear the area. Beregovoy calls to the chief, "We're clear and evacuating the area." He tosses the headset down and follows the others out the hatch. When he is clear, they dog the door closed. The bomb swings clear as the bow begins its dive into the next wave. It swings to the left and hits some twisted metal.

The men on deck fight the movement of the ship and the oscillation of the bomb. They signal the chief to lower it to the deck, so they can push it over the side. The beast is lowered and lies on the slick deck. One of the men moves to disconnect the winch as the bow dives into the water. As he pulls the pin to release the shackle, a four-foot wall of water rushes over him and the others. They all are pulled to the ends of their safety lines and are left sprawling on the raising deck. The bomb rolls towards the super structure and catches two of the men in its path. Their screams of pain are lost in the spray and wind.

"Shit." Sokolov watches out the front of the bridge. "The bomb is running free on the deck."

Yefimov calls down to the chief, "What the hell is going on?"

"When they pulled the pin, they got hit with a flood of water off the bow. We may also have two men down; they're not getting up."

The bomb rolls to the side of the ship and catches in the railing. Beregovoy and the others move to help the two men down. As they reach the first one, they can see that he is dead. Two men grab him and pull him towards the door near the chief. The other has crushed legs, and two others grab him under the arms and pull him into the super structure. Beregovoy is alone on the deck. The rolling deck and the rising bow throw him off his feet, but he pulls himself towards the bomb. His safety line stops him, three feet away. He stretches but cannot reach it. He looks forward as the bow climbs into the sky. He reaches back and unclips his safety line. He sticks a crow bar under the nose, and as the ship begins to roll right he pries up.

The chief, seeing what is going on, yells from the hatch at Beregovoy. "Sir, don't disconnect your line. We'll get you more help." He waves him off and keeps prying at the bomb.

"Sir, Lieutenant Beregovoy has released his safety line and is trying to pry the bomb off the starboard railing."

"What?" Sokolov walks out onto the starboard flying bridge. The rain slashes across his face. He can see the lone figure bracing himself on the rail and prying with the crow bar. His eyes track to the bow, which is falling back into the sea. In his heart, he knows there is no chance for the brave young officer. He watches as the bow dives deep and scoops a huge draft of water. As it begins to rise, the ship rolls to starboard. As Beregovoy pries with the help of the right hand roll, the bomb breaks free and slides over the side. A six-foot wall of water rolls over Beregovoy.

"Man overboard!" the chief yells in the headset.

The admiral looks over the empty deck, scourged clean by the wave. Yefimov moves towards the door to the outside as the admiral comes back in. "Sir, we have lost...." He does not finish the sentence. As he looks into the admiral's eyes, he sees the look of a father who has lost his son. Their depth seems endless.

"I know, Mr. Yefimov. Enter it in the log. Mr. Beregovoy's act of devotion and bravery deserves the highest honor. We are all humbled by his selfless act of courage."

About 200 feet behind the *Moskva*, a huge column of water erupts from the depths and cascades into the sky. The concussion can be felt throughout the ship.

"Apparently it was not a dud."

"Yes, sir."

Pstygo comes up from the combat center. "Sir, there has been a large detonation to the stern of the ship."

"Yes, Pstygo."

"Sir, the *Sovremennyy* has begun to take the men off the *Otlichnyy*. As soon as they are loaded, they will cut the hawsers."

"Very well. Tell her to stand off while we clear, and then torpedo her to the bottom. Then rejoin us."

"Aye, aye, sir."

THE OUTSKIRTS OF NEW ORLEANS

The two Hummers maneuver around fallen trees and downed power lines. The lead vehicle comes to a stop at an intersection, and the sergeant checks his map. "We're on the right track. Hang for a second. I need to check the PLRS." He keys the codes into the position location reporting system, and then waits for the read out. He checks it with the map. "All right, we're about ten miles out. We'll go up about two intersections and then turn left for about five miles. We'll hit a secondary road out into the swamps. There is a sheriff's unit out there who will meet us. Let's move."

The two vehicles move up the street, driving up onto lawns and through fences to get around fallen debris. They check in with the base and push farther out into the country.

AIRFIELD
GUANTÁNAMO BAY

The base commander waits in front of the tower as the Cuban airliner lands between the two F-18s. As it taxies to the front of the tower, two F-18s and the A6 Prowler jet land and taxi up next to the liner. The ground crew moves in the ramp as Colonel Bergmen walks over from the waiting vehicles. The door on the liner is opened, and Fidel's staff begins unloading. They are directed to the waiting vehicles as Fidel's personal aide talks with Colonel Bergmen.

"Colonel, your assistance in this matter is greatly appreciated. The president will be coming off soon, and would like to thank the pilots personally."

"That's fine. Mr. Diez," Bergmen calls over on his radio. A sergeant goes out to the jets and brings the pilots over to the ramp. Fidel comes to the door and walks down to the tarmac. Bergmen salutes him as he walks up. Fidel nods his head and extends his hand, "Thank you, Colonel."

"We're glad to have been of service, sir."

He walks over to the pilots and shakes their hands; they talk for a minute. Then he goes with Bergmen to the waiting cars. The convoy of six vehicles moves through the base to the front gates.

The guards salute them as they pass; they drive out onto the road and turn left. About a mile up the road, a line of Cuban military vehicles waits for them. They pull up next to them and stop. The doors to the vehicles are opened, and they climb out onto the asphalt. A Cuban colonel moves up to Fidel and salutes.

"Sir, we are ready to escort you to the air base at Santiago de Cuba. They have a helicopter waiting to fly you to Matanzas. On the way, we will bring you up to date on the events that have occurred."

"Thank you, Colonel." He turns back to Bergmen.

"When you report my arrival to your command center, extend my personal thanks to President Wayne for his assistance. Good night, Colonel."

"Good night, sir." Bergmen salutes and goes back to the vehicles. They drive back onto the base as the Cuban vehicles head for the airport.

ULTIMA
WASHINGTON, D.C.

Captain Van Nar is at the podium. "Gentlemen, we have touchdown of the Cuban airliner at Guantánamo. President Castro is being escorted to a meeting with his forces outside the perimeter of the base.

"He has the responsibility of his own forces now, Mr. President."

"You're right, Mr. Brant."

"At least one of the situations tonight has been brought to a close. We would hope this might ease the tension between our two countries."

"Sir." Commandant Swane stands up at his seat. "I have just finished speaking with Colonel Bergmen at Guantánamo. President Castro requested him to pass on his personal thank you for your assistance."

The president sits up a bit in his chair. "Well, there is a new wrinkle. This may prove to be an opportunity to finally bring some lasting peace to the area."

"Sir, while I was base commander at Guantánamo, I worked with then-Captain Quintano. He is an intelligent officer, and would, I believe, put a more moderate command structure in place. Mr. Castro will be served well by his counsel."

"Thank you, Commandant Swane. Mr. Brant, I believe that we should get a group together, one that can evaluate the changes in Cuba, which will occur after the fighting. If there is any form of contact that can be established, we'll be ready to respond."

"Yes, sir." Brant picks up the phone and makes a couple of calls. He looks up at the screens as he listens to the man on the other end of the phone. In the area that is considered a best location for bomb seven, a red rectangle sits on the map. He watches as four yellow squares enter the area in the red box. As they move forward, a white dotted line appears through the box. Van Nar sees him looking at the screen and orders it enlarged. He looks over and nods his head at her, and she returns a nod and goes back to work. The yellow squares come to a stop at a road junction, and the party on the other end of the call hangs up.

He turns back to the president. "Sir, I spoke with Secretary Drake. The foreign office will begin immediately to have their contact team brought up on-line with the latest events. They will meet with you at your convenience."

"Thank you, Mr. Brant. Let's hope that something positive comes out of this incident."

The room is quiet as they watch two of the yellow boxes form parallel to the white line. Captain Van Nar looks up at the screen and back at the others. "The white dotted line through the red rectangle is the flight path of the TU-26 Backfire bomber. The marine recon unit is now sitting parallel to its track." The yellow squares begin moving eastward along the track. As the two Humvees move up the road, they pass construction yards filled with equipment, oil company storage areas for mobile derricks, and large warehouses for businesses that need large areas for their records storage. They come around a slight curve in the road and a large heavy truck repair facility sits at their left. The road ends at the gates of a huge wrecking yard.

Spotlights from the two vehicles shine through the chain link fence, and they highlight stacks of cars five and six high. A light in the office just off the gates catches the eye of the sergeant. He calls back for one of the sheriff's cruisers to join them. A cold stiff wind blows around the recon group as they walk up to the gates. The sergeant knocks on the outside door with the butt of his flashlight. A man looks out a side window and then unlocks the door. As the door opens, the light from the lantern on the desk floods out on the sergeant and two of the men. "Sir, there is an evacuation going on for this area. You need to head for the stadium in New Orleans."

"Yeah, I know. I needed to close down the place and get my paperwork out. I'll be leaving in about five minutes." He looks at the collar of the man in the doorway. "The truth is, Sergeant, I needed to get this paperwork, but I also wanted to pick up the dogs out here. We have six of these old junkyard dogs, but they don't deserve to get killed out here." He looks him in the eyes and smiles.

Sergeant Bonds smiles back. "Yeah, I know what you mean. Do you mind if we take a look around?" The man looks at them puzzling. "I'm Bert Cassidy. I own the place. Ah, is there something wrong? There are no people out there, just wrecked cars and trucks."

Over Bond's shoulder the lights of an approaching police car blink vividly in the dark. The lights flash and fade off the fronts of the buildings along the street. It pulls in next to the two military vehicles. A large deputy gets out and walks up to the open door of the office.

The deputy, who stands about six feet, six inches, moves between the recon men and comes into the office; his raincoat and smoky bear hat enhance his large look. He addresses the group in great southern style. "Gentlemen, Bert, boy. What the hell you doing here?"

"Hi, Bo, I came back to pick up more paperwork and get the dogs."

"Shit, boy. Them damn hounds will be here after we're gone. Well, let's get you loaded, Bert. That storm is still cutting a mean path to us." Bo picks up a box on the desk and nods towards the back door.

Bert leads the way out the back door with Bo and Bonds following with boxes. He goes over to a Suburban parked near the gate and opens the side door. The dogs are barking and snarling in the side windows of the vehicle as they walk up.

"I had better load these. Them dogs are a bit wired up." He opens the side door and pushes his box in on the back seat. A wire barrier across the back of the seat keeps the dogs in the very back. As he puts the box in, the last place is filled. "Shit, I have to open the back. You boys had better let me load these."

"Shit, Bert. Open up the back of this thing."

Bert lifts the back open, and Bo steps in directly behind the open door. A lightning flash streaks across the sky behind the deputy as the door raises. His huge form catches the dogs by surprise as they quietly sit and stare at the huge apparition in wet yellow. Bert takes the box and slides it in, and he loads the one from Bonds. Then he closes the door.

Bert shakes his head. "Shit, Bo. I never have seen anything like that before."

A deep base laugh flows from the darkened figure. "Hell, same damn thing happens when I have to arrest people too."

"Shit, I believe that, Deputy."

Bond shakes his head. They walk back inside the office. Bert turns to Bonds. "You said you wanted to look around the place, right?"

"Yes, Mr. Cassidy."

"I saw that news conference with the president. About that Russian bomber dropping some kind of mines. You think there may be one out in the yard?"

"We're not sure. But we think the bomber may have come almost directly over your yard here."

"Shit, boy. You don't have to think it. I saw the bastard come over and there was a big crash in the back part of the yard."

"You saw it?"

"Yeah, it was so low and making so much noise with those other jets with it. You'd have to have been deaf to have missed it."

"Yeah," Bo cuts in. "Bert told me this morning he had seen the bomber last night. That was when we were getting everyone out of here."

"Yeah, Officer Bo and I talked about it earlier. I had to stay with the mechanics last night. They were trying to fix the big shredder out here. They didn't get done till about 5:30 in the morning. That bomber came over between 4:00 and 4:30, flying southwest."

"And the crash you heard? Where was that?"

"Out in the back. You think one of those mines landed back there?"

"It may have. We need to take a look. All right?"

"All right. Let me open the gates and you can bring your vehicles in. We'll take a ride out back." He gets his keys and heads for the back door.

"Can we just walk there?"

Bonds looks at Cassidy. "Boy, you don't know how big this place is, do you?"

Bonds shakes his head. "No."

"I have 150 acres of cars and trucks out here. Shit, boy. We'd be walking all night. Besides where you want to go is all the way in the back." Bert opens the gate and the two Hummers drive in. Bonds goes over to the men and posts a guard of two marines at the front. Bert and Bo climb into the back of the Hummer. Bonds slides in, and they pull out into a broad open area. "Take that road to the left and just follow it to some large cranes in the middle of the yard." As they drive along the road, they pass between stacks of cars and buses. The stacks rise high above the road on each side. Bonds has the feeling of driving through a narrow canyon. "Shit, I have never seen so many wrecked cars." He turns back in his seat to face the back.

"Yeah," Officer Bo jumps in. "Old Bert here run the largest auto recycling business on the Gulf."

"Yeah." Bert looks out the side window. "We do it all. Strip them for parts, and shred them for scrap. The stuff is shipped all over the world. I guess third world countries find it cheaper to melt down this old iron and reuse it, rather than having to produce it all themselves." They come out into a large cleared area with about six cranes sitting silently. Some have big round electron magnets hanging from them, while others have big buckets used for loading. "OK, work your way around that second crane, and go up the road to your right." The Hummer moves between the big pieces of equipment and begins driving down the road. They pass back into another canyon of vehicles.

Bo looks around. "Yeah, stacked as high as these things are, I don't think you want to be here in the coming high winds."

"I was just thinking the same thing." Bonds nods his head. "That is one of the reasons I sent everyone home. We lost power, and with the high winds, you're running a high risk of an accident." They break into another open area; hundreds of engines sit on the ground. A long open-faced shed has cars and trucks on racks, being stripped.

"That road over to your left. We're just about there." The Hummer drives by stacks of carburetors and other engine parts. As they head up the road, they begin passing by huge mounds of shredded steel. As they pass around the base of one of the mounds, a huge machine three stories high looms above them.

"That's the shredder. That bad boy can tear anything apart. We were working on it over by the dump belts when the power went out." They stop the vehicles and get out. A smell of wet rust and metal fills their nostrils. Bert goes over to the machine and the others follow. "We can walk from here. The crash we heard was from one of the stacks down this way." He takes off down a side road between stacks, with the others following. The vehicles slowly pull in behind and shine their lights over the group. As Bert rounds a corner, he stops and looks around. Fallen vehicles block the way. The stack they formed has been knocked into the road.

"Shit, we can't get through here. But this is what made the crash. But it could have been just the wind."

Bonds gets the men out and they play flashlights over the vehicles. "Corporal, take two men and get up on these cars, and see if you can see anything. And be careful. Shit, this whole group of stacks seems to be swaying."

The three men climb up slowly. Some of the cars they climb over teeter from their weight. They move out of sight over the vehicles, the beams of their lights shining against the wet metal bodies. "I have some fork lifts back down the road. We could pull some of these out of here."

"Well, let's wait and see what they find. This may be only the work of the storm."

"You know, something is not right here." Bert puts his hand to his chin. "It just doesn't look right."

"What's that Bert?" Bonds looks over to where he is standing. "I'm not sure. I need to get back a little and take a look." Bo walks along the edge of the stack, shining his light through windows and between cars.

Bert climbs up about two cars, on a stack that looks down the clogged road. "Give me some light on the stack to the right." They back up one of the Hummers and turn all its lights on high. It floods the area around Officer Bo, so he moves back over to where Bonds is.

"See anything, Mr. Cassidy?" Bonds yells up to him.

"Well, you notice that on the stacks to your left, they're mostly vans. And the stacks to your right are mostly cars."

"Yeah." Bonds plays his light from left to right.

"OK, the vans on the left have all fallen down into the road, where your men are looking."

"All right."

"OK, the stacks of cars on your right. Look at them in the lights. Everything above the first car is tilted towards the gate. Toss me a light, Sarge."

Bonds walks over to him and tosses the flashlight up to him. He looks back at the car stack on the right. As Cassidy had said, every car above the first one was pushed back. The higher up the stack, the more it was pushed. Bert shines the light over the cars and moves over to his left. He plays the light across the back of the stack and can see the three marines climbing over the vans in the road. Their lights go up and down as they raise and lower themselves from vehicle to vehicle. Bo shines his light up the stacks and climbs up on the side of a van lying at the bottom. As he shines his light on the stacks, they seem to be pushed into an arc. He yells over to Bonds. "Hey, Sarge, have your boys out here shine their lights over on to this stack of cars. Maybe Bert can see something."

Bonds calls the men on the radio and tells them what they want. They climb up on the backs and sides of the wrecked vans and shine their lights on the stack across from them. Bert moves over a couple of cars and can now see the whole arc of the stack. "Well, I can tell you one thing that is out of place. That white van does not belong in the middle of that stack."

"I'll check it." Bo climbs up on the next level of cars and moves over the tops of cars on the second row. About halfway, he climbs up another level. He can feel the stack sway beneath him.

"Be careful, Bo. I don't want to have to explain to your daddy how you got crushed by a pile of wrecked cars."

"I'm all right. You boys over there keep your lights on the van." Bond climbs up on the van in front of him to see how Bo is doing.

He watches as Bo climbs up one more level. The cars shimmy with each step he takes. He gets to the side of the van; it teeters as he approaches. The front of the van is facing away from him and their are no windows in the back. He grabs the handles on the back doors and pulls. The whole van rocks in place, but the doors are crushed shut.

"The doors are mashed shut. We'll need a crow bar on them. I'll check the front."

Officer Bo holds on to the side of the van as he carefully works his way to the front. As he moves, the van rocks in place. Any missed step will send him on a twenty-five-foot fall into tangled car metal. He reaches the door handle and tries it. As he pulls it open, the van slips a few inches towards him.

"Holy shit, the metal around here is all wet and covered with oil. Shit, this thing almost went." He climbs up into the front seat and pushes back a curtain hanging behind the two bucket seats. His light shines back into the dark cavity and is reflected off a large white cylinder, which is sticking through the van.

"Bonds, Bonds." He swings back to look out the door and back at the others. "I think your bomb is in the back of this van. A large white cylinder with Russian writing on it."

"You got it, Bo."

"Stay there. I'm coming up."

The three marines below climb across the roofs of fallen vans and begin the climb up towards Bo. Bonds works his way up the levels of cars, to just below Bo. He can feel the shaking of the stack as the others climb up to the van. "You guys hold where you are. This whole goddamn stack is shaking. Let me check with Bo. Then we're getting down. You guys start down one at a time, now." The lowest marines begin to climb back to the vans in the road. Bonds climbs up near the front window of the van. He looks through the broken glass at Bo in the front driver's seat. Bo pulls the curtain aside. Bonds shines his light on the white cylinder with the red lines on it. "You found it, Bo. We need to get down and wait for the disposal team."

"Sounds good to me, Sarge. Let's get the hell out of here." When he slides his feet to the door in order to get out, the van tilts and slides a few inches. The loud grinding noise fills the air. The van has pivoted on the bomb, and the front of the van is now hanging out in the air. Bonds is holding onto the front of the van. He is almost pushed over the side.

"Fuck this, I want out of here." Bo looks to climb over to the passenger side to get out. The van slips a few inches forward.

"Bo, don't move. This fucker is going to fall. We're going to have to brace this thing." As the last marine climbs down, a screeching sound fills the air and a section of the stack falls away. Bonds looks behind him. Two cars over, a huge void now exists.

"Shit, you guys get back to the Hummers and call Bulldog. Tell them that we have found the bomb, but we need help fast. We're going to have to hang loose up here. If we try and get down, we'll lose the thing." The corporal runs to the Hummer and calls back to base.

"Touchdown, this is Recon 1. Over."

"Roger, Recon 1. This is Touchdown."

"We have field goal at our site. Over."

"Roger, Recon 1. Field goal acknowledged. Hold one." The comm officer at the base has the call transferred to Captain Nelson's office. Chief Lang answers the phone and talks to the officer. "Sir, Nelson and Val are looking over a map on the table."

"Yes, chief."

"Sir, this is comm. They have contact with Recon 1. They have a field goal."

"Yes!" Nelson slaps the table and shakes Vals hand. "Let me talk to them." She hands the phone over to him.

"Patch me through to the recon unit, Mr. Chase. Recon, this is Touchdown. What is your status at the location."

"Touchdown, we need help. We are in a bad way. Over."

"Recon, just hang on the radio. We'll have the people you need assembled. We'll get back to you in a few minutes. Touchdown out." Nelson flashes the phone hooks. "Mr. Chase, put me through to Ultima. This is a flash message."

ULTIMA
WASHINGTON, D.C.

"This is Admiral Hillings." He listens as Nelson goes over his plans for the retrieval team. "It sounds great, Captain. We'll get back to you in thirty minutes. Good luck."

"Yes!" he calls out as he hangs up the phone. The others in the room look at him.

"I take it we have some good news, Admiral?"

"Yes sir, Mr. President. That was Captain Nelson. They have located bomb number two." As they all look at the screen, a large blinking yellow "X" appears on the screen.

"I agree with you Admiral. Yes, we have another one." Those in the room all cheer.

NELSON'S OFFICE
NAS, NEW ORLEANS

"Chief Lang, we need to wake the ladies. I need Commander Marino here as soon as possible. And we had better get the marine officers and senior NCOs." Nelson looks at his watch. "It's 2210. We'll have a staff meeting at 2230. We'll need the extra things for the meeting, Chief."

"Aye, aye, sir. I'll have the coffee and other things sent in. I'll go wake the ladies myself. I have sent runners to wake the others."

"Outstanding, Chief. I couldn't do this without you."

"Yes, sir. I try to do my best."

CHAPTER 16

NAS
NEW ORLEANS

Chief Lang makes some calls to the mess hall and the different barracks. Men are sent in to wake the officers. She then goes out the side of the building and walks over to the BOQ. She checks in with the front desk and walks up the hall to the room marked "Dr. Davies." She turns the handle and knocks as she enters the darkened room.

"Ladies, you need to get up. The recon team has found the second bomb. Dr. Davies." She hears a rustling of blankets and a low moan. "Susie, it's time to get up."

Laura gets up and turns on a table lamp. The soft yellow glow frames her as she puts her feet on the floor, and stands up to stretch. "I'm up, Chief. Is Susie up?"

"Not yet."

Lang walks over to the foot of the bed and gently shakes the bed. "Doctor, we need you at a meeting." Susie rolls over and can just make out the chief standing there. Behind her, Laura walks by with a towel over her shoulder. "Oh God, Chief. Do I have to get up?"

"I'm afraid so. Captain Nelson has called for a meeting in thirty minutes. They've located bomb two. They are going to send Commander Marino out to the site. There seems to be some kind of problem."

Susie sits up in bed and stretches. "I was having a dream about a fantastic cowboy out in New Mexico."

Lang smiles. "You know I think I've had that dream before. I have food and drinks being sent over to the office. I'll tell Captain Nelson you're on your way. "

"Thank you, Chief. It was nice of you to come over and wake us."

"I thought it would be better than having some 'rating' throw the door open and turn on the lights. Efficient but a little nerve racking. We'll see you at the meeting." She leaves as Susie gets to her feet and uses the bed to steady herself. She can feel the aches and pains of being wet and cold for long periods.

"Oh," She belts out as she yawns. "I am sore over ninety percent of my body." She collects her toothbrush and a towel and goes into the bathroom with Laura.

On her way back to the office, Chief Lang runs into Marino coming up the walk. She quickly salutes him as they meet. "Good evening, sir."

He returns the salute, and puts his arm around her shoulders. "Well, Chief? What's it look like?"

"I'd say you're on your way out to the site, sir. Apparently they have run into some kind of problem. And given the fact that you are our handsome troubleshooter, I wouldn't get to comfortable."

"I love it, Chief. It's why I'm here."

"Yes, sir. It's not just a job." They both laugh as Marino opens the door for her, and they head for Nelson's office.

As the chief hangs up her raincoat, Marino knocks on the door to Nelson's office.

"Just go on in, Mr. Marino. He is waiting for you." The chief follows him into the office as others set up coffee, and rolls. Nelson looks up as they enter. "Excellent, Commander. We have a problem at site two." He looks around at the chief. "And what did Chief Lang tell you?"

"Not to get comfortable, sir."

"She is right on the number. Grab something quickly to take with you. I need your expertise on this one. We seem to have two men trapped with the bomb. I have alerted the Seabee unit to stand by. We'll wait for your evaluation at the site. There is a helicopter standing by to take you to the site. The recon unit will have a vehicle for you at the front gate. They seem to be a little concerned about having the helicopter get too close."

Marino grabs a couple of cinnamon rolls and a cup of coffee. "I'm heading out now, sir. I'll call you from the site."

"Very good, and Mr. Marino, be careful on this one. You're too good an exec to lose in a junkyard."

"Thank you, sir." He heads out the door to a vehicle waiting to take him to the helicopter.

Val looks up from the donuts. "Mr. Marino is a very good officer, Captain Nelson. I would have such a man on my team."

"Well, I can tell you I'm glad he is with us on this operation."

The Blackhawk takes off and heads towards the east. Marino eats his rolls and drinks his coffee as the helicopter shudders from the winds and drizzle of the storm.

Susie and Laura walk from the BOQ and meet Lieutenant Neal and Johnson on the walkway. Johnson has a slight limp as he heads into the building. "Well, Mr. Neal and Mr. Johnson. It looks like we have a few more problems to take care of."

"Yes, ma'am." Johnson opens the door to the command building. "We're hoping that the next two will be more mundane than the others."

"I hope so, too, Mr. Johnson." They go up the stairs to Nelson's office. The smell of fresh donuts and rolls fills their nostrils. Chief Lang catches them as they come into the outer office. "Ladies and gentlemen, please help yourselves. We're waiting for the rest of the people to arrive." Susie and the others all walk over to the table and begin gazing over the different pastries. She picks up a cinnamon roll and goes to get a cup of orange juice. "I know I just ate a while ago, but I feel like I need a boost or something."

Neal chuckles. "I know what you mean. I think it's a sugar high or something." They all pick up some pastries and drinks and sit down in the outer office to wait for the others. Johnson rubs his leg and sits back in a stuffed chair. He has to hold the leg straight out because of the bandages.

Susie sits next to him. "How are you feeling, Captain?"

"Pretty good. They sewed it up and gave me some shots. The pain is light. It's just every now and then, I get a flash of heat in my cheek. Wow, it lets me know it there."

"Are you sure that you should be going out in the field?"

"I'll be all right, Susie. I have no intention of missing the finish of this weird night."

The chief comes in from Nelson's office. "Gentlemen and ladies, the captain would like you to join him and Mr. Val in his office. The others should be here shortly. And Captain Johnson, I took the liberty of sending for Gunny Marshall and Sergeant Cabolero."

They all get up to walk in. "That's great, Chief. I had someone go after them, too." Nelson is on the phone as they come in, and Val is leaning over a map.

He looks up as they take their seats. "Welcome back, everyone. I'm sorry you didn't get more rest."

"So they found another one, Mr. Val?" She takes a drink of juice and looks over the edge of her cup.

"Yes, Dr. Davies. But there is some type of problem at the site. Mr. Marino has already left and will contact us from there."

"How is your wound, Mr. Johnson?" Nelson walks up to the head of the table.

"Good, sir. It won't be a problem."

"Very good. As Val has said, we're waiting for a call in from Mr. Marino."

A radio from the recon group is brought into the conference room and set up on a table against the wall. A speaker is plugged in, and soon crackle and static fill the room. The operator adjusts some knobs and the set goes silent. Nelson waits for the operator to get the set quiet. "All right. We'll wait for Commander Marino to see what the problem is, and we'll have a better idea of what we're up against."

Marshall and Cabolero stop look at the pastries and then head into the office. They come to attention. "Master Gunnery Sergeant Marshall and Gunnery Sergeant Cabolero, reporting as ordered, sir."

Nelson nods. "At ease, Gunnies. This will be a very informal meeting. Please go back out and get something to eat and drink."

"Thank you, sir." They both go out and get donuts and coffee, then join the others in the room.

"While we're waiting, I have the privilege of passing on the news that Major Rice has been promoted to lieutenant colonel. He will replace Colonel Knight as regimental commander back at Lejeune."

"He is a good officer and leader. I've had the privilege of working with him over the last couple of years."

"Well, Mr. Johnson, he must feel the same as you. He said that these had fared well with him, and asked me to give them to you, Major Johnson." Nelson hands him the two gold oak leaves.

"Congratulations, Major." Nelson shakes his hand. Johnson starts to stand. "Thank you, sir."

"Please remain seated. You're going to have a long night. I was also asked to pass on some news to you, also, Mr. Neal. They didn't send anything over, but congratulations, Captain."

"Thank you, sir." Neal stands and shakes his hand.

"I was told by Colonel Rice that the full blown promotion ceremony will be held when you get back to base. And I quote him, 'It will not be pretty.'" They all laugh as the others congratulate them on their promotions. Johnson puts on the oak leaves and hands his twin bars to Neal. "You can use these if you would like, Captain."

"Thank you, sir. I will wear them proudly."

"Also, apparently you must have gotten on the wrong side of someone, Gunny Marshall. You are now the regimental first sergeant. These were sent over for you, Top." Marshall stands at attention, and shakes hands with Nelson. "You had better stand also, Gunny Cabolero. It seems with Gunny Marshall's promotion, your unit needs a new master gunnery sergeant. These were sent over for you. Congratulations." Everyone congratulates everyone else around the table. They all get more coffee and pastries.

"Now that we have had some good news, we have to get back to the bad news. As Val has stated, we have the bomb. But it sounds like were going to need some major construction to keep it from falling. It's pinned in a van, on top of a stack of junk cars."

"What?" Susie looks at the others.

"That's all we have until we hear from Commander Marino." Johnson and Neal talk as they get some more coffee. They walk back in the room and take Marshall and Cabolero off to the side. They talk in low tones and then go back to the table.

"Sir. Captain, we have decided to take the Third Platoon out on this bomb and leave the First and Second Platoons to get some rest. Both Captain Neal and myself will be in command, with Top Marshall and Gunny Cabolero as our senior NCOs."

"Very good. Your marines have definitely earned their rest. Because of the storm and the conditions approaching, we'll only be using the Sea Stallions. One for command and control, and one for your troops. The third is for support equipment."

"Aye, aye, sir." Johnson turns to Marshall and nods. He and Cabolero finish their coffee and get ready to leave. Captain Neal finishes his coffee and joins them.

"Sir, we'll leave now and secure the area at the site. It will give us all a chance to bring the troops up to speed."

Susie finishes her juice. "Captain, I would like to check on Dr. Reddeer's condition before we leave."

"Yes, ma'am. You will be going out with Major Johnson and Colonel Val. We'll have someone come and get you when they are ready to go."

"Thank you, Captain." Susie and Laura leave for the hospital.

The radio comes to life. "Touchdown, this is Recon. Over."

Nelson walks over and picks up the handset. "This is Touchdown. Over."

As they talk, the commander of the Seabee unit arrives and is waved over to the radio by Nelson. He listens as Marino describes the situation and a possible means of stabilizing the van. "Sir, I have talked with a Mr. Cassidy at the site. He has cranes and heavy forklifts, but no drivers. We'll need some welders and some lights."

"Marino, I have Lieutenant Buckley with me. He has been writing down the things you need."

"May I speak with him, sir?"

"Roger."

Buckley gets on the handset. "Yes, sir, Commander."

"Buck, do you have any kind of sling that would hold the weight of the vehicle?"

"Yes, sir. We'll load it on with the other stuff. I'll get the drivers and lights. We're pretty much prepackaged, so we should be on our way shortly."

"Outstanding. Do get here as soon as possible. Recon out."

"If you will excuse me, I'll get this stuff loaded."

Nelson nods. "Buck, we'll move one of the stallions over to your location. Good luck."

"Thank you, sir." He moves out of the room and disappears.

"Well, Mr. Val, we had better get going ourselves. We'll give you a call from the site, sir."

They get their stuff together, and move towards the door. "Good luck, gentlemen. This weather is giving us a short break, but it will not last. Good hunting."

"Thank you, sir."

The marine radioman packs up his gear and joins them as they leave. On their way out, Johnson turns to Chief Lang. "Thank you for the coffee and donuts, Chief. They were much appreciated."

"You're welcome, sir. Good luck."

They walk outside. The rain has stopped. But a brisk wind blows in from the southeast. They get into a Hummer and head for the waiting helicopters. When they arrive at the field, lights from the helicopters and the hangars shine off the wet concrete. The marines of the Third Platoon are being loaded as they drive up. Gunny Cabolero stands at the base of the ramp, directing the men aboard. Johnson watches as another Stallion taxies off towards the Seabee area. He walks over and joins Marshall and Sergeant Quan near the open hangar. Both men salute as he walks up. "At ease, gentlemen."

Sergeant Quan extends his hand. "Congratulations, Major Johnson."

"Thank you, Quan. How are we doing?"

"Fine, sir. We're waiting for Captain Neal. He ran over to the dispensary. We're short one corpsman. And he wanted to let Dr. Davies know we're ready to roll."

Cabolero walks up and salutes. "Sir, we have the men on board, and we're ready to roll as soon as the captain gets back."

"Good. We'll pack up, too, as soon as Dr. Davies gets here."

Johnson looks down the hangar at the two Cobra gunships parked there. He sees Captain Flint waving his hands towards his Cobra, and the marine crew chief and the navy line chief holding their hands up and shrugging. He watches as the maintenance officer joins them. "I need to have this thing back up, Commander." Night Moves looks into the man's face, looking for support.

"Captain Flint, I understand your situation. But you have to understand our problems. We have a major storm about to hit us and a Cobra with fourteen holes in it. We see both as dangers, and we're doing what we can to make sure they don't do any damage."

"But, sir." He looks into his eyes. No hope.

"Captain, not only is your Cobra deadlined, your two Harrier buddies accounted for eighteen holes in the airframes of their jets. So this is the end of the subject. They're down, and they will stay down."

"Aye, aye, sir."

He walks out the front of the hangar and looks across the wet concrete at a loaded Cobra. "Life is a bitch." He keys his radio. "Waco, this is Night Moves."

"Roger, sir."

"I'm going to borrow your ride. I want you to help the crews with their assignments here on the base."

"Aye, aye, sir. Sir, don't break it."

"Waco, it will be in the hands of a musician. When this is over, I'll show you that killer move I have invented." He waves his gunner over, and they walk out to the Cobra.

"We will again be the supreme beings of the air, guarding the very essence of American ideals."

"Yes, my leader. I will follow you into the jaws of death."

"A slight correction, in that you sit in front of me."

"Correct, supreme flying dude. I will go first to prepare the way."

"Have you ever thought of the kindness of the almighty, to allow you to be in the same aircraft as the maestro."

They check the helicopter as they walk around it. Down the line, two A-10s sit half in the shadows.

"Now, check these things out, Ratchet." The gunner joins him after checking a rocket pod. "I'll give them one thing. They are ugly."

"Yes, ugly. But can they tear up the countryside. I went to a demonstration of them down in Texas. That damn gun they have cut through a tank like butter. That aircraft is definitely an E-ticket ride."

"Yes, sir. We're locked and loaded. It's time to return to our element."

"You are correct. A fearful minion of the night belongs in the sky." They get on board and go through their preflight check. Flint keys his radio. "Bulldog, this is Night Moves. Over."

Johnson takes the handset. "Roger, Night Moves. This is Bulldog."

"Bulldog, we're strapped and ready to rock. Over."

"Roger. We're waiting for Dr. Davies and Captain Neal. It should only be a few minutes. Over."

"Roger, Bulldog. We'll stand by."

Ratchet keys his mike. "That Dr. Davies is a pretty ballsy babe. Oh, chosen one, who flies by the force."

"You're right. When we were talking, she told me that if she had not been a nuclear scientist, she would have been a marine."

"Your shitting me."

"I heard it straight from her. Her and I have this kind of special karma thing."

"No shit."

Neal catches sight of Susie and Laura down the hall talking to the head nurse. They peek into a room and then turn towards him.

"Doctor." Neal gets up to them. "We're going to be lifting off in a few minutes. They're loading now. How is Dr. Reddeer?"

"He is doing fine. They have him sedated. He was torn up pretty badly by the explosion. He just needs to get some rest."

"How about Chief Turvey?"

"Well, Laura checked on him. He is still in critical condition. They have him in ER. They think he is going to be fine."

"Great. Commander, we were short one corpsman. Have you got a replacement?"

"Yes, Captain. Dr. Rollens has decided to send one of the staff out with you." She raises her voice. "Which I personally think is a bone head idea."

"I heard that, Commander." Captain Rollens appears at the doorway of his office in full camos. He puts his medical bag over his shoulder and puts on his helmet. He walks up to the group. The others are stunned. "You're going out with the troops?"

He smiles. "Captain, I cut my teeth in Nam in the bush. We have all of the staff in, and the commander here is the best operator in the business."

"Don't give me that shit. I totally disagree about you going into the field on a night like this."

"I understand, Mary."

A tear rolls part way from her eye, she catches it with a Kleenex. "Well, then. You're blocking this hall. You need to be going, anyway." She leans over and kisses Rollens on the cheek. "You had better take care of yourself. Or I'll give you an enema with a fire hose."

"I will, Commander. I'll be back before four o'clock." They all start laughing as they head for the door; another corpsman is waiting and joins then. Neal calls forward to Johnson to let him know they are on the way. He hands the handset back to the radio operator. "They're on their way. Let's get loaded."

"Good luck, sir." Quan salutes as Johnson waves Agent Owens and Val to load.

"Well, take good care of those marines, staff."

"You know I will, Top. And by the way, neither of you better get dusted out there. You fuckers are buying the drinks back at the EM club when we get home." They all laugh and shake hands. Then Marshall and Cabolero run to the back of the helicopter and board. Johnson waits at the bottom of the ramp and watches the crewmen from his and the troop's helicopter. They check around the helicopter and talk with the pilot on their headsets.

Men run up the ramp at the Seabee yard, and the big door closes. It begins to taxi out onto the field. Night Moves's Cobra comes to life and begins to move out towards the field. The lights of the Hummer swing around the hangar and head for the rear of the helicopter. Neal jumps out and helps Susie and Laura out. He takes the corpsman with him and heads for his helicopter. The ramp is closing as they begin to taxi.

Susie and Laura run up the ramp and get to their seats. Dr. Rollens and Johnson clear the top of the ramp. The helicopter is already beginning to move. "This is a surprise, sir." Johnson points Rollens to a seat.

"You guys seem to need more medical help as the night gets older."

Johnson smiles. "Well, welcome to the team, sir." The helicopters taxi to the end of the runway and get their final clearance.

Their engines rev up, and the big Stallions roll forward and rise into the air. The Cobra settles in beside them as they all head eastward.

RUSSIAN SUBMARINE
THE GULF

The Russian submarine moves slowly in a circle at the contact point. The captain rechecks his position at the plotting table. The boat holds at 100 feet. "Sir, we continue to pick up random explosions from the southeast. We believe they are coming from the *Moskva* squadron."

"All right, let out the antenna. We'll attempt to contact the *Moskva*." Slowly, an antenna wire is released from the stern of the boat. It pays out to 1,000 feet behind the sub. It breaks the surface, and those on the boat listen for any air traffic. "Sir, we're clear and ready to transmit."

"Contact the *Moskva*."

Pstygo is near the radio when the first call comes in from the submarine. The men in the center look at each other and then cheer. Pstygo calls for silence. The radio operator calls out their response. Pstygo runs to the ladder and up to the bridge to get the admiral. The fires on the *Otlichnyy* flare up as the ship continues to list to port. The light of the fires is reflected from the lenses of the admiral's binoculars. He watches as the *Sovremennyy* destroyer pulls off about 200 yards to the starboard side of the sinking ship. The port side torpedo tubes are run out and prepared to launch. Pstygo passes out of the bridge to the port side flying bridge. "Sir, we have a contact with the submarine."

Sokolov lowers his binoculars but does not take his eyes off the burning ship. "All right, Pstygo. I will join you in the combat center in a minute." He readjusts his binoculars as two torpedoes are fired at the burning *Otlichnyy*. The ship seems serene as it drifts to the stern of the *Moskva*. In a split second, they hit one after the other. Two huge explosions burn into the night sky. The ship rolls bottom up and dives for the cool deep water of the Gulf. The admiral and the others with him salute the fallen warrior.

"Now, Mr. Pstygo, let's go talk with the submarine commander."

They move down to the combat center and over to the radio. "Sir, we are having some difficulty at our end because of the damage on the antennas. You're on the scrambler." The admiral talks with the submarine commander and brings him up to speed on what has happened. He explains the latest explosions that the boat keeps picking up at random. He passes on the information from the Americans about the two Cuban submarines, and that they believe one has moved out of the Frozen Forest, while the other is waiting to pick up the pieces. "Because of your situation, Comrade Admiral, we should return to provide security for those of you left."

"Just a moment." The admiral moves over to the plotting table. Pstygo points to their location and the location of the Kilo boat of the Cubans in the Frozen Forest. He then marks the location of the Russian submarine and a guess as to the possible location of the loose Cuban boat.

"Sir, the submarine is fifty miles in front of us. At our present rate of speed, it would take us four hours to reach him. We are barely getting out fifteen knots." The admiral runs his finger along the line of his ships. He stops his finger at the suggested location of the Cuban. He gets back on the radio.

"Commander, in all probability, the Cuban boat has passed your location and will reach us in about two and a half to three hours. You can be at the Frozen Forest in about one and a half hours. We should be back in operation well before the sub gets into firing range. So I am ordering you to go after the second submarine and then continue on to the Americans' picket line. If both of us are successful, you will have cleared the last obstacle in our path."

"I understand, sir. I wish you luck, Comrade Admiral."

"Good hunting, Commander." He hands the handset back to the operator. "I hope we are up in time for our visitor."

"I do, too, sir."

The commander hangs the mike up. "Bring the antenna in and set a depth of 400 feet." He and the executive officer look over the maps of the seabed in front of them. The Frozen Forest is towards the top of the map. From the direction they are coming, a deep channel runs up the middle of the formations. Along the channel, three deep valleys run off each side. At the end of the channel, a high ridge line cuts across the channel. The commander points to the valleys. "In one of these, the little Kilo boat will be hiding. Set course at 320 true, and give me full speed ahead." The order is repeated and the submarine pushes forward in the inky depths. About five miles north of their location, another submarine slides through the darken depths.

"Captain, we have a transmission being sent about five miles south of us. We would guess it to be the Russian submarine in contact with the squadron. They are now heading northwest at speed."

"Good." The captain looks at his charts. "From that last explosion, I would guess the squadron to be about here. We will reach them in about three hours. The number two boat will deal with the Russian submarine. We will deal with the remaining ships." They turn the boat a few degrees farther south and continue on their mission.

ULTIMA
WASHINGTON, D.C.

"Mr. President." Van Nar motions towards the screen. "We have received confirmation that her sister ship has sunk the Russian destroyer *Otlichnyy*. Communications between the Russian Sierra submarine and the *Moskva* has sent the submarine after the number two Cuban boat. The ships' movements and positions are on the screen. We believe that the Cuban number one boat is somewhere in this area." A yellow marker appears on the screen, and a proposed course is plotted. "Also, we have the bomb recovery team en route to the number two bomb site. They should be on the ground in about fifteen minutes." Admiral Hillings receives a call and talks in low tones with the other party. He hangs up and calls an aide over, who goes up to Van Nar. She gets on a phone.

"Mr. President. I just got off the phone with submarine command. We have a call coming in from a boomer, coming in from the south Atlantic. It's an Ohio class sub, the USS *Georgia*. She was returning to base and detoured around Cuba. She is in a position to reach the eye of the storm in about two hours."

"Will that be in time to save the men in the rafts?" The president looks at the screen. The rafts are marked in red in the swirl of the storm clouds. The red circles seem to be drifting farther apart.

"It is believed that the rafts will arrive in the eye first. We should have Captain Emmett give us his best guess."

Emmett goes to the podium. He points up to the swirling mass of the storm. "Evita's eye is now thirty miles across. The pull on the rafts is about fifteen knots, although that changes as the winds change." The picture is brought down to the eye itself. "The rafts will have about an hour in the eye for rescue. The boomer will have to get them before they reach this point."

A green line cuts across the eye at fifteen miles. "At this point, they will be running at fifteen knots." A yellow line appears at ten miles from the trailing edge. "At this point, the pull will increase to twenty knots." A red line appears at five miles. "We believe that the rate of pull from the whirlpool will be sufficient enough to pull them at up to twenty-five-plus knots. If the boomer is in this zone, he will need flank speed to contend with the current and will be in extreme danger."

"My God." The president shakes his head. "And the weather at the bomb sites, will it hold?"

"Sir, they have about an hour and a half. The weather will then turn ugly till around 0300. After that, there will be a strange stillness for about forty-five minutes. Then the full fury of the leading edge of the eye will hit."

"Thank you, Captain. Mr. Brant, where do we stand with the evacuation?"

Brant turn in his chair. "I have been talking with General Becker. He has been called away for a short time. But from what he is showing me, it is going great and will meet the time frame to clear the area south of the city. I will have him bring us up to date as soon as he gets back."

"Very good. Could I talk with you for a few minutes Mr. Brant?"

"Yes, sir." He gets up and goes over to the president's desk. He gets up, and they go out into the hallway. A marine guard closes the door behind them.

QUINTANO'S COMMAND
CUBA

"General, please sit down so that the doctor can finish with your wound." Quintano sits on the step on the back of the MT-LB tracked vehicle. He looks over the area on top of the mesa. Burning tracks and trucks smolder everywhere. Tanks and field pieces are cast about in bent and torn shapes. He watches as an ACRV-2 command track moves up the road, then pulls off to the side and heads for his location.

The track commander walks up to Quintano. "Sir, your new ride is coming over now. It's been a pleasure having you on board."

"Thank you, Lieutenant. You can rejoin your outfit."

The back of the command track opens up. Vargas jumps out and runs up to him. "Shit, sir. We thought we had lost you. We have some great news for you."

"Do you have something to drink? Water is getting a little old."

"Get the general a cup of coffee." One of the aides brings him a cup of coffee, and they bring him a folding chair. He takes a deep drink and moves his head to stretch his neck. He forgets about the wound, and it stings with pain.

"Sir, the president is in Matanzas. He landed at the airbase a short time ago. He has made contact with Colonel Augular. The forces out of Pinar del Rio are now with us. They have made contact at San Antonio de los Banos. And Colonel Zino has moved his forces around Havana. They are attacking from the rear of the forces to our front."

"Thank, God. There has been too much killing this night. Let's move up to meet with Zino for the final push into the city."

Quintano is helped into the track, and the others climb in and shut the rear doors. As the track pulls back to the main road, they join the column of vehicles moving north.

COMMAND CENTER
CUBA

"General Morales, we have confirmed that our units are trapped between Quintano and Zino's units. And the city is surrounded. We have the two Hinds fueled and ready to fly."

"Very well. Get my things loaded. We'll wait to see what their next move will be. I know that Fidel is on his way to Matanzas. Some time soon, he will be moving up to Havana. We may intercede in that plan."

"Sí, sir. We'll be prepared to leave at a moment's notice."

Morales moves a glass over to the center of his desk, and pours it half full of dark rum. He lifts it to his lips and drinks it down. His eyes are fixed on the opposite wall.

ULTIMA
WASHINGTON, D.C.

Captain Van Nar walks to the podium as the president and Secretary Brant come back into the room. "Gentlemen, we have confirmed that Havana is now surrounded. The forces of General Quintano are consolidating their positions, with Colonel Zino's command now in a blocking position. The fighting south of the city is now sporadic. We believe that individual units are surrendering to Quintano's forces. It is now 2300 hours. We believe that General Quintano will enter the city proper by 0100 our time."

Brant sits back down. "Thank you, Captain."

"Gentlemen, the president has asked me to present a worst-case scenario. If we are unable to disarm the last bomb, specifically, what would be the aftermath of a five-kiloton bomb going off so close to land? And what would be our response to such a situation? Please have your staffs work up possible contingency plans.

"It is to be understood, that we have the utmost optimism that Dr. Davies and the marines will be able to disarm the last bomb. And all available resources will be put at their disposal.

"President Wayne has a meeting with the ambassadors from the Gulf area at midnight. With all the fighting and actions spread across the entire area, they're to be briefed on the situation. Please have some of your staff members ready to accompany us to the meeting for specific questions.

"Thank you, everyone." Brant goes back to his paperwork and snatches a quick glance at the moving screens.

NEWS STATION KNLT
NEW ORLEANS

At the TV station, the eleven o'clock news is just coming on. The weatherman at the station is going over the latest pictures of the storm. They are showing a list of things about the approach of Evita. The anchorman takes a cue. "Thanks, Ken. We have a live report from out at the naval base. We'll go to Darin Bodine at the location." Bodine comes up on the screen, standing in front of a chain link fence. The lights in the background shine from the hangars.

"This is Bob Maxwell standing in for Darin Bodine here at NAS New Orleans. The base is still closed to reporters, and flights out have fallen to a minimum. Because of the activity in the Gulf, a flight of jets will leave and relieve another group out in the Gulf. We did have a pair of air force A-10 all-weather aircraft fly in earlier. The base liaison said that they had flown in some whole blood and other medical supplies from their base in Georgia.

"Since around eight o'clock, it has been pretty calm. But about twenty minutes ago, three of the marines' big Jolly Green Giants were suddenly moved up to the forward hangars. They were loaded with what looked like a platoon of armed marines. They took off to the east with a Cobra gunship as escort. We'll run the film."

The film shows the marines loading and the three helicopters taking off and heading east. "OK, we're back. That happened just a little while ago. I talked with the liaison officer. He would not confirm or deny that they were after another of the Russian mines.

"There are also a lot of rumors going around that a large group of dead and injured marines and navy personnel were brought in earlier. The liaison office did say that at one of the locations, the recovery team had come upon a large smuggling operation, that they were forced to return fire, and that some casualties are confirmed. The base is now getting set for Evita. This is Bob Maxwell for KNLT news, at the naval base."

"Thanks, Bob, for that live report."

"In other news around the city...." The anchor moves on with the day's news.

NEWS VAN
NEW ORLEANS SUBURBS

"From the police calls, we know they met them at this intersection. So keep an eye out for any sheriff units."

"Right, Marcey. Now sit down for a few minutes so I can drive safely to wherever we're going." The news van cruises down the side streets going north. Some flares being put out off to their right front draw all eyes forward. "That might be it, Marcey." They pull down the road and pull up to the sheriff's car in the road.

Marcey slides the side door open and gets out. "Hi, Deputy. We heard there was some kind of activity out here and came out to get it for the evening news."

"Hi, Marcey. I watch you on the TV." They shake hands.

"Is there something going on out here?"

"I don't really know. They called and asked me to put out some flares at my location. Another deputy is up at the CES yard, but I haven't heard from him in a little while. They're some marines up there also. And a helicopter came in earlier."

"Is it all right for us to go up and take a look?"

"Well, they didn't tell me that you couldn't."

"Thanks, Deputy. We'll go up and see what's going on." She gets back in the van and slides the door shut. "Yes, we're on our way. This may be a bomb site." The van moves up the street and passes the closed buildings along the route. "If I remember right, CES is at the very end of the street." They pull around the curve in the road and see a Hummer parked up at the entrance of the CES premises.

The other guard gets on the radio and calls in to the site. He speaks for a few minutes and puts the radio down. "Ma'am, there is a party coming up to the gates. You can talk with the officer in charge. So if you would please return to your van and wait for him." She looks by the men into the yard. The only lights on are at the very back of the facility.

"All right, thank you. We'll wait over here." She walks back to the people at the van. The man inside flips some switches, and the panel in front of him lights up. He talks to someone back at the station as the man on top finishes up. "Len, you and Cary get ready to go. I think we have come up on something big." Len adjusts his camera on his shoulder, and Cary plugs in a cord and hands Marcey her mike. "We're ready to rock. Let's step behind the van and get everything set properly."

Marcey walks out into the darkness behind the van a few paces. Len turns on the light above the camera and hits the trigger. "Man, that light is bright out here." Marcey gets her bearings and begins talking into the mike. The others set their exposures and levels for the sound.

The man inside the van leans out the door. "You're up, babe." As they stand in the darkness, lights from a vehicle inside the fence light up the two marines at the gate.

"Let's get it." Marcey walks to the side of the van with the gates to her back. The camera goes on.

Back at the station, the anchorman is given a prompt and a hand signal. "Ladies and gentlemen, we have a breaking story coming in from Marcey Lane out at the CES company site. So were going live with her."

"This is Marcey Lane, out at the CES company site. We believe that this is one of the sites where a Russian mine fell. We are trying to get continuation from the commanding officer. As you can see, the marines are already here." As the camera focuses on the gates, two Hummers drive through and out into the street. One continues down the street about 100 yards. The other one pulls off to the side, and men get out and begin running along the side of the street, putting out flares. The men in the Hummer down the road run a line of flares across the road. They then begin walking back towards the others, putting out flares every ten feet. Marino talks to the guards and then walks over to the van.

Marcey turns to meet him as he walks up. "Commander, we're live. I'm Marcey Lane with KNLT. Is this one of the sites where one of the weapons from the Russian bomber fell?" The light of the camera catches Marino.

"Ma'am, you're going to have to leave this area." Their attention is drawn to the sound of a large helicopter passing overhead and turning to their right. The Stallions swing around and begin coming down onto the road. The cameraman catches the event as the three helicopters settle to the ground, and their ramps are lowered. From the lead helicopter, marines unload. Some go up and through the front gate. Others move out around the perimeter of the helicopters. Their movement and weapons are caught on the camera.

A Hummer pick-up truck is unloaded from the third helicopter, and a load of navy men are driven in through the gate. As the engines die on the helicopters, the ramp on the second Stallion is lowered. "Marcey, wait here." Marino moves by the first helicopter and disappears behind it. He catches Johnson and Owens coming down the ramp. "Mr. Johnson, we have a news team that got this far. They're off to the side. I need to get with Buckley on the equipment."

"Yes, sir. We'll deal with it." Marino catches a ride on another Hummer and heads for the site.

A Cobra circles the group and then lands towards the front of the road. The camera catches the entire show.

Johnson walks around the back of the first helicopter and sees the news van. He and Owens walk up to them. "Major, is this one of the bomb sites?" Johnson and Owens reach the van. "We're live," Marcey looks at his nametag, "Major Johnson. Could you explain what is going on?"

"Miss Lane, you will have to leave this area. Yes, this is a site. One of the mines landed in Mr. Cassidy's yard here. We have a team in to defuse it and move it back to the base."

"Major, we are receiving word that at one of the other sites, the marines took some casualties. And I noticed that you were limping as you came up. We're you there?"

"Yes, ma'am. We did sustain some casualties. Some shrapnel hit me. We must get inside to remove the mine. You will be escorted back out to the main road."

"I noticed that this gentleman is with the DEA. Why is he with your group?"

"I'll let Mr. Owens explain that."

"Mr. Owens, what part is the DEA playing in these bomb recoveries?"

"I work out of our New Orleans office. We're more familiar with the surrounding areas, so our office was asked to assist the marines where we could."

"We also have a report that one of your agents was killed at one of the other sites. Is that true?"

"Yes. Agent Sandovol was killed at one of the other sites. The marines accidentally ran into a large smuggling operation. Agent Sandovol was killed in the ensuing gunfight. I would like to add that Agent Sandovol was a good agent and friend."

Susie and Laura walk around the helicopter with Dr. Rollens. They see Johnson and Owens with the TV crew. As they continue to walk towards the gate, Marcey calls out to them.

"Dr. Davies, Dr. Davies. Could we please speak with you?"

"Well let's make it quick." She walks over with Johnson and Owens. Marshall joins her and the others.

"Doctor, I'm Marcey Lane from KNLT. I had a chance to interview you last year."

"Right. How are you doing, Marcey?"

"I'm fine, Doctor. Could I ask you a few questions? What is America's top nuclear weapons person doing here?"

"I'm here as an adviser to the marines detachment. Because of this new type of mine, they asked if I would assist them in their disposal efforts."

"So these are not nuclear weapons?"

"Correct, but they do have a large warhead. I would guess about 2,000 pounds. So they could be relatively nasty if they went off."

"Is this the last of the bombs or mines?"

"I believe there is one more to disarm. But with the storm coming in, we are in a hurry to complete the task."

"I understand, Doctor. Thank you for talking with us."

"Well, there you are. Confirmation from Dr. Susie Davies that the weapons are not nuclear, and they are down to the last two. We have been advised to pull back to the main road in case there is an explosion. With all of the scrap metal in there, everything for about a mile around could be hit with shrapnel. This is Marcey Lane at one of the bomb sites for KNLT."

"Let's pack it up. We got the story." They move their stuff back into the van and lower the dish. A Hummer pulls up next to them, and they follow it back to the main road. They notice that the Hummer pulls in beside one of the deputies and relieves him in the road. His lights soon join theirs as they both drive back into town.

Back at KNLT, the anchor says, "That was live from Marcey at the bomb site. We'll have today's sports up next." A commercial comes on, and they all relax. The producer in the booth picks up his phone and talks to someone. He nods his head. "Get me Marcey on the radio." The radio in the van blares, and Marcey picks up the mike.

"Yeah, Larry. I'm going to put you on the speaker." She flips a switch.

"All right everyone. I have good news for you guys. First, we have a call about a large fire down near Bourbon Street from fallen electrical wires. And the other is that we had a call from CNN. They are picking up your live segment from the bomb site. So congratulations." Everyone in the van cheers as Marcey and Len high-five in the back.

BOMB SITE, NUMBER TWO
JUNKYARD IN LOUISIANA

Marshall gets out of the Hummer and helps Susie and Laura out. There are men setting up lights, and big forklifts bring in pallets from the helicopters. Two large cranes are coming up the road, and Marino and another man are directing them to certain spots. She sees Johnson and another man talking off to the side of a large pile of cars. He shines his light up the back of the stack and talks some more. "So where is the bomb?"

"I think it is up this way, Susie." Marshall leads them around men setting up lights to where Johnson and the other man are talking. "Well, Susie." Johnson motions her over. "This is Mr. Cassidy. He owns this yard. He and the others are the ones who found the mine."

"How do you do, ma'am." They shake hands.

"So where is it?"

"Right up there, ma'am." He turns his flashlight up the stack of cars. It stops at the van.

"All I see is that van."

"Yes, ma'am. It's stuck in the roof. Sergeant Bonds is next to it, and big Bo the deputy is inside."

"Holy shit." Susie looks in disbelief.

"My sentiment totally, ma'am."

Marshall and the others laugh. "Well put, Susie."

They watch as Marino and Buckley direct two cranes in behind the stack. The two sixty-foot squirt booms move up into the night air. Two large forklifts run their tines through junk cars and lift them up under the leaning stack. They position the cars under the top of the stack and lock the lift in place. They climb out and run over to the end of the cables banging from the two cranes. A harness is hooked on one of the cranes and lifted back up and over the top of the stack. The floodlights are beginning to come on-line, and the area of the van is suddenly bathed in light.

Marino runs up on top of one of the cars at the bottom of the stack, and lifts a bullhorn up to talk with Bonds. "Sergeant, we're going to lower a harness down to you. Slip it on and we'll lift you off the stack. Wave your hand if you understand." Bonds slowly lifts his right hand and gently waves. Marino leans back and tells Buckley to go ahead. The crane swings over the top of the stack and stops above the van. The cable is slowly lowered towards Bonds. "Tell me when you can reach it, Sergeant."

It lowers to within five feet of the top and stops; Marino calls out directions as the ball at the end of the cable moves over a few feet. He has it lowered to within two feet of Bonds. He slowly reaches out and pulls the harness to him. He slides his arms through the loops and fastens the belt around his waist. He signals that he is in. "Slowly, up ten feet." The harness goes tight around Bonds, and he is gently lifted straight up. The stack trembles just a little. The crane lifts him up over the top of the stack and lowers him off to the side near Buckley. The navy men help him unbuckle, and he moves over to Susie and Johnson.

"That is some damn crane work. Hell, those boys got a job here anytime. Good work, Navy," Cassidy calls out.

Bonds joins Johnson and Susie. He salutes and tells them of the bombs position and the situation with the deputy. "And sir, it is real rickety up there. You have the feeling it could go any minute."

"It looked that way from here, Sergeant." Johnson looks back up at the van. A navy man is lifted in the harness and lowered towards the van. The other crane lifts a sling with two large metal bars at its bottom.

Neal joins them. "Sir, I was going to leave for the last site. I'll take Gunny Cabolero with me, and four men. Mr. Owens has asked to go with us, also."

"That sounds good, Captain. You're taking the Blackhawk, right?"

"Yes, sir. They have a grid marked about fifteen miles east of here. It's in some kind of natural flood plan."

"All right, call me as soon as you get on site."

"Yes, sir. Gentlemen, let's go. Bonds will drive us out to the gate, and he and the two gate guards will head back to the base to help Sergeant Quan."

"Very good." Johnson watches the men load Hummers and head for the gate. "God, I hope these last two go good."

Susie grabs his arm and squeezes it. "I hope so, Major Johnson."

Johnson turns back to Cassidy. "Mr. Cassidy, I think it is time to let you get back to your family. We much appreciate your assistance in this matter."

"You're right, Major. My wife is probably worried sick. Good luck." They shake hands as a Hummer is brought up to drive him back to the office to get his truck.

As the Hummer pulls away with Cassidy, the others watch as a Blackhawk rises into the sky and flies off towards the northeast.

BOMB SITE, NUMBER ONE
LOUISIANA

In a log block house near bomb site one, six men sit drinking and sweating in the confines of the logs. Behind them towards the west, a twenty-eight-foot cruiser sits waiting. It is pulled up under a series of camouflage nets that rest down on the water level.

At a table in the center of the room, a woman rests her head in her hands trying to catch a bit of sleep. The red of her hair is caught in the light of a lantern, its straight follicles combed back. It runs half way down her back and is cut off straight across the bottom.

"This is bullshit, waiting here all day while this bitch tries to guess as to the arrival of some asshole from Texas. The least she could do is service a few of us while we wait. Shit, she has fucked every asshole with money from Dade County to New Orleans."

"Knock the shit off, Bryan, before you get your ass blown off."

"Well, Bob, that wasn't the particular place I intended to have blown."

"I'm warning you, Bryan, knock it off."

He walks over to the table near the sleeping figure. He stands looking down at her. "I don't think a blow job is out of the question."

He suddenly tenses up; he can feel the push of a 9 mm Glock at the base of his penis. He freezes and looks down at the sleeping figure. Her head lifts from her arms, and Natalie stands up. At five feet, eight inches, she almost looks him directly in the eyes. Her white tee-shirt fails to hide her full breasts. Sweat emphasizes her nipples.

"So you want some action?" Her green eyes twinkle in the lantern light. "If I pull this trigger and blow your dick and balls off, I guess you will have a cunt? Right?"

"Yes, ma'am. I was only kidding."

"Oh, just kidding. Well, I'm not. You fucking sorry piece of shit. Let me lay this out for you. You get within ten feet of me, and I will turn you into a girl. Then I will have the other guys do you on the table here for me. So have a clue, here, asshole."

"Yes, ma'am. I understand."

"Bob, get this piece of shit out of here."

"All right, Natalie. He just has a little cabin fever."

She withdraws the gun. "Get the shit out of here. Bob, how many men are outside?"

"We have eight on guard, and two waiting with the jet skis to do the pick up. We have two standing by with the boat. And these four to guard the block house."

"Get them out on guard. We should get a call from the plane soon." She goes over to a refrigerator, takes out a beer, and takes a long drink. She lets some of it dribble down her chin on to her tee-shirt. She looks at Bob. His eyes are glued on the falling droplets.

"See something you like, *Bob*?"

He shakes his head. "Man, you are a real piece of work. I have to admit, you got one hell of a body on you."

"Well, thank you. Now let's get going so we can get back to Miami. And the good life."

"Right, don't forget your night vision stuff for outside."

She smiles as she slips on the night camouflage jacket and tucks in the bottom. She finishes her beer and grabs her helmet.

BOMB SITE, NUMBER TWO
JUNKYARD IN LOUISIANA

Bo watches out the side window as a man is raised over the top of the stack. He loses sight of him and sees the sling lifted up behind the stacks. It disappears.

"Hello, Deputy."

The voice catches Bo off guard. "Holy shit." He grabs his chest as the man at the passenger side window smiles.

"I'm sorry I startled you. I'm Chief Ashman. We are going to try and slip a sling under the van. It will stabilize it. So just hang in there."

"Damn, Chief. You almost made me shit my pants." The chief swings gently in the harness as he works his way to the front of the van. He uses hand signals and his throat mike to communicate with Buckley, who is up on the car with Marino. Buckley calls the moves of the crane back to the operator.

The chief is lowered to look under the front of the van. It sits high enough to get the sling under. He signals for the sling to be brought down. It is lowered to about two feet above the van. Ashman is raised and grabs a nylon strap attached to the front bar. He is swung back into position at the front. Both he and the sling move as one. Bo watches as Ashman is lowered parallel with the stack and disappears down the front of the van. He watches as a metal bar is pulled down, and can hear the chief working under the front. Ashman slides the bar under the front of the van, up against the front rims. The cables attached to the ends of the bar swing loosely by the two side windows.

Ashman raises back up by the front window and gives Bo a thumbs up. He is lifted up and moves to the back of the van. He calls down on his throat mike. "Sir, I'll need some help getting the bar under the back. We may need to cut some metal away."

"Hang in there. I'm coming up." Buckley hands the radio over to Marino and jumps down from the car. The others watch in silence as the crane with the sling slowly lowers to the top of the van. Ashman is lifted up and detaches the sling. Bo can hear the metal ring on the sling bump up against the top.

Buckley gets into a harness and has a compact cutting torch attached to a nylon sling at his waist. The crane comes over and down to him, and he is hooked up. In a few seconds he is rising into the air with the cutting torch hanging a couple of feet below him. As he comes over the top of the stack, he tells Marino to position him behind the chief. Soon both are hanging near the back of the van. They discuss their next move.

Ashman takes the torch and begins to cut away metal crushed under the back of the van. Buckley is moved up to the passenger side of the van. "Hi, Deputy. I'm Lieutenant Buckley. We're going to have to cut away some of the metal at the back of the van. As soon as we can get the bar positioned, we'll get a harness up to lift you out."

"Hell, that sounds good to me, Lieutenant. My butt is getting sore sitting here."

"All right, Bo. We'll get it as fast as we can."

Buckley lifts up, over the stack, and down to the ground. He tells them which tools he will need, and the men run to retrieve them from the trucks and pallets. A bag is filled with the tools and is attached to his harness. Again he lifts up and over to the van.

Susie and the others sit on a crushed car and watch the show. "You know, if this wasn't so deadly, it'd be kind of pretty. Like watching Peter Pan or something."

"You know, Susie." Marshall looks over at her. "That same thought just passed through my mind."

The others all laugh. As a well-placed elbow catches him in the side. Marshall tightens up from the impact. "You butt."

Buckley moves back in and takes a large set of pliers out of the tool bag. He grabs a piece of loose metal and pulls it back as the chief cuts it off at the bottom. They work together, and pieces of the smashed cars are pulled and thrown down the stack. A sudden gust of wind slams into the back of the stack. As they all watch, the huge mound of metal shakes and moves slightly.

"Did you see that?" Laura grabs Susie's arm.

"Yeah, this looks like it's going to be a real fun one. Right, Top Sergeant?"

"Yes, ma'am. Susie, our hearts and thoughts will be with you up there, as you save America."

Susie laughs out loud. "Oh, no! I wouldn't go anywhere with out your support, Top. You had better get your wings on, because we're going flying."

Another gust of wind rocks the stacks. The torch flickers and sparks as Ashman works deeper under the rear of the van. Buckley continues to pull out cut pieces. They glow in the darkness as they fly through the air. Bo can see sparks flying in the rearview mirror as Ashman cuts metal away on his side. He cuts a slot in the metal back to the rear drums. "I think I got it, sir." Buckley comes in close with his flashlight. He runs the beam under the back. "It looks good, Chief. Let me get the sling down."

They raise him up, and he pulls the metal bar to the back of the van. "Are you ready, Chief?"

"Yes, sir." Buckley slides the bar off the top, and the chief grabs one side as Buckley grabs the other. They work the sling down and push it into the slot cut under the back of the van. When they get it in place, they check the fit.

"It looks good. I'll check the one in front." Buckley is moved around to the front of the van and lowered to check the sling. "All right, I'm out of here, Chief. I'll send the ball back up."

"Aye, sir."

Ashman watches as Buckley flies over the top and disappears. As he hits the ground, one of his men takes the tool bag. As another helps Buckley get un-snapped from the ball and out of the harness. He runs over to the front and climbs up next to Marino. "We should be ready to put tension on the sling, sir."

"Good job, Buck." They watch as the ball is lowered to Ashman, and he works it over to the top of the van. He hooks the sling up and signals for the lift. The cable moves slowly up until the steel cables on each side of the van pull tight. "That's it."

Ashman signals down to Marino. Marino calls over and has the crane locked in position. A third crane moves into position and begins extending its boom. It lowers the ball, and a harness is fastened on. It rises up and is lowered next to the van. The cables from the sling block the two front doors. Ashman moves around to the back and tries the rear doors. The doors are jammed and crushed in place. He calls down to Marino and Buckley.

Marino and Buckley confer on the top of the car, and then Marino calls up to Ashman. "Chief, go ahead and cut them off." He relights the torch and begins cutting the hinges at the back of the van. As he cut through the top hinge, the door slides down and falls on the stack below. As soon as both doors are removed, he brings the harness around.

"All right, Bo. Here's the harness. You'll have to climb back here and get it on. We'll have you down in just a few minutes."

"That's great. Can I move now?"

"Yeah, work your way around the bomb.

Bo climbs back over the seats and squeezes by the body of the bomb. The van squeaks as he moves inside. He slips the harness on and sits on the back of the van. His feet dangle out as Ashman signals for the line to be brought up. Bo is lifted up and out the back of the van. He swings about six feet out as the chief makes some last minute checks. "OK, Bo. We're out of here." He calls down to Marino and both men are lifted over the top of the stack and lowered to the ground. Navy men help Bo out of the harness. Two corpsmen take him over to a Hummer and have him sit down. They check him out.

"We're ready for your people, Mr. Johnson."

"Yes, sir." He slides off the top of the car and lands on his bad leg. "Shit." He rubs it as the others climb down. One of the sailors and Chief Ashman bring over the harness.

"Well, Top, it's your turn to fly."

"Thanks, Chief. You guys did a good job."

"That's what they pay us for." He helps Marshall into the harness and describes the layout of the van. Laura helps Susie into her harness and adjusts some of the straps. The chief looks both of them over and checks the harnesses. 'They have to be tight, or they will cut into you." They move over to the side of the car that Marino and Buckley are standing on. "Sir, they're ready to go."

"Thanks, chief." Buckley describes how to move around in the harness. He has them both check their radio mikes. He turns around to Marino. "They're ready, sir."

"Very good, Buck. I'll be in contact with you from here. Be careful, Susie, and you, too, Top."

"We will, Mr. Marino. Just don't let that thing fall." Susie and Marshall walk around the stack. The Seabees hook them up and await the command to lift.

"I'll go first, Susie, with the tool bag."

"What a gentlemen. Be careful, Top."

The man in front of him signals up. His voice trails behind him as he is lifted into the air. "I will." Marshall comes over the top of the stack and talks with Marino to position him at the side of the van. They move him to the back, and he climbs in, trailing the steel cable. He calls down to Susie. "Susie, I'm next to the bomb. The retard fins have crushed the roof in about two feet. And the end of the bomb is stuck through the bottom of the van. The access panel is turned to the side and the van kind of shimmies when you move. We'll need another hand light." One of the men hands her another light, and she clips it on her harness.

"You're just full of good news, Top. Here I come."

She sails straight up about forty feet, and then is swung over the top of the stack. She glides over the van and is lowered near the rear door. She can see Marshall reaching out to help her in. She talks her way to the edge of the doorframe and grabs Marshall's hand. He pulls her into the van and helps get her cable slacked. The crushed roof makes it hard to move around, and the panel is on the tight side of the bomb. Deep scratches run up the side where the casing tore through the metal top. Susie and Marshall take up places around the casing. He moves to an area near the back doors. She slides up against the side of the van on the passenger side. Her hand passes down the black stripe to the access plate, and she verifies the number two with Marshall. He calls back to the command helicopter with the information.

Johnson talks with Bo and thanks him for his help. He has a Hummer brought up and arranges for him and Val to ride back to the main gate. Bo shakes their hands and goes over to Buckley and Chief Ashman. "I wanted to thank you boys for getting me out of that thing." He shakes their hands then gets in the Hummer.

"We're glad you're all right, Bo." He waves goodbye, and the Hummer moves out. When they reach the front gate, Bo is surprised to see the three big helicopters parked in the street. "Holy shit! When did these big boys show up?"

"While you were up in the van." Val shakes his hand and heads for the command helicopter as Bo gets into his cruiser and begins working his way around the helicopters and off down the road. As Val walks up the ramp, the radio operator hands him a headset. "Sir, the link is up now. Just hit the button, and you're on the air." Val puts on the headset and keys the mike. He is instantly in contact with the war room in Moscow.

WAR ROOM
MOSCOW

In the war center in Moscow, Shagan nods to General Kuznetsov. The seventh envelope is opened and he is ready to begin sending the numbers for the bomb. He and Val check the number of the bomb that Susie has called down and verify the codes. He calls out the first number to Val as Shagan talks with Admiral Sokolov on the *Moskva*.

"I understand, Admiral. We will be in touch with the Americans if things continue to deteriorate. As I told you, they are now disarming the seventh bomb. And Morales is about to be thrown out in Cuba. This has been a costly night for all concerned. I will pass on your messages to Secretary Sholenska. We continue to wish you the best, Admiral."

Shagan hangs up the phone and looks up at their tracking screen as the numbers are read off to Val. He fights off a feeling of impotence, caused by not being able to send Sokolov anything other than words of confidence. He walks back to the table and picks up some notes. "I will be with Secretary Sholenska. I am to be informed of any changes that may occur."

COMMAND HELICOPTER
OUTSIDE JUNKYARD

Val calls the first number up to Marshall and he gives it to Susie. Marshall marks the number on a pad. Susie turns the first screw and backs it out. As she hands it to Marshall, a gust of wind rocks the stack and the van. "Wooo." Susie grabs on to the bomb and waits for the movement to quit.

"Damn." Marshall looks out the back at the stack. "This thing feels like it's alive." The second number is called up to them and verified. It is quickly removed and given to Marshall. Susie takes the third number.

"There is one screw on here that was hit by the metal when it came through the roof." A deep scar runs across the panel and passes through the screw head. Marshall moves over and takes a look at the screw. The van moves with his movement. "We'll probably need a drill to get that one. "I agree, and please try not to shake us off the pile." She smiles and hands him the screw.

Johnson watches from the ground as they work in the van. "Sir, you have a call from Bulldog 2."

"Roger, Bulldog 1."

"Sir, we're down. We just got to the top of a finger of land about 400 feet long, sticking out into a salt marsh. There is water and tall grass north of us, and Owens says there's a channel about 300 feet east that runs into the Gulf. We can hear waves breaking south of us, and there is another finger of land about 500 feet northwest of us. We all have a funny feeling about this place. Like that feeling you got when they told you scary stories late at night."

"Roger. Are there any signs of anyone having been around there?"

"Owens and Cabolero are working their way out to the point. Owens has us all looking like crazy for snakes and anything else that moves."

"Very good. The alert force can be loaded and sent."

"We're OK. I'll get back to you if we find anything."

"Bulldog 2 out." Johnson hands the handset back. "Get me the Cobra."

The operator calls out to the helicopters, "Sir, I have Night Moves."

"Night Moves, this is Bulldog."

"Roger."

"I just talked with the recon team at the next site. Nothing is going on, but they all seem to have a bad feeling about the area. I would like you to be ready to move at a minute's notice. I'll send you in first, for fire support."

"Roger. We're ready to fly."

"Bulldog out."

The wind gusts and blows water spray into the air. A gentle rain begins to fall on the site. Lightning sparks to the east. Johnson watches Marino talk with Buckley. He jumps down and runs to the back of the stack. He walks over to the side of the car. "Is there a problem?"

"Just a small one. They have requested a drill to remove one of the screws. It got crushed when the bomb came through the roof. We'll have to pull Top Marshall out to get it up there." The wind gusts harder as Johnson climbs up next to Marino.

"They're going to pull me out. I'll be right back with the drill."

"All right, I think I'll just wait here till you get back." He slides to the back of the van and prepares to lift out. The cable goes tight, and he is lifted out and up at the same time. As he swings above the van, he sees Johnson and Marino on the car at the base of the stack. He then begins to move up and over the top. They lower him down, and Buckley clips the drill onto his harness. He is immediately lifted back up and over to the van. As he comes down to the back of the van, he grabs the side and pulls himself in.

"Lucy, I'm home." He unclips the drill and places it in the waiting hand.

A look of disapproval on her face, she places the drill on the screw and pulls the trigger. "We get this one and one more screw, and we're halfway there." The stack moves again, and the casing slips a few inches lower.

"Shit." They both look up at the top of the van. The weight of the bomb is ripping the sheet metal on the top. Susie readjusts her self towards the back of the van because of the movement. "I don't like this, Top."

A cold gust of wind blows in the back of the van. "I'm with you on that."

The drill bit bites into the screw. She stops and reverses the motor. The screw is slowly retracted.

"Whew. That got it. We have one more." They verify, and Susie begins removing the last screw. She hands it to Marshall. As she removes the access plate, commercial power suddenly comes on. The lights around the perimeter of the yard flash on, and the huge chipping machine roars to life. A loud screaming noise catches everyone off guard as the huge toothed rollers on the machine pull in a car and tear it apart.

Everyone hits the deck. Johnson and Marino both kneel down on the top of the car. The crane operator for Marshall is caught by reflex action, and pushes the control lever forward. Susie slams back against the side of the van, the access plate and its wiring in her hand. As she looks towards Marshall, he suddenly flies out the back of the van. Her right hand comes up to her mouth. "My God, Gunny."

"Turn off that goddamn machine!" Johnson jumps down and runs towards the screaming giant. Buckley and two of his men run towards what looks like a control panel. They can feel the rumbling in the ground beneath their feet as another car is fed into the grinder. Johnson and Buckley reach the control panel at the same time. "Jesus, how do we turn this thing off?"

"Just start pulling levers, Major, and hope they're the right ones." They start pulling handles and throwing levers. Johnson slams a power lever down and the huge giant goes quiet. "Man, that scared the shit out of me." Johnson shakes his head.

"Me too, sir." They both pant as they take a moment to catch their breath.

"Run, run, get out of the way."

Johnson and Buckley turn around. The stack supporting the van teeters and then seems to just flatten out. The stacked bodies were shaken by the rumbling machine, and a block-long stack of cars falls into the next row. It, too, collapses under the weight.

"What the fuck?" Johnson runs to Marino and hops up on the car. "What the hell happened?"

"It was that machine. It just rattled the whole thing to pieces. But look up there." The van gently sways in the sling. Marshall swings up above it. "Well, I'll be damned." Everyone on the ground stands silently and stares at the van, hanging thirty feet above the smashed pile.

"Marshall, where the hell are you?" It is so quiet that Susie's words echo over the stunned people on the ground. They all suddenly start laughing. Buckley runs over to his men. "Quickly get another fork up here to clean some of this shit out of the way. And get those cars off the cranes."

Two more big forks are brought up, and they start lifting cars off the cranes. Marshall swings gently in the air above the van. He is amazed how the stack under the van just seemed to melt away. He yells down to Susie, "I'm above the van. I'll get back down as soon as they can get back to the crane."

"What happened? The bomb slipped another three or four inches."

"Well, let me put it this way. Other than the sling, there is nothing holding the van up."

"What? Get the hell back in here."

He sees the boom begin to move. "I'm on my way, Doctor." Marshall is lowered to the back of the van and pulls himself in. "I'm home, Lucy." He smiles at Susie.

"So we're just swinging up here, and you're out playing Peter Pan?"

Marshall looks up at the roof. The rips in the metal are getting worse.

"Here's the access panel." Susie moves farther towards the back and lies on the floor of the van. She shines the light into the casing and begins working on the motion device. "This doesn't look good, Susie. The roof is going to cave in at any minute."

"I just need a little more time." She puts her full attention on the bomb.

"Mr. Marino, this is Marshall. The bomb is caving in the roof. Sir, if I yell 'pull,' have the cranes pull us both out of the back."

"Roger, Top. On your call."

Marino gets the crane operator standing by and waits for the call. Susie pushes the button to deactivate the movement mechanism. She unscrews the harness caps and reaches for the wire bridle. Marshall watches the roof. A ripping sound fills the van, and the cracks in the roof begin to come in. "Now, sir. Now."

The cables from the cranes tighten. Susie and Marshall are pulled quickly out the back, and then up. They swing in the air. Susie waves the wire harness at Marshall. "I got it."

The retard fins on the bomb rip through the top of the van and slam into the floor. The entire bomb hangs from the bottom of the van, the fins caught on the metal of the floor. "Damn." Marino and Johnson just stand and stare at the van with the large white cylinder hanging down. In the air above the van, Susie strikes a Peter Pan pose. Commercial power is lost again, and the portable spotlights shine up on her. She holds the wiring harness in her hand above her head. Everyone on the ground breaks into a roaring cheer as Susie and Marshall are lowered to the ground.

As Susie is helped out of the harness, those around her applaud. She performs a slight curtsey. She hands the harness to Johnson, and he gives her a big hug. "Damn, we thought that it was the end when that thing came through the bottom."

Marshall walks up to her. "Well, we made it through another one."

"You're right." Susie hugs him as a light rain begins to fall.

Laura comes up, and she gives her the once over. "Are you all right, Susie?"

"Yeah, I'm fine, Laura. That sling really stretches you out good, let me tell you. I think I lost my panty shield a couple of times." She hugs Laura.

Marino and Buckley join them. "Is it OK to move the bomb?"

Susie looks up at the van. "Yes, I just need to disable the timer. If you can set it over here." She points to an open area.

"You got it, ma'am." Buckley calls over to the operator, and the van is swung over the stacks and lowered into the clearing. It is brought down so only the point is touching the ground. One of Buckley's men brings a stepladder over and sets it under the access hole.

"Well, let's finish this thing up." Susie climbs the ladder and in just a few minutes, hands the timer harness to Marshall. He gives her the spanning wrench, and she digs back into the bomb's interior. After a few minutes, she extracts the detonator. She hands it to Marshall as she climbs down.

"This beast is dead." Another cheer goes up from the men around her. The rain is beginning to fall harder, so Susie and Laura go over to a Hummer and climb in. They watch as the van is lowered onto its side. Men with torches begin cutting the body of the van in half. Sparks fly into the falling rain as Marshall joins them in the Hummer.

"Susie, do you want to move back to the helicopter?"

"Yes, we're through here."

Marshall tells Johnson, and a driver is sent over to take them out to the command Stallion. As they drive, Susie looks at her watch. "Damn, it's 12:05. I hope they find something soon."

Marshall turns back in his seat. "Yeah, we're still looking at an 0200 deadline. From the description of the next site, it could get real hairy out there."

"I love it when you're so optimistic, Top."

ULTIMA
WASHINGTON, D.C.

Captain Van Nar walks to the podium. "Gentlemen, we have just confirmed with Captain Nelson that bomb number two has been deactivated by Dr. Davies." The men around the table applaud as the cross marking bomb two goes green.

"The recon team is at the last site." The screen moves to the next location with a rectangular red box around it. "As you can see from the map," the topographical image of the area is brought up in white, "the recon group is shown with seven circles.

"We hope to hear from the team soon. The safety window from Captain Emmett is 0200 hours. Word from the second site is that they will be ready to move in about thirty to forty-five minutes."

"Thank you, Captain." Brant turns to a marine near him. "Corporal, I need this message delivered to the president." He writes the note and hands it to the corporal, who leaves the room to go to the president's meeting with the ambassadors.

"Mr. Brant." General Becker turns to him. "We have now moved all personnel to a point ten miles south of New Orleans. We see the completion of the evacuation by 0030 our time."

"General Becker, your alert team has done an outstanding job against adversity of both logistics and weather. Please pass on a job well done from me. And the president will call the commanders down the road. An excellent job." The others in the room applaud, led by Secretary Brant.

RUSSIAN SUBMARINE
OUTSIDE THE FROZEN FOREST

The submarine comes to a complete stop. "Sir, we are two miles off the entrance to the Frozen Forest, or gateway three."

"Roger, helm." The captain and the executive officer look over the map of the area. In some parts the depth is over 1,000 feet. The rift runs about five miles. From the entrance, there are three deep valleys to the south. The north side has two deep scars. The rift runs for about a mile, then turns sharply to the northwest, and like a serpent, coils twist off towards the continental shelf.

"Comrade, where would you put your submarine?" The captain takes a drink of tea.

"Here, sir. In the third valley on the south side. The only way out is either up or to the northwest in the rift. Either way, he would not escape."

The captain smiles. "Very good. I would do the same. You are more than ready to command your own boat, my friend."

"Thank you, sir."

"But I think the little Kilo boat will be here." His finger points to the first canyon south. "He will be up against the east wall. When we pass, he will fire at least two torpedoes. His nose is sticking out right now to try and pick us up. He will back up and wait for us."

The executive nods his head. "We will let him know we're coming. Give me full power astern. That should alert them."

"Yes, sir. Helm, give me full astern." The order is repeated, and the propeller claws at the still water. The cavitation is not missed by the smaller boat. Its sonar in the nose picks up the sudden sounds.

"Captain, sir. The Russians are here. They're about four kilometers out."

"Very good." The Cuban captain grabs the rail and nods his head. "We will have them. They have no knowledge that we are here. We'll dispatch them and then join our sister boat in the final battle. Bring us back slowly, so they will not have a clue until the two torpedoes are racing up their ass." Those in the control room laugh in muted tones.

ULTIMA
WASHINGTON, D.C.

Van Nar steps up to the podium. "Gentlemen, on screen one is the track of the Russian Sierra submarine. We have the outline of the Petrified Forest, and a possible location of the Cuban Kilo submarine." The red triangle appears in the third canyon. "The Russian boat is now two miles from the entrance of gateway two. The SOMAS system will track them in the rift." The yellow circle of the Russian boat is suddenly highlighted. Van Nar picks up the phone near her. "Gentlemen, the Russians have suddenly brought their submarine to full astern. The Cubans cannot help but pick up their location."

The president looks at the admiral. "Why would they do that, Admiral?"

"I don't know, sir. But as I have said, these are crafty captains. They are left to their own devices. We'll have to wait and see."

RUSSIAN SUBMARINE

The captain looks over at the executive officer. "Ivan, I want full speed ahead. I will call the commands, and I want them complied with at that instant. Load two of the NX-5 decoys in the aft tubes. I want everyone at battle stations."

"Aye, aye, Captain"

The klaxon horn bellows throughout out the boat. Men run to their stations. "Battle stations, battle stations."

"Helm, give our captain 100 percent power. Full speed ahead." The order is repeated. The men in the hull can feel the submarine picking up speed. They look at each other and nod; they have full faith in their captain.

ULTIMA
WASHINGTON, D.C.

"Gentlemen, the Russian submarine is making its move toward the Petrified Forest."

The yellow circle begins moving towards the entrance of the rift. They watch as the speed increases on the monitor.

RUSSIAN SUBMARINE
THE GULF

"Sir, we are approaching twenty-eight knots and continuing to gain speed."

The captain looks up from the chart. "Very good. We will enter the rift in twenty seconds. Timer stand by."

A sailor near the sonar scope begins calling out the heading to enter gateway two. "Comrade Captain, I must remind you that we will be entering the gateway twelve knots faster than the norm. We are recalculating the distances as we go. We are going too fast to make the first turn safely. Sir, we are running at thirty-four knots. We are passing the first valley to the south."

"Stand by."

In the dark water, the Kilo fires its torpedoes. They begin pursuing the speeding Russian sub.

"Sir, we have two homing torpedoes fired. They are 500 yards astern."

The captain looks at the speed of the boat; it is almost thirty-eight knots. "Hold our course, and release the decoys."

"Aye, aye, sir." The chief hits a button and releases two decoys. "Sir, we are passing the second canyon. The first turn is now 9,000 yards. We are now eighteen knots faster than the safe passage speed. It will be impossible to make the first turn."

The pinging of the torpedoes fills the submarine as they race through the water. A vertical wall that rises almost 1,000 feet from the seabed looms ahead of them on the sonar scope. The speed now hovers at forty knots. "Sir, the Cuban torpedoes have disregarded the decoys and are now 400 yards astern and gaining."

"Hold our course and speed." The pinging is the only sound in the submarine as the captain looks around the room at the men at their stations.

"We are 7,000 yards from the wall and 300 yards ahead of the torpedoes."

"Chief, release two more decoys."

"Yes, sir."

Outside the submarine, the decoys are shot from each side. They began to bubble and transmit a signature as they fall for the abyss. The seeker heads on the torpedoes scan the decoys and then the fleeting submarine; again they hold their original course.

The Cuban submarine pulls out into the main channel and begins chasing the other submarine. They pull up to fourteen knots and hold that speed as they move towards the first turn. "Captain, the torpedoes are still on course. The Russians have reached almost forty knots. They are going too fast to make the first turn. If the torpedoes don't get them, the wall will."

"Very good. Hold our course."

ULTIMA
WASHINGTON, D.C.

"Your attention, gentlemen. The Russian submarine is now pinned between the two torpedoes of the Cubans and the wall of the first turn. The Cuban was hiding in the first canyon and is now following the fleeing Russian. They have released two sets of decoys, which have had no effect." The yellow circle races at the solid white line of the cliff face as the red triangle follows slowly. Two white dotted lines continue to pursue the fleeing yellow circle.

RUSSIAN SUBMARINE

"Sir, we are 3,000 yards from and wall and 200 yards ahead of the torpedoes. Speed is holding at 39.4 knots." Sweat beads form on the foreheads of all on the submarine; they roll down chiseled faces. The captain slowly drinks his last bit of tea and sets the cup down. "Comrade Ivan, at 300 yards from the wall, I want a total blow of all tanks and full right rudder."

"Aye, aye, sir." The command is repeated, and all falls silent. "Sir, we have passed 1,000 yards. The torpedoes are now 100 yards astern. On my count we will reach the 300-yard mark. Stand by."

Men on the submarine grab hold of anything that is available. They await the coming maneuver. "Stand by. Eight, seven, six, five, four, three, two, one." The word is lost in the execution of the order. The tanks are suddenly pumped full of air, and the helm is thrown totally to the right. The nose begins to come around, and the boat begins to rise. "Prepare to fire the NX-5 decoys out the back." The chief has his hand near the button, waiting for the order.

The propeller fights to get around and pushes the submarine at an angle parallel to the wall. The torpedoes fight to make the turn at forty-five knots. They slide sideways, slam into the cliff face, and detonate. "Fire the decoys."

Two large containers are ejected from the rear torpedo tubes. The Russian submarine races towards the surface, and slides sideways. Suddenly, collision alarms sound in the boat. "Stand by for collision."

The full left side of the submarine slams into the cliff face, it crushes the outside hull into the inner hull, and shears off the tail plane in the back. It scraps along the side of the cliff and continues to rise.

In the depths behind them, the two decoys come to life. They dispense sounds and bubbles into the surrounding water, as they sink into the abyss.

CUBAN SUBMARINE

The exploding torpedoes come over the sound system. "Sir, we have hit the Russians, and they have slammed into the cliff face. They are sinking." A loud cheer is heard throughout the boat. "Captain, you have defeated the superior vessel with cunning and intelligence."

"Thank you. We will continue to the wall face to make sure." Over the intercom comes the sound of secondary explosions, the eerie sound of steel twisting in the depths, and the sound of the boat imploding.

ULTIMA
WASHINGTON, D.C.

"Mr. President, it would appear that the Russian submarine has been lost. These are the sounds from the SOMA sites in the rift." They all listen as the sounds of explosions and the twisting and creaking of metal fill the room. "God bless them. Amen."

OUTSIDE HAVANA
CUBA

Quintano's track pulls in next to another, parked on the outskirts of Havana. He climbs out and is met by Zino from his track. "My General, we stand ready to enter the city."

"Zino." They hug each other. "You have done an outstanding job, my Colonel." Another command track pulls up to the others and stops. The doors are opened and Captain Ruiz climbs out with Brock right behind him. Ruiz salutes as he walks up. "Sir, I heard that you had been killed in that attack up to the top of the mesa. We are glad that they were wrong."

"So am I, Mr. Ruiz." He bursts into a laugh. "My comrade Brock."

"General." They shake hands and then hug.

"You still have that damn shotgun."

"Yes, sir, and it's been well used."

"All right, Colonel, bring us up to date on what is happening."

An aide sets up a map on an easel. "It seems that General Morales has not left the command center at this time. I have positioned a company of tanks at the base of Avendia de la Revolución. They will cut the city in half. A group from Ruiz will enter the city from here on the west side. They will cut off the oceanfront and meet up with my group here at the docks. We are about to close the trap on General Morales."

"That looks good, Colonel. Send the units in. I don't want Morales to escape."

"Where is Fidel now? I heard him on the radio earlier."

"He is en route to the radio station. He has his car and is being escorted by tracks and tanks."

"Sir." An aide leans out of the track. "Sir, there is a call for you from President Castro."

"Quintano, this is Fidel. I'm on my way to the TV station. Are you entering the city now?"

"Yes, sir. But I must ask you not to transmit on the TAC frequency. The command center can pick you up. We have still not nullified the city."

"Very good, General. I will sign off."

"Get me the commander of the escort of the president. Have him switch to an alternate frequency." The radioman contacts the commander's track and has them change to another frequency.

"General, we're up with the escort."

Quintano grabs the handset. "Captain, move the president to one of the tracks and do not let him on the radios. Have him escorted away from your group. You continue on to the station, at full alert."

Outside of Havana, the convoy is stopped and Fidel moved from his car to a MT-LB track. It and two others take a side road towards the station as the main group continues on.

MORALES LEAVES HAVANA COMMAND CENTER

Morales smiles to himself. He looks over at the officer near him. "He is on his way to the TV station. I think we are ready to leave."

"Yes, sir. Forces are moving down the coast road, and the Avendia de la Revolución. We must hurry."

Morales puts on his jacket and walks out his office. He looks around the room at the upturned faces. "I want you to continue the fight. To the end."

"Yes, sir." One of his captains steps forward and salutes.

Morales returns the salute and leaves with the aircrew and one of his aides. He gets aboard one of the Hind helicopters, and they both lift off into the dark sky. As they fly out over the ocean, they pass over the forces moving along the waterfront. They continue out to sea. The ground forces do not know that their prey has passed out of their grasp. As soon as the helicopters lift off with Morales, the captain calls his men together in the front courtyard. "He is gone. Change out of your black uniforms and into regular army uniforms. We will leave immediately."

The special guard leaves in tracks and trucks into town. Their uniforms are thrown out the backs of the trucks. They abandon their vehicles and hide in the building for the next move of the attacking forces. A lieutenant in the command center casually goes out to the front of the building. He runs back inside, and orders the radio operator to contact Quintano's forces.

ZINO'S TRACK
OUTSIDE OF HAVANA

"I have the command center on the line, sir."

Zino goes to his track and takes the handset. "This is Colonel Zino."

"Sir, this is Lieutenant Munoas. Morales's guards have fled from the building. We will surrender the command center to your troops as soon as they arrive. I assure you, there are none of Morales's men left."

"Where is General Morales?"

"He left about ten minutes ago. They are in two Hind helicopters. They flew towards the ocean."

"Shit. Go to the front gate, Lieutenant. I'll have the commander of the tank group meet you there. If you do not show or we receive any hostile fire, his group will level the command center. Do you understand?"

"Yes, sir. I will go to the gate now and be waiting."

Zino throws the handset back into the track. "Shit! Morales has just left in two Hind helicopters. They flew out towards the sea. The command center has been abandoned."

"Damn it." Quintano stands up. "Get me two attack helicopters ready to go after him."

"Yes, sir. I have a tank unit moving directly to the command center. I will go with them and secure it."

"Good, Zino. Ruiz, you take over here. Mr. Brock, you choose where you want to go."

"I'll go with you, General. Action just seems to follow."

"Very good." A car is brought up to take them to the waiting helicopters.

BOMB SITE, NUMBER ONE
LOUISIANA

Neal and the others jump down from the helicopter into about three feet of water. They climb up the side of the mound to a small clearing. They look around with their night vision scopes. They seem to be surrounded by water on three sides with the sand finger they're on sticking out about 400 feet into the wet land. The wind gusts across the bleak spit of ground are filled with the smell of salt.

"Captain, let me look around a bit before everyone goes tramping all over the place."

"All right. Take Gunny Cabolero with you. We'll wait here."

"Good, it should only take a few minutes. This area is a hot spot; a lot of drugs move through here. It's all marsh and swamp for about fifty square miles. The coast is only about a mile due south of us." He and Cabolero move out on the finger, with Owens at the lead. Neal gets the other marines together. "Set up a perimeter across this spit. And take a look over towards the west. See if there are any trails over there."

He looks back at the helicopter. The pilot and the co-pilot stand towards the front, the crewman off to their right with a rifle. The radio operator with Neal gets under a small tree and pulls his poncho top over his head. The wind directly off the sea chills to the bone on exposed skin. Neal looks around with his night vision; a hedgerow about a half-mile to the south blocks their vision of the coast. North is marsh with tall grass, and to the west is another finger of land about 400 feet away. At least it has some small trees and bushes. He turns back towards the point and watches Owens and Cabolero poking around in the grass and brush. He pulls his poncho tighter as the rain gets heavier.

Natalie's green eyes flash in the light from the lantern. "Well, what the hell is going on?"

"We have a helicopter down on the other side of that finger of land east of us. There seems to be about six to eight people over there. One of the guys has DEA stamped on his back."

"Fuck." She swings around. "We're about to score one of the biggest loads brought in, and we have the butthole DEA out snooping around. We know that the plane is due here in about thirty minutes. If they're not out of here in about twenty minutes, the fuckers are going down." She turns around and looks directly into Bob's eyes. Even for him, a cold chill seems to emanate from the dark green orbs.

"You got it, Natalie."

He contacts the men out on the knoll. They hold their positions in the brush. Their night camos blend with the shadow. The lead man watches as the marines take up positions next to a trail. He is so close that he can hear them talking between each other. Across the open water area, a Russian Dragunov sniper rifle scans the area at the front of the spit. The cross hairs stop at a man holding a flashlight. He lowers the cross hairs to the man kneeling near him with another light. Cabolero looks around in the darkness. Something in him tells him to be aware. It is an old feeling that seems to have been in hibernation. But this night has brought back the feel.

"You know, Owens, something is definitely wrong out here. I can't put my finger on it, but there is something."

Owens looks up at him. "I feel it, too. Let's kill these lights." He stands up next to Cabolero. In the darkness, he leans over and whispers to Cabolero. "We're not alone out here."

"Shit." Cabolero looks around. "Let's get back to the captain."

They walk bent over back to Neal. "Captain, Mr. Owens has some bad news for you."

"What is it, Owens?"

"I checked some tracks out on the point. They can't be more than twelve hours old. Maybe it was just some swamp nut. But I have a feeling we're near something else. Maybe drugs."

"Shit, I've felt uneasy ever since we got here. Call the others back. We need a defensive plan. Climb down and let the helicopter guys know."

The marines near the trail are contacted. "We have to fall back The captain thinks there is someone else out here." They move back down the trail to Neal.

The man in the brush keys his mike. "Bob, they know we're out here. The DEA guy was looking around on the point. He probably found Paul's tracks out there."

"All right," Bob signs off. "Shit. Len thinks that the DEA guy may have found some tracks out there. They have pulled back into a position near the radio."

"Shit. Now how in the fuck did they find tracks out there?"

"Earlier, before you got here, Paul walked out there to check it. When that plane flew over early this morning, they heard something hit out in that area. So he went to check."

"I thought that no one was supposed to be out on that point, just for that reason."

"Right, Natalie. He just didn't think."

"Oh, oh. Now why doesn't that surprise me about this bunch."

"Well, they have about fifteen more minutes. And no one will give a shit."

"Yeah, Bob. You had better hope so." She slips on a shoulder holster and checks her Glock. She pulls a 9 mm submachine gun over to her. "I don't want anymore screw-ups." She hangs the submachine gun over her shoulder. "Turn the lights on, in case the plane gets here early." Bob goes over to a panel and flips a switch. Out in the marsh, infrared lights go on under the water.

BOMB SITE, NUMBER TWO
JUNKYARD IN LOUISIANA

Johnson watches as the men cut through the sides of the van. They hook up chains and begin to pull the body apart. The rain gets stronger. The sparks fly as the body is ripped apart. The bomb lies on its side; they hook a sling around it and lift it out of the wreck. Johnson calls a sergeant over and has him move half of the security force back to the helicopters.

"I think we have it, Major. We'll run it out to the Stallion on a fork."

"That sounds great to me, Commander."

Johnson gets in a Hummer, and they head back to the helicopters. He rubs his legs as they drive through the yard. The cold has caused it to numb up. "Sir, you have a call from Bulldog 2."

"This is Bulldog. Over."

"This is Bulldog 2. Mr. Owens believes we are not alone. And Sergeant Cabolero has this real funny feeling. We have not seen anything and will continue the search."

The Hummer pulls up to the back of the command helicopter. Marshall is standing at the base of the ramp, having a cup of coffee and talking with a sergeant, when the Hummer pulls up. Johnson opens the door. "Top, could I speak to you?"

Marshall moves over to the side of the Hummer. "Yes, sir."

"I have Bulldog 2 on the horn. Mr. Owens thinks there is someone else out there. And Gunny Cabolero has a funny feeling. I think I'm going to send the Cobra out to them."

"Sir, I would agree. Gunny Cabolero has made some pretty scary calls with his funny feelings. Do you want me to take the men out?"

"Not until we have a better idea of what is going on."

"Bulldog 2, you have the Cobra coming at you. Set your position, Neal."

"Roger. Bulldog out."

"Night Moves, this is Bulldog. You're out of here. They think there may be someone out there with them."

"Roger, Bulldog. We'll contact Bulldog 2 at the location. Out."

While they wait for the bomb to be brought out, the Cobra whines to life. Its lights come on, and it lifts into the night sky and heads towards the northeast. Marshall and Johnson watch it race out of sight.

"Let's get inside and get a look at the area near them." They walk up the ramp into the warmth of the big Stallion.

CHAPTER 17

BOMB SITE, NUMBER ONE
LOUISIANA

The pilot and co-pilot get back in the Blackhawk. The crewman moves to the front, his rifle at the ready. Neal calls the helicopter on the radio and orders him to lift off, to clear the area. They move the radio farther out on the finger of land and take a position with their backs to the sea. Two of the marines take positions facing towards the west, into the brush. The other two take up positions looking out towards the north.

The Blackhawk's engine comes to life and blows water and mud in all directions. They signal the crewman back on board and lift off quickly. They back off towards the south.

The marines lay in the total darkness. They scan the area around them with their night-vision gear. All lights have been extinguished. Neal lies next to the radio with Cabolero at his side. Their rifles are pointed out into the swamp north of them.

"Well, nothing happened when the Blackhawk took off."

"Maybe they think we left. I don't see shit out here." Cabolero looks around in a 360-degree arch. "But I sure have this feeling were being watched."

"We're losing time though." Neal looks at his watch. "Shit, it's almost 12:30. And we still don't have a clue where the bomb is."

"How about if Owens and I work our way to the end of the point. Then we'll work our way back to you. If we don't find anything, we'll all move towards the west together."

"Sounds good, Gunny. We should have the gunship over us in just a few minutes."

"I'll feel a lot better with Night Moves up there."

"I agree, Gunny. We'll wait here."

Cabolero and Owens work their way down the path and reach a small area of flat ground with a small sand edge. The water beyond the end of the point flows by slowly. "Well, let's work our way around the north side of this thing. I didn't see shit on this side."

"I'll lead the way."

Owens works his way around a bush, with Cabolero following. The man behind the sniper rifle moves it slowly along the finger of land. He has lost the men around the radio. But his infrared scope picks up a figure coming around the point. The cross hairs move to the center of the target. He moves it over as another figure emerges. Bob turns towards Natalie. "Shit. The Blackhawk lifted off before we were in position."

Natalie moves in next to Bob. "How many are over there?"

"We have counted seven. They have moved to the south side of the point. They haven't made any moves towards us. I think they found some tracks. But they haven't found anything else. They're just being cautious."

"I can't see anyone."

Bob leans over. "Look out towards the point."

Natalie moves her head to the left. She sees two men moving along the north edge of the point. She watches them for a few moments. "I'd say they're looking for something."

"I agree. And I don't think it's us. They may just leave."

"Tell everyone to hold where they are until we hear from the plane."

"I have one of the guys here and one on the point with Grail missiles. If the helicopter comes back, they'll smoke it."

Natalie nods her head. "Good."

"Bob, this is Pete. The plane just called. They're about twenty miles northwest and are inbound."

"Right. Natalie, the plane has called. They're inbound about twenty miles north. They're going to come in low and fast."

"Well, I think it's time to get rid of our friends."

"All right. We'll go in.". He stops talking as the sound of an approaching helicopter makes him look up into the sky. "From the sound, it's not the Blackhawk."

The helicopter flies around their position with its thermal site. It turns to the right and picks up the row of lights across the swamp. "Bulldog, do you have lights running north your position in the swamp?"

"Lights, no." Neal looks over the top of the mound towards the north. All he can see in his gear is the water and grass.

"Well, there is a line of lights running from your position north to a canal. And they're infrared. We're going to move. Keep your heads down."

The Cobra moves to the left and gains some altitude. The gunner scans the area on the south side of the position. The imager picks up two men in the water, and a group of six spreads out across the spit of land about 100 feet in front of Neal. "Bulldog, how many men do you have with you?"

"There are seven, including Owens. Over."

"You have two bad guys in the water southwest of your position. And six working their way towards you due west. We're going hot."

"Roger, Night Moves." Neal calls Cabolero. "We got bad guys due west."

The Cobra shifts position to the north on the other side of the small peninsula. As he swings around to fire, a man kneeling on the land spit 500 feet away sits in the imager. The gunner opens fire with the 20 mm canon. The first rounds hit in front of the mound to the west and begin walking up the side. Night Moves pulls up to maneuver. "We have a guy with a rocket due north." The flash from the launch lights up the area to their north. Ratchet yells over the intercom. "Save us, boss."

Night Moves swings the Cobra to the south as the missile hits near the base of the rotors. The cannon continues to fire in a descending arc as the Cobra falls from the sky and lands on it left side. The rocket pod on the right side fires. The rockets blast from the pod and fly eight feet over the water and explode into the brush at the base of the western knoll. Night Moves reaches up and hits the explosive jettison system. The doors are blown off of him and Ratchet, as water runs into the cabin. He fights his harness to free himself. The engine behind him is beginning to burn. The heat is getting intense as he rolls over into the cool water. Owens and Cabolero watch as the Cobra hits about 200 feet north of them in the swamp.

The sniper behind the SVD rifle picks the forward target and fires. The 7.62 mm round catches Owens in the chest and spins him around into the brush behind him. He moves his site and catches Cabolero as he begins to go to the ground. He is thrown over backwards by the hit. The sniper watches through the scope. Nothing moves on the north side of the knoll.

The marines hug the ground as the Cobra is blasted from the sky. They open fire on the north finger of land. Neal calls for the gunny, but no one answers. "Shit. Cabolero, are you out there?" Still only silence. A burst of gunfire from the south side of the knoll rakes through their position. Neal rolls down by the water and fires a half clip along the south side of the knoll. A flash down the knoll sends a streaking line of light towards the hovering Blackhawk. As he starts to move, the missile catches them head-on. There is a bright flash, and burning pieces fall into the swamp.

Neal goes to a kneeling position and catches one of the men in the water going up the bank. A quick burst throws him back into the swamp, face down. Gunfire from the men west of them rakes the position, catching one marine in the legs. Two other marines fire 40 mm grenades into the brush. The explosions flair, and the yells of men can be heard. They rake the area with rifle fire.

A marine at the top of the knoll fires off two 40 mm grenades at the knoll northwest of them. They hit against the face and explode. Natalie lifts her face back up and empties a clip. "Kill these sons of bitches." She rolls on her back and loads another clip.

Neal moves up towards the radio, firing into the brush. As he goes to reach for the handset, something heavy lands next to him. He looks to his side at the grenade. "Grenade!" He picks it up and tosses it into the water at their feet. They all hug the ground. The explosion rips the water apart as mud and shrapnel are hurled into the air.

"Aaaaaaaah!" Neal grabs his legs and rolls down into the water.

Corporal James jumps into the water and pulls him back up on the shore. He yells out to the others. "Get the wounded and move out to the end of the point. I'll cover you from here."

The other two marines grab Neal and a private and drag them to the crescent shaped area on the south side of the point. They lay them back against the face of a small cliff. One covers them to the north, as the other one works to stop the bleeding on Neal's legs and arms. He also bandages the marines hit in the legs. He gives them each a shot of morphine. Neal is still out, the other marines gets up in a seated position, his back on the cliff He checks his rifle. "I'll cover us east, and look after the captain." "Good, I'll cover James's move back to us."

He moves to the south side of the crescent. "James, Corporal James. We're clear. I'll cover you in."

James slaps in another clip. "All right, I need to get the radio." He pulls the pin on a grenade and tosses it into the brush to the west. He grabs the radio and moves farther to the east on the knoll. He grabs the handset.

"Bulldog, this is Recon 3. Over."

"Roger, Recon 3. This is Bulldog."

"Sir, we are pinned down at the end of the point. We have three casualties and two dead. The captain is down, and also Gunny Cabolero."

"Where is Night Moves?"

"They have AA missiles. They gunned both of the helicopters."

Johnson raises his arms in frustration. "Corporal James is this you?"

"Yes, sir."

"We're on our way, secure your position."

"Sir, this is a hot LZ. You have no where around us you can land. We will set zzzzzzzz."

"James, James." The radio is quiet.

The sniper's bullet catches the radio near the top and blows it off the knoll into the water. "Shit." James looks at the handset in his hand and tosses it aside. He fires a clip into the brush and moves to the point. The sniper scans the knoll around the position of the radio. He sees nothing, so he moves towards the point. As he scans with the scope, it quickly passes over something on the north face of the knoll. He swings back to get a bead on the target.

"I got one." Natalie looks over at him, just as the round hits him in the throat. His neck explodes from the impact, and he slides backwards, dragging his rifle.

Blood from the sniper splatters on to Natalie. "Oh, shit." She rolls back wiping her face.

"Fuck you, asshole." Cabolero, in a kneeling position, lowers his rifle. He reaches down and grabs Owens by the collar and drags him to the end of the point. They give him covering fire as he drags Owens up next to Neal.

"Shit." He looks down at the captain.

"A grenade got him, Gunny. I'm glad you're back."

Cabolero looks around. "Well, you got us secured, James. You did a good job."

"Thanks, Gunny. I lost the radio. Some asshole put a round in it."

"Well, I think I nailed that bastard." A hole in his utility top and a rip in his vest show where the round hit him. "I think the cocksucker broke my collar bone. He slammed Owens dead center in the chest. He broke some thing on him. He can hardly breathe."

"I'll take a look." James moves over and opens Owens's jacket. His vest is rip across the front. "The bullet may have broken his sternum and some ribs. Some ribs may be jammed into his lungs. Shit, I don't know." Blood trickles from his mouth. "Did you get a call out before the radio got killed?"

"Yeah, I talked to Major Johnson. He said that the alert group is on its way."

"Good, let's hope soon." Cabolero looks out over the swamp. The wind gusts, and rain begins to fall. It gets heavier by the minute. Soon, a full-blown cloud burst falls.

LEAVING BOMB SITE, NUMBER TWO

Johnson tosses the handset to the operator. "Keep trying to contact the recon group. Top," he waves Marshall over, "the recon group has been jumped. We have people down. Cabolero and Owens are presumed down. The LZ is hot."

"Shit, who is it out there?"

"I don't know. Owens thought it might be drugs."

Johnson opens a map, and they look at the terrain. "Shit. James was right. They're surrounded by swamp."

"We could do a hot drop, sir."

"You're right. We could do a line north to south behind the point."

"Yes, sir. I'll head for the other ship. This rain isn't going to help, either."

Water runs off the back of the helicopter and drops in rivulets around the ramp. Marshall runs through the rain and up the ramp of the Sea Stallion with the Third Platoon. The big engines kick in, and the rotors wipe the air into a frothy swirl. They lift off.

Johnson moves towards the front. "We're out of here." Their engines come on, and the rotors slice through the rain. "Get me Captain Nelson at base. We'll see if we can get some air cover."

IN THE SKY OVER THE SWAMP

"Lance leader. This is Touchdown. Over."

"Roger, Touchdown."

"Lance, we have a bogie northeast. It appeared and began a turn to the southeast. Over."

"Roger, Touchdown. We'll investigate." The F-18 pilot keys his look-down radar and picks up a blip moving north of the city. "Touchdown, I have your bogie. We'll advise."

The fighter rolls to its left and drops down from 5,000 feet. It aligns with the unknown plane and continues to drop in altitude. He holds at 500 feet and closes on the bogie.

"Touchdown, you have a twin engines civilian plane. He is making a southeast turn. I have tried to hale him. No response."

"Roger, Lance. We have tried to contact unknown with no success. He continues to move deeper into a secured area. You are advised to intercept. He is required to turn due west and land at base. Over."

"Roger. Intercept."

"Lance, you are advised. Hot, I repeat hot, on contact, if unknown refuses to comply."

"Roger, Touchdown. Hot. Lance out."

The F-18 quickly closes the distance between the two aircraft. He arms his outboard missiles. Again he calls out to the plane now only a mile in front of him. "Hey, Jeff. We have a fighter coming in behind us."

"I know, you asshole. He keeps calling for us to land over at the navy base in New Orleans. We are on the end run now. We should pick up the lights in a minute."

"Shit, I hope so. He is coming in closer." The man in the back watches as the lights of the fighter draw near. They have six large bundles in the middle of the plane. The seats have been removed, and a set of runners lead to the side door. "Open the door and get ready to push them out."

"Touchdown, I have a Gulfstream Twin Turboprop. Its designation numbers are taped off. I'm off the left side at 290 knots. Over."

"Lance, we have no record of this aircraft. They filed no flight plan with civilian authorities. They are presumed runners. Over."

"Roger. Continuing to hail. No response."

"Stand by." The pilot throws the agile Gulfstream into a diving right turn and heads for the deck. He looks forward with infrared goggles and picks up the lights in the swamp.

"We're in. On my count, push that shit out the door." The big plane drops to 100 feet above the swamp and begins his in-run. They pass over the swamps north of the lights and fly directly towards the lights.

The F-18 rolls over and picks up the diving plane. He falls in behind it at 500 yards. He flips a switch and arms a Sidewinder on the port wing. The pilot listens as the seeker head is engaged. He hears the "growl" of the missile in his earphones as it locks onto the Gulfstream.

"Lance, bogie is inbound into hot LZ. We have forces under attack, reporting AA missiles shooting down two helicopters. Over."

The Gulfstream passes over the canal at the north end of the field. "Now, drop." The men in back push the bundles forward, and they fly out the door. They pull the door shut as the plane, less 1,800 pounds, maneuvers over the south end of the field. The 300-pound bundles careen into the water at 200 miles an hour.

They hit and bounce into the air and slam into the still water. They float, bobbing up and down.

"What the shit?" The Gulfstream roars across the field and flies over the marines on the point. They duck down as the big plane comes over at fifty feet. Almost instantly, the Hornet fighter screams across their position. As he crosses them, the Sidewinder missile slides off its rail. The pilot pulls the nose up as a Grail AA missile is fired from the northwest point. As the Hornet pulls up, flares are dispensed out behind it. The missile explodes in the trail of the fighter.

"We're out of here. We made the drop."

The tone in the pilot's ears increases. "Yeah, Jeff, we made the drop."

The Sidewinder hits the Gulfstream in the right engine and blows the wing off. The plane is thrown into a massive right turn and cartwheels into the swamp south of the marines.

Cabolero and the others sit mesmerized. "Holy shit, I don't believe this." Cabolero looks at the others.

"Touchdown, this is Lance. Over."

"Roger, .Lance."

"Bogie is down. I'm resuming my patrol altitude. Over."

"Roger, Lance. We confirm bandit down. Well done. Over."

Natalie and Bob slide back down the knoll to the bunker. "Bob, get the jet skis going and make the pick up. Have them haul the stuff to the north end. We'll load the boat there."

"This thing is going to shit, Natalie. That's not DEA over there. We're in a fight with marines. They just flamed the delivery plane with a fighter. I say we cut our losses and haul ass."

"Fuck you, Bob. There is 100 million worth of cocaine floating out there. This is it for me. No more of this shit for me. Now, if you can't tell them to get going, I will."

He looks at Natalie. "You're right. Fuck it. It might as well be here as anywhere else."

"I'm glad you arrived at that decision." She lowers her pistol.

He runs to the back of the bunker. "Get the boat fired up. We're moving to the canal on the north end to load the bundles." The cigarette boat comes to life and sits idling under the camouflage nets. Two men bring in the wounded from the southern knoll and lay them in the bunker. They moan in pain on the floor.

Bob runs back out to Natalie as she empties a clip into the marines position. "We're out of here. Get on the boat, and we'll move to the canal."

Natalie throws the sub-machine gun down and moves back inside the bunker as Bob gives the pick-up men their instructions. Two men off the boat are putting bandages on the wounded as Natalie stands behind them. She is drinking a beer. Bob joins her in the bunker. "We need to get these guys loaded and moving."

"Get on the boat, asshole." Natalie prods the man bandaging the wounded with her pistol.

"But ma'am, these men are hurt." He looks in her eyes and cuts his next sentence. "Yes, ma'am." He runs to the boat and climbs aboard.

Bob steps in. "Natalie, we need to load these guys on the boat. They fought for you. We owe them that."

She walks over to the feet of the two men. Her pistol hangs in her right hand. She finishes her beer and throws it against the wall. She leans over the first figure.

"Hi, Brian. Still want a piece of ass? Well, come on big guy. It's all right here." She smiles into the bloody face as she lifts her tee-shirt, exposing her breasts.

"Fuck you, you bitch." His body twitches as two rounds from her pistol tear into his chest. She leans over the unconscious man next to him and fires two more rounds into him. She steps back and slips the pistol back into her holster.

"I guess we don't have a situation anymore. Now get on the boat." She laughs out loud as they head for the boat.

HAVANA, CUBA

Quintano climbs into a seat near the right side so he can look out the window. As Brock climbs in beside him and belts in, he slips on his helmet and adjusts the mike. "Let's get airborne and get a fix on Morales." The two Hinds lift into the air and fly west over the outskirts of the city. "Contact Matanzas and Buta, and see if they have anything on radar."

The radio operator is calling out and checking, when a call breaks in. "Sir, you have a call from the commander of the convoy." Quintano keys his mike.

"General, we have two gunships coming down the road from the TV station towards us. They are not answering our calls. Did you send them to assist us, sir?"

Quintano looks over at Brock. He shrugs his shoulders. "I have not sent any airborne assistance. If they do not respond, consider them hostile."

"Yes, sir."

Quintano swings around in his seat. "Do you think it could be them?"

"Well, it sure sounds like something Morales would pull." He calls to the pilot. "Let's head over in that direction." As they cross over the docks, the pilot makes a slow right hand turn towards the east.

The convey pulls to a stop. "This is Captain Fuentes to the two gunships flying down Avendia de la Revolución. Break off and return to your units. That is a direct order from General Quintano. Over."

"Captain Fuentes, we were sent by Colonel Zino to assist you. Over"

"We require no assistance. If you do not break off, we will consider you hostile. Over."

The big gunships fly down the street side-by-side. "This is General Morales. You can die with Fidel, Captain." Fuentes drops the mike and turns to yells to the others. "Open fire! They are after the president." Guns on the tracks turn to fire on the approaching gunships. Their tracers fly down the street. The Hinds lock on targets, and Swatter AT missiles fire from the outboard rails on the weapons wings. The under-nose, four-barreled canons on both gunships lock and fire along the line of the vehicles. The four AT missiles find their marks. The tracks in the column are hit and explode in the street. The forward canons continue to rake the column as both gunships fire two pods of unguided rockets into the killing zone.

Explosions rack the column from front to back as the Hinds pull up and away from the burning piles of twisted metal in the road. "I see the limousine. It is torn apart." Morales looks out the side window as they pass over the wreckage.

"Very good, Captain. You will be rewarded for your proficiency. Now head back out to sea. We will rendezvous with the boat off Cayo Coco. From there on, we will all be able to relax in great comfort." They fly back out over the water and head east, staying low to evade radar.

"Sir, we're turning onto Avendia de la Revolución now." Quintano looks out the window and sees the TV station on top of a two-story building glowing with lights. They head down the street. The pilot calls ahead and gets a radio operator from one of the tracks.

"Sir, they were hit just a few minutes ago. They had the hell blown out of them. The radio operator thinks all the officers are dead. Sir, I can see the fires from here."

"All right, Captain. Land at the front of the column." They pull up about 200 feet from the lead vehicle and land in the broad avenue. Before the doors are opened, the glare from the fires shines off the glass of the buildings lining the street.

As Quintano and Brock jump down, the wail of sirens fills the air. The city's firefighters are responding to the blaze. Ordnance in the tracks continues to explode as the heat cooks it off. They move up to a group of officers and firemen near the lead vehicle. As they walk up, a pair of tanks and some other tracks emerge from some side streets. They pull up and stop near them. A lieutenant is talking with the fire captain as they walk up. He turns and sees him coming.

"Sir." He salutes. "We have a bad situation going here. The fireman can't get too close to the middle vehicles because of the exploding ammunition."

Rounds go off and fly into the buildings lining the street. The fire captain turns to Quintano. "We have a problem with the magnesium flares in your tracks. And fires are starting in the side buildings; we can't get near to them."

"I can understand." They hunch down as a series of rounds fly over their heads.

"Sir." A crewman from the helicopter runs over. "You have a call from Colonel Zino, sir."

"Right." Quintano runs back to the helicopter as a fire pumper pulls up and the nozzle at the front sends a stream of water into the flames. The nozzle at the back of the truck comes to life and sends a second stream of water into the burning vehicles.

"This is Quintano."

"Sir, we are at the command center. The lieutenant is at the main gate. From the looks of the place it is abandoned. We're going in now."

"Good, Zino. Morales's attack downtown, it's a mess. Once you get control of the center, I want all ships, boats, and aircraft to return to their bases or land at appropriate sites. Get me a track on the two Hinds."

"Yes, sir. Zino out."

Zino leans out the back of his track. "You walk ahead of us, up to the main doors."

"Yes, sir. I say again, none of Morales troops are here."

"I understand, Lieutenant. But you have to understand that I have seen a lot of good men killed this night. So please proceed."

"Yes, sir."

He walks slowly through the front gates and across the courtyard to the steps leading up to the main entrance. He turns at the step and watches as men pile out of several tracks and take up positions around the entrance. A tank pulls in and sets up a clear field of fire for its main gun.

Zino climbs out, and with his pistol drawn, he walks around the side of his track and joins the lieutenant on the steps. As they walk up to the main doors, Zino can see the bodies of the men shot in the courtyard. A group of soldiers joins them, and they go into the building. The men spread out and begin searching the interior.

Three soldiers move down the hall to the command center. They yell to those inside and open the door. The people inside the center are under their desks and behind filing cabinets for protection. A solider sticks his head out the door and calls to Zino. "Sir, the command center is clear."

"Let's go, Lieutenant." Zino walks through the center and into Morales's office. Blood on the rugs and on a plotting table tell him of the ruthless killing that went on.

"Lieutenant, get your people up to their stations. I want a message sent out telling all forces to stand down. General Quintano and another helicopter are down in the city. I want all helicopters to land in safe areas, designated by their commanders."

"Yes, sir." The messages begin going out. "Sir."

Zino walks over to a radar screen. "Yes."

"We now show twenty helicopters airborne in the western sector."

Zino calls his aid over. "Have the troops secure the town and place any of Morales's special guard under arrest."

"Sir." The air traffic controller calls Zino from his scope.

Zino moves over and looks at a blank screen. "What is it?"

"Sir, all of our attack aircraft have gone into the sea. They are spread out on a line from here to here. No effort has been made to try and rescue them.

"Shit! Get me the navy base at Dimas. Have them send out rescue craft to search the area. And have two of the Bandeirantes sent out to search the area." Zino moves around the room and looks over the activities of the others. "Get me General Quintano."

"Sir," the air controller calls back. "We have eight aircraft down; we still show twelve airborne."

"This is Quintano." He listens as Zino tells him of the situation and what he has ordered done. He watches as fire units begin to move along the sides of the streets to attack the fires in the buildings lining the street. The tracks in the center of the street continue to burn.

"We still have four helicopters in the air. We should have them pin-pointed soon."

"Very good. We'll be ready to leave as soon as we have them."

"We do have one problem, General. We are unable to recall the submarines. They were ordered into the attack." "Damn, we'll have to deal with that issue. I'll talk to Fidel. We may have to request some help. Keep me informed."

Brock walks up, his shotgun slung over his shoulder. "These firemen are brave men."

"Comrade, we are unable to recall the submarines. The squadron remains in peril."

"I understand, General. Is it possible to get a call out to Marshal Shagan?"

"We're going over to the TV station. I'll have a secured line set up for you. Let's get over there and meet with Fidel."

"Thanks, General." They climb on board, and the two gunships wait to lift off.

ULTIMA
WASHINGTON, D.C.

Van Nar goes to the podium. "Mr. President, we have intercepted radio messages from the central command center in Havana. General Quintano has ordered all military units to step down. They are in control of the center, and are in pursuit of General Morales, who we believe was responsible for the attack in central Havana on President Castro's motorcade."

"Do we have any word on Fidel?"

"Not at this time, sir."

Admiral Hillings hangs up his phone. "I just talked with Captain Nelson at the base. They are grounding everything except essential aircraft. All cap aircraft over the Gulf are being moved east and west of the storm with alternative landing sites. They are getting gusts up to ninety miles per hour and rising."

"Thank you, Admiral." Brant turns in his seat and looks over at Wayne. "Sir, we are still holding with the 2:00 shut down of the bomb recovery unit."

"Right, Mr. Secretary. Where do we stand with the recon group?"

General Swane walks up to the podium. "The recon unit is pinned down at this point of land." His light pointer shows on the screen. "We have casualties. Captain Neal is down. We have lost two helicopters to rocket fire. Contact was lost due to hostile fire. Major Johnson and Third Platoon are en route. We will receive some pictures as the satellite comes over them soon. They had not located the bomb."

"Damn. We're so close." The president rocks back in his chair.

BOMB SITE, NUMBER EIGHT
LOUSIANA

As Cabolero and the others crouch down, tracer rounds fly over the north edge of their position. "Marines! Don't shoot!" The voice comes out of the darkness to their east. Their eyes strain to see anything in the inky blackness.

"What the fuck?" Cabolero lowers his rifle at the surface of the water. "Identify yourself, or you're dead."

"Cabolero, it's Night Moves."

"Shit, come on in."

"I have Ratchet with me; he has a broken leg and some other injuries."

In his night gear, a head and then shoulders emerge from the swamp grass. The form is pulling something behind him. James moves into the water to help. He gets Ratchet under the arms and pulls him up next to Owens. Night Moves drops in next to the gunny.

"Fuck, is this shit for real, Gunny?"

"I'm afraid so, sir. We're in a bad way. We made contact with Bulldog, then lost the radio. We have dead and wounded. And were pinned down by the bastards from the other knoll."

"Maybe I can help." Night Moves removes his emergency radio and pulls the antenna out. "If it didn't get screwed up in the crash, we may have a chance." He keys the radio to life.

"Bulldog, this is Night Moves. Over."

"Sir, we have Night Moves on the radio."

Johnson moves over and gets the handset. "Night Moves this is Bulldog. Over. We've got contact with them, Gunny."

"Thank God. We're in a bad way. Bulldog, we're taking fire from machine guns north of us and from the knoll northwest of our position. They have us pinned down. They have some kind of small powered boats out picking up packages in the swamp. Over."

"Roger. We're going to come in from the south. The command helicopter will be on a line north-south, dispensing flares. That should blind them and throw off any missiles. The other helo will come in west to east behind your position. They will hot drop and move up to your location. Over."

"Roger, one."

"Gunny they're going to do a hot drop in a line west to east behind the knoll here. The other helo is going to blow flares right through the center of this shit hole."

"Well, we have practiced it. This should get exciting in a real big hurry."

"You're right there."

"Bulldog, we are ready. I will take one of the guys with me and work our way down the south side of the knoll. We'll throw flares to mark our positions. Over."

"Roger, Night Moves. We'll be on your position in ten minutes, at 0105. We are requesting air support. Over." The wind rakes their position.

"Bulldog, tell the pilots there are gusts of wind here that have to be in the seventy to ninety mile per hour range. Over."

"Roger. Bulldog out."

"Gunny, James and I will work our way down the south side of the knoll and throw flares; you pop one here. We go at 0105."

James moves over next to them. "Sir, are you sure you don't want me to go alone? You could cover me from the edge of the position over here."

"Corporal, even thou I happen to be a phenomenal air ace, all marines are basic 0300 MOS. Just get me a rifle and we're on our way."

"Yes, sir."

They move to the south side of the position. "Good luck, Gunny."

"And to you too, sir."

Night Moves and James move down the side of the knoll. Their eyes try to see beyond the range of their night gear. They reach the area where the radio lies shattered near the water. James looks over at Night Moves. He signals with his hand and moves farther down the knoll. As they cut through some tall grass, Night Moves suddenly trips and goes sprawling to the ground. He hits and rolls to the edge of the water.

"What the fuck?"

"Fucking roots." He gets to his knees and looks back at James.

James pushes the grass aside. A bent metal bar two feet long protrudes from the mud. He slides down next to the captain. "Shit, sir. I think you just found the bomb."

"What?" He climbs back up the side of the knoll and pulls the grass apart. "No shit, that's it." He pulls a dye marker from his leg pouch, and throws the contents around the area. He slides back down with James. "Well, if anything happens to us, I marked the area. Let's move down this way."

They move along the water's edge. Night Moves stops and goes to his knees. James kneels down and traverses his rifle across their front. Two bodies lay in the grass, and one floats in the water nearby. Night Moves checks them, and they move up to a trail about six feet wide that leads up over the top towards the north. He checks his watch. It's 0102.

They move up the trail to the top of the knoll. It runs along the top of the knoll and then across an open stretch of water to the north knoll. He sends James back down to the water's edge and positions himself to protect their front from behind a fallen tree.

Rain begins to fall, and lightning strikes slash across the sky to the south. The wind gusts across them like a cold hand, pushing everyone to hug the ground. At 0105, flares begin to burst to life along the south side of the knoll from the point to the trail.

The radio comes to life in Cabolero's hand.

"Recon, we're inbound. Have spotted flares. Bulldog out." Johnson turns to the others in the cabin. "Make sure you're strapped in. We're going in hot."

In the other helicopter, Marshall gets the men ready. They form two lines leading to the back of the aircraft. He walks over next to Rollens. "Sir, I don't think throwing a doctor out of a perfectly good plane is a real good idea. You may want to remain aboard until we secure the area, sir."

"Thank you, Sergeant. But from the reports from the ground, they need help now."

"Very good, sir. When you exit the aircraft, just step out. Gravity will get you down. You will hit on your backpack, at about forty knots or more. The men on each side of you will check for you on the ground."

"Very good." The stress in his voice is lost as the rear doors begin to open. A bone-cold blast of air rushes in and hits the men in the cabin. Rollens shivers from the cold blast.

"I have to give the army credit for naming that particular phenomenon. You have just met the hawk, sir."

A yellow light goes on at the rear of the cabin. Marshall moves to the front of the line. "Stand by. Lock and load. Check your fire. Our people are in the zone also."

Rollens gets in line about the third man back. He can feel the helicopter sinking in height as they move. His eyes strain to see out in the inky blackness. A lightning strike from the side throws a silver-blue light across the rear of the helicopter. They are about fifteen feet off the water. The image disappears as fast as it came. The engines seem to shift gear, and the helicopter loses more height. Above them a light goes green. "Semper fi." The line moves forward. Rollens watches as Marshall disappears into the void. He is pushed forward by the men behind. Far too soon, his time at the brink arrives. He steps off into the void. Rollens feels the rush of cold air as he clears the ramp. His mind quickly flashes. "Is the water cold?"

As their helicopter moves across the swamp, the other Jolly Green crosses behind them. As it passes over the knoll, it begins dispensing flares out the side. The marines on the peninsula take off their night vision gear as the world in the swamp is bathed in the glow of magnesium. It catches the smugglers near their bunker and on the boat off guard. Their night vision is filled with a blinding white glare. A missile from the knoll fires blindly into the night sky. It streaks in front of the Jolly Green and disappears into the night. As the missle firer shades his eyes to see if he's hit, two round from the side tear into his body. He falls back down the side of the knoll.

"That's for Ratchet and my ride, asshole." Night Moves empties the rest of the clip along the top of the knoll to keep them down. The huge apparition takes a hard left banking turn, and disappears over the swamp to the west.

"Is everyone all right?" Johnson looks over the unbelieving faces of the others in the cabin.

"My God, I have never seen anything like this." Susie and the others stay glued to their portals. The flares continue to light the area as they turn towards the south to join the other helicopter.

His back hits first, and Rollens is sent bouncing over the water and wet grass like a skipping stone. The drag of his medical kit pulls at his shoulder. His body pushes into the water, knocking his breath out. As he gasps for air, the taste of wet grass and mud rushes across his taste buds. Settling his feet to the muddy bottom, he stands and spits out the muddy water.

"Doc, Doc, you all right?"

"Holy shit, what a rush." The two marines on each side of him begin heading for the knoll. Others are working their way out of the swamp. In the falling light of the flares, figures begin appearing out of the darkness, working their way up to James and Cabolero's position.

"Recon." Calls come from the approaching figures. James and Cabolero call back. "Recon, come on in."

As the flares begin hissing to death in the swamp, the men immediately begin setting up guns and positioning themselves along the top of the knoll.

Marshall works his way down the knoll, making sure everyone made it. He joins Cabolero at the point. "God, I'm glad to see your ugly face."

"Why should you have all the fun? There, bring the corpsman up behind me. We'll take it from here." Cabolero leans back on the wet mud of the knoll and takes a deep breath as the corpsman begins working on the others.

ON THE SMUGGLER BOAT

"Natalie, we have to get out of here. This isn't DEA. We're up against a fucking marine group. I saw the tack marks on the helicopter. I don't know what they're doing out here, but let's move."

"Shut up, Bob." They both watch as a third bundle is hoisted up onto the deck by a temporary hoist mounted at the back of the boat. It is dropped onto a mover's dolly, and two men push it forward into the front of the boat.

Natalie leans over the stern of the boat to talk to the two men in wet suits on jet skis. "We have three more bundles out there. Bring them in, and I'll double your share."

"All right." The two men lower their night vision scopes and dart out into the swamp beyond the bow of the boat. "Now there is a couple of stupid fucks. They will never make it back." Bob turns to the two men on the bow with an M-60 machine. "We're going to back the boat up a little, so that they can't get a shot at it. Get out on the knoll and keep them down."

They jump over the side into the water, and move up to the top. The boat backs behind the protective cover of the point.

"One more run, and then we're out of here, Bob. You forget how much money is floating out there."

"I didn't forget, but for every second we stay, our chance of getting out of here goes up in smoke. Even if we get by them, we still have the fucking storm to contend with."

"Bob, get me out of this, and you can name whatever it is you ever wanted to do with a women. All right?"

"Hey, I like a piece of ass. But I sure don't want to die for it." He jumps over the side of the boat and joins the men at the machine gun.

MARINES ON THE SOUTH KNOLL

"Gunny, we have two of those jet skis in the water looking for something. They're about sixty yards out."

A stream of machine gun rounds walks along the edge of the point as they all duck down. Marshall joins him and takes a look into the swamp. He can see the two jet skis moving back and forth. One of them pulls up next to a bundle floating in the water, and he buckles a strap on it and begins to pull it towards the channel to the north.

"Get a laws up here and see if we can interrupt his delivery." Marshall gets on the walkie talkie. "All right, let's get control of this situation."

The machine guns begin firing at the men near the bunker, and on the north point, rifleman join in and M-40 grenades are launched at the bunker. No incoming fire hits the south knoll.

A lance corporal moves up next to Marshall. "Where's our target, Top?"

"He is heading towards the north point. We'll put up a flare and light him up.

"Right." He moves away from the others and un-cases the laws.

"I'm ready when you are, Top."

Two men fire flares out over the swamp. As they burst to life, dangling from their parachutes, the area around the north point is lit up. "Clear." He raises up and aims at the man on the jet ski. He squeezes the trigger, and the missile thumps out of the casing.

Bob looks over the edge of the knoll. He watches as the missile catches the jet ski dead center. The explosion vaporizes the bike and the man.

SMUGGLERS ON THE BOAT AND NORTH KNOLL

"Holy shit." He turns towards Natalie on the boat. "You can scratch one bundle and the recovery guys. They just fucking disappeared." He slides down the side of the knoll to the water's edge and climbs back on the boat.

"Natalie, we have to get going. By now the marines are moving on the bunker. They're going to block the channel."

A laws rocket hits the top of the north knoll and blows the two men at the machine gun into the air. Their twisted bodies land in the water as a second rocket hits the water about thirty feet in front of the boat. Mud and water rain down on the boat.

"Damn." Natalie brushes mud and slim off her as she stands back up. They can hear gunfire farther down the peninsula near the bunker

"They're attacking the bunker. It's only a matter of time."

Natalie holds up a radio detonator. "Yeah, but they're going to get a major surprise when we shove that bunker up their ass."

"Save it for now. We can us it as a diversion when we run for it."

"All right." Natalie puts the detonator back in her pocket.

MARINES ON THE SOUTH KNOLL

"Bulldog, this is Recon. Over."

"Roger, Recon."

"Bulldog, we have control of the south knoll. We are receiving fire from the bunker and the north point of the north knoll. Night Moves and a fire team are crossing a stream to attack the bunker position. We have fire superiority but are unable to get at the boat behind the north knoll. Over."

"Roger. These choppers are beginning to lose to the gusts of wind. We'll need to secure the area and dust off the wounded. I'm trying to get some air support now from Touchdown. Over."

"Roger, Bulldog. Captain Rollens has advised me that we have to get these men out or they will be KIAs soon."

"Roger. Bulldog out."

SMUGGLER BOAT BEHIND NORTH KNOLL

The second jet ski driver dodges rifle fire and pulls his bundle around the north knoll. He pulls up to the back of the boat.

"Shit, did you see what happened to Greg? Fuck this. I'm not going back out."

The bundle is hoisted up onto the boat and pushed forward.

Natalie leans over the back of the boat. "We have one more bundle. Have some balls and go get it."

"Balls have nothing to do with it. Plant your cunt on this thing, and you go get it." He slips into the water and pushes the jet ski away from the boat. He climbs up the ladder on the back of the boat. As he goes to throw his leg over and get on board, a round hits him square in the chest. His arms fling out, and he falls back into the dark water. He floats face down beside his jet ski.

"Goddammit, Natalie. Knock that shit off We could have used him on the machine gun."

"He didn't deserve his share." She slips her pistol back into a holster at her side. She takes out the detonator. "Let's get ready to go."

MARINES ON THE SOUTH KNOLL

"Touchdown, this is Bulldog. Over."

"Roger, Bulldog."

"Touchdown, we need air support. Over."

"Bulldog, this is Touchdown. You have winds gusting between seventy-five and ninety miles per hour. We're recalling all aircraft and diverting aircraft to alternate fields. Over."

"Touchdown, this is Vampire flight. We can take your strike. Over."

Nelson turns to his executive office. "Who the hell is Vampire flight?"

"It's those two army A-10s that flew in the blood. They took off just a little while ago. Their flight path would put them just northwest of the marines."

"Bulldog, hold."

"Vampire leader, this is Touchdown."

"Roger."

"You're cleared to assist. Use your own discretion regarding conditions at site. Over."

"Roger, Touchdown. We'll contact Bulldog at site. Vampire leader out."

"Bulldog, you're running out of time and have still not located the package. Over"

"I just received word from Recon. Package eight has been found. Over."

"Excellent, Bulldog. You have till 0200 hours. Deadline is not changing. Prediction is that weather in your area will be at over 100 miles per hour with heavy rain. Touchdown out."

"Susie, as you heard, they found the bomb. As soon as the site is secured, were going in hot."

ULTLMA
WASHINGTON, D.C.

Admiral Hillings jumps to his feet. "Yes!" Everyone in the room looks silently at him.

"Mr. President, I have just got off the phone with Captain Nelson. He received word from Bulldog. They have found the last bomb."

A cheer goes up from the others. "Excellent, Admiral." Wayne looks at the clock and up at the storm on the screen. "Will they have time to secure the bomb?"

"We can only hope so, Mr. President." Brant turns back to the men at the table. "Whatever the outcome of the next hour, each service has performed in the highest possible manner to this situation. We could ask no more of them."

"Yes, sir." The men at the table answer in unison.

THE BRIDGE OF THE *MOSKVA*
THE GULF

"Admiral." Sokolov looks up at his aid from behind his coffee cup. "Sir, the damage to the forward sections is more severe that thought. Cables are being laid on the second level deck to try and get power back to the forward sonar. And one of the feed ramps for the forward anti-sub missiles has been bent out of shape."

"Can the SUW be cleared soon?"

"They think so, sir. It is believed we will have limited range from sonar."

"Thank you." He takes another sip of coffee. Sparks continue to fly from welding torches on the other slips. They continue north at eighteen knots.

Deep inside, Sokolov has an uneasy feeling. He has been unable to shake it for the last half-hour. His feeling is like a buck holding its muzzle into the air to sniff the breeze. He has a sense that something is not right, but he can't see anything. The hunter's scope keeps positioning him in the cross hairs.

TELEVISION STATION
HAVANA

"General, we'll be landing at the TV station. The president is inside under security."

"Very good." Quintano looks out the window as the Hind settles to the ground. "Brock, would you get a hold of Zino and see if they have located Morales's helicopters?"

"Yes, Comrade." Quintano goes inside to brief Fidel on the situation. He passes through the armed security men in the lobby. He enters a side office and sees Fidel behind the desk on the phone. His personal body guards are on each side of him. He waves Quintano to a chair.

Brock gets with Zino on the radio. "Have they isolated their two Hinds yet?"

"Malangas has picked up two boogies about fifteen miles out at sea. Their flying almost due east. Also, we had one of the Bandeirante patrol planes get a fix on Morales's yacht off Cayo Coco. If I were to guess, he is heading for it now."

"I agree. I'll tell the general. Out."

Brock jumps from the helicopter and runs up to the building. The security guards stop him at the doors to the building. A guard goes into the building to get the general. Quintano comes out of the office and sees Brock at the door. He waves him in.

"General, they have them spotted off Malangas. They're heading due east. Also, Morales's yacht is parked off Cayo Coco."

"Excellent. Send word to Zino to have the missile batteries there try and knock them down. Also, have the closest naval base send out a couple of the OSA boats to intercept the yacht."

"Yes, sir." Brock turns to head for the helicopter.

Quintano yells after him. "Have the Hind ready to leave. I'll inform the president and be right there."

"Right, Comrade."

Brock relays the information on to Zino. The missile batteries at Malangas are ordered to fire on the two boogies to their front. Quintano comes out of the building and jumps in next to Brock. "Let's go. If the missiles don't get them, we'll pick them up near Cayo Coco." The two Hinds lift off and head northeast.

At Malangas air base, the two tracked vehicles holding the SA-6 missiles slowly raise their missiles into firing position. Suited more for high altitude targets, the lower it depresses, the shorter its range.

"Set your track." The missile commander looks over at the radar operator. "Range fifteen miles, course due east."

"Missiles ready to fire, sir."

"General Morales, you have a call from the other helicopter."

"This is Morales."

"General, we have suffered some damage from the attack in Havana. We're losing hydraulic pressure. We'll need to head into the coast and land on the beach. We can then join you in your helicopter. Over."

Morales slowly keys his mike. "Wait one, Captain." The pilot breaks in. "General, we are just passing the airfield at Malangas. We are being scanned by high frequency radar."

"What is it?"

"I believe the missile batteries are preparing to fire."

"Can you keep us behind the other helicopter?"

"Yes, sir."

"Good, then use it as a shield. Maybe the lock on is only on them."

"Roger."

"Captain, hold your course until we get beyond the air base. Then we will go into the coast and off load you and your men."

"Yes, sir. We're picking up tracking radar from the coast."

"Don't worry about it. They won't fire on us."

In the missile command center, a man says, "We have a lock on the nearest helicopter. We are unable to get a steady fix on the other one."

"We'll fire two missiles on my count." The firing boards light up. "Clear the area. We're preparing to fire." The commander calls out one more time over the loud speakers.

"Radar."

"We have a lock, at sixteen miles."

The commander looks around the area. "Fire."

Two of the Gainful missiles are boosted from their launchers. The boosters fall away as the rockets accelerate and their ramjets take over. They lock on their target.

"General, Malangas has fired. We are tracking two missiles inbound. We believe they are locked on the other Hind."

"General, we have missiles inbound. We are unable to evade."

His next words are lost in the explosion as the two warheads smash into the side of the Hind. It explodes in a yellow-orange ball. Morales's helicopter dives for the ocean surface, and levels off just above the wave tops. It races east at full speed.

"Contact the command center. Inform them we have one confirmed kill. But the other one dove below our radar."

The message is relayed to Quintano. "Very well, inform the batteries that we will be passing south of their position. And to check their fire. Over."

"Well, Comrade Brock. The game is a foot."

"Yes, sir.

NORTH COAST
CUBA

A form suddenly appears at the opening of the cave. "Everyone come with me. We must move quickly. The boat will meet us in fifteen minutes." Luís and the other three grab their belong-ings and follow the older man out of the cave and down a path to the beach.

They move quickly down the darkened beach. The cold wind engulfs them, and they pull their jackets tighter around their necks. "We are almost there. Just a little farther." As they trudge through the sand, the old man encourages them to hurry. As they move around a large group of rocks, half in the water, a flashlight catches them all in its beam. They all freeze, staring at the light.

"Come on. We only have a short amount of time to clear the outer islands. The patrol boats have all been called back to base along with the aircraft."

The others wade out into the water to get on the boat. Another man pulls them on board. The twenty-four-foot bay liner bobs back and forth in the surf. The old man grabs Luís's arm. "Señor, I do not know what you and your friend have done, and I do not want to know. But he will not be joining us. The military caught him at the blue house, and he was killed. I only hope it was worth a young man's life."

"It was, Grandfather. We both knew that death was a possibility."

"Go quickly. Your chance for life lies to the north." He pats Luís on the shoulder and disappears into the darkness. The water is cold as he wades out to the boat. A helping hand pulls him up onto the deck.

"You're the last one, right?"

"Yes."

"Good, go into the cabin and have some coffee. And stay out of the way."

As Luís makes his way in to the cabin, the engines on the boat come to life. They begin moving away from shore towards the Archipelago de Sabana. Once they have cleared this obstacle, they will have a clear run to south Florida. The coffee warms his hands and throat. As Luís looks out the small porthole, the boat picks up speed.

HELICOPTER
NORTH COAST OF CUBA

Quintano looks at his map. "If we go south of Cardenas, we may be able to catch him near the islands in de Sabana."

The pilot cuts in. "Sir, we have a report from Caibarien and Punta Alegre. Both bases have put *OSA* boats to sea. They are heading for Cayo Coco."

"Excellent." Quintano goes over the course he wants with the pilot. The Hind makes a slight adjustment and plows into the night.

"He is going to break for the Bahamas. Then on to the Dominican Republic, General."

"Maybe, Comrade Brock. But not if I can help it." They both laugh.

BOMB SITE, NUMBER EIGHT
LOUISIANA

"Bulldog, this is Vampire. Over."

"Roger, Vampire."

"Bulldog, we're about five miles southwest of your position. We'll only have time for one pass. This weather is turning to shit fast."

"Roger that. Do you want us to mark their position? We have a bunker and some type of boat."

"Roger, and get your people out of the way. We're coming in with guns. We have no other ordnance."

"Roger. I'll contact our team to mark your targets."

"Roger. Vampire out."

"Recon, this is Bulldog."

Marshall answers at the point. "Roger, Major." He listens to Johnson. "Yes, sir. We have the boat to the north pinned down behind the knoll. And Night Moves has five men with him. They are crossing over to the north knoll to attack the bunker."

"Top, we have two army A-10s coming in with guns. We'll need to get the men back from the bunker."

"Roger, sir. Hold one."

Night Moves and the men with him move across the creek and up the side of the knoll in front of them. Men on the south point keep the men at the bunker down. Night Moves calls back on the radio, "Check your fire. We're moving on the position."

The firing from the other marines ceases, and they move forward. "Shit. They're moving on us. Get everyone back into the bunker."

They move off the top of the knoll as the first rounds from Night Moves's group begin to hit around them. Three men get up and sprint for the door to the bunker. They dive through the door and move towards firing slits in the front. One of them stays by the door and calls for the other two to make a run for it.

"Come on, you assholes." The two men roll over and begin running crouched over. The marines catch them in a withering fire. Their bodies are flung aside by the multiple hits.

"Fuck it." He slams the door and slides a bolt home. The other two fire into the brush south of their position. Rifle grenades explode around the bunker.

"Bob, there are three of us in the bunker. We are in a bad situation here. We're fighting the fucking marines out here."

Bob keys his radio. "Dave, get the fuck out of the bunker. It's set to go. We were waiting for them to get in there."

"Roger. We're out of here."

"Let's get the fuck out of here." They run back to the covered boat dock and jump onto an airboat. One gets in the seat as the others kneel down in the boat.

"Get us out from under this shit." The two men oar them out from under the camouflage. As soon as they're clear, the driver hits the starter, and the engine comes to life. They speed away from the bunker. When they reach the end of the side channel, they can see the boat behind the knoll.

"That stupid bitch is going to try and run the channel. Fuck that." He turns the airboat to the left, and races up a channel into the swamp.

Natalie watches as the airboat turns to the left and disappears into the swamp. "You chicken-shit bastards."

"Natalie, they may have the right idea. This channel run is a kamikaze run."

"Shut up, Bob. We have about seventy-five million worth of shit here. And you think we should leave it. Fuck you." Bob jumps over the side and moves up to the top of the knoll to see what is happening.

Marshall is kneeling next to Owens when he suddenly snaps awake and the pain in his chest hits him. "Oh, my God. I feel like I have an elephant on me."

Cabolero, sitting next to him, holds him down with his left arm, as the corpsman finishes bandaging his shoulder. "Owens, hang on. We're all right. A sniper hit you. They think it broke your sternum and cracked some ribs."

"Shit." His hands rest over his heart. A bandage holds him firmly.

"I hope you got the bastard?"

"I did, but he nailed me, too."

"Did I hear something about a bunker?" Marshall looks over at him. "Yeah, we have guys assaulting one now."

"Tell them not to go in. These fucking drug guys booby trap them. When you get near or in them, they blow the shit out of you."

"We have an air strike coming in."

"That's what we need. These assholes have so much fucking money, they have all the new high tech shit. I must say, it's more fun having you guys out here. Shit, you got the fucking power."

Rollens move up to his side. "Mr. Owens, you need to quit talking and stay calm, or you're going to cause more problems."

"God, do you have anything for the pain?"

"Yeah, but I didn't give it to you while you were out. As soon as the air strike is over, you and the others are being dusted out of here."

"Captain, you need to pull your men back. Owens says not to try and enter the bunker. It's a trap. When you're clear, you need to mark the bunker for the A-10s."

"Got you, Top. We're pulling back across the creek. On your count we'll light it up."

"Roger." Marshall moves two men to the front of the knoll. "When I give you the word, I want flares over the top of the north point." The two marines load the grenade launchers on their M-16s.

Night Moves and his men run down the knoll into the creek and back up onto the south knoll.

"Top, we're clear and ready to light up the bunker."

"Roger, Captain."

"Bulldog, we're in position. We'll illuminate on your call."

"Roger. Wait one."

"Vampire, we are ready to illuminate the targets. Your call."

"Roger. Vampire 2 is coming in east to west for the bunker. I'll be coming in south to north. We can only give you one pass, but it will be a thrill."

Rain adds to the misery of the situation, and gusts of wind blow in cold off the Gulf.

"Bulldog, this is Vampire 2. Light up your target. I'm inbound now."

"Light up the bunker."

Night Moves and the others fire flares around the bunker. Over the wind the whine of the engines on the A-l0s reaches the men on the point. The huge Avenger 30 mm cannon flares to life out over the swamp. The men on the point stare in disbelief at the huge fireball preceding the plane. The shark's mouth and eyes are visible in the light. It passes their position at 200 feet from east to west. The noise rises even above the winds.

Night Moves and the others hug the ground as the rounds from the cannon start at the base of the knoll and walk through it to the bunker. As they tear through the walls of the bunker and explode, the charges set earlier explode. A huge fireball lights up the night. The pilot pulls up and through the rising fireball. Night Moves and the others are screwed into the mud by the concussion. Debris falls all around them.

Night Moves lifts his head. "Holy shit. I have to have one of these babies."

"Bulldog, this is Vampire 1 inbound. Illuminate target."

"Holy shit." Bob slides back down from the knoll. "Get the fuck off the boat." He runs up the side of the knoll as two flares burst above the boat.

Natalie looks in disbelief at the disappearing figure. The second A-10 opens fire behind the marines on the south knoll. They hug the ground as it passes over them. The north end of the knoll is lost in explosion and smoke as the rounds hit. They tear through the sand and mud, and rip the fragile hull of the boat to pieces. The gas tanks on the boat explode in a yellow ball of fire. The pilot turns towards the west to rejoin his wingman. "Bulldog, good luck. Vampire out."

"Roger, Vampire. Great work. Thanks."

The two A-l0s meet over the swamp and head north at full speed.

"Recon, this is Bulldog. We're coming in." The two helicopters head for the point.

Night Moves and his men cross back to the northern knoll, to check the bunker. All they can find is a smoking crater and a huge chunk of the bank torn out.

"Jesus, is that a fucking gun or what? It tore the shit out of this place." They move through the bunker area and walk along the edge of the knoll towards the location of the boat.

"This is Night Moves. Check your fire. We are on the side of the knoll, moving towards the point. We have a path clear."

"Roger. Bulldog is inbound. Do you want flares?"

"Roger. Light up the point."

Marshall turns to the two marines at the north edge of their position. "Give the recon group illumination at the point." They aim their rifles into the air and fire the 40 mm grenade launchers. They shoot up into the air and burst high above the point. As the flares come to life, a figure comes across the top of the knoll. He empties a magazine in the direction of the marines at the south point. His burnt hand reaches down and pops the magazine into the mud. He slides a second one home. Dazed and stumbling, Bob moves down the side of the knoll towards the bunker. He fires a burst over the heads of Night Moves and his men. His wounds and burns make it hard for him to focus as he moves forward. He fires a second burst into the air. He suddenly flies backward as the rounds from Night Moves's group and the men on the south knoll hit him at one time. The recon group moves past him and up and over the north point.

Three bodies float in the water, and pieces of the boat are scattered everywhere. The cannon fire blew half of the point away.

"Top, we're at the north point."

"Roger, sir. Anything left?"

"Not really. Some bad guys in the water. It's clear."

"Good. Bulldog is on the way in. I suggest your team rejoin us."

"Roger. We're on our way."

The helicopters turn on their lights and move in to the point. The command helicopter moves to the south side of the knoll and settles down half in the water. The other Jolly Green moves around to the point and lands in the water. As soon as the ramp is lowered, marines begin carrying the wounded aboard. The dead are wrapped in ponchos and are prepared to be loaded.

Marshall walks down the knoll and meets Johnson and the others. They have to yell over the whine of the helicopter engines.

"Top, these helicopters are out of here. We need to load the wounded and get everyone except for a fire team loaded."

"They're loading the helicopter now, and Night Moves and the others are heading back now. I'll pick five men to stay and get the others on the command ship."

"Excellent, Top. Do you know where the bomb is?"

"They say it's this way, sir. Night Moves threw a bunch of dye marker around the area." The gusts of wind seem to increase, and the rain blows in stinging droplets. Susie and Johnson follow Marshall down a trail. As he passes marines along the top of the knoll, he has them head back towards the point.

Their lights search the ground in front of them, and they catch sight of the fluorescent green. "I think we have found it." They gather around the protruding tail fin.

They turn their backs towards the south as the rain-washes over them. Susie kneels down and pushes some of the mud aside.

"This is going to be a real bitch. It's in there deep." Marshall kneels down beside her. "We'll get some men to start digging. We're running out of time."

Johnson joins them. "The Coast Guard cutter *Eastwind* is sending in a special kind of boat to pull us out. We have to send the helicopters out now. So let's get some men working on this thing right away."

"Aye, aye, sir." Marshall walks back to the point.

They are carrying the dead aboard. "We're going to keep the fire team from the north knoll here for security. So staffs, get your men loaded."

The staff sergeants make a head count and begin loading the command ship. "I'll stay, Top."

Marshall puts his hand on Cabolero shoulder. "Hey, old buddy. You've done all you can. This is just a clean up from now on. So get your ass on the helicopter, and we'll see you back at the base."

"All right, but you owe me a tall Bushmill at the CPO mess."

"Shit, after this, you and I will get a couple of bottles."

Cabolero walks towards the ramp and turns. "Hey, all kidding aside, watch your ass, Top."

Marshall nods in the light from the helicopter.

"Top, I'm sending the other corpsman back with the wounded. Laura and I will remain with you."

"Very good, Dr. Rollens. You need to join the others at the bomb site. I'll show you where it is."

They meet Johnson near the command ship as Night Moves and his team come in.

Marshall gets with the fire team and takes them up to the bomb site.

"Sir, are you sure you want to stay?"

Rollens shields his face from the rain. "Yes, Major. I've done all I can for the men here. They need to get back to the hospital as soon as possible."

Johnson looks at Night Moves. "Well, Captain, they have loaded your gunner. And you need to head back on the command ship."

"Yes, sir. It's been a thrill." As he moves to the ramp, Johnson calls after him. "I hope you will join me for a drink when this is over. You did a hell of a job, Marine."

"Thank you, sir. I'll even buy. You have a good team here." He throws a quick salute as he moves up the ramp. Both helicopters close their ramps.

"Bulldog, we're out of here. Good luck."

"Roger. You did a great job." The big Jolly Greens lift up into the pouring rain and head west for the base. When Johnson gets back to the bomb site, men are already beginning to dig around the bomb. The rain pounds steadily as they scoop away the mud. It immediately fills any holes dug in the embankment.

Susie, Laura, and Dr. Rollens sit to the side on a tree trunk. Their ponchos are pulled tight around them. Marshall and Johnson stand to one side with their lights on the men digging. The radio operator kneels nearby. He talks to someone and moves up to Johnson.

"Sir, I have contact with the Coast Guard boat. They are in the channel, due east of us."

"Guardian, this is Bulldog. Over."

"Roger, Bulldog. We're out from your position about 100 yards east of you. Check your fire. We'll come in on the north side of the knoll."

"Roger, we're glad to hear from you. Bulldog out."

He walks over to Susie and the others. "We have the Coast Guard boat coming in. You may want to wait on board, while we get the casing cleared."

Susie's hair sits wet in strings around her face as she peeks out the front of her poncho hood. "That sounds great." The marine closest to the point calls back to the dig site.

"Sir, we have a boat coming in from the channel."

"Right." Johnson moves over next to him. They both watch the lights out on the swamp getting larger as they maneuver into their position. It skirts the point and moves down the north side of the knoll. Johnson strikes a flare and guides them into the shore. As the boat gets into the light of the flare, Johnson gives it a curious look. One of the crewman jumps from the deck and moves by him to secure the craft. The bow nudges into the sand as another man climbs out a side hatch and jumps down.

"Bulldog, I'm Lieutenant Childes." He holds his arm up. "We can't stay to long. All ships have been sent north. And you have eight to ten-foot breakers hitting the coast. They're breaking over another spit of land south of you. My orders are to remove your party no later than 0200, sir."

"Very good, Lieutenant. They're digging the bomb out now. We're hoping thirty minutes will give us enough time."

They walk up the knoll towards the bomb site. "By the way, what kind of boat is that thing?"

Childes chuckles. "It's called a Keslinger boat. It is used in hard-to-get-at places and extremely rough seas. It will roll over and right itself. It's like a sealed kayak."

"Well, let's hope we don't need that feature."

Johnson introduces Childes to Susie and the others. He asks if they can get on board to get out of the rain.

"Sure, I can also get you a couple of men to help with the digging. We were told that you would be using the on-board radio to contact Touchdown, sir."

They all head for the boat and climb inside. They're offered hot coffee as Johnson calls in to the base.

U.S. SUBMARINE
THE GULF

"Captain." The watch officer walks over to him. "Sir, communications has us on GPS, just entering the eye."

"Good. Bring us up to sixty feet."

"Aye, aye, sir."

As they reach sixty feet, the diving officer calls to the captain, "Sixty feet, sir."

"Very good. Up periscope."

The periscope breaks through the surface and turns a slow 365 degrees. "Surface, I want look-outs up."

"Aye, aye, sir." The diving officer hits the klaxon, and the boat begins to rise.

When the huge hull breaks the surface, the hatch on the sail is opened, and men begin climbing out. The men take up positions on the diving planes as the captain joins them. They are all drawn back by the sight. A low patchy fog surrounds them, but above a million diamonds sparkle in the sky. For a quiet moment, all stand and just look around. The captain shakes his head and then picks up a phone nearby.

"Commander, all on and hit the fog horn. Also, send up some flares. Have the deck party come out of the hull."

Men emerge from the base of the sail and connect safety lines. They are struck by the quiet beauty around them. Flare guns are handed out to the men standing on the dive planes. They fire out to the front of the sail.

"Sir, radar has a contact about three miles off the starboard side."

Corrections in the course are made, and their speed picks up. More flares are fired into the mist. Suddenly, a red dot rises in the mist and explodes into three red balls.

"There they are, sir," the man on the starboard side calls out. He points into the mist.

The captain calls down to Commander Blakely. "Get your people ready to take the raft down the port side."

Men in wet suits climb onto the hull from the hatch at the rear of the missle tubes.

"There she is, Captain." The look-out points just off the bow.

"Stand by to recover the raft. Bring the hull to a stop." The men on the hull space themselves out with ropes to throw, and the divers check their safety lines.

As the raft passes down the side of the submarine, men at the front hatch attempt to throw lines to the person near the raft opening. He tries to hold on but can't. They slip towards the next group down the hull.

A diver is lowered over the side to the water line. He waits for the raft and jumps for the opening. A hand from inside helps to pull him in.

As the submarine comes to a full stop, the phone on the sail rings.

"This is the captain."

"Sir, we are being pulled sideways at fifteen knots."

"Roger."

He watches as other ropes are thrown to the diver to secure the raft. A safety line is attached to the hull, and a line of sailors is positioned to help the wounded onto the hull.

Blakely calls down to the diver. "How many are in there, and what is their condition?"

"Sir, there are sixteen people on board. Four are dead, and the others are all injured. Their captain is on board. We'll bring out the most injured first."

"All right. Let's get going." Blakely calls up to the captain on his radio. "Sir, we have twelve casualties and four dead. We're moving them now."

"Very good, Commander. We need to hurry."

The first of the Russians is helped down into the hull. The last to leave the raft is the captain; he wears his ship's log book around his neck in a waterproof bag. As he gets on the hull, he is saluted by Commander Blakely. "Welcome aboard, sir."

The diver makes one more check. "That's it, sir. The others are all dead."

Blakely orders him off the raft, and the attaching lines are cut. The raft is quickly dragged away by the strong current. Blakely quickly checks the hull and orders all hatches secured.

USS *GEORGIA*
THE GULF

"Sir, the hatches are secured."

"Very good. Give me 100 feet." The *Georgia* begins to slide under the waves and starts to pick up speed. "Give me flank speed to the second target." The captain picks up a phone. "Engine room, stay on-line. We'll need power at a moment's notice." He hangs up the phone and goes over to the plotting board.

"Sir, we should have an intercept at this point." The navigation officer stops his finger on the map. "We'll be within ten miles of the whirlpool, and we'll have the French Shoals at our back. We have run the data from NavOps weather. We're in agreement with them."

"Very good." He picks up a phone, the exec answers at the base of the sail.

"Sir."

"We're not going to have much time at the next site. Is everything ready?"

"Yes, sir. We have had extra stretchers brought up. We put the overflow in the crew mess and the wardroom. The dispensary is pretty full."

"How is their captain?"

"He'll be fine. He has a broken arm and some cracked ribs."

"I'll visit him later. You sound like you're all set. We'll give you the intercept time as we close."

The captain hangs up the phone and takes a cup of coffee from a mess steward. "Thanks, Thomas. You guys had better keep the pot boiling. I think this is going to be a high caffeine night."

"Aye, aye, sir."

The big boomer races through the water at over thirty knots.

ULTIMA
WASHINGTON, D.C.

"You were right, Admiral." The president leans back in his chair.

"Yes, sir. I told you about these submarine captains. They're the sneakiest and most well trained officers in the service."

Secretary Brant looks at the screen. "Mr. President, the rescue submarine is heading for the second raft. Do they have the time to save these men, Admiral?"

"To be honest, Mr. Secretary, I'm not sure."

"I wonder if we are not putting a great many men and equipment in harm's way, Admiral? They seem to be heading directly for the whirlpool. We may consider, Mr. President, the option of ordering them out."

The president watches the submarine submerge on the screen next to the satellite pictures. A graphic shows the whirlpool and the raft. A red line shows the position and path of the raft. A yellow spiral shows the whirlpool and its path. A blue line represents the submarine. It moves slowly towards the other two.

"It is a consideration that we should look at, Admiral. They have performed outstandingly. In trying to comply with our order, though, maybe they are taking on too great a risk?"

"Sir, as I have stated, these captains are some of the most highly trained professionals in the service. Their entire reason for being is to outwit a mirror image of themselves. They are in a position to make life and death decisions on a twenty-four hour basis. I would go with the captain. If his decision is to go after the second raft, that means that he has weighed all possibilities and has determined that the rescue is possible." Both the president and Brant sit quietly and look at the admiral and the screen.

"Mr. President, I would have to agree with Admiral Hillings. Our trust in the abilities of these men would be undermined if we presumed to order them out."

"I agree, Mr. Brant. We should go with the captain and crew of the *Georgia*. I wish them luck."

"Gentlemen." Van Nar points to the map showing the last bomb. The outline of the fingers of land into the swamp is shown, and the site of the bomb appears in red. "We now have word that the communications circuit has been established. We have Mr. Val at the naval base and Major Johnson on the rescue boat. As soon as the panel is exposed, Dr. Davies will begin to disarm the bomb."

"Excellent." Wayne looks at the others. "Gentlemen, we may just pull this off."

Brant looks at the clock. "They will have less than thirty minutes before the pull-out time at 0200. We hope for good luck."

MORALES'S HELICOPTER
NORTH COAST OF CUBA

"General."

Morales keys his mike. "Yes."

"Sir, we have a contact about six miles ahead. It is a small boat moving between the shoals. It is just off our line of flight. We believe it is a smuggler. It poses no threat."

"Roger." Morales shakes his head and tries to remember something. "Wasn't Quintano chasing those two techs who blew up the bomber? This could be them."

The big gunship seems to come out of nowhere. It flies over the top of the boat and begins a turn to come around. "Shit." The man at the helm throws the levers forward and races for some rocks sticking out of the water. "He is running, General."

"Roger. Blow him out of the water."

They lock the cannon on the moving target and fire. A hail of tracers fly into the night as the boat pulls behind the rocks. They ricochet in different directions as they hit the stones. The boat races for a small island just ahead.

"Damn it." The pilot keys the rocket pods. He turns the helicopter to follow the boat and fires a salvo. Six rockets fly from each pod. They slam into the sand and rocks as the boat darts for another sandbar with trees. The explosions tear the little island in half.

"Did you get him?"

"No, General. We are coming around for a frontal attack." As they swing around, two blips show up on their scope. The pilot brings the helicopter up to face the two new threats.

"General, we have two aircraft coming in from the southeast at eight miles. They are showing as two of our Hinds. They are now splitting to attack us at two angles."

"Damn it, get me out of here. We need to make it to the boat."

"Yes, sir." The pilot pulls the helicopter around and heads due east.

QUTNTANO'S HELICOPTER

"Could you see the rockets, sir?"

Quintano keys his mike. "Yes, what are they firing at?"

"Our scan shows a small boat running between the rocks. He is heading due north."

Quintano looks over at Brock. "You don't think that this might be our other bomber?"

"It could be, General. He has had time to get to this location to get the boat." They feel the helicopter maneuver to attack. The other helicopter moves away in the other direction.

"General, they have spotted us and are breaking off to the east."

"Roger. Bring the other Hind in front of the boat. We'll come in from the rear."

"Roger." They get a track on the boat and move in behind him. The boat reaches open water and begins to race forward. The people on board work to seal holes and other damage from the attack. Suddenly in front of them, the forward lights of the gunship come on. They are flooded in the brilliant light. The trailing gunship turns its lights on also. The boat comes to a stop; they all raise their hands over their heads.

They come to a hover off to one side. Quintano and Brock look down on the people on the deck. Quintano pulls out a picture of Luís and hands it to Brock.

"The guy standing near the cabin door."

"You got him, General. It's our man."

"Damn it, we don't have time for this right now. We have to get Morales."

"Hell, from the damage, they will be lucky to make it." Quintano tells the pilot to key the outside speakers. The squawk startles the people in the boat.

"This is General Quintano. Have a good day, Luís." They watch through the windows as his mouth falls open. The others on the boat look at him. The lights on the helicopters go out, and they both turn and fly to the east.

Those on the boat stand in shock. They look from one to the other. "I don't know what that was all about. But we're getting our asses out of here while we can."

The captain pushes the throttles forward, and the boat pushes out into the Gulf. "Put something in those holes. We'll need God's help to get through."

ULTLMA
WASHINGTON, D.C.

Van Nar moves to the podium. "Gentlemen, on screen four is what we perceive as the pursuit of General Morales by General Quintano." White lines outline the islands and shoals of the area. "The red circle is Morales's helicopter. And the two yellow circles are General Quintano's. The smaller blue circle is a small craft of some kind. We think it may be a smuggler or escaping refugees. We'll show you what has just transpired."

The circles begin to move and show the attack on the boat. "We don't know why General Morales attacked this boat. But as you can see, the other helicopters drove it off. They actually stopped the boat, then left it and resumed their pursuit."

"A recon flight out of Florida has confirmed a large civilian craft parked off Cayo Coco. We believe this to be General Morales's personal yacht. From the course flown so far, he is heading directly for it."

Two green circles appear on the screen. "The two green circles are two *OSA* boats sent out from the naval station. They are on a course to intercept the yacht." An aide walks up to Captain Van Nar and hands her a message. "We have an intel from Sky 1. They are monitoring a speech from President Castro in Havana. They are recording it and will have it for you in just a few minutes."

"Well, he made it." Wayne runs his hand through his hair.

"Yes, Mr. President. Let's hope that this incident will bring on a softening of his policies."

"Amen, Mr. Brant."

QUINTANO'S HELICOPTER

Quintano calls to the pilot, "What is our status?"

"Sir, we're about ten miles behind them. They're going at full speed. We're picking up a homing beacon about twenty miles out."

"Good. Contact the surface units and give them the co-ordinants. I believe that whatever is sending out the beacon is where Morales is heading."

"They must have realized that we were following. They have turned off the beacon. But the Hind is still holding its course. General, I'm picking up a transmission from Havana. It is President Castro. I'll put it through."

Quintano and the others listen as Fidel covers the events of the day. He reassures them that all is in good hands and that General Morales is being hunted down. He also thanks the American forces at Guantánamo and President Wayne for their assistance.

"Sir, his helicopter has come to a hover. They are near a boat off Cayo Coco."

"Of course, it's Morales's boat. The bastard is going to run."

"What do you think: Haiti or the Dominican Republic?"

Brock thinks for a minute. "I'd say Dominican."

"I agree. Well, let's hope we can put a damper in his plans."

"Sir, the helicopter has left the ship. It is on a head-on course with us."

"Inform the other Hind and take appropriate action. This is a hostile engagement."

"Roger."

The two helicopters separate, forcing the attacking helicopter to choose whom to face. The men in the back are thrown against their seat belts as the helicopter begins to maneuver.

"Sir, he has picked our other ship as his primary target. They have gone to guns."

Streaks of tracers fly in the dark sky as the two adversaries maneuver. The pilot of Morales's helicopter suddenly turns towards Quintano's ship. It fires a volley of un-aimed missiles, which blast from its wing pylons. Then it resumes its attack on the other ship.

The helicopter gyrates, throwing everything not tied down around the cabin, as the pilot maneuvers out of harm's way.

As the other two fire and maneuver, Quintano's pilot brings the gunship around and locks onto Morales's helicopter with his Swatter missiles. He goes to guns and fires two of the missiles.

The gunner fires the missles at the moving target. Morales's helicopter is just beginning to turn to face his other adversary when the missiles hit. One hits just below the pilot and the other in the back cabin space. The gunship rolls hard to its right and dives for the sea. It crashes into the black water below.

"Sir, I think we have a first here. We just shot down an aircraft with two anti-tank missiles."

Brock chews on his lip for a second. "Shit, I think they're right, General. I've never heard of it happening before."

"Sir, the boat is pulling away to the northeast."

"Let's move in." The two gunships continue their chase after the boat.

"General, I have a call coming in from the boat." Quintano looks over at Brock. "I wonder who would be calling us from the boat?" His hand rubs his injured shoulder.

"Are you all right, General'"

"Yeah, just every once in a while, it lets me know it's there." He keys his mike.

"This is General Quintano."

"This is General Morales. Break off your pursuit. If you get within six miles, we'll shoot you down. I have six SA-7 missiles staged around the boat and more in the hold. You know they sell well around the world."

"You're not getting away. Your traitorous act has cost the lives of a lot of good men."

"If I had been successful, you would have been one of them. I would have raised Cuba to a power in the Caribbean. Not the economic cripple with its hand raised for hand outs from others."

"Give up now. You will get a fair trial by a military tribunal."

"You're kidding me. You always were one for the right way to do things. Go to hell, Quintano."

"No, Morales. But I foresee you going with honors. You have shamed the officers and men of the Cuban military. You tried to construct a madman's reality. And you will pay."

The radio goes dead. "Sir, we can test the boat. We'll hit the six-mile radius at an angle. If they fire we'll evade out of range."

"Let's see if they are lying."

The helicopter dips into the six miles, moving at an angle. Brook and Quintano watch out the side windows. Off to their right, flashes appear in the darkness.

"We have inbound missiles."

The pilot takes a sharp left turn and races into the western night. Flares burst to life in their wake. One of the missiles hits the flares and explodes. The other one burns out and explodes as it begins to fall.

"I would say he isn't kidding about the missiles, sir."

"Right, contact the boats and let me know how far out they are."

"Sir, we have them about sixteen miles southwest of our position."

"Can we give them command guidance?"

"Yes, sir."

"Then give them the coordinates. Let us know when they are ready to fire."

The two *OSA* boats begin running side by side. They lock in the coordinates. "Contact the general. We are ready to fire."

"General, the boats are ready to fire. Each boat will launch two missiles."

"Very good. Contact Morales."

"This is General Morales."

"This is your last chance to turn back to port."

"Go to hell, Quintano."

"Then meet your fate." He points to Brock who calls to the pilot to have them launch.

In the darkness south of them, the tube caps on the Styx launchers are blown off. A huge flame erupts from the launch tube as each boat fires their first missiles. In a few seconds, the second missiles are fired. They light up the boats as they race away to the north.

"General Quintano, we have two, correct that, four missiles inbound. They will be picking them up soon."

They watch out the side windows. Missiles are fired towards the south. One, then two. Three more are fired. They scream into the night. In the dark night south of the boat, a large yellow and orange fireball erupts.

"Well, it looks like they got one of them, General." They watch as a second volley of missiles fly from the yacht. "Yes, Brock, but I don't think they will be as successful with the other three."

MORALES'S YATCH

"We got one, General."

Morales walks to the stern of the boat as more missiles are fired. The *swoosh* of the firing missiles fills the air. He looks up at the stars and then back at the face of death coming from the south.

He lifts his glass up into the night air. "To Cuba." He drinks the dark rum. "Fuck you."

The missiles bracket the boat in one huge explosion. The fireball rises high into the dark night.

QULNTANO'S HELICOPTER

"Sir, radar shows nothing left. Should we investigate?"

"Roger, one quick pass over the area. Then back to Havana. Contact the naval boats to return to port with a job well done."

They move in over the area of the yacht. Small pieces of wreckage float in the sea. The lights from the two helicopters play over the area.

"Let's head back, Captain." The two helicopters join up and begin flying east.

"This has been one hell of a night, General."

Quintano stretches out on the seats. "That is true, Comrade. And tomorrow we will need our strength to help put Cuba back on the right path." He lays his head on a rolled-up field jacket and drifts off to sleep.

ULTIMA
WASHINGTON, D.C.

"Gentlemen, missiles have been fired from two Cuban *OSA* attack boats. They are inbound to the yacht." They watch the screen as dotted lines from the boats move towards the circle of the yacht. One flares and disappears. They watch as the remaining three hit their target.

"My God, that's it?"

Brant looks from the screen towards the president. "Yes, sir. Cuba is once again back in the hands of Castro. But this time we will be dealing with a much more moderate military staff And from the message that Fidel sent out, there may even be a chance to finally bring peace to the area."

"God, let's hope so, Mr. Brant."

BRIDGE OF THE *MOSKVA*
GULF

"Admiral, the forward work parties are reporting that the forward sonar is in pretty bad shape. The near misses and the hits on the forward deck have penetrated the hull. Water has filled the forward LF sonar spaces. They are continuing to replace the wiring."

Sokolov lowers his binoculars slowly. His eyes are still focused on the *Sovremennyy* and the *Osmotritelnyy*. Sparks fly from both welders working at different locations along the length of the ships. He turns slowly to the assistant weapons officer. The young man's face betrays his age.

"Thank you, Lieutenant. And what of the forward SUW launcher?"

"Sir, Comrade Kniglov says they are finishing the wiring. The terminals in the forward areas are pretty well gone."

"Please inform me when they are ready. I'll be in the control room."

The admiral puts his hand on the young officer's shoulder. "Lieutenant, unbutton your tunic and tie your life jacket on properly. Keep Comrade Yefimov informed of the situation."

Like a father, his hand pats him on the shoulder As the admiral reaches the bottom of the ladder, a call breaks in over the speakers.

"This is R-1. Over."

The admiral and Pstygo look at each other. "Admiral, it's the submarine. They're coming in on a satellite channel."

"Roger, R-1. This is pack leader. Over."

"Put me through to Admiral Sokolov. Over."

He picks up a handset. "This is Sokolov."

"Sir, we have sunk the Cuban submarine in the Frozen Forest. We will turn back to try and assist you with the other one."

"What is your condition, Captain?"

He moves over to the plotting table as Pstygo shows their location. Pstygo slowly shakes his head. "We have sustained some damage. But we can still fight."

"An excellent job, Captain. My compliments to you and your crew. But you are too far out to help us. I am ordering you to proceed on to the American demark point. We will fight the other submarine with the resources we have here."

"Very good, sir. But we may still be able to assist you. We will leave the circuit open. If you can give us a position, we will send some of the SS-N-2Is to assist."

"Outstanding, Captain. That may be all we have to throw at them."

"Comrade Admiral, I wish you good luck."

"Thank you, Captain. I hope to see us all get home safely."

Handing the handset back to the radio operator, he joins Pstygo at the plotting table. He watches as Pstygo puts a red transparency over their location.

"Admiral, according to the information we have, we will enter the torpedo danger zone within the hour. We are totally blind as far as sonar goes. They're trying to get it up now, but from the reports we have been receiving, we don't hold out much hope."

"Both of the destroyers are in bad shape. We may be fighting with only the RBUs. I would say about ten degrees off the bow for the first attack."

"I agree, sir."

"Comrade Pstygo, they are ready to test the forward sonar." Both he and the admiral move over to a sonar position, surrounded by techs. "Have them bring it up." They all watch the screen.

In the forward compartment, the repair crew is ordered to move back into the next compartment. The officer in charge stands in the hatchway as the men file by. They look like they have all been shoveling coal. The soot has blackened the interiors of the compartments, and oily water splashes over their shoes.

"Stand by. I'm going to throw the switch."

He snaps a fuse lever over. Sparks pop from connections on the wall and the cables lying on the deck. The men in the compartment can feel the tingle of electricity on their skin as it races in all directions.

"Shit." As the officer reaches for the panel, it explodes in a flash of silver-blue light.

"Ahhhhhh." He grabs his face and falls to the deck. The others move up to him; one of them pulls off the sweat soaked bandanna around his neck. He dips it into the oily water at his knees and folds it over the officer's eyes.

"Get a stretcher. We need to get him to the doctors."

He holds his burned hands in the air as the men lift him onto the stretcher. They move him back towards the belly of the ship.

Pstygo and the admiral watch as the screen comes to life and then crashes. They stare at the solid green tube.

"Sir, the feed panel blew up. The cables are burned. They lost the repair officer; he is badly burned. They say there are shorts all through the system. Do you want them to try again?"

"Tell them to concentrate on the forward SUW launcher."

"Yes, sir, Comrade Pstygo."

"Admiral, I have been talking with some of the sonar techs. They believe they could hook up a temporary system using one of the dunking sonars off the KA-27s. They think they can drop it over the side and hook it directly into the screen."

"Can that be done, Pstygo?"

He smiles and shrugs. "It's worth a try, Admiral."

"Do we have any of the units left?"

"Yes, sir. We checked already. We had it moved up to the main deck just in case we couldn't get the main unit up."

"Very good." The admiral smiles. "Hell, I'll take anything that will give us a track on that submarine."

"Aye, aye, sir." Pstygo points to a group of techs. They begin laying a cable out the side hatchway and up the ladder towards the main deck. They climb up the two decks to the hatchway to the starboard side of the ship. A group of crewmen muscles the unit towards the side of the ship. They hook it up on a small hoisting arm at the rail. The techs plug in a cannon plug and feed the tail back to the hatchway. They connect it to the feed cable, and the deck crew hoists the unit up and begins lowering it into the sea. The men at the hatch slowly feed out the cable.

The admiral watches as men remove the back of the sonar unit and begin sliding panels out. One man sits on the deck connecting wires as two of the others pour over a wiring schematic of the units.

One of the techs from the deck joins the others. "Sir, we'll have about 100 feet of cable over the side."

"Very good. Pstygo, I'll be on the bridge. Let me know if it works."

"I will, Admiral."

Sokolov climbs the ladder back up to the bridge.

ULTIMA
WASHINGTON, D.C.

"Gentlemen, we have made contact with the Russian submarine." Van Nar points to an area map. "They are proceeding to this point of contact. They have sustained some damage but feel they are still sea worthy." The screen showing the location of the submarine begins drawing lines showing its path to the American ships.

"On screen three is the path of the raft and the supposed path of the *Georgia*. Captain Emmett will give an updated report on the storm."

Brant's phone rings, and he picks it up. He talks in muffled tones and puts the line on hold. Standing, he walks back to the president and leans down to talk privately. The president listens and nods his head. He reaches over, presses down the flashing button, and they begin talking with Air Marshal Shagan. As he talks, he catches Admiral Hillings's eye, and motions for him to get on the line with him and Brant.

They listens as Shagan tells them of the plan passed on to him from Admiral Sokolov, regarding the missiles. He also tells them of the plight of the squadron.

"Sokolov has short range guidance. They are blind on sonar and have either lost by damage or fired all of the ordnance for the main 130 mm guns on the destroyers. The *Sovremennyy* has four HE rounds and fifty star shells. They are down to twelve knots to provide the *Osmotritelnyy* with some protection."

"Marshal Shagan, this is Admiral Hillings. We have been informed that the submarine R-1 has contacted the picket ships just north of them. We will relay the information that it may be required to fire missiles."

"Thank you, Admiral."

Hillings drops off, leaving the president and Brant discussing other issues.

He turns towards Van Nar. "Captain, give me a view of the picket ships north of the Russian submarine."

Van Nar picks up a handset and calls the control room. A position map of the western area comes up. It shows the four picket ships and their names. The admiral looks over the names.

Wayne and Brant hang up their phones. They look up at the screen. The class of ship and its name are displayed under the white squares on the screen.

"As you can see, Mr. President, we have two Spruance class destroyers, the *Deyo* and the *Young*, and also two sea-going tugs."

He turns to Van Nar. "Contact the *Deyo* and inform them that the Russian sub may be firing missiles in support of the Russian squadron. Otherwise, they may misinterpret the firing and sink the thing.

"Will do, Admiral."

MOSKVA
THE GULF

The men in the forward compartment of the *Moskva* pull the cable for the missile launcher up to the firing panel on the wall. A weapons tech pulls the burnt wiring off the panel and brushes off some of the soot. He splits the cable open and begins to connect the control cable. Water sloshes around their feet, and they can hear the sea slamming into the bow. The ship dips and raises in the rollers.

Lieutenant Kruglov watches the men working on the panel as others remove debris from the loading shoots and inspect the rails.

A chief on a ladder looks closely at the rails as they reach the top of the compartment.

"Comrade Kruglov, I think we have a problem up here. The rail to the left missile is bent, probably from the heat."

"Let me take a look at it, Chief" The chief climbs down and lets Kruglov climb up to look. He passes his flashlight along the rail until he sees the bend. He runs his hand over it. "Shit, give me a hammer, Chief. I might be able to get it straight enough to pass the missiles."

They hand a hammer up to him, and he begins beating on the rail. The dull metallic clanks fill the compartment. The techs finish putting in the temporary wiring.

"We're ready to try it, sir."

"All right, get everyone else out of the compartment. I don't know if this is going to work." He climbs down, and they move out of the way.

"Inform the bridge we are ready to try the SUW launcher. Have the lieutenant stand ready to turn it off."

"Admiral, Comrade Kruglov's men are ready to try and load the forward launcher."

"Good." Sokolov lifts his binoculars up to get a close look at the launcher.

The lieutenant throws a switch, and the panel in front of him comes to life. He pushes a button that activates the auto loader. The light above it goes green.

In the forward compartment, plates in the deck open. Two SS-N-16 anti-submarine missiles rise from below. They slide up the rails as the two doors on the main deck open. They rise up through a torrent of water from the open doors. The left missile twists on the rail and is pushed against the jagged side of the opening. The sound of metal against metal fills the room.

A point of torn metal rips into the side of the missile. It tears a one-inch gash in the side twelve feet long. Water over the bow smothers any chance of an explosion as it runs down into the compartment from above. The left missile is pulled part way off the rail.

"Shit, close the outer doors." Kruglov runs under the missile on the left and shines his light up into the falling water. The doors close and seal the room from the outside. Kruglov shines his light on his arm. He sees propellant from the rocket, mixed with the seawater. It runs down the side of the missile like brown syrup and drips on his arm.

"Damn it, Chief. Clear this compartment and the next one. Dog the doors shut, and no one goes back in. We have rocket fuel mixing with the water. It's all over the place. We won't be loading any more missiles."

The sweaty, soot-covered men work their way back into the ship. Kruglov checks the two compartments and moves down the passageway. Behind him, the chief and one of other men dog the doors closed.

"Chief, I'm going up to the bridge to tell the admiral. Post a guard here to keep everyone out.

Kruglov climbs the ladders to the bridge. He sees the admiral off to the side. He is looking over the bow into the raining night.

"Sir, we will not be able to load a second set of missiles. The one on the left is damaged. It will probably not fire."

Sokolov looks over the weapons officer. His face and arms are covered in soot and grease. His shirt is torn from working with jagged pieces of metal.

"Comrade Kruglov, you and your men have done an outstanding job. From the forward damage, I am amazed that you were able to load at all."

"It doesn't give us much of a chance against the sub."

"I saw that the left missile is twisted on the rail. We will have to go with what we have. The R-1 sub may be able to assist us with some long-range cruise missiles."

"We're going for the long shots. Right, sir?"

"I'm afraid so, Comrade Kruglov. It's about all we have. I talked with Marshal Shagan. All other Cuban forces have been recalled. And the Americans are working to disarm the last of the bombs. Apparently, things are getting better in other areas. You and your men should get some food and rest. I fear that this night is not over for us."

"Aye, aye, Comrade Admiral."

BOMB SITE, NUMBER EIGHT
LOUISIANA

As the men dig around the bomb casing, the rain hits them in the back like pea gravel. They get the mud dug away past the access plate. The rain washes the white body of the bomb clean.

Marshall licks his lips. "Shit, I taste salt in the water."

"It's the spray. This isn't swamp water anymore. It's coming in from the Gulf."

As the two men digging at the bomb finish up, Marshall shines his light down the knoll to the edge of the water. It suddenly seems to just swell up to the edge of the bomb hole. It covers the feet of the two kneeling figures.

"What the fuck?" It drops back down just as fast. The lieutenant from the boat runs up to them. "We're getting some large surges. How close are you to getting done?"

"We just finished, sir."

"Move these men onto the boat. We have to be ready to clear out of here at a moment's notice, Sergeant."

Marshall goes back with the men to the boat. They all climb on board to escape the rain. Marshall grabs a quick cup of coffee. "We're ready here, Top."

"Yes, sir. It is turning to shit outside. The water is raising up around the bomb. And the wind and the rain are the worst I have ever seen."

Johnson looks over the men packed into the boat. "How many men do you want out with you?"

Marshall gulps down his coffee. "None, sir. I'll go out with Susie, and we'll try and knock this thing out. The only bad guy left out there is the storm."

"Major, I think we should put life lines on both the doctor and the sergeant. These surges we're getting are only the beginning. You will have about thirty minutes, and we're out of here.

We will have to be in the channel to have a chance against this storm."

"Good idea, Lieutenant. Let's get you guys hooked up."

One of the crewmen gets them a web belt with a D-ring on the back. Two coils of rope are laid out near the hatchway.

The boat is suddenly rocked by a wave. The windows out the front are a solid torrent of water. Marshall adjusts his poncho, and Susie does the same. Marshall adjusts his radio mike on his web gear. They both stand near the hatch.

"Good luck." The lieutenant opens the hatch, and rain is blown in as if from a fire hose. Marshall climbs out and jumps down on the knoll. He helps Susie off the boat, and they both fight their way up to the top of the knoll. The wind-blown rain stings any exposed skin.

Marshall helps her up the slippery path. She pulls herself up near his ear. "This sucks big time."

"You're right, ma'am."

ULTIMA
WASHINGTON, D.C.

"Gentlemen." Van Nar moves to the podium. "We will have an update by Captain Emmett on the storm."

Emmett moves to the podium and looks up at the displays on the screens. A screen comes up showing the position of the raft and the purposed intercept of the *Georgia*.

"Mr. President, gentlemen, this update is to bring us up to speed on the events occurring at this time with the storm, and its possible affects on the bomb site and the southern Louisiana coast."

He takes out a pointer and aims it up at the screen. "So far, we have been able within certain parameters to make very accurate assessments of the storm's path and nature. This information is being sent through the national hurricane center and fed directly to the bomb site and the submarine *Georgia*. All ships in the path of the storm have been sent to safe positions. All aircraft in southern Louisiana have been grounded.

"We are holding with the 0400 arrival time of Evita's eye on the coast of Louisiana." He points to a spot just south of the bomb site. New Orleans sits in its proposed path.

An area map of Louisiana comes up. His pointer moves along the eastern coast of the state. "These areas are receiving storm surges and heavy rain. Wind speeds have been measured at between seventy-five and 100 miles per hour. This will intensify as the storm gets nearer to the coast. All of the east-facing coastal area is under a brutal attack by the storm. With the evacuation of General Beck's troops, loss of life will be minimal. But property damage will probably set new insurance records."

"Excuse me, Captain Emmett."

"Yes, sir."

The president turns towards Brant. "Mr. Secretary, are all services in place for the rehabilitation of the area?"

"Yes, sir. With the warning from Captains Emmett's group and the excellent job done by General Beck's forces, we will be able to move in as the storm dissipates."

"Excellent. Thank you, Mr. Emmett."

"Sir, as you can see, the bomb site is being hit with surges and increasingly foul weather. We would recommend holding with the 0200 pull out of the bomb site forces." He moves his pointer to the screen with the raft on it.

"We will add some topographical features." A group of small islands, like a necklace, lie spread out in a crescent shape, its points facing east. The pointer comes to rest on the crescent.

"These, gentlemen, are the French Shoals. They form this crescent with a conglomerate of small islands and rocks above water. This is considered by the Coast Guard as one of the most dangerous locations in the Gulf. It is riddled with freak tides and strong currents. This particular area now sits at the back of the rescue submarine. The whirlpool is heading right for it. If the submarine falls within three miles of the shoals and three miles of the vortex, we believe he will be trapped. He will run out of sea bottom and be thrown onto the shoals. This information has been passed on to the captain of the *Georgia*."

Admiral Hillings cuts in. "Sir, again, I have faith in the performance of the skipper of the *Georgia*. We can only wish them good luck."

"We pray for their success, Admiral." The president speaks as he watches the screen.

"We see a breaking down of the Sanboro effect. As the storm nears land, the jet stream is being pulled farther north."

"Will that lessen the effects of the storm?" Brant keeps looking at the screen.

"No, Mr. Secretary. From the reading we are receiving from the *Georgia*, they are operating in a twenty-two-knot pull to the east, into the vortex. This will amplify the closer they get. Our estimates are that the speed of the water entering the whirlpool is reaching above sixty knots. The maw of the thing is over 500 feet wide. If trapped, it will pull the *Georgia* in and then smash it on the shoals."

"My God, this storm is unbelievable." The president shakes his head.

"Yes, sir. But there is one more thing."

"Good, I hope, Captain."

"I'm afraid not, sir."

Wayne looks at him along with the others. "What more can this thing do?"

"Sir, the French Shoals form a barricade between the vortex and the coast of Louisiana. The ocean bottom is getting shallower the farther west it moves. This anomaly is packed with energy. When it breaks on the shoals, it will focus its energy and send it into the coast directly in front of it."

Emmett moves his pointer from the shoals to the point directly in front of it. It stops on the red marker of the bomb site.

"So what will this do to the bomb site?"

"Well, Mr. President, we believe it will cause a tsunami, like those caused by underwater earthquakes."

"So what are your predictions for the coast and bomb site?"

"We are guessing at a tidal bore of between thirty and sixty feet."

"Holy shit, Captain Emmett." The president gets to his feet. "You're predicting a sixty foot tidal wave will hit the bomb site?"

"Yes, sir. At somewhere around 0230 hours."

The president runs his hands through his hair as he looks at the screen. "God help them if they take too long."

BOMB SITE, NUMBER EIGHT
LOUISIANA

Susie can feel the tug of the rope as she follows Marshall up the knoll. The footing is slippery and the rain intense. As they reach the top of the knoll, a bolt of lightning seems to cover the sky above them. The concussion almost drives them to their knees. Marshall holds her hand to help her down the far side. His foot gives way, and he is thrown on his back. It pulls his hand forward, sending Susie down the slope, head first. She hits on her stomach and slides down the incline.

Marshall gets to his feet to help her up. She is covered in mud from head to toe. She looks up into his face. A big smile crosses his wet face.

"Sorry, Susie. I lost my footing in the mud."

A sarcastic smile comes out of the muddy face. "I think when this is over, I'm going to kill you."

"Yes, ma'am. But we made it to the bomb." She shines her light on the white casing sticking in the mud.

"You're lucky, Marshall." She turns to face the incoming rain and allows it to wash her off. Then she kneels down next to the casing and checks the number on the bomb. Marshall passes the number on to Johnson, and he relays it to Val at the base. In the war room in Moscow, the last envelope is opened and the first number sent on its way.

Susie takes out the ratchet and begins to turn the first screw. The rain stings the back of her hands as she works. Marshall holds his flashlight on the panel. As she gets the first screw out, she slides backwards a few inches in the flowing mud. Water runs around the bomb, eroding the bank. Marshall yells out the second number over the crash of another bolt of lightning.

USS *GEORGIA*
THE GULF

"Captain, we're one mile off the second target and closing."

"All right, COB, give them the fog horn as soon as we surface."

"Aye, aye, sir."

"Inform Mr. Blakely to stand by."

"Stand by to surface."

"Sir, we have a twenty-four knot current hitting the port side."

"Right, bring us up."

"Surface, surface." The klaxon rings through out the boat. The Russians in the mess hall look up; they, too, know the meaning of the klaxon. The big boomer breaks the surface and cool wind blows across its wet skin. The foghorn blares into the night as the captain and others climb out the top of the sail. Men climb up onto the top of the sail and out onto the stubby diving planes.

They use night scopes to scan the area around the sub. "Give me some flares over in this direction." The captain points to a spot just off the bow on the left side.

A haze over the water limits their ability to see more than 100 yards out. Two flares burst to life a couple of hundred yards in front of the bow. They cause the mist to glow silver-blue. A red spark flies into the sky, and bursts into three glowing red balls.

"We have them, sir. Just off the port bow. It's hard to tell, but the raft looks in pretty bad shape." The captain brings his binoculars to the spot. A dark form lies low in the water. He grabs a handset. "Hold this course. We'll bring them down the port side. Have the helm match the speed of the current."

A spotlight is aimed at the raft as men open the hull hatches and emerge onto the deck. They prepare the throwing lines and stand by. The exec calls up to the sail from the deck.

"It looks in bad shape, Captain. It looks half sunk." Slowly turning, it hits near the bow and begins passing down the port side. An arm rises out of the broken hatch, and waves in the air. The men on the bow throw their lines at the arm. They hit the raft and fall into the sea.

The next group at the base of the sail throw their lines, and again they fall off into the sea. The man on the raft near the open hatch yells to the men on deck. One of the crewmen moves along the hull, towards the stem. The men at the rear hatch throw their lines and watch them slide out of the grip of the man on the raft.

"Shit." The captain watches as the raft slides along the hull and passes between the exposed hull and the tail plane. It moves quickly astern of the boat. He grabs a handset.

"Bring us around. We'll try and get them on the starboard side." The man who had run down the hull yelling to the Russians comes back up to the executive officer.

"Sir, the Russian at the hatch opening was yelling that he had a broken arm and was unable to grab the ropes. He said they have dead and wounded on board."

The exec grabs a handset and calls up to the captain. "Sir, Wilson says that they're all injured on board and can't get the ropes pulled in. I have two divers suited up. We'll try and get them on board."

"Very good, Mr. Blakely. We're going to bring them along the starboard side."

The divers come out of the hull and put harnesses on. They tie ropes to the backs of the harnesses, and the men get into position at the bow and at the sail locations.

"Sir, we're four miles to the vortex on the port side. The current is now running twenty-eight knots and increasing. We have moved to within five miles of the French Shoals."

"Roger. Keep us operating ahead of it."

The submarine makes a tight starboard turn and pushes forward after the raft. The men on deck stand poised to react.

The *Georgia* pulls around and lines up on the raft. "She is about 100 yards off the bow."

They pull up alongside the raft and turn the bow to run them down the starboard side.

They all watch as the first diver leaps to grab the raft. He lands and his hands grab the side. He is pulled along with it, half in the water. "Hold on." The raft passes the side of the sail and the second diver leaps for the hatch. His arm goes through the hatch opening and the man inside grabs him. The tug on the rope pulls at his stomach. He works his way up into the opening. He grabs the hand of the other diver and pulls him on board. The ropes are pulled tight, and the raft is held near the rear hatch. They catch the ropes thrown by the men on the hull and tie them off on hard points on the raft. The men on deck pull the rafts up to the base of the sail and secure it.

The exec is lowered near the hatch to talk with the divers. He can see bodies floating in water inside the raft. "It looks bad in there."

"Yes, sir. They went through some major shit. We have six dead in the back, and the rest are all injured. We'll need all the stretchers."

"Right, let's start moving them." He is pulled back, and the crewmen form a human chain up to the sail. The divers move the injured to the hatch, and they are lifted up to the deck by rope.

CHAPTER 18

EYE OF THE STORM
THE GULF

"Sir, we're running at thirty knots. We will cross the three mile mark to the vortex in less than five minutes."

"Roger, have navigation continue to send updates to NavOps on the storm. We'll secure the hull hatches, fore and aft, and get prepared to dive."

The captain climbs back down to the control room and goes down to the hatch with the exec. He stands to the side as a stretcher is passed through the hatch. He climbs out on the hull with the exec.

"Sir, they're all in bad shape. We have four on board so far. There are eight left, and all have to come out on stretchers."

"Very good, Mr. Blakely. As soon as they're all on board, we'll submerge." In the vacuum of the eye, a roaring sound get louder and louder. The captain looks into the darkness east of them.

"It's the whirlpool, sir. We heard it when we first came out." A crewman signals the captain near the hatch. He walks over and grabs the handset.

"Sir, we have crossed the three mile mark to the vortex, and the shoals are four miles to starboard. We are now pushing thirty-two knots and holding."

"Roger. I'm heading back in."

The captain looks up at the stars above them. They sit stationary in the heavens; he can see the froth from the prop in the stern. The boat sits dead still at full power.

"I'm going back in the hull. As soon as you're able, secure for diving."

"Aye, aye, sir."

As the captain gets back in the control room, he picks up a cup of coffee. He takes a drink and looks over the men working at their positions. The howl of the whirlpool comes into the hull from the long tendril on the seabed.

"Sir, the vortex is less than three miles to port. The tendril is on the bottom. At 550 feet, we're over a sea mound. We're running recordings off to NavOps. Ultima is providing us with satellite navigation. We're holding our own." The tension in the control room can be felt as the howl grows louder. The chief of the boat walks back to his position behind the helm.

"Gentlemen, continue to do the jobs we're trained for. We'll concern ourselves with the operation of the boat and let the skipper concern himself with the forces beyond the hull." He nods as he passes the captain. "Sir."

"Thank you, COB. Secure the men on the sail. And have the boat ready to dive as soon as the hatch is secure."

The Russian captain comes to the hatch of the control room. The captain looks up from the plotting board and nods his head. "Captain."

"I do not mean to bother you at this time, Comrade Captain, but I know the danger that you and your men have put yourselves into. If you broke off the rescue in order to save yourselves and this ship, we would all understand."

"Thank you, Captain, for your concern. The safety of this hull and my men is paramount. The remainder of the men on the raft will be brought on board. I have no intentions of losing this boat. It would be a very bad career move."

The sonar speakers are now full of the howling sound of the vortex funnel. It hisses and screams in the dark waters beyond the hull.

"Sir, we are three miles from the French Shoals and two miles from the vortex. We have a running sea on the hull of thirty-five knots and gaining. We are dead calm in the water at flank speed."

"All right." The captain takes another drink of coffee and listens as the sound of the whirlpool blots out the world around him.

The captain's eyes look at the red lights glowing on the panel. They show the unsecured hatches on the hull. The lights for hatches at the base of the sail and mid-way on the hull burn like rubies. The phone rings next to him, and he picks it up.

"Sir, we have the last two stretchers coming off the raft now. We had to start putting the men on mattresses in Sherwood Forest."

"Very good. Get a quick head count and button it up."

"Aye, aye, sir."

Blakely hangs up the phone and watches as the last man is lifted off the raft and passed up to the hatch. "Sir, there are six dead left."

"We have to leave them. Get on the hull, so we can cut this thing free."

The crewmen help the divers out of the raft, and they begin cutting the ropes. The sound of falling water fills the air around them. Blakely looks back towards the stern, and then at the bow. He shines his light along the hull. "Sir, we're in."

His light catches the raft as it slips towards the stern and disappears quickly into the darkness. As he climbs down the hatch, it is slammed shut, and the dogs are spun home. He calls to the captain. "We're secure."

The captain's eyes look at the panel as the ruby light goes green. "Dive, dive. Give me 150 feet and full speed. Bring the bow to ten degrees off the funnel." The klaxon blares through out the hull.

"Sir, we have now passed forty knots and gaining. The current is pushing us forward."

The executive officer rejoins the captain in the control room. "I think were in for one hell of a ride, Mr. Blakely."

"Yes, sir, Skipper." They both hold on to the rails at the plotting table. The sound of rushing water fills the boat.

ULTIMA
WASHINGTON, D.C.

"Gentlemen, the *Georgia* has just submerged and is heading for the vortex." The president and the others watch as the symbol of the submarines and the whirlpool race at each other. "I would think he would have pulled away to the side."

The admiral looks at the screen. "Well, Mr. Secretary, I can only say he must have a plan. This is either a heroic move or a kamikaze run." The others around the table chuckle.

USS *GEORGIA*
THE GULF

"Sir, we are passing fifty knots. And we are still on course."

"Very good. Keep us at flank speed. Give me a call on our distance to the vortex."

"Sir, we are one mile and closing, maintaining ten degrees off the bow."

The huge boat waffles in the current as the hull speed increases. The sonar in the bow is filled with only the tracing of the funnel. "Sir, we're at fifty-three knots and maintaining course. We are holding the vortex at ten degrees off the bow."

"I'd say we have to send a case of champagne to Electric Boat in Groton. Their hull is setting a new underwater speed record."

The COB calls back to the captain. "Yes, sir. We have definitely passed their optimum safe speed."

The hull twists slightly in the rushing current as the sea quickly searches the hull for weak spots. The hull sends out its moans and creeks as it pushes back against the pressure. It seems to be stretching itself from stem to stern; the interior sounds are the same as those heard by the first submariners. They are odd haunting noises known only to the men who seek the depths as their hunting ground.

"Sir, we are at fifty-five knots and holding. The vortex is 200 yards off the port side. We will be parallel with the funnel in one minute."

The helmsmen and the planesman feel the shudder in their yokes. The forces outside the hulls try to pull them into the center. "Sir, the vortex is directly to port at 100 yards." He has to yell to get above the crashing sound of the funnel.

"Hold steady." The captain watches the diving officer; their eyes lock.

"Sir, we are coming around the back side of the funnel."

The captain yells to the diving officer, "Hard right rudder, flank speed."

The helmsman throws the yoke all the way to the right. It snaps and jerks as his hands fight for control. The diving officer lends a hand to hold it steady. The great hull tills ten, then fifteen degrees over. The forces outside push against the rudders and the hull, trying to feed it to the vortex. "Sir, fifty-five knots and holding."

The bow slowly nudges its way to starboard. As if helped by a giant hand, the huge bulk of the *Georgia* is hurled out into open water behind the eye. The still waters act like a brake to slow the speeding giant. The men inside are thrown forward by the still water impact.

"Sir, forward speed down to forty-five knots and falling. The vortex is now 500 yards astern and dropping back. We're free."

"Yes!" The captain raises his hand above him and brings it back to his side. A roaring cheer echoes through out the hull. The Russian sailors join their American comrades in the cheering. "Bring us back to a northeast course and send a message to Ultima. Tell them that the rescue is a success."

"My God." Blakely salutes the captain. "That was one hell of a ride, Skipper."

"Thank you. I thought that if a satellite can bounce off the spinning earth, we could use the vortex for speed and bounce off it."

"I wouldn't have thought you could do it, sir."

The captain leans over and whispers in Blakely's ear. "I didn't think you could either." They both laugh out loud as the radio antenna from the sail rises to the surface.

ULTIMA
WASHINGTON, D.C.

Near the president's desk, he and Brant sit discussing something in low tones. The others in the room work with their staffs. The sound of the numbers being sent from Moscow to Val in New Orleans comes over the speakers.

Van Nar takes a call near the screens and holds her hand over her other ear. "Yes!" The word fills the room. She hangs up the phone and goes to the podium. "Mr. President, we have just had contact with the *Georgia*. They have completed the rescue and are en route to the naval station at Mobile."

"Yes!" The president stands and claps his hands. The others in the room join in.

"Gentlemen, from the information sent to NavOps, we can now show the path of the *Georgia* after it submerged."

On the screen, a dotted line appears. It shows the path of the submarine near the vortex and then its exit point. Readings of its speed are flashed below the line.

Brant watches the screen. "My God, it looks like a space shot."

"Correct, Mr. Secretary." Admiral Hilling stands and leans forward over the table. "What a ballsy move. Look at those speeds. He used the vortex like we have used the earth to send rockets into space. I told you these guys were good."

"Admiral, please send the *Georgia* a job well done message from us."

"Yes, sir, Mr. President. They did a hell of a job."

BOMB SITE, NUMBER ONE
LOUISIANA

Wind and driving rain sweep across the knoll. Marshall leans closer to Susie and yells the next number to her. She puts the head of the ratchet in the screw head and begins to turn it out. Marshall holds his light closer as a bolt of lightning tears through the sky. The thunder claps seem to push them deeper into the mud.

Water running around the bomb slowly erodes the mud holding the bomb fast. Susie extracts the screw, tosses it over her shoulder, and looks over to Marshall. He gets the next number from Johnson. As he goes to tell her, a swell suddenly rises up to the middle of Susie's back, and she and Marshall are swept forward towards the boat.

"Goddammit." Marshall lets the light fall from his hand and digs his fingers into the soft mud of the knoll. Susie is lifted to the side and gently pushed to the top of the knoll. The bomb is lifted up to her height, and it strains at its tethers.

"Shit." Her hands grab an exposed root, as the swell passes on. She is left lying prone, grasping the root. "Susie, are you all right?"

"Yeah, just my pride. What the hell was that?"

Childes jumps down from the boat and comes up the knoll behind them. He helps Susie to her feet. The rain slams against his yellow slicker. "We're getting storm surges from Evita. They're hitting up and down the coast. We're lucky because we're about a mile inland. We have the swamp absorbing most of the force. The peninsula south of us is taking a beating. It's going to get worse, so I brought another light out. We need to move soon, or we will not be able to get away."

Susie leans forward to yell in his ear. "We have half the screws out now. It'll be just a little longer. I have to get to the movement switches. The rain is eroding the mud from around the casing. If it falls over, we won't have to worry about getting out."

"Let's hit it." They move back to the casing and shine their lights on the gleaming white cylinder.

"Shit." Marshall moves to the far side. "Half the casing is exposed. We have a problem."

"Give me the next number."

He yells it to her, and she begins removing the screw. As soon as it's clear, she tosses it and goes for the next one. Behind her, the surging sea sends its growls and snarls towards them as the water churns and swirls in the swamp.

Susie unscrews the last fastener and tosses it. She lifts the panel and reaches in and disconnects the harness. She leans back and throws it behind her.

"We have the panel off. I'm going for the anti-movement switches." Marshall passes the news on to Johnson. He relays it to Val. Susie holds a pen light in her teeth and looks into the maw of the beast. She begins to reach in as a sudden swell of water catches all three. They are swept over the knoll and into the swamp on the other side. The safety lines around them go tight. The force of the wave passes on. The men on the boat fight the lines and are thrown about as the boat is lifted and pulled away from the knoll. A sudden back surge hits the side of the boat, as it is lifted and dropped up the side of the knoll. As the water recedes, they are all sprawled along the side; the boat is half out of the water.

Marshall pulls himself up out of the water swirling around him. Childes is pulling himself backward from the swamp. Susie lies in the mud at the base of the slope, her poncho hood pushed off her head. She pushes herself up to her knees and looks at the boat high up on the side of the knoll. Johnson and Rollens jump down from the boat and slide down the side of the knoll.

"Is everyone all right?" Johnson looks around and helps Rollens to his feet. Johnson's light finds Susie. "Doc, check Susie. I'll check on Marshall." They move, slipping on the bank. Rollens reaches Susie and helps her to her feet. "Are you all right, Susie?"

"Yeah, I think I hit something on my side."

"Let's take a quick look." Rollens holds his light as Susie lifts the side of her poncho. On her left side a large bruise is forming. Rollens touches the area as Susie winches. He leans in close to her ear. "I don't think anything is broken, but you took a nasty hit. It will be sore." Her hair hangs down in strings. She pushes it back out of her face and pulls the hood back over her head.

"I'll be all right. I need to get back to the bomb." Johnson and Marshall join them near the boat as Childes inspects the situation.

"Major." He waves Johnson and the others over to him. "Sir, we have got to get out of here. One more of these and we are done for." He holds his watch up and checks the time. "This situation is going to get worse, and we have the vortex in the storm about to hit on the French Shoals. Within ten minutes of that, there is no hope. We have to leave."

Johnson looks at Susie and Marshall. "Go for it while we get the boat off the knoll." The marines get off the boat and join the boat crew in trying to push the boat back into the water. Childes gets back on board and starts the engines. He leans out the hatch and yells to Johnson.

"Major, while your men push, I'll try to back this thing off the knoll. Make sure everyone is clear."

"Right." The men on shore put their shoulders against the hull and wait for the command.

"All right, push." Childes throws the control into reverse and pushes the throttle forward. The engines rev up as the props churn into the mud. The water is whipped to froth and quickly turns brown from the mud. Lights are pointed at the stern as mud is thrown in every direction. The boat settles deeper by the stern. Childes backs the engines down; he leans out to look.

"Shit, we're held fast by the mud. The engines are just digging us in deeper. We'll have to time our next try with the surge and hope we can get clear."

Susie and Marshall work their way back to the bomb. The wind and rain try to keep them back. They reach the crest of the knoll. Their lights seem to only reach out a few feet in front of them. "Let's get this thing done so we can get out of here."

"Right, Gunny. Let's go." They lean into the storm. Near the point, two eyes glare in the darkness. They watch the two lights at the top of the knoll begin working their way down the side. The figure pulls herself up and begins working her way towards the lights. The stinging rain is is not noticed by her burnt arms and face. Only rage burns in the heart of the figure moving along the edge of the knoll.

Susie and Marshall reach the bomb. The water has cut a crescent around the bomb. The mud holds it fast.

"Damn." Susie works her way around to the panel. Marshall takes up a position to her left. He shines his light on the dark opening. He can see small red and yellow lights blinking inside. They both are concentrating on the bomb and fail to see the dark figure rise up to their right. "You fuckers are dead."

The sudden voice catches them off guard. Susie instinctively backs away from the sound and leans against Marshall.

"What the hell?" He points his light up into the face of a woman.

"Get that light out of my face, asshole." He drops the light. The beam rests on the barrel of a 9 mm Barretta.

"Keep your hands where I can see them." Natalie steadies herself with her right hand. She holds onto an exposed root. Susie and Marshall can see pink stains around the wounds up her left side. Her hands and the right side of her face are burnt and charred. Her clothes were shredded by the blast.

"We need to disarm this bomb." Susie leans forward.

"How about if I put a round in it, bitch."

"You don't understand."

"No, you don't understand. You and your fucking group have cost me 100 million dollars and the rest of my life. So it's your turn to hurt."

"Your only way out of here is with that boat over the knoll." Marshall leans forward. "The storm is coming in. We have a doctor on board who will look at your wounds."

"Oh, I'll use the boat." Her red hair hangs to one side like red licorice. Pain shoots through her like an icy wind. She takes a couple of deep breaths to clear her head.

Johnson holds his hand to his ear. He can't quite understand the words coming over his headset. "Top, what's going on over there?"

He can hear Marshall talking to someone. "Just throw your gun in the water, and I'll take you over to the boat and the doctor."

"How about I kill both of you and go take the boat for myself?"

"It will never happen."

"Oh, yeah? Time to die, bitch."

As the barrel moves to center on Susie, Marshall tosses his body across hers. Natalie fires two rounds. One hits Marshall in the back, and the other in his right thigh.

"Aaaah, my leg." Marshall grabs his leg. His weight pushes Susie deeper in the mud.

"Corporal, grab your rifle. They have trouble at the bomb." Johnson and James move up the knoll. Their feet slip and slide in the running mud. They fight for the crest. Natalie picks up Marshall's light and shines it into Susie's face. She moves the gun to point directly into her face. Just as she goes to squeeze the trigger, two lights coming over the top of the knoll distract her.

Natalie swings the light towards the top of the knoll; she catches James in its beam. She fires twice, and the figure is thrown back. James is hit in the chest by the two rounds. His flack jacket absorbs the shock, but he is thrown backwards into Johnson. They slide back down the side of the knoll. Johnson regains his feet. "Are you all right?"

"Yes, sir. There is a women standing over the bomb."

"Let's get back over there." They again fight their way up the side of the knoll. Johnson digs his feet in and pushes for the crest.

As Natalie deals with the new threat, Susie rolls Marshall forward and grabs his Beratta. Natalie swings the gun back to Susie and shines the light down on her.

"So long, bitch."

"You're right." Susie fires two rounds into her chest. Blood covers the front of her tee-shirt. She falls backwards, firing her two rounds into the air.

Johnson's light crests the hill and sweeps the area. It stops on the woman's body floating in the water. "Are you all right?"

"Yeah, but Marshall has been hit in the leg and back."

Johnson and James pull Marshall off Susie and lay him next to the bomb. Susie still holds the automatic pointed into the swamp. Rollens comes over the top of the knoll with Laura. He slides down the side of the knoll to Marshall's side. Laura moves over to Susie.

"Susie, give me the gun." She puts her hand over the gun and takes it from Susie. She hands it to Johnson. "Susie, are you all right?" Laura quickly checks her.

"I had to do it, Laura. I had to kill her."

"I know." She pulls Susie to her and they hug. Susie squeezes her hard.

"How is Gunny?"

"They're working on him now."

Rollens cuts away Marshall's trousers. Blood flows from the exposed wound. The rain quickly dilutes it. Rollens gives him a shot. "James, press here on the artery while I get a tourniquet on him."

"Major, we need to get him on the boat and to the hospital."

"Right. We'll get a stretcher over here and get him out." He calls back to the boat, and two other marines bring a stretcher. They load Marshall and begin working their way up the knoll. "Susie, are you OK?"

"Yeah, let's get this thing done with."

"Laura and I will stay with you. They're getting everyone else loaded on the boat."

"All right. I need a light."

Laura holds the light as Susie disarms the movement device and uncouples the connector. She removes it and tosses it behind her. A loud snarling sound comes from behind them. Laura swings the light into the swamp. The beam hits on a solid wall of water twelve feet high. "Oh, God."

The wave crashes at the base of the knoll. Air caught in the curl fires a fine spray at them. It is quickly followed by the liquid monster. The force of the wave lifts all three up and throws them like broken toys over the top of the knoll.

Someone brushes by Susie, and she grabs them. They are rolled over and over, and are caught by the safety lines. Johnson is pushed over the knoll and hits an uprooted tree; it rakes his lower body and reopens his leg wound. Laura is pushed into the mud, then picked up and hurled inside the swirling water.

Rollens is in the boat pulling Marshall aboard as the wave crests the knoll. The men outside are swept away, and the boat is tilted high into the air. The stretcher, Rollens, and everyone on board are thrown to the rear of the cabin. They are lying in a heap as the boat tugs at the ropes securing it to the knoll. Two of the deck cleats are torn out and the boat is slammed as the last rope holds.

Childs regains his feet. "Shit, get everyone on board." As quickly as it came, the wave is gone to pursue its path of destruction deeper into the swamp. Johnson lies at the base of the knoll; the pain in his leg rips through his body. Laura is in a pile of broken bushes near him. She can't get up; a searing pain in her back holds her fast.

Susie floats to the surface out in the dark water, still holding onto the other person.

"Help us." Susie calls from the dark. A bright light comes on at the boat. It shines out and catches her in its beam.

"We'll be right there."

"This person is hurt." Susie looks at the person she has grabbed. Natalie's red hair shines in the beam. "My God." She pushes the body away from her. It slowly rolls over, the cold dead eyes starring up into the falling rain.

More lights come on as men from the boat try to retrieve the wounded. James swims back to the knoll, dragging a dazed crewman from the boat. He hands him over to Childs and another marine. "Major." He runs up the edge of the knoll to Johnson. He pulls his helmet off and rests his head in his lap. "Sir, sir."

Johnson drifts in and out of consciousness. "James, is that you?"

"Yes, sir."

"Take command of the men. I...." Johnson drifts off again.

"Corpsman, corpsman!"

Rollens reaches them and quickly looks him over. "Shit, he reopened his leg wound. We need to get him on the boat." Rollens cuts his trousers and puts a compress on the bleeding wound.

Others come to help as Rollens moves over to Laura. A crewman is removing brush from around her. "Sir, I think she may have a broken back." Rollens kneels next to her as the other man holds a light. His hands quickly feel her neck and back. "Can you move, Laura?"

"No, sir. I hit my neck or back."

"No self diagnosing, corpsman." He places a neck brace on her and a stretcher is brought over. He gingerly puts a poncho under her. They grab the edges of the poncho. Two marines and Rollens lift her onto the stretcher. As they lift her up, she grabs Rollens's hand.

"I'm sorry, sir. I can't help."

Rollens puts his hand over hers. "Sailor, you have done a hell of a job. Now it's our turn to take care of you."

"Get her on board." As they carry her to the boat, Rollens moves over to Susie.

"Are you all right, Susie?"

"I think so. I'm a little beat up and stiff."

"That's good enough. Let me tell you something. You're one hell of a lady. It's an honor to work around you."

"I need that, Doctor." They hug in the rain.

"The bomb. I need to disarm the timer." Childes joins them. "We're out of here." Blood trickles down his face from a cut over his eye.

"Lieutenant, I need to do one more thing to the bomb and we're done."

"Doctor, you have until we get everyone on board. If you're not back, you'll be standing here alone."

James grabs her hand. "Let's go, Doc. I'll help you." They work their way up the knoll as the others lift the wounded on board. They get to the top and shine their lights down the other side.

"Oh, God, no." The words slip from Susie. They slide down the knoll to the pit. Where the bomb was is nothing but a jagged scar cut into the knoll. They shine their lights out into the swamp. All they see are the swirling waters.

Susie stands up and yells into the wind. "Why, damn it! This isn't fair. Too many good people have died this day."

"Ma'am." James grabs her hand. "You have done all you can. We have to get the hell out of here." He pulls her up the knoll, and they slide down to the side of the boat. Childes and Rollens help Susie on board. They pull James up into the cabin.

"Corporal, you're in charge. Do you have all your people on board?"

He looks around the lit cabin. "Yes, sir. All accounted for."

"Good. We're getting the hell out of here." The last rope is cut as the engines begin backing the boat away from the knoll.

"Did you get the bomb disarmed?" Those in the cabin look at Susie.

She lifts her head. "The bomb is gone."

"Holy shit, you mean...."

"It is best to clear the area. We have a five kiloton bomb ticking away out here somewhere."

"Get a message off to base. Tell them we're on our way out."

NAS
NEW ORLEANS

Nelson and Val get the news at the base. "God, we came so close." Val pounds his fist on to the table. "I'll inform Marshal Shagan."

"Right. I'll call Admiral Hillings."

They each inform their superiors of the situation.

ULTIMA
WASHINGTON, D.C.

Admiral Hillings takes the call and speaks in low tones. He shakes his head and hangs up. He stands and walks up to the podium.

"Mr. President, Mr. Secretary. I just got off the phone with Captain Nelson. They have received a call from the bomb site. Dr. Davies was able to disarm the tamper panel and the movement mechanism. They have been hit with some major surges from the storm. The bomb has disappeared."

"My God." The president gets to his feet. "Disappeared? How?"

"Sir, the surges dug it out and pulled it into the swamp. The boat is trying to fight its way out of the area. Its chances are not good."

"Admiral, has Marshal Shagan been informed?"

"Sir, Colonel Val is contacting him from the base."

"My God." The president turns towards the men at the table. "What do we do now?"

Brant arranges his papers in a stack. "Sir, we are helpless to prevent the detonation of a five kiloton bomb off our coast. We need to come up with a cover story."

"I think I have an answer, sir."

Everyone's eyes are drawn to the man who has just entered the room. Captain Emmett walks up to the podium. "The stage is yours, Captain."

"Thank you, Mr. Brant. I came in to update everyone on the storm. As we speak, the whirlpool and the full forces of the storm are breaking on the French Shoals."

EVITA
AT THE FRENCH SHOALS

Out in the dark sea, the full fury of the storm moves against the shoals. The depth falls away as the rising seabed compresses the whirlpool's long funnel. Its fury is pushed up, and a huge mound of water bulges up. Its tremendous force smashes into the shoals. A half-mile section holds back the fury for a short time, then buckles under the relentless attack. The rocks and sand of the shoals are pushed out of the path of the storm. The seabed rocks from the impact. A shock wave is sent racing ahead.

ULTIMA
WASHINGTON, D.C.

"Gentlemen, we have censors all along the Louisiana coast. They have been giving us reading of the surges hitting the coast. It is bad. But with the evacuation by the army personal, loss of life should be small. Property damage is going to be high. On screen three, we have a radar view of the French Shoals." On the screen, the shoals are highlighted. The swirling whirlpool moves on the screen. "We'll have an opportunity to see the force of the storm. It is moving directly on the shoals."

They watch as the swirling mass hits the shoals. It seems to stop, and then suddenly a section of the shoals is gone from the radar image.

"My God." Emmett turns to his assistant. "Get a reading on the damage to the shoals." He runs some figures. "Sir, we just lost a half mile of the French Shoals."

"It's just gone?" The president looks dumbfounded.

"Yes, Mr. President. On the bottom of the screen are readings from the seismic equipment on the sea floor. As you can see, they're registering high seismic activity. We have just seen the birth of a tsunami. The tidal wave is on its way to the coast. It will hit the bomb site in about eight minutes. These waves have been clocked in the open ocean at between 400 and 500 mile per hour. God help them at the bomb site."

"Any predictions on its size?"

"An educated guess is between fifty and 100 feet, Mr. President."

"And what of the bomb?"

"In that area, I would advance an old theory. Some think that by exploding a nuclear weapon in the path of an oncoming storm, you could dissipate the force of the storm by the blast effects."

"Would it work?"

"We don't know, Mr. President. Most of the weather community doesn't think so. But of course the theory has never been tested. I think we may be able to test the theory and cover the rogue missile politically."

"Sir." Brant gets to his feet. "I would be in full agreement with Captain Emmett. If we release a news brief, it should be in a form that would state that you have chosen this action because of the ferocity of the storm. It would cover our political responsibilities."

The president runs his hand over his head. "My God, you may be right. Have someone get started on a release. It will have to be presented by 0300."

"Yes, sir. We're on it."

"Very good work, Captain Emmett. Your suggestion will cover all aspects of the situation."

"Yes, sir." Emmett goes back to the weather office to track the storm.

CUBAN SUBMARINE
THE GULF

The Kilo boat hangs in the water next to the cliff face. Their equipment searches the area around them for any sign of a possible escape by the Russians. They ping the water openly in defiance. Nothing appears.

"Señor Captain, I must report that the water is clear in all directions." The captain looks around the control room and nods his head. "Gentlemen, we should be proud of our achievement. We will leave the Frozen Forest and join with our sister boat. We have completed our assignment." Cheers erupt throughout the boat as they slowly pull away from the wall and head back up the rift to the east.

ULTIMA
WASHINGTON, D.C.

Van Nar is at the podium. "Gentlemen, apparently the Russian boat was lost. The Cuban submarine is leaving the Petrified Forest. As you can hear, they are playing music that the SOSA system is picking up." They listen and the notes of Latin music can be heard. The red triangle begins moving out to open water.

CUBAN SUBMARINE
THE GULF

The music plays throughout the boat, as they are many miles from the oncoming task force. The rich heavy coffee is seasoned with a little rum, and battle stations are relaxed as men return to their bunks to get some sleep. The smell of cooking begins to fill the boat. "Commander, when we're about ten miles out, surface and recharge the batteries. I'm going to get some rest."

"Very good, sir."

After reaching his cabin, the captain removes his shoes and has a drink of ice water. He lays back on his bunk and is soon drifting away.

RUSSIAN SUBMARINE
THE GULF

In the darkness, a huge predator lies motionless. It listens to the music from the passing Kilo boat to its front. Two doors slowly open. The beast doesn't move. "Sir, the target is crossing the bow at 500 yards."

"Thank you, Comrade. Set the safeties on the torpedoes. We're using the wire guides." The men in the Russian submarine go about their business like a well-oiled machine. "Sir, everything is set to fire."

"Thank you. On my command—but first I want one loud ping sent to the Cuban boat."

"Yes, sir." The executive officer hits a lever. *Ping.*

"Fire."

CUBAN SUBMARINE
THE GULF

The men in the control room relax, listing to the music. Suddenly from beyond the hull, a loud ping hits the boat. They all look at each other, then in the direction of the sound. On the speakers the sound of running torpedoes fill the control room. The captain rushes to the control room in his bare feet. "We're dead!"

The torpedoes hit the hull in front and behind the sail. The submarine is torn into three sections, which sink into the depths.

"Sir, we have two hits. The Kilo boat is going to the bottom."

"I don't hear any Latin music now. Set a course for the American ships." The captain takes a drink of his tea and toasts the men around him.

ULTIMA
WASHINGTON, D.C.

Van Nar is talking on the phone when the yellow circle again appears on the screen. She drop the handle. "Gentlemen, the Russians are back." A loud ping comes out of the speakers. "We have torpedoes in the water." They all watch as the two dotted lines converge on the red triangle. After the explosion, the cracking of the hull sounds in the room. "The Russians are now moving towards the picket ships."

RESCUE BOAT
LOUISIANA SWAMP

Childes maneuvers the boat around fallen trees and other debris swirling around the boat. They head for the main channel.

"Get everyone secured. This is going to be a bumpy trip." Crewmen make sure that everyone who is able is buckled down in their seats. They take nylon straps and tie down the wounded on the floor. "Everyone is secured, sir."

Childes tightens his seat belt. The sound of objects bumping off the hull fills the cabin. An urgent call is received. "Rescue One, this is Touchdown. Be advised. Strong seismic activity at French Shoals. The focus is headed directly for you. Predictions are tsunami waves. Advise clear area as soon as possible."

"Roger, Touchdown. Rescue out."

"Well, that's good to know. And here we thought we were in a bad situation."

"Sir, radar shows multiple squalls coming in from the south." Childes looks out the windows. The lights from the boat shine on the swirling waters. Trees and bushes float by and bump into the boat. They work their way to the main channel. The water around them flows back to the sea.

"Positioning is correct, sir."

Childes turns to the others. "We're in the main channel. But we have a tidal wave coming at us. And the main channel inland is full of debris. We're going to have to work our way clear."

"Sir, look at the scope." As the sweep of the radar crosses the scope, a large crest is outlined. It keeps moving towards them, slowly filling the screen.

"Shit, what's it height?"

"Sir, eighty feet." The water outside begins to drop in height as it is sucked into the plying water. "We can't out run it. And we can't survive getting caught in the wash from it." He looks around the cabin.

"We're going for it. It's our only chance. Get ready for the ride of your life."

Childes throws the throttles forward and the boat lunges forward. It joins the waters around it, rushing for the building behemoth. The boat rushes at full speed towards the forming giant. Spotlights on the top of the boat light the way. They cut through the night, their beams reaching out a quarter mile ahead of the boat. Childes stares out the front windows. The beams of light have formed into round spots on the side of the undulating beast.

"My God. Stand by. We're going up the face of this thing." Looking up, they can't see the top. The water wall disappears into the night above them. The engines drive the boat forward, as the giant pushes inland. The angle of the boat begins changing. "Sir, we're at a twenty-degree angle and increasing. Correction, thirty degrees." The boat continues to climb the giant. They all hold on to the side as they push up the face.

"Sir, forty-degree angle." Their bodies lean forward as the belts around them tighten. Anything not tied down slides to the rear of the cabin. Marshall, Johnson and Laura hold each other's hands. Their stretchers tug at the tie down straps. A voice comes out of the darkness. "God protect us."

The bow tears through the top of the wave and the boat is pushed half out of the water. "Hang on." Childes yells out. It slams down behind the crest. The engines pull the boat to escape the crashing monster. It explodes behind them, and the force tries to drag them over the falls. The boat seems to sit dead in the water as machine fights nature. This time the machine wins; the surging wave moves inland.

"We made it! We made it!" Childes and his chief high-five at their success.

"We're going to follow the surge in. It will have pushed most of the debris in front of it. We'll try for the main channel."

Rollens unbuckles and goes to check Johnson and the others. The lights from the boat shine out over a shimmering sea. All the land seems to have disappeared. "It's not over yet. All this water is going to come running back at us. And there is a real good chance of more waves."

Rollens gets back in his seat and secures his seat belt. The rain outside abruptly ends. The lights from the boat cut through drifting wafts of fog. It seems that they had been thrown back in time into some primordial world. The chief checks their position on his GPS terminal.

"Sir, we're on course." The terminal screen displays a map of the area as their radar gives a true picture of their surroundings. "Sir, all of the primary markers on the map are gone."

Childes looks over at the screen. "The wave."

"Yes, sir. It's created a whole new area."

"Hang on everyone, we're not done with the wave yet. It is going to be coming back at us from the other direction. This thing is far from over."

One of the crewmen passes a blanket to Susie. "Thanks." She wraps it around her; her wet clothes cause her to shiver. "Is there any sign of the bomb?"

"No, Doctor. Not only did we lose the bomb. We lost the whole knoll. Everything is gone."

"Sir, we have a twelve foot wall of water coming at us from the front. It's about 500 yards out."

"Get ready. We're going to take this one on." The lights on the top of the boat catch it 200 yards in front of the boat. The churning wall of foam rushes towards them. "Stand by."

The swirling waters lift the bow high in the air, and turn it to the side. A tree trunk in the morass acts like a lever and pushes the boat over. It rolls to the right, on its top.

"Holy shit." The words echo in the cabin. Everyone is turned up side down; they strain at the seat belts. Those on the floor hang from the deck on their safety straps. The pain rushes through them. "Ahhh, shit." The boat rolls to right itself. Everyone is snapped back into their seats. Again the boat rolls to the right and goes over. A tree branch breaks through the window on the right side. It bursts, sending a blast of water on everyone in the cabin. "Ahhhh, God."

The boat seems to stay up side down for a long period, then takes a snap roll back to up right. Everyone is slammed into the side of the boat. Childes fights for control of the boat. He gets it back in the center of the channel. The angry water still rushes by. Water sloshes around in the bottom of the boat. The red lights inside the cabin add to the eerie situation.

"Is everyone all right?"

Moans seem to come from everyone. Rollens looks around the cabin, checking to see if there are any major injuries. Susie can taste blood in her mouth. "Are you all right, Susie?"

She wipes her lips. "Yeah, but I think I bit my tongue."

Rollens uses a pen light to see. "Yeah, it will be all right."

Others in the cabin complain of the same problem. As the chief tries to block the broken window with some rags, Rollens unbuckles and checks the people on the floor. He moves around the cabin and checks the others. Another crewman helps the chief plug the hole. The water in the cabin is slowly pumped out. The boat moves quickly up the channel. Two of the lights on the top have been torn away; the other two cut the night in front.

"Sir, there is a bend in the channel ahead. And it narrows. Radar is showing some kind of obstacle across the channel."

"Sir, the second wave has entered the main channel. Radar gives it at thirty-five to forty feet. It will be coming up behind us."

"Roger." Childes maneuvers the boat around a bend in the channel. The lights stop on a solid wall of broken trees, and mud. "Shit." The boat is brought to a halt. They sit about thirty feet from a huge pile of broken trees and brush.

"We have a dam of debris about twenty feet high. It is blocking the channel. There is no way around it." The chief shines a spotlight along the length of the dam. Tree trunks jut out like punji sticks from its side. As he moves the light from left to right, an airboat hull protrudes from the stack. Its engine and metal framework are off to the side. Near it is a part of a body in a diving suit. "How the hell did he get out here?"

"He was probably with the drug group and got lost. Then the wave caught up with him."

"What will we do now, Lieutenant?"

"I'm not sure, Major. We're trapped against this thing. And we don't have anything to blow it out of the way."

"Sir, the second wave is moving up the channel. It seems to be about thirty-five to forty feet. We'll get the wash up the channel in a few minutes."

"Right, let me know when it breaks." Childes looks up at the top of the debris dam, and towards the back of the cabin. His mind races for a solution. Rollens joins them at the front. He looks out at the twisted pile of trees.

"Are you guys all right?"

"Yeah, Captain."

"Sir, the wave is breaking in the channel. It's on its way."

Rollens watches as the huge crest on the radarscope seems to defuse. The crest moves in towards their direction.

"I had better belt back in."

"Yes, sir."

Childes turns back to the others. "The way I see it, we have two choices. One is that we sit here and get crushed against the dam. Or we move back up the channel and take on the surge. We then let it blow this thing apart and work our way through."

"Stand by. We're coming around. We'll move back up the channel to give us some maneuvering room."

Childes brings the boat about, and they race back up the channel. "Sir, the wave is about 400 yards dead ahead." The lights catch sight of the twenty-foot churning head of the wave. "Stand by. We're in it."

His words die in the cabin. The boat suddenly points its bow up into the sky. It then dives into the swirling mass and the bow digs out a chunk. It hurls it into the air as it comes up. The water blows the rags stuffed in the side window out. Again water sprays the inside. The boat rocks from side to side and up and down. The ride is like a runaway elevator. Childes turns the boat around in the swirling water and races towards the dam. The wave hits the dam; spray is fired high into the air. It holds its ground. The boat races across the surge as they approach the dam. Only the very top can be seen. Childes quickly picks a spot and steers the boat for it.

"Hang on! We're going flying."

They hit the top of the dam, and the boat rides up over the trunk of a tree. It moans and scrapes at the hull as they are catapulted into the void behind the dam. The entire boat is suddenly airborne. It tilts to the left and dives into the waiting channel below. Every one is thrown back and then forward by the impact. Childes regains control of the boat and slams the throttles forwards. The log dam strains and then yields to the pressure. It explodes backwards from the onslaught. The loud cracking fills the cabin as the water chases after the escaping boat.

Using radar and the remaining lights, Childes runs the boat at full speed. They snake around corners and sprint up straight sections. The ride is like a Jet Ski gone mad.

"Sir, we have a lake coming up. I think we can make it." Even over the sound of the engines, a snarling and cracking sound comes from behind them. They rush a hundred yards ahead of the foaming mass. It destroys everything along the sides of the channel. It seems to scream in frustration at the fleeing boat. The boat slices over a large sand bar. It tries to hold it for the rushing waters. But the momentum of the boat carries it clear. "Sir, around the next bend. It's about 200 yards to the lake."

"We're going too fast for this turn, so hang on."

Childes throws the boat into a sliding right turn. The right side dips sharply. Susie and those on the left side look down on the others, as water sprays in from the broken window. The boat careens off the side of a broken knoll of mud and sand. It claws at the water, fighting for its life. It starts to come back as the front lights fall on a large open stretch of water.

"It's the lake. We're going to make it." A cheer goes up from the people in the back.

As they hit the lake, the banks move a quarter mile to the sides. The foaming wave hits the lake and dissipates in a rippling arch as the boat races for the channel ahead.

"We're clear. We beat the bastard."

"Thank God."

"We're about and hour out. We'll be in New Orleans at around 0300. We'll call ahead for transportation and medical units." Rain begins to fall as they move forward. It slashes from the sky, and the wind buffets the boat. The boat speeds into the night.

ULTIMA
WASHINGTON, D.C.

Captain Thorp's phone rings in the control room. He answers and talks to the station on Lake Pontchartrain. He smiles and hangs up the phone.

"Mr. President, I an proud to announce that the Coast Guard rescue unit has extracted the members of the bomb party. They are on their way to the station in New Orleans."

The president claps his hands. "Yes, some great news. I want that boat and crew to be recognized when this thing over."

"Yes, sir." Brant walks over to Thorp and shakes his hand.

"They have upheld the highest traditions of the Coast Guard."

"On behalf of the crew, thank you, gentlemen."

Captain Emmett comes into the room. He walks over to Van Nar. They talk for a few minutes, and she walks to the podium.

"Mr. President, gentlemen. Captain Emmett would like to update you on Evita's progress."

"Gentlemen, we have a radar make up of the storm around the bomb site area. Screen two, please." A radar drawing of the area appears. It shows the topography of the area and pertinent landmarks. This is a depiction of the area prior to the storm. We'll now roll a computerized rendering from our radar reports."

White lines draw the land and water areas; the bomb site is shown with a red circle.

The action of the waves on the area begins to change the topography. It then shows the tidal wave and its push into the delta. The wave is shown as a yellow line as it crashes into the region.

"As you can see, gentlemen, the onslaught of these waves has recarved over twenty miles of coast line. In this particular area, the waves have obliterated over two miles inland." As the yellow line moves across the white outline, it seems to disappear. It pushes far up the streams and channels.

"From the force of the waves, we have tried to guess at where the bomb may have gone." The bomb site is enlarged. Moving from the bomb site, a red cone shape leading to the sea is drawn. "This is the primary area in red." A second area is added at the back of the cone in yellow. And a third area is shown in green.

"Each of these areas is a possibility. We believe that most likely, the bomb is in the red zone within one mile of the site. The yellow line extends out to three miles into the Gulf, but less than 100 feet of water. The green zone is out to six miles, below 100 feet of water.

"The importance of this is the capability of the weapon. This is not our expertise. Others here would be able to define the impact of the weapon under these conditions.

"We still predict that the eye will make landfall at 0400. On screen one are the latest reports out of New Orleans on CNN."

The screen comes alive. A woman in a raincoat is standing on a roof overlooking the city. "This is Marcey Lane on the roof of the KNLT station. As you can see, we are getting intense rain and winds up to ninety miles per hour. The storm is about fifty miles off the coast. Lowland areas are being hit by huge waves. There has been a report by the weather service of a tidal wave hitting the swamps. With the evacuation by the army and other local authorities, the death toll is expected to be very low. We have received some reports of cars being hit by trees in the southern areas of the city, and of power outages from trees being uprooted and falling on power lines."

A bolt of lightning breaks across the sky. It seems to cover the entire skyline. She ducks from the concussion.

"Wow, that seemed close. We have received news from our correspondent in Washington that the president will be issuing an important message at 3:00 A.M. our time. It is related to the storm. We will bring you the news conference live. We're going back inside, and we'll show emergency numbers and station setting for radios. This is Marcy Lane with KNLT."

The thousands of people in the stadium watch the big screen. The winds and rain outside lash and blow at the huge structure.

"Mr. President, we have the first draft of your 0300 news conference." Brant hands it to him, and he rocks back in his chair to read it.

A call comes in for Brant. "This is Secretary Brant."

"Mr. Secretary, this is Air Marshal Shagan."

"Marshal Shagan, you have probably heard the news?"

"Yes, I spoke with Secretary Sholenska. We regret that the last bomb has not been defused. We wonder what the reaction by the American people will be."

"We were going to call you in just a few minutes. We believe we have a solution to our problem."

Brant goes over their plan, and reads a short summary of the proposed speech. "We believe this will satisfy both critics in the United States, and protect the anonymity of the bombs."

"Mr. Secretary, please hold on. I would like to have Secretary Sholenska join us."

"Good. I'll get the president on the line." Wayne joins the others on the line, and they discuss the plan. They speak in hushed tones as Wayne covers the plan.

"Mr. President, the plan is brilliant." Sholenska takes a deep breath. "I was working on a draft of my own to try and explain how these weapons got into Cuba. This event will close the file on these last weapons.

"We have kept the president intentionally out of this affair, so that he would remain neutral if the situation became untenable. He is aware of your assistance on this matter. President Wayne, your assistance will not go unappreciated. A special delegation and myself will make arrangements to visit Washington soon."

"You are always welcome in Washington, Secretary Sholenska. I'll alert the state department that you will be arranging a visit soon."

"I must leave now and go tell the president of your plan. This one event may have saved the move towards democracy by not causing a civil war."

They all hang up. Wayne and Brant go back to working on the news release. Brant looks at his watch. "We have fifteen minutes to get to the conference room. We can finish the speech on the way, Mr. President."

"You're right, Mr. Secretary." The president gets up, and they start for the door.

"Gentlemen, we will be back soon. General Becker will field any urgent requests."

They go up the corridor with two marine guards.

COAST GUARD BOAT
LOUSIANA

The boat races up the estuary, working its way out of the swamps. "We should hit the main channel in just a few minutes. They will have a car waiting for you at the docks, Dr. Davies."

"Great. I hope they have some dry clothes and some food also."

Childes looks back over his shoulder. Susie looks like an Indian with the blanket pulled up over her head and the edges all tucked in.

"Sir." Childes looks over at the chief. "Yeah."

"We're receiving a Ultima priority message. It is for Dr. Davies. It's coming in scrambled."

"All right. Dr. Davies, you have a message coming in from Ultima. You need to come up to the screen."

"Damn, I was just getting warm."

"Don't be a weenie, Doctor."

She looks out from under her blanket, at Marshall. "You didn't have to go and get yourself shot on my account." Susie gets to her feet and drops the blanket back on the seat. She walks over to the foot of his stretcher, and looks into the mud-stained face.

"But I'm glad you did. You're a special hero in my eyes."

"Why, thank you, Dr. Davies."

She kicks the bottom of the boot on his good foot. "I told you to knock that shit off, Top Gunny."

"Leave me alone, Susie. I'm a wounded swamp veteran."

"Yeah." She works her way up to the data console next to Childes.

"I'll run it up for you now, Doctor." He hits a button, and the screen goes blank. A leader pops up on the screen. "TOP SECRET. EYES ONLY DR. DAVIES. ULTIMA OUT."

After Susie reads the message, she pushes a button, and the message disappears. She bites at her lip as she mulls over the message. "How soon will we be at the base?"

Childes looks at the clock above his head. "We're about thirty-five or forty minutes out. We have to be careful in this rain."

"All right." She walks back to Marshall's stretcher and sits down next to him. Both he and Johnson watch her in the dull light of the cabin.

Marshall grabs her hand. "Is everything all right, Susie."

"I'm not sure. The president is releasing a statement that we have decided to fire a tactical nuclear weapon into the storm to stop it."

Johnson chuckles. "Susie, it's a cover story. They have to say something."

"Yeah, I know. It's only that the theory they're working under is thin at best. There are others who have argued that the blast would only intensify the situation. Another event that will happen will be the effects of the EMP on the surrounding area."

"EMP? What the hell is an EMP?"

"An EMP, Mr. Top Sergeant, is an electromagnetic pulse. It will destroy all electric components in the blast area, such as radars, computers, aircraft controls, and power plant switching systems. Anything unprotected using modern semi-conductors will be destroyed."

"What a pleasant device."

"Yeah, we developed it. The thing that bothers me is that I have argued for years that these weapons were becoming so commonplace. We have relaxed in how we safeguard them. An article in the *Bulletin of Atomic Scientists* listed fifty lost nuclear weapons. Both the Soviets and we share this. They lost thirty-four in a single submarine. If our safety policies are somewhat lacking, theirs are totally incompetent." She shakes her head. "I'm starting to get on a soap box on this issue. I'm sorry."

"Hey, you're the one who knows about these things. And the one who knows their effects. If you're concerned, we should all be concerned."

"You should, Major. Their account of fifty lost weapons is low. And doesn't include the disasters with reactors."

"Dr. Davies, we're tuning the radio to pick up one of the stations in New Orleans. It will carry the president's message."

"Good, maybe they'll have some music, too."

Susie joins Childes at the front of the boat. He deftly turns the wheel and slips the boat around a bend in the channel.

"The main channel is just ahead." Childes checks his instruments as the sound of Dixieland music fills the cabin.

ULTIMA
WASHINGTON, D.C.

Brant checks his watch. "We have one minute, Mr. President." They quickly go over the final draft; they can hear the reporters talking together in the next room. Brant leaves and goes into the room. The press quickly assails him.

"Please, everyone. We apologize for the late hour. But the president will be addressing an event that is on-going. We have all been following the progress of hurricane Evita. According to the weather service and the hurricane watch out of Florida, this is the biggest and possibly most disastrous storm to ever hit the American mainland. Through the efforts of General Beck and the army react force, the evacuation of the southern peninsula has been accomplished. Working with local authorities, all efforts have been made to lessen the possible loss of life."

"What about the bombs or mines that the Russian bomber dropped?"

Brant takes a quick sip of water. "All weapons from the bomber have been recovered. They are being stored at the naval base in New Orleans. As you may have heard, there has been loss of life in this recovery effort. A platoon of marines from Camp Lejeune suffered the brunt of injuries. This will all be covered in a news conference later today. Right now, we ask that you hold all your questions. The president will brief you on his response to the storm."

"Ladies and gentlemen, the president of the United States." Wayne moves quickly to the podium. The reporters sit back down as he pours a glass of water.

"Ladies and gentlemen, again I must apologize for this late hour. But events sometimes dictate their own agenda. As Secretary Brant has outlined, this killer storm will arrive on the coast of Louisiana within the hour. The National Weather Service and naval units have been following Evita since it left Cuba.

"They have clocked winds at over 300 miles per hour around the eye. The storm surge that is hitting the coast at this time is proving to be disastrous. A tidal wave was generated with the collapse of the whirlpool earlier. It threw an eighty-foot wave, which fortunately hit in a swamp area. It was followed by other waves not quite as large." Wayne takes a quick drink of water.

"I have been conferring with the weather service and my science adviser. They believe that the storm will bring winds of over 250 miles per hour down on the city of New Orleans. Guesses of damage and probable loss of life are astronomical. I have conferred with Dr. Davies in New Orleans and Drs. Choy and Miano here in Washington. After long deliberation, I have decided to use a radical tactic that has never been tried to stop or dampen the storm.

"A few minutes ago, I ordered Admiral Hillings to position one of our nuclear submarines into a firing position. At 0400 hours, they will launch a tactical nuclear weapon into the path of the storm."

The reporters look at each other, and a flurry of discussions erupts. "Mr. President, you're going to bomb Louisiana?"

"Please, everyone. The president must get back to the command center. All of your questions will be answered later today."

"Thank you, Secretary Brant. The missile will be detonated off shore to get the best chance of defusing the eye. The city of New Orleans is in no danger. We have monitoring teams en route to the scene. All military personal and equipment are being moved out of the area. The theory is that the sudden blast will disrupt the wall of the eye and downgrade the storm's intensity."

"What about radiation?" A reporter yells from the group.

"All of these things will be covered later. I must get back to the center. We pray to God that this action will stop this storm. If not, you will be reporting on one of the world's greatest natural disasters. Thank you."

The president and Brant leave the room and head for the center.

"Well, Mr. Brant, we have set our sails. I only hope we're not headed for the rocks."

Brants nods. "Yes, sir."

BRIDGE OF THE *MOSKVA*
THE GULF

"Admiral." Pstygo walks across the bridge. "We have entered the torpedo danger zone. The techs believe they will have the sonar up in just a few minutes."

He lowers his binoculars. "Good, Pstygo." He rubs his chin and looks around the bridge. "Contact the other ships. We will secure from any exterior work activities. The flash from the welders is a great beacon."

"Yes, sir. I talked with the chief engineer. At best, we'll be able to run at fourteen knots. We're not going to have any blazing avoidance speed."

"Let's hope that the launcher works on the first try." He walks over to Yefimov. "We should get all ships up to general quarters."

"Yes, Admiral. I'll have the RBUs brought up also."

The admiral nods. "Very good."

COAST GUARD BOAT
LOUSIANA

The boat swings around a bend and enters a wide channel. Childes pushes the throttles forward. "We're in the outlet channel. We can pick up some speed. We'll follow it around to the Nay Channel and head down to the river. Then we'll go down to the outlet cannel that runs parallel with the 406. We'll hit the base around Peter's Road. They will have the cars and ambulances waiting."

Dr. Rollens joins them at the front. "Can I get a call through to the hospital?"

"Yes, sir." The chief calls out to Touchdown and has them patched through to the hospital. Rollens covers them on the types of injuries to those on the boat. They bring him up to date on the status of the men from the bomb sites.

"That is great to hear. Laura will be happy. I'll see you soon."

Rollens moves back next to Laura. "I just talked to the hospital. They said that Chief Turvey is doing fine and will recover completely."

She looks up into his eyes as tears well up in hers. "I'm so glad. He is such a good guy."

"Well, he must feel the same about you. He wrote a note to inform the head nurse that one of our own is inbound and that she had better get the best from the medical unit."

Rollens gently grabs her hand. He can feel the squeeze as she smiles. Tears roll down the sides of her face.

"We should be there in about fifteen minutes, everyone."

CHAPTER 19

BRIDGE OF THE *MOSKVA*
THE GULF

Pstygo climbs to the top of the ladder. "Admiral, they got the sonar working."

"Excellent." He joins Pstygo, and both go down to the combat center. They stand up behind the others and watch the green bar sweep the scope.

"It's not the greatest. But at least we have a view around the ships. Targeting may present a problem."

"It's better than nothing." They walk over to the plotting table. The red circle follows their track. The admiral looks at his watch. "Its 0315. So far we have been lucky."

Suddenly, on the scope four parallel lines burn into the screen. The operator yells out into the room. "Torpedoes inbound, four."

"God, they're heading right for us. Torpedoes."

They run over to the scope. "Distance is 5,000 yards."

The admiral puts his hand on the young man's shoulder. "All right, let's see what we can do, son. Get the bearing sent to the forward launchers and make sure the bridge is updated."

"Yes, sir."

Sokolov runs for the ladder and climbs up to the bridge. Already, Yefimov is ordering the ships to a position thirty degrees off the course of the torpedoes. The first flashes from the forward RBUs light up the bow and fly to the right front. The *Osmotritelnyy* fires her RBUs in suit. They arc through the air and dive into the waves. A volley of six explodes beneath the water. They are followed by the explosion of the torpedo warhead. White water is blown high into the sky. "We got one, sir."

More rockets fire from both ships. "The firing point is in the computer. We're ready to launch." Kruglov looks out the window towards the launcher. He looks back at the admiral and shrugs his shoulders.

"Gentlemen, I would suggest that we get down lower than the forward wind screens." Everyone squats down.

"Prepare to fire." The young lieutenant turns a key and the light goes green. He puts his finger over a large red button. "Fire, fire."

He pushes his finger down on the button. Both rockets ignite. The one on the left bursts into flames. As the missile on the right starts to leave the launcher, the warhead on the left explodes. The right missile is hit with burning shrapnel. It gets airborne about 200 feet from the ship when the second warhead explodes. The launcher is ripped off the deck, and the cover plate is blown off the deck. The cabin below burns furiously.

"Shit." Kruglov is looking at the floor. "Don't," he looks over at the young lieutenant, "reload."

He looks at Kruglov's mouth. The concussion is ringing in his ears. He reads his lips. "Reload."

His finger finds the switch and he throws it. Kruglov's eyes seem to expand. "God, what are you doing?" He jumps to the panel and resets the switch. But the indicator still burns.

"Everyone down." The plate covering the bottom of the cabin opens and two new missiles are sent upwards. They enter the blazing room. The rams move upward, and the missiles are shoved into the twisted steel of the deck. The doors in the floor close quickly as the first warhead explodes. The second warhead quickly follows the blast. The deck is split open and erupts in a huge fireball. The rear bulkhead is crushed, and the force of the explosion blows the hatch off the second room. A tongue of incandescent flame is pushed back into the spaces that the men are in. In an instant, twenty men are killed in the passageway.

"Goddammit, I said don't reload." Kruglov pushes him away from the panel. He turns a key and secures the board. The others on the bridge were knocked off their feet. The admiral pulls himself up to the forward windscreens. A fire blazes from the rip in the deck. The launcher and the two RBU launchers are gone. An explosion off the starboard side flashes in the night. "The *Osmotritelnyy* got another one, sir."

"We still have two inbound at 500 yards."

"Sir, the *Osmotritelnyy* is changing course."

Sokolov looks through his binoculars and watches the stricken destroyer maneuver away from him. "They're putting themselves in the path of the last two torpedoes."

The crippled ship fights to come over and get ahead of the *Moskva*. They fire one last salvo of rockets, which hit and have no effect.

The two torpedoes catch the destroyer about sixty feet back from the bow. Sokolov watches as the front of the ship seem to just break away. The forward momentum of the ship drives it into the depths. In an instant, a valiant fighter is gone. His glasses hang from his neck as the admiral puts his hands on the back of his neck. He stretches as he looks out the window.

"Sir, the *Sovremennyy* is coming around astern of us."

"Right." He press the palms of his hands together.

"Sir, we have a contact at 7,000 yards. It's passing down the starboard side."

"Contact the submarine. Have them prepare to launch their missiles. Give them your best coordinates. We'll make any last minute corrections here."

"Aye, aye, sir."

ULTIMA
WASHINGTON, D.C.

Captain Van Nar walks to the podium. "Gentlemen, we are bringing up shots from the satellite over the Russian fleet. They have come under attack by the second Cuban submarine."

The screen changes from the coast of Louisiana to the squadron. The president and Brant walk back into the room as the view of the ships is focused. They look up at the screen and go back to their seats.

"Next to the live pictures, we are running a tape of the last fifteen minutes." The video begins to run.

Van Nar looks up at the screen. "This, we believe, is the initial attack. As you can see, the ships are starting to maneuver. The torpedoes are coming from the upper right hand corner. They are beginning to fire their RBU rockets to intercept the torpedoes.

"The forward launcher on the *Moskva* is coming around to fire. This type of launcher is similar to our ASROC system." They all watch as the rockets ignite. Suddenly, a huge bright light covers the front of the ship.

"My God, it's exploded." The admiral leans forward on to the table. A second explosion racks the ship.

"What's happened?" Brant turns towards Hillings.

"They tried to reload the launcher. They must have been unaware that the launcher was destroyed. The air attacks really did a number on them."

"Gentleman, the *Osmotritelnyy* is beginning to maneuver away from the others. She is putting herself into the path of the oncoming torpedoes. Their RBUs have scored a second torpedo." A flash erupts at the right of the ship. It fires one more salvo of rockets and is hit. They watch it split at the bow and dive for the depths.

"Holy shit." Hillings rubs the back of his neck. "They have sacrificed themselves to save the others. I tell you, gentlemen, we should be grateful we never had to go one-on-one with this type of fighting sailors. I am totally impressed with their fighting spirit."

The screen goes blank. "That was the last of the tape. We are now seeing the situation on real time. Sky 1 has picked up a transmission from Admiral Sokolov to the submarine. They have informed their escorts that they are moving into a firing position."

The president looks at the picture. "Are they going to fire some ASROC type missiles at the Cuban submarine?"

"They're out of range of their SS-N-15 missiles, Mr. President."

Van Nar flips the pages on a binder in front of her. "Sir, I believe they are about to launch some SS-N-21 cruise missiles. They are similar to our Tomahawk. These are surface anti-ship weapons."

"Are they effective against a submarine?"

"Excuse me, Captain Van Nar." Hillings walks up to the podium. "They would only be effective if the sub were on the surface. I'm not sure what Admiral Sokolov is trying to do. Maybe they will try and bait it to the surface."

"This has got to be confusing to the Cuban captain, right, Van Nar?"

'Yes, Admiral. He would expect the RBUs against the torpedoes, but with no response to the sub itself. I think they are figuring out that the Russians have been mauled by the air attacks. It is possible that the sub may come to the surface and fire at will on the last two ships while he recharges his batteries."

"You know, you might be right, Captain. They have no ASW response. He is faster than they are. The bastard may be moving to the rear of the ships. He can sit back and bag them in the ass." .

"I must say, Admiral, your descriptions of different tactics is always right up front."

"Thank you, Mr. President."

CUBAN SUBMARINE
THE GULF

"Captain, there is nothing from the ships?"

"Sí, up periscope."

As the top breaks the surface, he scans the ships as they pass down their right side. He can see the fire blazing on the bow of the *Moskva*.

"We sank one of the escorts, a destroyer. The other one is moving around the stern of the carrier. Down scope." The Cuban captain looks around the control room. He rubs his lips with his right hand.

"I don't understand, Captain. They have not attempted to attack us."

"I'm not sure, but the air attacks may have knocked out their weapons. Both ships are heavily damaged, and the *Moskva* is burning at the bow."

"They're only doing twelve knots." He walks over to sonar and watches as the second destroyer comes to the right rear of the *Moskva*.

He turns back to the others and raises his open hand like a claw. He crushes his fingers into a fist. "We may have them, totally. Our brave airman may have knocked them down. But we will knock them out."

He goes over to sonar and checks the scope. "Release a buoy, but don't activate it. Give us about 1,000 yards."

"Sí, Captain."

A signaling buoy is released, and it floats to the surface. The submarine continues by the ships and takes up a position 1,000 yards astern of the ships.

"Up periscope." He waits until he has a clear view of the ships. "Activate the buoy."

The buoy comes to life 1,000 yards to starboard of the ships. The forward gun on the destroyer locks and fires. It quickly sends six 130 mm star shells at the target. Their flat trajectory blazes in the darkness. All hit around the buoy in a shower of magnesium sparks.

"Gentlemen, our prey has had their claws pulled. Are the forward tubes reloaded?"

"Sí, Captain. We are ready for the kill."

RUSSIAN SUBMARINE
THE GULF

To the northwest, the Russian submarine makes a starboard turn to the southeast. It slowly submerges, and moves away from the escorts. It holds a position 300 yards from the others. The captain brings the submarine to a dead stop.

"Are the firing coordinates set?"

"Yes, sir."

"Open outer doors." At the front of the hull, the doors slides slowly open.

"Prepare to fire." The captain looks at the firing board and quickly around the center. "Sir, we are ready to fire."

"We will fire in five second intervals. Stand by." A final check is quickly made. "Fire."

At the weapons panel, the first tube is fired. The missile casing is shot into the water and rushes towards the surface. As it breaks the surface, it is ejected into the air. The casing is blown off and the rocket motors cut in. The missile waffles in the air and then heads southeast, its tail plume shining in the night. In seconds the next missile breaks the surface. The others quickly follow.

The captain grabs a phone. "Inform the admiral that the missiles are on their way. We wish you luck."

The submarine resurfaces and joins the other ships as they continue north.

ULTIMA
WASHINGTON, D.C.

"Gentlemen, as you can see, the Russian submarine has launched four SS-N-21 cruise missiles. They are inbound towards the *Moskva*."

On a wide screen view, the tracks of the four missiles are shown in white dotted lines. The ships are shown as squares, and the submarine is a red circle. The lines march across the screen.

"Well, Mr. President. Whatever Admiral Sokolov's plan is will shortly be shown."

Van Nar goes back to the real time screen. "That firing by the destroyer *Sovremennyy*—we believe that it was aimed at a sounder released by the Cubans. We think that they were testing the Russian defenses. And have probably figured out that they have no ASW capability. We believe they are preparing to attack from the rear of the ships." They all watch as the white dots continue towards the ships.

COAST GUARD BOAT
LOUISIANA

"Doctor, we're just clearing the Nay Channel." Childes pulls the boat to the left, and they move out onto the Mississippi River. The main channel is empty of all shipping. The rain falls steadily. The wind and lightning disrupt the skies. As they head down the river, the lights of the city can be seen. Buildings on both sides of the river seem to glow in the darkness.

"Doctor Davies, we have called ahead. They are clearing the Algiers locks, so we can head straight down the channel. We'll turn in just a few minutes."

"That's great, Mr. Childes." She goes back to some figures that she has written down on a note pad. She can feel the movement of the boat as Childes turns it into the channel. They pass through the locks and race under the Woodland Drive bridge. They pick up speed and run down the channel.

"Call ahead and let them know were about three miles out. We're just passing Fort St. Leon." The chief calls forward. The response breaks suddenly on the quiet interior of the cabin.

"Rescue, this is Medivac. We're at the Peter's Road landing. We are prepared to receive you. Orders from Touchdown are that you will secure the boat and join the others at the control center."

"Roger, Medivac. We are showing all lights that are left." Ambulances and other vehicles are parked near the docks. Men standing near some Hummers search the dark waters for the lights of the boat. As the boat rounds a bend in the channel, they are a little over a mile from the docks.

"We have them. They're about a mile out."

"Rescue, we have you in sight. You're about a mile out." An ambulance is backed down the dock; a flare is lit, and swung slowly in the air.

"Medivac, we have you visual. Stand by."

Childes locks on the swinging red light and guides the boat in from the middle of the channel. As they get close, he can see people moving around the ambulances and the other trucks. One of the crewmen climbs onto the deck and gets a mooring line ready at the bow. A second man moves to the stern. As Childes eases the boat in to the dock, men on shore catch the lines and secure the boat.

A female nurse climbs on board and leans into the hatch. "Hi, everyone. You all made it. We're going to remove the injured first." She climbs down into the cabin.

"Doctor Rollens?"

"I'm back here with the stretchers."

She moves back and joins him next to Laura. Others climb in and move to pick up the stretchers. They load Johnson out first and then Marshall. "Doctor Rollens, we have a seat for you in the lead ambulance. I'll be staying with Laura."

"Very good." Rollens climbs out and is helped to the ambulance. It moves up the dock and disappears. A second ambulance is backed down.

The nurse grabs Laura's hand as they lift her. "Well, Corpsman, real navy nurses have got you now. Everything is going to be fine."

Laura smiles. "Thanks, Lisa." She squeezes her hand. They lift her off the boat and load her in the ambulance. The nurse checks others and sends some out to the ambulance.

"Dr. Davies, are you all right?"

"Yeah, I'm all right."

"They have a Humvee waiting to take you to the control center."

As Susie climbs out, she looks over at Childes. "This has been the very worst boat ride I have ever been on. You did a fantastic job getting us back, Mr. Childes."

"Thank you, Doctor." He shakes her hand. "Anytime."

"That was one hell of a ride, sir. A real E-ticket from hell."

Childes laughs. "Thank you, Corporal James. Make sure you get that shoulder looked at."

"Aye, aye, sir."

Childes and his crew secure the boat and head for the waiting vehicles. As he reaches the back of the vehicle, Childes looks back at his boat. A lightning flash dances high over its head. Childes nods towards it. "You did a hell of a job, funny boat." They head for the control center.

BRIDGE OF THE *MOSKVA*
THE GULF

"Admiral, the missiles are inbound."

"Good, inform *Sovremennyy* to zigzag with us. I'll be in the combat center."

Sokolov joins Pstygo at the plotting table. The submarine is working his way to the rear of the ships. A marker plots his location.

"That buoy he let go was a test of our defenses. He has got to know by now that we are defenseless."

"True. When you get control of the missiles, drop them around him in as tight a pattern as you can."

"Yes, Admiral. Our ability to be precise is somewhat limited."

"I know. Just do the best you can. It is our only hope at this time. I'll be on the bridge. Inform me when the attack begins."

"Yes, sir." In the night sky, the four missiles skim along at fifty feet above the surface of the Gulf.

CUBAN SUBMARINE

"Captain, we are reloaded and ready to fire. The ships have gone into a zigzag pattern. They are holding at twelve knots."

"Very good." The captain goes over to the intercom and talks to the crew. "We have sunk one of the escorts. We will now dispatch the other two ships. This is a great day for the naval forces of Cuba."

"Up periscope and open the outer doors."

The periscope moves upward to the surface. The captain presses his face against the soft rubber molding around the eyepiece. He can still see the fire burning at the front of the *Moskva* and just make out the shape of the escort. He adjusts the focal length.

"I have the *Moskva* at 5,100 yards, running true to the bow." His executive officer checks the settings, and they are passed on to the torpedo room. The guidance information is fed into the fire control system.

"Stand by to fire. Down scope."

"Captain, the torpedoes are ready."

"Stand by to fire two. Up periscope." The captain takes one more look and makes some slight corrections on the angle.

ON THE RUSSIAN SHIPS

On the *Moskva*, they are able to pinpoint the location of the sub.

At the rear of the destroyer *Sovremennyy*, a decoy is released. It is paid out to 200 yards behind the ship. The destroyer zigzags behind the *Moskva*. The decoy begins sending out ship propeller sounds and also transmits wave signals.

"Admiral, we are acquiring the missiles. They're about fifteen miles out."

Pstygo and his team send the target coordinates corrections to the inbound missiles. They make small adjustments. On the submarine, the order is given to fire. Two torpedoes are ejected from the tubes and race for their target. "We have them."

"Sir, we have two torpedoes running at 5,050 yards. Firing point is almost due astern." Two tracks appear on the scope. Next to them at another workstation, final corrections are sent to the missiles. At five miles, all four missiles rise into the sky. At 500 feet, they level off.

The admiral goes to the flying bridge and looks back behind the ship. The destroyer is firing its RBUs out into the night. He just picks up the sound of the missiles as they dive into the sea. They bracket the submarine. One hits twenty yards off the bow. A second and third hit thirty yards off each side. The fourth missile hits within twenty yards of the stern. The explosion tears the port side diving plane off. The rudders are jammed, and the submarine is thrown into a long arching turn to the right.

The two torpedoes are lured to the decoy, and explode at the rear of the destroyer.

Pstygo runs up the ladder to the bridge. "Admiral, we caught them by surprise. We may have hurt him. The submarine has taken a slow turn to starboard and is now 6,000 yards astern."

"Excellent, maybe he'll break off. Our luck can't last forever."

"Yes, sir."

CUBAN SUBMARINE

Just after they fire the torpedoes, the men on the submarine seem to be caught in a giant gripping hand. The exploding missiles rip apart the silent waters around them.

"Captain, we have water coming in the forward torpedo room." Slightly dazed, his mind races to explain the event his submarine just endured.

"Sir, steering is jammed to port. They're taking water along the main shaft. Engineering reports some cracked battery cases. They are requesting to surface and vent the rear spaces."

"What the hell did they shoot at us?"

"It must have been some kind of missile or mine. Whatever it was, it was not designed as an ASW weapon."

The captain looks around. "Sonar, anything?"

"No, sir. I'm still tracking the two ships. They're at 7,000 yards."

"Goddammit, what the hell hit us?"

"Bring us up to periscope depth and all stop."

The submarine comes to a stop and hovers in the water as the captain turns the periscope in a full circle.

"Bring us up. Surface." The command echoes as the main tanks are blown.

ULTIMA
WASHINGTON, D.C.

Hillings chews on his lip and shakes his head. "Well, that was the Russian's last hope. The only thing they can do now is either ram the sub or hope for some divine intervention."

Van Nar points to the submarine. "Gentlemen, the submarine is now heading back for the ships. They are on a intercept course."

"Admiral." General Lang walks up to him as they both look at the screen.

"We have Sky 1 tracking both the Russians and the sub. We also have the satellite setting over everything. And at 0400, one of your submarines will be firing a missile into the storm. That will cover the new release."

The admiral smiles as he looks at his air force counterpart. "And General?"

"Well, Admiral, that divine intervention could come in the form of a Tomahawk that is a little off course."

Brant looks at both of them. "General, are you suggesting that we attack the Cuban sub?"

"Well, Mr. Secretary, yes. The missile will be fired into the detonation area and lost in the explosion. If it were to veer farther south, Sky 1 can give it any command changes. If the submarine is on the surface, we can take it out. As far as anyone else knows, the Russians knocked it out. If we do nothing, we will sit and watch the demise of the last two ships."

Brant chuckles to himself, and turns to the president."You know, Mr. President. We could do this."

The president rubs the back of his head. "Mr. Brant, there is nothing that is going to come easy this day, is there?"

"I don't believe so, Mr. President."

Wayne looks at his watch. "It's twenty minutes to four." He takes a deep breath and exhales.

"So how does everyone else feel about this plan? I know that Secretary Brant and the navy and air force are for it."

General Becker stands. "Sir, the army is in full agreement."

Commandant Swane stands. "Sir, the Marine Corps agrees. If we do nothing, they are surely lost."

The phone rings, and the president picks it up. He looks at the men around the table. "Secretary Sholenska." He listens intently to the conversation, nodding as it progresses. He then hangs up.

"Well, gentlemen. That was Secretary Sholenska. They have been in contact with General Quintano's headquarters. They were able to reach the submarine when it surfaced. It was ordered to return to base and break off the attack."

Wayne takes a drink of juice. "They have refused to break off the attack. General Quintano has urged the Russians to use whatever is at their disposal to destroy it."

Brant looks back at the president. "Sir, we seem to have a consensus from all parties concerned that the Cuban sub must be destroyed by whatever means."

Wayne takes another drink. "I agree, Mr. Secretary. Proceed with the submarine launch. The missile is to be directed to the Cuban sub."

"Yes, Mr. President." Brant turns back to Hillings. "Admiral, the ball is in your court. Please proceed with the necessary arrangements."

"Yes, sir." Hilling gets on a phone and requests a direct line to the captain of the submarine.

NAS
NEW ORLEANS

Upon Susie's arrival at the headquarters building, she is given some fresh clothes, and she changes in Captain Nelson's bathroom. She discards her wet things and dries off, then quickly puts on the clean warm camouflage utilities. She dries her hair and looks in the mirror. "Oh, my God."

The chief calls through the door. "Is everything all right, Doctor?" Susie coils the towel around her head and opens the door. "Chief, I have no make-up on, and my hair looks like a rat nest. My skin has been in so much water that I look like a corpse. Other than that, I'm fine."

"Susie, you look fine. All of your stuff is over at the BOQ. I took the liberty of having your make-up case sent over."

"Thank God for women in the service." She takes the case and goes back into the bathroom. "I'll just be a second."

She quickly puts on lipstick and some foundation. She runs a comb through her hair. It lays back flat and still wet. She opens the door, and she and the chief head for the conference room. As she opens the door, Captain Nelson and a guard are talking. He looks up and sees her come in. "Well, Doctor. Welcome back."

"Thank you, Captain Nelson. Where is my terminal?"

"Over here, Doctor. You are in direct contact with Ultima." Susie gets to the terminal and keys it. The screen displays a diagram of the blast radius of the bomb at different distances from the site. She puts on a headset. "This is Susie. Who's on the line?"

"Susie, this is Dr. Miano. I'm here with Dr. Choy."

"Good, we'll have to get right to it. There is something about this bomb that doesn't fit right to me. If they intended to use them across the path of the army in Western Europe, conventional warheads would be too destructive and deniable."

"We see what you mean. I take it you are suggesting that these may be neutron bombs."

"If I were designing the thing, that's how I would have made them. Commander Val is out right now. We need to confirm the type."

"Hold on, Doctor. I'll ask Secretary Brant to confirm the type of weapons these are."

Miano talks to Brant. He then picks up the phone to contact Marshal Shagan. They talk for a minute, and he hangs up. "Shagan has verified them as neutron weapons."

Miano goes back to the terminal. "Susie, you were right. We'll have to rethink the blast zones. Hang on. We'll have them up on the screen in just a minute."

Val comes into the room." Dr. Davies, I came back as soon as I heard you were here."

She leans back in the chair. "We just verified that the weapons were neutrons with Marshal Shagan."

"I didn't know that."

"That changes our areas of saturation. I think basically they were looking at a five mile overlap."

"You're probably right."

"Doctor." Nelson joins them. "We have NBC units out placing monitors as close as they can to the blast site. They're working their way back into the city. They're putting them down at one-mile markers. They started earlier; they should be back on base in just a few minutes."

Susie looks up at the clock. The hands sit at 0340 hours.

Chief Lang joins them. "Susie, here is some hot soup. I hope you like chicken noodle?"

"It's exactly what I need, Chief. Thanks."

OFF LOUISIANA COAST

In the Gulf, at fifty feet under the surface, the white case of the bomb rolls along a strip of open sand. It rolls against a rocky outcropping and is pinned there. It lies silently three miles from the bomb site.

A hermit crab scurries along the rocks to escape the surging waters. He reaches a small cave and runs in. His antenna flurry about in the small cave. His eyes at the end of stocks can sense the blinking red light. He backs up against a curved metal structure and retreats back into his shell. The water surges about outside his little haven. He is secure.

HEADQUARTERS
NAS, NEW ORLEANS

Susie drinks some soup and sits thinking. Next, she keys the computer up and enters some figures. Along a line representing forty miles, she marks a bomb location. Lines are extended from their apex out to 4,200 yards. She types in another command, and a circle in red is drawn from each center on the line. It appears on the computers at Ultima.

"It looks like a string of pearls." Brant looks over the shoulders of the other two scientists. "Yes, Mr. Secretary. But probably the most deadly string you could ever imagine."

He turns to Van Nar. "Could we get a map of the East German border?"

"Yes, sir." She calls up to the control room, and a map of the German-Russian border comes up.

"Gentlemen, I will now superimpose Dr. Davies' detonation line on a choke point." He keys his computer, and the string of circles is placed on the main screen. "As you can see, gentlemen, this group of weapons would decimate an area forty miles long and five miles wide. With this particular device, the crews of armored vehicles, aircraft, etc., could not survive the radiation. The EMP would knock out electronics at an even greater range.

"The Russian armored units that were moved back are all NBC-proofed. And they have mobile decontamination vehicles with them. Within minutes, they would roll forward at top speed to close with weaker rear echelon units. This would prevent us from retaliating because of our own troops. Their plan would be to break out behind our forces, and then drive forward. They would probably send units to each side to knock out supply and command units."

The room remains quiet for a minute. Then General Becker turns towards Brant.

"What Dr. Miano has just described would be considered the modern nuclear blitzkrieg. By continuing to use this tactic, they could leap frog deep into Western Europe.

"The weapon is, in all probability, under the water. This will have a direct effect on the efficiency of the weapon." The screen of the bomb site comes up, and red circles are placed at different points on a line leading from it to the Gulf.

"We're concerned about a power sub-station in Pointe à la Hache, and there may be some effects felt in Davant or Bohemia. Dr. Davies has left the naval station with NBC—nuclear, biological, and chemical—personnel and Captain Nelson. The winds have died down enough to allow a Jolly Green to make it to Davant. They will observe the explosion from there."

"Is it safe?" The president looks over at Brant.

"Yes, sir. Susie believes that the bomb is in Black Bay."

"Well, it's 0345. We'll be able to pinpoint its location in about fifteen minutes." The president lowers his watch.

THE GULF, SOUTH OF ALABAMA

The captain of the USS *Tunny*, a Sturgeon class attack submarine, looks over the shoulder of his weapons officer as he puts in the final targeting information. It is sent to the guidance controls of the Tomahawk. The weapon is then slid into the torpedo tube. The boat hangs at sixty feet under the Gulf, just south of Biloxi. He looks at his watch. "Gentlemen, we will fire in ten minutes, at 0355. I'll be in the control room."

He works his way back to the control center. The light above the number one tube is green. The weapons officer takes his place, ready to push the button on command.

BRIDGE OF THE *MOSKVA*
THE GULF

Pstygo walks up to the admiral. "Sir, the submarine is slowly closing the distance with us. We must have hurt it. It has remained on the surface."

"I have received word from Marshal Shagan that the Cubans made contact with the submarine captain. They ordered him back to base and to break off the attack."

"That's great news, Admiral."

"Well, maybe not. He refused. He told them he would return a hero with the sinking of three Russian capital ships."

Pstygo blows his breath out. "Just what we need. A rogue captain with torpedoes."

"What is their range?"

"About 10,000 yards and closing. I would guess they will move in to 5,000 or 6,000 yards for their next shot."

"I think so, too. The *Sovremennyy* will engage them at 9,000 yards with star shells. Maybe it will discourage them."

"If it does, Comrade Admiral, it will set a new precedent for night engagements between ships and submarines."

They both chuckle. "That it might, Comrade Pstygo."

The admiral can feel the ship pull into its next turn as the ships continue to zigzag forward. He walks outside on the starboard side as Pstygo goes back to the command center.

Sokolov raises his binoculars and looks back at the trailing destroyer. Its forward gun mount quickly fires two rounds back into the black void. They form two parallel streaks of light. He follows them out into the darkness. Suddenly they both explode against a dark form; the sail of the submarine is showered with magnesium sparks. They disappear as quickly as they appeared.

The admiral shakes his head as two more rounds fly from the destroyer. "What I wouldn't give for one good round."

CUBAN SUBMARINE

The Cuban seaman on the sail see the guns fire on the destroyer. The glowing balls hit at the base of the sail and shower them with sparks. Two heavy thud sounds are transmitted through the boat as the two star shells hit.

"What the hell was that?" The captain looks around the room. The exec grabs a phone. He talks with one of the men on look-out.

"Sir, the destroyer has just fired two star shells at us."

"What do they expect them to do? Scare us off?"

"I think they are desperate, sir."

"I think they are pissing me off. How far out are they?"

"About 9,000 yards, Captain."

"We'll fire at 5,000 yards. Get me a good track."

Suddenly two more star shells hit the sail and fill the night with magnesium fireflies.

NAS
NEW ORLEANS

Susie follows Nelson and four armed marines up the ramp into the helicopter. Its spinning rotors disperse spray.

The crewman checks everything outside and runs up the ramp. He raises the ramp and tells the pilot that everyone is on board. They taxi out from the hangars and lift into the night. The winds still buffet them as they head for Davant, southeast of the base.

Susie talks with the NBC personnel. She is shown some of the equipment they will deploy as soon as they're down. Nelson joins them. "Doctor, we have a site picked out on the top of a ten story hotel. It should give us a good field of view of the entire area east."

"That sounds great, Captain. We're going to cut this pretty close."

"We'll off load on top of the building. The army units have already been working on the place. So we'll just have to join them. These people will get their stuff set up, and we're on for the show."

The crewman walks over to them. "Sir, the captain says were coming in to the hotel. It should be just a couple of minutes." Nelson looks around. "Everyone, we're landing in just a minute. Get ready to off load as quickly as possible."

As the helicopter nears the hotel, the wind fills with rain. The landing lights try and cut through the slashing silver sheet. Lightning crashes above them and floods the roof with silver light. The pilot calls down to the cabin that they will have to off load in the street below. He pulls the helicopter up and begins the descent to the parking lot in front of the hotel. "Captain Nelson, the pilot can't land on the roof. He is going to put down in front of the hotel."

"Very good. I would have been surprised if we were able to land up on top. This weather is bad."

They can feel the descent of the helicopter, and they prepare for the landing. He brings it down and moves closer to the entrance. The ramp is lowered and men and equipment pile off.

Army NBC personnel inside take Susie and Nelson to the main elevator. They ride up to the tenth floor; the doors open to an empty restaurant. Army personnel are working across the room, setting up some equipment.

"Captain Nelson?" A lieutenant walks up to them and salutes. "Sir, I'm Lieutenant Berry. We have a great vantage point here. If you will come this way." He leads them across the dining room to some sliding glass doors. They open out onto a covered verandah. "We have cameras set up at two locations on the wall. The rest of the equipment is spread along the roof."

Men work on equipment. Susie crosses her arms across the front of her field jacket, trying to fight the cold. Berry looks over at her.

"It is chilly, Doctor. The roof keeps the rain out, but it doesn't slow down the cold. We have some special binoculars for you. And if there is anything else you want, just let us know."

"Thank you, Mr. Berry. Everything looks good. There is one thing. Do you have any hot chocolate?"

"Yes, ma'am. Your Chief Lang sent a message down that you would like some."

Nelson laughs. "I swear, sometimes it's the chiefs of the navy that run the show. The officers are just there to sign the requisitions."

"I agree, sir. Sergeants do the same for the army." Nelson looks at his watch. "It's 0355. The *Tunny* will be firing her missile about now."

Susie's binoculars hang heavy around her neck as she takes a drink of chocolate.

CONTROL ROOM, USS *TUNNY*
THE GULF

"Sir, the outer doors are opened and locked."

"Very good. Stand by."

The captain watches the second hand on his watch as it passes thirty seconds.

"Prepare to fire." The weapons officer positions his hand above the button.

"On my count. Ten, nine, eight, seven, six, five, four, three, two, *fire!*"

The button is pushed, and the missile is jettisoned from the tube in a cloud of compressed air. It pushes to the surface and is ejected fifty feet into the air. The booster motor cuts in, and it seems to ride on a tail of flames. The missile separates from the launching capsule and fins deploy. The booster rocket falls away and the turbo jet starts. The missile descends to its cruising altitude just above the waves.

ULTIMA
WASHINGTON, D.C.

"Mr. President. The *Tunny* has just launched its missile."

Van Nar points to a circle just south of Biloxi. A red doted line begins appearing from it, heading south.

"Well, gentlemen. Our course is now set in stone on the submarine matter. I had hoped that we could remain neutral in the situation."

"We had all hoped that, Mr. President." Brant turns back to the screens.

"Gentlemen." Van Nar draws their attention to screen three. "The satellite is focusing down to five miles off the eastern Louisiana coast. We will be able to acquire the bomb on detonation. If the timing is correct, we have two minutes to detonation."

White caps can be seen on the water as the satellite view narrows. On the lower right hand corner, the leading edge of the eye moves into view.

STADIUM
NEW ORLEANS

In the stadium, all eyes are on the big screen. They watch as Marcey Lane gets in front of the camera. "We have set up two cameras here on the top of the KNLT station. We have them looking out to the southeast. We have received word from Washington that the missile has been launched. There should be an impact in less than two minutes. I'll be back, following the explosion." She ducks off camera, and runs for cover with some others. "Does anyone know if we should be looking at it?"

"The warning said not to look directly at it until after the flash."

"My God, this has got to be my ticket to the big time."

ULTIMA
WASHINGTON, D.C.

Those in the control room at Ultima sit quietly watching the satellite image. Their eyes are drawn over for an instant as the red dotted line continues to travel south on the Gulf map.

The people in the dome stare transfixed at the huge screen. The cameras show only a black void with rain slashing across it. Sky 1 has backed off to a safe distance and continues to track the Tomahawk and the bomb site. Cameras on the plane are turned to the west. Susie and the others gather at the wall edge and look out into the night towards the northeast.

The hermit crab pokes his head out from under his shell; some ancient sense disturbs his rest. His antennae test the water, and his eyes search about him for danger. His eyes are drawn to the blinking light that suddenly goes solid red. He cocks his head. The bottom of the casing blows off, and the payload is fired straight up. It is suddenly pushed through the surface and begins a flight into the night sky. For a second, the little hermit crab sees the light from a distant city, and a lightning stroke lights the great swamp to the west. They reach 500 feet, and his essence is sent on a journey to the stars. His molecules will reach Mars before any man's.

The fireball spreads in all directions; an elliptical shape is formed in the seabed a mile across. As the core of the explosion reaches the temperature of the sun, the sand around the base is fused into glass. A huge dome of living fire rises into the air. The earth shakes in all directions. The fiery display would cause even Thor to be envious.

At Ultima, the satellite picture suddenly goes white. The rising dome of fire is centered on the screen. "My God." The words fall to the floor, unanswered. Everyone sits focused at the screen. The people in the stadium watch silently. The dome of light is like a rising sun to the east.

Susie stands pressed up against the wall. She leans on her elbows to steady the binoculars. Instruments around her hum and click as they scan the explosion.

"Holy shit." The words drift past her. Nelson and the others are all looking out at the fireball. Her mind races to keep ahead of the events that the bomb has put into effect— expanding heat and the blast and concentrated radiation, plus the expanding ring of the electromagnetic pulse.

Miles from the blast, birds drop out of trees. Wild pigs fall at a dead run. Alligators on the shore and in the ponds and streams suddenly cease to live as the radiation from the bomb kills all in its path.

At Ultima, the satellite shows the perfect circle of the concussion wave as it radiates from the focus. With it travels the heat from the core.

At the stadium, they feel the ripple of the blast beneath their feet. They watch the huge dome of fire just drift away.

Men at the main power station in New Orleans quickly detach from the grid. The EMP pulse reaches some of the high-tension wires from the south. The convenient carrier allows it to run in both directions. Transformers on poles boil and explode.

Switching equipment is welded in place. The pulse hits the power sub-station at Delacroix. Their microswitches are seared away. Control panels burn and fuse in the sudden onslaught. Removed from the grid earlier, the station is left as a sacrificial lamb to the bomb.

The wind around the eye of Evita crashes into the mile-wide fire storm. The counterclockwise winds traveling at 200-plus miles per hour are sucked skyward by the rising heat. A pillar of flame spins thousands of feet upward.

Susie's elbows are shaken by the passage of the seismic waves in the ground. The spreading fireball transfixes her. It suddenly is swirled up into the fiery funnel. "Holy shit, do you see that?" The voice comes out of the crowd pressed against the wall.

Her mind searches its core to explain the rising yellow, orange, and red edifice. It reminds her of iridescent cotton candy as the top spreads out in the upper atmosphere. The winds fall away on the south side as their force is dissipated into the rising column on the north side. Nature tries to regain its hold on the situation. Lighting tears into the column. It spreads out in all directions; its cold blue-silver fingers cover the sky. The rolls of thunder recapture preminence in the heavens.

As the funnel dies away, the air around it rushes in to fill the vacuum. The resulting boom would be the envy of Zeus. The sound rushes in all directions. Susie drops her binoculars. "Everyone down. We're going to get hit hard with the boom."

As they drop, the impact of the compressed air blows the window out behind them. A sudden weight pushes them into the floor, and the sound deafens them. Everyone slowly begins to move. Susie can feel the ringing in her head, and the sudden lightness of her body. "Is everyone all right?" Nelson gets to his feet, looking around.

"My God, what a rush." Berry shakes his head. Army medics begins moving through the group. Two men in the restaurant were hit by flying glass. They are brought downstairs to waiting ambulances. "Susie, are you all right?" Nelson helps her to her feet.

"Yes, it's just this ringing in my head." They all speak louder to overcome the ringing.

"I know what you mean. That was one hell of a boom." The people in the stadium are presented with a fantastic display: the rising column of fire. As they watch, the sound of the imploding air reaches them. It booms like a hundred sonic booms. The dome is shaken by the impact.

"What a sight." Marcey stands to the side so that the camera can get both her and the fire column. It slowly dims away. "That was a spectacular site with all the lightning." The big boom hits their location.

"We will be covering the—" *Boom*. Marcey is knocked off her feet, and the camera shakes violently. The audio buzzes from the loud noise. Marcey slowly picks herself up. "My God, what happened? Was it a sonic boom or something?"

She walks back in front of the camera. "I'm sorry, everyone. We just got hit by some sort of sonic boom from the blast." Her ears ring from the sound.

ULTIMA
WASHINGTON, D.C.

Van Nar puts up a screen showing the CNN broadcast from KNLT. Next is the satellite picture. On the third screen, the red dotted line continues to move south.

Captain Emmett is at the podium. "This is fantastic. The blast has transformed into a huge column of swirling air. The clockwise movement of the storm has been cut with the bomb. And the winds coming into the blast area from the north are being shot into the upper atmosphere." As the column collapses, a second shock wave appears. "They're going to hear this clap of thunder a

100 miles away." He points to the southern portion of the eye. "The eye is collapsing as the winds are fed upwards at the explosion. The rest of the eye is collapsing behind it. Shit, it really worked."

"You mean we have stopped the storm?"

"Yes, Mr. President. Not the storm totally, but as you can see, it is falling back into the zone of a strong tropical storm."

The president and the others applaud. "You have done it, Mr. President. You have used a tactical weapon for good."

"It looks that way, Mr. Brant. Let's hope that the dangers are now over."

Brant turns to the two other scientists. "Gentlemen, what about radiation?"

"From the readings were getting so far, the water and the rain have absorbed most of the lethal dosages. The site is being scoured by the wave action, and the water is being carried out into the Gulf. We're not sure about the moisture-laden winds thrown up into the stratosphere.

"I might point out, gentlemen, that with all of the moisture suddenly thrown high into sub-zero temperatures, there is an outside chance of sleet or snow in New Orleans."

"Snow." Brant looks at Emmett in amazement.

"Look at the CNN broadcast." The president walks towards the screen. "I may be wrong, but that sure looks like snow falling around Marcy Lane?"

Marcey suddenly begins looking around her. "My God, it's snowing." White snowflakes begin drifting down across the city. The president and the others begin laughing. "We have finally brought snow to the deep south."

Dr. Miano walks over next to the president. "From the readings we're getting off the monitoring equipment, the background radiation is a little higher than normal. But it's well within tolerance levels. Mr. President, the danger has passed." They all breathe a sigh of relief as General Lane joins them.

"Mr. President, we have two air force jets flying in towards the detonation site. They will be taking readings on their passes. And I talked with Dr. Davies. As soon as they get some additional read outs, she will take a team to the actual site. She said that so far the bomb has performed about like they thought it would."

"That is great news, Mr. President. We'll schedule a news conference as soon as possible."

"Very good, Brant. We have only one more loose end."

They both look up at the red dotted line moving south.

"That will soon be over, too, Mr. President."

BRIDGE OF THE *MOSKVA*
THE GULF

"Admiral."

Sokolov lowers his binoculars as two more star shells are fired into the night. "Yes, Mr. Pstygo."

"Sir, the submarine will reach the 5,000-yard marker in three minutes. I believe they will attempt to sink the *Sovremennyy* first. Then they will pick us off."

"Your probably right. I'm sure they are not real happy with the bombardment from the destroyer. My God, I don't think that a commander could ask for any better group of men to fight with."

"Yes, sir." They both look back in the direction of the submarine as two more shells are fired. They hit and explode in an explosion of sparks.

The admiral lifts his binoculars. "At least we can go to the bottom with the knowledge that we have given them one hell of a headache."

CUBAN SUBMARINE

The captain looks through the periscope. "We'll take a final bearing on the destroyer and blow our antagonist to the bottom. Then we'll take our time and dispatch the *Moskva*." He lines the cross hairs on the destroyer as a star shell temporarily blinds him. "Shit." He gets the bearings. "Open the outer doors. We'll fire two into him. Stand by to fire." The lights on the firing panel go green above the two tubes. The captain takes a last look through the periscope.

"Stand by."

"Sir, radar has a missile inbound. Due north."

BACKFIRE

"Shit! Dive, dive. We'll take them down from below." Men slide down the ladders and secure the hatch. The submarine begins its dive to escape, and the hull begins to slide under the waves.

The Tomahawk missile jumps up at five miles to correct its bearing and to center the submarine. Its cross hairs scan the boat and pick out the sail. It aligns itself with the center of the sail. The cool waters of safety are just reaching the bottom of the sail as the Tomahawk hits it dead center. The explosion tears the sail completely off the hull as the now headless cylinder dives to its death.

BRIDGE OF THE *MOSKVA*

As Sokolov looks at the sub, he can see it beginning to dive. Suddenly a huge fireball decapitates the hull. "What the hell?" He looks around.

Pstygo runs to his side. "Did you see it, sir?"

"Yes. What happened?"

"Radar picked up a missile at about five miles out. It locked on the submarine as it was diving."

"Was it one of ours?"

"No, sir, I don't think so. Its path was coming from the north. My guess is that it was an American missile."

"My God." The admiral grabs his hand and shakes it. "Get me through to Marshal Shagan, Pstygo." Sokolov talks with Shagan for a few minutes and hangs up the phone. He calls Yefimov and Pstygo to him.

"Gentlemen, it seems our saviors in this engagement were the Americans. Admiral Hillings informed Marshal Shagan that they would fire a cruise missile to stop the sub. Also, Admiral Hillings has ordered rescue vessels to proceed for us. We will be escorted to a safe harbor. Our ordeal, it seems, is over. I want the captain of the *Sovremennyy* informed. And tell the crews about the coming vessels. And tell them a well done from me."

They both salute. "With pleasure, Admiral."

ULTIMA
WASHINGTON, D.C.

"Gentlemen." Van Nar goes to the podium. "Missile impact is in two minutes." They watch as the red dotted line collides with the round circle of the submarine. It disappears. Van Nar picks up a phone and talks with Sky 1. "Gentlemen, it is confirmed by Sky 1. The submarine has been destroyed."

"Yes!" Admiral Hillings thumps his hand on the table. "What a shot."

"Be sure and send a letter of commendation, Admiral."

"I believe that the men aboard the *Tunny* have just become celebrities, Mr. President."

"You're right, Admiral. They will be known as the storm busters, I'm sure."

Brant walks over to the president. "Sir, we have a press conference scheduled for five o'clock. And Admiral Hillings has ordered the rescue ships to head for the Russians. We have covered both captains of the submarines to expect a hardy welcome when they enter port. Per your earlier request, you will leave for New Orleans on *Air Force One* at ten A.M."

"Well, it looks like we're going back to the regular activities of running the government, Mr. Brant."

"Thankfully so, Mr. President."

DOME
NEW ORLEANS

As the sun begins to lighten the eastern horizon, the people in the dome go outside to see the snow. Serving lines set up in the parking lot begin feeding them. Children play in the white wonder. Snowmen begin appearing, and impromptu snow ball fights erupt. Marcey Lane continues her updates on CNN.

Susie looks at her watch. "We'll be going to the site around 5:30. The readings continue to show improvements."

Nelson nods his head. "I'm going to head back to the base." He looks up into the slowly lightening sky. "We will be back in operation at the base by 9:00 A.M. We'll send any material you need out to the site."

Susie begins getting into a protective suit. "That sounds good. Most of the radiation seems to have been blown into the Gulf. The aircraft readings are lower than expected."

The men and women going in with Susie begin to load their equipment up the ramp into the Jolly Green Giant.

Nelson climbs into a Humvee. "I'll see you back at the base, Doctor."

She waves as he drives off.

NEW ORLEANS

Army and navy teams begin moving through the city and out onto the highways. They take measurements and samples. Their equipment stays within the safe zones as they move down highway 23 and east on 39. As they reach a town, it sits silently in the morning sun. The rain moves quickly northward. Golden shafts of light cut through the dissipating clouds.

Aircraft begin taking off from the base to get pictures and take readings. Helicopters are sent to check damage from the storm and alert the civilian authorities of any major problems.

By noon, the first of the people at the dome begin moving south towards their homes. Susie and her team move over the bomb site. A shaft of light breaks through and shines down on a huge bowl shape cut into the seabed. Coast Guard ships begin moving into the area. They will provide living spaces for Susie and her team for the next few days.

The president arrives in the afternoon. The Joint Chiefs accompany him. They go to the Dome and address those still waiting to leave. He holds a press conference at the base. General Becker joins forward army units down the coast. Commandant Swane visits the men at the base hospital. Secretary Brant joins him; they thank the men for their exceptional job. The president makes it a point to visit each of the commands before they leave for Washington that evening.

NAS
NEW ORLEANS

Two days after the blast, the marines are loaded on a C-130 to go back to Camp Lejeune. Captain Rollens rides out to the plane in the ambulance. The men store their gear in the plane as the ambulances line up to unload. Johnson, Cabolero and Marshall wait to the side as the others are loaded.

"Well, Major." He shakes Johnson's hand. "It has been a pleasure to work with you and you men."

"Thank you, sir. We deeply appreciate your assistance with the men. Goodbye, Dr. Rollens." Johnson is lifted and carried onto the plane. Rollens walks over to the two sergeants. "Well, gentlemen. It was a pleasure to work with both of you. You rebuilt my faith that there still are hard-ass NCOs in the corps."

"Thank you, sir." They both shake his hand. As they're lifted to load, Marshall calls after Rollens.

"Anytime you want to do another butt jump with us, sir, you're always welcome with recon."

"I think that was probable my last, Top. But thanks." He waves them goodbye. A Humvee pulls in next to him, and Captain Nelson jumps out. "I'll give you a ride back to the hospital, Doctor." He runs up the ramp over to Johnson, who is lying on his stretcher.

"Mr. Johnson, I wanted to tell you what a honor it has been to have your elite group use my base during this operation. And tell these young men, they're one hell of a group of marines. You're always welcomed here. Have a good flight, Recon."

"Thank you, sir." Johnson shakes his hand.

He and Rollens watch as the plane taxies to the runway. It quickly lifts into the sky and turns towards the east.

Susie turns the site over to other scientists and flies back to the base. She showers and gets into a pants suit. She visits with Nelson and says goodbye to Chief Lang. She then heads for the hospital to say goodbye to Rollens and to see Laura.

A Humvee is brought around, and she is driven to the airport. She goes to the gate to wait for her plane to load. As she sits waiting, her eyes close and she thinks to herself that she was not able to say goodbye to Marshall and Johnson and the others. She would write them from home. The ticket agent interrupts her thoughts.

"Boarding for flight 106. We'll begin in five minutes. Rows one to ten will load first." She looks at her ticket. Nelson had her put in first class. Following others, she gets to her seat. Stretching out, she lays her head on the back of the seat. Her mind flashes back to the fact she had not been able to say goodbye to Gunny Marshall for saving her life. Her thoughts drift. He has probably already forgotten the crabby doctor. She is aware of the engines starting. The stewardess brings her a pillow and a cup of tea.

Susie watches the flight crew do a final count and start to close the door. The captain's voice comes over the intercom. "Ladies and gentlemen, we will be leaving in just a minute. We have been told to remain at the gate to receive a priority package. As soon as it arrives, we'll be taking off. Thank you for choosing Delta."

A knock sounds at the door, and Holly reopens it. A marine captain in dress blues holding a package walks in to the flight deck. He talks to Holly, and she walks him back to Susie.

"Dr. Davies?"

"Yes?" Susie sits up in her seat. "Is something wrong, Captain?"

"No, ma'am. I'm here to deliver a package to you from the commander of Second Recon. It was flown in from Camp Lejeune." He hands her the package.

"Thank you, Captain."

He salutes her, and Holly leads him back to the door. She closes it behind him. The plane begins to move away from the gate. The others watch her as she unwraps the package. Holly takes the paper. "It must be important to have them fly it in and hold our flight."

"I have no idea what it could be." She opens the box; a card sits on top of the white tissue paper. She opens the card.

Dear Susie,

It has been an honor for Second Recon to have been able to serve with you. You're one hell of a lady. We would like to make you an honorary marine. You will not be forgotten, and you are always welcome at Second Recon.

Major Johnson
Top Sergeant Marshall
Master Gunnery SergeantCabolero
The men of Second Reconnaissance

A tear comes to her eyes, as she unwraps the tissue. She lifts out a green tanker jacket. On the front is the patch for Second Recon. Her name is embroidered above it. On the back is a large Recon emblem. She squeezes it close to her. The smell of military clothing fills her nostrils. Holly leans over. "I'll put the box away for you, Doctor."

"Thank you, Holly." Her tears fall on the green fabric as the plane lifts off. Holly checks her again in a few minutes. Susie lays back in the chair with the jacket wrapped around her. Her thoughts are at peace. She thinks now of her home and her special cowboy.

EPILOGUE

QUINTANO AND BROCK
NORTHERN CUBA

Within a week, the battle cruiser *Frunze* arrives off the entrance to Havana harbor with its battle group. Their helicopters ferry personnel back and forth to the shore. General Quintano and Brock stand on the dock and look out at the flotilla. They visited the *Frunze* battle cruiser earlier.

"What a ship, amigo."

"Yes, sir. Her and her sister ship are at the front edge of the modern Russian navy." They walk back up the pier and climb aboard a Helix helicopter and fly back to the air base at Matanzas.

As they pass over the city, they can see construction crews clearing rubble from the downtown area. The main street is still scared by large burnt areas; they are soon flying over burnt armored vehicles and tanks along the road to the air station.

"This should not have happened, Comrade Brock." Quintano slowly shakes his head.

"I agree, my general. But where men and power meet, such men as Morales and Stalin are created. Their greatest casualties are their own people, so maybe we have stopped another harbinger of ethnic genocide."

Quintano looks over at his friend. "You are right, Comrade. Maybe we did some good." He pats him on the shoulder.

As they near the airbase, two Su-27 fighters race down the runway. They suddenly tilt their noses straight up and rocket into the sky. The helicopter flies down the side of the main runway. Six more Su-27 fighters sit parked in front of two burned-out hangers. As they land, the bodies of the Russians killed at the base are being loaded into the back of an Ilyushin Il-76. An honor guard of Spetsnaz troops lines the path of the coffins.

"I will say goodbye, my general. I leave with my men as soon as the planes are loaded. We return to Archangel and home."

"Goodbye, Brock. I wish you and Val the very best. And Cuba thanks you for your help." Their hands shake, and then Quintano pulls him in for a hug. "I have not forgotten my Russian training."

Brock steps back and laughs. "We will meet again, General. I can feel it."

He salutes and walks to the back of the huge plane. The last coffin is loaded, and the troops load. Quintano stops near the helicopter and looks back at the loading ramp. Brock waves to him from the rear doors. He quickly waves his hat to the disappearing figure. The plane has its engines running and begins to taxi for take off. Two more Sukhoi fighters taxi in front of the cargo plane. They race into the air and are gone. The big cargo jet rolls down the runway and lifts into the air. As it gains altitude, the four fighters join up around it.

They fly to the west for a while, and then turn to the southeast. They drop down to 1,000 feet and fly towards the Russian ships. As they approach, all hands are called on deck. The ships blow their horns and fire cannons to salute their fallen comrades. Over the intercom, a command is issued. "All hands, salute."

As they approach, the two fighters in the front go to afterburners and rocket over the ships. The boom of the jets overpowers the cannons. The other two pull up off each wing tip; they accelerate forward and cross in front of the Ilyushin. The men on the ships all cheer as they fly off to the east and soon disappear.

BRANT, SOLOLOV, AND VAL
COAST GUARD STATION

Farther north off the Coast Guard station on Grand Isle, Secretary Brant steps out onto the helicopter deck. The huge hole in the deck is just in front of him.

"Good God. This is unbelievable; the amount of damage is overwhelming." He looks beyond the rails of the *Moskva* and can see the battle cruiser *Kirov* and its squadron anchored. "What now, Val?"

"Sir, Admiral Sokolov has gone through the ship with our marine engineers. The *Moskva* cannot be saved. She will be towed into deep water and honorably sunk. The *Sovremennyy* will join up with the *Kirov* battle group and return home."

"Very good, Val."

They leave the ship and return to the Coast Guard base where Brant's helicopter is waiting to take him to NAS New Orleans. A color guard from the Coast Guard stands next to a color guard from the *Moskva*. Brant walks up to a podium.

"Gentlemen, both American and Russian sailors have distinguished themselves in the highest traditions of naval forces. The president has authorized me to present presidential citations to the Coast Guard base here and at NAS New Orleans." Everyone comes to attention as the secretary walks up to the base commander and shakes his hand. He then removes a blue and gold ribbon from a box and walks up to the unit flag for the station. The flag is dipped and the ribbon attached. Brant steps back and is saluted by the base commander. He walks back to the podium.

"Today also marks a time to salute our Russian comrades for their bravery and heroism. Admiral Sokolov, if you would join me." The admiral moves over and stands next to the podium. "By order of the president of the United States, a unit citation is presented to you, Admiral Sokolov, and to your ship's company." He salutes as Brant hangs the ribbon around his neck; the silver medal shines at its apex. He walks with the admiral to the color guard. They dip their battle flag. Brant secures the ribbon. As it lifts, the blue and gold ribbon waves in the breeze.

As Brant reaches the steps of the helicopter, he turns to Val. "Well, Val. The president wants me to thank you for your services."

They shake hands. "Thank you, Mr. Secretary."

"Will you be leaving with the ships or flying back?"

"I will head up to the naval base in a few hours and catch a flight out with the injured."

They shake again. "Good luck, my friend."

ADMIRAL SOKOLOV IN THE GULF

A week later, Admiral Sokolov stands on the deck of the *Kirov*, and watches as the *Moskva* is released from the tow vessels. As soon as they are clear, an Oscar class submarine fires a spread of four torpedoes at the side of the *Moskva*. As they tear into her, she slowly rolls but fights to remain afloat. Then she gives a blowing geyser of water and air. She slides into the waiting waves and disappears. Cannon fire and salutes send her home.

CAMP LEJEUNE MARINE BASE

A month later, Secretary Brant arrives at Camp Lejeune. He joins the base commander, and they drive over to the parade grounds. There the Second Platoon of the recon battalion stands in front of the reviewing stands. The rest of the battalion and groups from the Second Division fill the grinder.

On the reviewing stand, the base commander introduces Brant. He walks up to the mike as the entire parade ground come to attention. "Thank you, General Hays, and thank you, gentlemen. Please, at rest." The order for parade rest is given.

"I have been sent here to present in the name of the president of the United States a unit citation for Second Platoon, Alpha Company, Force Recon." He describes the events and the many actions the marines fought that night.

As he prepares to go down off the reviewing stand, he turns back to the mike. "For the marines of Second Platoon, the president has asked me to bring a special guest to do the medal presentations. Gentlemen, Dr. Susie Davies."

She walks with him down the stairs as Major Johnson orders the platoon to attention. She walks up to Johnson and is handed a medal on the end of a blue and gold ribbon. He leans forward to let her put the ribbon over his head. With it in place, she kisses him on the cheek and whispers in his ear. "Thank you, from me."

"It was an honor to serve with you, Doctor."

She moves next to Gunny Cabolero. He leans down, and she places the ribbon around his neck. Again she kisses him on the cheek. "Thank you, from me."

"You made for an exciting night, Doctor."
She moves in front of Top Sergeant Richard Marshall. He leans down, and she places the ribbon around his neck. She puts her arms around his neck. "Thank you for my life, and this is from me and my husband, who also thanks you." She kisses him on the cheek and hugs him. They look into each other's eyes; they are misty and laden with tears.

"I would follow you to the brink of hell. Well, we kind of did that. You're a very special woman, Dr. Susie Davies. It's an honor to know you."

Brant ties the commendation ribbon on the battalion flag. It furls in the breeze with many others. As they reach the top of the reviewing stand, Susie steps up to the mike. "Thank you all, from your country."

The entire parade ground comes to attention and yells in one huge voice. "Doctor Davies, MARINE!!!"

ABOUT THE AUTHOR

Steve Simmons grew up in Chula Vista, California. He attended Southwestern Junior College in 1962, then volunteered for the Marine Corps. He served with the First and the Third Marines. He left to return to college in 1965.

Steve married his high school sweetheart, Susie, in 1963. They raised four sons: Steve, Brad, Jason and Zack. Steve and Susie will celebrate thirty-nine years of marriage this year.

Steve worked with Pacific Bell for twenty-six years before retiring as a manager in 1990. He wrote this book while following his wife, who worked for Price Club/Costco, to Houston, Texas. They lived there for two years, then they moved back to California. They stayed there for a year before moving to Arizona.

In 1996, Steve went back to work with Lucent Technologies in Tucson, Arizona. It was in Tucson that he put the final touches on this manuscript. He and his wife live with two Morgan horses, Blaze and Mia, and a big fat Maine-coon cat named L.C.

Steve's first published work was "Mystic Dweller," a poem printed in *Poetry Publications Book 2000*.

Military history and the technologies of war have always intrigued Steve. He hopes you enjoy this book.

Printed in the United Kingdom
by Lightning Source UK Ltd.
100786UKS00002B/15